Enid Blyton

Enid Blyton, who died in 1968, is one of the most popular and prolific children's authors of all time. She wrote over seven hundred books which have been translated into many languages throughout the world. She also found time to write numerous songs, poems, and plays, and ran magazines and clubs. She was always very concerned for the welfare of children in need, and the Enid Blyton Trust, set up after her death, is very active in raising funds for sick and disabled children.

All eight titles in the Adventure series
are available from Macmillan Children's Books:

1. The Island of Adventure
2. The Castle of Adventure
3. The Valley of Adventure
4. The Sea of Adventure
5. The Mountain of Adventure
6. The Ship of Adventure
7. The Circus of Adventure
8. The River of Adventure

Enid Blyton

Adventure Series 2

including

The Sea of Adventure
The Mountain of Adventure
The Ship of Adventure

MACMILLAN CHILDREN'S BOOKS

The Sea of Adventure first published 1948 by Macmillan and Co. Ltd
Revised edition published 1988 by Pan Books Ltd

The Mountain of Adventure first published 1949 by Macmillan and Co. Ltd
Revised edition published 1988 by Pan Books Ltd

The Ship of Adventure first published 1950 by Macmillan and Co. Ltd
Revised edition published 1988 by Pan Books Ltd

Omnibus edition published 1990 by Pan Books Ltd
This revised omnibus edition published 1994 by Macmillan Children's Books
a division of Macmillan Publishers Limited
25 Eccleston Place, London SW1W 9NF
and Basingstoke
13 15 17 19 18 16 14

ISBN 0 330 31631 1
Printed and bound in Great Britain by
Mackays of Chatham PLC, Chatham, Kent

The Enid Blyton Trust for Children

We hope you will enjoy the adventures of the children in this book. Please think for a moment about those children who are too ill to do the exciting things you and your friends do. Help them by sending a donation, large or small, to the ENID BLYTON TRUST FOR SICK CHILDREN. The trust will use all your gifts to help children who are sick or disabled and need to be made happy or comfortable.

Please send your postal orders or cheques to:
The Enid Blyton Trust for Children
98 Bonneville Gardens

Enid Blyton

The Sea of Adventure

Contents

1

No governess, thank you!

'Do you know, it's May the fifth already!' said Jack, in a very gloomy voice. 'All the fellows will be back at school today.'

'What a pity, what a pity!' said Kiki the parrot, in just as gloomy a voice as Jack's.

'This awful measles!' said Lucy-Ann. 'First Philip had it as soon as he came home for the hols, then Dinah, then she gave it to me, and then you had it!'

'Well, we're all out of quarantine now,' said Dinah, from her corner of the room. 'It's just *silly* of the doctor to say we ought to go away and have a change before we go back to school. Isn't it enough change to go back to school? I do so love the summer term too.'

'Yes – and I bet I'd have been in the first eleven' said Philip, pushing back the tuft of hair he had in front. 'Golly, I'll be glad to get my hair cut again! It feels tickly, now it's grown so long!'

The four children had all had a bad attack of measles in the holidays. Jack especially had had a very nasty time, and Dinah's eyes had given her a lot of trouble. This was partly her own fault, for she had been forbidden to read, and had disobeyed the doctor's orders. Now her eyes kept watering, and she blinked in any bright light.

'Certainly no school work for Dinah yet,' the doctor had said, sternly. 'I suppose you thought you knew better than I did, young lady, when you disobeyed orders. Think yourself lucky if you don't have to wear glasses a little later on!'

'I hope Mother won't send us away to some awful boarding-house by the sea,' said Dinah. 'She can't come with us herself, because she's taken on some kind of important job for the summer. I hope she doesn't get us a governess or something to take us away.'

'A *governess*!' said Philip in scorn. 'I jolly well wouldn't go. And anyway she wouldn't stay now that I'm training young rats.'

His sister Dinah looked at him in disgust. Philip always had some kind of creature about him, for he had a great love of animals. He could do anything he liked with them, and Lucy-Ann secretly thought that if he met a roaring tiger in a jungle, he would simply hold out his hand, and the tiger would lick it like a dog, and purr happily like a cat.

'I've told you, Philip, that if you so much as let me *see* one of your young rats I'll scream!' Dinah said.

'All right, then scream!' said Philip obligingly. 'Hey, Squeaker, where are you?'

Squeaker appeared above the neck of Philip's jersey collar, and true to his name squeaked loudly. Dinah screamed.

'You beast, Philip! How many of those things have you got down your neck? If we had a cat I'd give them all to her.'

'Well, we haven't,' said Philip, and poked Squeaker's head down his collar again.

'Three blind mice,' remarked Kiki the parrot, with great interest, cocking her head on one side and watching for Squeaker to appear again.

'Wrong, Kiki, old bird,' said Jack, lazily putting out a hand and pulling at his parrot's tail feathers. 'Far from being three blind mice, it's one very wide-awake rat. I say, Kiki, why didn't you catch measles from us?'

Kiki was quite prepared to have a conversation with Jack. She gave a loud cackle, and then put her head down to be scratched. 'How many times have I told you to shut the door?' she cried. 'How many times have I told you to wipe your feet? Wipe the door, shut your feet, wipe the . . . '

'Hey, you're getting muddled!' said Jack and the others

laughed. It was always comical when Kiki mixed up the things she loved to say. The parrot liked to make people laugh. She raised her head, put up her crest, and made a noise like a mowing-machine outside in the garden.

'That's enough,' said Jack, tapping her on the beak. 'Now stop it, Kiki!'

But Kiki, pleased with the noise, flew up to the top of the curtains, and went on being a mowing-machine, one that wanted oiling.

Mrs Mannering put her head in at the door. 'Children! *Don't* let Kiki make such a noise. I'm interviewing someone, and it's very annoying.'

'Who's come for an interview?' said Philip at once. 'Mother! You haven't gone and got a governess or something awful to take us away for a change, have you? Is she here?'

'Yes, she is,' said Mrs Mannering. All the children groaned. 'Well, dears, you know I can't spare the time to take you myself,' she went on. 'I've taken on this new job, though, of course, if I'd known you were going to be measly for so long, and then be so peaky afterwards . . . '

'We're *not* peaky!' said Philip indignantly. 'What an awful word!'

'Peaky Squeaky,' said Kiki at once, and cackled with laughter. She loved putting the same-sounding words together. 'Peaky Squeaky!'

'Shut up, Kiki!' called Jack, and threw a cushion at her. 'Aunt Allie – we can quite well go away by ourselves. We're old enough to look after ourselves perfectly.'

'Jack, as soon as I let you out of my sight in the holidays, you plunge into the middle of the most hair-raising adventures,' said Mrs Mannering. 'I shan't forget what happened in the last summer holidays – going off in the wrong aeroplane and being lost for ages in a strange valley.'

'Oh, that was a *marvellous* adventure!' cried Philip. 'I

wish we could have another. I'm fed up with being measly so long. Do, do let us go away by ourselves, Mother, there's a darling!'

'No,' said his mother. 'You're going to a perfectly safe seaside spot with a perfectly safe governess for a perfectly safe holiday.'

'Safe, safe, safe!' shrieked Kiki. 'Sound and safe, sound and safe!'

'Other way round, Kiki,' said Jack. Mrs Mannering put her fingers to her ears.

'That bird! I suppose I'm tired with nursing you all, but honestly Kiki gets dreadfully on my nerves just now. I shall be glad when she's gone with you.'

'I bet no governess will like Kiki,' said Jack. 'Aunt Allie, have you told her about Kiki?'

'Not yet,' admitted Mrs Mannering. 'But I suppose I'd better bring her in and introduce her to you all and to Kiki too.'

She went out. The children scowled at one another. 'I knew it would happen. Instead of having fun at school we shall mope about with somebody we can't bear,' said Dinah gloomily. 'Phil – can't you do something with those awful rats of yours when she comes in? If she knew you were the kind of boy that likes mice and rats and beetles and hedgehogs living down his neck and in his pockets, she'd probably run for miles.'

'Jolly good idea, Dinah!' said everyone at once, and Philip beamed at her. 'It's not often you get a brainwave,' he said, 'but that's one all right. Hey, Squeaker! Come along out. Woffles, where are you? Nosey, come out of my pocket!'

Dinah retreated to the furthest corner of the room, watching the young white rats in horror. However many had Philip got? She determined not to go near him if she could possibly help it.

'I think Kiki might perform also,' said Jack, grinning. 'Kiki – puff-puff-puff!'

That was the signal for the parrot to do her famous imitation of a railway engine screeching in a tunnel. She opened her beak and swelled out her throat in delight. It wasn't often that she was begged to make this fearful noise. Lucy-Ann put her hands to her ears.

The door opened and Mrs Mannering came in with a tall, rather stern-looking woman. It was quite plain that no adventure, nothing unusual, would ever be allowed to happen anywhere near Miss Lawson. 'Perfectly safe' was written all over her.

'Children, this is Miss Lawson,' began Mrs Mannering, and then her voice was drowned in Kiki's railway-engine screech. It was an even better imitation than usual, and longer drawn-out. Kiki was really letting herself go.

Miss Lawson gave a gasp and took a step backwards. At first she did not see Kiki, but looked at the children, thinking that one of them must be making the terrible noise.

'KIKI!' thundered Mrs Mannering, really angry. 'Children, how could you let her? I'm ashamed of you!'

Kiki stopped. She put her head on one side and looked cheekily at Miss Lawson. 'Wipe your feet!' she commanded. 'Shut the door! Where's your handkerchief? How many times have I told you to . . . '

'Take Kiki out, Jack,' said Mrs Mannering, red with annoyance. 'I'm so sorry, Miss Lawson. Kiki belongs to Jack, and she isn't usually so badly-behaved.'

'I see,' said Miss Lawson, looking very doubtful. 'I'm not very much used to parrots, Mrs Mannering. I suppose, of course, that this bird will not come away with us? I could not be responsible for pets of that kind – and I don't think that a boarding-house . . . '

'Well, we can discuss that later,' said Mrs Mannering hastily. 'Jack, did you hear what I said? Take Kiki out.'

'Polly, put the kettle on,' said Kiki to Miss Lawson, who took absolutely no notice at all. Kiki growled like a very fierce dog, and Miss Lawson looked startled. Jack caught the parrot, winked at the others and took Kiki out of the room.

'What a pity, what a pity!' mourned Kiki as the door shut behind them. Mrs Mannering gave a sigh of relief.

'Jack and Lucy-Ann Trent are not my own children,' she said to Miss Lawson. 'Lucy-Ann, shake hands with Miss Lawson. Lucy-Ann and her brother are great friends of my own children, and they live with us, and all go off to boarding-school together,' she explained.

Miss Lawson looked at the green-eyed, red-haired little girl and liked her. She was very like her brother, she thought. Then she looked at Philip and Dinah, each dark-eyed and dark-haired, with a queer tuft that stuck up in front. She would make them brush it down properly, thought Miss Lawson.

Dinah came forward politely and shook hands. She thought that Miss Lawson would be very proper, very strict and very dull – but oh, so safe!

Then Philip came forward, but before he could shake hands, he clutched at his neck. Then he clutched at one leg of his shorts. Then he clapped a hand over his middle. Miss Lawson stared at him in amazement.

'Excuse me – it's only my rats,' explained Philip, and to Miss Lawson's enormous horror she saw Squeaker running round his collar, Nosey making a lump here and there over his tummy, and Woffles coming out of his sleeve. Goodness, how many more had the awful boy got!

'I'm sorry,' said Miss Lawson faintly. 'I'm very sorry – but I can't take this post, Mrs Mannering. I really can't.'

2

A glorious idea

After Miss Lawson had hurriedly said goodbye to Mrs Mannering, and the front door had shut after her, Mrs Mannering came back into the children's playroom looking very cross.

'That was too bad of you, really! I feel very annoyed and angry. How *could* you let Kiki behave like that, Jack! – and Philip, there was no need at all for you to make those rats all appear at once.'

'But, Mother,' argued Philip, 'I can't go away without my rats, so it was only fair to let Miss Lawson know what she was in for – I mean, I was really being very honest and . . . '

'You were being most obstructive,' said Mrs Mannering crossly. 'And you know you were. I consider you are all being really unhelpful. You know you can't go back to school yet – you all look thin and pale, and you really must pick up first – and I'm doing my best to give you a good holiday in the care of somebody responsible.'

'Sorry, Aunt Allie,' said Jack, seeing that Mrs Mannering really was upset. 'You see – it's the kind of holiday we'd hate. We're too big to be chivvied about by Miss Lawson. Now – if it was old Bill . . . '

Old Bill! Everyone brightened up at the thought of old Bill Smugs. His real name was Cunningham, but as he had introduced himself as Bill Smugs in their very first adventure, Bill Smugs he remained. What adventures they had had with him!

'Golly, yes! – if we could go away with Bill,' said Philip, rubbing Squeaker's nose affectionately.

'Yes – and dive into the middle of another dreadful adventure,' said Mrs Mannering. 'I know Bill!'

'Oh no, Aunt Allie – it's us children who have the adventures, and drag old Bill into them,' said Jack. 'Really it is. But we haven't heard from Bill for ages and ages.'

This was true. Bill seemed to have disappeared off the map. He hadn't answered the children's letters. Mrs Mannering hadn't heard a word. He was not at his home and hadn't been there for weeks.

But nobody worried much about him – Bill was always on secret and dangerous missions, and disappeared for weeks at a time. Still, this time he really had been gone for ages without a word to anyone. Never mind – he would suddenly turn up, ready for a holiday, grinning all over his cheerful ruddy face.

If only he would turn up now, this very afternoon! That would be grand. Nobody would mind missing the glorious summer term for a week or two if only they could go off with Bill.

But no Bill came – and something had to be decided about this holiday. Mrs Mannering looked at the mutinous children in despair.

'I suppose,' she said suddenly, 'I suppose you wouldn't like to go off to some place somewhere by the sea where you could study the wild sea-birds, and their nesting habits? I know Jack has always wanted to – but it has been impossible before, because you were all at school at the best time of year for it . . . and—'

'Aunt Allie!' yelled Jack, beside himself with joy. 'That's the most marvellous idea you've ever had in your life! Oh, I say . . .'

'Yes, Mother – it's gorgeous!' agreed Philip, rapping on the table to emphasise his feelings. Kiki at once rapped with her beak too.

'Come in,' she ordered solemnly, but no one took any notice. This new idea was too thrilling.

Lucy-Ann always loved to be where her brother Jack

was, so she beamed too, knowing how happy Jack would be among his beloved birds. Philip too, lover of animals and birds, could hardly believe that his mother had made such a wonderful suggestion.

Only Dinah looked blue. She was not fond of wild animals, and was really scared of most of them, though she was better than she had been. She liked birds but hadn't the same interest in and love for them that the boys had. Still – to be all by themselves in some wild, lonely place by the sea – wearing old clothes – doing what they liked, picnicking every day – what joy! So Dinah began to smile too, and joined in the cheerful hullabaloo.

'Can we really go? All by ourselves?'

'When? Do say when!'

'Tomorrow! Can't we go tomorrow? Golly, I feel better just at the thought of it!'

'Mother! Whatever made you think of it? Honestly, it's wizard!'

Kiki sat on Jack's shoulder, listening to the Babel of noise. The rats hidden about Philip's clothes burrowed deeply for safety, scared of such a sudden outburst of voices.

'Give me a chance to explain,' said Mrs Mannering. 'There's an expedition setting out in two days' time for some of the lonely coasts and islands off the north of Britain. Just a few naturalists, and one boy, the son of Dr Johns, the ornithologist.'

All the children knew what an ornithologist was – one who loved and studied birds and their ways. Philip's father had been a bird-lover. He was dead now, and the boy often wished he had known him, for he was very like him in his love for all wild creatures.

'Dr Johns!' said Philip. 'Why – that was one of Daddy's best friends.'

'Yes,' said his mother. 'I met him last week and he was telling me about this expedition. His boy is going, and he wondered if there was any chance of you and Dinah going, Philip. You weren't at all well then, and I said no at once. But now . . . '

'But now we can!' cried Philip, giving his mother a sudden hug. 'Fancy you thinking of somebody like Miss Lawson, when you knew about this! How could you?'

'Well – it seems a long way for you to go,' said Mrs Mannering. 'And it wasn't exactly the kind of holiday I had imagined for you. Still, if you think you'd like it, I'll ring up Dr Johns and arrange for him to add four more to his bird-expedition if he can manage it.'

'Of course he'll be able to manage it!' cried Lucy-Ann. 'We shall be company for his boy, too, Aunt Allie. I say – won't it be absolutely lovely to be up so far north, in this glorious early summer weather?'

The children felt happy and cheerful that teatime as they discussed the expedition. To go exploring among the northern islands, some of them only inhabited by birds! To swim and sail and walk, and watch hundreds, no, thousands of wild birds in their daily lives! . . .

'There'll be puffins up there,' said Jack happily. 'Thousands of them. They go there in nesting time. I've always wanted to study them, they're such comical-looking birds.'

'Puff-puff-puffin,' said Kiki at once, thinking it was an invitation to let off her railway-engine screech. But Jack stopped her sternly.

'No, Kiki. No more of that. Frighten the gulls and cormorants, the guillemots and the puffins all you like with that awful screech when we get to them – but you are not to let it off here. It gets on Aunt Allie's nerves.'

'What a pity, what a pity!' said Kiki mournfully. 'Puff-puff, ch-ch-ch!'

'Idiot,' said Jack, and ruffled the parrot's feathers. She sidled towards him on the tea-table, and rubbed her beak against his shoulder. Then she pecked a large strawberry out of the jar of jam.

'Oh, Jack!' began Mrs Mannering, 'you know I don't like Kiki on the table at mealtimes – and really, that's the third time she's helped herself to strawberries out of the jam.'

'Put it back, Kiki,' ordered Jack at once. But that didn't please Mrs Mannering either. Really, she thought, it would be very very nice and peaceful when the four children and the parrot were safely off on their holiday.

The children spent a very happy evening talking about the coming holiday. The next day Jack and Philip looked out their field-glasses and cleaned them up. Jack hunted for his camera, a very fine one indeed.

'I shall take some unique pictures of the puffins,' he told Lucy-Ann. 'I hope they'll be nesting when we get there, Lucy-Ann, though I think we might be a bit too early to find eggs.'

'Do they nest in trees?' asked Lucy-Ann. 'Can you take pictures of their nests too, and the puffins sitting on them?'

Jack smiled. 'Puffins don't nest in trees,' he explained. 'They nest in burrows underground.'

'Gracious!' said Lucy-Ann. 'Like rabbits!'

'Well, they even take rabbit burrows for nesting-places sometimes,' said Jack. 'It will be fun to see puffins scuttling underground to their nests. I bet they will be as tame as anything too, because on some of these bird-islands nobody has ever been known to set foot – so the birds don't know enough to fly off when people arrive.'

'You could have puffins for pets, easily, then,' said Lucy-Ann. 'I bet Philip will. I bet he'll only just have to whistle and all the puffins will come huffing and puffing to meet him.'

Everyone laughed at Lucy-Ann's comical way of putting things. 'Huffin and puffin,' said Kiki, scratching her head. 'Huffin and puffin, poor little piggy-wiggy-pig.'

'*Now* what's she talking about?' said Jack. 'Kiki, you do talk a lot of rubbish.'

'Poor little piggy-wiggy-pig,' repeated Kiki solemnly. 'Huffin and puffin, huffin and . . . '

Philip gave a shout of laughter. 'I know! She's remembered hearing the tale of the wolf and the three little pigs – don't you remember how the wolf came huffing and puffing to blow their house down? Oh, Kiki – you're a marvel!'

'She'll give the puffins something to think about,' said Dinah. 'Won't you, Kiki? They'll wonder what sort of a freak has come to visit them. Hallo – is that the telephone bell?'

'Yes,' said Jack, thrilled. 'Aunt Allie has put through a call to Dr Johns – to tell him we'll join his expedition – but he was out, so she asked for him to ring back when he got home. I bet that's his call.'

The children crowded out into the hall, where the telephone was. Mrs Mannering was already there. The children pressed close to her, eager to hear everything.

'Hallo!' said Mrs Mannering. 'Is that Dr Johns? – oh, it's Mrs Johns. Yes, Mrs Mannering here. What's that? Oh . . . I'm so dreadfully sorry. How terrible for you! Oh, I do so hope it isn't anything serious. Yes, yes, of course, I quite understand. He will have to put the whole thing off – till next year perhaps. Well, I *do* hope you'll have good news soon. You'll be sure to let us know, won't you? Goodbye.'

She hung up the receiver and turned to the children with a solemn face. 'I'm so sorry, children – but Dr Johns has been in a car accident this morning – he's in hospital, so, of course, the whole expedition is off.'

Off! No bird-islands after all – no glorious carefree time in the wild seas of the north! What a terrible disappointment!

3

Very mysterious

Everyone was upset. They were sorry for Mrs Johns, of course, and for her husband – but as they didn't know them at all, except as old friends of Mr Mannering long ago, the children felt far, far more miserable about their own disappointment.

'We'd talked about it such a lot – and made such plans – and got everything ready,' groaned Philip, looking sadly at the field-glasses hanging nearby in their brown leather cases. 'Now Mother will look for another Miss Lawson.'

'No, I won't,' said Mrs Mannering. 'I'll give up my new job, and take you away myself. I can't bear to see you so disappointed, poor things.'

'No, darling Aunt Allie, you shan't do that!' said Lucy-Ann, flinging herself on Mrs Mannering. 'We wouldn't let you. Oh dear – whatever can we do?'

Nobody knew. It seemed as if their sudden disappointment made everyone incapable of further planning. The bird-holiday or nothing, the bird-holiday or nothing – that was the thought in all the children's minds. They spent the rest of the day pottering about miserably, getting on each other's nerves. One of their sudden quarrels blew up between Philip and Dinah, and with yells and shouts they belaboured one another in a way they had not done for at least a year.

Lucy-Ann began to cry. Jack yelled angrily.

'Stop hitting Dinah, Philip. You'll hurt her!'

But Dinah could give as good as she got, and there was a loud crack as she slapped Philip full across his cheek. Philip caught her hands angrily, and she kicked him. He tripped her up, and down she went on the floor, with her brother rolling over and over too. Lucy-Ann got out of their way, still crying. Kiki flew up to the electric light, and cackled loudly. She thought Philip and Dinah were playing.

There was such a noise that nobody heard the telephone bell ringing again. Mrs Mannering, frowning at the yells and bumps from the playroom, went to answer it. Then she suddenly appeared at the door of the playroom, her face beaming.

It changed when she saw Dinah and Philip fighting on the floor. 'Dinah! Philip! Get up at once! You ought to be ashamed of yourselves, quarrelling like this now that you are so big. I've a good mind not to tell you who that was on the telephone.'

Philip sat up, rubbing his flaming cheek. Dinah wriggled away, holding her arm. Lucy-Ann mopped her tears, and Jack scowled down at the pair on the floor.

'What a collection of bad-tempered children!' said Mrs Mannering. Then she remembered that they all had had measles badly, and were probably feeling miserable and bad-tempered after their disappointment that day.

'Listen,' she said, more gently, 'guess who that was on the telephone.'

'Mrs Johns, to say that Dr Johns is all right after all,' suggested Lucy-Ann hopefully.

Mrs Mannering shook her head. 'No – it was old Bill.'

'Bill! Hurrah! So he's turned up again at last,' cried Jack. 'Is he coming to see us?'

'Well – he was very mysterious,' said Mrs Mannering. 'Wouldn't say who he was – just said he might pop in tonight, late – if nobody else was here. Of course I knew it was Bill. I'd know his voice anywhere.'

Quarrels and bad temper were immediately forgotten. The thought of seeing Bill again was like a tonic. 'Did you tell him we'd had measles and were all at home?' demanded Philip. 'Does he know he'll see us too?'

'No – I hadn't time to tell him anything,' said Mrs

Mannering. 'I tell you, he was most mysterious – hardly on the telephone for half a minute. Anyway, he'll be here tonight. I wonder why he didn't want to come if anyone else was here.'

'Because he doesn't want anyone to know where he is, I should think,' said Philip. 'He must be on one of his secret missions again. Mother, we can stay up to see him, can't we?'

'If he isn't later than half-past nine,' said Mrs Mannering.

She went out of the room. The four looked at one another.

'Good old Bill,' said Philip. 'We haven't seen him for ages. Hope he comes before half-past nine.'

'Well, I jolly well shan't go to sleep till I hear him come,' said Jack. 'Wonder why he was so mysterious.'

The children expected to see Bill all the evening, and were most disappointed when no car drove up, and nobody walked up to the front door. Half-past nine came, and no Bill.

'I'm afraid you must all go to bed,' said Mrs Mannering. 'I'm sorry – but really you all look so tired and pale. That horrid measles! I do feel so sorry that that expedition is off – it would have done you all the good in the world.'

The children went off to bed, grumbling. The girls had a bedroom at the back, and the boys at the front. Jack opened the window and looked out. It was a dark night. No car was to be heard, nor any footsteps.

'I shall listen for Bill,' he told Philip. 'I shall sit here by the window till he comes. You get into bed. I'll wake you if I hear him.'

'We'll take it in turns,' said Philip, getting into bed. 'You watch for an hour, then wake me up, and I'll watch.'

In the back bedroom the girls were already in bed. Lucy-Ann wished she could see Bill. She loved him very much – he was so safe and strong and wise. Lucy-Ann had no father or mother, and she often wished that Bill was her father. Aunt Allie was a lovely mother, and it was nice to share her with

Philip and Dinah. She couldn't share their father because he was dead.

'I hope I shall keep awake and hear Bill when he comes,' she thought. But soon she was fast asleep, and so was Dinah. The clock struck half-past ten, and then eleven.

Jack woke Philip. 'Nobody has come yet,' he said. 'Your turn to watch, Tufty. Funny that he's so late, isn't it?'

Philip sat down at the window. He yawned. He listened but he could hear nothing. And then he suddenly saw a streak of bright light as his mother, downstairs, pulled back a curtain, and the light flooded into the garden.

Philip knew what it was, of course – but he suddenly stiffened as the light struck on something pale, hidden in a bush by the front gate. The something was moved quickly back into the shadows, but Philip had guessed what it was.

'That was someone's face I saw! Somebody is hiding in the bushes by the gate. Why? It can't be Bill. He'd come right in. Then it must be somebody waiting in ambush for him. Golly!'

He slipped across to the bed and awoke Jack. He whispered to him what he had seen. Jack was out of bed and by the window at once. But he could see nothing, of course. Mrs Mannering had drawn the curtain back over the window, and no light shone out now. The garden was in darkness.

'We must do something quickly,' said Jack. 'If Bill comes, he'll be knocked out, if that's what that man there is waiting for. Can we warn Bill? It's plain he knows there's danger for himself, or he wouldn't have been so mysterious on the telephone – and insisted he couldn't come if anyone else was here. I wish Aunt Allie would go to bed. What's the time? The clock struck eleven some time ago, I know.'

There came the sound of somebody clicking off lights and a door closing. 'It's Mother,' said Philip. 'She's not going to wait any longer. She's coming up to bed. Good! Now the house will be in darkness, and maybe that fellow will go.'

'We'll have to see that he does,' said Jack. 'Do you suppose Bill will come now, Philip? – it's getting very late.'

'If he says he will, he will,' said Philip 'Sh – here's Mother.'

Both boys hopped into bed and pretended to be asleep. Mrs Mannering switched the light on, and then, seeing that both boys were apparently sound asleep, she switched it off again quickly. She did the same in the girls' room, and then went to her own room.

Philip was soon sitting by the window again, eyes and ears open for any sign of the hidden man in the bushes below. He thought he heard a faint cough.

'He's still there,' he said to Jack. 'He must have got wind of Bill coming here tonight.'

'Or more likely still, he knows that Bill is a great friend of ours, and whatever gang he belongs to has sent a man to watch in that bush every night,' said Jack. 'He's hoping that Bill will turn up sooner or later. Bill must have a lot of enemies. He's always tracking down crooks and criminals.'

'Listen,' said Philip, 'I'm going to creep out of the back door, and get through the hedge of the next-door garden, and out of their back gate, so as not to let that hidden man hear me. And I'm going up to watch for old Bill and warn him. He'll come up the road, not down, because that's the way he always comes.'

'Good idea!' said Jack. 'I'll come too.'

'No. One of us must watch to see what that man down there does,' said Philip. 'We'll have to know if he's there or not. I'll go. You stay at the window. If I find Bill coming along I'll warn him and turn him back.'

'All right,' said Jack, wishing he had the exciting job of creeping about the dark gardens to go and meet Bill. 'Give him our love – and tell him to phone us if he can, and we'll meet him somewhere safe.'

Philip slipped quietly out of the room. There was still a light in his mother's room, so he went very cautiously downstairs, anxious not to disturb her. She would be very scared if she knew about the hidden man.

He opened the back door quietly, shut it softly behind him, and went out into the dark garden. He had no torch, for he did not want to show any sign of himself at all.

He squeezed through a gap in the hedge, and came into the next-door garden. He knew it very well. He found the path, and then made his way quietly along the grass at the edge of it, afraid of making the gravel crunch a little, if he walked on it.

Then he thought he heard a sound. He stopped dead and listened. Surely there wasn't *another* man hiding somewhere? Could they be burglars, not men waiting for Bill, after all? Ought he to creep back and telephone to the police?

He listened again, straining his ears, and had a queer feeling that there was someone nearby, also listening. Listening for him, Philip, perhaps. It was not a nice thought, there in the darkness.

He took a step forward – and then suddenly someone fell on him savagely, pinned his arms behind him, and forced him on his face to the ground. Philip bit deep into the soft earth of a flower-bed, and choked. He could not even shout for help.

4

A visit from Bill – and a great idea

Philip's captor was remarkably quiet in his movements. He had captured Philip with hardly a sound, and as the boy had not had time to utter a single cry, nobody had heard anything at all. Philip struggled frantically, for he was half choked with the soft earth that his face was buried in.

He was twisted over quickly, and a gag of some sort was put right across his mouth. His wrists, he found, were already tied together. Whatever could be happening? Did this fellow think he was Bill? But surely he knew that Bill was big and burly?

Trying to spit out the earth in his mouth behind the gag, Philip wriggled and struggled. But it was of no use, for his captor was strong and merciless.

He was picked up and carried to a summer-house, quite silently. 'And now,' hissed a voice, close to his ear, 'how many more of you are there here? Tell me that, or you'll be sorry. Grunt twice if there are more of you.'

Philip made no answer. He didn't know what to do, grunt or not grunt. Instead he groaned, for his mouth was still full of earth, and it did not taste at all nice.

His captor ran his hands over him. Then he got out a small pocket-torch, and flashed it once, very quickly, on Philip's gagged face. He saw the tuft of hair standing straight up on Philip's forehead and gave a gasp.

'Philip! You little ass! What are you doing out here, creeping about in the dark?'

With a shock of amazement and delight, Philip recognised Bill's voice. Gosh, so it was Bill! Well, he didn't mind his mouth being full of earth then. He pulled at the gag, making gurgling sounds.

'Shut up!' whispered Bill urgently, and he took off the gag. 'There may be others about. Don't make a sound. If you've anything to say whisper it right into my ear, like this.'

'Bill,' whispered Philip, his mouth finding Bill's ear, 'there's a man hidden in the bushes at our front gate. We spotted him there, and I slipped out to warn you if I could. Be careful.'

Bill undid Philip's wrists. The boy rubbed them tenderly, Bill knew how to tie people up, no doubt about that! Good thing he hadn't knocked him out.

'The back door's open,' he whispered into Bill's ear. 'As

far as I know there's nobody waiting about at the back. Let's try and get into the house. We can talk there.'

Very silently the two made their way back to the gap in the hedge that Philip knew so well. Neither of them trod on the gravel, in case the slight crunch might warn any hidden watcher.

They squeezed through the gap slowly and carefully. Now they were in Philip's own garden. Taking Bill by the arm he led him slowly over the dark lawn, under the trees, towards the house. There was no light in it anywhere now. Mrs Mannering had gone to bed.

The back door was still unlocked. Philip pushed it open, and the two of them went in. 'Don't put on the light,' whispered Bill. 'We don't want anyone to know that we're awake here. I'll lock this door.'

They went cautiously upstairs. One of the stairs creaked loudly, and Jack, who was waiting in the bedroom, shot to the door. Luckily he didn't switch the light on.

'It's all right – it's only me,' whispered Philip. 'And I've got old Bill.'

'Good egg!' said Jack in delight, and dragged them into his room. Bill gave his hand a hearty shake. He was very fond of the whole family.

'I must rinse my mouth out,' said Philip. 'It's full of earth still. I didn't dare to do any spitting out in the garden, because of the noise. Ugh! It's horrible!'

'Poor Philip!' said Bill remorsefully. 'I didn't know it was you, old fellow. I thought it was somebody lying in wait for me, and I meant to get him, before he got *me*!'

'You did it jolly well,' said Philip, rinsing his mouth out. 'Now where's my tooth-paste? I really must clean my teeth! Oh, blow!'

His hand, seeking for his tooth-paste in the dark, had knocked over a glass. It fell into the basin and smashed. It made a tremendous noise in the silent night.

'Go and warn the girls not to put their light on, if this has waked them ' said Bill urgently to Jack. 'Quick! And see if it has waked Aunt Allie. If it has, warn her too.'

Lucy-Ann was awake, and Jack just managed to stop her switching on the light. His mother did not stir. Her room was further away and she had not heard the sound of breaking glass. Lucy-Ann was astonished to hear Jack's urgent voice.

'What's up?' she asked. 'Anything gone wrong? Are you or Philip ill?'

'Of course not,' said Jack impatiently. 'Get your dressing-gown on, and wake Dinah. Bill's here! But we're not to put on any lights, see?'

Something fluttered by his head with a low squawk. 'Oh, Kiki! I wondered where you were,' said Jack. 'What made you sleep in the girls' room tonight? Come along and see Bill!'

Lucy-Ann awoke an astonished Dinah. The two girls put on their dressing-gowns and went to the boys' room. Kiki was already there, nibbling Bill's ear in delight, making soft noises in his ear.

'Hallo! hallo!' said Bill, when the girls crept softly into the room. 'Which is which? I can only feel you. Ah, this must be Lucy-Ann – I can smell your freckles!'

'You can't smell freckles,' said Lucy-Ann, giggling. 'But you're right, it is me, all the same. Oh, Bill, where have you been so long? You didn't answer any of our letters at all.'

'I know,' said Bill. 'You see – I was on a peculiar job – hunting down a gang of rogues – and then, before I knew what was happening, they got wind of what I was doing – and began to hunt *me* down! So I had to go into hiding, and keep dark.'

'Why – would they have kidnapped you or something, Bill?' asked Lucy-Ann, scared.

'Oh, there's no knowing what they would have done to me,' said Bill airily. 'I should certainly have disappeared for good. But here I am, as you see.'

'So that's what that man at the front gate was there for – hoping to get you,' said Philip. 'Why have you come to see us now, Bill? Do you want us to do anything?'

'Well,' said Bill, 'I've got to disappear for some time, and I wanted to see your mother particularly, to give her a few things to keep for me – just in case – well, just in case I didn't turn up again. I'm what is called a "marked man" now, as far as this particular gang is concerned. I know too much about them for their own comfort.'

'Oh, Bill – but where are you going to disappear to?' asked Lucy-Ann forlornly. 'I don't like you to disappear into the blue. Can't you tell us?'

'Oh – I'll probably lead the simple life somewhere in the wilds,' said Bill. 'Till these fellows have given up hunting for me, or get themselves caught. *I* don't want to disappear – don't think that! I'm not afraid of any of them, but my chiefs can't afford to let anyone get hold of me. So I've got to vanish completely for a time – and not even get into touch with you or my family.'

There was a silence. It wasn't nice to hear all this, told in a low voice in the darkness of midnight. Lucy-Ann groped for Bill's hand. He squeezed her fingers.

'Cheer up! You'll hear from me again some day – next year, or the year after. I shall take some kind of disguise – become a miner somewhere in the wilds of Alaska – or – or a lonely ornithologist on some desolate island – or . . . '

Jack gave a gasp. Something clicked in his mind as a really brilliant idea slid into place there.

'Bill! Oh, Bill! I've thought of something grand!'

'Sh! Not so loud!' said Bill. 'And just take Kiki on your shoulder now, will you, before she nibbles away the whole of my left ear.'

'Listen, Bill,' said Jack urgently. 'I've thought of something. We had a great disappointment today – I'll tell you about it first.'

'Go on, then,' said Bill, thankful that Kiki was no longer on his shoulder.

'I don't expect you know, but we've all had measles pretty badly,' said Jack. 'That's why we're not back at school. Well, the doctor said we ought to go away for a change, and Aunt Allie decided we could go on a bird-watching expedition, with Dr Johns and his party, to some lonely coasts and islands off the north of Britain – you know, places that only birds live on, and only bird-lovers visit.'

'I know,' said Bill, listening intently.

'Well, Dr Johns got hurt in an accident today,' said Jack. 'So we can't go because there is nobody to take us. But – why can't *you* take us – disguised as some bird-man or other? – then we'd have a perfectly glorious holiday, you'd be able to get off into the unknown without anyone knowing – and we could leave you behind there when we come back – quite safe!'

There was silence. All the children waited breathlessly for Bill's answer. Even Kiki seemed to be listening anxiously.

'I don't know,' said Bill at last. 'It's too much like using you as a smoke-screen – and if my enemies saw through the smoke – well, things wouldn't be too good for you or for me either. I don't think it's possible.'

The mere thought of Bill's turning the wonderful idea down made the children more enthusiastic and urgent about it. They each had a few words to contribute.

'We were *so* disappointed not to go – and now this does seem a way – and after all, it would only be for about two weeks, as far as we're concerned. We'd be going back to school then.'

'You're awfully good at disguises. You could *easily* look like an ornithologist – sort of earnest, and always peering into the distance for birds, and with field-glasses over your shoulder . . . '

'Nobody could possibly know. We'd all be absolutely safe

up in the northern seas, so wild and desolate, with you. Think of May up there – the sea so blue, the birds all soaring and gliding, the sea-pinks out all over the place . . . '

'You'd be *safe*, Bill – no-one surely would ever dream of hunting for you in a place like that. And oh, we do want that kind of holiday. We've felt mouldy after measles.'

'Not so *loud*,' whispered Bill. 'I'll have to talk things over with your mother first – even if I think it's all right myself. It's a bold idea – and I don't think it would occur to anyone for one moment that I would go off openly like that. And I must say that a holiday with you four – and Kiki too, of course – is just what I'm needing at the moment.'

'Oh, Bill – I believe you'll do it!' said Lucy-Ann, hugging him with ecstasy. 'What a lovely ending to a horrid day!'

5

Exciting plans

Bill spent the night, unknown to Mrs Mannering, in the little spare room. He said he would talk to her the next morning. He was relieved to find that a daily maid came in each morning, but that no-one except the family slept in the house at night.

'We children do all the beds and things upstairs, now that we have recovered,' said Dinah. 'So you can stay up here unseen, if you like. We'll bring breakfast up.'

But the next morning everything was upset again. Mrs Mannering knocked on the wall separating the girls' room from hers, and Dinah went running in to see what the matter was.

'Dinah! The most sickening thing has happened!' said Mrs Mannering in disgust. '*I've* got measles now – look at my spots. I thought I'd had it when I was your age – but it's measles right enough. Oh dear, I wish I had engaged that Miss Lawson and let her take you off to Bournemouth or somewhere yesterday. Now what are we to do?'

'Oh dear!' said Dinah. Then she decided to tell her mother about Bill being there. Perhaps that would help. 'I'll get you your dressing-jacket and tidy the room,' she said briskly, 'because there's someone who wants to see you. He may help quite a lot. It's Bill!'

'Bill!' said Mrs Mannering, amazed. 'When did he come? I waited up till eleven, but I felt so terribly tired I just had to go to bed. Well, now – I wonder if old Bill would take you off my hands for a bit and leave Hilda, the daily, to look after me!'

'I'm sure he would,' said Dinah, delighted. 'Poor Mother! You feel worst the first two or three days and after that it's not so bad. There – are your pillows comfy? I'll send Bill in now.'

The news was broken to the others. The children were sorry and dismayed. Did grown-ups actually get measles then? Poor Mother! Poor Aunt Allie! She would certainly want them out of the house now.

'She's ready to see you, Bill,' said Dinah. 'I say – I suppose you've had measles all right, haven't you?'

'Oh, dozens of times,' said Bill cheerfully, going to Mrs Mannering's room. 'Cheer up – we'll get things right in no time!'

'But you can only have measles once,' began Lucy-Ann. Then the door was shut, and the children could hear only a murmur of voices in the room.

They went down to breakfast. The boys had more or less got back their ordinary appetites, but the girls still only picked at their food. Dinah looked at Lucy-Ann.

'Your freckles hardly show,' she said. 'Nor do Jack's. A bit of sun will do us all good. I don't feel like this bacon, do you? Oh dear – I wish Bill would hurry up and come down. I do want to know what they've decided.'

Bill did not come down. The children heard the door above opening, and then a soft whistle. Bill was evidently afraid the daily was about. But she had gone out to do the shopping.

'It's all right,' called Dinah. 'Hilda's out. Come down if you want to. We've saved you some breakfast.'

Bill came down. 'Your mother doesn't want any breakfast except toast and tea,' he said. 'You make the toast, Dinah. I see the kettle's boiling – we can make tea as soon as the toast is ready. Then I'm going to ring up the doctor, and then ring up Miss Tremayne, your mother's friend, and ask her to come along for a week or two to be with the invalid. She says she'll like that.'

The children listened in silence. 'And what about *us*?' asked Jack at last. 'Didn't you decide?'

'Yes, I decided,' said Bill. 'Your aunt begged me to take you away for two weeks – and I told her I was due to disappear for a while, so I'd go off to the northern seas with you. I didn't scare her with my reasons for disappearing – she's really feeling bad this morning – and she's so thankful to think you'll get away for a change that she hardly asked me any questions at all.'

'So we're to go?' said Jack, unable to keep the joy out of his voice, even though he was very sorry about Aunt Allie. 'How absolutely super!'

The four faces glowed. Kiki picked a piece of rind out of the marmalade and, as nobody said anything, took a piece of lump sugar from the sugar-basin.

'Mother will be quite all right, won't she, with Miss Tremayne?' said Philip earnestly. 'She wouldn't like one of us to stay with her, would she? I'll stay, if so.'

'She would be much better with you all out of the house,' said Bill, helping himself to bacon. 'She's tired out and wants a really peaceful time. Measles is beastly, but at least it will make her rest in bed for a while!'

'Well, then, we can really look forward to going off with a

light heart,' said Jack cheerfully. 'Oh, Bill – you always turn up just exactly at the right moment!'

'Here's Hilda!' said Philip suddenly. 'You'd better hop upstairs, Bill. Take your plate. I'll bring you more toast and tea when we take Mother's up. Isn't that toast finished *yet*, Dinah?'

'Just,' said Dinah, and put the last piece in the toast-rack. 'No, Kiki, leave it alone. Oh, Jack, look at Kiki's beak – just *dripping* with marmalade. There won't be any left for us. Greedy bird!'

Bill disappeared upstairs. Hilda went into the kitchen and began to fill up the kitchen stove. Dinah went out to tell her about Mrs Mannering having the measles. Hilda was most sympathetic, but looked very worried.

'Well, I daresay I can manage,' she said, 'but what with all you children here too . . . '

'Oh, but we shan't be,' said Dinah. 'We're going off on a bird-expedition, as soon as we can – and Miss Tremayne is coming to see to Mother – so . . . '

'Hilda! Hill-da! Hilllll-da!' called a voice, and Hilda jumped.

'My, that's the missus calling!' she said. 'And you told me she was in bed! Coming, Madam!'

But it was only Kiki, of course, doing one of her imitations. She cackled with laughter when Hilda came running into the dining-room.

'Wipe your feet!' she ordered. 'Don't sniff! How many times have I told you to . . . '

Hilda went out and banged the door. 'I don't mind taking orders from them as has the right to give them,' she said to a giggling Dinah, 'but take orders from that ridiculous bird I will not. I hope, Miss, that you're taking that parrot with you. I don't want the minding of her whilst you're gone. Drive me crazy, she would.'

'Oh, of *course* we'll take her!' said Dinah. 'Jack would never dream of going without her.'

The doctor came. Miss Tremayne arrived. Hilda agreed to sleep in. Everything seemed to be going well. Bill, ensconced in the spare room, whose door he kept locked in case Hilda should come barging in, made a few quick plans.

'Pack up your things. Order a taxi for eight o'clock tomorrow night. We'll catch the night train to the north. I'll slip out tonight and make the rest of the plans for the journey and the holiday. I'll meet you at Euston, and it won't be as the Bill Smugs you know! I shall then be Dr Walker, the naturalist. I'll come over and introduce myself in a loud voice as soon as I see you arrive, in case there's anyone about that know you – or me either! Then off we'll go.'

It all sounded very thrilling. What a mysterious way to begin a holiday! It sounded as if they were setting off for a first-class adventure, but of course they weren't. It would be fun if they were, but what could happen on lonely bird-islands? Nothing at all except birds, and more birds and yet more birds.

Bill slipped off that night. No one had known he was in the house, not even Miss Tremayne, who had been given the little dressing-room leading off Mrs Mannering's room. Mrs Mannering had promised not to say that Bill had been there, in case it meant danger to him. But she was so heavy and sleepy that day, that she really began to wonder if Bill *had* actually been there at all, or if she had dreamt it.

The children packed. No need to take best dresses or anything like that! Shorts and jerseys, rubber shoes, bathing-suits and mackintoshes were the things they would want. And a few cardigans, some towels – and what about some rugs? Were they going to sleep under a roof or not? Bill hadn't said. For all they knew they might be sleeping in tents. What fun! They decided not to take rugs. Bill would be sure to take things like that if they needed them.

'Field-glasses – note-books – pencils – my camera – and a

rope,' said Jack, trying to think of everything. Lucy-Ann looked astonished.

'A *rope*?' she said. 'Why a rope?'

'We might want to go cliff-climbing if we want to examine nesting-places there,' said Jack.

'Well, you can go cliff-climbing if you like. I shan't!' said Lucy-Ann, with a shiver. 'I'd hate to climb down steep cliffs with just a rope round me and hardly anything to put my feet on.'

'Kiki's taken your pencil,' said Dinah. 'Kiki, don't be such a nuisance. We shan't take you to see the puffins if you behave like this.'

'Huffin and puffin, puffin and huffin, muffin and puffin, muffins and crumpets,' pronounced Kiki, and cracked her beak in delight at having said something new. 'Huffin and puff—'

'Oh stop huffing and puffing,' called Dinah.

'God save the Queen,' said Kiki, and stood up very straight.

'Goodness knows what the birds up there will think of you,' said Lucy-Ann. 'Jack, shall we put her into a basket to take her with us on the train? You know how she will keep shouting "Guard, guard" and pretending to blow a whistle, and telling everyone to wipe their feet.'

'She can go on my shoulder,' said Jack. 'We shall be sleeping on the train, in beds or berths, and she'll be quite all right. Stop cracking your beak, Kiki. It's not clever to keep *on* making a nuisance of yourself.'

'Naughty Polly!' said Kiki. 'Sing Polly-wolly-oodle-all-the-day!'

Philip threw a cushion at her and she retired to the top of the curtains and sulked. The children went on discussing their coming holiday.

'Fancy having the luck to be with Bill after all!' said Jack. 'Much better than Dr Johns. I wonder if he'll have a boat and go exploring round. Golly, I'm going to enjoy the next week or two. We might even see a Great Auk!'

'You and your Great Auks!' said Philip. 'You know quite well they're extinct. Don't start all that again, Jack. We might find Little Auks up there, though – and razor-bills – and thousands of guillemots on the cliffs.'

The next day came at last and then dragged on till the evening. Mrs Mannering slept most of the time and Miss Tremayne would not let them go in and wake her to say goodbye.

'Better not,' she said. 'I'll say goodbye for you. Mind you write to her from wherever you're going. Is that the taxi I hear now? I'll come and see you off.'

'It *was* the taxi. They bundled in with all their luggage. Now to London – to meet Dr Walker – and to travel hundreds of miles to the north, to wild places where few people had ever been. No adventures this time, but just a glorious, carefree holiday with old Bill.

'All aboard!' said Kiki, in a deep voice that made the taxi-driver jump. 'One – two – three – OFF!'

6

Travelling far

Bill had told the children exactly where to wait for him at Euston Station, so, each carrying a bag and a mackintosh, they went to the spot.

They stood there waiting. 'Suppose,' said Philip, in a mysterious voice, 'just suppose that one of the gang that Bill is after, knew Bill was going to meet us here – and came up and told us he was Bill – and took us all off with him, so that we were never heard of again!'

Poor Lucy-Ann stared at him in the greatest alarm. Her eyes nearly popped out of her head. 'Oh, Philip – do you think that might happen? Gracious, I hope to goodness we recognise Bill when we see him. I shall be scared stiff of going with him if we don't.'

A very fat man approached them, smiling. He was big all over, big head, big body, big feet – and big teeth that showed when he smiled. Lucy-Ann felt her heart sink. This couldn't be Bill! Nobody could make himself as big as that, if he wasn't fat to begin with. She clutched Philip's hand. Was it one of the gang?

'Little girl,' said the big man to Lucy-Ann, 'you've dropped your mackintosh behind you. You'll lose it if you don't pick it up.'

Lucy-Ann had gone pale when he first began to speak. Then she looked round and saw her mac on the ground. She picked it up. Then, scarlet in the face, she stammered out a few words of thanks.

The big man smiled again, showing all his fine teeth. 'Don't look so scared,' he said. 'I shan't eat you!'

'He looks just as if he might,' thought Lucy-Ann, retreating behind Jack.

'Pop goes the weasel,' said Kiki, in a polite conversational tone. 'Pop, pop, pop!'

'What a remarkably clever bird!' said the big man, and put out his hand to pat Kiki. She gave him a vicious nip with her beak, and then whistled like an engine.

The big man's smile vanished and he scowled. 'Dangerous bird, that,' he said, and disappeared into the crowd. The children were relieved. They didn't think, of course, that he was one of the gang – that had only been Philip's make-up – but they were worried in case he kept them talking, and prevented Bill from coming up and fetching them.

They stood there, under the clock, looking all round for Bill. They couldn't see anyone even remotely resembling him. Then a rather shambling, round-shouldered man came up, wearing thick glasses through which his eyes peered sharply.

He wore a thick long coat, had field-glasses slung across his back, and a curious black-checked cap. He also had a black beard. But he spoke in Bill's voice.

'Good evening, children. I am glad to see you are punctual. Now at last we start on our little expedition.'

Lucy-Ann beamed. That was Bill's nice warm voice all right, in spite of the beard and the strange get-up. She was just about to fling herself on him, crying, 'Oh, Bill, it's good to see you,' when Jack, feeling sure that Lucy-Ann was going to do something impulsive like that, pushed her away and held out his hand politely.

'Good evening, Dr Walker. How are you?'

The others took their cue from Jack, and anyone looking on would have thought that here were four children greeting a tutor or a guardian who was going to take them on a journey somewhere.

'Come this way,' said Dr Walker. 'I have a porter for your things. Hey, porter, put these bags on your barrow, will you, and find our reservations in the ten o'clock train. Thank you.'

It wasn't long before they were all safely on the night train. The children were thrilled with their little 'bedrooms.' Lucy-Ann liked the way everything could fold down or fold back, or be somehow pushed out of the way.

'Now, you must sleep all night,' said Bill, his eyes smiling at them from behind his thick glasses. 'Dr Walker will see that you are awake in time for breakfast.'

'How do we get to the place we're going to, and where exactly is it?' asked Jack.

'Well, we get there by this train and another, and then by motor-boat,' said Bill. The children looked thrilled. They loved travelling.

'I've got a map here,' said Bill, making sure that the door was shut. 'It's a map of all the many little islands dotted off the north-west coast of Scotland – hundreds of them. Some are too small to map. I don't expect anyone has ever visited all of them – only the birds live there. I thought we'd make one of them our headquarters, and then cruise around a bit, taking photographs, and watching the birds in their daily life.'

The eyes of the two boys gleamed. What a glorious thing to do! They visualised days of sunshine on the water, chugging to and from tiny islands inhabited by half-tame birds, picnicking hungrily in the breeze, sitting on rocks with their feet dangling in the clear water. Their hearts lifted in happiness at the thought.

'What I should really like,' said Philip, 'would be a tame puffin or two. I've never seen a live puffin – only a stuffed one – but they look real characters.'

'I suppose you would teach them to sit up and beg,' said Bill, amused.

'Huffin and puffin,' announced Kiki. 'God save the Queen.'

Nobody took any notice. They were all too much absorbed in thinking of the unusual holiday.

'I shall remain behind there, once you have gone back,' said Bill. 'It'll be a bit lonely without you all, but no doubt you will leave me your tame puffins for company.'

'I shall hate leaving you,' said Lucy-Ann. 'Will you have to be there all alone for long, Bill?'

'A goodish time, I expect,' said Bill. 'Long enough for my enemies to forget about me, or to think I'm dead and gone.'

'Oh dear!' said Lucy-Ann. 'I wish you didn't have to lead such a dangerous life, Bill. Can't you do something else instead?'

'What? Be a gardener, or a tram conductor or something safe like that, do you mean?' asked Bill, grinning at Lucy-Ann's serious face. 'No, Lucy-Ann – this kind of life suits me. I'm on the side of law and order and right – and to my mind they're worth while running any risk for. Evil is strong and powerful, but I'm strong and powerful too, and it's good to try one's strength against bad men and their ways.'

'Well, I think you're marvellous,' said Lucy-Ann stoutly.

'And I'm sure you'll always win. Don't you hate having to hide now?'

'I'm furious about it,' said Bill, looking anything but furious, but with a note in his voice that made the others realize how desperate he felt, having to 'disappear' when there was work to be done. 'but – order are orders. And anyway, my disappearance means a perfectly glorious holiday for all of us. Well, boys, have you finished studying that map?'

The two boys had been poring over the map of islands. Jack put his finger on one. 'Look – that sounds a good one – the Isle of Wings – it must be full of birds!'

'We'll try and go there,' said Bill. 'We shall probably get well and truly lost, but never mind. Who minds being lost on the blue-green sea in May-time, with all kinds of little enchanted islands ready to welcome you?'

'It sounds glorious,' said Dinah. 'Oh, look at Kiki. She's trying to pull the plug off its chain in that basin.'

Kiki had thoroughly explored the whole of the 'bedroom,' and had had a good drink out of one of the water decanters. Now she settled down on the little towel-rail and, with a remarkably human yawn, put her head under her wing. At the same moment there came a loud banging of doors all down the train. She took her head out again.

'Shut the door,' she remarked. 'Pop goes the door. Send for the doctor.'

The whistle blew, and to Kiki's alarm the whole 'bedroom' suddenly shook as the train pulled out of the station. She almost fell off the towel-rail.

'Poor Kiki, what a pity, what a pity!' she said, and flew to Jack's shoulder.

'Now it's time we all retired to bed and to sleep,' said Bill, getting up. He looked very queer in his black beard and thick glasses. Thank goodness he had taken off the awful black-checked cap.

'Do two of us sleep here, or four of us?' asked Lucy-Ann, looking doubtfully at the small beds, one on each side of the 'bedroom.'

'Two of us,' said Bill. 'I've got a single room on the right of you – and to the right again is another compartment, or room, for the two boys. I'm in the middle of you, you see – and you've only to bang hard on the wooden wall between us, if you want anything, and I'll come rushing in.'

'Oh, good!' said Lucy-Ann. 'I'm glad you're so near us. Bill, are you going to sleep in your beard?'

'Well, as it's rather painful to remove at the moment, being well and truly stuck on, I think I will,' said Bill. 'I'll take it off when we're safely among our little islands. No one will see us there. Don't you like me in my beautiful beard?'

'Not much,' said Lucy-Ann. 'I feel as if you're not you when I look at you, but when I hear your voice, it's all right.'

'Well, my child, look at me with your eyes shut, and you'll have no horrid feelings,' said Bill, with a grin. 'Now good night, and sleep well. Come on, boys, I'll take you to your compartment. I'll wake you in the morning, and we'll dress and go along to the restaurant car for breakfast.'

'I feel a bit hungry now,' said Philip, 'although we had a jolly good supper. But that's ages ago.'

'Well, I've got some sandwiches and some bananas,' said Bill. 'I'll get them. But don't be long turning in, because it's getting late.'

'Only just gone ten,' said Dinah, but she yawned loudly as she spoke. Kiki promptly imitated her, and that set everyone else yawning too.

Bill went into his own compartment and fetched sandwiches and ripe bananas. Then he said good night to the girls and took the boys to their own 'bedroom.' It really was very exciting to go to bed in a train. It was queer undressing with the train swaying about, rushing through the night at sixty miles an hour.

It was nice to be in bed, listening to the 'tutta-tut-*tah*! tutta-tut-*tah*!' of the train wheels turning rapidly over the rails.

'Travelling *far*, travelling *far*, travelling *far*,' said the wheels to Lucy-Ann, as her eyes closed, and her mind swung towards sleep. 'Travelling *far* . . . '

In spite of all the excitement the four children were soon fast asleep and dreaming. What were they dreaming of? That was easy to guess. Blue-green water, clear as crystal, enchanting little islands, big white clouds flying across an enormous blue sky, and birds, birds, birds . . . travelling *far*, travelling *far*, travelling *far*.

7

On the sea at last

The journey was half over before the children awoke again. Bill banged on the walls, and they woke with a jump. They dressed and walked staggeringly along to the restaurant car, feeling very hungry. Lucy-Ann didn't much like walking across the bits that joined two carriages together. She clutched Bill's hand then.

'I'm always afraid the train might come in two, just when I'm walking through the bit where two carriages are joined,' she explained. Bill quite understood, though the others were very scornful of Lucy-Ann's extraordinary idea.

Kiki behaved very badly at breakfast, throwing the toast about, and squawking because she was not allowed any of the rather small helping of marmalade. She made rude noises at the sunflower seeds Jack offered her. The other passengers were amused at her and laughed – but that only made Kiki show off all the more.

'Stop it, Kiki,' said Bill, exasperated, and tapped her

smartly on the beak. Kiki screeched and made a pounce at his beard. A vicious tug and some of it came away. Kiki hadn't been able to understand why Bill had arrived with a strange mass of hair under his chin, and round his cheeks. Now, having got some of it, she retired under the table and began to peck it gently, separating the hairs one by one and murmuring to herself all the time.

'Let her be,' said Bill. 'She'll be happy pulling that bit of my beard to pieces.' He rubbed his chin. 'That hurt. I hope I don't look too peculiar now?'

'Oh no – it doesn't really show much,' Jack assured him. 'Kiki always gets excited on a journey like this. She's awful when I bring her back from school – whistles like the guard, and tells all the people in the carriage to blow their noses and wipe their feet, and screeches in the tunnels till we're almost deafened.'

'But she's a darling really,' said Lucy-Ann loyally, and didn't say a word about Kiki undoing her shoe-laces and pulling them out of her shoes at that very moment!

The journey was a long one. There was a change to be made at a very big and noisy station. The next train was not quite so long as the first one and did not go so fast. It took them to a place on the coast, and the children were delighted to see the blue sea shining like a thin bright line in the distance. Hurrah! They all loved the sea.

'Now I feel that our holiday has really begun,' said Lucy-Ann. 'Now that we've seen the sea, I mean. It gives me a proper holiday feeling.'

Everyone felt the same, even Kiki, who leapt about like a warrior doing a war-dance, on the luggage-rack above the children's heads. She flew down to Jack's shoulder when they got out of the train at a big seaside town.

The strong breeze blew in their faces, and the girls' hair streamed back. Bill's beard blew back too, and Kiki was careful to stand with her beak to the wind. She hated her feathers being ruffled the wrong way.

They had a very good meal in a hotel, and then Bill went down to the harbour to see if his motor-boat was there. It had just come in. The man who brought it knew Bill very well, and had been told in what disguise he was to be seen.

'Morning, Dr Walker, sir,' he said in loud tones. 'Fine weather for your expedition. Everything's ready, sir.'

'Plenty of provisions, Henty?' asked Dr Walker, blinking though his thick glasses.

'Enough to stand a siege, sir,' said Henty. 'I'm to pilot you out, sir – I've got a boat behind.'

Everyone went on board. It was a fine motor-boat, with a little cabin in front. Jack's eyes gleamed when he saw the stock of food – tins, tins, tins! The little refrigerator was full of stuff too. Good! There would be plenty to eat anyway, and that, in Jack's opinion, was one of the main things to be planned for, on a holiday. People always got so terribly hungry when they were holidaying.

Henty piloted them out of the harbour, his tiny boat bobbing about. When they were beyond the harbour Henty saluted and got into his boat.

'Well – good luck, sir,' he said. 'The wireless is O.K., sir – we'll be expecting a message regularly, to know you're all right. There are extra batteries, and a repair set as well. Good luck, sir. I'll be here in two weeks' time to pick up the kids.'

He rowed off, his oars making a soft plash-plash-plash in the water. He soon looked very small indeed, as Bill's motor-boat sped away.

'Well – we're off!' said Bill, with great satisfaction. 'And my beard can come off too – and my glasses, thank goodness. And my coat. Here, Philip, you know how to steer a motor-boat, don't you? Take the wheel whilst I make myself presentable again. No one is likely to see me now. Keep her going north-north-west.'

Proudly Philip took the wheel. The engine of the boat purred smoothly, and they sped fast over the blue water. It was a wonderful day, almost as hot as summer. The May sun shone down out of a sky flecked with tiny curly clouds, and little points of light danced on the waves.

'Gorgeous!' said Jack, sitting down with a grunt of joy near Philip. 'Simply absolutely perfectly gorgeous.'

'I've got such a lovely feeling,' said Lucy-Ann, looking the picture of happiness. 'You know – that feeling you get at the very beginning of a lovely holiday – when all the days spread out before you, sunny and lazy and sort of enchanted.'

'You'll end up by being a poet if you don't look out,' said Philip, from the wheel.

'Well, if a poet feels like I feel just exactly at this moment, I wouldn't mind being one for the rest of my life, even if it meant having to write poetry,' said Lucy-Ann.

'Three blind mice, see how they run,' remarked Kiki, and for one moment everyone thought that Kiki was joining in the talk about poetry, and giving what she thought was an example. But she was merely referring to the three tame rats that had suddenly appeared on Philip's shoulders. They stood there daintily, their pink noses raised, sniffing the salt sea air.

'Oh, blow you, Philip!' said Dinah, from her seat near Jack. 'I was hoping against hope you hadn't brought those detestable little creatures. I only hope the gulls eat them.'

But even Dinah couldn't feel annoyed for long as they glided over the green waves, leaving a white wake behind them, like a long feathery tail. When Bill appeared from the little cabin, they all hailed him in delight.

'Bill! Dear old Bill, you look like yourself again!'

'Oh, Bill – never wear a beard again. It does spoil your beauty.'

'Hurrah! We've lost Dr Walker for ever. Silly fellow, I never liked him.'

'Bill, you look nice again. I can see your mouth when you smile.'

'Pay the bill, pay the bill!'

'Shut up, Kiki, or the gulls will get you!'

'Ah, this is something like,' said Bill happily, taking the wheel from Philip. 'Golly, if we get this weather we'll all be quite sun-burnt in a day or two. Better keep your shirts on, boys, or you'll get blistered.'

Everyone had discarded coats and wraps at once. The breeze was cool, but the sun was really hot. The sea, in the distance, was unbelievevably blue, the colour of corn-flowers, Lucy-Ann thought.

'Now, my friends,' said Bill, his white shirt billowing in the breeze, 'this is a holiday, not a hair-raising adventure. You've had enough of adventures. We've had three together, and this time I want a holiday.'

'Right,' said Jack. 'A holiday it shall be. Adventures keep out!'

'I don't want any adventures either,' said Lucy-Ann. 'I've had plenty. This is adventure enough for me. I like this kind best – not the kind where we have to hide, and creep through secret tunnels and live in caves. I just want a sunny, lazy, windy time with the people I like best. It would be nice if Aunt Allie was here too – but perhaps she wouldn't enjoy it very much.'

'I hope she's feeling better,' said Dinah. 'I say, where's the land? I can't see a bit – not even an island!'

'You'll see plenty tomorrow,' said Bill. 'You can choose one for your own.'

That was a wonderful afternoon and evening. They had a fine tea on board, prepared by the two girls, who found new bread, strawberry jam and a big chocolate cake in the cabin larder.

'Make the most of this,' said Bill. 'You won't get new bread often now. I doubt if we shall find any farmhouses at all, among the lonely islands we shall visit. But I've brought tins and tins of biscuits of all kinds. And as for this chocolate cake, eat it up and enjoy it – I don't think you'll get any more for two weeks.'

'I don't care,' said Dinah, munching away. 'When I'm

hungry I simply don't mind *what* I eat – and I can see I'm always going to be hungry on this holiday.'

The sun went down in a great golden blaze, and the tiny curly clouds turned a brilliant pink. Still the motor-boat went on and on and on, over a sea that blazed pink and gold too.

'The sun has drowned itself in the sea,' said Lucy-Ann at last, as it disappeared. 'I watched the very very last little bit go down into the water.'

'Where are we going to sleep tonight?' asked Jack. 'Not that I mind – but it would be fun to know.'

'There are two tents somewhere in the bow,' said Bill. 'I thought, when we came to an island we liked the look of, we'd land, put up the tents and sleep there for the night. What do you say?'

'Oh *yes*,' said everyone. 'Let's look for an island – a really nice wild one!'

But at the moment there was no land in sight, not even a small rocky island. Bill gave the wheel to Jack, and looked at the chart. He pointed with his finger. 'We've been running in this direction. We should come on these two islands presently. One has a few people on it, and, I believe, a tiny jetty. We'd better go there tonight, and then set off to the unknown tomorrow. It's getting too late to go hunting for islands further away. It would be dark before we got there.'

'It's still very light,' said Philip, looking at his watch. 'At home it would be getting dark.'

'The further north you go, the longer the evening light is,' said Bill. 'Don't ask me why at the moment. I don't feel capable of a lecture just now.'

'You don't *need* to tell us,' said Philip loftily. 'We learnt all about it last term. You see, owing to the sun being . . . '

'Spare me, spare me,' begged Bill, taking the wheel again. 'Look, one of your inquisitive little rats is sniffing at Kiki's tail. There will be murder done in a moment if you don't remove him.'

But Kiki knew better than to hurt any of Philip's pets. She contented herself with cracking her beak so loudly in Squeaker's ear that he ran back to Philip in alarm, scampering up his bare legs and into his shorts in a trice.

Gradually the sea lost its blue, and became grey-green. The breeze felt cold and everyone put on jerseys. Then far away in the distance a dark hump loomed up – land!

'That's it, that's one of the islands we want for tonight,' said Bill, pleased. 'I consider I've done pretty well to head so straight for it. We'll soon be there.'

It certainly was not long before they were nosing alongside a simple stone jetty. A fisherman was there, in a long blue jersey. He was astonished to see them.

Bill explained in a few words. 'Och, so it's bairds ye're after,' said the fisherman. 'Weel, there's plenty for you out yon,' and he nodded towards the sea. 'Where will you be sleeping the night? My bit cottage won't tak' sae mony.'

Lucy-Ann couldn't understand him, but the others gathered what he meant. 'Bring the tents,' ordered Bill. 'We'll soon have them up. We'll ask the fisherman's wife to give us a meal. It will save our own provisions. Maybe we can get some cream too, and good butter.'

By the time that darkness came at last they had all had a good meal, and were bedded down in the two tents, comfortable on ground-sheets and rugs. The fresh air had made them so sleepy that the girls fell asleep without even saying goodnight.

'They're a' daft,' said the fisherman to his wife. 'Wasting a fine boat like yon, looking for bairds. *Bairds*! When there's good fish to be got! Well, they'll soon see bairds in plenty. Och, they're a' dafties!'

8

The island of birds

Next day, after a fine breakfast of porridge and cream, and grilled herrings, the tents were struck and the five went aboard their boat. It was called *Lucky Star*, which the children thought was a very nice name.

Kiki had not been popular with the old fisherman and his wife. They had never seen a parrot before, and they regarded Kiki with suspicion.

'God save the King,' said Kiki, having learnt by experience that most people thought this was a fine thing for her to say. But she spoilt it by adding. 'Pop goes the Queen, pop, pop, pop!'

Now she was aboard with the others, and once again the boat was skimming over the blue water. Once again the sky was blue and the sun was hot. True May weather, that made the sea a clear, translucent blue, and set thousands of little sparkles dancing over the water.

'I've still got that lovely feeling,' said Lucy-Ann happily, as she dangled her hand over the side of the boat and felt the cool, silky water catch hold of her fingers and trail them back. 'Now to find some bird-islands. We really are going to find some today, aren't we, Bill?'

'We certainly are,' said Bill, and gave the boat a little extra speed. Spray came up and fell lightly over everyone.

'Ooooh, lovely!' said Dinah. 'I was so hot. That cooled me beautifully. Let her out again, Bill! I could do with some more of that.'

For five hours they sped over the water, and then Jack gave a shout. 'The islands! Look, you can see little blobs here and there on the horizon! They must be the islands!'

And now the children began to see a great many different

birds on the water and in the air. Jack called out their names exitedly. 'There's a shearwater! Jolly good name for it. And look Philip, that's a razorbill! – and gosh, is that a Little Auk?'

The boys, well versed in the appearance of the wild sea-birds, almost fell overboard in their excitement. Many of the birds seemed to have no fear of the noisy boat at all, but went bobbing on their way, hardly bothering to swerve when it neared them.

'There's a shag diving,' shouted Jack. 'Look! you can see it swimming under water – it's caught a fish. Here it comes. It's clumsy getting out of the water to fly. Gosh, if only I'd got my camera ready!'

Kiki watched the many birds out of baleful eyes. She did not like the interest that Jack suddenly appeared to take in these other birds. When a great gull appeared, flying leisurely right over the boat, Kiki shot up underneath it, gave a fearful screech, and turned a somersault in the air. The gull, startled, rose vertically on its strong wings and let out an alarmed cry.

'EEE-oo-ee-ooooo!'

Kiki imitated it perfectly, and the gull, thinking that Kiki must be some strange kind of relation, circled round. Then it made a pounce at the parrot. But Kiki flipped round, and then dropped to Jack's shoulder.

'Eee-oo!' she called defiantly, and the gull, after a doubtful glance, went on its way, wondering, no doubt, what kind of a gull this was that behaved in such a peculiar manner.

'You're an idiot, Kiki,' said Jack. 'One of these days a gull will eat you for his dinner.'

'Poor old Kiki,' said the parrot, and gave a realistic groan. Bill laughed. 'I can't imagine what Kiki will do when we see the puffins, waddling about among the heather and sea-pinks,' he said. 'I'm afraid she will give them an awful time.'

As they came nearer to the first island, more and more birds were to be seen on and above the water. They glided gracefully on the wind, they dived down for fish, they bobbed along like toy ducks. There was a chorus of different cries, some shrill, some guttural, some mournful and forlorn. They gave the children a wild, exultant kind of feeling.

As they came near to the island the children fell silent. A tall cliff towered in front of them, and it was covered from top to bottom with birds! The children stared in delight.

Birds, birds, birds! On every ledge they stood or squatted, thousands of white gannets, myriads of the browner guillemots, and a mixture of other sea-birds that the boys could hardly make out, though they glued their field-glasses to their eyes for minutes on end.

'What a coming and going!' said Bill, staring with fascinated eyes, too. And it certainly was. Besides the birds that stood on the ledges, there were always others arriving and others leaving. That way and this went the busy birds, with a chorus of excited cries.

'They're not very careful with their eggs,' said Lucy-Ann, in distress, when she looked through Jack's glasses in her turn. The careless birds took off and knocked their precious eggs over the ledge and down the cliff, to be smashed on the rocks below.

'They can lay plenty more,' said Philip. 'Come on, Lucy-Ann – give me back my glasses! Golly, what a wonderful sight! I shall write this all up in my notes tonight.'

The motor-boat nosed carefully round the rocky cliffs. Bill stopped looking at the birds and kept a sharp look-out instead for rocks. Once round the steep cliffs the land sloped downwards, and Bill spotted a place that seemed suitable for the boat.

It was a little sheltered sandy cove. He ran the boat in and it grounded softly. He sprang out with the boys, and made it safe, by running the anchor well up the beach and digging it in.

'Is this going to be our headquarters?' asked Dinah, looking round.

'Oh, *no*,' said Jack at once. 'We want to cruise round a bit, don't we, Bill, and find a puffin island. I'd really like to be in the *midst* of the bird-islands, and be able to go from one to the other as we pleased. But we could stay here for tonight, couldn't we?'

That was a wonderful day for the four children, and for Bill too. With thousands of birds screaming round their heads, but apparently not in the least afraid of them, the children made their way to the steep cliffs they had seen from the other side of the island.

Birds were nesting on the ground, and it was difficult to tread sometimes, without disturbing sitting birds or squashing eggs. Some of the birds made vicious jabs at the children's legs, but nobody was touched. It was just a threatening gesture, nothing more.

Kiki was rather silent. She sat on Jack's shoulder, her head hunched into her neck. So many birds at once seemed to overwhelm her. But Jack knew that she would soon recover, and startle the surrounding birds by telling them to wipe their feet and shut the door.

They reached the top of the cliffs, and were almost deafened by the cries and calls around them. Birds rose and fell in the air, glided and soared, weaving endless patterns in the blue sky.

'It's funny they never bump into one another,' said Lucy-Ann, astonished. 'There's never a single collison. I've been watching.'

'Probably got a traffic policeman,' said Philip solemnly. 'For all you know some of them may have licences under their wings.'

'Don't be silly,' said Lucy-Ann. 'All the same, it *is* clever of them not to collide, when there's so many thousands. What a row! I can hardly hear myself speak.'

They came to the very edge of the cliff. Bill took Lucy-Ann's arm. 'Not too near,' he said. 'The cliffs are almost sheer here.'

They were. When the children lay down on their tummies and looked cautiously over, it gave them a queer feeling to see the sea so very very far below, moving slowly in and out, with only a far-off rumble to mark the breaking of the waves. Lucy-Ann found herself clutching the cushions of sea-pink beside her.

'I somehow feel I'm not safe on the ground,' she said with a laugh. 'I feel as if I've got to hold on. I feel sort of – well, sort of upside-down!'

Bill held on to her tightly after that speech. He knew that she felt giddy, and he wasn't going to risk anything with little Lucy-Ann! He liked all the children very much, but Lucy-Ann was his favourite.

The children watched the birds going and coming endlessly to and from the narrow cliff ledges. It was a marvellous sight. Jack looked through his glasses and chuckled at the squabbling and pushing that was going on, on some of the narrower shelves.

'Just like naughty children,' he said. 'Telling each other to move up and make room, or I'll push you off – and off somebody goes, sure enough. But it doesn't matter, because out go their wings and they have a lovely glide through the air. My word, I wouldn't mind being a sea-bird – able to stride along on the sea-shore, or bob on the sea, or dive for fish, or glide for miles on the strong breeze. I shouldn't mind be—'

'What's that?' said Philip suddenly, hearing a noise that wasn't made by sea-birds. 'Listen! An aeroplane, surely!'

They all listened, straining their eyes through the sun-washed air. And, far away, they saw a speck, steadily moving through the sky, and heard the *r-r-r-r* of an engine.

'A plane! Right off all the routes!' said Bill. 'Well – that's the last thing I expected to see here!'

9

Hurrah for Puffin Island!

Bill seemed so astonished that the children stared at him. Surely it wasn't so surprising to see an aeroplane, even near these desolate bird-islands?

Bill took Jack's glasses and looked through them, but it was too late to make out anything.

'I wonder if it was a seaplane or an ordinary plane,' he said, half to himself. 'How strange.'

'Why is it strange?' asked Dinah. 'Aeroplanes go everywhere now.'

Bill said no more. He handed back the glasses to Jack. 'I think we'd better have a meal, and then put up our tents,' he said. 'What about putting them by that little stream we saw on our way here? About a quarter of a mile from the shore. It wouldn't be too far to carry everything if we all give a hand.'

The tents were set up. The ground-sheets were put down and the rugs tumbled over them. Then, sitting on a slight slope, looking out to the blue sea, the five of them had a glorious meal. 'I always think', began Lucy-Ann, munching a couple of biscuits with butter and cream cheese between them. 'I always think . . . '

'You needn't go on,' said Jack. 'We know what you're going to say and we quite agree with you.'

'You *don't* know what I'm going to say,' said Lucy-Ann indignantly.

'We do,' said Philip. 'You say it every holiday when we have a meal out of doors.'

'You're going to say, "I always think food tastes *much* nicer when it's eaten out of doors," ' said Dinah. 'Aren't you?'

'Well, I was,' said Lucy-Ann. 'Do I really always say it?

Anyway, it's quite true. I *do* think . . . '

'Yes, we know,' said Jack. 'You're an awful repeater, Lucy-Ann. You tell us the same things over and over again. Never mind. We think the same, even if we don't keep on saying it. Kiki, take your fat beak out of the cream cheese!'

'Kiki's awful,' said Dinah. 'She really is. She's pinched three biscuits already. I don't think you give her enough sunflower seeds, Jack.'

'Golly, I like *that*!' said Jack. 'She won't even *look* at sunflower seeds when there's a spread like this. Anyway, Philip, your rats can always eat them. I found Squeaker in my pocket a little while ago, nibbling one of them as fast as he could.'

'I hope it won't make him ill,' said Philip in alarm. 'I say, look! – here comes a gull – tame as anything. It wants a biscuit too, I should think.'

It did. It had watched Kiki pecking at a biscuit and enjoying it, and it didn't see why it shouldn't have a share. Kiki saw the gull out of the corner of her eye and sidled away. The gull made a pounce, got the biscuit and rose into the air, making a loud laughing noise. 'Ee-oo, ee-oo, ee-oo!'

Kiki flew up angrily, calling out all kinds of things to the gull. They were meant to be very rude, but unfortunatley the gull didn't understand. Kiki could not catch the strong-winged bird and flew disconsolately back to the children.

'You can't complain, Kiki,' said Jack. 'You shouldn't have pinched that biscuit out of the tin – and the gull shouldn't have pinched it from you. It's six of one and half a dozen of the other.'

'What a pity, what a pity!' said Kiki, and sidled near the biscuit-tin again.

'That bird is a real clown,' said Bill, shaking the crumbs off his jersey. 'Now, who's coming back to the boat with me to hear the news on the radio? Also I must send out a few messages – especially one for your mother, Philip, who will be sure to want to know if we've got here safely.'

They all wanted to stretch their legs, so they walked back over the soft cushions of the sea-pinks, whose bold little pink heads nodded everywhere in the wind.

They watched Bill as he put up his little radio mast and fiddled about with the set. It was a transmitter as well as a receiver.

'I suppose if you send messages home every night, we shan't need to post letters off to Aunt Allie,' said Lucy-Ann.

Everyone roared. 'And where would you post a letter, pray?' asked Jack. '*I* haven't seen a pillar-box anywhere about. Lucy-Ann, you're an idiot.'

'Yes, I am!' said Lucy-Ann, going red. 'Of course we can't post anything here! How useful that you can send messages, Bill! Then if any of us wanted help, you could get it.'

'Quite so,' said Bill. 'But I hope if you wanted help I could whizz you off in the motor-boat. Anyway I wouldn't have consented to bring you all away into the wilds like this, if I hadn't a transmitter with me, so that I could send messages every night. I send them to headquarters, and they telephone them to your aunt. So she'll follow our travels and adventures each night.'

They watched for a while, and then listened to part of a programme. Then Lucy-Ann yawned and Kiki imitated her. 'Blow! You make me feel sleepy,' said Dinah, rubbing her eyes. 'Look, it's getting dark!'

So back they went to their tents, and were soon cuddled into their rugs. The birds called incessantly from the cliffs and the sea. 'I believe they keep awake all night,' thought Dinah. But they didn't. They slept too when the darkness came at last.

The next day was very warm and close. 'Looks to me like a storm blowing up sooner or later,' said Bill, screwing up his eyes and looking into the bright sky. 'I almost think we'd better try and find our headquarters today, so that we have some shelter if a storm does blow up. This sort of holiday needs fine weather if it's going to be successful – a storm wouldn't be at all pleasant, with only tents to sleep in – we'd be blown to bits.'

'I just want to take a few photographs of these cliffs and the birds on them,' said Jack. 'I'll do that whilst you're getting down the tents, if you don't mind my not helping you.'

So off he went with Kiki towards the steep cliffs. Bill called after him that he was not to try any climbing down the cliffs, and he shouted back that he wouldn't.

Soon everything was packed away again on the motor-boat, which was just being floated by the rising tide, and they waited paitently for Jack. He soon appeared, his glasses and his camera slung round his neck, and his face beaming.

'Got some beauties,' he said. 'Kiki was awfully useful to me. I got her to parade up and down, so that all the birds stayed still in amazement, watching her – and then, click! I got them beautifully. I ought to have some fine pictures.'

'Good!' said Bill, smiling at the enthusiastic boy. 'You'll have to have a book of bird photographs published. "*Masterpieces*, by Jack Trent, price thirty shillings." '

'I'd like that,' said Jack, his face shining. 'Not the thirty shillings I mean – but having a book about birds with my name on it.'

'Come on in,' said Philip impatiently, for Jack was still outside the boat. 'We want to be off. It's so warm I'm longing to get out to sea again, and feel the breeze on my face as the boat swings along.'

They soon felt it and were glad of it. It certainly was very hot for May. The boat went swiftly through the water, bobbing a little as it rode over the waves. Lucy-Ann let her fingers run through the water again – lovely and cool!

'What I should like is a bathe,' said Philip, little drops of perspiration appearing round his nose. 'Can we bathe from the boat, Bill?'

'Wait till we get to another island,' said Bill. 'I don't particularly want to stop out at sea, with a storm in the offing. It's so jolly hot I feel there must be thunder about. I'm anxious to run for shelter before it comes. Now – here are more islands bobbing up out of the sea. Let's see if we can spot a puffin island. That's what you want, isn't it?'

Lucy-Ann, still dangling her hand in the water, suddenly felt something gently touching it. In surprise she looked down, withdrawing her hand at once, afraid of a jellyfish.

To her astonishment she saw that it was a piece of orange peel, bobbing away on the waves. She called to Bill.

'Bill, look – there's a bit of orange peel. Now whoever in the world eats oranges in these wild little islands? Do you suppose there are any other bird-lovers somewhere about?'

Everyone looked at the tiny bit of orange peel bobbing rapidly away. It did seem very much out of place there. Bill stared at it hard. He was puzzled. The fishermen, if there were any on the islands they were coming to, would not be at all likely to have oranges. And naturalists surely would not bother to load themselves up with them.

Then how did that bit of peel come to be there? No ships went anywhere near where they were. It was a wild and lonely part of the sea, where sudden storms blew up, and great gales made enormous waves.

'Beats me!' said Bill at last. 'I shall expect to see a pineapple or something next! Now look! – here is an island – fairly flattish – probably has puffins on it all right. Shall we make for it?'

'No – cruise round a bit,' begged Jack. 'Let's have a look at a few of the islands here. There is quite a colony of them round about.'

They cruised round, looking at first this island and then that. They came to one that had steep cliffs at the east side, then ran down into a kind of valley, then up again into cliffs.

Jack put his glasses to his eyes and yelled out excitedly. 'Puffins! Plenty of them! Can you see them, Philip? I bet the island is full of their burrows. Let's land here, Bill. There'll be masses of birds on the cliffs, and hundreds of puffins inland. It's quite a big island. We could probably find good shelter here and water too. The cliffs would protect us from both the east and west. What ho, for Puffin Island!'

'Right,' said Bill. He looked all round and about, and guided the boat towards the island. There were many other islands not far off, but as far as he could see they were inhabited only by birds. The sea chopped about between the islands, making little rippling waves.

Round Puffin Island went the boat, and Philip gave a shout. 'Here's a fine place to put the boat in, Bill – see, where that channel of water goes into a cleft of the cliff! It'll be deep there, and we can just tie the boat up to a rock. We'll put out the fenders, so that she doesn't bump against the rock sides.'

The boat nosed into the channel. As Philip said, the water was deep there – it was a natural little harbour. There was a ledge of rock on which they could land. Could anything be better? Hurrah for Puffin Island!

10

A little exploring

'Isn't this a gorgeous place?' said Jack, as the boat glided gently into the little channel. There was just room for it. 'It might be a boat-house made specially for the *Lucky Star*.'

Bill leapt out on to the rocky ledge, which did very well for a landing-stage. Sheer above them on each side rose rocky cliffs. Rows and rows of birds sat on the ledges, and there was a continual dropping of eggs, knocked off by the careless birds. One broke near Bill, and splashed its yellow yolk over his foot.

'Good shot!' he yelled up to the circling birds, and the children roared.

They made the boat fast by tying the mooring-rope round a convenient rock. The boat bobbed up and down gently as waves ran up the little channel and back.

'Tide's up now,' said Bill. 'When it goes down there will still be plenty of water in this channel. The boat will look much lower down then. Now – is there a way up the cliff from here? We don't want to have to walk down the ledge and clamber round the cliffs over hundreds of rocks before we get on to the island proper.'

They looked round. Jack ran up the rocky ledge, and then turned and gave a shout. 'Hi! We can get up here, I think. There are rocky shelves, like rough steps, going up the cliff – and there's a break in it a bit above. We could probably clamber out all right, and find ourselves right on the island.'

'Well, you four go and explore,' said Bill. 'I'd better stay with the boat and see that she doesn't get her sides smashed in against these rocks. You look round the island and see if you can spot a sheltered cove somewhere, that I can take the boat round to.'

The children left the boat and followed Jack. Kiki flew on ahead, calling like a gull. Up the rocky ledges went Jack. They were almost like giant steps, roughly hewn by the great wintry seas for century after century.

As Jack said, the cliff had a deep cleft in it just there, and the children found that they could make their way through it, and come out on to the cushions of sea-pinks beyond. It needed a bit of clambering, and they were out of breath when they reached the top – but it was worth it.

The sea spread bright blue all round the island. The sky looked enormous. Other islands, blue in the distance, loomed up everywhere. A real colony of them, it seemed – and their island was in the centre.

Then Jack gave such a yell that everyone jumped. 'Puffins! Look! Hundreds and hundreds of them!'

The children looked to where Jack pointed, and there, among the sea-pinks and the old heather tufts, were the most curious-looking birds they had ever seen.

They were dressed in black and white. Their legs were orange – but it was their extraordinary bills that held the children's attention.

'Look at their beaks!' cried Dinah, laughing. 'Blue at the base – and then striped red and yellow!'

'But what *enormous* beaks!' cried Lucy-Ann. 'They remind me a bit of Kiki's.'

'Puffins are called sea parrots,' remarked Jack, amused to see the crowd of solemn-looking puffins.

'Their eyes are so comical,' said Philip. 'They stare at us with such a fixed expression! And look at the way they walk – so upright!'

The colony of puffins was as good as a pantomine to watch. There were hundreds, thousands of birds there. Some stood about, watching, their crimson-ringed eyes fixed seriously on their neighbours. Others walked about, rolling from side to side like a sailor. Some took off like small aeroplanes, eager to get to the sea.

'Look! – what's that one doing?' asked Lucy-Ann, as a puffin began to scrape vigorously at the soil, sending a shower of it backwards.

'It's digging a burrow, I should think,' said Dinah. 'They nest underground, don't they, Jack?'

'Rather! I bet this island is almost undermined with their holes and burrows,' said Jack, walking forward towards the colony of busy birds. 'Come on – do let's get near to them. Kiki, keep on my shoulder. I won't have you screaming like a railway engine at them, and scaring them all away.'

Kiki was most interested in the comical puffins. She imitated their call exactly. 'Arrrrr!' they said, in deep guttural voices. 'Arrrrrrrr!'

'Arrrrrr!' answered Kiki at once, and various birds looked up at her enquiringly.

To the children's huge delight the puffins were not in the least afraid of them. They did not even walk away when the children went near. They allowed them to walk among them, and although one aimed a peck at Philip's leg when he stumbled and almost fell on top of it, not one of the others attempted to jab with their great beaks.

'This is lovely!' said Lucy-Ann, standing and gazing at the extraordinary birds. 'Simply lovely! I never thought birds could be so tame.'

'They're not exactly tame,' said Jack. 'They're wild, but they are so little used to human beings that they have no fear of us at all.'

The puffins were all among the cushions of bright sea-pinks. As the children walked along, their feet sometimes sank right down through the soil. The burrows were just below, and their weight caused the earth to give way.

'It's absolutely mined with their burrows,' said Philip. 'And I say – it's not a very nice smell just about here is it?'

It certainly wasn't. They soon got used to it, but they didn't like it. 'Pooh!' said Lucy-Ann, wrinkling up her nose. 'It's getting worse and worse. I vote we don't put our tents up too near this colony of puffins – it's as bad as being near a pig-sty.'

'I don't mind it,' said Jack. 'Hey, come here, Kiki!'

But Kiki had flown down to make friends. The puffins gazed at her fixedly and solemnly.

'Arrrrr!' said Kiki politely. ARRRRRRR! God save the Queen!'

'Arrrrr!' replied a puffin, and walked up to Kiki, rolling from side to side like a small sailor. The two looked at one another.

'I shall expect Kiki to say how-do-you-do in a minute,' said Dinah, with a little squeal of laughter. 'They both look so polite.'

'Polly put the kettle on,' said Kiki.

'Arrrrr!' said the puffin, and waddled off to its hole. Kiki followed – but apparently there was another puffin down the hole, who did not want Kiki's company, for there was soon an agonised squeal from the parrot, who shot out of the hole much more rapidly than she had gone in.

She flew up to Jack's shoulder. 'Poor Kiki, what a pity, what a pity, what a pity!'

'Well, you shouldn't poke your nose in everywhere,' said Jack, and took a step forward. He trod on a tuft of sea-pinks, which immediately gave way, and he found his leg going down into quite a deep burrow. Whoever lived in it didn't like his leg at all, and gave a vicious nip.

'Ooooch!' said Jack, sitting down suddenly and rubbing his leg. 'Look at that – nearly had a bit right out of my calf!'

They went on through the amazing puffin colony. There were puffins on the ground, in the air – and on the sea too! 'Arrrrr! Arrrrr! Arrrrr!' their deep calls sounded everywhere.

'I'll be able to take some magnificent photographs,' said Jack happily. 'It's a pity it's too early for young ones to be about. I don't expect there are many puffin eggs yet either.'

The puffins were living mainly in the green valley between the two high cliffs. Philip looked about to see if there was any good place to pitch their tents.

'I suppose we all want to make Puffin Island our headquarters?' he said. 'I imagine that nothing will drag Jack away from here now. He's got cliffs where guillemots and gannets nest, and a valley where the puffins live – so I suppose he's happy.'

'Oh *yes*,' said Jack. 'We'll stay here. This shall be *our* island – we'll share it with the puffins.'

'Well, we'll find a good place for our tents,' said Philip. 'Then we'll bring our goods and chattels here and camp. We'd better find a place where there's a stream, though . . . if there *is* one on this island. We shall want water to drink. And let's look for a cover where we can put the boat. We can't very well leave it in that narrow channel.'

'Look – there's a dear little cove down there!' said Dinah suddenly, pointing to the sea. 'We could bathe there – and the boat would be quite all right there too. Let's go and tell Bill.'

'I'll go,' said Philip. 'Jack wants to stare at the puffins a bit more, I can see. I'll take the boat round to the cove with Bill, and you two girls can find a good place for our tents. Then we'll all help to bring the things there from the boat.'

He ran off quickly to find Bill and tell him where to put the boat. Jack sat down with Kiki to watch the puffins. The girls went to look for a good place to put up their tents for the night.

They wandered over the island. Beyond the puffin colony, just at the end of it, before they came to the high cliffs at the other side of the island, was a little dell. A few stunted birch-trees grew there, and banks of heather.

'This is just the place,' said Dinah, pleased. 'We can put up our tents here, be sheltered from the worst of the wind, watch the puffins, go down to bathe when we want to, and when we're tired of that, go cruising round the other islands.'

'A very nice life,' said Lucy-Ann, with a laugh. 'Now – is there any water about?'

There was no stream at all on the island – but Dinah found something that would do equally well. At least, she hoped it would.

'Look here!' she called to Lucy-Ann. 'Here's an enormous rock with a hollow in its middle, filled with water. I've tasted it and it isn't salt.'

Lucy-Ann came up, followed by Jack. Dinah dipped in her hand, scooped up a palmful of water and drank. It was as sweet and as pure as could be.

'Rain-water,' said Dinah pleased. 'Now we'll be all right – so long as it doesn't dry up in this hot weather. Come on – let's go back to the boat and collect all the things we want. We'll have to do a bit of hard work now.'

'We'll wait here a bit,' said Jack, coming up with Kiki. 'I expect Bill and Philip will be bringing the boat round to the cove over there – then we'll go and tell them we've found a good place, and help to bring the things here.'

It was not long before Bill and Philip ran into the cove with the boat. Bill leapt out, took the anchor well up the beach and dug it in. He saw Jack and the girls and waved to them.

'Just coming!' he cried. 'Have you found a good place for the tents?'

He and Philip soon joined the others, and were pleased with the little dell. 'Just right!' said Bill. 'Well, we'll bring all the things we want from the boat straight away now.'

So they spent quite a time going to and from the cove, laden with goods. It did not take quite as long as they feared because there were five of them to do it, and even Kiki gave a hand – or rather a beak – and carried a tent-peg. She did it really to impress the watching puffins, who stared at her seriously as she flew by, the peg in her big curved beak.

'Arrrrrr!' she called, in a puffin voice.

'You're showing off, Kiki,' said Jack severely. 'You're a conceited bird.'

'Arrrrr!' said Kiki, and dropped the tent-peg on Jack's head.

It was fun arranging their new home. The boys and Bill were to have one tent. The girls were to have the other. Behind the tents Lucy-Ann found a ledge of rock and below it was a very large dry space.

'Just the spot for storing everything in,' said Lucy-Ann proudly. 'Jack, bring the tins here – and the extra clothes – there's room for heaps of things. Oh, we *are* going to have a lovely time here!'

11

Huffin and Puffin

'Isn't it time we had a meal?' complained Jack, staggering over with a great pile of things in his arms. 'It makes my mouth water to read "Spam" and "Best Tinned Peaches" and see that milk chocolate.'

Bill looked at his watch and then at the sun. 'My word – it certainly is time! The sun is setting already! How the time has flown!'

It wasn't long before they were all sitting peacefully on tufts of sea-pink and heather, munching biscuits and potted meat, and looking forward to a plate of tinned peaches each. Bill had brought bottles of ginger-beer from the boat, and these were voted better than boiling a kettle to make tea or cocoa. It was very warm indeed.

'I feel so happy,' said Lucy-Ann, looking over the island to the deep-blue sea beyond. 'I feel so very very far away from everywhere – honestly I hardly believe there is such a thing as school, just at this very minute. And this potted meat tastes heavenly.'

Philip's white rats also thought it did. They came out from his clothes at once when they smelt the food. One sat daintily upright on his knee, nibbling. Another took his tit-bit into a dark pocket. The third perched on Philip's shoulder.

'You tickle the lobe of my ear,' said Philip. Dinah moved as far from him as she could, but, like Lucy-Ann, she was too happy to find fault with anything just then.

They all ate hungrily, Bill too, their eyes fixed on the setting sun and the gold-splashed sea, which was now losing its blue, and taking on sunset colours. Lucy-Ann glanced at Bill.

'Do you like disappearing, Bill?' she asked. 'Don't you think it's fun?'

'Well – for a fortnight, yes,' said Bill, 'but I'm not looking forward to living in these wild islands all alone, once you've gone. It's not my idea of fun. I'd rather live dangerously than like one of these puffins here.'

'Poor Bill,' said Dinah, thinking of him left by himself, with only books to read, and the radio, and nobody to talk to.

'I'll leave you my rats, if you like,' offered Philip generously.

'No, thanks,' said Bill promptly. 'I know your rats! They'd have umpteen babies, and by the time I left this would be Rat Island, not Puffin Island. Besides, I'm not so much in love with the rat-and-mouse tribe as you are.'

'Oh, look, do look!' suddenly said Dinah. Everyone looked. A puffin had left its nearby burrow and was walking solemnly towards them, rolling a little from side to side, as all the puffins did when they walked. 'It's come for its supper!'

'Then sing, puffin, sing!' commanded Jack. 'Sing for your supper!'

'Arrrrrrr!' said the puffin deeply. Everyone laughed. The puffin advanced right up to Philip. It stood close against the boy's knee and looked at him fixedly.

'Philip's spell is working again,' said Lucy-Ann enviously. 'Philip, what makes all animals and birds want you to be friends with them? Just look at that puffin – it's going all goofy over you.'

'Don't know,' said Philip, pleased with his odd new friend. He stroked the bird's head softly, and the puffin gave a little *arrrrr* of pleasure. Then Philip gave it a bit of potted-meat sandwich and the bird tossed it off at once and turned for more.

'Now I suppose you'll be followed round by a devoted puffin,' said Dinah. 'Well, a puffin is better than three rats, any day – or mice – or that awful hedgehog with fleas that you had – or that pair of stag-beetles – or . . . '

'Spare us, Dinah, spare us,' begged Bill. 'We all know that Philip is a walking zoo. Personally, if he likes a goofy puffin, he can have it. I don't mind a bit. It's a pity we haven't brought a collar and lead.'

The puffin said 'Arrrr' again, a little more loudly, and then walked off, perfectly upright, its brilliant beak gleaming in the setting sun.

'Well, you didn't pay us a very long visit, old thing,' said Philip, quite disappointed. The puffin disappeared into its burrow – but reappeared again almost immediately with another puffin, a little smaller, but with an even more brilliant beak.

'Darby and Joan!' said Jack. The two birds waddled side by side to Philip. The children looked at them in delighted amusement.

'What shall we call them?' said Dinah. 'If they are going to join our little company, they'll have to have names. Funny little puffins!'

'Huffin and puffin, huffin and puffin,' remarked Kiki, remembering the words suddenly. 'Huffin and . . . '

'Yes, of course – Huffin and Puffin!' cried Lucy-Ann in delight. 'Clever old bird, Kiki! You've been talking about Huffin and Puffin ever since we started out on our holiday – and here they are, Huffin and Puffin, as large as life!'

Everyone laughed. Huffin and Puffin did seem to be perfectly lovely names for the two birds. They came close to Philip, and, to the boy's amusement, squatted down by him contentedly.

Kiki was not too pleased. She eyed them with her head on one side. They stared back at her with their crimson-ringed eyes. Kiki looked away and yawned.

'They've out-stared Kiki!' said Jack. 'It takes a lot to do that!'

The three rats had prudently decided that it was best to keep as far away from Huffin and Puffin as possible. They sat round Philip's neck, gazing down at the two birds. Then, at a movement from Huffin, they shot down the boy's shirt.

Bill stretched himself. 'Well, I don't know about you kids – but I'm tired,' he said. 'The sun is already dipping itself into the west. Let's clear up, and turn in. We'll have a lovely day tomorrow, bathing and sunning ourselves, and watching the birds. I'm getting used to their eternal chorus of cries now. At first I was almost deafened.'

The girls cleared up. Lucy-Ann dipped a bowl into the clear pool of water and handed it round for washing in. 'We oughtn't to wash in that pool, ought we, Bill?' she said seriously.

'Good gracious, no!' said Bill. 'It would be absolutely black after the boys had gone in! We'll keep it for drinking-water only, or just take our water from it when we want it for boiling or washing.'

'I think I'll go and have a dip now,' said Jack, getting up. 'No, not in the rock-pool, Lucy-Ann, so don't look so upset – I'll go down to the little cove where the boat is. Coming, Philip?'

'Right,' said Philip, and pushed Huffin and Puffin away from his knees. 'Move up, you! I'm not growing here!'

'I'll come too,' said Bill, and knocked out the pipe he had been smoking. 'I feel dirty. You girls want to come?'

'No,' said Lucy-Ann. 'I'll get the rugs and things ready for you in the tents.'

Dinah didn't want to go either, for she felt very tired. Measles had certainly taken some of the energy out of the two girls. They stayed behind whilst the others set off to the cove to bathe. The valley sloped right down to the sea just there, and the small sandy cove was just right for bathing. The boys and Bill threw off their things and plunged into the sea. It felt lovely and warm, and rippled over their limbs like silk.

'Lovely!' said Bill, and began to chase the boys. With howls and yells and splashings they eluded him, making such a terrific noise that Huffin and Puffin, who had solemnly accompanied Philip all the way, half walking and half flying, retreated a little way up the beach. They stared at the boys fixedly and thoughtfully. Philip saw them and was pleased. Surely nobody had ever had two puffins for pets before!

The girls were setting out ground-sheets and rugs neatly in the two tents when Dinah suddenly stopped and listened. Lucy-Ann listened too.

'What is it?' she whispered – and then she heard the noise herself. An aeroplane again, surely!

The girls went out of the tent and looked all over the sky, trying to locate the sound. 'There! – there, look!' cried Lucy-Ann excitedly, and she pointed westwards. 'Can't you see it? Oh, Dinah – what's it doing?'

Dinah couldn't spot the plane. She tried and tried but she could not see the point in the sky where the aeroplane flew.

'Something's falling out of it,' said Lucy-Ann, straining her eyes. 'Oh, where are the boys' field-glasses? Quick, get them, Dinah!'

Dinah couldn't find them. Lucy-Ann stood watching the sky, her eyes screwed up.

'Something dropped slowly from it,' she said. 'Something white. I saw it. Whatever could it have been? I hope the aeroplane wasn't in any trouble.'

'Bill will know,' said Dinah. 'I expect he and the boys saw it all right. Maybe they took the glasses with them. I couldn't find them anywhere.'

Soon there was no more to be seen or heard of the plane, and the girls went on with their work. The tents looked very comfortable with the piles of rugs. It was such a hot night that Dinah fastened the tent-flaps right back, in order to get some air.

'That storm doesn't seem to have come,' she said, looking at the western sky to see if any big clouds were sweeping up. 'But it feels very thundery.'

'Here are the others,' said Lucy-Ann, as she saw Jack, Philip and Bill coming up from the shore. 'And Huffin and Puffin are still with them! Oh, Di – won't it be fun if we have two pet puffins!'

'I wouldn't mind *puffins*,' said Dinah. 'But I can't bear those rats. Hallo, Bill! Did you hear the aeroplane?'

'Good gracious, no! Was there one?' demanded Bill, with great interest. 'Where? How was it we didn't hear it?'

'We were making such a row,' said Jack, grinning. 'We shouldn't have heard a hundred aeroplanes.'

'It was funny,' said Lucy-Ann to Bill. 'I was watching the aeroplane when I saw something falling out of it. Something white.'

Bill stared, frowning intently. 'A parachute?' he said. 'Could you see?'

'No. It was too far away,' said Lucy-Ann. 'It might have been a parachute – or a puff of smoke – I don't know. But it did look as if something was falling slowly from the plane. Why do you look so serious, Bill?'

'Because – I've a feeling there's something – well, just a bit strange about these planes,' said Bill. 'I think I'll pop down to the motor-boat and send a message through on the radio. Maybe it's nothing at all – but it just *might* be important!'

12

Bill goes off on his own

Bill went off down the valley to the cove where the motor-boat was moored. His feet sank deeply into the soft earth. The children stared after him.

Lucy looked solemn – as solemn as Huffin and Puffin, who were leaning against Philip, standing upright, their big beaks looking heavy and clumsy.

'Oh dear – what does Bill mean? Surely we're not going to tumble into an adventure again! Up here, where there's nothing but the sea, the wind and the birds! What *could* happen, I wonder?'

'Well, Bill isn't likely to tell us much,' said Philip. 'So don't bother him with questions. I'm going to turn in. Brrrrr! It's getting a bit cold now. Me for that big pile of rugs! Huffin and Puffin, you'd better keep outside for the night. There'll be little enough room in this tent for you, as well as us three, Kiki and the rats.'

Huffin and Puffin looked at one another. Then, with one accord, they began to scrape the earth just outside the tent, sending the soil up behind them. Lucy-Ann giggled.

'They're going to make a burrow as near you as possible, Philip. Oh, aren't they funny?'

Kiki walked round to examine what the two puffins were doing. She got a shower of earth all over her and was very indignant.

'Arrrrrrr!' she growled, and the two puffins agreed politely. 'Arrrrrrr!'

Bill came back in about half an hour. All the children were cuddled up in their rugs, and Lucy-Ann was asleep. Dinah called out to him.

'Everything all right, Bill?'

'Yes. I got a message from London, to tell me that your mother is getting on as well as can be expected,' said Bill. 'But she's got measles pretty badly, apparently. Good thing you're all off her hands!'

'What about your own message, Bill – about the aeroplane?' said Dinah, who was very curious over Bill's great interest in it. 'Did that get through?'

'Yes,' said Bill shortly. 'It did. It's nothing to worry your head about. Good night, Dinah.'

In two minutes' time everyone was asleep. Squeaker and his relations were only to be seen as bumps about Philip's person. Kiki was sitting on Jack's tummy, though he had already pushed her off several times. Huffin and Puffin were squatting in their new-made tunnel, their big coloured beaks touching. Everything was very peaceful as the moon slid across the sky, making a silvery path on the restless waters.

The morning dawned bright and beautiful, and it seemed

as if the storm was not coming, for there was no longer any closeness in the air. Instead it was fresh and invigorating. The children ran down to the shore to bathe as soon as they got up. They ran so fast that Huffin and Puffin could not keep up, but had to fly. They went into the water with the children, and bobbed up and down, looking quite ridiculous.

Then they dived for fish, swimming with their wings under the water. They were very quick indeed, and soon came up with fish in their enormous beaks.

'What about giving us one for breakfast, Huffin?' called Philip, and tried to take a fish from the nearest puffin's beak. But it held on to it – and then swallowed it whole.

'You ought to teach them to catch fish for us,' said Jack, giggling. 'We could have grilled fish for breakfast then! Hey, get away, Puffin – that's my foot, not a fish!'

At breakfast they discussed their plans for the day. 'What shall we do? Let's explore the whole island, and give bits of it proper names. This glen, where we are now, is Sleepy Hollow, because it's where we sleep,' said Lucy-Ann.

'And the shore where we bathe is Splash Cove,' said Dinah. 'And where we first moored our motor-boat is Hidden Harbour.'

Bill had been rather silent at breakfast. Jack turned to him. 'Bill! What do *you* want to do? Will you come and explore the island with us?'

'Well,' said Bill, very surprisingly, 'if you don't mind, as you'll be very busy and happy on your own, I'll take the motor-boat and go cruising about a bit – round all these islands, you know.'

'What! Without *us*?' said Dinah in astonishment. 'We'll come with you, then, if you want to do that.'

'I'm going alone, this first time,' said Bill. 'Take you another time, old thing. But today I'll go alone.'

'Is there – is there anything up?' asked Jack, feeling that something wasn't quite right. 'Has something happened, Bill?'

'Not that I know of,' said Bill cheerfully. 'I just want to go off on my own a bit, that's all. And if I do a bit of exploring round on my own account, I shall know the best places to take you to, shan't I?'

'All right, Bill,' said Jack, still puzzled. 'You do what you want. It's your holiday too, even if it *is* a disappearing one!'

So Bill went off on his own that day, and the children heard the purr of the motor-boat as it went out to sea, and then set off apparently to explore all the islands round about.

'Bill's up to something,' said Philip. 'And I bet it's to do with those aeroplanes. I wish he'd tell us. But he never will talk.'

'I hope he comes back safely,' said Lucy-Ann anxiously. 'It would be awful to be stranded here on a bird-island, and nobody knowing where we were.'

'Gosh, so it would,' said Jack. 'I never thought of that. Cheer up, Lucy-Ann – Bill isn't likely to run into danger. He's got his head screwed on all right.'

The day passed happily. The children went to the cliffs and watched the great companies of sea-birds there. They sat down in the midst of the puffin colony and watched the colourful, big-beaked birds going about their daily business. Lucy-Ann wore a hanky tied round her nose. She couldn't bear the smell of the colony, but the others soon got used to the heavy sourness of the air, and anyway, the wind blew strongly.

Huffin and Puffin did not leave them. They walked or ran with the children. They flew round them, and they went to bathe with them. Kiki was half jealous, but having had one hard jab from Huffin's multi-coloured beak, she kept at a safe distance, and contented herself with making rude remarks.

'Blow your nose! How many times have I told you to wipe your feet? You bad boy! Huffin and puffin all the time. Pop goes huffin!'

The children sat in Sleepy Hollow after their tea and

watched for Bill to come back. The sun began to set. Lucy-Ann looked pale and worried. Where was Bill?

'He'll be along soon, don't worry,' said Philip. 'We'll hear his boat presently.'

But the sun went right down into the sea, and still there was no Bill. The darkness closed down on the island, and there was no longer any point in sitting up and waiting. It was four anxious children who went into their tents and lay down to sleep. But none of them could sleep a wink.

In the end the girls went into the boys' tent and sat there, talking. Then suddenly they heard a welcome sound – *rr-rr-rr-rr-rr!* They all leapt up at once and rushed from the tent.

'That's Bill! It must be! Where's a torch? Come on down to the cove.'

They stumbled through the puffin colony, waking up many a furious bird. They got to the beach just as Bill came walking up. They flung themselves on him in delight.

'Bill! Dear Bill! What happened to you? We honestly thought you'd got lost!'

'Oh, Bill – we shan't let you go off alone again!'

'Sorry to have worried you so,' said Bill. 'But I didn't want to return in the daylight in case I was spotted by an aeroplane. I had to wait till it was dark, though I knew you'd be worried. Still – here I am.'

'But, Bill – aren't you going to tell us anything?' cried Dinah. 'Why didn't you want to come back in daylight? Who would see you? And why would it matter?'

'Well,' said Bill slowly, 'there's something peculiar going on up here in these lonely waters. I don't know quite what. I'd like to find out. I didn't see a soul today, anywhere, though I nosed round umpteen islands. Not that I really expected to, because nobody would be fool enough to come up here for something secret, and let anything of it be seen. Still, I thought I might find some sign.'

'I suppose that bit of orange peel was a sign that some-one's here besides ourselves, on some other island?' said Lucy-Ann, remembering the piece that had bobbed against her fingers. 'But what are they doing? Surely they can't do much in this desolate stretch of waters – with nothing but islands of birds around.'

'That's what I'm puzzled about,' said Bill. 'Can't be smuggling, because the coasts of the mainland are very well patrolled at the moment, and nothing could get through. Then what is it?'

'Bill, you're sure nobody saw you?' asked Dinah, anxiously. 'There might be hidden watchers on one of the islands, you know – and one might see you, without you seeing him.'

'That's true,' said Bill, 'but I had to risk that. It's not very likely, though. The risk of anyone coming to these islands and disturbing whatever secret game is going on, is very remote, and I don't think there would be sentinels posted anywhere.'

'Still – you *might* have been seen – or heard,' persisted Dinah. 'Oh, Bill – and you were supposed to be disappearing completely! Now perhaps your enemies have spotted you!'

'They would hardly be the same enemies that I've disappeared from,' said Bill with a laugh. 'I don't think anyone else would recognize me here, seen at a distance in a motor-boat. In any case they would just think I was a bird-man or a naturalist of some kind, who likes the solitude of these seas.'

They were soon back in their tents again, happy to have Bill with them in safety. The stars shone down from a clear sky. Huffin and Puffin shuffled down their burrow, glad that their new family had gone to rest. They did not approve of these night walks.

Lucy-Ann lay and worried. 'I can *feel* an adventure coming. It's on the way. Oh dear – and I did think this would be the very very last place for one.'

Lucy-Ann was quite right. An adventure *was* on the way – and had very nearly arrived.

13

What happened in the night?

The next morning everything seemed all right. The children had forgotten their fears of the night before, and Bill joked and laughed as merrily as the others.

But all the same he was worried – and when an aeroplane appeared and flew two or three times over the islands, he made the children lie down flat, in the middle of the puffin colony, where they happened to be at that moment.

'I don't think our tents can be seen,' he said. 'I hope not, anyway.'

'Don't want anyone to know we're here, Bill?' asked Jack.

'No,' said Bill shortly. 'Not at present, anyway. If you hear a plane, bob down. And we won't light a fire to boil a kettle. We'll have ginger-beer or lemonade instead.'

The day passed happily enough. It was very hot again and the children went to bathe half a dozen times, lying in the sun to dry afterwards. Kiki was jealous of Huffin and Puffin because they could go into the water with the children. She stood on the sandy beach, her toes sinking in, shouting loudly.

'Polly's got a cold, send for the doctor! A-tish-*ooooo!*'

'Isn't she an idiot?' said Jack, and splashed her. She was most annoyed and walked a bit farther back. 'Poor Kiki! What a pity! Poor pity, what a Kiki!'

'Yes, what a Kiki!' shouted Jack, and dived under the water to catch Bill's legs.

They took a good many photographs, and Huffin and Puffin posed beautifully, staring straight at the camera in a most solemn manner.

'I almost feel they'll suddenly put their arms round one another,' said Jack, as he clicked the camera. 'Thank you,'

Huffin and Puffin. Very nice indeed! But I wish you'd smile next time. Kiki, get out of the way – and leave that tent peg alone. You've already pulled up three.'

That night the sky was full of clouds and the sun could not be seen. 'Looks as if that storm might be coming soon,' said Bill. 'I wonder if our tents will be all right.'

'Well, there's nowhere else to go,' said Jack. 'Sleepy Hollow is about the most sheltered place on this island. And, as far as I've seen, there are no caves or anything of that sort.'

'Perhaps the storm will blow over,' said Philip. 'Phew, it's hot! I really think I must have one last bathe.'

'You've had eight already today,' said Dinah. 'I counted.'

Darkness came earlier that night, because of the clouds. The children got into their rugs, yawning.

'I think,' said Bill, looking at the luminous face of his wrist-watch. 'I think I'll slip along to the boat and send a message or two on my transmitter. I might get some news too, for myself. You go to sleep. I shan't be long.'

'Right,' said the boys, sleepily. Bill slipped out of the tent. The girls were already asleep and did not hear him go. Philip fell asleep almost before Bill was out of the tent. Jack lay awake a few minutes longer, and pushed Kiki off his middle for the fifth time.

She went and stood on Philip's middle, and waited for a lump to come near her feet, which she knew would be one of the tame rats. When one did venture near, raising a little mound under the rug, Kiki gave a sharp jab at it. Philip awoke with a yell.

'You beast, Kiki! Jack, take her away! She's given me an awful peck in my middle. If I could see her I'd smack her on the beak.'

Kiki retired outside the tent till the boys were asleep again. She flew to the top of it, and perched there, wide awake.

Meanwhile Bill was in the cabin of the boat tuning in on

the radio. But because of the coming storm it was difficult to hear anything but atmospherics.

'Blow!' said Bill at last. 'I shan't get my messages through at this rate. I've a good mind to take the boat to the little channel – what is it the children call it? – Hidden Harbour. Maybe I could get the radio going better there – it's so sheltered.'

It was very important to Bill to be able to use the radio that night. He set the engine of the boat going, and was soon on his way to Hidden Harbour. He nosed in carefully and moored the boat.

Then he set to work on his radio again. After a while he thought he heard some noise out to sea – a noise getting nearer and nearer. Bill turned off his radio and listened, but the wind was getting up, and he heard nothing but that.

He tuned the knobs again, listening intently for any message. He had got one through, and now he had been told to stand by and wait for an important announcement from headquarters.

The radio fizzed and groaned and whistled. Bill waited patiently. Then, suddenly hearing a sound, he looked up, startled, half expecting to see one of the boys coming down into the cabin.

But it wasn't. It was a hard-faced man with a curious crooked nose who was staring down at him. As Bill turned and showed his face, the man uttered a cry of the utmost astonishment.

'*You*! What are *you* doing here? What do you know of . . .'

Bill leapt up – but at the same moment the man lunged out at him with a thick, fat, knobbly stick he held in his hand – and poor Bill went down like a ninepin. He struck his head against the edge of the radio, and slid to the floor, his eyes closed.

The man with the crooked nose whistled loudly. Another man came to the small cabin and looked in.

'See that?' said the first man, pointing to Bill. 'Bit of a surprise, eh, to find *him* up here? Do you suppose he guessed anything?'

'Must have, if he's here,' said the second man, who had a short thick beard hiding a very cruel mouth. 'Tie him up. He'll be useful. We'll make him talk.'

Bill was tied up like a trussed chicken. He did not open his eyes. The men carried him out, and took him into a small boat, moored beside the *Lucky Star*. It was a rowing-boat. Into it went poor Bill, and the men undid their rope, ready to row back to their own motor-boat, which lay, perfectly silent, a little way beyond the island.

'Do you suppose there's anyone else with him?' asked the man with the crooked nose. 'There was no-one on board but him.'

'No. When his boat was sighted yesterday, we only saw one man aboard – and it was him all right,' said the man with the beard. 'If there'd been anyone else we'd have seen them. He's all alone. Ho! He didn't know he was being watched all the way back here last night.'

'I suppose there really *isn't* anyone else here,' said the first man, who seemed very reluctant to go. 'Hadn't we better smash up the boat – just in case?'

'All right – and the radio too,' said the man with the beard. He found a hammer and soon there were crashing sounds as the engine of the motor-boat was damaged and the beautiful little radio was smashed to bits.

Then the men set off in their rowing boat with the unconscious Bill. They reached their motor-boat, and soon the purring of its engine getting fainter and fainter, sounded in the night. But nobody on Puffin Island heard it except Kiki and the sea-birds.

The children had no idea at all that Bill had not returned that night. They slept peacefully, hour after hour, dreaming of huffins and puffins, big waves and golden sands.

Jack awoke first. Kiki was nibbling at his ear. 'Blow you,

Kiki!' said Jack, pushing the parrot away. 'Oh, goodness, here's Huffin and Puffin too!'

So they were. They waddled over to Philip and stood patiently by his sleeping face. 'Arrrrrr!' said Huffin lovingly.

Philip awoke. He saw Huffin and Puffin and grinned. He sat up and yawned. 'Hallo, Jack!' he said. 'Bill up already?'

'Looks like it,' said Jack. 'Probably gone to bathe. He might have waked us up though! Come on. Let's wake the girls and go and bathe too.'

Soon all four were speeding to the sea, expecting to see Bill in the water. But he wasn't.

'Where is he, then?' said Lucy-Ann, puzzled. 'And good gracious – where's the boat?'

Yes – where was the boat? There was no sign of it, of course. The children stared at the cove, puzzled and dismayed.

'He must have taken it round to Hidden Harbour,' said Jack. 'Perhaps the radio wouldn't work or something. It still feels stormy, and that might have upset it.'

'Well, let's go to Hidden Harbour then,' said Philip. 'Perhaps Bill got sleepy down there in the boat and thought he'd snuggle up in the cabin.'

'He's probably there,' said Dinah. 'Fast asleep too! Let's go and give him a shock. We'll halloo down into the cabin and make him jump. The sleepy-head!'

'Oh, I do hope he's there,' said Lucy-Ann, shivering as much with worry as with cold.

They dressed quickly, shivering a little, for the sun was hidden behind angry-looking clouds. 'I do hope the weather isn't going to break up, just as we've begun such a lovely holiday,' said Dinah. 'Oh, Huffin, I'm sorry – but you got right under my feet. Did I knock you over?'

The puffin didn't seem to mind having Dinah tread on it. It shook out its wings, said, 'Arrrrr!' and hurried on after Puffin, who was trying to keep pace with Philip.

They went across the puffin colony, and came to the cleft

in the cliffs. There, below them, lay the motor-boat, swaying very gently as waves ran up under her, and then ran back again.

'There she is!' said Dinah in delight, 'Bill *did* take her round to the harbour!'

'He's not on deck,' said Jack. 'He must be in the cabin. Come on.'

'Let's call him,' said Lucy-Ann suddenly. 'Do let's. I want to know if he's there.'

And before the others could stop her she shouted at the top of her voice. 'BILL! OH, BILL, ARE YOU THERE?'

No Bill came out from the cabin, and for the first time a little uneasiness crept into the children's minds.

'*BILL!*' yelled Jack, making everyone jump violently. '*BILL*! Come on out!'

No sound from the boat. Suddenly panic stricken, all four children stumbled down the rocky ledge to the boat. They jumped on board and peered down into the little cabin.

'He's not there,' said Dinah, scared. 'Well, where is he, then?'

'He must be somewhere about, as the boat is still here,' said Jack sensibly. 'He'll come along soon. Maybe he's exploring somewhere on the island.'

They were just turning away when Philip caught sight of something. He stopped and clutched Jack, turning very pale.

'What?' said Jack, frightened. 'What's up?'

Silently Philip pointed to the radio. 'Smashed!' he said, in a whisper. 'Smashed to bits! Who did it?'

Lucy-Ann began to cry. Jack went up on deck and had a look round, feeling sick and upset. Then Philip gave an anguished howl from the cabin that sent the others running to his side.

'Look! The engine of the boat is smashed up too! Absolutely destroyed. My goodness – what's been happening here?'

'And where is Bill?' said Dinah, in a husky whisper.

'Gone. Kidnapped,' said Philip slowly. 'Someone came for him in the night. They don't know we're here, I suppose – they just thought Bill was alone. They've got him – and now we're prisoners on Puffin Island and we can't get away!'

14

A few plans

Everyone felt suddenly sick. Lucy-Ann sat down in a heap. Dinah joined her. The boys stood staring at the smashed engine as if they couldn't believe their eyes.

'It must be a nightmare,' said Dinah at last. 'It can't be true. Why – why, everything was right as rain last night – and now . . . '

'Now the boat's smashed up so that we can't get away, the radio is smashed so that we can't get a message through – and Bill's gone,' said Philip. 'And it isn't a dream. It's real.'

'Let's sit down in the cabin, all together,' said Lucy-Ann, wiping her eyes. 'Let's sit close and talk. Let's not leave each other at all.'

'Poor Lucy-Ann!' said Philip, putting his arm round her, as she sat down unsteadily. 'Don't worry. We've been in worse fixes than this.'

'We haven't!' said Dinah. 'This is the worst fix we've *ever* been in!'

Kiki felt the tenseness of all the children. She sat quietly on Jack's shoulder, making little comforting noises. Huffin and Puffin sat solemnly on the deck, staring fixedly in front of them. Even they seemed to feel that something awful had happened.

In the cabin, sitting close together, the children felt a little better. Jack rummaged in a tiny cupboard beside him and brought out some bars of chocolate. The children had had no breakfast, and although the shock they had had seemed to have taken their appetites away, they thankfully took the chocolate to nibble.

'Let's try and think out carefully exactly what must have happened,' said Jack, giving a bit of his chocolate to Kiki.

'Well – we know that Bill was worried about something,' said Philip. 'Those planes, for instance. He felt certain something peculiar was going on up here. And that's why he went out by himself in the boat. He must have been seen.'

'Yes – and maybe in some way his enemies got to know he was here,' said Dinah. 'They could have followed him a long way back, using field-glasses to keep him in sight. Anyway – it's quite clear that they came looking for him here.'

'And found him,' said Jack. 'What a pity he went off to tinker with the radio last night!'

'Well, if he hadn't, the enemy, whoever they are, would probably have searched the island and found us too,' said Dinah. 'As it is – they probably don't know we're here.'

'It wouldn't matter if they did know,' said Lucy-Ann. 'They'd be quite sure we couldn't do any harm, living on an island we can't get off!'

'They got here – in a motor-boat probably,' went on Jack. 'Left the motor-boat out beyond, somewhere – and slipped inshore quietly in a rowing-boat. They must know this little channel – or maybe they saw a light from the boat. Bill would be sure to have the cabin light on, and it's a pretty bright one.'

'Yes. And they surprised him and knocked him out, I suppose,' said Philip gloomily. 'They've taken him away – goodness knows what'll happen to him!'

'They won't – they won't hurt him, will they?' said Lucy-Ann in rather a trembly voice. Nobody answered.

'Cheer up, Lucy-Ann,' said Philip. 'We've been in worse scrapes before, whatever Dinah says. We'll get out of this one all right.'

'How?' asked Lucy-Ann. 'I don't see *how* we can! You don't either.'

Philip didn't. He scratched his head and looked at Jack.

'Well – we've got to make *some* kind of plan,' said Jack. 'I mean – we must make up our minds what we are going to do to try and escape – and what we are going to do *till* we escape.'

'Won't Bill's friends come and look for us when they don't get Bill's messages through?' asked Dinah suddenly.

'Pooh! What would be the good of *that*?' said Philip at once. 'There are hundreds of these little bird-islands here. It might take years visiting and exploring every single one to find us!'

'We could light a fire on the cliff and keep it burning so that any searcher could see the smoke in the daytime and the flames at night,' said Dinah excitedly. 'You know – like ship-wrecked sailors do.'

'Yes, we could,' said Jack. 'Only – the enemy might see it too – and come along and find us before anyone else does.'

There was a silence. Nobody knew who the enemy were. They seemed mysterious and powerful and frightening.

'Well, I can't help it – I think we ought to follow Dinah's plan and light a fire,' said Philip at last. 'We've got to run the risk of the enemy seeing it and coming to find us. But we simply *must* do something to help anyone searching for us. We can keep a look-out for the enemny, and hide if they come.'

'*Hide! Where* can we hide?' asked Dinah scornfully. 'There isn't a single place on this island for *anyone* to hide!'

'No, that's true,' said Jack. 'No caves, no trees, except for those few little birches – and the cliffs too steep to explore. We really *are* in a fix!'

'Can't we do anything to help Bill?' asked Lucy-Ann dolefully. 'I keep on and on thinking of him.'

'So do I,' said Jack. 'But I don't see that we can do much to help ourselves, let alone Bill. Now – if we could escape from here – or radio for help and get some of Bill's friends along – it would be *some*thing. But there doesn't seem anything at all to do except stay here and wait.'

'There's plenty of food, anyway,' said Dinah. 'Stacks of tinned stuff, and biscuits and potted meat, and Nestlés milk and sardines . . . '

'I think we'd better strip the boat of them,' said Jack. 'I'm surprised the enemy didn't take what they could with them. Maybe they'll come back for them – so we'll take them first. We can hide them down some of the puffin burrows.'

'Let's have a bit of breakfast now,' said Philip, feeling better now that they had all talked the matter over and made a few plans. 'Open some tins and get some ginger-beer. Come on.'

They all felt better still when they had had something to eat and drink. They had put a cover over the poor smashed radio. They couldn't bear to look at it.

Jack went up on deck when they had finished their meal. It was very close again, and even the wind seemed warm. The sun shone through a thin veiling of cloud, and had a reddish hue. 'That storm is still about,' said Jack. 'Come on, everyone. Let's get to work before it comes.'

It was decided that Philip and Dinah should hunt for driftwood to make a fire up on the cliff. 'We don't *know* that those aeroplanes we sometimes see belong to the enemy,' said Philip. 'If they don't, they may see our signal and come to circle round. Then they will send help. One might come today, even. So we'll get a fire alight. We'll bank it with dry seaweed. That will smoulder well and send up plenty of smoke.'

Jack and Lucy-Ann were to carry things from the boat to the tents in Sleepy Hollow. 'Take all the tins and food you can,' said Philip. 'If the enemy happened to come back at night and take it we'd be done. We should starve! As it is, we've got heaps to last us for weeks.'

The four children worked very hard indeed. Jack and

Lucy carried sacks of tins from the boat to Sleepy Hollow. For the time being they bundled them in a heap by the tents. Kiki examined them with interest, and pecked at one or two.

'It's a good thing your beak isn't a tin-opener, Kiki,' said Jack, making the first little joke that day, to try and make Lucy-Ann smile. 'We shouldn't have much food left if it was.'

Philip and Dinah were also very busy. They took a sack each from the boat and wandered along the shore to pick up bits of wood. They found plenty at the tide-line and filled their sacks. Then they dragged them to the top of the cliff. Huffin and Puffin went with them, solemn as ever, sometimes walking, sometimes flying.

Philip emptied his sack of wood on a good spot. He began to build a fire. Dinah went off to fill her sack with dry seaweed. There was plenty.

Soon Jack and Lucy-Ann, emptying their own sacks in Sleepy Hollow, saw a spiral of smoke rising up from the cliff-top. 'Look!' said Jack. 'They've got it going already! Good work!'

The wind bent the smoke over towards the east. It was good thick smoke, and the children felt sure that it could be seen from quite a distance.

'One of us had always better be up here, feeding the fire, and keeping watch for enemies or friends,' said Philip.

'How shall we know which they are?' asked Dinah, throwing a stick on the fire.

'Well – I suppose we shan't know,' said Philip. 'What we'd better do if we see any boat coming is to hide – that is, if we can *find* anywhere to hide – and then try and discover if the searchers are enemies or friends. We are sure to hear them talking. We'd better get lots more wood, Di – this fire will simply *eat* it up!'

Lucy-Ann and Jack helped them when they had finished their own job. 'We've taken every single tin and every scrap of food out of the boat,' said Lucy-Ann. 'We really have got plenty to eat – and that rock-pool to drink from when we've finished the ginger-beer. There aren't an awful lot of bottles left now. Wouldn't you like to have dinner soon?'

'Yes. I'm jolly hungry,' said Philip. 'Let's have it up here, shall we? Or is it too much bother to fetch a meal here, Lucy-Ann? You see, one of us must keep the fire going all the time.'

'Well, it won't go out for a while, anyhow,' said Lucy-Ann. 'Bank it up with some more seaweed. Honestly, we feel fagged out, carrying all that stuff. Let's go to Sleepy Hollow and have a good rest and a jolly good meal.'

So they all returned to Sleepy Hollow, where the two tents flapped in the little breeze. They sat down and Lucy-Ann opened tins, and ladled the contents on to plates.

'You've got tinned salmon, biscuits and butter, tinned tomatoes and tinned pears,' she said.

Even Huffin and Puffin came closer than usual, to share such a nice meal. They would have eaten every scrap of the salmon if they could. Kiki preferred the tinned pears, but the children would only allow her one.

'Well, things would be a lot worse if we hadn't got all this nice food,' said Jack, leaning back in the warm sun, after a big meal. 'An adventure without good food would be awful! Kiki, take your head out of that tin. You've had more than any of us, you greedy glutton of a parrot!'

15

A really terrible storm

The wind got up about five o'clock. It whipped the waves round the island until they towered into big white horses that raced up the beaches and broke with a sound of thunder. The sea-birds deserted the coves, and flew into the air, crying loudly. The wind took them and they soared for miles without beating a wing, enjoying themselves throughly.

Kiki didn't like so much wind. She could not glide or soar like the gulls and guillemots. It offended her dignity to be blown about too much. So she stayed close to the tents, which flapped like live things in the wind, and strained at the tent-pegs violently.

'Look here, we can't possibly watch the fire all night!' said Philip. 'We'll have to bank it up and hope for the best. Maybe it will send out a glow, anyway. Doesn't that seaweed keep it in nicely? My goodness, the wind tears the smoke to rags now!'

The sun went down in a bank of angry purple clouds that gathered themselves together in the west. Jack and Philip stared at them.

'That's the storm coming up all right,' said Jack. 'Well, we've felt one coming for days – this hot weather was bound to end up like that. I hope the wind won't blow our tents away in the night.'

'So do I,' said Philip anxiously. 'Honestly, there's a perfect gale blowing up now! Look at those awful clouds! They look really wicked!'

The boys watched the clouds covering the sky, making the evening dark much sooner than usual. Philip put his hand into one of his pockets. 'My rats know there is a storm coming,' he said. 'They're all huddled up in a heap together right at the very bottom of my pocket. Funny how animals know things like that.'

'Jack!' called Lucy-Ann anxiously. 'Do you think the tents are safe? The wind is blowing them like anything!'

The boys went to examine them. They were as well pegged as they could be, but in this gale who knew what might happen?

'We just can't do anything about it but hope for the best,' said Jack rather gloomily. 'Philip, have you got your torch?

We'd better be prepared to be disturbed in the night, if this gale goes on – we might have to re-peg one of the tents.'

Both boys had torches with new batteries, so that was all right. They put them down beside their beds when they cuddled up into their rugs that night. They all went early because for one thing it was getting very dark, for another thing it had begun to rain heavily, and for a third thing they were all very tired with the day's work. Kiki retired with the boys as usual, and Huffin and Puffin scuttled into their burrows nearby.

'Wonder what poor old Bill is doing,' said Jack to Philip, as they lay listening to the wind howling round them. 'I bet he's worried stiff about us.'

'It's a shame, just as we were all set for a glorious holiday,' said Philip. 'And now the weather's broken too! What on earth shall we do with ourselves if it goes on like this for days? It will be frightful.'

'Oh, it may clear up again when the storm is over,' said Jack. 'Golly, hark at the waves on the beaches round the island – and how they must be dashing against those steep cliffs! I bet the gannets and guillemots aren't getting much sleep tonight!'

'The wind's pretty deafening too,' said Philip. 'Blow it! I feel so tired, and yet I can't possibly sleep with all this din going on. And gosh – what's that?'

'Thunder,' said Jack, sitting up. 'The storm is on us now all right. Let's go into the girls' tent, Philip. Lucy-Ann will be pleased to see us if she's awake. A storm over this exposed little island won't be very funny.'

They crept into the other tent. The girls were wide awake and very glad to have them beside them. Dinah squeezed up into Lucy-Ann's rugs, and the boys got into Dinah's warm place. Jack flashed on his torch.

He saw that Lucy-Ann was very white. 'There's nothing to be frightened of, old thing,' he said gently. 'It's only a storm, and you're never frightened of those, Lucy-Ann, you know you aren't.'

'I know,' gulped Lucy-Ann. 'It's only that – well, the storm seems so wild and – and *spiteful*, somehow. It *tears* at our tent, and bellows at us. It seems alive.'

Jack laughed. The thunder came again and crashed more loudly than the waves on the shore. Kiki crept close to Jack.

'Pop, pop, pop!' she said, and put her head under her wing.

'Thunder doesn't pop, Kiki,' said Jack, trying to joke. But nobody smiled. The wind blew more wildly than ever and the children wished they had more rugs. It was very very draughty!

Then the lightning flashed. It made them all jump, for it was so vivid. For an instant the steep cliffs and the raging sea showed vividly. Then the picture was gone.

Crash! The thunder came again, this time sounding overhead. Then the lightning split the sky open again and once more the children saw the cliffs and the sea. They didn't seem quite real, somehow.

'Sort of unearthly,' said Philip. 'Gosh, hark at the rain! I'm getting spattered all over with it, though goodness knows how it's getting in here.

'The wind's getting worse,' said Lucy-Ann fearfully. 'Our tents will blow away. They will, they will!'

'No, they won't,' said Jack stoutly, taking Lucy-Ann's cold hand in his. 'They can't. They . . . '

But at that very moment there came a rending sound, a great flap-flap-flap, something hit Jack across the face – and their tent was gone.

The four children were struck dumb for a moment. The wind howled round them, the rain soaked them. They had nothing over them to protect them – their tent had vanished. Vanished with the wild wind in the darkness of the night.

Lucy-Ann screamed and clutched Jack. He put his torch on quickly.

'Gosh – it's gone! The gale has taken it away. Come into our tent, quickly!'

But before the children could even get up from their rugs,

the gale had taken the other tent too. It rushed by Philip, as he stood trying to help the girls up, and when he turned his torch to where his tent should be, there was nothing.

'Ours has gone too,' he cried, trying to out-shout the wind. 'Whatever are we to do?'

'We'd better get down to the boat – if we possibly can,' yelled Jack. 'Or do you think we shall be blown over? Had we better roll ourselves up in the ground-sheets and rugs and wait till the storm has blown itself out?'

'No. We'll be soaked. Better try for the boat,' said Philip. He dragged the girls up. Each of the children wrapped a rug round their shoulders to try and ward off the rain and the cold.

'Take hands and keep together!' yelled Philip. 'I'll go first.'

They took hands. Philip set off, staggering in the gale that was blowing in his face. Through the puffin colony he went, trying to keep on his feet.

Suddenly Dinah, who had hold of Philip's hand, felt him drag it away. Then she heard a cry. She called in fright.

'Philip! Philip! What's happened?'

There was no answer. Jack and Lucy-Ann came close to Dinah. 'What's up? Where's Philip?'

Jack's torch shone out in front of them. There was no Philip there. He had vanished completely. The children, their hearts beating painfully, stayed absolutely still in dismay and astonishment. Surely the gale hadn't blown him away!

'PHILIP! PHILIP!' yelled Jack. But only the wind answered him. Then all three yelled at the tops of their voices.

Jack thought he heard a faint answering cry. But where? It sounded at his feet! He swung his torch downwards, and to his immense surprise and fright he saw Philip's head – but only his head, on a level with the ground.

Dinah shrieked in fright. Jack knelt down, too dumbfounded to say a word. Just Philip's head – just Philip's . . .

Then he saw in a flash what had happened. Philip had trodden on soil so undermined by the puffins that it had given way – and he had fallen right through to a hole below. Jack could have cried with relief.

'Are you all right, Philip?' he yelled.

'Yes. Give me your torch. I've dropped mine. I've fallen through into a whopping big hole. There might be room for us all to shelter here for a bit,' shouted back Philip, the words being whipped away by the wind almost before Jack could hear them.

Jack gave Philip his torch. The boy's head disappeared. Then it came back again, looking very odd sticking up between some heather and a sea-pink cushion.

'Yes. It's an enormous hole. Can you all get down? We'd keep safe and dry here till the storm is over. Come on. It's a bit smelly, but otherwise not bad.'

Dinah slid through the opening of the hole and found herself beside Philip. Then came Lucy-Ann and then Jack. Jack had found Philip's torch and the two torches were now shone around the hole.

'I suppose the rabbits and the puffins together managed to burrow so much that they have made an enormous hole,' said Jack. 'Look, there's a puffin burrow leading out of it over there – and one of the puffins staring in astonishment at us! Hallo, old son. Sorry to burst in on you like this.'

The relief of finding that Philip was safe, and of being out of the wild noise of the storm, made Jack feel quite light-headed. Lucy-Ann's shivers stopped, and they all looked round them with interest.

'*I* should think this was a natural cavity of some sort,' said Philip, 'with a layer of good soil, held together by roots and things, making a surface above – but all that burrowing by the puffins made it give way when I trod on it – and down I fell. Well, it's just what we wanted, for the moment.'

Above them, deadened by tangled heather and sea-pinks, the storm raged on. No rain came into the cavity. The thunder sounded very far away. The lightning could not be seen.

'I don't see why we shouldn't sleep here for the night,' said Jack, spreading out the rug he had taken from his shoulders. 'The soil is dry and soft – and the air must be good enough, because that puffin is still there, gazing at us. I say – I hope Huffin and Puffin are all right.'

They all spread out their rugs and lay down, cuddled up together. 'Congratulations on finding us such a fine home for tonight, Philip,' said Jack sleepily. 'Very clever of you indeed! Good night, everybody!'

16

Next day

They all slept soundly in their unexpected shelter. They did not awake until late in the morning, because for one thing it was dark in the hole, and for another they had all been tired out.

Jack awoke first, feeling Kiki stirring against his neck. He could not think where he was. A little daylight filtered through the entrance of the hole, but not much. It was very warm.

'Arrrrrr!' said a guttural voice, and made Jack jump. 'Arrrrrr!'

It was the puffin which had come down its burrow to see them the night before. Jack switched on his torch and grinned at it.

'Good morning – if it is morning. Sorry to have disturbed you! I'll get Huffin and Puffin to explain to you, when we see them again.'

Philip woke and sat up. Then the girls stirred. Soon they were all wide awake, looking round the curious cavity, and remembering the events of the night before.

'What a night!' said Dinah, shuddering. 'Oh – when our tents blew away – I really did feel awful!'

'And when Philip disappeared, I felt worse,' said Lucy-Ann. 'What time is it, Jack?'

Jack looked at his watch and whistled. 'My word – it's almost ten o'clock. How we've slept! Come on, let's see if the storm is still going strong.'

He stood up and pulled away the overhanging heather that blocked up the narrow entrance to the hole. At once a shaft of blinding sunlight entered, and the children blinked. Jack put his head out of the hole in delight.

'Golly! It's a *perfect* day! The sky is blue again, and there's sunshine everywhere. Not a sign of the storm left. Come on, let's go up into the sunlight and have a look around.'

Up they went, giving each other a hand. Once they were out of the hole, and the heather fell back into place again, there was no sign of where they had spent the night.

'Wouldn't it make an absolutely marvellous hiding-place?' said Jack. The others looked at him, the same thought occurring to everyone at once.

'Yes. And if the enemy come – *that's* where we'll go,' said Dinah. 'Unless they actually walk over the place they can't possibly find it. Why – I don't know myself where it is now – though I've just come out of it!'

'Gosh, don't say we've lost it as soon as we've found it,' said Jack, and they looked about for the entrance. Jack found it in just the same way as Philip had the night before – by falling down it. He set an upright stick beside it, so that they would know the entrance easily next time. 'We might have to sleep down there each night now, as our tents have gone,' said Jack. 'It's a pity we've brought our rugs up. Still, they can do with a sunning. We'll spread them out on the heather.'

'Thank goodness that awful wind's gone,' said Dinah. 'There's hardly even a breeze today. It's going to be frightfully hot. We'll bathe.'

They had a dip in the quiet sea, which looked quite

different from the boiling, raging sea of the day before. Now it was calm and blue, and ran up the sand in frilly little waves edged with white. After their bathe the children had an enormous breakfast in the spot where their tents had been.

Huffin and Puffin appeared as soon as the children arrived and greeted them joyfully.

'Arrrrrr! Arrrrrrr!'

'They're saying that they hope we've got a good breakfast for them,' said Dinah. 'Huffin and Puffin, I wish you'd eat rats. You'd be very useful then.'

Philip's rats had appeared again, now that the storm was over, much to Dinah's disgust. They seemed very lively, and one went into Jack's pockets to find a sunflower seed. It brought one out, sat on Jack's knee and began to nibble it. But Kiki pounced at once, and snatched the seed away, whilst Squeaker scurried back to Philip in a hurry.

'You're a dog in the manger, Kiki,' said Jack. 'You don't really want that sunflower seed yourself, and you won't let Squeaker have it either. Fie!'

'Fie fo fum,' said Kiki promptly, and went off into a screech of laughter, right in Jack's ear. He pushed her off his shoulder.

'I shall be deaf for the rest of the day! Lucy-Ann, look out for that potted meat. Huffin is much too interested in it.'

'Really – what with Kiki pinching fruit out of the tin, and Huffin and Puffin wanting the potted meat, and Philip's rats sniffing round, it's a wonder we've got anything ourselves!' said Lucy-Ann. But all the same, it was fun to have the creatures joining in and being one with them. Huffin and Puffin were especially comical that morning, for now that they were really friendly, they wanted to look into everything. Huffin suddenly took an interest in Dinah's fork and picked it up with his beak.

'Oh, don't swallow that, silly!' cried Dinah, and tried to get her fork away. But Huffin had a very strong beak, and he won the tug of war. He waddled away to examine the fork in peace.

'He won't swallow it, don't worry,' said Philip, tossing Dinah his own fork. 'It'll keep him quiet a bit if he plays with it for a while.'

The children's fire was, of course, completely out. It had to be pulled to pieces and lighted all over again. This was not so easy as before, because everything had been soaked during the night. Still, the sun was so very hot that it wouldn't be long before the wood and the seaweed were bone-dry again.

The children missed out dinner completely that day, because it had been twelve o'clock before they had cleared up their breakfast things. 'We'll have a kind of high tea about five,' said Jack. 'We've plenty to do – look for our tents – light the fire – find some more wood – and go and see if the motor-boat is all right.'

Their tents were nowhere to be seen. One or two pegs were found but that was all. 'The tents are probably lying on some island miles and miles away,' said Jack. 'Scaring the sea-birds there. Well – shall we sleep in that hole to-night?'

'Oh no, please don't let's,' begged Lucy-Ann. 'It's smelly. And it's so very hot again now that surely we could put our rugs on cushions of heather and sleep out in the open. I should like that.'

Philip looked up at the clear blue sky. Not a cloud was to be seen. 'Well,' he said, 'if it's like this tonight, it would be quite comfortable to sleep in the open. We'll plan to do that unless the weather changes. Let's find a nice cushiony place, and put our rugs there, and our other clothes, with the ground-sheets over them. Good thing the ground-sheets only blew up against those birch-trees and got stuck there!'

They found a nice heathery place, not too far from where Lucy-Ann kept the stores beneath the big ledge of stone, and piled their extra jerseys, their mackintoshes, their rugs and their ground-sheets there. Lucy-Ann had stored their spare clothes with the food under the ledge, but the rain had driven in, and had made them damp. So it was decided that it would be better to use them as extra bedclothes at night, and keep them under the ground-sheets during the daytime.

After they had done all this they went to see their fire, which was burning well now. They sat on the top of the cliff, with the birds crying all round them, and looked out on the calm, brilliantly blue sea.

'What's that?' said Lucy-Ann suddenly, pointing to something floating not far off.

'Looks like a heap of wood, or something,' said Philip. 'Wreckage of some sort. Hope it comes inshore. We can use it for our fire.'

It came slowly in with the tide. Philip put his glasses to his eyes. Then he lowered them again, looking so taken-aback that the others were scared.

'Do you know,' he said, 'that wreckage looks awfully like bits of the *Lucky Star*. And there's more bits over there, look – and I dare-say we should find some down on the rocks.'

There was a shocked silence. Nobody had even *thought* that the motor-boat might have been taken by the storm and battered. Jack swallowed hard. That *would* be a blow! He got up.

'Come on. We'd better go and see. Of course I suppose it was bound to be smashed up, but anyhow we couldn't have moved it. Gosh – what bad luck if the boat's gone! Even if the engine was smashed, it was still a boat. We might have rigged up a sail – or something . . . '

In silence the children left the fire on the cliff and made their way through the cleft, and down the rocky ledges to the little harbour.

There was no boat there. Only a bit of the mooring-rope was left, still tied round the rock nearby, its ragged ends fluttering in the tiny breeze.

'Look!' said Jack, pointing. 'She must have been battered up and down by great waves rushing in and out of the channel – see the paint on the rocks – and look at the bits of wood about. When the rope broke she must have been taken right out of the channel, and then beaten to bits against the cliffs. What a frightful shame!'

The girls had tears in their eyes, and Philip had to turn away too. Such a lovely boat! Now she was nothing but masses of wreckage which they could burn on their fire. Poor *Lucky Star*. *Unlucky Star* should have been her name.

'Well, nothing we could have done would have helped,' said Jack at last. 'The storm would have wrecked her anyway – though if Bill had been here, and the boat was all right, he would have taken her round to Splash Cove and we could have dragged her right up the beach, out of reach of the waves. It wasn't our fault.'

They all felt sad and downcast as they left the little harbour and went back. The sun was going down now, and the evening was very peaceful and beautiful. There was hardly any wind at all.

'I can hear an aeroplane again!' said Lucy-Ann, her sharp ears picking up the distant throbbing before the others. 'Listen!'

Far away a small speck showed low down in the blue sky. The boys clapped their glasses to their eyes. Jack gave an exclamation.

'It's dropping something, look! Philip, what is it? Is it a parachute?'

'It looks like a small parachute – with something underneath it, swinging to and fro,' said Philip, his eyes glued to his glasses. 'Is it a man? No, it doesn't look like a man. Then what in the world is it? And why is the plane dropping things here? Gosh, I wish Bill was here to see this. There is something peculiar going on. Something the enemy are doing. I shouldn't be surprised if they get the wind up when they see our smoke and come along to search the island. Tomorrow one of us must always be on the lookout, from the cliff.'

Puzzled and anxious, the children went back to Sleepy Hollow. It was time for high tea, and Lucy-Ann and Dinah prepared it in silence. They were in the middle of an adventure again – and they couldn't possibly get out of it.

17

A boat, a boat!

'Do you think it's worth while keeping the fire going, if the aeroplanes belong to the enemy?' asked Lucy-Ann at last.

'Well, if we're *ever* to be rescued, we shall have to show some kind of signal,' said Jack. 'We'll have to risk the aeroplanes seeing it. Perhaps, when no messages come through from Bill, motor-boats will come looking for us. Then they will see our signal, and come to the island.'

'I hope they do,' said Dinah. 'I don't want to be here for months. And it would be awful in the winter.'

'Good gracious! Don't talk about being here for the *winter*!' said Lucy-Ann, in alarm. 'Why, it's only May!'

'Dinah's looking on the black side of things as usual,' said Philip.

Dinah flared up. 'I'm not! I'm being sensible. You always call being sensible "looking on the black side of things." '

'Oh, don't quarrel just now, when we all ought to stick by each other,' begged Lucy-Ann. 'And *don't* put those rats near Dinah, Philip – don't be mean just now!'

Philip snapped his fingers and the rats scurried back to his pockets. Kiki snorted.

'Three blind mice, see how they run, pop goes Kiki!'

'Arrrrr!' said Huffin, agreeing politely. It was really very comical the way he and Puffin seemed to talk to Kiki. They never said anything but 'Arrrr,' but they said it in many different tones, and sounded quite conversational at times.

That night the children slept out in the open. It was a beautiful calm night, and the stars hung in the sky, big and bright. Lucy-Ann tried to keep awake to watch for shooting stars, which she loved, but she didn't see any.

Her bed was very comfortable. The children had chosen

thick heather to put their groundsheets and rugs on, and had used their extra clothes for pillows. A tiny breeze blew against their cheeks and hair. It was lovely lying there with the stars shining peacefully above, and the sound of the sea in the distance.

'It's like the wind in the trees,' thought Lucy-Ann sleepily. 'And the wind in trees is like the sound of the sea. Oh dear, I'm getting muddled – muddled – mudd—'

The weather was still lovely the next day, and the spiral of smoke from the signal fire went almost straight up in the air, there was so little wind. Jack and Philip took a good many bird-photographs, and Jack looked longingly over the steep bird-cliff, wishing he could climb down a little way and take some photographs of the birds there.

'Bill said not,' said Philip. 'And I think we oughtn't to. Suppose anything happened to us, what would the girls do? We've got heaps of fine photographs without bothering to take the eggs and birds on those ledges.'

'I wish the puffins had laid eggs,' said Jack. 'I haven't found a single puffin egg yet. It's a bit too early, I suppose. How sweet baby puffins must look! I wish I could see some.'

'Well, you're likely to, as things have turned out,' said Philip, with a half-comical groan. 'We may be here for quite a long time.'

It was arranged that one or other of the children should always be on the look-out somewhere on the bird-cliff. From there it was possible to see nearly all round the island, and no enemy could approach without being seen when still far off. That would give plenty of time for the others to be warned, and for all of them to go into hiding.

'We'd really better hide all the tins and things that are under our ledge, down in that hole, hadn't we?' said Lucy-Ann, when the plans were made. 'They might easily be found.'

'We'll stuff heather round them,' said Jack. 'It would be an awful bore to have to keep going down into the hole to fetch all the food each time we wanted something to eat.'

So clumps of heather were most realistically tucked under the rocky ledge where Lucy-Ann kept the tins. Nobody would guess it wasn't growing, it looked so natural there.

'We'd have plenty of time to chuck our clothes and things down into the hidey-hole, if we saw anyone coming,' said Jack. 'I'll take first watch. I shan't be a bit bored, because there are so many birds up there – and Kiki is such a clown with them, it's as good as a pantomine to watch her.'

Two days went by without anything exciting happening at all. Once they heard another aeroplane, but didn't see it. More wreckage was thrown up on the beach from the unfortunate *Lucky Star*. The children bathed and ate and slept, and took it in turns to keep watch, but they saw nothing to worry them at all.

Kiki always kept watch with Jack. Huffin and Puffin kept watch with Philip. Once another puffin came too near Philip for Huffin's liking, and the bird ran at it with his head down, growling *arrrrrrr* like an infuriated dog. Their big beaks locked together, and Philip almost cried with laughter as he watched the curious battle.

'The battle of beaks,' he called it, when he described it to the others afterwards. 'Talk about stags locking their antlers together and fighting – those two puffins were every bit as fierce with their huge beaks.'

'Who won?' asked Lucy-Ann, with great interest. 'Huffin, I suppose?'

'Of course,' said Philip. 'He not only won, he chased the other one right into its burrow, and they both came out again at another entrance, with Huffin winning the race. I'm surprised the other poor bird had any feathers left by the time Huffin had finished with him.'

On the afternoon of the third day, Jack was sitting up on the top of the bird-cliff. It was his turn to look out. He gazed lazily out to sea. There was just a little more breeze that day, and the waves had frills of white as they came in to shore.

Jack was thinking about Bill. Where was he? What had happened to him? Had he been able to escape, and if so, would he come quickly to rescue the four children? And what was Aunt Allie thinking? Had she heard that there was no word from Bill, and was she worried?

Jack thought deeply about all these things, listening to the different cries of the sea-birds about him, and watching their graceful fight over the sea. Then his eyes suddenly picked out something far off on the water.

He stiffened like a dog that suddenly sees something unusual. He reached down for his field-glasses and put them to his eyes. He had soon got the something out there into focus – and he saw that it was a small motor-boat.

'Enemies,' he thought, and was about to leap to his feet when he remembered that whoever was in the boat might also have glasses, and might see him. So he wriggled away on his tummy, and not until he was well down into the little valley did he jump up and run to the others.

'Hi!' he called breathlessly, as he tore down to Sleepy Hollow, where the others were having a laze. 'There's a boat coming!'

They all sat up at once. Lucy-Ann's green eyes were wide with excitement and fright. 'Where? How far away?'

'Quite a way off. It will take them about ten minutes to come in and tie up. We'd better chuck everything down into the hole at once.'

'What about the fire?' said Dinah, grabbing her pile of jerseys and coats.

'Have to leave that. They've already seen the smoke anyway,' said Jack. 'Come on, quick! Get a move on, Lucy-Ann!'

It didn't take long to part the heather over the narrow entrance to the hole and hurl everything down. Jack removed the stick he had put there to mark the place.

'No good leaving a signpost for them,' he said, trying to make Lucy-Ann smile. She gave him a watery grin.

'No – everything cleared up?' said Philip, looking round. He pulled at the clumps of heather they had been lying on, which had got rather flattened, but the springy plants were already getting back into position themselves. Philip picked up a spoon that someone had left lying there and popped it into his pocket. There really did seem to be nothing left now that would show that the children had been there a few minutes before.

'Come on, Tufty! Don't wait about!' said Jack, in a fever of impatience to get below ground. The girls were already safely in the hole. Jack slid down himself and Philip followed almost at once.

Jack pulled the heather neatly over the hole. 'There! Now unless anybody actually treads in the hole, as Philip did the other night, we're safe. Nobody would ever know there was a big cavity underground.'

'I feel like a puffin,' said Philip. 'I feel I'd like to burrow. What about digging a nice little burrow for each of us to lie in?'

'Oh, don't make jokes now,' begged Lucy-Ann. 'I don't feel like jokes. I feel – I feel all sort of tight and breathless. And my heart simply *couldn't* beat any louder. Can you hear it?'

Nobody could. But then, their own hearts were beating so fast and so loudly that it was no wonder they could not hear anybody else's.

'Can we whisper?' asked Dinah, in a loud whisper that made everyone jump.

'I should think so. But don't talk out loud,' said Jack. 'And if we hear anyone coming, listen with all your might, so that we shall know if it's friends or enemies. It would be *too* awful if it was friends and we let them go away without finding us.'

That was indeed an awful thought – almost worse than the thought of being found by an enemy. Everyone sat quietly, holding their breaths, listening with all their might.

'Friend or enemy, friend or enemy, friend or enemy,' said a voice in Lucy-Ann's mind, and she couldn't stop it saying the words over and over again. 'Friend or . . . '

'Sh,' came Jack's whisper, suddenly. 'I can hear something.'

But it was only Huffin and Puffin arriving in the hole. They pushed the heather aside and flopped in, giving the children a terrible shock. The heather swung back, and the puffins stared in the darkness, trying to find Philip.

'You wretched birds!' scolded Philip. 'You might have shown them our hiding-place. Don't you dare to say a word!'

'Arrrrrr!' said Huffin deeply. Philip gave him an angry push, and the bird walked away in astonishment. It was the first time he had ever had an angry word or gesture from his beloved Philip. He hopped up to the beginning of a nearby burrow, followed by Puffin, and began to walk up it, very much offended. The children were glad to hear them go.

'Sh!' came Jack's whisper again, and the others clutched one another. 'They're really coming now! Shhhhhhhh!'

18

The enemy – and Kiki

The thud of footsteps could be felt in the dark hole below ground. Then came the sound of voices. 'We'll search the whole place. *Somebody* must be keeping that fire going!'

'There's nowhere much to hide on this small island,' said another voice. 'Nobody could get down those sheer cliffs, so that rules them out. And there's obviously nobody in this valley – except these ridiculous birds.'

There came the sound of a match being struck. One of the men was evidently lighting a cigarette. He tossed the match away – and it came trickling through the heather into the hole where the trembling children crouched. It fell on to Dinah's knee and she almost squealed.

'They're dreadfully near,' everyone was thinking. 'Dreadfully, dreadfully near!'

'Look here,' said one of the men's voices, suddenly. 'What's this? A bit of chocolate wrapping-paper! I bet the hiding-place isn't far off.'

The children's hearts almost stopped beating. Philip remembered that a bit of his chocolate-paper had blown away on the wind and he hadn't bothered to go and pick it up. Blow! Blow! Blow!

Jack felt about for Kiki. Where was she? She had slid off his shoulder, but he couldn't feel her anywhere near. He did hope she wouldn't suddenly make one of her loud remarks, just under the very feet of the men.

Kiki had gone up the burrow, after Huffin and Puffin. The two puffins were now staring at the men who had come to hunt. They stood at the entrance of a burrow, looking fixedly with their crimson-circled eyes.

'Look at those silly chaps,' said one man. 'Whatever are these ridiculous birds, with beaks like fireworks about to go off?'

'Don't know. Puffins or sea parrots, or something,' said the other man.

'Huffin and Puffin,' said Kiki, in a loud, conversational sort of voice. The men jumped violently and looked all round. Kiki was in the burrow behind Huffin and Puffin and could not be seen. She didn't want to push past them in case they nipped her.

'Did you hear that?' said the first man.

'Well – I thought I heard something,' said the other. 'But these birds all round make such a racket.'

'Yes – a frightful din,' said the first man.

'Din-din-dinner,' announced Kiki and went off into one of her cackles of laughter. The men stared in alarm at the two solemn puffins. 'I say – surely those birds can't *talk*?'

'It's a bit odd, isn't it?' said the first man, rubbing his chin and staring at Huffin and Puffin. It seemed as if it really must be the two puffins who were talking and coughing. Kiki could not be seen.

Huffin opened his beak. 'Arrrrrr!' he said solemnly.

'There!' said the man. 'I saw him that time. They *are* talking birds. Sea parrots perhaps – and parrots talk, don't they?'

'Yes, but they have to be taught,' said the other. 'And who taught these two?'

'Oh, come on – don't let's waste any time on the ridiculous creatures, said the first man, turning to go. 'We'll go down to the shore and walk along it to make sure there's no one there. Pity the boat's been smashed up in the gale. We could have taken off some of the food in it.'

Kiki gave an imitation of a motor-bike in the distance, and the men stopped suddenly in astonishment.

'I could have sworn that was a motor-bike!' said one, with a half-ashamed laugh. 'Come on – we're hearing things. Wait till I get hold of whoever is on this island – making us waste time hunting like this!'

To the children's enormous relief the men's voices got fainter and fainter and at last could not be heard at all. Kiki came back into the cave.

'What a pity, what a pity!' she said in a whisper, cracking her beak.

'Kiki, you awful idiot, you nearly gave the game away!' whispered Jack. 'Get on my shoulder – and I warn you, if you say just one more word, I'll tie your beak up with my hanky.'

'Arrrrrrrr!' said Kiki, and settled down with her head under her wing. She was offended.

For what seemed like hours the children sat silently in the hole underground. They heard no more voices, and no more footsteps shook the ground nearby.

'How long have we got to stay here like this?' whispered Dinah at last. She was always the first to get impatient. 'I'm cramped.'

'I don't know,' said Jack, in a whisper that seemed to fill the underground cavity. 'It would be dangerous to pop my head out and take a look-see.'

'I'm hungry,' said Lucy-Ann. 'I wish we'd brought something to eat down with us. And I'm thirsty too.'

Jack wondered whether or not to risk sticking his head out. Just as he was making up his mind that he would, everyone in the hole heard a far-off, very welcome noise.

'It's the engine of their motor-boat being started up,' said Jack in relief. 'They must have given up the hunt, thank goodness. We'll give them a few minutes, then I'll hop out.'

They waited for five minutes. The motor-boat's engine sounded for a little while, then grew fainter and finally could not be heard at all.

Jack cautiously put his head out. He could see and hear nothing but puffins. Huffin and Puffin were squatting nearby and got up politely when they saw his head.

'Arrrrrrr!' they said.

Jack got right out of the hole. He lay down flat, put his field-glasses to his eyes and swept the sea around. At last he spotted what he was looking for – the motor-boat going away at top speed, getting smaller and smaller in the distance.

'It's all right!' he called down to the others. 'They're almost out of sight. Come on out.'

Soon they were all sitting in Sleepy Hollow, with the girls getting a meal ready, for by this time they were once again ravenous. The ginger-beer had now all been drunk, so they drank the water from the rock-pool, which was rather warm from the sun, but tasted very sweet. The rain from the storm had swelled it considerably.

'Well, that was a jolly narrow escape,' said Philip, his spirits rising as he tucked into slices of 'Spam.' 'I really did think one of them would tumble in on top of us.'

'Well, what do you suppose *I* felt like when the match one of them used fell through the hole and bounced on my knee?' said Dinah. 'I nearly let out a yell.'

'Kiki almost gave the game away too,' said Jack, putting potted meat on a biscuit. 'Calling out "din-din-dinner" like that. I'm ashamed of you, Kiki.'

'She's sulking,' said Dinah, laughing. 'Look at her – standing with her back to you, pretending not to take any notice. That's because you were cross with her.'

Jack grinned. He called to Huffin and Puffin, who were, as usual, standing patiently beside Philip. 'Hey, Huff and Puff – come and have a tit-bit. Nice birds, good birds, dear Huff and Puff.'

Huffin and Puffin walked over to Jack, doing their sailor-roll from side to side. They solemnly took a bit of biscuit from Jack's fingers. But that was more than Kiki could stand. She whisked round and screeched at the top of her voice.

'Naughty boy, naughty boy, naughty boy! Poor Polly, poor Polly! Polly's got a cold, put the kettle on, naughty boy, naughty boy!'

She rushed at the startled puffins and gave them a sharp jab with her curved beak. Huffin retaliated at once, and Kiki stepped back. She began to screech like a railway-train, and the two puffins hurriedly returned to Philip's knees, where they stood and stared in alarm at Kiki, ready to dart down a burrow at a moment's notice.

The children roared with laughter at this little pantomime. Kiki went to Jack, sidling along in a comical manner. 'Poor Kiki, poor Kiki, naughty boy, naughty boy!'

Jack gave her a tit-bit and she sat on his shoulder to eat it, looking triumphantly at Huffin and Puffin. 'Arrrrrr!' she said to them, sounding like a snarling dog. 'Arrrrrr!'

'All right, Kiki. Don't *arrrrr* any more just by my ear,' said Jack. 'And I should advise you not to go too near Huffin for a bit. He won't forget that jab of yours.'

'Do you think it'll be safe to sleep out of doors again tonight?' asked Dinah, clearing up the meal. 'I don't fancy sleeping down that hole again, somehow.'

'Oh, I should think it would be all right,' said Jack. 'I don't somehow think those fellows, whoever they were, will come along in the dark of night. Pity we didn't catch a glimpse of them.'

'I didn't like their voices,' said Lucy-Ann. 'They sounded hard and horrid.'

'What a good thing that storm blew our tents away the other night!' said Dinah suddenly. 'If it hadn't, we wouldn't have stumbled on that hole, and been able to use it as a hiding-place. We wouldn't have known *where* to go, but for that.'

'That's true,' said Philip. 'I wonder if those men will come back again. We'll go on keeping watch anyway, and keep the fire going. It's our only hope of rescue – and Bill's only hope too, I should think – because if nobody comes to rescue us, certainly nobody will rescue Bill!'

'Poor Bill!' said Lucy-Ann. 'He wanted to disappear – and he has.'

'Those men must have put our fire out,' said Jack, suddenly noticing that there was no smoke. 'The wretches! I suppose they thought they'd put it out, and then, if it was lighted again, and the smoke rose up, they'd know for certain that somebody was here.'

'We'll jolly well go and light it again,' said Philip at once. 'We'll show them we're going to have our fire going if we want to. I guess they don't want it going, in case somebody does happen to come along and see it. They won't want people exploring this part of the world at the moment.'

So they all went up to the cliff-top, and set to work to light the fire again. The men had kicked it out, and the ashes and half-burnt sticks were scattered everywhere.

It didn't take long to get it going again. The children built it up carefully, and then Philip lighted it. It caught at once and flames sprang up. When it was going well, the children banked it with seaweed, and at once a thick spiral of smoke ascended in the air.

'Ha! You men! I hope you have caught sight of our signal again!' cried Jack, facing out to sea. 'You can't beat us! We'll get the better of you yet, you'll see!'

19

Someone else comes to the island

The children were now very brown with the sun. 'If Mother could see us now, she wouldn't call us "peaky",' said Philip. 'And you've got back all your freckles, Jack and Lucy-Ann, and a few hundreds more!'

'Oh dear!' said Lucy-Ann, rubbing her brown freckled face. 'What a pity! I did think I looked so nice when my freckles faded away during measles.'

'I seem to be losing count of the days,' said Jack. 'I can't for the life of me make out whether today is Tuesday or Wednesday.'

'It's Friday,' said Philip promptly. 'I was counting up only this morning. We've been here quite a time now.'

'Well – is it a week since we left home?' wondered Dinah. 'It seems about six months. I wonder how Mother is getting on.'

'She must be feeling a bit worried about us,' said Philip. 'Except that she knows we're with Bill and she'll think we're quite all right, even if she doesn't get messages.'

'And we're not with Bill, and we're not all right,' said Lucy-Ann. 'I wish I knew where Bill was and what was happening to him. If only we had a boat, we could go off in it and try to find where he was. He must have been taken to the west of us somewhere – because that's where the planes seem to be.'

'Well – we're not likely to get a boat,' said Philip. 'Come on – let's go up on the cliff-top and see to the fire. The smoke doesn't seem very thick this morning. Huffin and Puffin, are you coming?'

'Arrrrrrr!' said both Huffin and Puffin, and walked along beside Philip. Huffin had taken to bringing fish as a little present for Philip, and this amused the children immensely. The first time that Huffin had waddled up with the fish in his big beak, the children hadn't been able to make out what he was carrying. But when he came nearer they roared with laughter.

'Philip! He's got six or seven fish in his beak for you – and do look how he's arranged them!' cried Jack. 'Heads and tails alternately in a row all down his beak! Huffin, how did you do it?'

'Thanks awfully, old chap,' said Philip, as Huffin deposited the fish beside the boy. 'Very generous of you.'

Now Huffin brought fish two or three times a day, much to the children's amusement. Philip knew how to prepare it for cooking over the fire, and the children ate the bigger fish with biscuits and tinned butter. Huffin solemnly accepted a piece cooked, and seemed to enjoy it just as much as raw. But Puffin would not touch it.

'Well, as long as we've got Huffin to provide us with fish, we shan't starve,' said Jack. 'Kiki, don't be so jealous. If Huffin wants to be generous, let him.'

Kiki tried to head off Huffin when he arrived with fish. She could not catch fish herself, and did not like the way Huffin brought presents to the little company.

'Naughty, naughty, naughty boy!' she screeched, but Huffin took no notice at all.

The children were sitting by the fire, idly throwing sticks on it, and stirring it now and again to make it flare up a little. A spiral of smoke rose up, bent northwards. Jack took up his field-glasses and swept the lonely sea with them. You never know when friends – or enemies – might turn up.

'Hallo! There's a boat again!' cried Jack suddenly, his glasses focused on something small far away. 'Philip, get your glasses.'

The boys gazed through them, whilst the girls waited impatiently. They could see nothing with their bare eyes – not even a speck on the sea.

'Is it the same boat as before?' said Philip. 'It's getting nearer – we shall soon be able to find out.'

'It looks a different one to me,' said Jack. 'Smaller. And it's coming from a different direction. That might just be a trick though – to make us think it was a friend.'

'How shall we know?' said Lucy-Ann. 'Have we got to go and hide again'?'

Jack gave his glasses to her to look through. He turned to Philip, a gleam in his eye. 'Philip – there's only *one* man this time – he'll have to leave his boat moored somewhere, if he's come to look for us. What about capturing it?'

'Golly! If only we could!' said Philip, his face glowing. 'It's a motor-boat – a small one – but big enough to take us all easily.'

'Capture it! But how?' demanded Dinah, her eyes glued on the approaching boat. 'The man would see us easily, come running up, and capture *us*!'

'Here, let me have my glasses back,' said Philip, tugging them away from Dinah. 'That's the worst of you, Di – you will always make your turn so long!'

'Now let's think a bit,' said Jack, his eyes bright. 'That fellow can't be coming to *rescue* us, because anyone knowing we were all alone here would send a bigger boat, and probably more men, in case they had to tackle our enemy. If Bill had managed to get word to anyone, that's what they would do. Therefore, it seems to me that this boat is not one sent to rescue . . . '

'So it's probably a trick of the enemy's,' continued Philip.

'They may or may not know there are only children here – it depends on how much Bill has told them – but they might quite easily send someone who would pretend *not* to be an enemy, so as to take us in – and then we would be persuaded to get into his boat to go to safety – and he'd take us off somewhere to join Bill as prisoners.'

'Oh!' said Lucy-Ann, who didn't like the sound of this at all. 'Well, I certainly shan't get into his boat. Jack, what are we going to do?'

'Now listen,' said Jack. 'I really have got a good idea – but it needs all of us to carry it out, you girls too.'

'Well, what have we got to do?' said Dinah impatiently.

'We'll find out where he's going to moor his boat,' said Jack. 'He'll either go into that little channel where the *Lucky Star* was – or pull her up on a sandy beach. We shall soon know, because we shall watch.'

'Yes, what then?' asked Lucy-Ann, beginning to feel excited.

'Well, Dinah and I will hide nearby,' said Jack. 'The man will walk up on to the island, to look for us – and you and Lucy-Ann, Philip, must go and meet him.'

'Oh, I *couldn't*,' said Lucy-Ann, in alarm.

'All right then – you stay put somewhere,' said Jack, 'and Philip can meet him. And Philip, somehow or other you've got to get this fellow into that underground hole. We can easily keep him prisoner there – and if we can block him in somehow, with plenty of food, we can take the boat and go.'

There was a silence whilst everyone digested this remarkable plan. 'But how am I to get him into the hole?' asked Philip at last. 'It sounds a bit like " 'Won't you come into my parlour?' said the spider to the fly" – and somehow I don't think that the fly will oblige this time!'

'Can't you just take him through the puffin colony, and walk him near the hole – and then trip him up?' asked Jack impatiently. 'I'm sure *I* could do it all right.'

'Well, you do it then,' said Philip, 'and I'll hide near the boat to capture it. But suppose you don't trip the man up and make him fall into the hole and be a prisoner? What about the boat? What shall I do with it?'

'Well, silly, you'll hop into it, if you find that I haven't been able to manage the man, and you'll get out to sea,' said Jack. 'And there you'll stay till it begins to get dark, when you can creep in and see if you can find us and take us off. But you needn't worry – I shall get that fellow all right. I shall tackle him just like I tackle chaps at rugger, at school.'

Lucy-Ann gazed at Jack in admiration. She thought her brother was very clever!

'Well, I'll help too,' she said. 'I'll go and meet him with you.'

'We shall have to pretend to believe all he says,' said Jack. 'Every word! It'll be funny – him trying to take *us* in with a cock-and-bull story, and us doing the same!'

'I hope he won't be very fierce,' said Lucy-Ann.

'He'll pretend to be quite harmless, I expect,' said Jack. 'Probably say he's a naturalist, or something – and look very simple and friendly. Well – so shall I!'

'The boat's getting quite near,' said Philip. 'There *is* only one man. He's wearing dark glasses because of the sun.'

'To hide his fierce eyes, I expect,' said Lucy-Ann fearfully. 'Not because of the sun. Do we show ourselves?'

'Only two of us,' said Jack. 'You and I will get up, Lucy-Ann, and wave like mad, standing beside the fire. And mind, whatever story I tell, you've got to back me up. Philip, you and Dinah mustn't show yourselves.'

'Where's he going to park his boat?' wondered Dinah. 'Oh, he's making straight for the channel! He knows it then!'

'There you are, you see!' said Jack. 'Nobody would make straight for that hidden channel unless he had been here before. He's quite probably one of the men who came in that bigger boat.'

This did seem very likely indeed, for the boatman made

straight for the little channel as if he had been there before. Just as he came near the cliffs Jack and Lucy-Ann stood up and waved. The man waved back.

'Now, Dinah – you and Philip get down among the rocks that lead to the little harbour,' said Jack. 'There are some big ones there you can crouch behind till he's moored his boat, and comes up to find us here. Then down you must go and hop into the boat ready to go out to sea if we fail in *our* part. If we *don't* fail, things will be fine – we shall have a prisoner we can hold as hostage – and a boat to escape in!'

'Hurray!' said Philip, feeling suddenly excited.

'Hip-hip-hip-!' said Kiki, flying down to Jack's shoulder. She had been on an expedition of her own somewhere – probably chivvying the gulls around, Jack thought.

'You can join in the fun, Kiki,' said Jack. 'And mind you say all the right things!'

'Send for the doctor,' answered Kiki, solemnly. 'Pop goes the doctor!'

'He's going into the channel,' said Philip. 'Come on, Dinah – time we hid! Good luck, Jack and Lucy-Ann!'

20

Mr Horace Tipperlong gets a shock

The man guided the motor-boat expertly into the narrow channel of water, where the *Lucky Star* had been battered to pieces. He saw the bit of broken rope still round one of the rocks, and looked at it, puzzled.

Dinah and Philip were crouching behind two or three large rocks further up the cliff. They could not see what the man was doing, for they were afraid of being spotted if they peeped out.

Jack and Lucy-Ann were waiting on the cliff-top. Lucy-

Ann was nervous. 'My knees feel funny,' she complained to Jack. He laughed.'

'Don't worry. Buck up, knees! Now – here he comes. You needn't say a word if you don't want to.'

The man came up the rocky steps that led to the top of the cleft in the cliff. He was a thin fellow, rather weedy, with skinny legs. He wore shorts and a pullover. He had been burnt by the sun, and his skin was blistered.

He had a thin little moustache, and a high forehead on which the hair grew far back. He wore very dark glasses indeed, so that it was quite impossible to see his eyes. He did not look anybody to be very much feared, Jack thought.

'Hallo, hallo, hallo,' said the man, as he and the children met. 'I was astonished to know there were people on this island.'

'Who told you?' asked Jack at once.

'Oh, nobody,' said the man. 'I saw your spire of smoke. Whatever are you doing here? Is there a camp of you, or something?'

'There might be,' said Jack, airily. 'Why have you come here?'

'I'm an ornithologist,' said the man, very earnestly. 'You won't know what that means, of course.'

Jack grinned to himself. Considering that he and Philip thought themselves very fine ornithologists, this amused him. But he wasn't going to let this man know that.

'Orni-orni-ornibologist?' he said innocently. 'What's that?'

'Well, my lad, it's a student of bird life,' said the man. 'A bird-lover, one who wants to know all he can about birds and their ways.'

'Is that why you've come here, then – to study birds?' asked Lucy-Ann, thinking she ought to say something. Her knees had stopped shaking and feeling funny, now that she saw the man was not at all fearsome.

'Yes. I've been to this island before, years and years ago,

when I was a lad,' said the man. 'And I wanted to come again, though I had a job finding it. I *was* surprised to see your smoke going up. What's it for? Playing at shipwrecked sailors, or something? I know what children are.'

It was plain that the man knew very little about children, and thought the two to be much younger than they were. 'He'll be reciting "Humpty Dumpty" to us in a moment,' thought Jack, with a secret grin.

'Do you know a lot about birds?' said Jack, not answering the man's question.

'Well, I don't know a *great* deal about sea-birds,' said the man. 'That's why I've come to these islands again. I know more about ordinary birds.'

'Aha!' thought Jack, 'he says that because he is afraid I'll ask him a few questions about the birds here.'

'We've got two tame puffins,' said Lucy-Ann suddenly. 'Would you like to see them?'

'Oh, very much, my dear, very much,' said the man, beaming at her. 'By the way, my name is Tipperlong – Horace Tipperlong.'

'Tripalong?' said Lucy-Ann, with a giggle, thinking it was a very good name for this man, who walked with curious mincing steps. Jack wanted to laugh.

'No, no – Tipperlong,' said Horace, and smiled all over his face at Lucy-Ann. 'What is your name?'

'My name's Lucy-Ann,' she said. 'And my brother's name is Jack. Are you coming to see the puffins? It's this way.'

'I should also like to meet whoever is in charge of you,' said Mr Horace Tipperlong. 'And – er – where is your boat?'

'It was smashed up in a storm,' said Jack solemnly. Mr Tipperlong tut-tutted with sympathy.

'How dreadful! Then how were you going to get back home?'

'Look out,' said Jack, just saving Horace as he was about to plunge down a puffin's burrow. 'This place is undermined by the puffins. Mind where you go!'

'My word – what a lot of birds!' said Horace Tipperlong, standing still. He had been so engrossed in polite talk that he did not seem to have noticed the amazing colony of puffins. Another black mark against him! Jack could not believe that a real ornithologist would walk half-way through the puffins without exclaiming at them.

'Extraordinary! Most astonishing! I don't remember ever seeing so many birds together before,' said Horace. 'And all those thousands on the cliffs to. Well, well, well! And do you mean to say you really have got two tame puffins ? I can hardly believe it.'

'They're Philip's,' said Lucy-Ann, and she could have bitten out her tongue.

'I thought you said your brother's name was Jack,' said Horace enquiringly.

'She must have made a mistake,' said Jack, saying the first thing he could think of. They were getting very near the entrance of the underground hole now. Look out, Mr Horace Tipperlong!

Lucy-Ann began to feel nervous. Suppose this man Trip-along, or whatever his name was, didn't fall into the hole when Jack tripped him – suppose instead he went for Jack? Suppose – well, suppose he had a revolver? He didn't *look* a desperate sort of a man, but you never knew. Lucy-Ann looked at the pockets of his shorts to see if she could spy anything like a lump in the shape of a revolver there.

But his pockets were so bulged out with dozens of things that it was impossible to tell. Jack nudged her. 'Keep out of the way now,' he said in a very low voice. Lucy-Ann obediently slipped behind, her heart beating fast.

Jack came to the entrance of the hole. A stick marked it as usual, for it really was almost impossible to find without some sort of signpost. Horace tripped along, looking short-sightedly through his dark glasses – and then, to his enormous astonishment, Jack put out a leg, pushed him, and tripped him right over. He fell at the side of the hole – but before he could get up, Jack had given him a shove – and right into the hole he went, crash!

Jack had a stout stick in his hand, which he had picked from the pile beside the bonfire. He parted the heather and looked into the hole. In the dim light he could see Horace Tipperlong sitting up, and he heard him groaning.

Tipperlong looked up and saw Jack. 'You wicked boy!' he said angrily. 'What do you mean by this?'

His glasses had fallen off in his headlong dive. His eyes certainly did not look very fierce. They looked rather weak and watery. He held his head as if he had hurt it.

'Sorry,' said Jack, 'but it had to be done. Either you caught us – or we caught you. We needn't go on pretending any more. We know quite well what gang you belong to.'

'What are you talking about?' cried the man, and he stood up. His head popped out of the hole. Jack raised his stick at once.

'Get back!' he said fiercely. 'You're our prisoner. You took Bill, didn't you? – well, now we've taken *you*. If you attempt to clamber out, I shall hit you on the head with this. You just try it.'

Horace hastily retreated. Lucy-Ann looked white and scared. 'Oh, Jack – is he hurt? Jack, you won't really hit him, will you?'

'I jolly well will,' said Jack. 'Think of Bill, Lucy-Ann – and our poor *Lucky Star* – and us stranded here because of this fellow and his precious friends. Don't you realise that if he gets out and back to his boat, they'll send heaps more, and won't rest till they've got us? Don't be feeble!'

'Well – I don't want to see you hit him,' said Lucy-Ann. 'Dinah wouldn't mind a bit, but I'm not like Dinah.'

'Look here – will you kindly tell me what all this nonsense is about?' shouted Horace. 'I never heard of such a thing! Here I come to a bird-island, which, as far as I know, certainly isn't a crime – and you two kids lead me here, trip me up, and shove me down this hole. I've hurt my head badly. And now you say if I try to get out, you'll brain me. You nasty little creatures!'

'I'm really very sorry about it,' said Jack again, 'but there wasn't anything else to be done. You realize that with our boat gone – and Bill disappeared – we had to get a boat somehow. We can't stay here for the rest of our lives.'

Horace was so amazed and upset at this speech that he stood up again. He sat down hurriedly when he saw Jack's stick. 'But look here – do you really mean to say you're now going to take my boat? I never heard such brazen cheek. You wait till I get hold of the people in charge of you, my boy – you'll get the worst hiding you've ever had in your life.'

21

Horace does not like Puffin Island

'Lucy-Ann – see if you can spot either Philip or Dinah,' ordered Jack. 'Philip will probably be in the boat, ready to start her up, if he has to – but Dinah will possibly be looking out to see if there is any sign from us.'

Lucy-Ann stood up. She saw Dinah standing a good way off, waiting anxiously at the top of the cleft in the cliff. Philip was not to be seen. Presumably he was down in the boat.

Lucy-Ann waved violently. 'It's all right. We've got him in the hole!' she yelled.

Dinah waved back, then disappeared. She had gone to tell Philip. Soon the two appeared again, and came through the puffin colony at top speed to hear what had happened.

'We got him,' said Jack proudly. 'Easy as pie. Down he went, plonk!'

'Who's there?' enquired Horace plaintively. 'Is that somebody else? Look here – you've just *got* to tell me what's going on here. I'm all at sea.'

'That's where we'll be soon, I hope,' grinned Jack. 'And in your boat! Philip, meet Mr Horace Tripalong.'

'Gosh – is that really his name?' said Philip.

The incensed Mr Tipperlong roared up the hole. 'My name is TIPPERLONG and I'll thank you to remember it. Ill-mannered children! You wait till I make a complaint about you, and get you punished. I never heard of such behaviour in all my life.'

'You can't blame him for being wild,' said Jack. 'He says he's a-a-I say, Mr Tripalong, what did you say you were?'

'An ornithologist, ignorant boy!' yelled Mr Tipperlong.

'Golly, what's that?' said Philip innocently, and the others giggled.

'You let me out of this,' commanded Mr Tipperlong, and his head appeared cautiously near the entrance of the hole, ready to bob back if necessary.

It *was* necessary. 'Look here,' said Jack, exasperated, 'do you want me to give you a good old conk on the head before you know I mean what I say? Because I will! I don't *want* to; but I will! I bet you gave old Bill a few blows before you captured him. What's sauce for the goose is sauce for the gander.'

'You're talking double-Dutch,' said Horace, in a disgusted voice. 'I think you must be mad. Do you mean to tell me you kids are all alone on this island? I don't believe a word you say. You tell whoever is in charge of you to come and have a word with me. If you think I'm going to stay here much longer, you're mistaken. I've never met such unpleasant children in my life. I suppose you're all playing at being Just Williams. *Pah!*'

This was a lovely noise. Kiki, who had been listening with surprise and enjoyment to the animated conversation, now joined in.

'Pah! Pooh! Pah! Pop!'

She flew to the edge of the hole and looked in. 'Pah!' she

said again, and went off into a cackle of laughter.

Horace looked up in fresh alarm. Was that really a parrot at the hole entrance – saying 'pah' and 'pooh' to him in that rude way?

'Is that – is that one of the tame puffins you told me about?' he asked doubtfully.

'I thought you were an ornithologist,' said Jack in scorn. 'Kiki is a parrot. I should have thought anyone would have known that!'

'But – how can a parrot live here?' said Horace. 'It's not a sea-bird. Oh, this is all a dream. But what a very silly dream!'

At that moment a puffin came down the end of the burrow that led into the back of the hole.

'Arrrrrrr!' it announced in a deep and guttural voice. Mr Tipperlong jumped violently. All he could see in the dimness of the hole was a baleful eye and a big and many-coloured beak.

'Go away,' he said weakly. 'Shoo!'

'Shoo!' said Kiki from the hole entrance in great delight. 'Pah! Pooh! Shoo! Arrrrrrrr!'

'You're all mad,' said poor Horace. 'I'm mad too, I suppose. Shoo, I tell you!'

The puffin said *arrr* again and then went back up its burrow. Judging by the flow of *arrrrs* that came down the hole, it was telling its wife all about the peculiar puffin-man it had just seen in the hole.

'What are we going to do now we've got him?' said Philip in a low voice. 'I suppose he *is* an enemy? I mean, – he does sound rather a goof, doesn't he?'

'All part of a clever plan,' said Jack. 'He's no ornithologist. He's been told to dress up like a goofy one and act the part. Some bird-men *are* awful goofs, you know. We've met them. Well, this one is just about too goofy for words – he's over-acting, if you know what I mean. I'm glad he hasn't got a revolver. I've been afraid of that all the time.'

'Yes. So was I,' admitted Philip. 'There may be one in the boat. I hope there is. It might come in useful. Well, what are we going to do?'

'Do you think he can hear what we're saying?' said Lucy-Ann, looking frightened.

'No, not if we talk as low as this,' said Philip. 'Jack, the boat is a nice little bit of work. Smaller than the *Lucky Star*, but it has a little cabin and will easily take us all, and some food.'

'Are there oars in it, in case we want to cut out the engine and go in quietly to shore anywhere?' asked Jack.

'Yes,' said Philip. 'I noticed those. Have you got a good plan, Jack? I keep on and on thinking, but all I can make up my mind about is to sail off in the boat – but where to I don't know. We want to escape – but we want to escape *to* somewhere. And not out of the frying-pan into the fire, either. We'd better do it soon, too, because if dear old Tripalong doesn't get back to the gang with news pretty soon they'll send others here.'

'Yes, I'd thought of all that too,' said Jack, and the girls nodded. 'The thing is – shall we try to make for the outer islands and find one where a few fishermen live, and try to get help? Or shall we try for the mainland? Or shall we hunt for Bill?'

There was a silence. Everyone was thinking hard. Lucy-Ann spoke first.

'I vote for hunting for Bill,' she said. 'We could try that first, anyway – and then make for safety afterwards if we're not successful. But I do think we ought to try to find Bill first.'

'Good for you, Lucy-Ann,' said Jack. 'That's what *I* think. Now for some more planning.'

Horace Tipperlong suddenly demanded their attention again. 'Stop all that talk, talk, talk,' he cried fretfully. 'I'm ravenous – and thirsty too. If you're going to try and starve me to death, say so. But at least let me know.'

'We're not going to starve you. Don't be an ass,' said Jack. 'Lucy-Ann, open some tins and give them to him. And chuck him down some biscuits too. Dinah, fill a pan with water from the pool.'

'Right, chief,' grinned Dinah, and went off to the pool in the rocks. Horace was handed down the full pan of water, and some tins and biscuits. He began to eat hungrily. The sight of the food made the others feel hungry too.

'We'll have a feed as well,' said Philip. 'Shall I take a turn at holding the stick and sitting by the hole, Jack?'

'Yes,' said Jack. 'But mind – give him a good old conk if he so much as shows a hair!'

This was said in a very loud voice, so that Horace was sure to hear. But Horace said nothing. Apparently he was willing to bide his time now.

The children were soon devouring a tinned chicken, tinned peas which they ate without heating, and a tinned fruit salad with tinned cream, washed down with water from the pool.

'Jolly good,' said Jack, with a comfortable sigh. 'I feel better. Wonderful what food does to you!'

'It would make me sick if I ate as much as you've just eaten,' said Dinah. 'You're a greedy pig. You ate twice as much as anyone else.'

'Can't help it,' said Jack. 'I was twice as hungry. Now then – lower your voices, please – we'll make our plans.'

'Shall we set out at night?' said Philip in a low voice.

'No,' said Jack at once. 'We'd never see our way, even in the moonlight. We'd better set off first thing tomorrow morning, about dawn. We'll hope old Tripalong is asleep then, so that we can get a good start without his interrupting us.'

'Yes – because we'll have to leave the hole unguarded when we all go to the boat,' said Lucy-Ann.

'I'd thought of that,' said Jack. 'You three can go to the boat, take food with you, and our clothes and rugs – get everything absolutely ready – and then, when you're ready to start, give me a yell and I'll come tearing along to join you. You can send Dinah up to the top of the cleft to wave.'

'And by the time Horace has realized nobody is on guard to conk him on the head, we'll be out to sea in his boat!' said Dinah, enjoying the thought. 'Poor old Horace! I feel quite sorry for him.'

'I don't,' said Jack unfeelingly. 'If he's Bill's enemy, he's jolly well mine. He deserves all he's got – honestly, except for being tripped into the hole, he's got nothing much to complain about. I shan't block him in, when we leave, and put food there, as I thought we would at first. It won't matter if he gets out once we're gone. And I shouldn't think it will be long before some others of the gang come along to see why he hasn't turned up at home – wherever that is!'

'It seems a bit of a wild-goose chase to try and find Bill, with all these scores of islands to choose from,' said Philip. 'But I shouldn't feel comfortable if we didn't have a shot, anyway.'

'Nor should I,' said Jack. 'Bill's often come to *our* rescue, in other adventures. It's time we went to his – if only we can find him. I suppose there's no doubt but that the enemy have taken him to their headquarters on some island or other here.'

'Don't you think it would be a good idea if we got everything ready this evening?' said Dinah suddenly. 'You know – all the food in the boat – and rugs and clothes and things – so as not to have to waste a single minute getting ready tomorrow morning. You said you wanted to set off at dawn.'

'Yes – that's a good idea,' said Jack. 'I'll take a turn at the hole with the stick now if you like, Philip – and you help the girls carry things down to the boat. What a bit of luck capturing one like that! I must say I think we've been pretty clever.'

'Pah!' said Kiki. 'Pooh! Pah!'

'Sorry you don't agree, old thing,' said Jack. 'Very sorry. But I still think we *have* been very clever!'

'We'd better leave some food for Tripalong, hadn't we?' asked Dinah. 'I mean – I know the gang will be along in a day or two to see what has happened to him – but he'll have to have things to eat till they come.'

'Yes. Leave him some tins and a tin-opener,' said Jack. 'And, Philip, were there any rugs in the boat, belonging to him?'

'Yes,' said Philip. 'I'll bring them back here, after I've taken some food to the boat. We'll chuck them down to him. I think we're being awfully kind to our enemy.'

Horace didn't think so. He got all upset again after a bit, and began to shout wildly down in the hole.

'This has gone on long enough. You let me out, you little villains! Wait till I get my hands on you! What is the meaning of this, I'd like to know!'

'Oh, don't keep up the pretence any more, Mr Horace Tripalong,' said Jack, bored. 'We're enemies, both of us, and you know it. You open up a bit and tell me where Bill is and a few things more. You might get off more lightly in the end, if you do.'

'Who's this Bill you keep talking about?' said Horace in an exasperated tone. 'Look here, are you playing at pirates or bandits or what? I never heard of anyone being kept prisoner down a hole like this, by a pack of villainous children!'

'No – I never heard of it either, now I come to think of it,' said Jack. 'Well, dear Horace, if you won't admit what we all know, keep quiet.'

'Pah!' said Horace, aggravated beyond words.

'Pah!' said Kiki at once, and went to the hole entrance. She looked down.

'Pah! Naughty boy! Pop goes the weasel! How many times have I told you to shut that door? God save the Queen! Pah!'

Mr Tipperlong listened in amazed horror. Was he really and truly mad? *Could* that be a parrot talking to him so rudely?

'I'll wring that bird's neck,' he said fiercely, and got up.

'Ring the bell, please!' said Kiki, and went off into one of her cackles. Then she poked her head in again and screeched like a railway engine in a tunnel. It was absolutely deafening in the hole below, and Horace fell back on the ground defeated.

'Mad! Quite mad! All mad!' he muttered, and, putting his head in his hands, he said no more.

22

The enemy

The three children, accompanied by Huffin and Puffin, made various journeys to and from Sleepy Hollow with food, rugs and clothes. Philip brought back a pile of rugs from the boat and thrust them down the hole entrance. They descended on poor Horace and enveloped him. He was very much startled, but glad to find in a moment or two that his captors were actually offering him something warm and soft to lie on.

He arranged them underneath himself. Ah, that was more comfortable. He began to think longingly of all the things he would do to those children, once he got free.

At last everything was in the motor-boat, ready for the early start. It was now getting dusk. Philip, Lucy-Ann and Dinah came and sat beside Jack.

'I suppose one or other of must keep watch over the hole all night, in case Horace escapes?' whispered Philip. Jack nodded.

'Yes. We can't risk his getting out, just as we've got

everything set. You take first watch, Philip. We won't ask the girls to watch, because I'm pretty sure they wouldn't enjoy hitting Horace good and hard if he popped his head out.'

'I would!' said Dinah indignantly. 'Lucy-Ann is kind, but I'm not.'

Lucy-Ann said nothing. She felt sure she wouldn't like to hit Horace hard. Anyway the boys decided that only they should keep watch, so that was all right.

The sun had gone down into the sea. The sky was pricked with the first few stars. The children lay about comfortably on the heather, talking in low voices. There was no sound from Horace. Perhaps he was alseep.

Philip's three rats, which had suddenly begun to look very grown-up, came out to sniff the evening air. Dinah removed herself at once. Huffin and Puffin regarded the rats with fixed eyes. Kiki yawned and then sneezed. Then she coughed in a very hollow manner.

'Shut up, Kiki,' said Jack. 'If you want to practise your awful noises, go up on the cliff and make the seagulls and guillemots listen.'

'Arrrr!' said Huffin solemnly.

'Huffin agrees with me,' said Jack.

'Pah!' said Kiki.

'And pah to you,' said Jack. 'Now shut up, Kiki, do. It's a lovely evening. Don't spoil it with your pahing and poohing.'

Just as he finished speaking, there came a noise from far out to sea – a very small noise at first, hardly heard above the sound of the sea and the wind – but becoming quite unmistakable after a while.

'A motor-boat!' said Jack, sitting upright. 'Now what in the world . . . '

'Have they come to look for Horace already?' said Philip, in a low voice. 'Blow! This upsets our plans like anything!'

Nothing could be seen on the darkening sea, but the noise

came nearer and nearer. Jack clutched Philip and spoke in his ear.

'There's only one thing to do. We must all go and get into our boat now, this very minute – and get out to sea. We mustn't let the enemy see the boat in the channel there, or they'll take it, and our only chance will be gone. Come on, quickly!'

Silently the four children rose to their feet. Kiki flew to Jack's shoulder, not uttering a sound. Huffin and Puffin, who had retired to their burrow, came out again. They flew beside the hurrying children, not even remarking *arrrr* to one another.

Across the puffin colony they went, stumbling and staggering between the hundreds of burrows. Up the little slope of the cliff and over to the cleft in the rock. Down the rocky ledges, be careful, be careful! And into the rocking boat, their breath coming fast and their hearts beating like hammers.

'Start her up,' ordered Philip, and Jack started the engine. Philip threw off the mooring-rope and it skittered into the boat by the girls' feet. In a moment more they were backing gently out of the little channel.

Soon they were right out of it. Philip went to the east a little. It was almost dark now.

'We'll stop the engine,' said Philip. 'And wait here till the other boat goes into the channel, because I expect she'll make for it. I don't want to bump into her. And the men on board her might hear our engine.'

So the engine was stopped, and the motor-boat swung up and down gently as waves ran beneath her to the rocky cliffs some way off.

The sound of the other boat's engine was now very loud. Philip wished he had gone a bit further off after all. But the bigger boat swung by without stopping and then nosed its way into the hidden harbour. The children, crouching in their boat, straining their eyes, had just been able to make out a dark shape and that was all.

The other boat's engine stopped and peace came back into the night. Some of the sea-birds, disturbed, uttered a few wild cries and then flew back to their roosting-places on the ledges.

'Horace will be glad to be rescued,' said Dinah at last.

'Yes, he'll probably be out of the hole already,' said Jack. 'He'd soon know when we were gone. I've no doubt there'll be a lot of bad language going on when they find out how we imprisoned poor Horace – and gosh, when they find out we've taken his boat . . . '

'Arrrrrr!' said a deep voice from the rail round the deck.

The children jumped in the darkness. 'Oh – it must be Huffin or Puffin,' said Philip, pleased. 'Fancy them coming with us. I do think that's friendly of them.'

'They're sweet,' said Lucy-Ann, and put out her hand to Huffin. Both the puffins were there, sitting side by side in the darkness. Kiki flew to join them.

'What are we going to do now?' said Dinah. 'Dare we go off in the dark? We might bump into rocks and wreck the boat.'

'We'll have to stay here till the first light of day,' said Philip. 'Then we'll set off, and hope the men on the island won't hear our engine, and come after us!'

'We shall have got a good start,' said Jack. 'Well, what about having a snooze, if we're going to stay here? Where's the anchor? Shall we let it down? I don't fancy drifting about at the mercy of the waves all night long.'

Whilst the boys were busy, the girls laid out rugs, mackintoshes and jerseys to lie on. It was a lovely warm night, and nobody minded.

'It's so nice to have the stars above us instead of a ceiling or a tent roof,' said Lucy-Ann, snuggling down. 'I don't feel a bit sleepy, somehow. I suppose it's all the excitement. I've got used to this adventure now. Oh dear, how glad I am that I didn't have to hit Horace on the head! I should have dreamt about that for ages.'

They lay for some time, talking. They all felt very wide awake indeed. Huffin and Puffin appeared to be awake too, because they occasionally remarked *arrr* to one another. Kiki was on Jack's feet.

She was also wide awake, and began to recite the nursery rhymes she knew: 'Humpty Dumpty, puddingy pie, ding dong bell, ring his neck!'

'Shut up!' said Jack. 'We're trying to go to sleep, you tiresome bird!'

'I hope Huffin and Puffin stay with us,' said Lucy-Ann. 'Wouldn't it be lovely if we could take them home with us?'

'Shut up!' said Kiki, and cackled.

'Parrots are not allowed to say that,' said Jack severely, and sat up to tap her on her beak. But she had promptly put her head under her wing, so he couldn't.

'Artful creature,' said Jack, and heard a faint 'Pah!' from under Kiki's wing.

Just as Lucy-Ann was falling off to sleep, the others sat up so suddenly that she was jerked awake. 'What's the matter?' she began. And then she knew.

The engine of the other motor-boat was going again. Lucy-Ann sat up with the others, her eyes straining through the darkness.

'They must have found Horace, heard his report, and all have gone back on board,' said Jack. 'They are evidently not going to spend the night here. Look – here they come – gosh, they've got their lights on this time.'

'Jack – Jack! They'll be going back to their headquarters,' said Philip urgently. 'Let's follow them. Get the anchor up, quick. They won't hear our engine because theirs makes such a row. Come on, let's follow them! They'll take us to where Bill is!'

The men's motor-boat had swung round when it had come from the channel, and was now headed out to sea. It was not long before the children's boat set off in its wake.

They could not hear the other boat's engine because of their own, and they knew that theirs would not be heard by the men for the same reason.

Huffin and Puffin were still on the deck-rail. Clearly they meant to go wherever the children went. Lucy-Ann thought it was nice to have such staunch, loyal friends, even if they were only puffins. Kiki was on Jack's shoulder again, her beak to the breeze.

'All aboard,' she kept saying. 'All aboard. Pah!'

The first boat sped along quickly. It was easy to follow because of its light. The children stood with their noses to the wind in silence. Lucy-Ann spoke first.

'This adventure is getting more adventurous,' she said. 'Oh dear – it really is!'

23

The secret lagoon

For a long time the two boats sped across the sea. 'It's the Sea of Adventure!' Lucy-Ann thought. 'Anything might happen here. Oh, I do hope we find Bill. Things always seem right when he's with us.'

'You girls had better have a nap,' said Jack at last. 'You'll be tired out. Philip and I will keep awake and take turns at the wheel. You snuggle down and go to sleep.'

So they did, and it wasn't long before both girls were asleep and dreaming of swings and hammocks, because of the swinging, swaying motion of the boat they were in.

After a good long time, Jack spoke to Philip. 'Tufty – do you see the light flashing over there? It must be a signal of some sort, I should think. The boat in front is heading towards it. I hope we're soon coming to our journey's end, because the moon will be up soon, and we might be seen.'

'That light must be a guide to the boat – or perhaps to an aeroplane,' said Philip. 'Blow, here comes the moon! – out of that bank of clouds. Well, she's not very bright, that's one good thing.'

By the light of the moon the boys could see an island looming up in front of the boats. To the left was another island, two or three miles away from the first, or so it seemed to the boys.

'Look here, Jack – we don't want to drive right into the jaws of danger,' said Philip, 'which is what we shall do if we follow the first boat right up to that island it's heading for. I think it would be better to go to that other one, over there, look – we could probably see enough in the moonlight to make out a cove to land in. We could pull this boat into safety between us.'

'Right,' said Jack, swinging the wheel round. Now they were no longer following the first boat. It was soon out of sight, and was probably by now safely in some little harbour. Their own boat headed for the further island. By the time they got there their eyes were used to the moonlight, and they could see everything fairly clearly.

'Doesn't seem very rocky,' said Jack, nosing in gently. 'No – all sand and fine shingle. I'll run her straight up this beach, Philip. Be ready to jump out as soon as she stops.'

The girls awoke and scrambled out of their wraps. Jack ran the boat straight up the shingly beach. It drove into the fine shingle and stopped. Philip sprang out.

'Can't shift her at all,' he panted, when he and the others had tried to pull the boat further up. 'Let's chuck out the anchor and let her be. It's nearly low tide now, so we'll just paddle out and drop the anchor, and give the boat a push – it will be quite all right then, if the sea keeps calm.'

The boys did this and then lay on the shingle to get their breath. They were both very tired. They almost fell asleep as they lay there.

'Come on, boys,' said Dinah, at last. 'Bring some rugs and

find a sheltered place somewhere. You're half asleep.'

'Well, we're safe till the morning anyway,' said Jack, as he stumbled up the beach with the others, almost asleep as he walked. 'Nobody knows we're here. Another bird-island, I suppose.'

They came to a low cliff. Lucy-Ann saw a dark cave at the foot. 'Put your torch on,' she called to Philip. 'We might be able to sleep here.'

It proved to be a small cave, with a soft, dry sandy floor. It smelt a little of seaweed, but nobody minded that. They dragged their rugs in, and flung themselves down. Huffin and Puffin squatted at the opening of the cave, as if they had put themsleves on guard.

Almost before their heads touched the rugs the boys were alseep. The girls followed suit, and soon there was nothing to be heard but tiny snores from Jack, who was flat on his back. Kiki examined his face in the darkness to find out why her beloved Jack was making such queer little noises, then decided they weren't worth bothering about. She sat herself down in the middle of his tummy and went to sleep too.

The next morning Huffin and Puffin walked over to Philip and stood heavily on him. 'Arrrr!' they said, meaning 'Come on, wake up!'

Philip awoke. 'Get off,' he said. 'Don't copy Kiki's bad ways, Huffin and Puffin. Oh, I say – thanks for the fish – but don't put them all over my chest, Huffin!'

Huffin had been diving for fish. He now deposited them carefully on Philip, opened and shut his mouth a few times, and made his one and only remark, in a deep and satisfied voice. 'Arrrrrrrrrr!'

The children laughed when they heard about Huffin's morning offering. They rubbed their eyes and decided to have a dip in the sea, for they all felt dirty.

'Then we'll have breakfast,' said Jack. 'Gosh, I wish I wasn't always so frightfully hungry. I say, this is rather a nice island, isn't it? Look, you can see the enemy's island on the horizon over there. Wonder if Bill is there.'

'Well go up to the highest point on this island after breakfast, and have a good look round at all the others,' said Philip. 'Let's go and get some food from the boat.'

The boat was afloat on the high tide. The children had to swim out to her. They rifled her for food – and whilst she was looking for a tin of salmon she knew she had put in, Lucy-Ann found something that made her shout.

'I say, look! – a radio! Do you suppose it is a transmitter as well as a receiver? Can we send a message on it?'

'Don't know,' said Jack, examining it. 'It's not a bit like Bill's. If only we knew! Anyway, even if we *could* send out messages on it, I wouldn't know how to. I expect it's just some sort of portable radio. Come on, let's have breakfast. Phew, this sun's hot.'

With Huffin, Puffin, Kiki and the three rats all sharing their breakfast, the four children made a very good meal on the boat. 'Now, what next?' said Jack. 'Shall we go up to the topmost height in this island and see what's all round us?'

'Yes,' said the others, so, leaving the boat by itself, they made their way up the low cliff and on to the grass-grown land behind. It was not so heathery as Puffin Island had been, nor were there many birds on it.

'It's funny. You'd think there would be plenty on a nice little island like this,' said Jack. 'Look, there's a hill at the other end of the island! – let's climb it.'

They climbed to the very top – and then they stood still in astonishment. Beyond them, sparkling blue, was a lagoon, flat and still as a mirror. It lay between two islands, but the islands were joined by broad strips of rocks that enclosed the whole lagoon, so that it was impossible to say which island it really belonged to. The rocks ran out from each one, in some places as high as cliffs – and there between them lay this unbelievably lovely sea-lake.

'Look at that!' said Jack in awe. 'We've seen some wonderful sights – but never one as beautiful as that blue lagoon. It can't be real.'

But it was. It stretched out below them for about a mile and a half, so sheltered and protected that not a ripple broke its calm blue surface.

And then something happened that gave the children a shock of amazement. They heard the low hum of an aeroplane. They saw it coming towards them. Jack pulled them down flat in case they were seen. It flew right over the lagoon, and as it flew, something dropped from it – something that opened out, billowed white, and had something else fixed below it.

The children watched in amazement. All sorts of ridiculous things flashed through their minds – was it a scientific experiment – bombs – atom bombs – what was it?

A little parachute had opened, and was swinging down to the lagoon. The package underneath it was wrapped in glistening stuff – some kind of waterproof material, Jack thought. It reached the water and disappeared. The parachute spread itself out on the calm surface and lay still. But as the children watched, it seemed to dissolve and finally it too disappeared into the water.

'Look – the plane is circling the lagoon again. It's going to drop another,' said Philip. They all watched as the plane once more dropped a parachute, and the same thing happened.

Down to the water it floated with its unknown package, and in a few minutes all trace of it had disappeared. A third one was sent down and then the aeroplane circled round once and headed away. Soon it was lost in the distance.

'Well, whatever in the world was it doing, dropping things into this lagoon?' said Jack in astonishment. 'What a strange thing to do! What's in those enormous packages the parachutes carry?'

'And why drop them into the lagoon?' wondered Dinah. 'It seems so silly. Do they want to get rid of something? What a strange way to do it!'

'Let's take the boat and go and sail over the lagoon to see if we can see down into the depths,' said Lucy-Ann.

'And how do you think we are going to get *in*to the lagoon, idiot?' said Jack. 'No boat can get into that water – unless it's dragged over that barrier or rocks surrounding it.'

'Yes – of course – how silly of me!' said Lucy-Ann. 'I do wish we could see down into that water though – and find out what secrets it is holding, down in the blue depths.'

'Arrrrr!' said Huffin and Puffin, and, their wings vibrating quickly, they sailed down to the lagoon as if to say 'You want to go there? Well, it's easy.'

They bobbed there on the lagoon, very small specks indeed, diving under the water for fish. The children watched them.

'I don't see why we can't go and have a bathe there,' said Jack at last. 'We could swim a good way out and then dive down to see if we could find out anything. You never know!'

'Well, let's go now then,' said Dinah eagerly. 'I feel as if I simply *must* find out what all this is about. It's the most peculiar secret, I must say!'

They began to scramble down the hill. It grew rocky as they got lower down, but there were plenty of sea-pink cushions to soften the way for their feet. At last they reached the edge of the calm blue water.

They undressed and went in. The water was very warm indeed, and rippled like soft silk over their arms. They swam out slowly, enjoying the warmth of the lake and of the sun on their shoulders.

'Now I'm going to dive down and see if I can make out anything,' said Jack, and turning himself up like a duck, down he went, down and down and down. What would he find at the bottom?

24

An amazing discovery

The lagoon was quite deep. Jack could not swim to the bottom, because he couldn't possibly hold his breath long enough. He came up, gasping.

'All I could see was a pile of silvery stuff lying on the bottom,' he gasped to the others. 'Nothing else at all. I couldn't go right down to it, because I hadn't enough breath.'

'Well, that's not much use,' said Dinah. 'We want to see what's *inside* the waterproof wrapping – tear it off, so that we can see what it holds.'

'We wouldn't be able to do that very easily,' said Philip. 'I bet it's sewn up pretty tightly – or sealed in some clever way. I'll go down, Jack – perhaps I can get near enough to *feel* what's inside.'

'Oh dear – do be careful,' said Lucy-Ann. 'You don't know *what* might be inside!'

'Well – it's hardly likely to be anything that will eat us,' grinned Jack. 'Kiki, why don't *you* do a little diving, like Huffin and Puffin do – you could be a bit of help then!'

But Kiki did not approve of all this love of bathing. She flew about above the children in the water and tried occasionally to perch on a bare shoulder. Huffin and Puffin loved having the children in the water, and swam and dived beside them, uttering deep *arrrrrs* of satisfaction.

Philip dived under, and swam rapidly downwards, his eyes wide open in the salt water. Far below him he saw the silvery mass, gleaming dimly on the lagoon bed. He swam right down to it, and put out his hand to touch it. Beneath the wrapping he felt something very hard indeed.

Then, his breath giving out, he rose up to the surface,

almost bursting. He took in great gulps of air.

'I felt something hard,' he said at last. 'But it was impossible to tell what it was. Blow! Isn't it sickening to be right on top of a mystery like this, and not be able to solve it?'

'We shall have to give it up,' said Jack. 'I know perfectly well I haven't enough breath to go down and probe the wrappings. I should burst for want of breath.'

'I do hate giving things up,' said Dinah.

'Well, swim under the water yourself and see if *you* can find out anything,' said Philip.

'You know I can't hold my breath even as long as you can,' said Dinah. 'So what's the good of that?'

'I'm going to swim back to shore,' said Lucy-Ann. 'There's a nice sunny rock over there, covered with seaweed. I shall have a sunbathe there.'

She swam slowly over to it. Huffin and Puffin dived under, just beside her. 'I wonder what they look like when they swim under water,' thought Lucy-Ann. 'I'd love to see them chasing a fish.'

She turned herself up, and duck-dived under the water. Ah, there was Huffin, using his wings to swim swiftly through the water after a big fish. Quick, Huffin, or you'll lose it!

Just as she was going to swim upwards again Lucy-Ann noticed something below her. The lagoon was not nearly so deep just there, for a shelf of rocks ran out into the water, making it fairly shallow, although it was much too deep still for Lucy-Ann's feet to touch the bottom.

The little girl took a quick glance to see what it was on the rocks below the water, but then her breath gave out, and, half choking, she rose up to the surface, gasping and spluttering.

When she had got her breath again, down she went – and then she realized what it was she saw. One of the parachuted packages, instead of falling into the deeper waters of the lagoon, had fallen on to the shallow rocky bed just below her. The package had split open – and all its contents were spread and scattered on the rocky bottom below.

But whatever were they? Lucy-Ann could not make them out at all. They looked such peculiar shapes. She rose up to the surface again and yelled to Jack.

'Hi, Jack! One of those secret packages has split open on the rocky bottom just here – but I can't make out what was in it!'

The boys and Dinah swam up in great excitement. They all duck-dived and down they went, down, down, down. They came to where the silvery wrapping was split open, moving gently up and down with the flow of the water. All around it were the split contents.

The boys, almost bursting for breath, examined them quickly, then shot up to the surface, gasping.

They looked at one another, and then both shouted the same words.

'Guns! Guns! Scores of them!'

The children swam to the sunny rock that Lucy-Ann was now sitting on, and clambered up.

'Fancy that! Guns! What in the wide world do they want to drop guns down in this lagoon for? Are they getting rid of them? And why?'

'No. They wouldn't wrap them up so carefully in waterproof stuff if they were just dumping them,' said Philip soberly. 'They're hiding them.'

'*Hiding* them! But what a very peculiar place to hide guns in!' said Dinah. 'What are they going to do with them?'

'They're probably gun-running,' said Jack, 'bringing hundreds of guns here from somewhere, and hiding them till they're ready for them – ready for some revolution somewhere – South America, perhaps.'

'Something like that, I bet,' said Philip. 'There are always people stirring up trouble *some*where, and wanting weapons to fight with. Those who can supply them with guns would make a lot of money. Yes, that's what it is – gun-running!'

'*Well!*' said Lucy-Ann, 'to think we've dropped right into an awful thing like that! I expect Bill guessed it – and they saw him snooping round – and captured him so that he couldn't give the game away.'

'However do they get the guns away from here?' wondered Jack. 'I mean – they can't be got away by boat, because this lagoon is absolutely enclosed by rocks. Yet the guns must be taken out of the water, to be sent to wherever they are wanted. It's jolly strange.'

'Well, now we *do* know what that aeroplane was dropping,' said Philip. 'My word – this lagoon must be full of armaments! What an absolutely wonderful hiding-place – nobody to see what happens, nobody to discover the guns at the bottom . . . '

'Except us,' said Lucy-Ann promptly. '*I* discovered that split package. I suppose it hit the rocks just below the surface and split open at once.'

They lay basking in the sun, talking over the curious discovery. Then Kiki suddenly uttered an astonished cry, and the children sat up to see why.

'Goodness – there's a boat coming,' said Jack in dismay. 'Coming towards this very place, too, from the seaward side of the rocky barrier.'

'What shall we do?' said Lucy-Ann, frightened. 'There's nowhere to hide, and we haven't time to make our way back without being seen.'

The boys gazed round in desperation. What could be done? Then Philip suddenly grabbed up a great armful of seaweed and flung it over the surprised Lucy-Ann.

'We'll cover ourselves up with this!' he said. 'There's stacks of it! Quick! Pull it up and cover yourselves with it. It's the only way we can hide.'

Their hearts thumping loudly again, the four children piled the thickly growing seaweed, with its great ribbon-like fronds, all over themselves. Jack peered through his and spoke urgently to Dinah.

'One of your feet is showing, Di. Put some seaweed over it, quick!'

Huffin and Puffin were amazed at this sudden seaweed game. They decided which lump was Philip and went to perch solemnly on him. He felt their weight, and almost laughed.

'Nobody could possibly guess there was a boy under these two puffins and all the seaweed,' he thought. 'I only hope the others are really well covered.'

The boat grounded not far off. The voices of two or three men could be heard, coming nearer and nearer. The children held their breath. 'Don't tread on us, oh, don't tread on us!' prayed Lucy-Ann, feeling quite sick, especially as there was a great flabby piece of seaweed across her mouth.

The men did not tread on them. They came and stood quite nearby, however, and all of them lighted cigarettes as they stood there.

'The last lot of stuff came today,' said one man, in a husky, deep voice. 'This lagoon must be almost full now.'

'Yes. Time we got some of it away,' said another voice, a sharp, commanding kind of voice. 'We don't know how much information that fellow we've got has passed on to his headquarters. He won't talk. Better send a message through to the chief, to tell him to collect as much as he wants, in case anyone else is sent along to snoop.'

'What about the second fellow? He won't talk either,' said the first voice. 'What are we going to do with them?'

'They can't remain up here,' said the commanding voice. 'Put them on the boat tonight, and we'll dump them somewhere where they won't be heard of again. I'm not going to waste my time on that first fellow any more – what's his name? – Cunningham. He's been enough trouble to us, poking his noise into all we do for the last year. Time he disappeared.'

The four hidden children, feeling very damp and cold under their seaweed, shivered to hear all this. They knew perfectly well what was meant. They, these men, were Bill's bitter enemies, because he had been successful in keeping on their track – now they had got him, and they were afraid he knew too much, though actually it was likely that Bill didn't know as much as they, the children, did.

'And so they are going to remove all these guns and then dump poor Bill somewhere so that he never *will* be heard of again, because he will be drowned,' thought Jack desperately. 'We shall *have* to rescue him. And as quickly as possible too. I wonder who the other fellow is they are talking about. Surely it can't be Horace. I thought he was one of the enemy.'

The men wandered away over the rocks. Evidently they had come to survey their extraordinary hiding-place though they could see very little of its contents. The children lay perfectly still, not daring to move, in case they should be noticed. They got very tired indeed of lying there, and Lucy-Ann was shivering.

Then they heard the sound of the motor-boat's engine starting up again. Thank goodness! They waited a while, and then Jack sat cautiously up. He looked round. There was no-one to be seen. The men had gone back to the boat by a different way, and it was now some distance out to sea.

'Phew!' said Jack. 'I didn't like that at all. Another inch or two nearer, and one of the men would have trodden on my foot!'

25

Another surprise

They all sat up and removed the slippery seaweed from themselves. Huffin and Puffin walked down Philip's body, where they had perched the whole time. Kiki, to her fright and dismay, had been covered with seaweed by Jack, and forced to stay beside him, for he was afraid she might give them away by talking. She talked angrily now.

'Poor, poor Polly! Send for the doctor! What a pity, what a pity, ding dong bell, Polly's in the well!'

The children looked at one another solemnly when they had finished uncovering themselves. Bill was in great danger, there was no doubt of that at all.

'What are we going to do?' said Lucy-Ann, with tears in her eyes. Nobody quite knew. There seemed to be danger wherever they turned.

'Well,' said Jack at last, 'we've got a boat of our own, that's one thing – and I think when it's dark tonight we'd better set out for the other island, the one the men are on, and see if we can't find where they keep their motor-boat. We know that Bill will be there.'

'And rescue him!' said Dinah, thrilled, 'But how shall we get close in to shore without being seen or heard?'

'We'll go when it's dark, as I said,' said Jack, 'and when we get near to the shore, we'll stop our engine and get the oars. Then we can row in without being heard.'

'Oh, yes. I'd forgotten there were oars in our boat,' said Dinah. 'Thank goodness!'

'Can't we get back to our little cave, on the shore at the other side of the island?' asked Lucy-Ann. 'I don't feel safe here, somehow. And I'd be glad to know our boat was all right.'

'Also, we can't have anything to eat till we get back there,' said Philip, getting up. 'Come on, I'm frozen. We shall get warm climbing up the rocks, on to the height over there, and then over the island to the boat.'

So they went back over the rocks, and found their clothes where they had left them. They stripped off their wet suits and dressed quickly. Philip's rats, which he had left in his pockets, were extremely pleased to see him again, and ran all over him with little squeals of delight.

Huffin and Puffin accompanied the children as usual. All of them were secretly relieved to find their boat was safe on the shingly beach. They went to her and chose some tins of food.

'Better have something with lots of juice to drink,' said Jack. 'There's no fresh water here as far as I can see, and I'm awfully thirsty. Let's open a tin of pineapple. There's always lots of juice in that.'

'Better open *two* tins if Kiki's going to have any,' said Dinah. 'You know what a pig she is over pineapple.'

They all tried to be jolly and cheerful, but somehow, what with their strange discovery of the guns in the lagoon, and the news that Bill was in real danger, none of them could talk for long. One by one they fell silent, and hardly knew what they were eating.

'I suppose,' said Dinah at last, after a long silence in which the only noise was the sound of Kiki's beak scraping against the bottom of one of the pineapple tins, 'I suppose we had better set out as soon as it's dark – but I do feel quaky about it!'

'Well, look here,' said Jack, 'I've been thinking hard – and I'm sure it would be best if Philip and I went alone to get Bill. It's very risky, and we don't know a bit what we shall be up against, and I don't like the idea of you girls coming.'

'Oh, we *must* come!' cried Lucy-Ann, who couldn't bear the thought of Jack going off without her. 'Supposing something happened to you – we'd be here on this island all alone, and nobody would know about us! Anyway, I'm going with you, Jack. You can't stop me!'

'All right,' said Jack. 'Perhaps it would be better if we stuck together. I say – I suppose that other fellow they spoke about couldn't be Horace? We couldn't have made a mistake about him, could we?'

'Well, I did think he was too idiotic for words,' said Dinah. 'I mean – he *looked* it, not only acted it. I believe we did make a mistake. I think perhaps he really was a bird-lover.'

'Gosh! He must have thought we were frightful!' said Jack, horrified. 'And we took his boat too – and left him to be taken prisoner by the enemy!'

'And they must have thought he was Bill's friend, and have been wild with him when he said he didn't know Bill or anything about him,' said Philip.

Everyone thought solemnly about poor Horace. 'I'm jolly glad none of us hit him on the head, after all,' said Jack. 'Poor old Horace Tripalong!'

'We'll have to rescue him, too,' said Lucy-Ann. 'That'll make up a bit for taking his boat. But won't he be *furious* with us for all we've done!'

Huffin appeared at this moment with his familiar gift of half a dozen fish, neatly arranged head and tail alternately in his large beak. He deposited them at Philip's feet.

'Thanks, old man,' said Philip. 'But won't you eat them yourself? We daren't make a fire here to cook anything on.'

'Arrrrr!' said Huffin, and walked over to have a look in the empty tins. Puffin took the opportunity of gobbling up the fish, and Kiki watched her in disgust. Kiki had no use for fish fresh from the sea.

'Pah!' she said, in Horace's voice, and the children smiled.

'Kiki, you'll have to be jolly quiet tonight,' said Jack, scratching her head. 'No pahing or poohing to warn the enemy we're near!'

When the sun began to sink the children took the motor-boat a little way out to sea, to make sure that there were no rocks about that they must avoid when setting out at night. Far away on the horizon line they saw the island of the enemy. Somewhere there was Bill – and perhaps Horace too.

'I hope to goodness we see some kind of light to show us where to go inshore,' said Jack. 'We can't go all round the island, looking for the right place. We'd be heard. And we couldn't possibly row round.'

'Well, we saw that light that was signalling to the other boat last night,' said Philip. 'Maybe it will be signalling again. Let's go back now. There doesn't seem to be any rock to avoid tonight. We'll set out as soon as it is dark.'

They went back – and no sooner had they got to their little beach than they heard the humming of an aeroplane.

'Surely they're not going to drop any more packages!' said Jack. 'Lie down flat, all of you. We don't want to be spotted. Get near those rocks.'

They crouched down near a mass of rocks. The aeroplane made an enormous noise as it came nearer and nearer.

Jack gave a cry. 'It's a seaplane! Look, it's got floats underneath!'

'What an enormous one!' said Dinah. 'It's coming down!'

So it was. It circled the island once and then came lower as it circled it again. It seemed almost to brush the hill that towered at the other end of the island, the hill that overlooked the lagoon.

Then the engines were cut out, and there was a silence.

'She's landed,' said Jack. 'She's on the lagoon! I bet you anything you like that's where she is!'

'Oh, do let's go and see, as soon as dusk comes,' begged Dinah. 'Do you think she's going to get up the hidden guns?'

'However could she do that?' said Jack, rather scornfully.

'Well, she's pretty big and hefty,' said Philip. 'It's possible she's got some sort of apparatus on her for dragging up the hidden armaments. If the men think there's a danger of our Government sending patrols up here to look into the matter, always supposing that Bill has sent a message through to his headquarters, then our enemy will certainly try to remove the guns as soon as possible. It rather looks, seeing that this is a seaplane, as if the guns are going to be flown to South America – or somewhere far across the sea.'

As soon as it was dusk the children could not resist the temptation to go across the island and climb up the heights to peep over and see the lagoon. Even in the twilight they might be able to see something interesting.

They were soon on the cliff overlooking the lagoon. They could just make out the great shape of the giant seaplane in the middle of the sea-lake. Then suddenly lights shone out from it, and a noise began – a grating, dragging noise, as if some kind of machinery was being set to do some heavy work.

'I bet they're dragging up the packages of guns,' whispered Jack. 'We can't very well see – but we can hear enough to know something is at work, something needing winches, I should think.'

Lucy-Ann couldn't see any winches, but she could quite well imagine the kind of machinery that would send hooked cables overboard to drag up the heavy bundles of guns. Then the seaplane, when loaded up, would fly off again. And another would come, and another! Or maybe the same one would come back again and again.

The lights showed the children the vast shape of the seaplane. It looked weird lying quietly there in the middle of the dark lagoon. Lucy-Ann shivered.

'It's awful to be up against enemies who have boats and aeroplanes and seaplanes and guns,' she thought. 'We haven't anything except poor Horace's little motor-boat, and our own wits.'

They went back soberly to their boat. The tide had taken

it out a little way, but as they had tied a rope to a convenient rock, they pulled it in without difficulty. They all got on board.

'Now this is the greatest adventure of all,' said Jack, rather solemnly. 'Hiding is an adventure. Escaping is an adventure. But rescuing somebody else from the very jaws of the enemy is the greatest adventure of all.'

'If only we don't get captured ourselves!' said Lucy-Ann.

Jack started up the engine. The little boat nosed out to sea, leaving the lagoon island behind. Huffin and Puffin settled themselves on the deck-rail as usual, and Kiki sat on Jack's shoulder. Philip's rats, frightened at the sudden noise of the engine, twined themselves together in a large bump in the hollow of Philip's back. 'You tickle me!' he said, but the rats took no notice.

'Well, good luck to us all!' said Dinah. 'May we rescue Bill – and Horace too – defeat the enemy – and get back home in safety!'

'God save the Queen!' said Kiki devoutly, in exactly the same tone of voice, and everyone laughed. Funny old Kiki!

26

Off to the enemy's island

The little boat sped along in the darkness. Philip was at the wheel. He took a large star as guide, and kept the boat well on its course.

After a while Jack touched his arm. 'See that light? It must come from the enemy's island. It's not the bright signalling light we saw before, but it certainly comes from the island.'

'I'll set course for it,' said Philip. 'You'll make certain Kiki doesn't go off into one of her cackles or screeches, won't you, Jack? Any noise out here on the water would be easily heard on land. Sound over water carries such a distance. I'll have to shut off the engine soon, or that will be heard.'

'Kiki won't make a sound,' said Jack.

'Shhhhhhh!' said Kiki at once.

'Yes. Good bird! Shhhhhhh!' said Jack. Philip shut off the engine and the boat gradually lost way until it was just drifting on. Then it came to a gentle stop on the restless sea.

Jack looked through his glasses at the light he could see on the island. 'I think it must be some sort of harbour light,' he said. 'Perhaps they have a small harbour there – they may have quite a fleet of motor-boats, you know, continually patrolling to make sure no-one visits islands near here. It's quite a steady light.'

Philip fumbled for the oars. 'Now for a spot of hard rowing!' he said. 'What's the time, Jack? Can you see by your wrist-watch? It's got a luminous face, hasn't it?'

'It's almost eleven o'clock,' said Jack. 'Just about right. We shall be nearing land about midnight, when we can hope that the enemy won't be wide awake.'

The boys took an oar each. Splish-splash! the oars went in and out of the water as the boys pulled with a will, and the boat glided smoothly along.

'We'll take turns when you're tired,' said Dinah. 'Philip, where are your rats? Something brushed against my leg just now. I shan't be able to help squealing if you let them run about.'

'They're in my pocket,' said Philip. 'You're imagining things as usual. And if you dare to squeal, I'll jolly well tip you overboard!'

'She won't, she won't,' said Lucy-Ann. 'It's only Huffin and Puffin walking about the deck, Dinah. One of them perched on my leg just now.'

'Arrr!' said a guttural voice from the deck-rail.

'Shhhhhhh!' said Kiki at once.

'She doesn't understand that it doesn't in the least matter Huffin and Puffin *arrr*ing all they like,' said Jack. 'They make a natural bird-noise that wouldn't put anyone on guard.'

'Shhhhhh!' said Kiki reprovingly.

The light from the shore gleamed steadily. 'Must be from a lantern,' said Jack, in a low voice, pulling hard at his oar. 'Probably a guide to any motor-boat going in or out. Philip, let's have a rest. I'm getting puffed.'

'Right,' said Philip. The girls wanted to take a turn, but Jack wouldn't let them. 'No, we're just having a rest. There's no hurry. The later we are the better, in a way.'

They soon took the oars again, and their boat moved steadily over the water towards the light.

'No more talking now,' whispered Jack. 'Only tiny whispers.'

Lucy-Ann's knees went queer again. Her tummy felt peculiar too. Dinah was strung up and her breath came fast, although she was not rowing. The two boys were tense with excitement. Would they find the enemy's motor-boat there, with Bill already in it, ready to be 'dumped,' as the man had said that day? And would there be many men on guard?

'Whatever's that noise?' whispered Dinah at last, as their boat drew nearer to land. 'It does sound queer.'

The boys paused in their rowing, and leaned on their oars to listen.

'Sounds like a band playing,' said Jack. 'Of course – it's a radio!'

'Good!' said Philip. 'Then the enemy won't be so likely to hear us creeping in. Jack, look! – I think that's a little jetty there – you can just make it out by the light of that lantern. Can we possibly creep in without being seen or heard? And look! – is that a boat lying under the lantern?'

'I'll get the glasses,' said Philip, and felt about for them. He put them to his eyes. 'Yes – it *is* a boat – quite a big one. I should think it's the one the enemy came to our island in. I bet Bill is on it, battened down in the cabin!'

The band continued playing on the radio. 'Somebody on

board has got it on,' said Jack. 'The guard, I should think. Will he be on deck, then – the guard, I mean? There's no light there.'

'If you ask me, he's having a nice lazy time, snoozing on deck with his radio playing him nice tunes,' whispered back Philip. 'Look! – can you see that little glow, Jack? I bet that's the end of a cigarette the guard is smoking.'

'Yes, it probably is,' said Jack.

'I don't think we dare go in any closer,' said Philip. 'We don't want to be seen. If the guard gives the alarm, we're done for. I wonder how many there are on the deck. I can only see one glowing cigarette-end.'

'What are you going to do?' whispered Lucy-Ann. 'Do do something. I feel awful! I shall burst in a minute.'

Philip put out his hand and took hers. 'Don't worry,' he whispered. 'We shall have to do something soon! It looks to be rather a good time. If only that guard would fall asleep!'

'I say, Tufty – do you know what I think would be much the best thing to do?' said Jack suddenly. 'If you and I swam to the harbour, climbed up, got on the boat and surprised the guard, we could probably tip him into the water, and before he could raise the alarm, we'd open up the hatch and get Bill out. Why, we could probably drive the motor-boat off too – then we'd have two!'

'Sound a good plan,' said Philip. 'But we don't know yet if Bill is there – and it's quite likely we couldn't tip the guard overboard – especially if there are more than one. We'd better do a little exploring first. Your idea of slipping overboard and swimming to the harbour is jolly good though. We'll certainly do that. We can clamber up a part where there are shadows, away from that light.'

'Oh dear – must you go swimming in the dark?' said Lucy-Ann, looking at the black water with a shiver. 'I should hate it. Do, do be careful, Jack!'

'I'll be all right,' said Jack. 'Come on, Philip. Strip off your clothes. We'll swim in our pants.'

It wasn't long before the boys silently slid overboard and entered the water. It was cold and they drew their breaths in sharply. But they soon felt warm as they swam rapidly towards the harbour. They could hear the radio more plainly as they came near. 'Good thing,' thought Jack. 'They won't be able to hear us coming at all.'

They avoided the light, and clambered up the part of the jetty where there were black shadows. It was not easy. 'The boat's just there,' whispered Jack in Philip's ear. 'Not right under the light, thank goodness!'

A sound made them stop suddenly. A loud and prolonged yawn came from the deck of the boat. Then the radio was snapped off and silence came back to the night.

'He may be going to sleep,' hissed Jack. 'Let's wait.'

They waited in complete silence for about ten minutes. The man tossed a glowing cigarette-end overboard but did not light another. The boys heard him give several grunts as if he was settling down comfortably. Then he gave a loud yawn again.

Still the boys waited, shivering in the darkness of the jetty, keeping close to one another in order to get a little bit of warmth from each other's bodies.

Then, on the night air, came very very welcome sounds. 'He's snoring,' whispered Jack, pressing Philip's arm in joy. 'He's asleep. I'm sure there's only one guard, because otherwise they would have been talking together. Now's our chance. Come on – but quietly, so as not to wake him!'

The two boys, shivering now with excitement as much as with cold, crept along the jetty to the boat. They climbed cautiously on board, their bare feet making no sound at all. On the deck lay the sleeping guard – if he was a guard!

Then another sound stopped them. This time it came from beneath their feet. Philip clutched Jack's bare arm and made him jump violently. They stood and listened.

It was somebody talking, down below in the cabin. Who was it? Could it be Bill? And who was he with? Horace perhaps. But maybe after all it wasn't Bill down there, maybe it was the enemy, playing cards, and perhaps the sleeping man wasn't a guard. It would be very foolish to toss him overboard and open the cabin hatch to find the enemy down in the cabin.

'We'd better listen and find out if it's Bill,' said Jack, right in Philip's ear. The boys could see thin streaks of light where the hatch was fitted down into the deck, covering in the little cabin; so they knew exactly where it was. They crept forward and then knelt down by the closed hatch. They put their ears to the cracks and strained to listen to the voices talking.

They could not hear what was being said – but, when one of the talkers suddenly cleared his throat and gave a little cough, the boys knew who it was all right! It was one of Bill's little ways. Bill was down there. It was Bill who was talking. Both boys felt a surge of tremendous relief. If only they could get Bill out, and let him take charge of things!

'If we throw this fellow overboard, we may find he raised the alarm so quickly that we shan't be able to get Bill out and explain things to him fast enough,' said Jack, in Philip's ear. 'As he's so fast asleep, what about unbolting the hatch and letting Bill see we're here? Then he could help us with the guard, and take charge of the boat.'

'You undo the hatch, and I'll stand by the guard, so that if he wakes I can knock him overboard,' said Philip. 'Go on. Quick!'

Jack felt for the bolt. His fingers were trembling and he could hardly pull it. He was afraid it might make a grating noise, but it didn't. It slid back easily and smoothly. Jack felt for the iron handle that raised the hatch, and then lifted up the hatch itself, so that a bright mass of light came up from the cabin below.

The men in the cabin heard the slight noise and looked up. One was Bill – and the other was Horace. When Bill saw Jack's face peering down out of the darkness he leapt to his feet in amazement. Jack put his finger to his lips, and Bill bit back the exclamation on his tongue.

'Come on out,' whispered Jack. 'Quick! We've got to deal with the guard here.'

But Horace spoilt everything. As soon as he saw Jack, the hated boy who had shut him into the hole on Puffin Island, he sprang up furiously. 'There's that villainous boy! Wait till I get him!' he shouted.

27

Escape

'Sh!' said Jack fiercely, and pointed over his shoulder towards the guard. But it was too late. The man awoke with a jump, as the shouting penetrated into his dreams. He sat up blinking, and then, seeing the brilliant light streaming up from the open hatch, he leapt to his feet.

Bill had the sense to switch off the light. Now all was darkness. Bill began to climb up the hatchway, and the guard began to shout.

'What's all this? Hi, what are you doing? Who's there?'

Philip sprang at him and tried to push him overboard, but the man was strong and began to struggle. In the end it was poor Philip who was thrown overobard, with a most terrifc splash. Then Bill came up and, guided by the sound of the panting of the guard, hit out with his right fist. The surprised guard felt the sudden blow and reeled over. Bill put out a foot, hoping to trip him, and down he went to the deck. In a trice Bill was on top of him, and Jack came to help. 'Who was that going overboard?' panted Bill.

'Philip,' answered Jack, sitting firmly on the guard's legs. 'He's all right. He can swim to the other boat.'

'Get the guard down into the cabin,' ordered Bill.

'Where's the other fellow – Tipperlong? The idiot spoilt the whole show.'

Horace was standing well out of the way, wondering what was happening. He could hear pants and groans and strugglings, and he was scared. Then there came another yell from the guard, and down the man went into the cabin, slithering sideways down the steps.

Bang! The hatch shut down on him and Bill slid the bolt across.

'He's safe for the moment,' said Bill grimly. 'Now let's get the boat going, quick! We'll be off before the enemy know what we're up to!'

'That's what I planned we'd do!' panted Jack, thrilled that his wildest hopes seemed to be coming true. 'How do we start up the engine? Blow this darkness! I haven't a torch on me.'

The guard below was kicking up a terrific row. He was yelling and banging for all he was worth. Bill made his way in the darkness to the wheel of the boat.

And then things began to happen. Lights sprang up on shore, and voices began to shout. There came the sound of running feet.

'We shan't have time to get her free from her moorings and start her up before they're on us,' groaned Bill. 'Did you say you've got another boat here, Jack? Where is it? And what about Philip? Quick, answer me!'

'Yes – there's a boat off the end of the jetty there – with the girls in it – and Philip will probably be there by now, too,' said Jack, his words falling over one another in his excitement. 'We'd better swim for it!'

'Overboard then!' said Bill. 'Tipperlong, where are you? You'd better come too.'

'I c-c-c-can't swim,' stammered poor Horace.

'Well, jump overboard and I'll help you,' commanded Bill. But the thought of leaping into the dark cold water in the middle of the night, with enemies all round, was too much for Horace. He crawled into a corner and refused to move.

'Well, stay where you are, then,' said Bill scornfully. 'I'll have to go with these kids – can't let them down now!'

Overboard went Bill and Jack. Horace heard the splashes and shivered. Nothing would have induced him to do the same. He trembled in his corner, waiting for the enemy to come pounding down the jetty.

And come they did, with torches flashing, and voices that urgently demanded from the guard what all the noise was about. They swarmed on board the motor-boat, and found Horace at once, shivering in the corner. They dragged him out.

The guard was still hammering down in the cabin, getting hoarse with fury. The enemy, not really certain of what had happened, flung questions at poor Horace.

Bill and Jack, swimming swiftly through the dark water, heard the excited voices, and prayed that Horace would not give them away. The guard would soon tell them all they wanted to know, but perhaps the few minutes' start they had would be all they needed.

Philip was already on board the boat, reassuring the two frightened girls. When he heard the splash of Bill and Jack jumping overboard from the other boat, he strained his eyes to watch for them. As he caught the sound of their swift armstrokes through the water, he cautiously held his torch down over the sea, and flicked it on once or twice, to mark their way for them.

They saw the slight flashes of light and thankfully swam towards them. Jack had been afraid of missing the boat altogether in his excitement. Soon they were clambering up, and Lucy-Ann and Dinah caught hold of Bill's wet, hairy arms, so strong and firm and comforting.

'Come on – we must get going,' said Bill, giving each girl a quick pat. 'My, what a row there is on that boat! They've let the guard out now. Come on, before they know where we are.'

'The engine will tell them, when we start it up,' said Jack. 'We've got oars. Shall we row?'

'No,' said Bill. 'We must get away as quickly as possible. They'll chase us, and we *must* get a good start. You girls lie flat on your tummies, and you boys lie on top of them There'll be bullets flying after me in a tick!'

Bill started up the engine. Lucy-Ann and Dinah lay down flat. The boys lay on top of them, almost squeezing the breath out of the girls. It was most uncomfortable.

Oddly enough not one of the children felt frightened They all felt a terrific excitement, and Lucy-Ann had a mad feeling that she would like to yell and dance about. It was hard to have to keep flat on the deck, with Jack squashing her breath out of her.

As soon as the engine of the motor-boat started up, there came an astonished silence on board the other boat. Plainly the guard had not gathered that there was a second boat not far off, and had not told his friends about it. The enemy had thought that Bill and his rescuers were swimming somewhere about, and they were still quite in the dark about what had happened.

But when the engine of Bill's (or rather Horace's) boat purred out in the night, the enemy knew that they must stop it somehow. That boat could not be allowed to get away!

Crack! Somebody's revolver went off, and a bullet sped over the sea, towards the boat.

Crack! Crack! Crack! Bill crouched as low as he could by the wheel, as he heard a bullet whizz much too near the boat for his liking.

'Keep down, you kids!' he ordered anxiously. 'We'll soon be out of reach.'

Crack! Another bullet went pinging by, and struck the water beyond the boat. Bill said several things under his breath, and wished the motor-boat would go a little faster.

R-r-r-r-r-r went the engine steadily, and the boat swung over the waves out to sea.

Crack! Crack!

There came a sudden squeal from Kiki, who was sitting on top of Jack, puzzled by all the noise and excitement. Then she screeched wildly.

'Oh! Kiki's hit!' shouted Jack, and sat up in anxiety, feeling for his beloved parrot.

Kiki didn't say a single word, but continued to screech as if she was in the most terrible pain. Jack was beside himself with grief.

'Keep down, you idiot!' roared Bill, sensing that Jack was not lying flat. 'Do you hear what I say?'

'But Kiki,' began Jack, only to be drowned by an even more furious roar from Bill.

'Kiki's all right! She couldn't screech like that if she was really hurt. Lie down flat, and do as you're told!'

Jack obeyed orders. He lay down again, and listened with anxiety to Kiki's screeching. The others, quite certain that the bird was wounded, were very anxious too.

Lucy-Ann wondered what had happened to Huffin and Puffin. She had not heard them say *arrrrr* for a long time. Perhaps they were shot too! Oh dear, when would they be out of reach of the enemy, and safe?

The shooting stopped – but another noise came, sounding faintly over the chugging of their own boat. Bill's sharp ears heard it.

'They're after us!' he called. 'They've started up their own boat. Thank goodness it's a dark night. We must just go on and on till our petrol gives out, and hope for the best.'

The motor-boat chasing them switched on a powerful searchlight. It swept the sea all round.

'We're just out of reach,' said Bill thankfully. 'This little boat can certainly get a move on. Kiki, shut up screeching! You're NOT hurt!'

'Bill, we might have enough petrol to get to the island we came from, over to the east there,' said Jack suddenly. 'The men would probably think we'd try and make for safety miles away, and if we do, we shall certainly be overtaken. Their boat is more powerful than ours, and as soon as we get within the range of their searchlight, we'll be seen. Let's swing off to the left.'

'What island did you come from?' demanded Bill. 'And what's been happening to you all since I was fool enough to let myself get captured? I've been worrying my head off about you!'

'We were worried about you, too,' said Jack. 'Swing her to port, Bill – we'll make for the lagoon-island, and hope that the men won't guess we're there.'

The boat set course for the other island, across the dark, heaving sea. Far behind them the searchlight was still sweeping the waters, but it was plain that the enemy's motor-boat was now going off in the other direction. Another few minutes and they would be out of sight and hearing.

'Arrrrrrr!' said a guttural voice from just beyond Bill. He jumped. Then he laughed.

'My goodness – have you still got Huffin and Puffin? Now don't start screeching again, Kiki. I'm absolutley certain you're not hurt.'

'Can I sit up now and just *feel* if Kiki is hurt?' begged Jack anxiously. 'They're not doing any more shooting.'

But before Bill could answer, the engine of the motor-boat gave a series of coughs and wheezes, and then, with a curious sound like a tired sigh, stopped altogether.

'Petrol's run out,' said Bill bitterly. 'It would, of course! Now we'll have to row, and it won't be long before the enemy catch us up!'

28

A night of talking

The children all sat up at once, and the girls thankfully stretched their arms and legs. 'You are heavy, Philip,' grumbled Dinah. 'Oh Bill – what awful bad luck to have no petrol just as we must be so near shore!'

Jack reached out for Kiki. His hands felt over her body anxiously, and down her legs, and over her beak. Where was she hurt?

Kiki nestled close to him, murmuring funny little words that had no sense. 'You're not hurt, silly bird,' said Jack thankfully. 'You made a fuss for nothing. I'm ashamed of you.'

'Poor Kiki, poor Kiki, send for the doctor,' murmured Kiki, and put her head under her wing.

'She's not hurt, as far as I can make out,' said Jack to the others, 'but she must have had an awful scare. Perhaps a bullet zipped very near her.'

'Oh, forget Kiki for a moment and let's talk about ourselves,' said Dinah. 'Bill, what are we going to do?'

Bill sat lost in thought. What was the best thing to do? It was no joke to be in charge of four children, with such dangerous enemies so near. Would it be best to make for this lagoon-island, whatever it was? It should at least be within rowing distance. Or would it be best to row further on?

'We'll make for your lagoon-island,' he said at last. 'It's the best idea.'

'It can't be far away,' said Jack, straining his eyes in the darkness. 'I think I can make out a dark shape over there. Can you, Philip?'

'Yes,' said Philip. 'Look, over there, Bill! Can you see?'

'Not a thing,' said Bill. 'But I'll take your word for it. You youngsters have got such sharp eyes and ears. Now, where are the oars?'

They were soon found, and the slow splish-splash of rowing came to the ears of the girls, as they sat huddled together for warmth.

'Yes – it *is* land of some sort,' said Bill, after a while, with satisfaction. 'We'll be ashore soon. I only hope there are no rocks to run aground on.'

'Oh no,' said Jack. 'We'll be all right. There aren't any rocks near the lagoon-island. At least, not the part where we should be coming to now.'

But hardly were the words out of his mouth before there came a horrid grinding noise, and the boat shivered from end to end. Everyone got a terrible shock. Whatever was happening now?

'On the rocks!' said Bill grimly. 'And I don't somehow think we'll get her off! She means to stay here all right!'

The boat could not be moved. Jack anxiously switched on a torch, and tried to see what had happened. It was only too plain!

'There are rocks all round,' he said dolefully. 'We haven't come to the right part of the island at all. Goodness knows where we are.'

'Let's see if we're holed,' said Bill, and took Jack's torch. He examined the boat thoroughly, and gave a sigh of relief. 'No. It looks as if we're safe so far. She must have run right on to a shallow ledge of rock. It's no use doing anything about it now. We'll have to wait till it's light and then see if we can shift her. If we mess about now and do get her off, we shall only get on to other rocks at once.'

'Well, let's snuggle down in rugs and have something to eat, and talk then,' said Lucy-Ann. 'I should never, never be able to go to sleep.'

'None of us could tonight,' said Jack. 'I've never felt so wide awake in my life. I'm going to get some clothes on first. I haven't had time to put any on. Wasn't I glad to get some rugs round me, though!'

'I'm pretty wet through myself,' said Bill. 'I'll have a few rugs too, I think.'

'There's some clothes of Horace's in that locker,' said Dinah. 'The one behind you. We gave him all of his, as we thought, but I found some more yesterday, tucked away there. They won't fit you, Bill, but at least they'll keep you warm.'

'Good,' said Bill, and opened the locker. 'I'll put them on now, if I can feel what they are in the dark. You girls get some food, if you've got any. Pity we can't boil a kettle and get something hot into us!'

Soon Bill and the boys had dry clothes on. Then all five of them sat close together for warmth, and ate biscuits and chocolate hungrily.

'Now suppose we tell each other what's happened since I so hurriedly departed from Puffin Island,' said Bill.

'You tell your tale first,' said Lucy-Ann, pressing close to him. 'Oh, Bill, it's good to have you back! I was so scared when we found you were gone, and the engine of the motor-boat smashed up, and the radio too.'

'Yes. They told me they'd done that,' said Bill. 'Apparently they didn't know you kids were on the island at all – so I didn't say a word, of course. Well – to make a long story short, when I was fiddling about with the radio that night, on our boat, trying to get a message through – and not succeeding, unfortunately . . . '

'Oh, Bill – then we shan't be rescued!' said Lucy-Ann at once. 'Oh, we did hope you would have sent a message for help or something! . . . '

'Well, headquarters knew that I was on to something up here, but no more than that,' said Bill. 'Anyway, as I say, I was fiddling with the radio – when I suddenly got a blow on the head, and down I went. Then I knew nothing more at all until I woke up on some other island, a prisoner in a shack!'

'The enemy didn't hurt you, did they?' asked Lucy-Ann anxiously.

Bill didn't answer that. He went on with his tale. 'They questioned me, of course, and got nothing out of me at all. The queer part was that the very men I'd been told to disappear from, because they were after me, were the very men we bumped into up here! *This* was where they were carrying on their activities! I had thought it was somewhere in Wales – but they made me think that by laying false clues.'

'Oh, Bill – and to think this wild desolate sea, with all its little islands, was the very place they had chosen, and *we*, too, chose to come to!' said Jack. 'They must have thought you'd found out their hiding-place, and had come to track them down.'

'Just what they did think,' said Bill. 'And what's more they imagined that one or other of their men must have given their secret away, and they wanted to find out from me who it was. That was why they held me for questioning, I imagine – instead of bumping me off at once.'

'Humpy-dumpy-bumpy,' said Kiki, taking her head out from under her wing. But nobody paid the slightest attention. Bill's story was too absorbing.

'They wanted to know *how* much I knew, and *who* had told me,' said Bill. 'Well, I didn't actually know very much, and what I did know nobody had told me, so they didn't get a great deal out of me – and they were not pleased.'

'Didn't you *really* know very much then?' said Philip, astonished.

'I knew this gang were up to something illegal – I knew they were getting a lot of money from somewhere – I guessed it was something to do with guns,' said Bill. 'I tried to put several spokes in their wheel, and they got wise to the fact that I was after them. I'd cleaned up a nasty little business of theirs once before – though we didn't get the chief ones then – so I wasn't popular.'

'And they decided to track *you* down and bump you off!' said Jack. 'So you were told to disappear – and lo and behold! you came here to disappear . . . '

'And walked right into the hornets nest,' agreed Bill. 'And took you with me too! How is it you kids always attract adventures? As soon as I go near you, an adventure leaps up, and we all get caught in it.'

'It *is* very peculiar,' said Jack. 'Go on, Bill.'

'Well, then my guards suddenly brought Mr Horace Tipperlong to my shack,' said Bill. 'They appeared to think that he was a pal of mine, and was up here among these islands to help me in my snooping. He was just as bewildered as I was. I couldn't make him out at all. But when we were alone, he began to tell me about you kids, and I guessed what had happened. You were absolute little demons to him, according to his story.'

'Yes, we were,' said Jack remorsefully, remembering their treatment of the puzzled and angry Horace. 'You see, we honestly thought he was one of the enemy, got up to look like a rather goofy ornithologist, sent to capture us and make us get into his boat – so . . . '

'We captured him instead, and pushed him down a hole we found, and kept him there,' said Dinah.

'And conked him on the head every time he popped up, it appears,' said Bill. 'I shouldn't have thought you were so bloodthirsty. He said even the girls took turns at hitting him.'

'*Well!*' said everyone, in shocked astonishment at such colossal untruths. 'Bill! We never hit him once!'

'I wouldn't have been surprised at the boys giving him one or two knocks, if they really thought he was one of the enemy sent to capture them,' said Bill, 'but I simply could not *imagine* the girls hitting him. He said Lucy-Ann was the worst.'

'*Oh!* And I was the only one that said I couldn't possibly,' said Lucy-Ann, really shocked at such wicked statements.

'Anyway, apparently you gave him an awful time, and then made off with his boat, leaving him to be captured by the enemy,' said Bill. 'You know, I couldn't help grinning when I heard it all. There's plenty of pluck in you kids! The enemy took him off in their boat and didn't believe a word of his story about your taking him prisoner. They really thought he was a pal of mine. Of course, I pretended not to believe his tale about there being children on the island either, because I didn't want you captured as well. But I did wonder what was happening to you when I heard you'd taken his boat. Horace said it was no longer in the little harbour when he was yanked on board the enemy's boat.'

'I don't like Horace,' said Lucy-Ann. 'I hope the enemy give him an *awful* time! He's silly and he's untruthful and he's a coward.'

'And if he hadn't yelled out when he did tonight, just after I'd opened the hatch of the cabin to let you out, Bill, we'd have been able to capture that big fast motor-boat, and get right back to the mainland,' said Jack gloomily. 'Silly idiot – yelling like that!'

'Yes, that was a great pity,' said Bill. 'Now you tell me *your* story.'

So the children told it, and Bill listened with interest and amazement. When they came to the bit about the lagoon, and what was hidden there, he held his breath in astonishment.

'So *that's* where they put the guns – dropped them by parachute into a secret lagoon – and then meant to get them up again as soon as the time was ripe – and take them away by seaplane. Gun-running on the grand scale!'

'We were jolly astonished when we watched it all happening,' said Jack.

'I should think so!' said Bill. 'It's beyond belief! And to think you children stumbled on the whole secret. My word, if only I could get a message through to headquarters, we'd catch the whole gang red-handed!'

'It's been pretty thrilling,' said Philip. 'We had some scares, I can tell you, Bill.'

'You're good kids,' said Bill. 'Good and plucky kids. I'm proud of you. But there's one thing I don't understand. Why didn't you make for safety, when you captured Horace's boat? Why did you mess about here?'

'Well . . . ' said Jack, 'you see – we had the choice of making for safety – or trying to find you. And we chose to try and find you, Bill. Even Lucy-Ann voted for that.'

There was a silence. Then Bill put his big arms all round the huddled-up four and gave them such a hug that Lucy-Ann gasped.

'I don't know what to say,' said Bill, in a queer sort of voice. 'You're only kids – but you're the finest company of friends anyone could have. You know the meaning of loyalty already, and even if you're scared you don't give up. I'm proud to have you for my friends.'

'Oh, *Bill*!' said Lucy-Ann, tremendously thrilled to hear such a speech from her hero. 'You *are* nice. You're our very very best friend, and you always will be.'

'Always,' said Dinah.

The boys said nothing, but they glowed inwardly at Bill's praise. Friendship – loyalty – staunchness in face of danger – they and Bill both knew these things and recognised them for the fine things they were. They felt very close to Bill indeed.

'Look!' said Lucy-Ann suddenly. 'The dawn! Over there, in the east. Oh, Bill – I wonder what's going to happen today?'

29

Bill makes a grand find

The sky grew silvery in the east. Then a golden glow spread slowly upwards, and the sea became a milky colour that gradually turned to gold.

Almost at once there came a crying of seabirds as guillemots, gannets, cormorants, puffins and gulls came from their roosting-places to greet the new day. Soon the sea around the children was dotted thickly with hundreds of birds eagerly seeking fish for food. Huffin and Puffin joined them.

Jack gave an exclamation as he looked all round him. 'This isn't the lagoon-island. There were no rocky cliffs to it like this, facing the sea. This is another island we've come to!'

'Yes, it is,' said Philip. 'One I don't remember to have seen before. Blow! Where are we?'

'I should think it must be the island we once noticed on the chart,' said Lucy-Ann, remembering. 'The Isle of Wings. Just *look* at the mass of birds on the waters round us! It's more than we've ever seen before!'

'Extraordinary!' said Bill, amazed. 'There must be millions of birds. Some of them are so close that they bob against each other.'

Not only the sea was full of birds, but the air too, and the screaming and calling was deafening. Soon one bird after another flew up from the water with fish in its beak. Huffin flew to the boat and presented Philip with his usual beakful of neatly arranged fish.

'Kiki's very quiet,' said Philip, looking at her. 'What's the matter with her? Kiki, put up your crest, you ridiculous bird!'

'Send for the doctor,' said Kiki mournfully. Jack looked at her closely. Then he gave an exclamation.

'She's lost some of her crest! She's hardly got any! Oh, Bill – that's what she screeched for last night! A bullet must have zipped through her crest – right through her top-knot – and taken some of the feathers off with it.'

'Poor Polly, poor Polly, what a pity, what a pity!' said Kiki, glad to be the centre of attention.

'Yes, poor old Kiki!' said Jack, and he stroked her. 'What a shock you must have got! No wonder you screeched. Never mind, old thing – the crest will grow again. You'll look a bit mangy for a while, but *we* shan't mind.'

Bill had been looking to see exactly what had happened to the boat. It had run on to a shelf of rock, and had settled there so firmly that until high tide came there was no hope of getting off. They were not on the mainland of the island, but on an outcrop of tall rocks, hung with thick seaweed, and inhabited by about two hundred or more birds. They did not seem to mind the boat and its load of people in the least. In fact, seeing Huffin and Puffin perched there, some of the birds came on deck too. Jack was thrilled.

'I don't think the boat's damaged at all,' said Bill. 'Once she gets afloat again with the tide, she'll be all right. But the thing is – what in the world are we going to do if she does get afloat?'

'Row to safety,' said Lucy-Ann promptly.

'Sounds easy,' said Jack regretfully. 'But you don't realize what a wild and desolate sea this is, Lucy-Ann, or how few people ever come to these little bird-islands. We couldn't possibly row to the mainland, for instance, could we, Bill?'

'No. I don't think so,' said Bill. 'I'm glad to see we've got a good store of food. That's something. But what about drinking-water?'

'We'll have to drink pineapple juice or something like that,' said Dinah. 'And if it rains we'll catch rainwater.'

'What *is* the best thing to do?' said Bill, talking to himself, with a frown. 'They'll be looking for us, I expect. They'll know we couldn't get far. They'll send out patrols – probably even an aeroplane. They can't afford to let me get away now.'

The children knew that 'they' meant the enemy. Dinah looked all round them. 'If the enemy do come round this island, they can't help seeing us. We'd be spotted at once in our boat.'

'Well – we'll make up our minds what to do when the boat's afloat again,' said Bill at last. 'What about a spot of sleep? Lucy-Ann is looking as white as a sheet. She's had no sleep at all.'

'I do feel awfully sleepy,' admitted Lucy-Ann, trying not to yawn. 'But I feel dirty and sticky too.'

'Let's have a quick dip in the sea, and then have a snooze,' said Jack. 'We can take it in turn to keep watch for the enemy.'

'I don't want a dip,' said Dinah. 'I'm too sleepy. You three and Bill have a dip, and I'll make up our beds again and get the rugs and things set out comfortably.'

'I'll help you,' said Lucy-Ann. 'I'm too tired to bathe.'

Bill and the boys soon slipped into the water. The girls watched them. 'You know,' said Lucy-Ann, after a while, 'it's almost impossible to see the boys and Bill among all those birds bobbing about. Once I lose sight of them I can't spot them again.

It was quite true. There were so many birds bobbing about on the water that the boys' wet dark heads, and Bill's, could hardly be picked out from the crowd.

'Let's tell Bill when they come back,' said Dinah, a sudden idea sliding into her head. 'I bet if we all slid into the water if the enemy came, nobody would ever spot us among the birds there.'

'No, they wouldn't,' agreed Lucy-Ann. 'It would be a marvellous idea, Dinah!'

They told the others when they came back, glowing from

their bathe. Bill nodded, pleased. 'Yes – a fine idea. If the enemy comes in sight, that's what we'll do. Our heads would be completely lost among the bodies of the swimming birds.'

'What about the boat though?' said Jack.

'We could do what we did for ourselves, when we were on the rocks beside the lagoon,' said Philip. 'Drape it with seaweed so that it looks like a rock!'

'You're full of bright ideas, you kids,' said Bill. 'Whilst you're all having a snooze I'll do a little boat-draping. If the enemy come, they'll come soon. They won't waste many hours before they try to find us. I'll wake you if I see or hear any sign of them, and you must all be prepared to drop over the side of the boat. Better sleep in your undies, so that you don't wet all your clothes. Your bathing-suits are wet.'

'Ours aren't,' said Lucy-Ann. 'Oh dear – I'm so awfully sleepy. I do hope the enemy don't come yet. I'm not at all sure I shall wake if they do!'

Bill tucked them all up in rugs. They were asleep in a moment or two, tired out. Bill began to do a little boat-draping. He pulled great fronds of seaweed off the nearby rocks and hung them over the boat-sides, till the little vessel looked like a boat-shaped rock.

Having finished his task, Bill sat down in the cabin. He idly removed a cover from something there – and then stared in surprise.

A radio! Was it a transmitter too? Surely Horace going off all alone into the wilds, would have had the sense to take a transmitter with him, in case he got hurt, or became ill? With trembling hands Bill began to examine the radio.

He gave a loud exclamation that woke up Jack. The boy sat up in alarm. 'Is it the enemy, Bill?'

'No. But look here – why on earth didn't you tell me there was a radio in this boat? I can get a message through, with luck.'

'Golly, I forgot all about it!' said Jack. 'But is it a transmitter, Bill?'

'Yes. Not a very good one – but I'll do my best to try and work it so that I can send a message to headquarters,' said Bill. 'There's always someone standing by there, hoping to hear from me. I haven't reported for days.'

Bill began to hunt about and Jack wondered why. 'What are you looking for, Bill?' he asked.

'The aerial,' said Bill. 'There must be an aerial somewhere, for the transmitter. Where on earth can it be?'

'I remember seeing something on a shelf at the back of the cabin,' said Jack sleepily. 'It was about six feet long.'

'That would be it!' said Bill, and went to look. He pulled out something long and slender. 'Good! Here it is. I can soon fix it up.'

Jack watched Bill for a few minutes, then he felt his eyes closing and he slumped down in his rugs again. It was very, very exciting to watch Bill putting up the aerial and trying to make the transmitter work – but not even that excitement could make Jack's eyes keep open. In half a second he was fast asleep again.

Bill worked and worked, groaning occasionally with disappointment as first one thing failed and then another. Curious sounds came from the radio, and little lights glowed here and there within it. There was something the matter with it, and Bill didn't know what. If only he knew! Oh, if only he could get the thing to work, just for a minute or two!

At last he thought he had got it fixed. Now to send a message through. Now to send out his code number and wait for a reply.

He sent out his code time and again. There was no reply. The radio seemed to be quite dead at his end. There was nothing for it but to send a message and hope it would be received – but Bill had grave doubts about it.

He rapidly sent a message through in code, asking for

immediate help. He repeated the message time and time again, but got no reply at all. He gave the lagoon-island as a guide to their whereabouts, knowing that they must be somewhere near it. Surely it must be on some map, and could be located?

He was so busy trying to send his message and listening for a reply which never came, that he almost didn't hear the distant purr of a powerful motor-boat. But the sound did at last penetrate his mind and he looked up with a start.

He shouted to the children. 'Wake up! Quick! Into the water with you – the enemy are here! WAKE UP!'

They all woke up with a jump. The enemy! Splash! Into the water they slid, all five of them, the two girls hardly awake. The enemy! Yes, there was the motor-boat heading straight for them all!

30

Ahoy there! Show yourselves!

There was a sudden flash of sunlight on the lenses of a pair of field-glasses. They were being levelled at the island, on whose rocks the children's boat had been grounded. The glasses swept the rocks and the island, and then came back to the rocks again.

The boat was there, draped end to end with seaweed. The glasses rested on it for a few moments. Then they swept the sea, but among the bobbing birds it was impossible to pick out the five wet heads.

The children kept as close to swimming birds as possible. Philip was all right because Huffin and Puffin perched on his head, and hid him beautifully. Lucy-Ann was near a big cormorant, who eyed her with interest but did not swim away from her. Dinah and Jack were among a crowd of bobbing, diving puffins, and Bill, fearful of his big, somewhat bald head being spotted, kept bobbing under the water, and holding his breath there as long as he could.

After what seemed an age the enemy's motor-boat swung round and went away, going right round the island – or so Bill thought. They heard the sound of its engine growing fainter and fainter.

Not until it had completely died away did Bill let the children get back into the boat. Then, when he thought it was quite safe, they all clambered back, wet and hungry, but no longer sleepy.

'How slippery the boat is, with all this seaweed!' said Jack. 'Dinah, your idea worked well. I don't think the enemy even *guessed* there was anyone here – and there were five people and a boat within easy sight of their glasses.'

'Yes, a very fine idea, Dinah,' said Bill. 'Now – what about breakfast? I'm starving!'

They sat down and opened a few tins. Kiki screeched with delight when she saw the chunks of pineapple in one of them. She tried to raise her crest, but as she had only one or two feathers left in it, it was not a very successful effort.

Jack suddenly thought of something. 'Bill! Do I remember something – something about you and Horace's radio – or did I dream it? Yes, perhaps I dreamt it.'

'You certainly didn't, said Bill. 'I found Horace's radio – most unexpectedly, I must say – and discovered to my joy that it was a transmitter as well as a receiver – so that I ought to be able to send messages as well as receive them.'

'Oh, *Bill*! So you've radioed for help – and we shall be saved!' said Lucy-Ann joyfully.

'Unfortunately there's something wrong with the thing,' said Bill. 'Couldn't get a chirp out of it – and whether or not my messages have gone through I can't tell. But probably not. It's not a very good set, this one of Horace's.'

'Oh – so it's not very likely it was of much use,' said Dinah, disappointed.

'Not very,' said Bill. 'By the way, did anyone feel a slight upward lift then? I have an idea the boat is coming off the rocks.'

He was right. It was soon afloat, and Bill took the oars. He rowed for some distance away from the island, and then a thought struck him.

'Look here – Horace couldn't possibly have come all the way up here – and hoped to get back again – without a store of petrol. Have you examined this boat thoroughly?'

'No, not really thoroughly,' said Jack. 'It isn't much of a boat.'

'I grant you that – but there really *should* be some petrol somewhere,' said Bill. 'Philip, pull up those piles of rope and stuff. There would be room under the board there for tins of petrol.'

Philip and Jack did as they were told. They hauled up three loose boards – and there, neatly arranged below, was Horace's store of petrol!

'Gosh!' said Jack. 'What a find! *Now* we'll be all right. We'll be on the mainland in no time. Good old Horace!'

They handed Bill a tin. He emptied it into the petrol tank of the engine and then took another tin. That was emptied in too. Hurrah! Now they could really make headway.

Soon the engine was purring happily away and the little boat was speeding over the waves. No more rowing! Bill set his course for the south-east.

'Hark! There's an aeroplane about somewhere!' said Lucy-Ann suddenly. 'I can hear it.'

They all looked up into the sky. Soon they saw the plane, coming from the north-east. It was flying low.

'Looks as if it's trying to spot us,' said Bill uneasily.

'It belongs to the enemy then!' said Jack. They all looked intently at the approaching plane. It seemed suddenly to see them, and veered in their direction. It flew down very low, circled round them, and then made off.

'Blow!' said Bill. 'Now we're for it! They'll send out their most powerful motor-boat – or maybe one of the seaplanes they seem to use – and that'll be that!'

'Well, we've got plenty of petrol,' said Jack, 'so we can keep on quickly for miles. We'll be well away from here before long.'

The boat sped on, Bill giving her her top speed. When he reckoned that her petrol would soon be running out he called to Jack, 'Get out the other tins, Jack. I'll put some more in before she's empty.'

But what a shock for the boys! All the other tins were empty! Bill stared in dismay.

'Gosh! Somebody has swindled Horace properly! He probably gave orders for all the tins to be filled – and somebody took the money for the lot, and only filled half. What a dirty trick!'

'But just the sort that *would* be played on poor silly Horace!' said Philip. 'Oh, Bill – we're out on the open sea now, miles away from any island. What will we do if the petrol gives out before we've reached anywhere?'

Bill wiped his forehead. 'I don't like this,' he said. 'There's not much left in the tank now. Once we run out, we can't get far with oars, and we shall be at the mercy of any fast motor-boat sent out to catch us. I think perhaps one of the bullets must have glanced off the petrol tank and made it leak a bit.'

Nobody said anything. 'Oh dear,' thought Lucy-Ann, 'just as we think things are all right, they turn out all wrong again.'

After a while the engine stopped with a series of coughs and splutters. 'No more petrol,' said Jack gloomily.

'Send for the doctor,' said Kiki.

'Wish we could,' said Philip.

'Arrrrr!' said Huffin from the deck-rail. Both Huffin and Puffin were still with the little company. Lucy-Ann had begun to hope that they would travel right home with them. What excitement they would cause!

'This is really disgusting,' said Bill. 'So near and yet so far!'

There was a dead silence, and only the plish-plash of the sea against the sides of the boat could be heard. Philip's rats, surprised at the quiet, ran out of the various hiding-places in his clothes, and sniffed the air. Bill hadn't seen them since he had been captured from Puffin Island, and he stared in surprise.

'My word – how they've grown! Well, well, who knows, we may have to eat them in the end!'

He meant this as a joke, but both Lucy-Ann and Dinah squealed in horror.

'Ugh! Bill! How could you say such a horrible thing! Eat a *rat*! I'd rather die!'

'Shall we row, just for something to do?' said Jack. 'Or have a meal? Or what?'

'Oh, have a meal,' said Philip. Then a thought struck him. 'I say, Bill – I suppose we oughtn't to start rationing ourselves, ought we? I mean – do you think we may be marooned out here on this lonely sea for days on end?'

'No,' said Bill, who privately thought that before the day was up they would all be back on the island in the hands of the enemy, now that their plane had spotted them. 'No. We really don't need to think of things like that at the moment. All the same – I wouldn't have headed out for the open sea as we have done, if I'd thought the petrol was going to give out – I'd have kept near the islands.'

It was a boring and anxious day. The four children were still very tired, but refused to try and sleep. No motor-boat appeared in chase of them. The sun began to sink in the west, and it looked as if the little company was going to spend a night out on the open sea.

'Well, thank goodness it isn't cold, anyway,' said Dinah. 'Even the wind is warm tonight. Don't we seem a long long way from home – and from school – and from all the ordinary things we know?'

Lucy-Ann gazed round her at the vast open sea, green

near the boat, but a deep blue beyond. 'Yes,' she said, 'we're far away from everywhere – lost on the Sea of Adventure.'

The sun slid down further still. Then, on the evening air, came a familiar sound – the throb-throb-throb of a powerful engine.

Everyone sat up straight at once. Motor-boat? Aeroplane? Seaplane? What was it?

'There it is!' cried Jack, making everyone jump. 'Look, over there!' Golly, what a big one! It's a seaplane.'

'It must be the one we saw on the lagoon the other day,' said Dinah. 'They've sent it after us. Oh, Bill – what can we do?'

'All lie down flat,' said Bill at once. 'You've got to remember that if it's the enemy they don't know I've got children with me – they probably think there are three or four men in the boat – and they may shoot, as they did before. So lie down flat and don't move. Don't show your heads at all.'

Lucy-Ann's knees began their familiar wobbly feeling. She lay down flat at once, glad that Bill had not suggested that the boys should squash on top of them again. Bill put his arm over her.

'Don't you worry, Lucy-Ann,' he said. 'You'll be all right. They won't hurt children.'

But Lucy-Ann didn't want 'them' to hurt Bill either, and she was very much afraid they would. With her pale face pressed into the rugs, she lay as still as a mouse.

The roar of the seaplane came much nearer. It circled just overhead. Then its engine cut out and it landed not far off. Waves from it rippled under the boat and sent it up and down.

Nobody dared to look overboard and see the great seaplane. Bill was afraid of a bullet if he did.

Then a colossal voice came booming over the sea, the voice of a giant: 'AHOY THERE! SHOW YOURSELVES!'

'Don't move,' said Bill urgently. 'Don't move. Don't be frightened, Lucy-Ann. They're using a megaphone, that's why the voice sounds so loud.'

The giant voice came again: 'WE'VE GOT OUR GUNS ON YOU. ANY FUNNY BUSINESS AND YOU'LL BE BLOWN TO SMITHEREENS. SHOW YOURSELVES!'

31

Over the sea of adventure

'It's no good,' said Bill, in a low voice. 'I must stand up. I don't want them to machine-gun the boat.'

He stood up and waved, then put both hands up to show that he surrendered. A boat put off from the seaplane and came rapidly towards Bill's boat. In it were three men, one of them holding a revolver in his hand.

The children waited, panic-stricken, fearing to hear a shot at Bill. They had none of them raised their heads, but they could picture all too plainly what was happening.

The boat came near – and then there came a loud cry of amazement from it.

'BILL! By all that's wonderful, it's BILL! Why on earth didn't you welcome us, instead of making us think you were part of the gang!'

'Good heavens! It's you, Joe!' yelled Bill, and the relief in his voice brought all the children to their feet at once. 'Look here, kids – it's Joe – my colleague. Hey, Joe, you got my message then, all right?'

The boat came alongside with a gentle bump. Joe put away his revolver, grinning. 'Yes, I got your radio message all right – but I guess you didn't get ours. We kept asking you questions, and all you did was to go on repeating the same old thing. So this seaplane was sent out and we were just cruising along looking for the lagoon you told us about, when we spotted your boat here. So down we came to investigate.'

'Thank goodness,' said Bill. 'We'd run out of petrol. We were expecting the enemy to send a plane or a boat out after us at any moment!'

'Come along to the seaplane,' said Joe, who had bright-blue eyes and a very wide grin. 'Will the kids mind flying?'

'Oh no. We're used to it,' said Jack, and helped the girls into the boat where Joe stood.

'Are we rescued?' said Lucy-Ann, hardly believing it could be true, after all their alarms and fears.

'You are,' said Joe, and grinned at her. 'Sent one of our biggest seaplanes after you, to take you home! Have to do that for Bill here, you know. He's a V.I.P.'

'What's that?' asked Lucy-Ann, as they sped towards the seaplane.

'Very Important Person, of course,' said Joe. 'Didn't you know he was?'

'Yes,' said Lucy-Ann, beaming. 'Oh yes. I always knew he was.'

'We've left Huffin and Puffin behind,' suddenly wailed Dinah.

'Good heavens! Was there somebody else in your boat then?' said Joe in alarm. 'Never saw them!'

'Oh, they're only puffins,' said Jack. 'But awfully nice ones, quite tame. Oh, there they are, flying after the boat.'

'Can we take them with us?' begged Lucy-Ann. But Bill shook his head.

'No, Lucy-Ann. They'd be miserable away from their home here in the islands. Soon they will nest again and lay an egg. Then they will forget all about us.'

'I shall never, never forget them,' said Lucy-Ann. 'They kept with us all the time!'

'Here we are,' said Joe, as they came to the enormous seaplane. They were helped into it, and then the plane took off smoothly and sweetly, circling into the air like a broad-winged gull. Horace's boat was left bobbing alone, waiting for one of the police boats to collect it.

'What about that lagoon?' said Joe suddenly. 'I'd like to spot it, and plot it on our maps. I think we can find it. Will these kids know it if they see it?'

'Oh *yes*, said Jack. 'You can't mistake it. It's a most extraordinary sea-lake, and much bluer than the sea. I shouldn't be surprised if you can see some of the packages under the water, if you go down low. The water's so clear there.'

The seaplane roared through the sky. The children were thrilled. Down below was the blue sea, looking smooth and still. Then, as they looked, they saw little islands coming into view. What hosts of them there were!

Then Jack caught sight of the lagoon. 'There it is, there it is!' he shouted. 'Look down there! You can't mistake it, lying between those two islands, shut in by a reef of rocks all the way round.'

The seaplane circled round the surprising lagoon. It dropped lower. The children watched to see if they could make out any of the underwater packages – and sure enough, through the clear water glimmered the silvery-grey wrapping that covered the hidden guns.

'That's where the guns are,' said Philip. 'Look, Bill – you can see the waterproof wrappings! They had already begun to lift the packages from the water and load them on to seaplanes. We watched them loading one.'

Bill and Joe exchanged glances. 'We've got some pretty good witnesses then,' said Joe. 'Good bunch of kids, this, Bill. Are they the ones you've gone adventuring with before?'

'They are,' said Bill. 'You can't keep them out of adventures, you know. And they will drag me into them too!'

They left the lagoon with its sinister secret behind them and flew over the island where Bill had been a prisoner.

'There's the little jetty,' said Jack, as they flew low. 'And look, there are *two* motor-boats there now! I say, Bill – what about Horace?'

'Horace will be rescued when we clean up these scoundrels,' said Bill. 'They're the men who make fortunes when one country goes to war with another, or when civil war is fought – because they get the guns and sell them to each side. We try to stop it by all kinds of international treaties – but these men are against the law, and scorn it. That's where I come in – to stop them!'

'How will you stop them now?' asked Jack. 'Will you raid the island – and capture the men? And destroy all the hidden guns? Suppose they escape by motor-boat or plane?'

'Don't you worry about that,' said Joe, with his wide grin stretching across his brown face. 'We've got messages through already. There'll be a fleet of our seaplanes up here in a few hours – and armed boats patrolling all round. There's no hope for any of the gang now.'

Except for the little jetty, which would hardly have been noticed if the children and Bill hadn't known it was there, there was nothing to see on the enemy's island at all.

'Everything well camouflaged,' said Bill. 'A clever lot, and I've been after them for a long time. They sent me off on all kinds of false trails and I'd almost given up hope of finding their lair. But there it is.'

'They *must* have been surprised to see you up here, Bill!' said Lucy-Ann, as the seaplane left the enemy's island behind.

'Oh, look – there's the island where we landed with Bill!' cried Dinah. 'Puffin Island! Do look! There's the bird-cliff – and you can just see the little narrow channel going into the cliff – only you have to look hard to see it. And there's where we had our signal fire.'

'And there's where we had our tents that blew away in the storm – by those few trees,' said Jack. 'And look, there's the puffin colony!'

The seaplane flew down as low as it dared. It flew low enough for the children to see a moving mass of birds, scared of the enormous noise made by the seaplane's powerful engines.

'I can see Huffin and Puffin!' cried Lucy-Ann. The others roared with laughter.

'You can't, you fibber!' said Dinah.

'No, I can't really. I'm pretending to,' said Lucy-Ann. 'I want them to be there always. I want them to have their own burrow, and a nest – and an egg! I want them to have a lovely baby puffin that would be tame too. Goodbye, dear Huffin and Puffin! We did so love having you for pets.'

'Arrrrrrr!' suddenly said Kiki, for all the world as if she understood what Lucy-Ann was saying.

'Kiki's saying "goodbye" in puffin language,' said Lucy-Ann. 'Arrrrr, Huffin and Puffin! I'm saying goodbye too.'

And from the scared puffin colony rose a medley of deep guttural *arrrrrrrs* as the birds settled down once more. Those that had run down burrows popped up again and added their *arrrrr* to the chorus.

'What a lot we shall have to tell Mother,' said Philip. 'I wonder how she is?'

Joe smiled at him. 'Getting on fine, except for worrying about you four,' he said. 'She'll feel better still when she gets our radio message.'

'Oh, have you sent one already?' asked Dinah. 'Oh, good! Now she'll know we're all right. Goodness – won't it be strange to go back to school after all this?'

School! Sitting at a desk, learning French grammar, getting into rows for leaving tennis racquets about, playing silly tricks, having music lessons, going to bed at the proper time – how very, very strange it would all seem!

Only Lucy-Ann thought of it with real pleasure. 'It'll be so nice to wake up in the mornings and know there's only lessons and tennis and things to worry about,' she said to Bill. 'Instead of wondering if the enemy is coming, and seeing planes parachuting guns down into lagoons, and rushing about in motor-boats, and . . . '

'Conking poor Horace on the head,' said Bill, grinning.

'Well, we *didn't* do that, whatever he said to you,' said Lucy-Ann. 'And if ever I see him again I'm going to tell him I'm sorry we made such an awful mistake – but that honestly he deserves a good old – a good old . . . '

'Conk,' said Philip, chuckling.

'Well, conk if you like,' said Lucy-Ann. 'A good old conk for telling such awful stories.'

The seaplane was flying south now. It had left behind all the exciting little islands, and all the millions of noisy sea-birds. The sun was now almost gone and the sea was shadowed a deep blue. In a few minutes the first stars would prick through the evening sky, as bright as diamonds.

'We'll be over the mainland soon,' said Bill. 'Thank goodness it's all ended up well! I thought it was the finish of everything when this seaplane landed beside us and hailed us. Another adventure to talk over when we see each other in the holidays. What a lot we've had together!'

'I think I've liked this one the best,' said Jack thoughtfully, and he scratched what was left of Kiki's crest. 'All those islands – and this lonely sea, with its blues and greens and greys.'

'The Sea of Adventure,' said Lucy-Ann, looking down at its vast expanse of dark blue, touched here and there with the golden reflection of the sky. 'Goodbye, Sea of Adventure! You're a lovely place – but *much* too exciting for me!'

Enid Blyton

The Mountain of Adventure

Contents

1

All set for a summer holiday

Four children were singing at the tops of their voices in a car that was going up a steep mountain-side road.

A parrot was also joining in, very much out of tune, cocking up her crest in excitement. The man at the wheel turned round with a grin.

'I say! I can't even hear the car hooter. What's the matter with you all?'

Philip, Jack, Dinah and Lucy-Ann stopped singing and shouted answers at him.

'It's the beginning of the hols!'

'And we're going to have a donkey each to ride in the mountains!'

'Pop goes the weasel!' That was Kiki the parrot, of course, joining in.

'We've got eight weeks of fun all together.'

'And you'll be with us, Bill, as well as Mother! Mother, aren't you excited too?'

Mrs Mannering smiled at Philip. 'Yes – but I hope you're not going to be as noisy as this all the time. Bill, you'll have to protect me from this rowdy crowd of children.'

'I'll protect you all right,' promised Bill, swinging the car round another bend. 'I'll knock all their heads together once a day at least – and if Lucy-Ann starts getting tough with me I'll . . . '

'Oh, *Bill!*' said Lucy-Ann, the youngest and least boisterous of the lot. 'Jack's always saying I'm not tough *enough*. I ought to be by now, though, considering all the adventures I've been through.'

'Tough enough, tough enough!' chanted Kiki the parrot, who loved words that sounded alike. 'Tough enough, tough . . . '

'Oh, stop her,' groaned Mrs Mannering. She was tired with their long car journey, and was hoping it would soon be over. She had eight weeks of the children's holidays before her, and was quite sure she would be worn out before the end of it.

Philip and Dinah were her own children, and Jack and Lucy-Ann, who had no parents, lived with her in the holidays and loved her as if she were their own mother. Bill Cunningham was their very good friend, and had had some hair-raising adventures with them.

He had come with them on these holidays to keep them out of any more adventures – or so he said! Mrs Mannering vowed she was not going to let them out of her sight for eight weeks, unless Bill was with them – then they couldn't possibly disappear, or fall into some dreadful new adventure.

'They ought to be safe, tucked away in the Welsh mountains, with both you and me, Bill, to look after them,' said Mrs Mannering. Mr Mannering had been dead for many years and Mrs Mannering often found it difficult to cope with so many lively children at once, now that they were growing older.

Philip loved any animal, bird or insect. His sister Dinah didn't share this love at all, and disliked most wild animals, and hated quite a number of harmless insects, though she was certainly better than she used to be. She was a hot-tempered girl, as ready to use her fists as Philip, and they had many a battle, much to gentle Lucy-Ann's dismay.

Lucy-Ann and Jack were brother and sister too. Kiki the parrot was Jack's beloved parrot, usually to be found on his shoulder. In fact, Mrs Mannering had once actually suggested that she should put a little leather patch on the shoulders of each of Jack's coats to stop Kiki from wearing thin places there with her clawed feet.

Jack was fond of birds, and he and Philip spent many an exciting hour together bird-watching, or taking photographs. They had a marvellous collection of these, which

Bill said was worth a lot of money. They had brought cameras with them on this holiday, and, of course, their field-glasses for watching birds at a distance.

'We might see eagles again,' said Jack. 'Do you remember the eagle's nest we found near that old castle in Scotland once, Philip? We might see buzzards too.'

'Buzz-z-z-z-z-z,' said Kiki at once. 'Buzz! Buzz off!'

'We might even have an adventure,' said Philip, with a grin. 'Though Mother and Bill are quite certain they will guard us from even the smallest one this time!'

Now here they were, all set for a wonderful holiday in the Welsh mountains, in a very lonely spot, where they could wander about with cameras and field-glasses wherever they liked. Each child was to have a donkey, so that they could ride along the narrow mountain paths as much as they wished.

'I shan't always come with you,' said Mrs Mannering, 'because I'm not so thrilled with donkey-riding as you are. But Bill will be with you, so you'll be safe.'

'Ah – but will Bill be safe with *us*?' said Jack, with a grin. 'We always seem to drag him into something or other. Poor Bill!'

'If you manage to pull me into an adventure in the middle of some of the loneliest of the Welsh mountains, you'll be clever,' said Bill.

The car swung round another bend and a farmhouse came into sight.

'We're nearly there,' said Mrs Mannering. 'I believe I can see the farm-house we're going to stay at. Yes – there it is.'

The children craned their necks to see it. It was a rambling old stone place, set on the mountain-side, with barns and out-buildings all around. In the evening sunset it looked welcoming and friendly.

'Lovely!' said Lucy-Ann. 'What's it called?'

Bill said something that sounded like 'Doth-goth-oo-elli-othel-in.'

'Gracious!' said Dinah. 'What a name! Not even Kiki could pronounce that, I'm sure. Tell her it, Bill. See what she says.'

Bill obligingly told the name to the parrot, who listened solemnly and raised her crest politely.

'Now you just repeat that,' said Jack to Kiki. 'Go on!'

'This-is-the-house-that-Jack-built,' said the parrot, running all the words together. The children laughed.

'Good try, Kiki!' said Jack. 'You can't stump Kiki, Bill – she'll always say something. Good old Kiki!'

Kiki was pleased by this praise, and made a noise like the car changing gear. She had been doing this at intervals during the whole of the journey and had nearly driven Mrs Mannering mad.

'*Don't* let Kiki start that again,' she begged. 'Thank goodness we are here at last! Where's the front door, Bill – or isn't there one?'

There didn't seem to be one. The track went up to what appeared to be a barn and stopped there. A small path then ran to the farmhouse, divided into three and went to three different doors.

The children tumbled out of the car. Bill got out and stretched his legs. He helped Mrs Mannering out and they all looked round. A cock near by crowed and Kiki promptly crowed too, much to the cock's astonishment.

A plump, red-faced woman came hurrying out of one of the doors, a welcoming smile on her face. She called behind her to someone in the house.

'Effans, Effans, they have come, look you, they have come!'

'Ah – Mrs Evans,' said Bill, and shook hands with her. Mrs Mannering did the same. A small man came running out of the house, and came up to them too.

'This iss Effans, my husband,' said the plump woman. 'We hope you will be very happy with us, whateffer!'

This was said in a pleasant sing-song voice that the

children liked very much. Everybody shook hands solemnly with Mrs Evans and her husband, and Kiki held out a claw as well.

'A parrot, look you!' cried Mrs Evans to her husband. 'Effans, a parrot!'

Mr Evans didn't seem to like the look of Kiki as much as his wife did, but he smiled politely.

'It iss very welcome you are,' he said in his sing-song voice. 'Will you pleass to come this way?'

They all followed Effans. He led them to the farm-house, and, when the door was flung open, what a welcome sight met the children's eyes!

A long, sturdy kitchen table was covered with a snow-white cloth, and on it was set the finest meal the children had ever seen in their lives.

A great ham sat ready to be carved. A big tongue garnished round with bright green parsley sat by its side. An enormous salad with hard-boiled eggs sprinkled generously all over it was in the middle of the table. Two cold roast chickens were on the table too, with little curly bits of cold bacon set round.

The children's eyes nearly fell out of their heads. What a feast! And the scones and cakes! The jams and the pure yellow honey! The jugs of creamy milk!

'I say – are you having a party or something?' asked Jack, in awe.

'A party! No, no – it is high tea for you, look you,' said Mrs Evans. 'We cannot do dinners for you at night, we are busy people! You shall have what we have, and that is all. Here is high tea for you today, and when you have washed, it iss ready!'

'Oh – have we got to wash?' said Philip with a sigh. 'I'm clean enough. Golly, look at that meal! I say, if we're going to have food like this these hols I shan't want to go donkey-riding at all. I'll just stay here and eat!'

'Well, if you do that you'll be too fat for any donkey to

carry,' said his mother. 'Go and wash, Philip. Mrs Evans will show us our rooms – we can all do with a wash and a brush – and then we can do justice to this magnificent meal.'

Up some narrow winding stairs went the little party, into big low-ceilinged rooms set with heavy old-fashioned furniture. Mrs Evans proudly showed them a small bathroom, put in for visitors to the farm-house.

There were four rooms for the party. Bill had a small one to himself. Mrs Mannering had a big one, well away from the children's rooms, because they were often so noisy in the mornings. Philip and Jack had a curious little room together, whose ceiling slanted almost to the floor, and the girls had a bigger one next door.

'Isn't this going to be fun?' said Jack, scrubbing his hands vigorously in the bathroom, whilst Kiki sat on a tap. 'I'm longing to get at that meal downstairs. What a spread!'

'Move up,' said Dinah impatiently. 'There's room for two at this basin. We shall have to take it in turns to come in in the morning. Oh, Kiki, don't fly off with the nail-brush! Jack, stop her.'

The nail-brush was rescued and Kiki was tapped on the beak. She didn't mind. She was looking forward to the food downstairs as much as the children. She had seen a bowl of raspberries which she meant to sit as near to as possible. She flew to Jack's shoulder and muttered loving things into his ear whilst he dried his hands on a very rough towel.

'Stop it, Kiki. You tickle,' said Jack. 'Are you ready, you others? Aunt Allie! Bill! Are you ready? We're going downstairs.'

'Coming!' cried the others, and down they all went. Now for a proper feast!

2

At the farmhouse

That first meal in the Welsh farm-house was a very happy one. Mrs Evans was excited to have visitors, and Effans, her husband, beamed all round as he carved great slices of ham, tongue and chicken. There were a lot of 'look yous' and 'whateffers,' and Kiki was especially interested in the up-and-down song-like way the two Welsh folk talked.

'Wipe your feet, whateffer,' she said to Mrs Evans suddenly. Mrs Evans looked surprised. She hadn't heard the parrot speak before.

'Shut the door, look you,' commanded Kiki, raising her crest. The children squealed with laughter.

'She's speaking Welsh already!' said Dinah. 'Hey, watch her, Jack – she's absolutely wolfing those raspberries!'

Jack put a plate over the bowl, and Kiki was angry. She made a noise like the car changing gear and Effans looked startled.

'It's all right – it's only Kiki,' said Jack. 'She can make all kinds of noises. You should hear her give her imitation of a train whistling in a tunnel.'

Kiki opened her beak and swelled up her throat as if she was about to make this horrible noise. Mrs Mannering spoke hastily. 'Jack! Don't let Kiki make that noise. If she does you'll have to take her upstairs and put her in your bedroom.'

'Bad Kiki, naughty Kiki,' said the parrot solemnly, recognizing the stern tone in Mrs Mannering's voice. She flew to Jack's shoulder and cuddled there, eyeing the plate that he had put over the bowl of raspberries. She gave his ear a little nip.

What a meal that was for six very hungry travellers who

had had nothing but sandwiches all day long! Even Mrs Mannering ate more than she had ever eaten before at one meal. Mrs Evans kept beaming round as she filled the plates.

'There iss plenty more in the larder, look you,' she said. 'Effans, go fetch the meat-pie.'

'No, no!' said Mrs Mannering. 'Please don't. We have more than enough here – it's only that we are extra hungry and the food is so very very good.'

Mrs Evans was pleased. 'It iss plain country food, but it iss very good for the children,' she said. 'They will soon have good appetites in this mountain air, look you.'

'Indeed to gootness they will,' agreed Effans. 'Their appetites are small yet. They will grow.'

Mrs Mannering looked rather alarmed. 'Good gracious! I've never in my life seen them eat so much – if their appetites get any bigger I'll never be able to feed them at home!'

'And we shall *starve* at school,' grinned Jack.

'The poor boy!' said Mrs Evans. 'It iss a big ham I must give him to take back, whateffer!'

At last nobody could eat any more. They sat back from the table, looking out of the wide, low windows and the big open door. What a view!

Great mountains reared up their heads in the evening light. Deep shadows lay across the valley, but the mountains still caught the sunlight, and gleamed enchantingly. It was all so different from the country round their home, and the children felt that they could never look long enough on the mountain-tops and the shadowed valleys below.

'You are very lonely here,' said Bill. 'I can't see a single house or farm anywhere.'

'My brother lives on the other side of that mountain,' said Mrs Evans, pointing. 'I see him at the market each week. That is ten miles away, or maybe eleven. And my sister lives beyond that mountain you can see there. She too has a farm. So we have neighbours, you see.'

'Yes – but not next-door ones!' said Dinah. 'Don't you

ever feel cut-off and lonely here, Mrs Evans?'

Mrs Evans looked surprised. 'Lonely? Indeed to gootness, what iss there to be lonely about, with Effans by my side, and the shepherd up on the hills, and the cow-herd and his wife in their cottage near by? And there iss plenty of animals, as you will see.'

Hens wandered in and out of the open door, pecking up crumbs fallen from the table. Kiki watched them intently. She began a warm, clucking noise, and the hens clucked back. A cock came strutting in and looked round for the hen that had a cluck he didn't quite know.

'Cock-a-doodle-doo!' suddenly crowed the cock defiantly, catching sight of Kiki on Jack's shoulder.

'Cock-a-doodle-doo!' answered Kiki, and the cock immediately jumped up on to the table to fight the crowing parrot.

He was shooed down and ran out indignantly, followed by a cackle of laughter from Kiki. Effans held his sides and laughed till the tears ran down his cheeks.

'That is a fine bird, look you!' he said to Jack, quite losing his heart to Kiki. 'Let her help herself to the raspberries again.'

'She's had enough, thank you very much,' said Jack, pleased at Effans' praise of Kiki. People sometimes didn't like the parrot, and when she went away with him Jack was always anxious in case anyone should object to her.

They all wandered out into the golden evening air, happy and well satisfied. Bill and Mrs Mannering sat on an old stone wall, watching the sun sink behind a mountain in the west. The four children went round the farmhouse and its buildings.

'Pigs! And what a marvellous clean pig-sty,' said Dinah. 'I've never seen a clean pig before. Look at this one, fat and shining as if it's been scrubbed.'

'It probably has, in preparation for our coming!' said Philip. 'I love these little piglets too. Look at them rooting round with their funny little snouts.'

'Kiki will soon have a wonderful collection of noises,' said Lucy-Ann, hearing the parrot giving a very life-like grunt. 'She'll be able to moo and bellow and grunt and crow and cluck . . . '

'And gobble like a turkey!' said Dinah, seeing some turkeys near by. 'This is a lovely farm. They've got everything. Oh, Philip – *look* at that kid!'

There were some goats on the mountain-side not far off, and with them was a kid. It was snow-white, dainty and altogether lovely. Philip stood looking at it, loving it at once.

He made a curious little bleating noise and all the goats looked round and stopped eating. The kid pricked up its little white ears, and stood quivering on its slender legs. It was very young and new.

Philip made the noise again. The kid left its mother and came leaping to him. It sprang right into his arms and nestled there, butting its soft white head against Philip's chin.

'Oh, Philip – isn't it sweet!' said the girls, and stroked the little thing and rubbed their cheeks against its snow-white coat.

'I wish animals came to me like they come to you, Philip,' said Lucy-Ann enviously. It was amazing the attraction that Philip had for creatures of any kind. Even a moth would rest contentedly on his finger, and the number of strange pets he had had was unbelievable. Hedgehogs, stag-beetles, lizards, young birds, mice, rats – you never knew what Philip would have next. All creatures loved him and trusted him, and he in turn understood them and loved them too.

'Now this kid will follow at his heels like a dog the whole time we're here,' said Dinah. 'Well, I'm glad it will be a kid, not a cow! Do you remember that awful time when Philip went into a field with a herd of cows in, and they all went to him and nuzzled him and followed him about like dogs. They even tried to get over the gate and through the hedge when he went out. I was awfully scared they would.'

'You ought to be ashamed of being afraid of cows,' said Philip, stroking the kid. 'There's no reason to be, Di. It's surprising you're not afraid of this kid. I bet you'd run if the goats came near.'

'I shouldn't,' said Dinah indignantly, but all the same she moved off hurriedly when the herd of goats, curious at seeing the kid in Philip's arms, began to come nearer to the children.

Soon they were all round Philip, Lucy-Ann and Jack. Dinah watched from a distance. The kid bleated when it saw its mother, but as soon as Philip put the little thing down to run to her, it leapt straight back into his arms!

'Well! You'll have to take it to bed with you tonight, there's no doubt about that,' said Jack, grinning. 'Come on – let's go and see the horses. They're the kind with shaggy hooves – I just love those!'

The goats were shooed off, and the children went to look at the great horses standing patiently in the field. There were three of them. They all came to Philip at once of course.

He had put down the little kid, and now it followed so close to his heels that, every time he stopped, it ran into his legs. At the first possible chance it sprang into his arms again. It followed him into the farmhouse too.

'Oh! You have found little Snowy!' said Mrs Evans, looking round from her oven with a face redder than ever. 'He has not left his mother before, look you!'

'Oh, Philip, don't bring the kid in here,' said Mrs Mannering, seeing at once that yet another animal had attached itself to Philip. She was afraid that Mrs Evans would object strongly to the kid coming indoors with Philip – and once it had felt the boy's attraction nothing would stop it from following him anywhere – even upstairs!

'Oh, it iss no matter if a kid comes into the house,' said Mrs Evans. 'We haff the new-born lambs in, and the hens are always in and out, and Moolie the calf used to come in each day before she was put in the field.'

The children thought it was a wonderful idea to let creatures wander in and out like that, but Mrs Mannering thought differently. She wondered if she would find eggs laid in her bed, or a calf in her bedroom chair! Still, it was a holiday, and if Mrs Evans like creatures wandering all over her kitchen, the children would like it too!

Lucy-Ann gave an enormous yawn and sank down into a big chair. Mrs Mannering looked at her, and then at the grandfather clock ticking in a corner.

'Go to bed, all of you,' she said. 'We're all tired. Yes, I know it's early, Philip, you don't need to tell me that – but we've had a long day, and this mountain air is very strong. We shall all sleep like tops tonight.'

'I will get ready some creamy milk for you,' began Mrs Evans, 'and you would like some buttered scones and jam to take up with you?'

'Oh, *no*,' said Mrs Mannering. 'We simply couldn't eat a thing more tonight, thank you, Mrs Evans.'

'Oh, *Mother*! Of *course* we could eat scones and jam and drink some more of that heavenly milk,' said Dinah indignantly. So they each took up a plate of scones and raspberry jam and a big glass of creamy milk to have in bed.

There came the scampering of little hooves, and Snowy the kid appeared in the boys' bedroom. He leapt in delight on to Philip's bed.

'Gosh! Look at this! Snowy's come upstairs!' said Philip. 'Have a bit of scone, Snowy?'

'I say – did we hear the kid coming up the stairs?' said Lucy-Ann, putting her head round the door of the boys' room. 'Oooh, Philip! You've got him on your bed!'

'Well, he won't get off,' said Philip. 'As soon as I push him off, he's on again – look! Like a puppy!'

'Maa-aa-aa!' said the kid in a soft, bleating voice, and butted Philip with its head.

'Are you going to have it up here all the night?' asked

Dinah, appearing in her pyjamas.

'Well, if I put it outside, it'll only come in again – and if I shut the door it will come and butt it with its head,' said Philip, who had quite lost his heart to Snowy. 'After all, Jack has Kiki in the room with him all night.'

'Oh, *I* don't mind you having Snowy,' said Dinah. 'I just wondered what Mother would say, that's all – and Mrs Evans.'

'I shouldn't be at all surprised to hear that Mrs Evans has got a sick cow in her room, and half a dozen hens,' said Philip, arranging Snowy in the crook of his knees. 'She's a woman after my own heart. Go away, you girls. I'm going to sleep. I'm very happy – full of scones and jam and milk and sleep.'

Kiki made a hiccuping noise. 'Pardon!' she said. This was a new thing she had learnt from somebody at Jack's school the term before. It made Mrs Mannering cross.

'I should think Kiki's full up too,' said Jack sleepily. 'She pinched a whole scone, and I'm sure she's been at the raspberries again. Look at her beak! Now shut up, Kiki, I want to go to sleep.'

'Pop goes the weasel, look you,' said Kiki solemnly and put her head under her wing. The girls disappeared. The boys fell asleep. What a lovely beginning to a summer holiday!

3

The first morning

The next day the two girls awoke first. It was early, but somebody was already about in the yard. Lucy-Ann peeped out of the window.

'It's Effans,' she said. 'He must have been milking. Dinah, come here. Did you ever see such a glorious view in your life?'

The two girls knelt at the window. The sun was streaming across the valley below through the opening between two mountains, but the rest of the vale was in shadow. In the distance many mountains reared their great heads, getting bluer and bluer the further they were away. The sky was blue without a cloud.

'Holiday weather – real holiday weather!' said Dinah happily. 'I hope Mother lets us go picnicking today.'

'There's one thing about *this* holiday,' said Lucy-Ann, 'we shan't have any awful adventures, because Aunt Allie is absolutely determined to go with us, or send Bill with us, wherever we go.'

'Well, we've had our share of adventures,' said Dinah, beginning to dress. 'More than most children ever have. I don't mind if we don't have one this time. Hurry, Lucy-Ann, then we can get to the bathroom before the boys. Don't make too much row because Mother doesn't want to be wakened too early.'

Lucy-Ann popped her head in at the boys' room on the way to the bathroom. They were still sound asleep. Kiki took her head from under her wing as she heard Lucy-Ann at the door, but she said nothing, only yawned. Lucy-Ann looked closely at Philip's bed.

Snowy the kid was still there, cuddled into the crook of

Philip's knees! Lucy-Ann's heart warmed to Philip. What an extraordinary boy he was, to have every creature so fond of him, and to be able to do anything he liked with them. The little kid raised its head and looked at Lucy-Ann.

She fled to the bathroom and washed with Dinah. They soon heard the boys getting up, and Kiki's voice telling somebody to wipe his feet.

'She's probably teaching a few manners to Snowy,' giggled Lucy-Ann. 'Kiki always tries to teach things to all Philip's pets. Oh, Dinah – do you remember how funny she was with Huffin and Puffin, the two puffins we found when we had our last adventure?'

'Arr,' said Dinah, making the noise the puffins used to make. Kiki heard them. 'Arrrrr!' she called from the boys' bedroom. 'Arrrrr!' Then she went off into a cackle of laughter, and Snowy the kid stared at her in alarm.

'Maa-aa-aa!' said the kid.

'Maa-aa-aa!' said Kiki, and the kid looked all round for another kid. The boys laughed.

Kiki, always encouraged when people laughed, swelled up her throat to make the noise of a car changing gear, her favourite noise of the moment, but Philip stopped her hurriedly.

'Stop it, Kiki! We've had enough of that noise. Do forget it!'

'God save the Queen!' said Kiki, in a dismal voice. 'Wipe your feet, blow your nose.'

'Come on,' said the girls, putting their heads in. 'Slowcoaches!'

They all went downstairs just as Mrs Evans was setting the last touches to the breakfast-table. It was loaded almost as much as the supper-table the night before. Jugs of creamy milk stood about the table, warm from the milking, and big bowls of raspberries had appeared again.

'I shan't know what to have,' groaned Jack, sitting down with Kiki on his shoulder. 'I can smell eggs and bacon – and there's cereal to have with raspberries and cream – and ham – and tomatoes – and gosh, is that cream cheese? Cream cheese for breakfast, how super!'

Snowy the kid tried to get on to Philip's knee as he sat down to breakfast. He pushed him off. 'No, Snowy, not at meal-times. I'm too busy then. Go and say good morning to your mother. She must wonder where you are.'

Kiki was at work on the raspberries. Mrs Evans had actually put a plate aside for Kiki's own breakfast. She and Effans beamed at the bird. They both thought she was wonderful.

'Look you, whateffer!' said Kiki, and dipped her beak into the raspberries again. It was rapidly becoming pink with the juice.

The children had an extremely good meal before Bill or Mrs Mannering came down. The Evans' had had theirs already – in fact they seemed to have done a day's work, judging by the list of things that Evans talked about – he had cleaned out the pigs, groomed the horses, milked the cows, fetched in the eggs, been to see the cow-herd and a dozen other things besides.

'Mrs Evans, do you know where the donkeys are that we arranged to have, for riding in the mountains?' asked Philip, when he had finished his breakfast and Snowy was once more in his arms.

'Ah, Trefor the shepherd will tell you,' said Mrs Evans. 'It iss his brother, look you, that has the donkeys. He is to bring them here for you.'

'Can't we go and fetch them and ride them back?' said Jack.

'Indeed to gootness, Trefor's brother lives thirty miles away!' said Effans. 'You could not walk there, whateffer. You go and see Trefor today and ask him what has he done about your donkeys.'

Mrs Mannering and Bill appeared at that moment, looking fresh and trim after their good night's sleep in the sharp mountain air.

'Any breakfast left for us?' said Bill with a grin.

Mrs Evans hurried to fry bacon and eggs again, and soon the big kitchen was full of the savoury smell.

'Golly, if I stay here and smell that I shall feel hungry all over again,' said Philip. 'Bill, we're going up to see Trefor the shepherd to ask about our donkeys. Mother, can we have a picnic in the mountains as soon as the donkeys come?'

'Yes – when I'm sure I can keep on my donkey all right,' said his mother. 'If mine's a very fat donkey I shall slide off!'

'They are not fat,' Effans assured her. 'They are used in the mountains and they are strong and small. Sometimes we use ponies, but Trefor's brother breeds donkeys, and they are just as good.'

'Well, we'll go and have a talk with Trefor,' said Philip, getting up and letting Snowy fall off his knee. 'Come on, everyone! Kiki, do you want to be left with the raspberries? You greedy bird!'

Kiki flew to Jack's shoulder, and the party set off up the path that Effans had pointed out to them. Snowy bounded with them, turning a deaf ear to his mother's bleats. Already he seemed one of the company, petted by them all, though Kiki was not altogether pleased to have another creature taking up so much of the children's attention.

They went up the steep little path. The sun was up higher now and was hot. The children wore only thin blouses or shirts, and shorts, but they felt very warm. They came to a spring gushing out of the hillside and sat down to drink, and to cool their hands and feet. Snowy drank too, and then capered about lightly on his strong little legs, leaping from place to place almost as if he had wings.

'I wish I could leap like a goat,' said Jack lazily. 'It looks so lovely and easy to spring up high into the air like that, and land wherever you want to.'

Philip suddenly made a grab at something that was slithering past him on the warm bank. Dinah sat up at once. 'What is it, what is it?'

'This,' said Philip, and showed the others a silvery-grey, snake-like creature, with bright little eyes.

Dinah screamed at once. 'A snake! Philip, put it down. Philip, it'll bite you.'

'It won't,' said Philip calmly. 'It's not a snake – and anyway British snakes don't bite unless they're adders. I've told you that before. This is a slow-worm – and a very fine specimen too!'

The children looked in fascination as the silvery slow-worm wriggled over Philip's knees. It certainly looked very like a snake, but it wasn't. Lucy-Ann and Jack knew that, but Dinah always forgot. She was so terrified of snakes that to her anything that glided along must belong to the snake family.

'It's horrible,' she said with a shudder. 'Let it go, Philip. How do you know it's not a snake?'

'Well – for one thing it blinks its eyes and no snake does that,' said Philip. 'Watch it. It blinks like a lizard – and no wonder, because it belongs to the lizard family.'

As he spoke the little creature blinked its eyes. It stayed still on Philip's knee and made no further attempt to escape. Philip put his hand over it and it stayed there quite happy.

'I've never had a slow-worm for a pet,' said Philip. 'I've a good mind . . . '

'Philip! If you dare to keep that snake for a pet I'll tell Mother to send you home!' said Dinah in great alarm.

'Dinah, it's *not* a snake!' said Philip impatiently. 'It's a lizard – a legless lizard – quite harmless and very interesting. I'm going to keep it for a pet if it'll stay with me.'

'Stay with you! Of course it will,' said Jack. 'Did you ever know an animal that wouldn't? I should hate to go to a jungle with you, Philip – you'd have monkeys hanging lovingly round your neck, and tigers purring at you, and snakes wrapping themselves round your legs, and . . . '

Dinah gave a little scream. 'Don't say such horrible things! Philip, make that slow-worm go away.'

Instead he slipped it into his pocket. 'Now don't worry, Dinah,' he said. 'You don't need to come near me. I don't expect it will stay with me because it won't like my pocket – but I'll just see.'

They set off up the hill once more, Dinah hanging back carefully. Oh dear! Philip *would* go and spoil the holiday by keeping something horrible again!

4

Up on the mountain-side

Trefor the shepherd had a small cabin-like cottage a good way up the mountain-side. Around him for miles grazed the sheep. Nearer in were that year's lambs, now grown into sturdy little beasts, their woolly coats showing up against the sheared bodies of the older sheep.

The shepherd was having a simple meal when they got to his hut. He had bread, butter, cream cheese and onions, and beside him a great jug of milk that he had cooled by standing in the stream that ran down the mountain-side near by.

He nodded his head to the children as they came up. He was a curious-looking old fellow, with longish untidy hair, a straggling beard, and two of the brightest blue eyes the children had ever seen.

He spoke Welsh, which they didn't understand. 'Can you speak English?' asked Jack. 'We can't understand what you say.'

Trefor knew a few words of English, which, after much thought and munching of onions, he spoke.

'Donkeys. Tomorrow.'

He added something the children didn't understand, and waved his hand down the mountain-side towards the farmhouse.

'He means the donkeys will arrive tomorrow at the farm,' said Jack. 'Good! Perhaps Aunt Allie and Bill will come for a picnic on the donkeys.'

Trefor was very interested in Kiki. He had never in his life seen a parrot. He pointed at Kiki and laughed a hoarse laugh. Kiki at once copied it.

Trefor looked startled. 'Wipe your feet,' said Kiki sternly. 'How many times have I told you to shut the door? Three blind mice!'

Trefor stared at the parrot, amazed. Kiki cackled loudly. 'Look you, whateffer, look you, whateffer, look . . . '

The children laughed. Jack tapped Kiki on the beak. 'Now, now, Kiki – don't show off.'

Snowy butted against Philip's legs. He didn't like so much attention being given to Kiki. Philip turned, and the little creature leapt straight into his arms. Trefor seemed most amused and sent out a flood of Welsh words that nobody could understand at all. He tapped Philip on the arm, and then pointed to the ground to show the children that he wanted them to sit down.

They sat down, wondering what he wanted. He went a little way down the hillside, making a soft baaing noise. From everywhere around the woolly lambs looked up. They came running to the shepherd, bleating, and even little Snowy left Philip and ran too. The shepherd knelt down and the lambs crowded round him, nuzzling against him. Trefor had had them when they were tiny – he had looked after them, even fed some of them from bottles if their mothers had died, – and when they heard his soft call that once they had known so well, they remembered and came to him, their first friend.

A lump came into Lucy-Ann's throat. There was something very touching in the sight of that solemn, lonely, long-haired old shepherd, calling to his lambs and being answered. Snowy the kid, eager to get close to him, leapt on to the woolly backs of the lambs, and butted his head against him.

'Look at Snowy! Isn't he a cheeky rascal of a kid!' said Dinah. 'My goodness, you can hardly see Trefor now, he's so surrounded by lambs!'

Trefor came back, smiling, his eyes very blue in his old brown face. He offered the children some bread and onions, but the onions were big and strong-smelling, and Jack felt certain Mrs Mannering wouldn't approve if they all came back smelling strongly of Trefor's onions.

'No, thank you,' he said politely. 'Will you be down to see your brother tomorrow, when he brings the donkeys?'

Trefor seemed to understand this. He nodded. 'I come. Tomorrow. Donkeys.'

'Getting quite talkative, isn't he?' said Jack to the others. 'Right, Trefor. See you tomorrow then.'

They set off down the hill again. They stopped once more at the little spring to drink. They sat on the grass, looking at the towering mountains round them.

'Effans says that all those mountains over there have hardly anyone living on them, because they are difficult to get at,' said Jack. 'I bet there are some interesting animals and birds there. Wish we could go and see.'

'I don't see why we shouldn't if Bill and Mother would come with us,' said Philip, trying to stop Snowy from walking on his middle. 'Stop it, Snowy. Get off my tummy. Your hooves are sharp. It would be fun to go off into the mountains on donkeys and take food with us for a few days.'

'And have tents, do you mean?' said Jack. 'I say – that's an idea, Philip. We could take our cameras and get some fine pictures. I might see some rare birds.'

'I bet you would!' said Philip. 'Hallo, here comes Sally Slither!'

Out of his pocket glided the slow-worm, and curled itself up in the crook of Philip's elbow, in the sun. Dinah removed herself to a safe distance at once. Kiki looked down with interest from her perch on Jack's shoulder.

'Sally Slither! What a nice name!' said Lucy-Ann, running her finger down the slow-worm's silvery back. 'Look – my finger's tickling her – she's going all dithery!'

'Slithery dithery,' said Kiki, at once. She had a real talent for putting together words of the same sound. 'Dithery slithery, slithery dithery . . . '

'All right, all right,' said Philip. 'We don't want to hear it again, Kiki. You're a clever old bird, we all know that. Jack, look at this slow-worm. It's not a scrap frightened now.'

'I do think you're mean to keep it,' began Dinah, from a safe distance. 'You know how I hate snakes. All right, all right, I *know* it isn't a snake – though I wouldn't be a bit surprised if it bit me if I came near it, so there!'

'I wouldn't be surprised at anything biting you when you're so nervous,' said Philip crossly. 'I feel like biting you myself. Come here, Dinah. Run your fingers down Sally Slither's back – look at her sharp little eyes. . . . '

Dinah gave a scream. 'I couldn't bear it! No, don't come near me, Philip. It's worse than those awful white rats you had a few months ago. But at least they grew up and you let them go!'

'Sally can go whenever she wants to,' said Philip. 'I never keep any pet when it wants to go. Do you want to go, Sally Slither?'

'Slithery dithery, musty dusty fusty,' said Kiki, trying to remember the various collections of words she had picked up at one time or another. 'Huffin and Puffin.'

'Come on – let's go,' said Dinah. 'Perhaps that horrible thing will go back into your pocket if we go. And I'm getting hungry.'

The slow-worm slid back somewhere in Philip's clothes. He got up and Snowy bounded round him. 'Now just see if you can walk without getting your head between my legs all the time,' said Philip to Snowy. 'You'll send me flying in a minute. You're a bit *too* friendly at times, Snowy.'

They went back to the farmhouse, enjoying the sunshine and the constant breeze that blew over the mountain-side. By the time they reached the farmhouse they were all terribly hungry, and visions of ham, chicken, salad and and raspberries and cream kept coming into their minds.

Bill and Mrs Mannering had been for a walk too, but down the mountain, not up. They had been back for a little while, and were just beginning to wonder where the children were. Snowy went bounding up to them.

'He's a pet!' said Mrs Mannering. 'I suppose we shall have him at our heels the whole of this holiday now. It's a pity kids have to grow up into goats. Don't think you're going to take Snowy back home with you, Philip. I'm not going to have a goat in the garden, whilst you're at school, eating the vegetables out of the beds, and the clothes off the line!'

'Mother, Trefor says his brother will arrive at the farmhouse tomorrow with the donkeys,' said Philip. 'Can we each choose our own? How many will there be?'

'Yes, you can choose your own if you want to,' said Mrs Mannering. 'I don't know how many there will be – six, I suppose. I only hope I choose a sure-footed one!'

'They'll all be sure-footed,' said Jack. 'As sure-footed as goats. But not so leapy. I shouldn't care to ride one of these mountain goats, and find myself leaping about from rock to rock.'

'Good gracious, what a horrible thought!' said Mrs Mannering. 'I shall choose the quietest, staidest, placidest, best-tempered donkey of the lot – one without a single bound or leap in him.'

Everyone laughed. Effans came over to them, beaming to see them happy. 'It iss dinner-time,' he said. 'Mrs Effans has it ready.'

'I shall soon begin to talk in a sing-song voice myself,' said Lucy-Ann, getting up from the stone wall. 'Indeed to gootness I shall!'

They all laughed at the lilting way she spoke. Snowy galloped ahead into the kitchen. Mrs Evans didn't seem to mind at all, but she shooed him down when he leapt into a chair. A hen scuttled out from under the table. Kiki went up to a rafter, sat on a ham wrapped up in a cloth, and cocked her eye down to the table to see what fruit there was.

'Pop goes the weasel,' she announced, and made a popping noise like a cork coming out of a bottle. Effans looked up in admiration.

'Such a bird!' he said. 'Never have I seen such a bird, look you!'

Kiki began hiccuping, and Effans went off into a roar of laughter. Mrs Mannering frowned.

'Kiki! Stop that! How many times am I to tell you I don't like that noise?'

'How many times have I told you to wipe your feet?' retorted Kiki, and screeched. Effans almost died of laughter. Kiki began to show off, snapping her beak open and shut, putting her crest up and down and making peculiar noises.

'Kiki! Come here!' said Jack sternly, and Kiki flew down to his shoulder. Jack tapped her smartly on her beak. 'Any more nonsense from you and I'll shut you in the bedroom upstairs. Bad bird! Silly bird!'

'Poor Polly! Bad Polly!' said Kiki, and nipped Jack's ear. He smacked her on the beak again.

'Be quiet! Not another word!' he ordered. Kiki put her head under her wing in disgrace, and various whispering sounds came to everyone's ears. But nobody could hear what she said, though Effans strained his ears hopefully. What a bird! He wished he could have one like it.

The dinner was as good as the high tea and breakfast had been. The children set to work and Mrs Evans felt very pleased to see how much her good food was appreciated. She kept pressing second and third helpings on everyone, but soon even the boys could eat no more.

'There iss no four o'clock tea,' she kept saying. 'Nothing till six o'clock. So eat, look you, eat!'

'Dithery slithery,' announced Kiki suddenly, and Dinah gave a scream. The slow-worm was gliding out of Philip's sleeve! He pushed it back hurriedly, hoping that no one had seen it. Bill had. His sharp eyes had caught sight of it at once. He grinned.

'Another member added to the family?' he said. 'Very nice too! What with Snowy and Kiki and – er – Slithery, we look all set for a most interesting holiday.'

5

Arrival of the donkeys

The next excitement, of course, was the arrival of the donkeys. The children had waited expectantly for them all the following morning, not liking to go for a walk in case they missed the donkeys' arrival. Lucy-Ann saw them first.

She gave a yell that sent the slow-worm back into Philip's pocket, and startled Snowy so much that he leapt four feet in the air. Even Kiki jumped.

'The donkeys!' cried Lucy-Ann. 'There they come, look, up the mountain-path.'

Soon all four children were tearing down the path to the donkeys. There were eight of them, strong, sturdy little creatures, with big bright eyes, and long tails that whisked the flies away. They were all grey, and their long ears twitched to and fro as they came steadily up the steep path.

Trefor's brother David was with them, an elderly man rather like Trefor but with tidier hair and beard. He had the same bright blue eyes, but he looked timid and shy, as if the world had not been kind to him.

He smiled faintly at the lively children. 'Can we ride four of the donkeys now?' asked Philip. 'We know how to ride. Come on, Lucy-Ann, up with you!'

He gave Lucy-Ann a shove and she was up on a donkey's back. Dinah needed no help. With a leap like Snowy's she was up at once.

The donkeys ambled up the steep path with the children, refusing to trot now that they had heavy weights on their backs. Snowy galloped beside Philip's donkey, half jealous of it, butting it in the legs.

'Hallo! Here we are!' cried Jack, ambling up to Mrs Mannering and Bill. 'Eight donkeys to choose from! Which are you going to have, Aunt Allie?'

David stood by smiling whilst his donkeys were examined and tried. Trefor the shepherd arrived, and the two old brothers chatted together in Welsh. Effans and his wife came along, and soon there was quite a company in the farmyard, discussing the donkeys.

'We badly want to go off on the donkeys into the mountains, Mother,' said Philip coaxingly. 'Can we? With you and Bill, of course. To stay a few nights, I mean. Jack and I think there should be a fine lot of rare birds over there in those lonely mountains – and there will be lots of animals too.'

'It *would* be rather fun,' said his mother. 'I haven't camped out for ages, and in this weather it would be lovely. What do you say, Bill?'

'I say yes!' said Bill, who loved outdoor life and was an old hand at camping. 'Do you good, Allie. We could take a couple of extra donkeys to carry the things we want.'

'Oh, *Bill*! Can we really go?' said Lucy-Ann, overjoyed, and Dinah danced round him too. To go off on donkeys into the mountains, and take tents and food – what could be more fun?

'It will be an adventure!' said Dinah. 'Not one of our usual ones, of course, but a really nice one. You'll like that, Lucy-Ann, won't you?'

'Oh, *yes*,' said Lucy-Ann, who never really enjoyed a proper adventure whilst it was happening. 'I'd like *that* kind of adventure. When can we go?'

'Well, we'd better get used to our donkeys before we think of going,' said Bill. 'I'm not used to donkey-riding, nor is

Aunt Allie. We shall be stiff at first, so we'd better get over that stage before we go. Say next week?'

'Oh – I can't wait that long!' said Dinah, and the others laughed at her long face.

'Effans, where is a nice place to go?' asked Jack, turning to him. Effans considered. He spoke to Trefor in Welsh and the old shepherd answered him.

'He says the Vale of Butterflies in a good place,' said Effans. 'It is full of birds as well as butterflies.'

'The Vale of Butterflies – that sounds gorgeous,' said Jack, pleased.

'Super!' said Philip. 'Absolutely wizard! We'll go there. Is it far?'

'Two days on donkeys,' said Effans.

Bill calculated. 'We shall want a guide – either Trefor, Effans or Trefor's brother – and two donkeys at least to carry our tents and food – and six donkeys for ourselves. That's nine. We've only got eight here. Effans, ask this fellow if he's got another donkey.'

It turned out that Trefor's brother had meant to ride home on a donkey himself, and take another donkey back with farm produce to sell, leaving only six. Effans bargained with him to come back the next week, complete with three donkeys to add to the six left behind.

'Then you can act as guide to these people, look you,' he said. 'That will be money. You will have one donkey, they will have six, and there will be two for loads. That is much money for you, David, indeed to gootness!'

David agreed. He would come in the Wednesday of next week, bringing three donkeys to add to the six he would leave behind. Two to carry loads, one for himself, and six for the children, Mrs Mannering and Bill.

The children were very excited. They ran round the donkeys, patted them, rubbed their long noses and sat on their broad backs. The donkeys seemed to like all the fuss. They stood stolidly there, their tails whisking, following the children with their eyes. Snowy darted about, running under first one donkey and then another, acting like a mad thing.

Trefor helped his brother to load up a donkey with packages of all kinds. Heavier and heavier grew the load, but the donkey stood patiently, seeming not to mind at all. Then, eager to be gone, it suddenly brayed.

Kiki had never heard a donkey bray before and she sailed straight up into the air with fright.

'Ee-ore, ee-ore!' brayed the donkey, and stamped his foot.

'Gracious! Now I suppose Kiki will practise braying too,' said Jack. 'We shall have to stop her firmly if she does. It's bad enough from a donkey – but brays from Kiki would be frightful.'

The donkey was loaded at last. David mounted his sturdy little beast, said a polite goodbye to everyone and rode off down the path, the loaded donkey being led after him by a rope he held in his hand.

'Now we can choose our own donkeys!' said Lucy-Ann in delight. 'Aunt Allie – you choose first.'

'Well, they all look *exactly* alike to me!' said Mrs Mannering. Bill spoke to Effans, asking him if he knew which donkey was the quietest. Effans turned to Trefor.

Trefor knew. He pointed out a little creature with a patient expression in its eyes, and said a few words in Welsh.

'He says that is the one for you,' said Effans. 'It is quiet and good. Its name is Patience.'

'Oh, good – I'll choose her then,' said Mrs Mannering. 'This is mine, children – the one with the black mark on her forehead.'

'I want this one,' cried Lucy-Ann, pulling at a sturdy animal that threw his head back continually, and stamped now and then. 'I like him. What is his name, Trefor?'

Trefor said something nobody understood. Effans translated. 'His name is Clover. This one is Grayling, and that one is Dapple. The other two are Buttercup and Daisy.'

Lucy-Ann had Clover. Jack had Grayling, and Dinah had

Dapple. Bill had Buttercup, and Philip had Daisy. Each of them was delighted with his or her own special donkey.

'Let's ride them now,' said Jack, mounting his little beast. 'Come on, Bill. Aunt Allie, get on. We'll go for our first ride now – up the path and back again.'

With Effans and his wife looking on in delight, the six rode off on their donkeys. They would not go fast uphill, and Bill warned each child not to try and make them. 'They'll trot coming down all right,' he said. 'But it's heavy going for them uphill, with our weight on their backs.'

It was great fun riding the grey donkeys up the steep mountain path. Mrs Mannering was nervous at first when she came to the rocky bits, but her donkey was as sure-footed as the others, and went steadily along on even the stoniest parts.

Bill rode close by in case Mrs Mannering needed help, but she didn't. The four children, of course, would have scorned any help. They were all used to riding horses, and the donkeys were very easy to manage.

'Now we'll turn back,' called Bill. So they all turned and went homewards. Snowy came too, of course, having leapt and bounded ahead of them all the way, apparently under the impression that he was leading them.

'That was fun,' said Lucy-Ann, as they trotted homewards, the donkeys going faster now that they were on a downhill road. Mrs Mannering didn't like the trotting so much as the ambling.

'My donkey is a very bumpy one,' she said to Bill. 'When I go down he comes up and when I go up he goes down, so we keep meeting with a bump!'

Everyone laughed. They were all sorry when they reached the farmhouse, for by that time they felt as if they could go trotting on for ever. But a meal was ready for them on the table, and Mrs Evans was beaming at the door, so they didn't lose much time in taking the donkeys to the field and carrying their harness to the stables.

'You'll be quite used to riding a donkey by next week,' Bill said to Mrs Mannering. 'By the time Wednesday comes you'll be ready to set off and you'll feel as if you'd ridden a donkey all your life!'

'Oh, yes, I'm sure I shall,' said Mrs Mannering. She felt something pecking at her foot and looked under the table. She saw a fat brown hen there and pushed it away. 'Shoo! Stop pecking my foot!'

The hen shooed, only to be replaced by Snowy, who, pushed off Philip's knee as he sat at table, was amusing himself by trying to eat shoe-laces under the table. Mrs Mannering pushed him him away too, and Snowy went to chew the hem of Mrs Evans' dress. She never noticed things like that, so Snowy had a nice long chew.

The next day the girls and Mrs Mannering were so stiff with their donkey-ride that they could hardly walk. The boys and Bill were all right, but Mrs Mannering groaned as she came down the stairs.

'Good gracious! I feel like an old old lady! I'll never be able to ride a donkey again!' she said.

But the stiffness wore off, and the six of them soon got used to riding their donkeys day after day into the mountains. There were some lovely rides and magnificent views. Snowy came with them always, never tired, leaping along gaily. Kiki rode on Jack's shoulder, occasionally taking a flight into the air to scare any bird that happened to be flying overhead. They flew off quickly, full of astonishment when Kiki told them to wipe their feet.

'Two days more and it's Wednesday,' said Lucy-Ann happily. 'We'll be quite ready then – able to ride for hours and hours.'

'Yes – off to the Vale of Butterflies!' said Jack. 'I wonder what it's like! I imagine it to be full of wings of all colours. Lovely!'

'Oh, hurry up and come, Wednesday!' said Dinah. 'Only

forty-eight hours – and then, off we go!'

But something unexpected happened in that forty-eight hours – something that quite upset their lovely plans!

6

Off to the Vale of Butterflies

It happened the very next day. It was when Mrs Mannering had gone with Mrs Evans to the big barn. The door suddenly blew shut, and caught her hand in it, trapping it tightly.

Mrs Mannering screamed. Mrs Evans ran to open the door, but poor Mrs Mannering's hand was badly bruised and crushed.

Bill was very concerned. 'I must take you down to the doctor,' he said. 'I'll get the car. Where are the children? Out on their donkeys? Tell them where we've gone, Mrs Evans, when they come back. They needn't worry. I'll have Mrs Mannering's hand seen to, and properly bandaged. I don't expect it will be very much, but I'd like her to have it X-rayed in case any small bone is broken.'

Looking rather white, Mrs Mannering was driven off by Bill, down the steep mountain road to the town that lay some way off in the next valley. It was about fifteen miles and soon Mrs Mannering was in hospital having her hand X-rayed and bound up.

The children were very upset when they heard what had happened. 'Poor Mother!' said Philip. 'It must have hurt dreadfully when her hand got caught in that heavy door.'

'Indeed to gootness, it did,' said Mrs Evans, who looked quite upset too. 'She gave one scream, poor soul, and then made not a sound, whateffer. Now don't look so sadly – she'll be back tonight.'

'Will she be able to go off to the mountains tomorrow?' asked Lucy-Ann. 'How can she ride with a bad hand?'

'Well, there now, she can't,' said Mrs Evans. 'But she can stay here with me and I'll look after her for you. You can go with Mr Cunningham and David.'

'But will Bill go if Mother's hurt?' wondered Philip. 'He thinks the world of her. Oh, blow! It's bad luck for this to happen just when we had such a lovely plan. Poor Mother! I do hope her hand's better now.'

Mrs Mannering arrived back in Bill's car that evening, just before high tea. She looked better, and made light of her hand.

'We've had it X-rayed,' said Bill. 'She's broken a tiny bone just here,' and he showed them where, on the back of his hand. 'It's got to be bandaged and kept at rest. I'm to take her down to have it seen again in three days' time.'

'I'm so sorry, dears,' said Mrs Mannering. 'And Bill, you don't need to take me down, you know. I'm quite able to drive myself down even with an injured hand. Take the children on their trip tomorrow. I can't bear to have them disappointed.'

'What! And leave you like this!' said Bill. 'Don't be silly, Allie. I shall take you down myself in the car on Friday. The children can go with David, if he'll take them on by himself. It's a perfectly ordinary trip, and they'll be back in a few days' time. They can all ride their donkeys as easily as David – and probably they'll enjoy a trip without us!'

'We'd *much* rather you and Aunt Allie came,' said Jack. 'But as you can't, it's decent of you to let us go alone. We'll be perfectly all right, Bill. David knows the way, and we can all look after ourselves.'

So it was settled that the four children should go by themselves on the donkeys with their guide David, taking with them tents, bedding and food. Philip questioned Bill to make sure that his mother's hand was not seriously hurt.

'Oh, no – it will soon be right,' said Bill. 'But I want to be sure she doesn't use it, and I want to take her down to the doctor in three days' time. I'm sorry not to come with you – but you'll be all right by yourselves. I don't see that you can get into any trouble, or any startling adventure, going donkey-riding in the mountains with David. Maybe we can all go together, later on.'

The children were very excited that night, getting ready the things they wanted to take. They had two small tents, a sleeping-bag each, two ground-sheets, cameras, field-glasses, a change of clothes – and food.

The food was Mrs Evans' care. Bill watched her packing up what she thought they would eat in the next few days.

'I didn't like to stop her,' he told the others. 'But, honestly, she's packed enough for a month. She's put in a whole ham!'

'Golly!' said Jack. 'What else?'

'A tongue or two, hard-boiled eggs, tins of all kinds, plum-cake and goodness knows what!' said Philip. 'We shall feast like kings.'

'Well,' began Lucy-Ann, 'I always think that we eat twice as much in the open air, because food tastes so . . . '

'Much nicer!' chorused everyone. Lucy-Ann always said that at least a dozen times each holidays. She laughed.

'Well, anyway, it will be nice to have as much as ever we can eat. There's David too – we've got to take food for him as well.'

'He doesn't look as if he'd eat much,' said Dinah. 'Skinny little fellow, he is!'

'You'd better go to bed early, children,' said Mrs Mannering a little later. 'You'll have a long ride tomorrow, according to Effans.'

'All right. It'll make tomorrow come all the sooner!' said Lucy-Ann. 'How's your hand feel, Aunt Allie?'

'It's quite comfortable, thank you,' said Mrs Mannering. 'I'm sure I could have gone with you tomorrow, really!'

'Well, you couldn't,' said Bill hastily, half afraid that Mrs Mannering would try to be foolish and go with the others after all. She laughed.

'Don't worry! I'm going to be sensible – and, dear me, it

will be quite a change to be rid of four noisy ruffians and an even noisier bird for a few days, Bill, won't it?'

All the children were awake very early the next day. Snowy the kid, who was a real sleepy-head in the mornings, didn't want to wake up at all, and snuggled deeper into Philip's blankets as the boy tried to get out of bed.

Kiki took her head from under her wing and scratched her poll. 'Dithery Slithery,' she remarked, which meant that she had spied Philip's slow-worm. It was coiled up in a corner of the room. It would very much have liked to sleep on Philip's bed, but it was afraid of Snowy, who had a habit of nibbling anything near him.

The boys got up and looked out of the window. It was a really perfect day. The mountains towered up into the fresh morning sky, as beautiful as ever.

'They look as if someone had just been along and washed them,' said Jack. 'The sky looks washed too – so very very clean and new.'

'I like the feel of an early morning,' said Philip, putting on his shorts. 'It has a special *new* feel about it – as if it was the first morning that ever happened!'

Snowy went over to the corner where Sally the slow-worm was, and the slow-worm at once wriggled away under the chest of drawers. Philip picked her up and she slid gracefully into his pocket.

'Have to get you a few flies for breakfast, Sally,' said Philip. 'Shut up, Kiki – you'll wake the rest of the household with that awful cough.'

Kiki could give a terrible, hollow cough at times, which she had copied from an old uncle of Jack's, and she was practising it now. She stopped when Philip spoke to her, and hopped to Jack's shoulder.

'Funny bird, silly bird,' said Jack affectionately, scratching her neck. 'Come on, Philip – let's see if the girls are up.'

They were just getting up, both of them thrilled at the fine day and the idea of going camping in the mountains. 'Have you got that horrid slow-worm on you?' asked Dinah fearfully, looking at Philip.

'Yes, somewhere about,' said Philip, feeling all over him. 'There's one thing about Sally Slithery – she does get about!'

Dinah shuddered and went to wash in the bathroom. Snowy the kid was there, nibbling the cork bath-mat, which he evidently thought was delicious.

'Oh, Snowy! Mrs Evans won't be at all pleased with you!' said Dinah, and shooed the kid out of the door. He went to find Philip. He was quite one of the family now.

Mrs Mannering's hand was stiff and sore that morning, but she said very little about it, not wanting to upset the children. She was glad it was such a lovely day for them, and watched with amusement as Mrs Evans carefully packed up all the food she had prepared for the children to take with them.

'If you eat all that you'll never be able to ride home on the donkeys,' she said. 'You'll be too fat.'

'They must not go hungry,' said kind Mrs Evans. 'There! I think I have thought of everything. Children, you must use one donkey for the food and the other for everything else, look you. I will see that David straps everything on well.'

The children listened to her kind, lilting voice as they sat at breakfast. They felt very happy, and the only thing that spoilt their pleasure was the fact that Bill and Mrs Mannering were not coming with them. On the other hand, they would be freer without grown-ups!

Kiki gave a hiccup, with one eye on Mrs Mannering. She looked at the parrot severely. 'Kiki! You did that on purpose. Do you want your beak smacked?'

'Pardon,' said Kiki, and went off into a cackle of laughter. Effans choked over his bacon, trying to laugh with his mouth full, and went purple in the face. His bacon went down the wrong way, and he got the hiccups too.

'Pardon, look you!' he said to Mrs Mannering, with such a horrified look on his face that everyone roared with laughter.

'Now here is David, all ready for you!' cried Mrs Evans from the door, where she had gone to chase away a turkey that had suddenly appeared. It made a gobbling noise that scared Snowy terribly. Kiki, of course, at once gobbled too, and the turkey looked into the kitchen in amazement. 'Shoo!' said Mrs Evans. 'Good morning, David, it's early you are, and a nice day you have brought with you!'

'Indeed to gootness I have,' said David and smiled timidly at the company in the big kitchen. His donkeys crowded round him, sturdy and patient, their harness clinking and glinting.

'Come on!' yelled Jack, suddenly feeling too excited to sit at the table any longer. 'Come on! Let's pack the things on the donkeys and go!'

They all rushed out. Soon David and Effans were strapping everything on two donkeys. One donkey had big panniers each side for food. The other had the things strapped across his broad little back. They stood perfectly still, their ears twitching as a fly or two settled on them.

'Well – are we ready to start?' said Philip. 'I think we've got everything. Oh, gosh, where are my field-glasses?'

At last everyone and everything was ready. It had been explained to David that Bill and Mrs Mannering could not come, and Effans had said he would care for the two extra donkeys till the children came back. David did not seem too pleased to think he was to go alone with the children. He looked rather alarmed, Bill thought. Poor fellow! Bill wished it was Effans who was going with the children, not David. Still, the children were used to camping out and could be trusted to be sensible.

'Goodbye!' called everyone. 'See you in a few days' time. Take care of your hand, Mother! Now we're off – off to the Vale of Butterflies! Goodbye, everyone!'

7

On the way

With Bill, Mrs Mannering, Effans and Mrs Evans waving and calling goodbye, the party set off on their donkeys. They had to go up by Trefor the shepherd's little cabin, and the donkeys picked their way steadily up the steep hillside.

Snowy ran beside them, bobbing about under the donkeys' bodies as he pleased. They seemed to like him, and Dapple kept putting his head down to the kid whenever he came near. Kiki was perched as usual on Jack's shoulder, jogging up and down contentedly, snapping her beak, and making a few quiet remarks into Jack's ear.

They came to Trefor's cabin. He was on the hillside, seeing to a sick sheep. He came to meet them, his untidy hair blowing in the wind, and his eyes shining as blue as forget-me-nots.

There was a conversation between the two men in Welsh. David sounded rather complaining. Trefor seemed to be pooh-poohing what he said. David got out a map that Bill had given him, and appeared to be saying that he didn't understand it at all.

Trefor then spoke earnestly, pointing in this direction and that, poking David with his finger every time he wanted to make a point go home. The children thought he must be telling David the exact way to go.

'I hope David really does know the way,' said Jack. 'He might have thought Bill would help him with the map if Bill had been going. It looks to me as if he's telling Trefor he's not too certain of the way.'

'Well, what does it matter?' said Philip, pushing Snowy off with his hand as the kid tried to jump up on to his donkey with him. 'I'd *like* to see the Vale of Butterflies – but so long as we go off camping in those gorgeous mountains, that's all that matters.'

'Yes. We shall see heaps of birds and animals anyway,' said Jack, feeling that Philip was right. 'Come on, David! Let's go!'

David leapt on to his donkey at once. He called goodbye to Trefor, and the little company set off once more, taking a narrow path along the mountain-side that went neither very far up, nor very far down.

It was glorious riding there, so high, looking down on the valley far below. It was partly in the sun and partly in the shadow, for the sun was not yet high. Swallows flew round them catching flies, their steel-blue wings gleaming in the sun. Kiki watched them out of her sharp eyes. She had often tried fly-catching herself, but she knew she was no good at it. Anyway, flies didn't taste as good as fruit!

They ambled on until everyone felt hungry and thirsty. They came to a copse of birch-trees with a small stream near by.

'Let's picnic here,' said Philip, sliding off his donkey. 'In the shade of those trees. I'm absolutely cooked with the sun.'

David saw to the donkeys, taking them to the stream for water. He then let them wander free, for they came most obediently at his call, and could be trusted not to go too far away. They went to the shade of the trees and stood there, swishing their long grey tails, enjoying the rest.

Snowy ran to them, and behaved like a spoilt child, letting the donkeys fuss him and stare at him. Dapple put down his big head to the little kid, and nuzzled him in the neck. When Snowy ran to the next donkey Dapple followed him.

'Dapple wants to be friends with Snowy,' said Dinah unpacking the lunch parcel from one of the enormous panniers. 'Here, Lucy-Ann – take this tin and fill it with water from the stream. It must be absolutely pure, I should think. We can put some of this lemonade essence with it. I'm so dreadfully thirsty!'

David was drinking at the stream, so the children felt that it must be all right. It gurgled along, fresh and clear, running through the pebbles and down the hillside at top speed. Lucy-Ann went to fill the tin.

There was a lovely lunch. The children had to call David to share it because he suddenly seemed shy. He came and sat down a little way away from them.

'No, David. Come here with us,' called Jack, patting the ground. 'We want to learn Welsh! Come and talk to us!'

But the old Welshman was very shy, and it was as much as the children could do to persuade him to eat his share of the lunch. It was such a good lunch too!

There were five different kinds of sandwiches, fresh lettuce wrapped in a damp cloth, hard-boiled eggs to nibble, and great slices of jam tart. Washed down with cold lemonade it was the finest lunch anyone could wish.

'Nobody in the whole world, not even the very richest king, can possibly have a nicer lunch than this,' said Lucy-Ann, munching a chicken sandwich.

'Or a nicer place to eat it in,' said Philip, waving his sandwich at the magnificent view before them. 'Look at that! No king could have a better view from his palace than that! Valleys and mountains, and yet more mountains, and then the clear blue sky! Marvellous!'

They all gazed at the unbelievable view that lay in front of them. A rustle of paper made them look round.

'Snowy! You greedy little kid! Look here, he's eaten the rest of the chicken sandwiches!' cried Jack indignantly, forgetting all about the lovely view. 'Philip, smack him. We can't let him do that or our food won't last out. He can jolly well eat the grass.'

Philip gave Snowy a smart tap on the nose. The kid retreated in a huff, taking with him a mouthful of sandwich papers, which he proceeded to eat with apparent enjoyment. But soon he was back with Philip, pressing against him affectionately, anxious to be back in his good books. Dapple the donkey moved over to Philip too, to be near the kid. He lay down beside him, and Philip at once leaned back against him.

'Thanks, old man! Very nice! Just what I wanted!' said Philip, and everyone laughed as he settled himself against the donkey's side.

'Have another sandwich, David?' asked Lucy-Ann, holding out a packet to him. David had not eaten nearly as much as they had, either through shyness or because he hadn't such an enormous appetite. He shook his head.

'Let's have a bit of rest now,' said Philip sleepily. 'There's no hurry. We can take all the time we like to get anywhere.'

Jack began to ask David the names of things in Welsh. It was silly not to be able to talk to David. David apparently understood more English than he spoke, but even the few English words he said were pronounced so differently that the children found it hard to puzzle out what he was saying.

'Come on, David, talk,' said Jack, who did not feel as sleepy as the others. 'What's this in Welsh?' He held out his hand.

David began to realize that Jack wanted a lesson in Welsh, and he brightened up a little. He was a trifle embarrassed by Kiki, who insisted on repeating all the words he said too, and added a few nonsense words of her own for good measure.

The girls and Philip fell asleep in the shade, Lucy-Ann sharing Philip's donkey to lean against. Dinah would have liked to do the same but she was afraid that Sally the slow-worm might come out of Philip's pocket if she did, and nothing would make Dinah go near the silvery creature!

Jack patiently tried to learn a few Welsh words, and then got tired of it. He threw a few pebbles down the mountain-side, and gazed round at the many summits towering up in the distance. There was one odd one, shaped like three teeth, that amused him. He decided to look it up on the map.

The map, however, was rather disappointing. It showed

very few names in the district where they were, probably because it had been very little visited, and there were no farmhouses or other buildings to put on record. Jack found a name that seemed to him to fit the mountain. 'Fang Mountain,' he read. 'That might be it. Gosh, what a lot of mountains there are about here! I bet nobody has ever explored them all. I'd like to fly over them in an aeroplane and look down on them. We haven't seen a plane since we've been here. Off the route, I suppose.'

David had gone to round up the donkeys. Jack woke up the others. 'Come on, lazy things! We'd better get on, or David will think we mean to camp here for the night. There's a heavenly wind got up now. It will be gorgeous riding this afternoon.'

Soon they were all on their donkeys again, jogging along round the mountain-side, enjoying the wind and the sun, gazing on the different vistas that opened up before them round every bend of the track. New mountains reared up far-away heads, new skylines appeared. For long stretches the children said nothing at all to one another, but simply drank in the beauty around them, and the sun and wind.

They travelled until six o'clock, having decided to keep to the high tea that Mrs Evans had at the farm. Jack spoke to David when six o'clock came.

'David! We stop at half-past six. Do you know a good place to camp for the night near here?'

David did not understand and Jack repeated it more slowly. David smiled and nodded.

'Iss! Iss!' This meant 'yes', and Jack looked as David pointed to a wooded spot some way ahead. David said something else in Welsh, and Jack caught a few words here and there which he understood. One was 'water', the other was 'trees'.

'David says there's a good place to camp in a little way off!' Jack shouted back to the others. 'There's water there, and trees.'

'Gosh! However do you understand him?' said Philip in admiration. 'Jolly clever of you, Jack!'

Jack grinned all over his freckled face. 'Oh, I just caught the words "water" and "trees", that's all! Come on, let's get there in time to watch the sun sink over the mountains. I'd like to have a sunset with my sandwiches!'

Philip laughed. They all ambled on towards the spot pointed out by David. It was a little further than they thought, but when they got there they all agreed it was just the right place to camp for the night.

A spring gushed out beside the small wooded patch, as cold as ice. The trees sheltered the campers from the night-wind, which could be very chilly at times. The donkeys were to be tied to trees so that they would not wander in the night. Everything was perfect!

The children were tired but happy. They slid off their donkeys' backs, and the little beasts, tired now too, were taken to the spring to drink. They stood patiently waiting their turn, whilst Snowy skipped about like a mad thing, not in the least tired with his long trip.

'We'll put up the tents after we've had a meal and a rest,' said Philip. 'Get out the food, Lucy-Ann and Dinah. There's a nice flat stone here we can use as a table.'

Soon the supper, or high tea, was spread out on the big flat stone, and mugs of lemonade were set by each plate. The children drained them at once, and Jack was sent to get more ice-cold water from the spring.

They all ate quickly, for they were very hungry again. They said very little until the first edge of their appetite had worn off, then they all talked with their mouths full, eager to make the others remember the lovely day.

David ate too and listened. The donkeys pulled at the grass. Snowy was with Dapple, and Kiki was eating a tomato and dripping the juice down Jack's neck. They all felt as if they couldn't possibly be happier.

'Now we'll put up the tents,' said Jack at last. 'Come on, Philip! It'll be dark before we've put them up if we don't make haste!'

8

First night in camp

The girls washed the dirty crockery in the cold spring water whilst David and the boys unpacked the tents from the donkey that carried them. They took off the whole of his pack, and also unstrapped the heavy panniers from the other donkey. Both were delighted to be rid of their loads. They lay down on the ground and rolled, kicking their legs up into the air.

Kiki couldn't understand this at all, and flew up into a tree. 'She thinks they've gone mad,' said Jack. 'It's all right, Kiki, they're only feeling glad because their packs have gone!'

Kiki made a noise like a train screeching in a tunnel, and the two rolling donkeys leapt to their feet in alarm and raced some way down the hill. David also jumped violently, and then called to the donkeys.

'Kiki, if you do that again I'll tie your beak up!' threatened Jack. 'Spoiling this lovely peaceful evening with that horrible screech!'

'Wipe your feet, wipe your feet!' screamed Kiki and danced from foot to foot on her branch.

The tents were soon put up, side by side. David did not want to sleep in one. He preferred to sleep outside. He had never slept in a tent, and he thought they were quite unnecessary.

'Well, I'd just as soon he slept outside,' said Jack to Philip.

'I don't believe there'd be room for one more in here, do you?'

'Let's leave the tent-flaps open,' said Lucy-Ann, coming up with the clean crockery. 'Then we can look out down the mountain-side. I wouldn't mind a bit sleeping in the open air, like David, as a matter of fact.'

'Wind's too cold,' said Jack. 'You'll be glad to have a cosy sleeping-bag, Lucy-Ann! David must be very hardy – he's only got a thin rug to cover himself with, and he's apparently going to sleep on the bare ground!'

The sun had now disappeared completely. It had gone behind the mountains in a perfect blaze of colour, and all the summits had gleamed for a while, and then darkness had crept up to the very tops, leaving only a clear sky beyond. Stars were now winking here and there, and a cold wind was blowing up the mountain.

The donkeys were tied loosely to trees. Some of them were lying down. Dapple was looking out for Snowy, but the kid had gone to Philip, and was waiting for him to go into his tent.

They all washed at the spring – but David seemed rather astonished to see the four children solemnly splashing themselves with the cold water. He had drawn his thin rug over him and was lying quite still, looking up to the starry sky.

'He's not what you might call a very *cheerful* companion, is he?' said Jack. 'I expect he thinks we're all quite mad, the way we joke and laugh and fool about. Buck up, Philip, and get into the tent.'

The girls were already in their tent. They had slid down into their sleeping-bags and tied them up loosely at the neck. Each bag had a big hood to come over the head. They were comfortable, quite roomy, and very warm.

Lucy-Ann could see out of the tent opening. Stars twinkled in the sky, looking very big and bright. There was no sound at all, except of the trickle-trickle of the spring, and the sound of the wind in the trees.

'We might be alone in the world,' said Lucy-Ann to Dinah. 'Dinah, imagine that we are. It gives you an awfully queer feeling. It's wizard!'

But Dinah hadn't got Lucy-Ann's imagination and she yawned. 'Go to sleep,' she said. 'Are the boys in their tent yet? I wish they were a bit further away. I've got an awful feeling that slow-worm will come slithering here in the night.'

'It won't hurt you if it does,' said Lucy-Ann, snuggling down in her sleeping-bag. 'Oh, this is super! I do think we have lovely hols, don't you, Dinah?'

But Dinah was asleep already. Her eyes had shut and she was dreaming. Lucy-Ann stayed awake a little longer enjoying the sound of the running spring and the wind. She still felt rather as if she was on her donkey, jogging up and down. Then her eyes closed too.

The boys talked for a little while. They had thoroughly enjoyed their day. They gazed out of the open flap of the tent. 'It's pretty wild and desolate, here,' said Jack sleepily. 'It's surprising there's a track to follow, really. Decent of Bill and Aunt Allie to let us come by ourselves!'

'Mmmmmmm!' said Philip, listening, but too sleepy to answer.

'Mmmmmmm!' imitated Kiki from the top of the tent outside. It was too hot for her in it.

'There's Kiki,' said Jack. 'I wondered where she was. Philip, aren't you hot with Snowy on top of you?'

'Mmmmmmm!' said Philip, and again there came the echo from the tent-top. 'Mmmmmmm!'

Snowy was almost on top of Philip. He had tried his hardest to squeeze into the boy's sleeping-bag with him, but Philip was quite firm about that.

'If you think you're going to stick your sharp little hooves into me all night long, you're wrong, Snowy,' he said, and tied up his bag firmly at the neck, in case Snowy should try any tricks in the night. The slow-worm was somewhere about too. Philip was too sleepy to bother to think where. Sally slid about where she pleased. Philip was now quite used to the sudden slithering movement that occurred at times somewhere about his body, which meant that Sally was on the move again.

There were a few more quiet remarks from Kiki, who was apparently talking to herself. Then silence. The little camp slept under the stars. The night-wind nosed into the tent, but could not get into the cosy sleeping-bags. Snowy felt too hot, walked over Philip, trod on Jack and went to lie in the tent opening. He gave a tiny bleat and Kiki bleated in answer.

David was up and about before the children the next day. He was looking at his donkeys when Philip put a tousled head out of the tent opening to sniff at the morning. 'Lovely!' he said. 'Stop butting me, Snowy! Your little head is jolly hard! Jack! Stir yourself. It's a gorgeous morning.'

Soon all the campers were out of their sleeping-bags and running about. They splashed at the spring, laughing at nothing. Snowy bounded everywhere, quite mad too. Kiki hooted like a car, and startled the donkeys. Even David smiled to see such early-morning antics!

They had breakfast – tongue, cream cheese and rather stale bread, with a tomato each. There was no lemonade left because they had been so lavish with it the day before, so they drank the cold spring water and vowed it was just as nice as lemonade.

'David! Shall we get to the Vale of Butterflies today?' asked Jack, and then repeated it again slowly, flapping his arms to show David that he was talking about butterflies. It took David a minute or two to realize this. Then he shook his head.

'Tomorrow?' asked Philip, and David nodded. He went to strap the packs on the donkeys again and to put on the big pannier baskets. All the little grey creatures were waiting impatiently to set off. Already the sun was getting well above the mountains, and, for David and the donkeys at any rate, it was late!

They set off at last, though Jack had to gallop back to get his field-glasses which he had left behind, hanging from a tree-branch. Then they were all in a line, one donkey behind the other, ambling over the mountains with the wind in their hair.

Jack felt sure he saw a couple of buzzards that day and rode most of the time with his field-glasses in his hand, ready to clap them to his eyes at the first sight of specks in the sky. The others saw red squirrels among the trees they passed, shy but tame. One shared the children's lunch, darting up for tit-bits, but keeping a wary eye for Kiki and Snowy.

'It wants to come with you, Philip,' said Lucy-Ann, amused when the red squirrel put a paw on Philip's knee.

Philip stroked the pretty little thing gently. It quivered, half frightened, but did not bound away. Then Kiki swooped down and the squirrel fled.

'You *would* spoil things, you jealous bird!' said Philip. 'Go away, I don't want you. Go to Jack, and let the squirrels come to me.'

Swallows flew round them once again, not attracted by the food, but by the flies that pestered the donkeys. The children could hear the snapping of their beaks as they caught the flies.

'We ought to get Jack to tame a few swallows and take them with us to catch the flies,' said Lucy-Ann, slapping at a big one on her leg. 'Horrid things! I've been bitten by something already. You wouldn't think there'd be any as high up as this, would you?'

Sally the slow-worm came out to eat the fly that Lucy-Ann had killed. She was getting much too tame for Dinah's liking. She lay in the sun, gleaming like silver, and then slid under Philip as Snowy came up enquiringly.

'Keep your nose out of things,' said Philip, pushing the kid away as it tried to nose under him to find the slow-worm. Snowy butted him hard and then tried to get on his lap.

'Too hot, too hot,' said Philip. 'Why did we ever bring a little pest like you, Snowy? You breathed down my neck all night!'

Lucy-Ann giggled. She loved Snowy. They all did. The kid was mischievous, given to butting, and didn't mind treading on anyone – but he was so lively, so full of spring and bounce, so affectionate that it was impossible to be cross with him for long.

'Come on,' said Philip at last. 'David's clearing his throat as if he's going to tell us we're too lazy for words.'

David had a habit of clearing his throat about a dozen times before he spoke. It was a nervous habit which Kiki copied to perfection. She would sit near him, and make a noise as if she was clearing her throat every time he did the same thing. Then she would go off into a cackle of laughter. David always stared at her solemnly when she did this.

They travelled well that second day, and went a long way. When the time came to camp again, David looked earnestly over the mountains as if he was searching for something.

'Lost your handkerchief, old chap?' said Jack, and everyone laughed. David looked solemnly at him, not understanding. Then he suddenly began to flap his arms like wings, and to say a few words in Welsh.

He looked comical standing there, flapping like that. The children had to turn away, trying not to laugh. 'He says tomorrow we shall see the butterfly valley,' said Jack. 'Good! It ought to be a real sight, if it's anything like I imagine it to be!'

They had a meal and prepared to camp out again. The evening was not so fine as the day. It had clouded over and there was no sunset to watch, and no stars to come gleaming out, one by one.

'If it rains, you'll get wet, David,' said Jack. David shrugged his shoulders and said something in his Welsh voice, then wrapped himself in his rug on the bare ground.

'It won't rain,' said Philip, looking at the sky. 'But it's much colder. Brrrrr! I'll be glad of my sleeping-bag tonight.'

'Good night!' called the girls. 'Sleep well.'

'Good night! It will be a lovely day again tomorrow! You just see!' called back Philip, who thought himself a good weather forecaster.

But he was wrong. When they awoke the next morning, they looked out on a completely different world!

9

A different world

Lucy-Ann awoke first. She was cold. She snuggled down into her sleeping-bag, and then opened her eyes. She stared out of the open tent-flap, expecting to see the green mountain-side, and the distant mountains towering up into the sky.

But they weren't there! Instead, a white mist swirled past the tent-flap, some of it putting thin cold fingers into the tent itself.

There was nothing to see at all except this mist. The mountains had gone, the trees by the camp were blotted out, even the donkeys couldn't be seen.

'What's happened?' said Lucy-Ann, astonished. 'Golly! It's a thick mist come up!'

She awoke Dinah and the girls peered out in dismay at the misty mountain-side. Now and again a tiny bit of view could be seen as the mist thinned a little – but it grew thick again at once.

'It's a cloud,' said Dinah. 'You know how we see clouds resting on mountain-tops – well, this is one. It's resting on *us*! It's like a thick fog we can't see through. Blow!'

The boys woke up then and the girls could hear their dismayed voices. They called to them.

'Jack! Philip! Isn't this sickening! We can't see a thing!'

'It may clear when we've had breakfast,' said Philip cheerfully, appearing out of the mist with Snowy at his heels. 'Gosh, it's chilly! I'm going to put on a warm jersey.'

David also appeared, looking very doleful. He swung his arm out towards the valley and poured out a torrent of Welsh.

'He's quite excited about it, isn't he?' said Jack. 'I wish I could follow him when he talks like that. I just don't understand a word.'

They decided to have breakfast in one of the tents because the mist made everything damp and chilly. David preferred to stay outside. Dinah didn't want to come into the tent because of Sally, and only agreed to if she was allowed to sit in the doorway, ready to escape if the slow-worm appeared.

It was not so cheerful a meal as usual. The children missed the magnificent view they had been used to, and were afraid perhaps David wouldn't take them on their way that day. But the mist cleared a little in an hour's time, and David seemed quite willing to go.

They loaded up the donkeys, mounted and set off down the track. They could see some way ahead of them now, for the sun was rising higher, and trying to dissolve the mist with its heat.

'It'll be all right,' said Jack. 'I *almost* caught sight of the sun then!'

But then the mist came down again and it was only just possible to see the donkey in front.

'I feel as if I ought to hold your donkey's tail, in case you disappear in the mist!' shouted Jack to Dinah. 'You know – like elephants do in circuses when they come into the ring all holding on to one another's tails!'

The mist thickened even more, and the little company stopped to discuss what to do. It was difficult to get anything intelligible out of David, who seemed suddenly to have forgotten any English words he knew.

Jack flapped his arms, raised his eyebrows and pointed in front of him, meaning to ask if they were near the butterfly valley. David understood, but he hesitated.

'I hope he hasn't lost the way,' said Jack to Philip. 'He seemed sure enough of the direction yesterday – now he doesn't seem very certain. Blow!'

'Well, we can't stop here,' said Dinah, shivering in the clammy mist. 'There's no shelter and it's jolly cold. Oh for the sun again!'

'Ride on!' said Jack to David. 'It's the only thing to do till we find some kind of shelter. It's too cold to hang about till the mist has gone. If we go the wrong way we can turn back and go right when the mist goes.'

So they went on, following David's donkey through the wet mist. Kiki was very silent. She didn't understand the mist and was afraid of it. Snowy kept close to Philip's donkey, and was not nearly so full of spring and liveliness. Everyone disliked the mist thoroughly.

'When we find a sheltered place we'll stop for lunch,' said Philip. 'I'm sure we're all getting frightfully hungry now, but we seem to be on quite a bare bit of mountain-side, hopeless to picnic in. We'd all be down with colds tomorrow!'

They ambled on, nose to tail, pulling their jerseys close, glad of their coats too. Jack began to look rather worried. He stopped his donkey and went to walk beside Philip's.

'What's up?' said Philip, seeing Jack's serious face.

'We've left the track,' said Jack. 'Haven't you noticed? We've followed some kind of track up till an hour or two back – but now I'm pretty certain we've lost it. Goodness knows where David's heading for. I doubt if he's even noticed we're not on any track at all.'

Philip whistled. 'Don't let the girls hear you. They'll be scared. Yes, you're right. There's not the vestige of a track here. David's lost the way.'

'Better ask him,' said Jack and rode to the front of the line. 'Is this the right way?' he asked David slowly, so as to be understood. 'Where is the track?' He pointed downwards to the ground.

David was looking solemn too. He shrugged his shoulders and said something in his sing-song voice. Jack rode back to Philip.

'I think he knows he's off the track, but he's hoping to pick it up further on. Anyway he doesn't seem inclined to stop or go back.'

'Well – he's our guide,' said Philip, after a pause. 'We'll have to trust him. He knows these mountains better than we do.'

'Yes. But he's so shy,' said Jack. 'He wouldn't be able to tell us we were lost. I wouldn't put it past him to go on losing us deeper and deeper in these mountains, once he'd begun! He just wouldn't know what else to do.'

'What a horrible idea!' said Philip. 'Good thing we've got so much food with us, if that's what he means to do!'

They came at last to a big outcrop of rocks, which would give them shelter from the wet, chilly wind. 'Better have a meal here,' said Philip. 'I'd like something hot to drink. Did Mrs Evans put in a kettle?'

'Yes. If we can find a stream or spring, we'll build a little fire and boil some water for cocoa or something,' said Jack.

But there was no spring and no stream. It was most annoying.

'Considering the *dozens* we've passed this morning, and waded through, I call it a bit hard that there's not even a tiny one here,' said Dinah. 'I'm jolly thirsty too.'

They had to have a meal without anything to drink. They were very hungry, and the food seemed to warm them a little. They played a game of Catch to get themselves thoroughly warm after the meal. David looked as if he thought they had gone mad. Snowy joined in wildly, neatly tripping everyone up. Kiki rose in the air and screamed.

'Look at David's face! He thinks we're all crazy!' giggled Lucy-Ann. She sank down on a rock. 'Oh, I can't run any more. I've got a stitch in my side.'

'Stitchinmyside, stitchinmyside,' chanted Kiki running all the words together. 'Pop goes the weasel!'

'The mist's clearing! Hurrah!' suddenly cried Jack, and he pointed upwards. The sun could quite clearly be seen, struggling to get through the clouds of mist.

Everyone cheered up at once. Even David looked less dismal. 'Let's try to get to the Butterfly Valley before the evening,' said Jack to David, doing the flapping business vigorously to make sure David understood. David nodded.

They mounted the donkeys again and set off once more. They could see much further in front of them now. Quite a big stretch of mountain-side was spread before them. The world suddenly seemed a much bigger place.

They rode on steadily. The mist thinned more and more rapidly, and the children felt the heat of the sun on their heads. They took off their coats, revelling in the warmth, after the chilliness of the mist.

'Look – we can see the nearest mountain-tops now,' called Jack. 'And the distant ones will soon be uncovered too. Thank goodness!'

'We ought to see the Vale of Butterflies soon,' said Lucy-Ann, eagerly. 'David said we'd get there today. I wonder where it is. Look, there's a butterfly, Philip.'

Philip glanced at it. 'Only a meadow-brown,' he said. 'We've seen heaps of those.' He looked before him searchingly and then put his field-glasses to his eyes.

'There's a valley which *might* be it,' he said, pointing. 'Hey, David! Is that the Vale of Butterflies?'

David looked where Philip was pointing. He shrugged his shoulders. 'Iss. No,' he said.

'Yes, no! Whatever does he mean by that?' said Philip in disgust. 'I suppose, in plain English, he means he hasn't the faintest idea. Well, we'll go on and hope for the best. It looks a nice sheltered kind of valley, the sort that might be hot enough for all kinds of insects and flowers.'

Picturing a perfect paradise of brilliant flowers and equally brilliant butterflies, the children rode on and on down towards the valley in the far distance. It was much further than they thought. That was the worst of travelling in mountains. Everywhere was about twice as far as you imagined it to be. Most disappointing!

It was late when they rode into the valley, which was really more of a shallow depression between two high mountains than a real lowland valley. Certainly it was sheltered, and certainly it had more flowers in it than they had so far seen – but there were no butterflies!

'This can't be it!' said Philip in disappointment. 'Is it, David?'

David shook his head. He was looking round in a puzzled manner, and it was quite clear that he really didn't know where he was.

'If this is *not* the Butterfly place, where is it?' asked Jack slowly and clearly. David shook his head again. It was really maddening, not being able to speak Welsh.

'Well,' said Philip, 'he's brought us the wrong way, to a place he doesn't know, but it's quite warm and sheltered, so we'll make the best of it tonight. Tomorrow we'll get the map from David, see if *we* can find out the way, and set off with ourselves as guides. He's as much use as Kiki to guide us in these mountains!'

They set up their camp again, feeling rather disappointed. They had so hoped to come to the place they wanted that night, and set up camp properly for a few days, to revel in hordes of common and uncommon butterflies. Now they would have to ride on still further, and goodness knew if they would ever find it!

They crawled into their sleeping-bags and called good night, just as the stars gleamed out. David was sleeping as usual outside.

But in the night the boys woke up suddenly. David was crawling into their tent. He was trembling with fright. 'Noises,' he said, in English, and then poured out something in Welsh. He was very frightened. 'Sleep here,' he said, and crept between the boys. They were amused and puzzled.

Whatever *could* have scared David so much?

10

A disturbing night

The sun was shining brightly when the camp awoke next day. It made them all feel cheerful and lively. Snowy, who had resented David sleeping with Philip and Jack the night before, and had butted him continually, bounded about lightly everywhere, butting David whenever he met him.

'What happened to you last night, David?' asked Jack, when they were all having a meal. 'Why were you so frightened?'

'Noises,' said David.

'What sort?' asked Philip curiously. '*We* didn't hear any.'

David made some surprising noises that sent Kiki sailing into the air and Snowy bounding away in fright. The children stared at David in astonishment.

By means of odd words and gestures David managed to convey to the children that he had gone to see if the donkeys were all right in the night, and had heard these noises near by where they were tethered.

'That explains why *we* didn't hear them, I suppose,' said Jack. 'David makes them sound like animal noises – fierce and savage!'

Lucy-Ann looked scared. 'Oh! You don't think there are wild animals anywhere about here, do you, Jack? I mean, *fierce* wild animals?'

Jack grinned. 'Well, if you are thinking of lions and tigers and panthers and bears, I think I can say you needn't be afraid of finding *those* here. But if, like Dinah, you include snakes, foxes, hedgehogs and so on in your list of fierce wild animals, then I should say, look out!'

'Don't be silly, Jack. Of course I don't mean those,' said Lucy-Ann. 'I don't quite know what I *did* mean. I just felt scared – and wondered what animal had made the noises David heard.'

'Probably his own imagination,' said Philip. 'Or a bad dream. That could scare him.'

David did not seem to want to go any further. He kept pointing back over the way they had come. But the children were not going to let their trip come to such a disappointing end. They meant to go and find the Butterfly Valley, if it took them all week! There was a lot of flapping to make David understand this.

He turned even more silent, but mounted his donkey to go with them. Jack now had the map, and examined it very carefully. It was annoying that the Butterfly Valley wasn't marked. Perhaps very few people knew about it.

They all set off across the valley and up into the mountains again. Perhaps the next valley would be the one they wanted, or the one after that. But although they travelled hopefully all the day, they did not find any valley full of butterflies. The children began to think it was all a fairy-tale.

There was no track to follow now, though they kept a keen look-out in case they should come across one again. When they camped that night, they discussed what they had better do next.

'If we go on any further we shan't know our way back,' said Jack. 'David would, perhaps, because he was born and bred among mountains, and, like a dog, could follow his own trail well enough, if we had to go back. But he's lost us once and I don't like to trust him too much. I wouldn't be surprised if he lost the way going back, if we take him much further!'

'Had we better go back then?' asked Lucy-Ann in disappointment.

'Or camp here for a few days,' said Jack, looking round. 'It's quite a good place.'

They were halfway up a steep mountain that rose very sharply from where they were, and looked quite unclimbable.

'What a peculiar mountain!' said Dinah, gazing up. 'I shouldn't think anyone ever climbed that to the top. It's all crags and rocks and jutting-out bits.'

'We'll camp here,' decided Philip. 'The weather looks quite settled. There's a spring near by. We can mess about with our cameras and field-glasses.'

They told David. He did not seem pleased, but went off to tether the donkeys for the night. They were all tired that evening, children and donkeys both, for they had had a very long day. They cut the big ham that Mrs Evans had provided for them, afraid that it might go bad if they didn't eat it soon.

David looked as if he thought he would sleep in the tent again that night, for he cast various longing glances in that direction. However, the night was hot, and he felt he couldn't bear to be under cover. So he arranged himself under his rug in the open, fairly near to the two tents. The donkeys were some way away, tethered to trees by long ropes.

That night there was a snuffling around the camp. Lucy-Ann awoke suddenly and heard it. She went right down to the bottom of her sleeping-bag, frightened. What could it be? Was it the wild animal that David had heard?

Then she heard a howl! The boys heard it too, and awoke. David, outside, was awake, having heard both the noises. He was shivering with fright, all kinds of fears coming into his mind at once.

The moon was up and everywhere was silvery bright. David sat up and looked down the hill. What he saw made his hair rise straight up on his head.

Wolves! A pack of wolves! No, no, it couldn't be wolves!

He was dreaming! Wolves had not been known in the mountains for hundreds of years. But if those creatures were not wolves, what were they? And that noise of snuffling he had heard. That must have been a wolf too! No, not a *wolf*. It couldn't have been such a thing.

David sat there, hugging his knees, his mind going round and round – wolves or not? Wolves or not? What were they doing near the donkeys?

Another howl came – half a howl, half a bark, a horrible noise. David shot into the boys' tent and gave them a terrible start.

He stammered something in Welsh, and then in English, 'Wolves!'

'Don't be silly,' said Jack at once, seeing that the man was badly scared. 'You've had a bad dream.'

David dragged him to the tent opening and pointed with a trembling finger to where the pack of snuffling animals stood, not far from the donkeys.

The boys stared as if they could not believe their eyes. They certainly *looked* like wolves! Jack felt a cold shiver down his back. Good gracious! Was he dreaming? Those creatures were more like wolves than anything else!

Snowy the kid was trembling as much as David was. The trembling somehow made the boys feel scared too. The only person who was not in the least scared was Kiki.

She too had caught sight of the wolves. She sailed out of the tent at top speed to go and investigate. Anything unusual always interested Kiki. She flew above the animals, whose eyes gleamed green as they turned at her coming.

'Wipe your feet!' screamed Kiki, and made a noise like a mowing-machine cutting long grass. It sounded really terrible in the still night air of the mountain-side.

The wolves started in fright. Then with one accord they all galloped away down the hillside into the night. Kiki shouted rude remarks after them.

'They've gone,' said Jack. 'Gosh, were they real? I can't understand it!'

When it was dawn, David got up to see if the donkeys were all right. Neither he nor the boys had slept again that night. David had been too scared to, and the boys had been too puzzled.

Daylight was almost on the mountain. David crept down quietly to the donkeys. They were all there, safe and sound but uneasy. David untethered them to take them to the stream to drink.

The boys were looking out of their tent, down the hillside to watch. There was no sign of any wolf now. Birds sang a little, and a yellow-hammer cried out for a little bit of bread and no cheese.

Suddenly something happened. David, who was taking the donkeys in a line to the stream, gave a terrified yell and fell to the ground, covering his face. The boys, holding their breath, thought they saw something moving in the bushes, but they couldn't see what.

David gave another yell and got to his feet. He mounted a donkey and rode at top speed up to the tent.

'Come!' he cried in Welsh, and then in English. 'Black, black, black!'

The boys had no idea at all what he meant. They stared at him in amazement, thinking he must have gone mad. He made a violent gesture to them, pointed to the following donkeys as if to tell the boys to mount and follow him, and then galloped off at breakneck speed.

They heard the hooves of his donkey echoing on the mountain-side for some time. The other donkeys looked doubtfully at one another, and then, to the boys' dismay, trotted after David!

'Hi! Come back, David!' yelled Jack, scrambling out of the tent. 'Hi, hi!'

One donkey turned and made as if to come back, but he was pushed on by the others behind. In a trice they had all disappeared, and the sound of their hooves grew fainter and fainter as they galloped away after David and his mount.

The two boys sat down suddenly. They felt faint. Jack

turned pale. He looked at Philip and bit his lip. Now they were in a terrible fix.

They said nothing for a moment or two, and then the girls' two scared faces looked out from their tent.

'What's happened? What's all the yelling? Was that David galloping away? We didn't dare to look!'

'Yes – it was David – running away from us – and all the donkeys have gone after him,' said Philip bitterly. 'We're in a pretty fix now!'

Nobody said anything. Lucy-Ann looked really alarmed. No David! No donkeys! What were they going to do?

Jack put his arm round her as she came and sat down beside him. 'It's all right! We've been in worse fixes than this! At the worst it only means a few days here, because as soon as he gets back to the farm, Bill will come and look for us.'

'Good thing we unloaded the donkeys and have got plenty of food,' said Philip. 'And our tents and sleeping-bags. Blow David! He's a nuisance.'

'I wonder what he saw to make him gallop off like that,' said Jack. 'All I could make out was "Black, black, black!" '

'Black what?' asked Dinah.

'Black nothing. Just black,' said Jack. 'Let's go down to the place where he got his fright and see if we can see anything.'

'Oh *no*!' said the girls at once.

'Well, I'll go, and Philip can stay here with you,' said Jack, and off he went. The others watched him, holding their breath. He peered all round and then turned and shook his head and shouted.

'Nothing here! Not a thing to see! David must have been seeing things! His bad night upset him.'

He came back. 'But what about those animals in the night?' said Philip, after a pause. 'Those wolves. We both saw those. *They* seemed real enough!'

Yes – what about those wolves!

11

A strange happening

It wasn't long before Dinah suggested having something to eat, and went to the big panniers that had been unloaded from the donkeys the night before. She pulled out some tins, thinking it would be a change to have sardines, and tinned peaches, or something like that. Anything to take their minds off David's flight, and the disappearance of the donkeys!

They sat down rather silently. Lucy-Ann kept very close to the boys. What with wolves and David's fright she felt very scared herself!

'I hope this won't turn into one of our adventures,' she kept saying to herself. 'They always happen so suddenly.'

Snowy the kid bounded up to Philip and knocked a tin flying from his hand. He nuzzled affectionately against him and then butted him. Philip rubbed the furry little nose and then pushed the kid away.

'I'm glad *you* didn't go off with the donkeys too!' he said. 'I've got used to having you around now, you funny aggravating little thing. Take your nose out of that tin! Lucy-Ann, push him off – he'll eat everything we've got!'

Kiki suddenly flew at Snowy, screaming with rage. She had had her eye on that tin of sliced peaches, and to see Snowy nosing round it was too much for her. She gave him a sharp peck on the nose, and he ran to Philip, bleating. Everyone laughed and felt better.

They sat there, eating by the tents, occasionally glancing up at the mountain that towered up so steeply above them. It had no gentle slope up to the summit, as most of the mountains around had, but was steep and forbidding.

'I don't much like this mountain,' said Lucy-Ann.

'Why?' asked Dinah.

'I don't know. I just don't like it,' said Lucy-Ann. 'I've got one of my "feelings" about it.'

The others laughed. Lucy-Ann often had 'feelings' about things, and really believed in them. It was just like her to start having 'feelings' about the mountain, when everyone was also having uncomfortable ideas about wolves and other things.

'Well, you needn't have any "feelings" about mountains,' said Philip. 'Mountains are all the same – just tops, middles and bottoms, sometimes with sheep on and sometimes without!'

'But not many have wolves,' said Lucy-Ann seriously, and that made the others feel uncomfortable again.

'What are we going to do today?' asked Jack, when they had finished their meal. 'I suppose we *must* stay here till Bill comes to find us. We can't try to walk back home, because for one thing we don't know the way, and for another we'd never be able to carry enough food to get there without starving.'

'We'd far better stay here,' said Philip at once. 'It's ten chances to one David will know his way back here all right, and can bring Bill and the donkeys. Whereas if we start moving about, they'll never find us.'

'Yes – it does seem the most sensible thing to do,' said Jack. 'We've got our camp here – tents set up and everything – so we might as well make the best of it, and enjoy the camping. I wish there was somewhere to bathe though. It's so jolly hot. That little stream's too small to do anything but paddle in.'

'Let's all keep together,' said Lucy-Ann. 'I mean – we could frighten those wolves away perhaps if we all screamed at them – but one of us alone might be – might be . . . '

'Gobbled up!' said Jack, and laughed. 'What big *eyes* you've got, Granny! And, oh, what big TEETH you've got!'

'Don't tease her,' said Philip, seeing Lucy-Ann's alarmed

face. 'It's all right, Lucy-Ann. Wolves are only really hungry in the winter-time and it's summer now.'

Lucy-Ann looked relieved. 'Well – I suppose if they'd been really hungry they would have attacked the donkeys, wouldn't they?' she said. 'Oh dear – I do think it's most extraordinary to find wolves here.'

They were just about to get up and clear away the picnic things when something curious happened that froze them to the ground.

First of all there was a grumbling, rumbling noise that seemed to come from the heart of the mountain itself – and then the ground shook a little. The four children distinctly felt it quivering beneath them, and they clutched at one another in alarm. Kiki flew straight up into the air, screaming. Snowy leapt to a high rock and stood there, poised on his four little legs as if to take off in the air like a plane.

The ground stopped shaking. The noise died away. But almost imediately the rumbling began again, a little louder, but very muffled as if great depths of rock separated it from the listeners. The ground quivered once more and Snowy took a flying leap into the air, landing on another rock. He was really terrified.

So were the four children. Lucy-Ann, very pale, clung to Jack and Philip. Dinah, forgetting all about the slow-worm, held on to Philip too.

There were no more rumblings, and the earth beneath them stayed still. The birds, which had stopped singing and calling, began to chirp again, and a yellow-hammer gave his familiar cry.

Snowy recovered himself and came bounding up to the others. Kiki landed on Jack's shoulder. 'God save the Queen,' she said, in a relieved voice.

'What in the *world* was that?' said Philip at last. 'An earthquake? Gosh, I *was* scared!'

'Oh, Philip! This mountain isn't a volcano, is it?' said Lucy-Ann, gazing up at it fearfully.

'Of course not! You'd know a volcano all right if you saw one!' said Jack. 'This is a perfectly ordinary mountain – and goodness knows why it should have rumbled like that, and trembled beneath us. It gave me a horrible feeling.'

'I told you I had one of my "feelings" about this mountain,' said Lucy-Ann. 'Didn't I? I feel very peculiar about it. I want to go back to the farmhouse and not stay here.'

'So do we all,' said Philip. 'But we shouldn't know the way, Lucy-Ann. It isn't as if we'd followed a track – we left the track as you know, and part of the way we were in thick mist – we shouldn't have the faintest idea of the way.'

'I know you're right,' said Lucy-Ann. 'But I *don't* like this mountain – especially when it starts to rumble and shake! What made it?'

Nobody knew. They got up, cleared away the meal and went to splash in the little stream. The wind suddenly began to blow rather chilly, and, looking up, the children saw that big clouds were coming up from the south-west.

'Looks like rain,' said Jack. I hope the wind doesn't get up much more, or it will blow our tents away. Do you remember how they were blown clean away from over us on our last adventure – on the Island of Birds? That was an awful feeling.'

'Well,' said Philip, 'if you really think the tents might blow away, Jack, we'd better find a better place to camp than this – somewhere not too far, though, because we don't want to miss seeing Bill and David when they come for us. A copse of trees or a cave or somewhere like that – right out of the wind.'

'Let's look now,' said Dinah, pulling on her coat. It was extraordinary how cold it got as soon as the sun went in and the wind blew up the mountain. 'We'd better take Snowy with us, or he'll eat everything we've left!'

Snowy had every intention of coming with them. He capered along by Philip and Jack, as mad as ever. He was now very annoyed with Kiki, and leapt at her whenever she came within reach, wanting to pay her back for nipping his nose.

When the girls had been left a little way behind, Philip spoke in a low voice to Jack. 'We'd better find a cave, I think, Jack – I don't like the idea of those animals prowling around us at night – wolves, or whatever they are. If we were in a cave we could light a fire at the entrance and that would keep any animal off.'

'Yes. That's quite a good idea,' agreed Jack. 'I hadn't thought of that. I can't say *I* like the idea either of wolves nosing round our tents when we're asleep at night! I'd feel much safer in a cave!'

They hunted about for some kind of rocky shelter or cave, but there seemed none to be found. The mountain was so steep that it really was difficult to climb, and Lucy-Ann was afraid of slipping and falling.

Snowy leapt ahead of them, as sure-footed as ever. The boys wished heartily that it was as easy for them to leap about the mountain as it was for the kid.

'Look at him up there, standing on that rock!' said Jack, feeling exasperated and far too hot with his climbing. 'Hey, Snowy, come and give us a leg up! If only we had four springy legs like yours!'

Snowy stood there, whisking his little tail, and then ran back and disappeared. 'Where's he gone?' said Jack. 'Oh, there he comes again. Philip, there must be a cave or overhanging rock up where he is – he keeps going back and disappearing into it, whatever it is!'

They climbed up to where Snowy was, and sure enough, just at the back of the overhanging rock was a long low cave, its roof made out of another overhanging rock, its opening fringed with ferns of all kinds.

'This would do awfully well for us,' said Jack, going down on hands and knees and looking in. 'We could light a fire on the rock outside – the one Snowy stood on – and feel quite safe tonight. Clever little Snowy! You found us just what we wanted!'

'But how in the world are we going to get everything up here?' said Philip. 'It was such a climb. It's not as if we are donkeys or goats, able to scramble up steep places quite easily, even with a load to carry. We need our hands to help us.'

This was certainly a problem. The boys hailed the girls and helped them up on to the rock where Snowy stood. 'Look,' said Jack, 'here's a good place to sleep in tonight. We can quite well see from here if Bill and David come – see what a good view we have from this rock – and we'd be safe from the wolves if we lighted a fire at the entrance to the cave.'

Oh, *yes*!' said Lucy-Ann, pleased. She went into the cave. She had to bend her head at the opening, but inside the roof grew higher. 'It's not *really* a cave!' she said. 'It's just a space under that big jutting-out rock – but it will do awfully well.'

They all sat down on the rock, wishing the sun would come out. Snowy lay down beside them and Kiki sat on Jack's shoulder.

But suddenly she rose up into the air and screeched loudly. Snowy leapt up and stood looking downwards. What was the matter?

'Is it the wolves again?' asked Lucy-Ann in alarm. They listened. They could hear a noise of some animal or animals down below in the thick bushes, under the birch-trees.

'Get back into the cave,' said Jack to the girls. 'And keep quiet.'

The two girls went silently back into the darkness of the cave. The boys listened and watched. What animal was it down there? It must be big, by the noise it made!

12

Wolves in the night!

Snowy suddenly bleated loudly and took a flying leap off the rock before Philip could stop him. He disappeared into the bushes below – and then a loud and welcome sound filled the air.

'Ee-ore! Ee-ore! Ee-ore!'

'Goodness! It's a donkey!' cried Jack and scrambled down to see. 'Have they come back? Is David with them?'

They soon found what they were looking for. Dapple the donkey was in the bushes, nuzzling Snowy, evidently full of delight at seeing him again. But there was no sign at all of the other donkeys or of David.

'Dapple! You darling!' said Lucy-Ann, running up to him in joy. 'You've come back to us.'

'Come back to *Snowy*, you mean!' said Philip. 'He was always fond of Snowy, weren't you, Dapple? So you came back to find him. Well, we're very very glad to see you, because you will solve a very knotty problem for us – how to get all our goods up to that cave!'

Dapple *had* come back to see Snowy, but he was also very pleased to see the children again. He was a quiet, stout little donkey, hard-working and patient. He kept close to the children, and had evidently made up his mind he was going to stay with them. Snowy was sweet with him, and trotted by his side all the time.

'Here, Dapple!' called Philip. 'Come and help us with these things, there's a good fellow.'

Dapple stood obediently whilst the boys strapped things on to his back. He took all the bedding up to the cave first, scrambling up the steep bits with difficulty, but managing very well indeed. Then he took up the panniers of food.

'Thanks, Dapple,' said Jack, giving him a pat. 'Now come and have a drink!'

They all went to the stream and drank and splashed. The sun had come out again and immediately it was very hot. The children flung off their coats and lay about basking.

'We must collect wood for the fire tonight,' said Jack. 'We shall need a good lot if we're going to keep the fire going all night long. We'll stack it in the big panniers and get Dapple to take it up for us.'

'Good old Dapple!' said Dinah.

They collected as much wood as they could, and soon it was all piled up on the rock outside the cave. The boys made a fire but did not light it. There was no need to do that till night.

The day soon went, and the sun sank behind the mountains in a blaze of crimson. As soon as darkness fell on the mountain-side, the children retired into the cave. The thought of wolves kept coming into their mind, and David's scream of terror, when he had seen something in the bushes, 'Black, black, black!' What *could* he have seen?

The children hadn't thought much of these things during the bright daylight, but they came back into their minds now it was dark. They debated whether or not to have Dapple in the cave with them.

But Dapple settled that idea by firmly refusing to go under the overhanging rock. He just stood outside stubbornly, his four legs set firmly on the ground, and no amount of pushing or pulling made the slightest difference. He was *not* going into that cave!

'All right, Dapple,' said Jack crossly. 'Stay outside and be eaten by wolves if you want to!'

'Oh, *don't* say things like that,' said Lucy-Ann. 'Dapple, do come inside! Please!'

Dapple lay down firmly outside, and the children gave it up. There would be no difficulty about Snowy or Kiki. One would want to be with Philip, the other with Jack.

'Now we'll light the fire,' said Jack, as stars began to glimmer in the sky. 'It's getting very dark. Got the matches, Philip?'

The fire soon burnt up, for the twigs and branches were very dry. The cheerful flames leapt and flickered, and the fire crackled merrily.

'That's very very nice,' said Lucy-Ann, pleased. 'I feel safe tucked away in this cave with a fire at the entrance. Philip, make Snowy go the other side of you. He's sticking his hooves into me. I wish he'd wear bedroom slippers at night!'

Everybody laughed. They all felt safe and comfortable, tucked up in their sleeping-bags, with the fire lighting up the cave, filling it with jumping shadows. Snowy was pressed against Philip, Kiki was on Jack's middle. Somewhere outside was Dapple. Lucy-Ann wished he was in with them, then the whole family would be safe.

They all watched the flames for a while and then fell asleep. The fire flickered down as the wood was burnt up, and soon only the embers glowed.

Philip woke up with a start a few hours later. He saw that the fire had died down, and he got out of his sleeping-bag to put on more wood. It would never do to let it go out!

Dapple was still outside, lying quietly. Philip saw him when the flames leapt up to burn the wood he piled on. The boy went back to his sleeping-bag. He found that Snowy had crept inside it whilst he was piling wood on the fire.

'You little scamp!' he whispered. 'Get out. There's not room for us both.'

There was quite a scuffle as he tried to get Snowy out of the bag. Fortunately the others were so very sound asleep that they didn't wake. Philip got Snowy out at last and slid in himself. He hastily laced up the neck of the bag before Snowy could try to squeeze in again. Snowy gave a sigh and lay down heavily right on Philip's middle.

Philip lay awake, watching the fire. The wind sometimes blew the smoke towards the cave, and for a moment or two the smell made Philip want to cough.

Then he heard Dapple stir outside, and he got up on one elbow to see why. His heart began to beat very fast.

Silent dark figures were slinking up to the cave! They did not pass beyond the fire, but they did not seem to be afraid of it. Philip felt breathless, and his heart beat even faster, as if he had been running.

What were those figures? Were they the wolves? The boy caught sight of two gleaming eyes, shining like the headlights of a distant car – but green as grass! He sat up quietly.

The wolves were back! They had smelt out the little company. What would they do? They had not attacked Dapple, thank goodness – and the donkey did not seem to be unduly frightened. He was only moving uneasily.

The slinking figures moved to and fro behind the fire. Philip couldn't think what in the world to do! He could only hope that the fire would frighten them enough to keep them out of the cave.

After a while all the animals disappeared. Philip breathed again! Gosh, what a horrible fright he had had! What a blessing they had thought of that fire! Philip made up his mind that he wasn't going to sleep again that night, in case the fire went out. At all costs he must keep that up.

So the boy lay wide-eyed, thinking of wolves, rumblings, earthquakes and 'Black, black, black.' There was something very unusual about all these things. Did they fit together, or didn't they? *Was* there something peculiar about this mountain?

The fire was dying down again. Philip got up cautiously to put more wood on. The moon was up now and he could see for miles. He piled wood on the fire and the flames shot up. He slipped out of the cave to Dapple.

Then the boy heard a sound. He looked up – and to his horror he saw a wolf between him and the cave! He had gone to pat Dapple – and in that moment the wolf had slunk in between fire and cave. Would he go in?

The wolf stood still, looking at Philip in the moonlight. Philip gazed back, wondering what to do if the creature attacked him – and as he looked, a very peculiar thing happened.

The wolf wagged its long tail! To and fro it went, to and fro, like a big dog's! Philip's heart leapt. The animal wanted to be friendly! All animals were attracted to Philip – but a wolf! That was extraordinary.

The boy held out his hand, half afraid, but bold and daring. The wolf trotted round and fire and licked Philip's hand. It gave a little whine.

The moon shone down brightly on the animal's dark coat, pointed ears and long muzzle. *Was* it a wolf? Now that he was close to it Philip began to doubt.

And then quite suddenly he knew what this friendly animal was!

'Why, you're an Alsatian *dog*!' he cried. 'Aren't you? Why didn't I think of it before? I *knew* there weren't wolves in this country! Where are the others? You're all Alsatians! Good dog! Fine dog! I'd like to be friends with you!'

The big Alsatian put his paws up on Philip's shoulder and licked his face. Then he lifted his head and howled. It was a wolf-like noise, but Philip no longer minded that!

It was a call to the other dogs, the rest of the pack. There came the sound of feet in the bushes below, and a crowd of dogs leapt up on to the rock. They clustered round Philip, and, seeing that their leader was so friendly with the boy, they pawed him and licked him.

The howl awakened all the three children in the cave, and they sat up in fright. To their unspeakable horror they saw, outside the cave, what looked like Philip being attacked by wolves!

'Look! They've got Philip! Quick!' yelled Jack.

All three children slid out of their sleeping-bags and rushed to Philip's aid. The dogs growled at the sudden commotion.

'Philip! We're coming! Are you hurt?' cried valiant little Lucy-Ann, picking up a stick.

'It's all right, it's all right!' yelled Philip. 'They're not attacking me. They're friendly. They're not wolves, but Alsatians! Dogs, you know!'

'Goodness gracious!' said Dinah, and came out into the moonlight, so glad that the dogs were not wolves that she didn't even feel afraid of so many big dogs!

'Oh, Philip!' said Lucy-Ann, almost in tears with the shock of delight at knowing the wolves were only dogs. 'Oh, Philip! I thought you were being attacked.'

'You were a darling to come to my rescue then,' said Philip, smiling when he saw the little stick that Lucy-Ann had meant to attack the wolves with. 'The leader of the dogs made friends with me – so all the others are doing the same!'

The dogs had apparently made up their minds to stay for the night. Philip debated what to do. 'We can't possibly go back into the cave,' he said. 'The whole pack will come crowding in, and it would be impossible to breathe.'

'Quite impossible,' said Dinah, filled with horror at the thought of so many dogs sleeping with them.

'So we'll bring our sleeping-bags out here on the rock beside Dapple, and sleep there,' said Philip. 'The dogs can stay if they want to – they'll be good guards! And if they don't want to, they can go. There are about ten of them! I wonder how it is they're wandering about here wild. Ten of them! It's extraordinary.'

They dragged out their sleeping-bags, and got into them. The dogs sniffed round in wonder. The leader sat majestically down by Philip, as if to say, 'This boy is my property. Keep off!' The others lay about among the children. Snowy was afraid of the big leader-dog and dared not even go near his beloved Philip. He went to Jack instead. Kiki stayed up in a tree. There were altogether too many dogs for her!

It was a curious sight the moon looked down on: four children, one goat, one parrot, one donkey – and ten dogs!

13

The face in the tree

When the morning came, Dapple awoke the children by giving a mighty sneeze. They woke with a jump, wondering what it was. Dapple gave another sneeze, and they knew!

'It's Dapple! Have you got a cold, Dapple?' asked Lucy-Ann anxiously. Then she remembered the happenings of the night, and looked round.

Everyone said the same thing at once.

'Where are the dogs?'

They had disappeared. Not one was there. The children looked at one another, puzzled. Where had they gone, and why?

'We couldn't *all* have dreamed them,' said Dinah, answering everyone's unspoken thought. 'They really were here. Ten of them. Most peculiar.'

'Yes, it *is* peculiar,' said Jack. 'Personally, I think they must belong to somebody. They didn't strike me as being a pack of *wild* dogs.'

'Nor me,' said Philip. 'But who could they belong to? There's not a house for miles! And why should anyone in this desolate mountain country keep ten man-hunting dogs?'

'Oooh – are they man-hunters?' said Lucy-Ann, startled.

'Well, the police use them for that,' said Philip. 'Don't they, Jack? They hunt criminals with them. Those Alsatians can smell them out and capture them. But there can't be any police here, with hunting-dogs! I mean – Bill would have had it reported to him, if they were. He's high up in the police organization himself, and there's not a thing he doesn't know about what's going on in the police world.'

'Where do the dogs come from then?' asked Dinah.

'Would they be kept as guards for anything – to frighten anyone off, or give the alarm, for instance?'

'Yes – but what is there to guard here, among these mountains?' said Jack. 'Nothing at all, as far as I can see!'

'Give it up!' said Philip, sliding out of his sleeping-bag. 'I'm going for a splash in the stream. Coming?'

'Yes. Then we'll open a tin or two,' said Dinah. 'I wish we'd thought of giving that ham-bone to the dogs, Jack. The ham's gone bad now – but they wouldn't have minded.'

'We'll give it to them next time we see them,' said Jack. 'I've no doubt they'll be along again!'

They all splashed in the stream, Snowy and Dapple too. Kiki sat apart, making sarcastic remarks, for she was not fond of water.

'Pooh! Gah!' she shouted, trying to remember all the rude words she knew. 'Gooh! Pah!'

'That's right. Mix your words up, Kiki,' said Jack. 'What about "piffle" and "bunk"? You used to know those too.'

'Pifflebunk,' said Kiki, and thought that was a good word. 'Pifflebunk, bifflebunk, pop goes the pifflebunk.'

The children laughed. Kiki laughed too and then began to give an imitation of Dapple braying. This was much too lifelike and Dapple started up, looking all round for the other donkeys.

'Ee-ore, ee-ore, ee-ore,' went on Kiki, till Jack threw a towel at her to make her stop. It fell over her head and she screamed in rage. Dapple and Snowy stared solemnly at her, puzzled and surprised.

They had a meal. Lucy-Ann volunteered to go down to the stream again and wash the dishes, whilst the others looked at the map, trying to find out exactly where they were. She went off to the stream, humming.

She knelt down by the water, scouring a dish, when a sound made her look up. She had heard something in the tree above, just by the water.

There was a big, leafy tree there, growing almost out of the stream. Lucy-Ann, thinking there must be a bird in the tree, peered up into the branches.

She got a terrible shock. Looking down at her was a face – and it was black.

The little girl sat there, petrified, the dish in her hand, unable to move or speak. The branches moved and she saw that the face was topped by black, thick hair, and had bright eyes and a cheerful expression.

'It's a black man!' she thought to herself. 'But here! Up this tree! What shall I do?'

The black face looked down on the little girl, and then the man's lips parted in a smile. The head nodded amiably. Then a black finger came up from among the leaves, and was put to the lips.

'Don't you make a sound, l'il gal,' said the man, in a hoarse whisper. He sounded like an American! 'Don't you say I'm here. I'm just a poor man, lost and alone.'

Lucy-Ann couldn't believe her ears. She felt that she simply must call the others. But they didn't hear her, and as soon as she had shouted, the man frowned fiercely and shook his head.

'L'il gal, you gotta git away from here. It's a no-good mountain, full of bad men. They'll git you if you don't git away. There's bad things here, l'il gal.'

'What are you doing here?' asked Lucy-Ann, in a scared voice. 'How do you know all this?'

'I've been in that there bad mountain, l'il gal. I've gotten away. But this poor fellah's gotten no place to go – and he's surely scared by those big dogs. I'm staying right here in this nice big tree. You git away, l'il gal, git far away!'

Lucy-Ann felt odd, standing there talking to a black stranger up a tree. She suddenly turned and ran back to the others. She ran fast, and arrived absolutely out of breath.

'What's the matter, what's the matter?' cried Jack, seeing from Lucy-Ann's face that she had had a shock. Lucy-Ann could only gasp out one or two words. She pointed back to the stream.

'Black man!' she gasped. 'Black!'

'Black! That's what David said!' cried Philip. 'Get your breath, Lucy-Ann! Tell us what you saw. Quick!'

Lucy-Ann panted out what she had seen and heard. The others listened in astonishment. A black man hiding in a tree – from the dogs! A man who said the mountain was bad – an American – whatever did it mean?

'Come on – we'll ask him what he knows!' cried Jack. 'There's something going on here. We'd better find out and then we can tell Bill when he comes. Quick!'

They all ran back to the stream and peered up the tree. But there was nobody there. The man had gone.

'Blow!' said Jack, in disappointment. 'He must have seen you scuttle back to us, Lucy-Ann, to tell us you had seen him – and he's scared, and now he's gone.'

'It's a wonder the dogs didn't find him last night – and before that, when David saw him up this very same tree,' said Jack.

'Well, he's been rather clever, I think,' said Philip, looking at the stream. 'You know, dogs can't follow scent through water. They lose it. And I reckon that chap was clever enough to wade up or down the stream to that tree, and hop up it from the water. The dogs couldn't possibly follow his scent through the stream. They would lose it wherever he entered the water. Still, he must have felt pretty scared when he saw the dogs milling around near here!'

'Were they hunting for him, do you think?' asked Lucy-Ann fearfully. 'He must have been awfully afraid. I should be terrified if I thought a pack of Alsatian dogs was after me.'

The children hunted for the strange man, but he was nowhere to be seen. They wondered what he ate. There was not much to eat on the mountains except bilberries, wild raspberries and grass.

'Do you think he really meant there were men inside this mountain?' asked Dinah, when they had tired themselves out looking for the American.

'It seems incredible – but if you remember those noises of rumbling we heard yesterday – and the way the earth shook beneath us – it seems as if there *might* be men working underground,' said Jack.

'What – as miners or something?' asked Dinah.

'I don't know. Possibly. Though goodness knows what could be mined inside this mountain, or how they would get the machinery there. There would have to be a road – and then everyone would know.'

'It's very mysterious,' said Dinah.

Lucy-Ann sighed. 'It's another adventure, that's what it is. It's fatal to go off together like this. We go to look for birds, or butterflies or something – and we always stumble into something peculiar. I'm getting tired of it.'

'Poor Lucy-Ann!' said Philip. 'We certainly do happen on strange things. *I* think it's very exciting. I love adventures.'

'Yes, but I don't,' said Lucy-Ann. 'I don't like that kind of thing at all.'

'*I* do,' said Dinah at once. 'I've enjoyed every single one of our adventures. And this one seems more mysterious than any other. What *is* going on inside this mountain? How I'd love to know! If only we could see that chap again, we could ask him to tell us all about it.'

'Oh, listen – I do believe that rumbling's going to start again,' said Lucy-Ann suddenly. 'See how frightened Snowy is! Yes – there it comes.'

They sat and listened. Jack put his ear to the ground. At once the rumblings became magnified, and sounded more puzzling than ever. Was something exploding down there, far in the heart of the mountain?

Then the earth quivered as it had done before and Lucy-Ann clutched at Jack. It was horrible to feel the firm solid earth quivering like a jelly.

It soon stopped. Dinah glanced up at the steep mountain, rearing up just behind them, wondering what its secret was. She suddenly stiffened, and caught hold of Philip's arm.

'Look!' she said, and pointed upwards.

They all looked. Out of the side of the mountain was drifting a small cloud of smoke. One puff came. Then another. But it was not ordinary smoke. It was a curious crimson colour, and it did not drift away like mist on the wind, but hung like a solid little cloud, close to the mountain, for some time. Then it suddenly became lighter in colour and disappeared.

'Well – whatever was *that*?' said Jack, in amazement. 'I never in my life saw smoke like that before. There must be a vent or something in the side of the mountain there, that lets out smoke or gases.'

'What's a vent?' asked Lucy-Ann, her eyes looking as if they would drop out of her head.

'Oh – a sort of chimney,' said Jack. 'Somewhere with a draught that will take up smoke or gases to the outer air. Whatever's going on in the mountain produces that smoke, which has to be got rid of. I wonder what else is being produced inside there!'

Nobody could imagine. They couldn't seem to fit together all the curious facts they knew – the pack of man-hunting dogs – the poor runaway – the noises, the earth's shaking, the crimson smoke. It didn't make any sense at all.

'If only Bill would come!' said Philip. 'He might be able to fit this jigsaw together.'

'Or if we could get hold of that chap Lucy-Ann saw,' said Philip. 'He could tell us a lot.'

'We may see him again,' said Dinah. 'We'll watch out for him.'

They did see him again, that very evening – but alas, he didn't answer any of their questions!

14

Plenty of things happen

They decided to go for a walk that evening. They would leave Dapple tied up to a tree by the stream, with a note on his harness to say they would soon be back – just in *case* Bill came when they were away.

'Though he couldn't *possibly* be here yet,' said Jack. Still, you never knew with Bill. He had a remarkable way of doing impossible things extraordinarily quickly.

They went off together, Snowy capering about, and Kiki on Jack's shoulder. They climbed up past the cave where they had slept the night before. Their sleeping-bags were still there, pulled into the cave out of the sun. They meant to sleep in them up on the rock again that night.

'Let's follow Snowy,' suggested Dinah. 'He always seems to know a way to go, thought I expect he only follows his silly little nose! But he usually chooses quite possible paths for us.'

So they followed Snowy. The little kid took it into his head to climb up the mountain, but at last they all came to such a steep cliff of rock, almost sheer, that they had to stop. Even Snowy was brought to a halt!

'I'm frightfully hot,' said Dinah, fanning herself. 'Let's sit down under those trees.'

The trees were waving about in the wind. Jack looked longingly up into the wind-blown branches. 'It would be lovely and cool up there, in the windy boughs,' he said. 'What about climbing up? They look pretty easy to climb.'

'A wizard idea!' said Philip. 'I love swinging in the branches at the top of a tree. Want a leg-up, Lucy-Ann?'

Lucy-Ann got a leg-up and soon they were all settled into forking branches, letting themselves be swung about in the wind, which was very strong just there.

'This is lovely,' said Dinah. 'Heavenly!'

'Super!' said Jack. 'Don't clutch my shoulder so tightly, Kiki. You won't fall off!'

Snowy was left down below, bleating. He tried his best to leap up into the tree but he couldn't. He ran round and round Philip's tree and then, in a rage, he tore up to a rock and leapt up it and down it without stopping. The children watched him, laughing at his antics.

Then, quite suddenly, a hullabaloo broke on their ears. It was the sound of excited barking and snarling, howling and yelping.

'The dogs!' said Jack, straining his eyes to see where the noise came from. 'I say – they're after that man!'

There came the crashing of bushes and twigs far below them on the mountain-side, accompanied by more howls and barks. Then the children caught sight of a man running across a bare stony part of the mountain-side below them – about half a mile away.

The dogs poured after him. Lucy-Ann almost fell out of her tree in fright at seeing a man chased by dogs. The children watched without a word, their hearts beating fast, anxious for the man to escape.

He came to a tree and flung himself up it just as the first dog reached him. He pulled himself up, and was lost to sight. The dogs surrounded the tree, clamouring loudly.

Lucy-Ann gulped. Tears ran down her face. She felt so sorry for the hunted man that she could hardly see through her tears. The others watched grimly. Philip debated whether to go down and see if he could call the dogs off.

Then another man appeared, walking leisurely across the mountain-side toward the tree and the dogs. He was too far away for the children to see what he was like, or to hear his voice.

But on the crisp air of the mountain came the shrill sound of a whistle. The dogs at once left the tree, and trotted back to the man. He stood not far off the tree, and evidently gave orders for the man to come down. But nobody came down from the tree.

The man waved his hand to the dogs and at once they streamed back to the tree again, clamouring and howling like mad. The man turned to go back the way he came.

'Oh! He's left the dogs to keep the poor man up the tree till he starves, or comes down to be set on!' sobbed Lucy-Ann. 'Philip, what shall we do?'

'I'll go down and call the dogs off,' said Philip. 'I'll give the man a chance to get right out of sight, so that he won't see me. Then I'll see if I can get the dogs away and give that chap a chance to escape from the tree.'

He climbed down his tree, after he had waited for twenty minutes, to give the second man a chance to go back to wherever he had come from. He made his way cautiously through the tall bushes.

And then something happened. A rough hand pounced down on his shoulder and he was held in a grip like iron. He was swung round – and came face to face with the man who had ordered the runaway to come down from the tree!

Philip wriggled, but he couldn't possibly get away. He didn't dare to yell for the others in case they got caught too. Blow! Why hadn't he waited longer before going off to the black man's rescue!

'What are you doing here?' said the man, in a strange, foreign accent. 'Who are you, boy?'

'I've only come to look for butterflies,' stammered Philip, trying to look as if he knew nothing about anything but butterflies. He didn't like the look of the man at all. He had fierce hawk-like face, overhanging eyebrows, and such a sharp look in his black eyes that Philip felt sure he would be difficult to deceive.

'Who are you with?' asked the man, digging his steel-like fingers into Philip and making him squirm.

'I'm alone, as you can see,' said Philip, hoping the man

would believe him. The man looked at him searchingly.

'My dogs would have got you if you had been here for long,' he said. 'And all your friends too!'

'What friends?' asked Philip innocently. 'Oh, you mean Snowy, my kid? He always comes with me.'

Snowy had bounded up at that moment, to the obvious surprise of the man. 'He's like a dog – never leaves me. Let me go, sir. I'm looking for butterflies. I'll be gone tonight.'

'Where did you come from?' asked the man. 'Do your parents know where you are?'

'No,' said Philip truthfully. 'I just went away to hunt for butterflies. I came from over there.'

He nodded his head vaguely behind him, hoping that the man would think he was a harmless nature-lover, and let him go. But the man didn't.

Instead he tightened his fingers on Philip's shoulders, and turned towards the tree where the black man was still hiding, surrounded by the dogs.

'You'll come with me now,' he said. 'You've seen too much.'

Just then there came a yelling and shouting from the tree. Evidently the runaway had given in. The man, still clutching Philip by the shoulder, and followed by a puzzled Snowy, went towards the tree. He took a whistle from his pocket and blew on it shrilly. As before, the dogs at once left the tree and came to him. The man shouted for the runaway to come down.

The poor man came down in such a hurry that he half fell. The dogs made no attempt to go for him. Philip saw that they had been extremely well trained.

The man fell on his knees and began to jabber something. He was terrified. The man told him to get up, in cold contemptuous tones. Surrounded by the dogs, the prisoner walked stumblingly in front of the man, who still held Philip firmly by the shoulder.

Up in their trees the children watched in horror, hardly

believing their eyes when they saw Philip held by the man.
'Sh! Don't make a sound,' commanded Jack. 'It's no good us being captured too. If the dogs go with Philip, he'll be all right. He'll have ten friends he can call on at any time!'

The little procession of men, boy, dogs and kid passed almost beneath the trees the children were in. Philip did not glance up, though he longed to. He was not going to give away the hiding-place of the others.

Jack parted the branches of his tree and followed the procession anxiously with his eyes. They were going in the direction of the steep wall of unclimbable rock. Jack took up his field-glasses, which were slung round his neck as usual, and glued them to his eyes, following the company closely. Where exactly were they going? If he knew, he might be able to go and rescue Philip and Snowy.

He saw Philip taken right up to the steep wall. Then, before his eyes, the whole company seemed to vanish! One moment they were there – the next they were gone! Jack took his glasses from his eyes and rubbed the lenses, thinking something must have gone wrong with them. But no – he saw exactly the same thing – a steep wall of sheer rock – and nobody there at all, not even a dog!

'Jack! Can you see what's happened to Philip?' came Lucy-Ann's anxious voice. 'Oh, Jack – he's caught!'

'Yes, and he's been taken into that mountain,' said Jack. 'Though how, I don't know. One moment they were all there, the next they were gone! I can't understand it.'

He looked through his glasses again but there was nothing to be seen. He suddenly realized that the sun had gone down and it was getting dark. 'Girls! It'll be dark soon. We must get down and go to the cave, whilst we can still see our way!' said Jack. They all climbed down quickly. Lucy-Ann was trying to blink back tears.

'I want Philip to come back,' she said. 'What's happened to him?'

'Don't cry,' said Dinah. 'Crying won't help him! You

always burst into tears when anything happens!'

Dinah spoke crossly because she was very near tears herself. Jack put his arm round both of them. 'Don't let's quarrel. That won't help Philip. Come on, let's get back quickly. I'll fetch Dapple from the stream, and bring her up to the rock.'

They made their way back to the cave they had left their sleeping-bags in. Jack fetched the patient Dapple. Kiki sat silently on his shoulder. She always knew when things had gone wrong with the children. She nipped Jack's ear gently to tell him she was sorry.

It was almost dark when they reached the cave. There was no need to make a fire tonight – they did not fear wolves any more. Indeed they would have been very glad indeed to see dark figures come slinking up to the cave. They would have welcomed the dogs eagerly.

'I miss Snowy,' said Dinah. 'It's queer without him leaping about everywhere. I'm glad he's gone with Philip. I'm glad the slow-worm's gone too!'

They didn't want to get into the sleeping-bags and go to sleep. They wanted to talk. A lot of things seemed to be happening very suddenly. Oh dear – when would Bill come? They could manage quite well without grown-ups in many ways – but just at the moment all three would have welcomed even David!

'Well – let's get into our bags,' said Jack. 'Isn't the moon lovely tonight?'

'Nothing seems very nice when I think of Philip being captured,' said Lucy-Ann dismally. All the same, the moon was glorious, swinging up over the mountains, and making everywhere as light as day.

They were just about to slide into their bags when Lucy-Ann's sharp ears caught an unfamiliar sound.

'Listen!' she said. 'What's that? No, not a noise underground this time – somewhere up in the sky!'

They went out and stood on the flat rock, listening, their

faces upturned to the moonlit sky.

'What a peculiar noise!' said Jack. 'A bit like an aeroplane – but *not* an aeroplane. What *can* it be?'

15

Behind the green curtain

The noise came nearer. 'Like a motor-bike in the sky,' said Jack.

'Or a sewing-machine,' said Dinah. 'Jack, look! What's that? That tiny speck up there?'

Jack fumbled for his glasses, which were still round his neck. He put them to his eyes, straining to focus the little black speck up in the moonlight. It came nearer.

'Well – whatever it is I do believe it's going to land on this mountain!' said Dinah. 'Isn't it going slowly? *Is* it an aeroplane, Jack?'

'No,' said Jack. 'Gosh – it's a helicopter! You know – they are just the thing for travelling in mountains. They don't fly fast but they can land in a very small space – on a lawn, or a roof even!'

'A *heli*copter!' cried Dinah, and took the glasses from Jack. 'Let me see.'

It was now near enough for Dinah to be able to see it clearly with the glasses. Jack and Lucy-Ann watched it with screwed-up eyes. It hovered over the mountain-top, and then flew slowly round it, appearing in sight again after a few minutes.

It then flew up a little higher, and descended slowly, almost vertically, its engine making a curious sound in the night. Then there was silence.

'It's landed,' said Jack. 'But where? Gosh, I wouldn't like to land on a mountain as steep as this one.'

'Perhaps there is a proper landing-place,' said Lucy-Ann. 'Right on the very top!'

'Yes. There may be,' said Jack. 'What a thing to do, though – land a helicopter on the very summit of a mountain like this! What for?'

Nobody knew the answer to that.

'Well,' said Jack, at last, 'if that helicopter *did* land up on top, that would be one way of bringing food and stuff to the men who are at work inside the mountain – they'd have to have food, and there's no way of getting it round about here!'

'I feel as if all this must be a dream,' said Lucy-Ann, in a small voice. 'I don't like it at all. I wish I could wake up.'

'Come on – let's get into our bags,' said Jack. 'We can't *do* anything. We'll just have to wait for Bill. We can sleep out on the rock tonight, if you like. It's got very warm again, and we're snug enough in our bags.'

Nibbling bars of chocolate the three of them slipped into the bags. Kiki flew up into a near-by bush. She cleared her throat as David had often done. 'Look you, whateffer, look you, whateffer,' she began, meaning to have a little practice of the new words she had learnt.

'Kiki! Shut up!' said Jack.

'Whateffer!' said Kiki, and hiccuped very loudly. 'Pardon!' she gave a cackle of laughter and said no more for a moment. Then she took her head out from under her wing. 'Pifflebunk,' she said, delighted at having remembered it, and put her head back again.

Jack woke several times in the night wondering about Philip. He also puzzled his head to think how the whole company of dogs, men and boy could possibly have vanished as they did, under his very eyes. He felt that he really would have to go and explore that steep wall of rock the next day. Perhaps he would find out where the company had gone – and *how* it had gone.

'Do you think Bill will come today?' asked Lucy-Ann,

next morning. Jack reckoned up and shook his head. 'No – perhaps he will tomorrow, though, if David got back quickly, and Bill came at once. Still – if we go far away from the stream, we'd better leave a note for Bill, in case he comes and we're not there. Like we did yesterday.'

They had taken the note off Dapple's harness the night before, when they had brought the donkey back from the stream, up to their sleeping-rock. Now Jack set to work to write another. In it he told the story of Philip's disappearance by the wall of rock, and he also wrote about the helicopter he had seen. He had a feeling that he had better tell all he knew in case – just in *case* – something happened, and he and the girls were captured too. So many strange things had happened on this mountain. It was quite likely that if the man got out of Philip the fact that he had friends near by the mountain, they would send to capture them too.

He took Dapple back to the stream, putting him in the shade, in some long lush grass, and near enough to the stream to stand in it, or drink if he liked. Dapple liked this kind of life well enough, but he stared anxiously all around, missing Snowy. Where was his tiny friend?

'Snowy will come back soon, Dapple,' said Jack, rubbing his hand up and down the long grey nose. 'You wait and see!'

'What are we going to do today?' asked Lucy-Ann, when Jack came back. 'I don't feel like doing anything now Philip's gone!'

'Well, – would you like to come with me to the steep rocky wall the others went to last night?' said Jack. 'Just to see if we can find out how they disappeared so suddenly. But if you come we'll have to keep a jolly good lookout in case we're taken by surprise!'

Lucy-Ann looked as if she didn't want to come at all, but nothing would stop her being with Jack if she thought there was any likelihood of danger. If they were going to be taken by surprise, then she would be there too!

So, taking some tins with them in case they didn't feel inclined to go all the way back to the cave in the heat of the day for a meal, the three of them set off. Kiki flew over their heads, annoying the swallows, and crying 'Feetafeetit, feetafeetit!' just as they did. They took not the slightest notice of her, but went on with their fly-catching deftly and serenely.

The three came at last to the little copse of trees where they had swung in the wind the evening before. 'Wait here a minute,' said Jack, and he leapt up into a tree. 'I'll just have a look round to make sure the coast is clear.'

He balanced himself in branches near the top of the tree and swept the countryside around with his glasses. Not a sound was to be heard except the wind, the trees and the birds. There was no sign of any human being, or of any of the dogs.

'It seems all right,' said Jack when he got down to the foot of the tree again. 'We'll go. Come on.'

Kiki began to bray like Dapple, and Jack turned on her fiercely. 'Kiki! Stop it! Just when we want to be quiet! Bad bird! Silly bird!'

Kiki raised her crest up and down, snapped her beak angrily, and flew up into a tree. It was almost as if she had said 'All right then – if you speak to me like that, I won't come with you!' She sat on a branch sulking, keeping one eye on the three children walking towards the wall.

They reached it and looked upwards. It towered up, steep and sheer. Nobody could climb that, not even Snowy!

'Now where were the others when they disappeared?' said Jack. 'About here, I think.'

He led the way to an uneven slab of rock. Hanging down in front of it, over the rocky wall, was a thick curtain of greenery, half bramble, half creepers of some kind, all matted together.

The children thought this mass of green was actually growing on the wall, in the same way that many other little plants and ferns grew. It was only when the wind blew strongly, and the curtain-like mass swung backwards and forwards a little that Lucy-Ann guessed it wasn't growing out of the wall – it was hanging down, covering it!

She caught hold of it. It swung back like a curtain! Behind it was the wall, right enough – but there was a split in it, a great crack that reached up about twenty feet.

'Look!' said Lucy-Ann. 'This is a kind of curtain, Jack. And look at the big crack in the wall behind. Is this where they went yesterday?'

'Gosh, yes! They must all have gone quickly behind this curtain of creepers,' said Jack. 'And I thought they had vanished! Hold it up, Lucy-Ann. Let's see the crack. I bet they went through that!'

All three passed easily behind the swinging curtain of creeper and bramble. They could slip through the crack without any trouble at all. Once through it they found themselves in an immensely high cave, very round, and with no roof that could be seen, though Jack flashed his torch up as far as he could manage.

'It's like a hole in the mountain,' he said. 'It goes up goodness knows how high!'

'Did the others come in here?' asked Dinah, staring upwards. 'Where did they go then?'

'Can't think,' said Jack, puzzled. 'I say, look here – look what's in the middle of the floor! I almost went into it!'

He flashed his torch on to the floor of the cave – but there was hardly any floor to be seen! Most of it was taken up by a silent black pool, whose surface had no wrinkle or ripple!

'It's not a nice pool,' said Lucy-Ann, with a shudder.

'This is a most peculiar cave,' said Dinah. 'No roof – no floor – only a deep pool! And no sign of where the others went yesterday.'

'There must be *some* way out,' said Jack, quite determined to search until he found it. He began to walk all round the cave, flashing his torch on it, inch by inch. But there was no opening anywhere, not even a tiny hole. The walls were absolutely solid.

'Well, there's no passage leading out of *this* cave!' said Jack, giving it up. He glanced up to the roofless top of the cave. 'The only way is up there! But there are no footholds to climb up – nothing! Nobody could possibly climb up these steep walls.'

'Well then – is there a way out through the pool?' said Dinah, half in fun.

Jack looked at the black pool. 'No, I don't see how that pool can possibly contain a way out of this cave. Still – it's the only thing I haven't examined. I'll have a swim in it – or wade across!'

But it was too deep to wade. Jack took two steps and the water came over his knees. He stripped off his clothes and plunged in. Lucy-Ann didn't like it much. She watched Jack anxiously as he swam across and back.

'Can't feel the bottom at all,' said Jack, kicking out with his legs. 'Must be awfully deep. A bottomless pool and a roofless cave – sounds odd, doesn't it? I'm coming out now. The water's icy cold.'

He found his footing almost at the edge of the pool, slipped and went in again. He reached out to grasp the edge and his hand found something else. It felt like a small steering-wheel, a foot under the water!

Jack got out and dressed. He was shivering too much to do any more investigation till he had some clothes on. Then he knelt down by the edge of the pool and put his hand in to feel the curious wheel-like thing again.

'Hold my torch, Lucy-Ann,' he commanded. 'There's something odd here!'

Lucy-Ann held the torch in trembling fingers. What was Jack going to find? 'It's a little wheel,' he said. 'Why is it here? Well, wheels are meant to turn, so I'll turn it! Here goes!'

He turned it to the right. It ran easily. And then he jumped violently because both the girls screamed loudly and clutched him hard!

16

Inside the mountain

'What's the matter?' shouted Jack, jumping up. 'What's happened!'

Lucy-Ann had dropped the torch in her fright. The light went out and they were in darkness. She clutched at Jack again and startled him.

'Something touched me!' she whispered. 'Something ran its fingers all down me. Oh, Jack, what was it?'

'Yes, and me too,' said Dinah, in a trembling voice. 'I felt them. They touched my shoulder softly and then ran all the way down to my feet. What is it, Jack? There's something here. Let's get out.'

'Where's the torch?' said Jack impatiently. 'Oh, Lucy-Ann, I hope it isn't broken. You idiot, dropping it like that.'

He groped about for it on the floor and found it. Luckily it hadn't rolled into the pool. He shook it and the light came on. Everyone was very thankful.

'Now what touched you?' demanded Jack. 'Nothing touched *me*!'

'I don't know,' said Lucy-Ann. 'I want to get out of here, Jack. I'm frightened.'

Jack swung his torch round behind the girls. He saw something that made him cry out in surprise. The girls didn't dare to look. They clung to him, trembling.

'See what touched you? A rope-ladder falling down just behind you!' laughed Jack. 'Well, what a surprise! You'd never dream of that!'

Dinah pulled herself together at once, and forced herself to laugh. 'Well! Fancy that! I really did think it was somebody touching me. It felt just like it.'

'It must just have run down quietly behind you from somewhere up high,' said Jack, flashing his torch upwards, and following the ladder with the beam as far as he could. 'Well, you made *me* jump all right when you yelled. I almost went head-first into the pool!'

'It happened when you turned that wheel down there,' said Lucy-Ann, still shivering a little.

'Yes. A very clever little idea,' said Jack. 'I must say this is a jolly well-hidden entrance to the mountain – better even than Ali Baba's cave! First there's the green curtain. Then just a crack in the rock. Then you come in and see nothing but a black pool and a roofless cave. Most people would just say, "How odd!" and go out again!'

'Yes. They would never, never guess about the ladder that comes tumbling down when you turn the wheel hidden so cleverly in the water,' agreed Dinah. 'Most ingenious, all of it. Somebody with brains lives in this mountain!'

'Yes,' said Jack thoughtfully. 'Brains that work and produce minor earthquakes and crimson smoke, and plan for landing-grounds for helicopters on mountain-tops – and keep packs of Alsatians that would terrorize anyone roaming too near the mountain. Very remarkable brains! I wonder exactly what those brains are after!'

The girls stared at him in the dimly lit cave, with the black pool glinting up at them. Jack sounded very serious. He felt serious too. There was something very strange about all this. Something very clever. Much too clever. What *could* be going on?

He stared up the ladder. He felt very much inclined to go up it. He longed to see what was inside the mountain – and he wanted to find Philip again too. Then a hollow voice made them all jump violently.

'Naughty boy! Pifflebunk!'

'It's Kiki,' said Jack, relieved. 'You wretched bird, you made me jump! What do you think of this cave, Kiki?'

'Pifflebunk,' repeated Kiki, and made a noise like a mowing-machine. It sounded terrible in that roofless cave. The noise seemed to go up and up endlessly. Kiki enjoyed the sound. She began all over again.

'Be quiet,' said Jack. 'Goodness knows what will happen if your noises arrive at the top of this ladder, and somebody hears them!'

'You're not going up, are you, Jack?' asked Lucy-Ann, afraid, as she saw Jack place a foot on the lowest rung of the rope-ladder.

'Yes. I'll just go up to the top and see what's there and come down again,' said Jack. 'I don't expect there'll be anyone on guard, because nobody would ever dream of us guessing the secret of getting the ladder down. You two go out into the sunshine and wait for me.'

'No. We're coming too,' said Lucy-Ann. They had lost Philip. She wasn't going to lose Jack! So she and Dinah began to climb up behind him.

The ladder was well made and strong. It swung to and fro a little as the three of them climbed it. Up they went, and up and up. There seemed no end to it!

'I'm stopping for a rest,' whispered Jack. 'You stop too. It's frightfully tiring, this.'

They clung to the rungs and rested, panting a little with their long climb. Lucy-Ann didn't like to think how far away the foot of the cave was. Nor did she like to think how far away the top of the ladder was!

They went on again. It was pitch dark, for Jack had put away his torch, needing both hands to climb with. Lucy-Ann began to feel that she was in a peculiarly horrid nightmare – one in which she would have to climb ladders in the dark until she awoke in the morning!

'I say – I can see a dim sort of light now,' whispered Jack. 'I believe we must be coming to the top. Don't make any noise.'

They got to the top just as Lucy-Ann felt that her arms would not hold on to the ladder any longer. As Jack said, there was a dim light there. He climbed off on to a rocky floor, and the girls followed. They all lay panting for a few minutes, unable even to look round and see where they were.

Jack recovered first. He sat up and gazed round him. He was in a little chamber, lighted by a dim lamp. Big stone jugs full of what looked like water stood at the back, with mugs near by. Jack's eyes gleamed. Just what they wanted after their terrible climb! He fetched a jug and three mugs and the three of them drank deeply of the ice-cold water.

'Now I feel better,' said Jack, with a sigh. He put back the jug and mugs. There was nothing else to see in the room at all. At the far end was an open passage-way, leading into the heart of the mountain.

Jack went to it. Lucy-Ann called softly to him. 'Jack! Aren't you coming back? You said you'd only go to the top and look!'

'Well, I'm looking,' said Jack. 'There's a narrow passage here. Come and see. I wonder where it leads to.'

The girls went to see. Jack wandered along a little way and the girls followed, not liking to be left alone. They came to another dim lamp, set on a rocky shelf in the passage wall. Jack went on and on, following the winding passage, coming to lamp after lamp that lighted the way.

'Come back now,' whispered Lucy-Ann, pulling at his sleeve. 'We've gone far enough.'

But Jack felt that he couldn't possibly go back now. Why, he might meet Philip round the next corner! So on he went.

They came to a forking of the passage, which suddenly divided into three. The children stopped, wondering where the three passages led to. They all looked exactly the same to them.

And then, out of one passage capered somebody they knew very well indeed. It was Snowy!

The kid was as delighted to see them as they were to see him. He butted them all, rubbed his nose into their hands, and bleated joyfully. Jack felt pleased.

'We'll follow Snowy,' he said to the girls. 'He'll lead us to Philip!'

So they let the little kid dance in front of them, leading the way. He led them down the passage, into a vast, hall-like cave, into another passage, and then, to their great surprise, they came to a most amazing place.

It was like a vast laboratory, a work-room set in the heart of the mountain. It lay below them, and they had to lean over a little gallery to look at it.

'What is it?' whispered Lucy-Ann, awed at the amount of curious things there. There was no enormous machinery – only a vast network of gleaming wires, great glass jars standing together, crystal boxes in which sparks and flames shot up and down, and rows upon rows of silently spinning wheels that shone strangely as they spun. The wires ran from these all over the place.

In the middle of the work-room shone a curious lamp. It had many sides, and it glowed first one colour and then another. Sometimes it was so dazzling that the children could hardly look at it. Sometimes it died down to a faint red, green or blue glow. It seemed alive – a monster eye that watched over everything in that secret laboratory.

The children gazed, fascinated. There was nobody there at all. Everything seemed to work on its own, never stopping. The wheels spun round, the wires gleamed, and nothing made any noise beyond a very quiet humming.

And then – and then there began that faint, far-off rumbling they knew so well. Far below the laboratory, deep

deep down, came a stirring and a groaning, as something happened in the depths of the mountain. Then, as had happened before, the mountain quivered a little, and shook, as if something tremendous had happened deep underground.

The great lamp in the middle suddenly grew bright, so bright that the children crouched back afraid. It grew crimson, the brightest crimson they had ever seen in their lives. It began to belch out tiny puffs of crimson smoke.

Jack began to choke. He pushed the girls back into the passage, and they breathed the fresher air there in relief. Snowy, frightened, crouched against them.

'That's the smoke we saw coming out of a hole in the side of the mountain,' whispered Jack. 'There must be a chimney-pipe built from that lamp, right away up the mountain to the hole, where the smoke can escape.'

'What's going on, do you think?' asked Dinah, in awe. 'What's all that wire for, and the crystal boxes and things?'

'I haven't the least idea,' said Jack. 'But it's plain that it's something very secret, or they'd never do all this here, in this lonely, inaccessible place.'

'Atom bombs or something, do you think?' asked Lucy-Ann, with a shiver.

'Oh, no – you want enormous buildings for that,' said Jack. 'No – it's something very odd and unusual, I should think. Let's go back and peep.'

They went back, but everything was just as it had been, the wheels spinning silently, the crystal boxes sparking and flaming up and down inside, the great lamp watching like an eye, now crimson, now blue, now green, now orange.

'Let's go round the gallery and see where it goes to,' whispered Jack. 'I feel as if I'm in some sort of Aladdin's cave now – the Slave of the Ring might appear at any moment!'

They wandered on and came to another extraordinary place. It was really only a high-roofed cave – but it was made into a great, sumptuous hall, with flights of steps leading up to what looked like a throne. Beautiful hangings hung down the walls from the roof, which glittered with shining lamps shaped like stars.

The floor was laid with a golden carpet, and ranged on each side were beautiful chairs. The children stared in astonishment.

'Whatever's all this?' whispered Dinah. 'Does some king live here? The king of the mountain!'

17

Philip again

'It's peculiar there's nobody about at all,' said Jack, staring round at the silent hall. 'Not a soul to be seen! I wonder where everyone is. All those wheels and wires and things whirring away busily by themselves, with nobody to see to them – and now this great empty place, with its throne and gorgeous hangings!'

'Jack!' said Dinah, pulling at his sleeve. 'Can't we find Philip now and rescue him? We've only got to go back through those long passages and down the rope-ladder! Snowy will take us to Philip, and we can take him safely to the entrance of the mountain.'

'Yes. That's a good idea,' said Jack. He stroked the little white kid by his side. 'Where's Philip?' he whispered, and gave Snowy a push. 'You show us, Snowy.'

Snowy butted Jack gently. He didn't seem to know what the boy meant. Jack gave it up after a bit. 'We'll wait and see if Snowy goes off by himself,' he said. 'If he does, we'll follow him.'

So they waited. Snowy soon became restive and set off down the big hall past the great throne. The children followed cautiously, keeping by the walls, as far in the shadows as possible. Snowy disappeared through some deep red curtains. The children peeped through them. On the other side was what looked like a small library. Books lined the walls. The children looked at the titles curiously. They could not understand what any of them meant. Most of them were in foreign languages, and all of them looked very learned and difficult.

'Scientific books,' said Jack. 'Come on. Snowy has gone through that opening.'

They followed him. He saw that they were coming and waited for them. They hoped he was taking them to Philip!

He was! He led them upwards through a curiously rounded tunnel-like passage, lit at intervals by the same kind of dim lamps they had seen in the first passages. It was weird going along in the half-dark, not able to see very far in front or behind. Snowy trotted in front like a little white ghost.

They passed big openings filled with what looked like stores of some kind. Boxes, chest, packages of all kinds were there, flung in higgledy-piggledy.

Jack paused to examine some. There were foreign labels on most of them. One had been opened, showing tins of food.

'Look,' said Jack, 'it's what I said. They have their food brought here – by the helicopter, I expect. I wonder what in the world they're up to.'

They came to some steps hewn out of the rock itself. These led upwards rather steeply in a spiral. Snowy bounded up lightly, but the others panted as they went up and up, twisting and turning with the spiral of the stairway.

They came to a door set fast in the side of the stone stairway. It was a stout wooden door, with great bolts on the outside. Snowy stopped beside this door and bleated loudly.

Then the children's hearts jumped as they heard a familiar

voice. 'Snowy! I'm still here! I can't get to you, Snowy, but never mind!'

'That's Philip!' said Jack. He knocked gently on the door. 'Philip! It's us! We're going to undo the bolts of this door.'

There was an astonished exclamation, and the sound of feet running across to the door. Then Philip's excited voice came through the door, eager and thrilled.

'Gosh, Jack! Is it really you? Can you let me out?'

Jack shot the bolts back. They were well oiled and went back easily. Philip pulled him into the space beyond as soon as the door was open. The girls followed too, with Snowy.

'Jack! How did you get here? I've been shut in this strange place with that black man. Look, there he is over there. He sleeps most of the time. He's the one the dogs were after.'

Sure enough, there was the man, lying against the side of the cave, fast asleep. Jack and the girls looked round Philip's prison in wonder.

It was nothing but a cave in the side of the top of the mountain. It opened on to the sky . . . or so it seemed! At first the children could see nothing but a vast expanse of blue when they gazed out of the opening opposite to the door.

'It's almost at the top, this cave,' said Jack. 'Isn't it a miraculous view? You can see right over the tops of the mountains yonder. I've never been so high in my life before. It makes me quite giddy to look out for long.'

Dinah stepped to the edge of the cave but Philip pulled her back. 'No, don't go too near. There's an almost sheer drop there. And if you look down it makes you feel very strange – as if you're on top of the world and might fall any minute!'

'Hold my hand then, whilst I look,' said Dinah, and Jack wanted to see too.

'Lie down on the floor of the cave and look out of it that way,' said Philip. 'You feel safer then.'

So all four lay down and peered over the edge of the cave

that was almost at the top of the mountain. It certainly gave them a curious feeling. Far far down below were the slopes of the mountain, and far below that the valley. Lucy-Ann clutched Philip tightly. She felt as if she was toppling over downwards! But she wasn't, of course. She was safe on the floor of the cave. It was just the terrific feeling of height that made her think she must be falling down and down!

'I don't like it,' she said, and came away from the ledge. The others were awed. They gazed until they too felt that they were going to fall, and then they pushed themselves back and sat up.

'Come with us quickly,' said Jack to Philip. 'We know the way out – and Snowy will guide us if we don't! We must go whilst there's a good chance. The whole place seems deserted. It's most peculiar.'

'Well, the men live on the very top of the mountain,' said Philip. 'The American has been telling me quite a lot. This cave is very near the top – so near that I can sometimes hear men talking and laughing. There must be a plateau on the summit – or some kind of flat place – because the helicopters land there.'

'Oh! Well, I suppose everyone must be up on the mountain-top then!' said Jack. 'We didn't meet a soul coming up here. Come on, let's go, Philip. Don't let's waste a minute. We can tell each other everything when we're safely out of this extraordinary mountain.'

They all went to the door – and then Jack pushed the others back quickly. He shut the door quietly and put his finger to his lips.

'I can hear voices!'

So could the others. Loud voices that were coming nearer their door. Would the owners of the voices spot that the bolts were undone?

The voices came nearer and nearer – and then passed! Evidently nobody had looked at the bolts of the door. The children breathed again.

'Thank goodness! They've gone past!' said Jack. 'Shall we wait for a few minutes and then run for it?'

'No. Wait till the men come back and go up to the roof,' said Philip. 'I think they are only the paratroopers gone to get some stores to take up to the top.'

Everyone stared at him. '*Para*-troopers!' said Jack, in amazement. 'What do you mean? Why should there be paratroopers here?'

'This chap told me. His name's Sam,' said Philip, nodding towards the sleeping man. 'Let's wait till those fellows come back with their stores, or whatever they've gone to fetch. I don't think they'll even look at this door. They don't know I'm here!'

'Well – for goodness' sake tell us all about everything then,' said Jack, filled with intense curiosity. 'Paratroopers! It sounds impossible.'

'Well, you know when I was caught, don't you?' began Philip. 'They took me to that steep wall, behind a thick screen of creeper, and in at an opening there. I was pushed up some kind of ladder in the dark – a rope-ladder, I should think, – and we went up for ages and ages.'

The others nodded. They knew all about that.

'We went through long passages, and came to a jolly frightening place – with wheels and things. . . . Did you see it too?'

'Yes. Most extraordinary. But there was no one there,' said Jack.

'I didn't have time to see much,' said Philip. 'Then we went round a gallery – the one that looks down on that place of wheels and wires and sparks and flames – and came into a most magnificent place – like a room out of a palace!'

'Yes – we saw it too. A room for a king, with throne and all,' said Jack. 'But nobody there!'

'Well, then I was pushed up passages and steps to this cave,' said Philip. 'And I was bolted in, and here I've stayed ever since! This man was pushed in too – but poor little

Snowy was bolted out! He's come and bleated outside my door dozens of times. I hated that. He sounded so lost and miserable.'

Snowy was very happy now, however! He was curled up on Philip's knee, occasionally butting him gently to get a little more attention.

'I've had food pushed in through the door – all tinned stuff,' said Philip. 'But nobody's said a word to me, not even that nasty foreign-looking fellow who caught me. You should see his eyes! You often read in books about people with piercing eyes. Well, he's *really* got them – they go right through you! I was glad he didn't question me much, because I felt as if he'd know everything by reading my very thoughts.'

The others had been listening intently. Jack nodded towards the sleeping man. 'What did he tell you?'

'Oh, a lot of peculiar things,' said Philip. 'He said he saw an advertisement in the paper asking for men who had been paratroopers – you know, men who are trained to jump out of planes high in the air, and parachute to earth.'

'Yes. Go on,' said Jack, impatiently.

'Well, the hawk-eyed man – the one who captured me – he goes by the name of Meier by the way – interviewed him at some office in Mexico, and offered him a terrific sum of money if he'd come and try some new kind of parachute-jumping.'

'What kind?' asked Dinah.

'I don't exactly know. Sam sounded a bit muddled when he told me – or else I didn't understand him,' said Philip. 'It's something to do with flying through the air on *wings* – wings fixed to his arms. Apparently you can't possibly fall to earth when you've got these wings on, and you can guide yourself where and how you like – just as birds do.'

'That's impossible,' said Jack at once. 'Quite mad.'

'Yes. That's why I think Sam got hold of the wrong idea,' said Philip. 'Well – this fellow Meier engaged a whole lot of ex-paratroopers, paid them fabulous sums, and brought them here, in helicopters, to the top of this mountain. And their job is to try out these wings – or so Sam says.'

'Has he tried them?' asked Jack.

'No. But three of his mates have. They had these peculiar wings fitted to their arms and were given orders to jump from the helicopter at a given moment – or else be pushed out,' said Philip.

'What happened?' asked Jack.

'Sam doesn't know,' answered Philip. 'You see, none of his mates came back. He's pretty certain they fell to their death. *He* didn't want to do the same – so he got away.'

18

A little exploring

There was a long pause after this strange story. It was very hard to believe – and yet they had seen and heard such strange things the last few days that they felt anything might be true of this lonely mountain.

'But what's the idea?' asked Jack, after a while. 'And why all the wheels and wires and things? I just don't get the hang of it all.'

'Nor do I. But Sam reckons that if the experiment came off, and men could really fly with these wings, somebody would make a most colossal fortune!' said Philip. 'Everyone would want them. Everyone would fly.'

'It sounds lovely,' said Lucy-Ann. 'I should love to fly like the birds do – much, much better than going in an aeroplane!'

They all felt the same – but nobody could really believe in these 'wings' that Sam had talked of.

'How did he escape?' asked Jack, nodding at the black man.

'He did an absolutely mad thing – as dangerous as

jumping off a helicopter to try the "wings," said Philip. 'He got a parachute out of the stores, came in here, fitted it on – and jumped!'

Everyone shuddered. 'What! Jumped out of this cave, right from the top of the mountain?' said Jack. 'Gosh, he's a brave man!'

'He is. His parachute opened, and he floated down to earth, landing with an awful bump. But of course he'd learnt how to fall, and he soon recovered. The next thing was – to find safety somewhere.'

'He couldn't have found a lonelier, more deserted bit of country than in these mountains,' said Jack. 'I suppose he didn't even know where he was.'

'He hadn't the faintest idea,' said Philip. 'I told him we were in Wales – but he didn't know where that was.'

'And then the dogs got after him, I suppose?' said Jack. 'Poor Sam!'

'Yes. He knew about them, because they live up on the mountain-top with the men. He says they're used to scare any possible wanderer who comes near this mountain – and, of course, to hunt anyone who does escape – or find anyone who crashes if the wings don't work.'

'That's more likely,' said Jack. 'Gosh, what a horrible, callous lot of men there must be behind all this! I never heard of anything like it in my life.'

'Sam says there's a king,' said Philip. 'The king of the mountain! Isn't it incredible? That throne must be for him. Sam's never seen him. He must be the spider at work, catching all these fellows and making them try out his mad experiments.'

'We thought there was some colossal brain behind all this,' said Jack. 'I suppose that hawk-eyed man – Meier – isn't the king, is he?'

'Oh, no! I don't know what you'd call him – sort of organizer, I suppose. He sees to everything – the stores – all the arrangements – shuts up the men when the helicopters arrive – and so on. There are two men, apparently, who work together on these things. The king is somebody who only appears on state occasions – such as when another pair of wings is produced, and the men have to go down to that great stateroom, listen to some speech they don't understand, and watch one of their number being picked to try out the wings.'

'Picking out a victim for sacrifice, it sounds like!' said Jack grimly. 'I don't like this at all. It's so *mad*.'

'Sam was ill the last time the king picked out his victims,' said Philip. 'So he hasn't seen the king of the mountain, as I said. He must be a twisted sort of chap – really callous and cruel, to make these fellows try out wings that can't possibly be any good.'

'I agree with you!' said Jack. 'And I think the sooner we get out of here and get into touch with old Bill the better. I don't feel safe in this mountain. No wonder Lucy-Ann got "feelings" about it. I've got quite a lot of feelings about it myself now!'

'Look – Sam's waking up,' said Lucy-Ann. They all looked at the man. He sat up, and rubbed his eyes. He looked across the cave and seemed surprised to see so many children.

Then he recognized Lucy-Ann as the little girl who had seen him up in the tree. He smiled, and then shook his head.

'Didn't I tell you to git away,' said Sam, looking solemn. 'This here is a bad mountain. Those men are bad, too.'

'We're going now, Sam,' said Philip. 'As soon as we think it's safe. Will you come too? We know the way out.'

Sam looked frightened. 'I'm scared of those dogs,' he said. 'I reckon I'm safe right here.'

'You're not. I bet you'll be the very next one chosen to try out the "wings" you told me about,' said Philip.

'The wings're better than those dogs,' said Sam.

Voices came past the door. The children fell silent and listened till they had gone past. Sam listened too.

'That was Pete and Jo,' he said.

'Well, Pete and Jo have gone up to the mountain-top again,' said Jack. 'Come on. It seems a good time to go now. We didn't meet anyone coming here – and the chances are we shan't meet anyone going back. What a tale we'll have to tell Bill!'

They opened the door cautiously. Snowy bounded out at once. Kiki was on Jack's shoulder, having kept silent for a surprisingly long time. She did not seem to like this peculiar mountain!

They went quietly down the spiral stairway, following its many turns round and round. They came to the openings where the stores were kept. It made them feel very hungry to see all the tins of food; but there was no time to think of eating now. They had to escape as quickly as possible.

Snowy led them down the dimly lit passages. The children expected to see the curious library of books at the end of them, but Snowy had apparently taken them a different way. They stopped after a while in dismay.

'I say – this isn't right. We didn't see that cave there before – I'm sure we didn't!' said Jack. They hesitated, not knowing whether to go on or go back. It would be awful to get lost in the heart of the mountain!

'I can hear some kind of noises,' said Lucy-Ann, listening. 'Let's creep on and see what they are.'

They went on down a wide passage that at times ran very steeply downhill. The air suddenly grew hot.

'Phew!' said Philip, mopping his forehead. 'I can hardly breathe.'

They came out on a kind of balcony that overlooked a great deep pit, so vast that it took the children's breath away. Far down in the middle of it men were at work, though what they were doing the children couldn't possibly tell. They were as small as ants.

Great lamps lit up the pit. The children gazed in astonishment. What *could* be going on down there?

Suddenly Jack nudged Philip. 'Look – the men have slid aside the floor of the pit – do you see? What's that under it?'

Philip might well ask! Out of the hole in the pit floor shone a brilliant mass of colour – but a colour the children did not know! It was not blue or green, not red or yellow, not any colour they had ever seen before. They gaped at it in surprise.

Then, suddenly they felt a curious feeling – a feeling of lightness, as if they were in a dream, and not quite real. They clutched the balcony rail, afraid. At the same moment the men down below slid the great floor over the hole in the pit again, and shut out the brilliant mass of unknown colour. At once the strange feeling passed away from the children, and they were themselves once more.

They felt a little weak. 'Let's go,' said Jack, scared. 'I don't like this.'

But before they could go there began that now familiar rumbling noise from the very depths of the mountain! The children clung to one another. It was so much louder now that they were *inside* the mountain. It was louder than thunder, an angry, unearthly noise. Then the balcony they were on began to shake.

Jack took one last look down into the strange pit. The men had disappeared – probably hidden safely behind rocky walls. Jack caught Lucy-Ann's hand and fled! After him came Philip and Dinah. Kiki clung to Jack's shoulder, more scared than any of them. Snowy had disappeared completely.

The four children tore up the steep wide passage that had led them down to the pit. The floor of it shook beneath their feet as they ran. The children felt sure that the whole of the great mountain was shaking. What powers were being used by these men? Surely they must have discovered some scientific secret unknown to anyone before!

The children did not stop running until they came to the end of the uphill passage. They were streaming with perspiration, and panting loudly. Snowy suddenly joined them and pressed against Philip's legs. All four children sank down in a heap and Snowy walked over them unheeded.

'For goodness' *sake* let's get out of here,' said Philip at last. 'I daresay if we were scientists we shouldn't be a bit scared, only intensely interested – but all I can say is – let's get out of here!'

Everyone agreed heartily. The only thing was – which was the way? They got up and walked along a twisty little passage. It forked into two after a bit, and the children, not knowing which to take, took the right-hand one. It led them to a cell-like cave with a narrow bed in it, a jug and basin, and a shelf. Nothing more.

'Funny!' said Jack. 'I expect it belongs to Meier, or one of the other men. Let's go back.'

They went back to where the passage forked, and took the left-hand way. To their great surprise they came to hanging curtains of purple silk, patterned with great red dragons!

They stopped. Philip put his hand on Snowy to prevent him from darting forward. Jack crept to the curtains on tiptoe.

Beyond was a cave so beautifully decorated, so profusely hung with curtains and spread with thick carpets that it didn't seem like a cave at all. A couch stood in one corner, covered with a purple silk quilt, worked with the same red dragons as on the curtains they had seen.

Jack stared. Perhaps this was where the king slept. It felt deliciously cool there. Where did the little cooling draught come from? He saw a narrow rod hanging on the wall near him, with slits in it all the way along. He put his hand up and felt a draught of air. How astonishing! It was only a rod fixed to the wall. How could fresh air come out of it? Again Jack felt that there were remarkably ingenious brains at work in this mountain.

He heard voices from a room further on, whose opening was hidden by the same kind of purple curtains that hung in other places. He tiptoed back to the others.

'We'll wait for a bit. There's somebody talking in the room beyond this one. This is the king's bedroom, I should think.'

They waited, peeping through the curtains every now and then. They all began to feel terribly hungry. They were very relieved when the voices stopped and there was silence. They tiptoed through the bedroom and into the room beyond.

They stopped in delight – not at the strange beauty of the room – but at the gorgeous food on the table!

19

The king of the mountain

'Look at that!' said Jack. 'Somebody's been having a meal here – three people – and look at what they've left!'

'Can't we have some?' said Lucy-Ann, eyeing a great bowl of fresh strawberries and a jug half full of cream. Near by was a plate of cooked lobsters, and two dishes of mixed salads.

It was clear that three people had been having a meal there, judging by the plates and glasses, all of which were really beautiful.

'I call this a feast – a royal feast!' said Dinah, and she picked up a cake with cream icing on the top in the shape of a rose, and dug her teeth into it. 'I don't know who this stuff belongs to – but there's nobody to ask permission to share it – and I'm too hungry to wait!'

'So am I! We'll get Bill to pay for it if anyone objects,' said Jack, and set to work on a lobster. There were dishes of things the children had never seen before. They tasted one or two, but they were spiced in a way they disliked.

There were peaches and nectarines, pineapples and plums of all kinds. 'The helicopter must be pretty busy bringing all these!' said Philip, biting into the sweetest peach he had ever tasted in his life. 'I must say the King of this mountain does himself proud!'

Nobody came to interrupt them at all. Kiki feasted well, enjoying the food as much as the children. Snowy ate all the salad offered him, and for a treat was allowed to be on Philip's knee, with his forefeet on the table. He badly wanted to get on the table itself, and could not understand why Kiki was allowed there when he wasn't.

'If you eat any more, Kiki, you'll get the hiccups properly!' said Jack. 'Stuffing yourself like that! Greedy!'

'Pop goes Polly,' agreed Kiki, and would have given a cackle of laughter if Jack hadn't shushed her.

'Well – what about trying to find our way out again?' said Jack at last. 'I don't know whether it's anything to do with that strange feeling we had when the floor of the big pit was pushed back, and we saw that extraordinary mass of brilliance below – but I feel rather don't-carish now – not scared any more. I don't even feel that it's terribly urgent to get out of here, though I know it is!'

'It was a very unusual feeling,' said Philip. 'I thought I was going to float up into the air the next minute! I hung on to that balcony for dear life!'

They had all felt the same – and now they felt as Jack did – very 'don't-carish.' But that wouldn't do at all – it was imperative that they should find their way out as soon as possible.

They left the curious dining-room, with its laden table. They went into a passage that was much more brightly lit than the others they had walked down. Hangings decorated the rocky walls, great curtains that swayed a little in the draught that ran through the passages.

'This must be the king's own quarters,' said Jack. 'Maybe we shall come to the throne-room soon.'

He was quite right. They did. But this time the throne-room was not empty. It was full!

Men stood there silently. There were all kinds and a tough-looking lot they were! They were of many nationalities. Some had the maroon beret that paratroopers have when in uniform. The peeping children thought that probably they were all old paratroopers. There were about twenty of them. Sam was there too, and Philip gave a little start when he saw him. Now it would be known that he, Philip, had escaped! Whoever had gone to bring Sam down here would have seen the unbolted door and found that he was gone.

Blow! Now he would be carefully hunted for, and it would be very difficult to escape. He nudged Jack and pointed out Sam to him. Jack, peeping through the curtains that hung before them, nodded and frowned. The same thought occurred to him as had occurred to Philip.

He debated whether to go off straight away now and try to find the way out. But either they would have to go back the way they had just come, which obviously would not take them to the entrance they knew – or else they would have to go into the throne-room – where they would certainly be seen. No – they would have to stop where they were till this meeting, or whatever it was, was over.

Besides the paratroopers there were guards, men who looked like soldiers standing in an elaborate uniform down each side of the great hall. The throne was empty. There was no sign of the man Meier.

But suddenly there came a whispering among the men gathered there. The great curtains near the throne were flung back by two soldiers and the king of the mountain entered!

He seemed very tall, for he had a great crown that stood up from his head, embroidered with glittering stones. He wore a rich suit and cloak, and looked more like an Indian prince at some splendid festival than anything else. He yellowish face looked out impassively from below his great crown, and a mass of black hair swung down on each side. He sat down on the throne.

Beside him stood two men. Philip was sure that one was Meier. He didn't know the other, but he didn't like the ape-like face and enormous, burly figure. Meier's hawk-like eyes swept the room. He began to speak in a penetrating, most incisive voice, in a language that the children did not know. Then he paused and spoke in English.

The children listened, spell-bound. Meier spoke of the king and the wonderful gift he was giving to mankind – the gift of flying. He spoke of the grand men who were helping them in their experiment – the paratroopers willing to try the 'wings.' He spoke of the great wealth the men would receive, the honours that would be piled on them. Then he said it all again in a third language and then in a fourth.

He seemed to hypnotize everyone as he spoke. Jack could not help feeling that a lot he said was sheer nonsense – but he couldn't do anything but believe it whilst he heard it, and it was obvious that all the men there drank every word in, whether it was spoken in their own language or not. What a spell-binder, thought Jack!

Then volunteers were called for. All the men stepped forward at once. The king then rose and, apparently at random, picked out two or three. He spoke a few inaudible words in an unexpectedly thin, reedy voice, that didn't seem to go at all with his kingly presence.

Then Meier took charge again. He said that these men, among the first to fly with wings, would be sent back to their own countries after the experiment, with wealth enough to last them for a lifetime. All the others who had tried out the wings were now safely back in their homes, and were rich and honoured men.

'I *don't* think!' muttered Jack to Philip, remembering what Sam had related.

The king then walked majestically out and Meier and the

other man followed. The guards ushered the paratroopers away and soon the great throne-room was empty.

When everyone had gone and there was complete silence, Jack whispered to Philip, 'We know the way out from here. Come on!'

They went to the huge laboratory, where the wheels and wires were still at their secret work. The children stood in the gallery above the big work-room and looked down at the strange lamp in the middle. Dinah suddenly clutched Jack and made him jump. He looked at her.

She pointed to where there was a great cluster of glass jars, with tubes running from one to the other. Jack saw somebody there.

It was an old man with a very large forehead, larger and rounder than any forehead Jack had seen in his life. The man was quite bald, which made his head seem more curious than ever. He bent over the glass jars and looked searchingly into them.

'Come on before he sees us,' whispered Jack, and pulled the others towards the passages that would lead them to the entrance. They went along them and at last came to the little chamber where the pitchers of water and the mugs were. Now to get down the rope-ladder and escape!

'What about Snowy?' whispered Dinah. 'How can we get him down?'

'I wonder how he got up before?' said Philip. 'And the dogs too. I never thought of that. I was just pushed up in the dark, and I was so scared I didn't think of Snowy or the dogs. They couldn't have climbed that ladder!'

'There's probably some hole somewhere that they went into,' said Dinah. 'A hole outside, I mean – too small for us, but big enough for Snowy and the dogs.'

As it turned out afterwards, Dinah was right. There *was* a small hole near the crack, and it was through this and up a narrow little tunnel that Snowy had passed with the dogs, who knew the way very well. The dogs' tunnel led eventually into one of the passages, and that was how Snowy had got into the mountain but had not been imprisoned with Philip.

Snowy was still with them. He knew the way he had come in by, but he wasn't going to leave the others. Jack switched on his torch and felt above for the rope-ladder.

'Where is the wretched thing?' he said. 'Surely it was just here!'

Snowy came and pressed close to him, and nearly sent him headlong down to the black pool. 'Hold Snowy!' he said to Philip. 'I almost went over then. I can't seem to find the ladder. It should be hanging down somewhere about here.'

'Let *me* look,' said Philip, giving Snowy to Dinah. He felt about too, and Jack flashed his torch all round and about to see if he could spy the rope-ladder up which they had all come.

But it wasn't there – or if it was, nobody could see it! Jack flashed his torch down into the hole as far as he could. No ladder at all!

'What's happened to it?' he said, exasperated.

'Perhaps someone has turned that little wheel in the pond the *other* way – and the ladder rolled up and put itself away,' suggested Dinah.

This was a dreadful thought. Jack began to look round the little chamber to see if the rope-ladder had been pulled up by the machinery set in motion by the wheel – but he couldn't see it anywhere.

His hand touched a spike on the wall. He focused his torch on it. 'This may be a lever!' he said to the others. 'Look!'

He pulled and pressed at the spike, and it suddenly gave way, pulling downwards. A slab of rock was moved smoothly – and there behind was the rope-ladder! How it worked with the wheel below the children could not imagine.

It certainly wouldn't work with them. It was evidently

coiled or folded neatly in the hollow behind the rock – but how to get it from there nobody could make out. It needed some machinery put in motion to set it free. Then, Jack supposed, it would come sliding smoothly out of the place it was in, fall over the edge of the rock, and uncoil all the way to the bottom – hanging ready for any climber to come up.

'How does it work from up here though?' said Jack, for the twentieth time. All of them had pulled and twisted and tugged at the ladder, lying so snugly in its hiding-place – but it was quite impossible to move it.

'Give it up!' said Jack gloomily at last. 'No good! We're done for. It's absolutely maddening, just when we are almost out of this beastly mountain.'

20

An amazing secret

They sat in the little room for some time, disappointed and puzzled. Time and again they tried to make the rope-ladder slide out of its secret place, but it wouldn't. In the end they got very thirsty and very hungry. They drank all the water left in the jugs, and wondered where they could get something to eat.

They could only think of the room where they had feasted before. 'Let's go back to it and see if the remains of that meal are still there,' said Jack. 'I could do with another lobster or two!'

'Poor Polly!' remarked Kiki, who always seemed to know when food was being talked about. 'Polly's got a cold. Send for the doctor.'

'Oh, you've found your tongue again, have you?' said Jack. 'I thought you'd lost it! Now don't start screaming or cackling, for goodness' sake, or you'll have us caught!'

They found their way back to the throne-room, which was still empty, and then to the room where the meal had been.

There were still the remains of the meal there. The children's eyes gleamed. Good! They felt better at once.

They sat down and reached for the food. Then suddenly Jack put his hand on Philip's arm and frowned. A noise had come from the next room – the beautifully furnished bedroom! The children sat as still as mice. Was anybody there?

Kiki suddenly saw Snowy with his front hooves on the table, reaching for the salad. In anger she flew at the kid and screeched.

'That's done it!' said Jack. And as he spoke, the hangings at the entrance to the room opened, and a face peered through.

It was the face they had seen down in the big work-room – the face with the enormous forehead. It had bulging eyes of a curious green-blue, a hooked nose, and sunken cheeks, yellowish in colour.

This face stared in silence at the four children, and they, in turn, stared back without a word. Who was this strange old man with the great forehead?

'Do I know who you are?' asked the face, a puzzled look coming over it. 'I forget, I forget.' The curtains were swung further apart and the old man came right through. He was dressed in a kind of loose tunic of blue silk, and the children thought he looked a pathetic old thing. He had a thin high voice that Kiki immediately copied.

The old man looked astonished, especially as he could not see Kiki, who was behind a great vase of flowers. The children didn't say anything. They were wondering if it was possible to make a dash and get away.

'What are children doing here?' said the old man, in a puzzled tone. 'Have I seen you before? Why are you here?'

'Er – we came to look for somebody who was lost,' said Jack. 'And now we can't get out again. Could you tell us the way?'

The old man seemed so lost and wandering that it seemed to Jack that he might quite well be foolish enough to show them the way out. But he was wrong.

'Oh no, oh no,' said the old fellow at once, a cunning look coming over his yellow face. 'There are secrets here, you know. My secrets. Nobody who comes in may go out – until my experiments are finished. I'm the king of this place – my brain runs it all!'

He finished up on a high shrill note that gave the children an odd feeling. Was the old fellow mad? Surely he couldn't be the 'king' they had seen in the throne-room?

'You don't look like the king,' said Lucy-Ann. 'We saw the king in the throne-room – he was tall and had a great crown, and black hair round his face.'

'Ah, yes. They make me appear like that,' said the old man. 'I want to be king of the world, you know, the whole world – because of my great brain. I know more than anyone else. Meier says I shall be ruler of the world as soon as my experiments are done. And they are nearly finished, very very nearly!'

'Does Meier dress you up like a king then, when you appear in the throne-room?' asked Jack, astonished. He turned to the others and spoke in an undertone. 'That's to impress the paratroopers, I suppose! He wouldn't cut any ice with them if they saw him like this.'

'I *am* a king,' said the old man, with dignity. 'Because of my great brain, you know. I have a secret and I am using it. You have seen my great laboratory, have you? Ah, my little children, I know how to use all the great powers of the world – the tides, the metals, the winds – and gravitation!'

'What's 'Gravitation'?' said Lucy-Ann.

'It is the power that keeps you on the earth – that makes

you come back to it when you jump, that brings a ball back when you have thrown it,' said the old man. 'But I – I have conquered gravitation!'

This seemed a lot of nonsense to the children. They were quite sure the poor old man was mad. He might have had a marvellous brain at one time – but he couldn't be much good now.

'You don't believe me?' said the old fellow. 'Well, I have discovered some rays that repel the pull of the earth. Do you understand that, my children? No, no, it is too difficult for you.'

'It's not,' said Jack, interested. 'What you mean is – you think you've got hold of some rays that, if we use them, will cancel out gravitation? So that if you used the rays say, on a ball, it wouldn't feel the pull of the earth to bring it back here, but would speed through the air and not fall to earth?'

'Yes, yes – that is it – very very simply,' said the old man. 'And now, you see, I have invented these wings. I send the rays through them. I imprison them in the wings. And then, when a man jumps from an aeroplane, he presses a button to release the power of the rays – and he does not fall to earth! Instead he can glide and soar, flap his wings, and fly like a bird until he tires of it – then he can imprison the rays again and glide to earth!'

The children listened to all this in silence. It was the most extraordinary thing they had ever heard.

'But – is it really true?' asked Lucy-Ann at last. The idea of flying like that was very tempting!

'Do you think we would have come here to this lonely mountain for our experiments, do you think Meier and Erlick would have poured out their money if they had not known I could do this?' demanded the old man, looking rather angry.

'Well – it just sounds so extraordinary, that's all,' said Lucy-Ann. 'It sounds perfectly *lovely*, of course – I mean, I'd give anything to be able to fly like that. How clever you must be!'

'I have the biggest brain in the world,' said the old man solemnly. 'I am the greatest scientist that ever lived. I can do anything, anything!'

'Could you show us the way out of here?' asked Jack, in an innocent voice. The old man looked uncomfortable.

'If you use my wings, then you can go,' he said at last. 'We are all prisoners here till then, even I! Meier has said this must be so. He says I must hurry, hurry to get my wings quite perfect – time is short. Then I shall be made king of the whole world, and everyone will honour me.'

'Poor old man,' thought Philip. 'He believes everything that rogue of a Meier says. Meier and Erlick are using his brains for their own purposes.'

As suddenly as he had appeared, the old man went. He seemed to forget they were there. He vanished through the curtains and left them alone. They looked at one another, feeling uneasy.

'I don't know how much to believe,' said Jack. 'Has he really got hold of the secret of how to cancel out the pull of gravitation? Do you remember how peculiar we felt when we were looking at that extraordinary brilliant mass down in that pit – we felt sort of light, as if we ought to cling on to the balcony, or we'd float off into the air? Well, I bet some of those rays he spoke of were flying loose then!'

'Gosh, yes – that was strange,' said Philip thoughtfully. 'And, of course, all this would have to be done underground – so that the rays couldn't go flying off everywhere! The heart of a mountain seems a jolly good place for a terrific experiment like this – walls of thick rock all round. No wonder we heard rumblings and felt the earth shaking! That old scientist knows a thing or two. I'd be scared stiff to meddle with all the powers that scientists use nowadays. This is more extraordinary than splitting the atom.'

'I don't understand about things like that,' said Lucy-Ann. 'I feel like the people of old must have felt towards their magicians – I don't understand what they're doing, but it all seems like magic, and I'm scared!'

'You wait till you put on a pair of non-gravitation wings or whatever he calls them,' said Philip, helping himself to a peach. 'That'll be magic if you like.'

'Meier and Erlick must believe in the ideas the old man has,' said Jack. 'Or they wouldn't go to all the terrific trouble they do – and try to keep everything such a secret. I suppose, if the idea really came to something, they'd make such a colossal fortune that they'd be the richest men the world has ever known – and the most powerful.'

'Yes. *They'd* be the rulers – not the old man,' said Philip. 'They're just using him, and stuffing him up with all kinds of stories. He's as simple as can be, though he's got such a brain. They would give out that *they* were the inventors, not the old man. Fancy keeping him a prisoner here like that – and everyone else too!'

'Us included,' said Dinah. 'Well, I'm beginning to see daylight a bit now – understanding what's going on here – but I just can't believe it. Nor will Bill!'

They finished a very good meal. Nobody came to interrupt them. There was no sound from the old man's room. The children thought perhaps he had gone to bed for a rest, or had returned to his weird underground pit. They all made up their minds that nothing would persuade them ever to go down there again!

'What shall we do now?' said Jack. 'Snowy, tell us! Kiki, you've had enough peaches.'

'Poor Polly,' said Kiki sorrowfully, and wiped her beak on the table-cloth.

'Someone's coming!' suddenly said Lucy-Ann. 'Quick, hide!'

'Behind the hangings on the wall,' whispered Dinah, and the four children fled to the loose hangings. They squeezed behind them and waited, holding their breath.

It was two of the soldiers who had entered the room to clear away the meal. They talked to one another in surprised voices, and indeed, they were filled with astonishment to see so much of the food eaten.

The children heard their light feet pattering to and fro. Then one of them gave a sharp exclamation, which the children didn't understand. They stood behind the curtains, their hearts beating fast. Kiki was on Jack's shoulder, silent and puzzled.

Suddenly Lucy-Ann gave a loud scream, and the two boys leapt out from behind their curtains at once. One of the soldiers had seen her foot below the hangings, and had pounced on her.

'Jack! Philip! Quick, save me!' she cried, and they rushed to her rescue.

21

On the mountain-top

Both the soldiers had got hold of poor Lucy-Ann. She was screaming wildly, and the two boys flew at the men. But to their great surprise they were thrown back as easily as if they had been feather-weights. Just a twist of the men's arms, and back they went, falling headlong to the floor.

They were up again in a trice – but this time one of the soldiers caught Philip in a vicious grip, and the boy found himself turning over in the air, and flying right over the man's head! He landed with a crash on the table, and sent all the dishes into the air.

What with Lucy-Ann's screams, the boys' yells, and the crashes of the dishes there was a terrific commotion. Kiki added to it by screeching loudly. Then she flew down and attacked one of the men. He fended her off.

Four more soldiers suddenly appeared, and that was the

end of the children's resistance. They were all captured. Kiki flew off somewhere, still screeching. Snowy had disappeared completely.

The four children were marched out of the room and taken to a bigger room, well furnished, but not nearly so elaborate as the king's rooms. Hangings covered the walls, but they were plain and simple. The roof of the cave was not covered, and the children could see the rough rock above their heads.

Lucy-Ann was sobbing. Dinah looked very pale and the boys were angry and defiant. They were all stood in a row against the wall. Philip felt in his pocket to see if his slow-worm was hurt in the scuffle. Sally Slithery had not liked life in the mountain. She had become lethargic and dull. But she would not leave Philip.

She was still there, coiled up. Philip wondered where Kiki and Snowy were. It was not like Kiki to fly off like that. She must have been very scared – or perhaps one of the dishes had struck her as it flew off the table.

In a few minutes Meier and Erlick, the two men who were the real power behind the poor old 'king,' came into the room. Meier was glowering, and his piercing eyes glanced from one child to another sharply.

'So! There are four of you! Three of you came to find this boy, I suppose – and let him out of the cave he was in. You thought you could all escape – you thought it would be easy, so easy. And it was not?'

He fired this question at them, with a twisted smile on his hawk-like face.

Nobody answered. 'How did you find the way to let down the rope-ladder?' The man fired this question at them so suddenly that they jumped. 'Who told you how to get it down?'

Nobody said a word. Meier's eyes began to narrow, and the girls felt uneasy. He was horrid!

'I asked you a question,' he said. 'You, boy, answer me!'

'I used my brains,' said Jack shortly, seeing Meier looking at him.

'Does anyone else know of that entrance?' said Erlick suddenly. The children looked at him with dislike. He was like an ape, they thought! Meier was bad enough – but Erlick was ten times worse.

'How do we know?' said Philip, beginning to boil at the way these two men spoke to them. 'What does it matter if they do? Is what you're doing here so shameful that you need to hide even the entrance to the mountain?'

Erlick stepped forward and slapped Philip across the face. Lucy-Ann stopped crying, in greater fright than ever. Philip did not flinch. He looked the man boldly in the face, and did not even rub his smarting cheek.

'Leave him alone, Erlick,' said Meier. 'There are better ways of bringing a boy like that to heel than by slapping his face. And now we will send out the dogs to scour the countryside. If these children have friends anywhere near, the dogs will find them, and bring them in.'

The children's hearts sank. Would the Alsatians capture Bill and David then – and bring them to the mountain to make them prisoners too? That would be dreadful.

From somewhere outside came a hollow cough. Meier and Erlick jumped. Meier went to the entrance to the cave and looked out. There was nobody there at all.

'Is there another of you?' asked Meier. 'Is it boy or girl?'

'Neither,' said Jack, who had recognized Kiki's cough, and was hoping she would keep out. It would be just like these men to wring her neck.

'Pooh! Gah!' came Kiki's voice, and then a cackle that was enough to make the men's blood curdle. They went to the entrance of the cave again, and had a good look round, but Kiki was safely perched on a shelf of rock above their heads, and they could not see her at all.

'Send for the doctor,' said Kiki, in a sepulchral voice, that sent shivers down the men's backs. 'Send for the doctor.'

'Good heavens! Who *is* it?' said Erlick. He looked threateningly at the four children. 'If that's another boy out there, being funny, I'll skin him alive!'

'There are only four of us, two boys and two girls,' said Jack.

'And here we all are,' said Philip, in an insolent voice. He knew it was foolish to talk like this to the two men, but he couldn't help it. Both he and Dinah were foolhardy when their tempers were up.

'Oh! And here you'll all stay!' said Meier. 'And I'll think up something to take the spirit out of you, my boy. You may have gone through your life cheeking everyone and throwing your weight about – but you won't do it with me. Now – walk in front of us, and keep going!'

The children were forced to walk out of the cave in front of the two men. They soon found themselves stumbling up the stone spiral stairs, going up and up. They came to the openings where the stores were, and then went on past those till they came to the door of the cave in which Philip had been bolted.

'Hey, you, boy! You're to go into that cave again,' ordered Meier. 'A few days without much to eat will soon take the insolence out of you. You others go on up.'

Poor Philip! He was shut once more into the cave that looked out to the sky – but this time he had no Sam to keep him company. He sat down, wishing he hadn't been so foolish as to cheek the two grim men. Then he was glad he had. *He* wasn't going to kow-tow to two rogues like that. All the same it was a pity he wasn't with the others – especially as now there was only Jack to be with the girls.

The other three were forced to go on higher, climbing steadily. And then – what a surprise!

They came up a broad flight of steps hewn out of the rock, on to the very top of the mountain itself. They stood there, catching their breath at the sight of the amazing panoramic view all round them. The top of the world! Surely they must be touching the sky itself!

The three forgot their troubles for a moment as they gazed round in wonder. Everywhere they looked were mountains, rising high. Valleys, deep in shadow, lay far far below. It was wonderful to be up there in the blazing sunshine and cool breeze, after being in the dark mountain for so long.

The top of the mountain was extraordinarily flat. On three sides rose steep rocks, like teeth. Jack knew in a flash what mountain it was – Fang Mountain, the one he had noticed when they had set out. He looked round the mountain-top. Nothing grew there at all. It was bare, flat rock, the size of a great courtyard. At one side, playing cards in the shade, were the paratroopers.

They stared in surprise at the children. Runaway Sam was with them and he pointed to Jack and was evidently telling his companions about him and the others. Jack was glad that Philip had told Sam so little about himself and the other three. He did not want Meier to know any more than he already did.

There was an awning rigged up on the side opposite the paratroopers. Meier pushed the children towards it.

'You will stay here,' he said. 'You will not talk to those men over there at all. You will not go near them. You are prisoners, you understand? You have forced your way in here, where you are not wanted, and now we shall keep you here as long as we wish.'

'Can't Philip come with us?' begged Lucy-Ann. 'He'll be so lonely away from us.'

'Is that the other boy? No. He needs a little punishment,' said Meier. 'A little starvation diet! Then we will see if he will talk civilly.'

Meier and Erlick then left the three and disappeared into the mountain again. Jack and the girls sat down looking doleful. Things weren't too good! It was a thousand pities that poor Philip was apart from them.

Evidently the paratroopers had been warned that they were not to go near the children, for they made no attempt even to shout to them. It was obvious that Meier and Erlick were used to being obeyed.

There was a natural parapet of rock near where the children were, that ran round the edge of the mountain just there. Jack got up and went to it. He sat on it and put his field-glasses to his eyes. If only he could spot Bill! And yet he was afraid that if Bill was there anywhere, the dogs might set on him and find him. He wondered where all the dogs were.

Then he sat up a little straighter on the parapet and focused the glasses on a small spot on the slope of the mountain. He had seen a movement. Could it be Bill and David and the donkeys?

No, it wasn't. It was the dogs! They had evidently already been let loose and were ranging the countryside. If Bill was anywhere about, they would soon find him! Blow! Then Bill would be captured too. Jack wished he knew some way of preventing this happening, but he couldn't think of anything.

He wondered about poor old Dapple. Thank goodness they had tied him up so very loosely. He had plenty of range, and there was grass and water for him. But how the donkey would wonder what had happened to everyone!

Something touched Jack's hand and he jumped and looked down. It was Snowy! The kid had found his way to them and was nuzzling Jack in a half-scared manner.

'Hallo, Snowy! Have you been looking for Philip?' said Jack, rubbing the kid's soft nose. 'He's in that cave again. You can't get to him.'

Snowy knew that very well. He had already been to bleat outside Philip's door. He looked so dismal that Jack took him to the girls and they all made a fuss of him.

'What do you suppose has happened to Kiki?' asked Lucy-Ann after a time.

'Oh, she'll turn up all right,' said Jack. 'She knows how to take care of herself. Trust Kiki for that! She's probably leading those two men a fine old dance, coughing and sneezing and cackling and making a noise like an express train screeching in a tunnel!'

Jack was perfectly right. Kiki had been playing a fine game with Meier and Erlick, and as they had no idea that the children had a parrot, they were two extremely puzzled men. A voice without a body to it – how very strange!

Nothing happened for some time. Then, when the sun was sinking, there came a clamour of howls and barks, and the pack of Alsatians was brought up to the top of the mountain by two of the soldiers. The children watched to see if Bill had been caught, but there was no sign of any prisoner with the dogs. They heaved a sigh of relief.

The dogs were taken to a big wire enclosure some way off the children. 'You be careful of dogs,' said one of the guards to the children. 'They bite hard. You be careful!'

22

The helicopter

The children, however, were not in the least afraid of the dogs, for had they not all slept together with them some nights before? They did not tell this to the soldiers, of course. They waited till the men had disappeared and then they went over to the dogs.

But Philip was not there this time, and the dogs did not feel the same towards the girls and Jack as they had done towards Philip. They growled when Jack came near to them, and one showed his enormous white teeth. Lucy-Ann and Dinah shrank back.

'Oh! How terribly fierce they look! They've quite forgotten us. Jack, be careful.'

Jack was not afraid, but he was cautious when he saw that

the dogs did not want to be friendly. They were strong, fierce creatures, disappointed in their hunting that day, hungry, and suspicious of Jack. Now, if he had been Philip how different their behaviour would have been! Philip's magic touch with animals would have put everything right. He had an irresistible attraction for all live creatures.

'Come away from them,' said Lucy-Ann, when she heard the growling taken up by most of the pack. 'They're making a perfectly horrible noise – just like wolves would, I'm sure.'

They went back to their own part of the mountain. 'A corner for the dogs, a corner for us, a corner for the men!' said Jack. 'Well – I wonder how long we're going to be here!'

Nobody brought them anything to eat at all for the rest of that day. They thought it was a very good thing they had had such good meals in the king's room! Jack wondered if they were supposed to lie on the bare rock to sleep. What brutes those men were, if they meant to keep them without rugs or food!

But just as it was getting dark three of the soldiers appeared. They carried rugs with them, which they threw down at the children's feet. One had brought a pitcher of water and mugs.

'What about something to eat?' asked Jack.

'Not bring,' said one of the men. 'Master say not bring.'

'Your master not nice,' Jack told him. 'Your master very nasty.'

The men said nothing. He and the others went away, soft-footed as cats. The children curled up in their rugs, wondering how Philip was faring alone in his cave.

The next morning was unbelievably beautiful when the sun rose and lighted up the mountain-tops one by one. The three children sat on the parapet and watched. They all felt very hungry indeed. Snowy was with them. Kiki had still not appeared and Jack was getting a little worried about her.

Snowy leapt up on to the parapet beside Jack. There was a

very steep drop from there, with a tiny ledge of rock jutting out some way below. Nobody could escape by climbing down, that was certain. He would just go slipping and sliding down the mountain and break all his limbs in no time.

Snowy stood there, his little ears pricked up as if he was listening. He suddenly bleated very loudly. And then, very muffled, hardly to be heard, a voice answered. Jack leapt up from the parapet. Was it Philip's voice? Where was his cave then? Anywhere near where they were?

Lucy-Ann and Dinah joined Jack, seeing his sudden excitement. Then Snowy gave them a really terrible shock. He jumped right over the mountain-top, off his perch on the parapet of rock!

'Oh!' shouted Lucy-Ann. 'He'll be killed!'

She wouldn't look to see what happened, but Dinah and Jack watched in horror. The little kid had leapt to the tiny ledge of rock jutting out some way below the parapet. He landed on it with all four tiny hooves close together! There was only just room for them – not half an inch to spare!

He stood balanced there, and then, when it looked as if surely he must topple off, he leapt to a small ledge lower down, slithered down a rough bit, and disappeared completely.

'Goodness gracious! What a thing to do!' said Dinah, taking a deep breath. 'My heart almost stopped beating.'

'Is Snowy all right?' asked Lucy-Ann, still not daring to look.

'Apparently. Anyway he's disappeared – and I should think he's probably found the cave where Philip is,' said Jack. 'All I hope is he won't try to get back the same way – or he'll certainly break his neck.'

But Snowy did get back the same way and appeared on the parapet about half an hour later, looking as frisky as a squirrel.

And round his neck was a note! It was tied there with string. Jack took it off quickly and opened it. He read it to the others.

How are you getting on? I'm all right except that I've nothing to eat, and only water to drink. I believe those brutes are going to starve me out! Can you send Snowy with anything for me to eat when you get a meal?
Cheerio!
Philip

At that moment the guards arrived with a meal for the children. It was all out of tins but there was plenty. With it was a loaf of fresh bread. Dinah said she thought perhaps the soldiers had an oven down in the pit somewhere to bake their bread.

They waited till the men had gone and then Jack debated how to send food to Philip. He made some sandwiches and wrapped them up firmly in the paper the soldiers had brought the bread in. He slipped a note inside the sandwiches to say they would send food by Snowy whenever they could. Then he tied the packet very firmly on to Snowy's back. Snowy smelt it and tried to reach it, but he couldn't.

'Now you go to Philip again,' said Jack and patted the parapet to show Snowy that he wanted him up there. As soon as he was up Snowy remembered Philip and down he went again on his clever little feet, landing on first one tiny ledge and then another.

The other three felt pleased to think that Philip was having a meal instead of being starved. Jack took a look round the countryside below with his field-glasses, as they sat and ate, wondering if Bill would come that day. Time was getting on now. Surely Bill would arrive soon!

The day passed very slowly. The paratroopers were taken off into the mountain by the soldiers and didn't come back. The dogs were also taken out and Jack was sure he could see them ranging the countryside again.

They sent food to Philip by Snowy each time they had a

meal. It was a help to exchange cheery notes with him even though nobody felt all that cheerful. Kiki hadn't yet returned and all the children were now very worried about her.

The evening came. The paratroopers had not come back and the children wondered why. The dogs came back, however, but this time the children did not go over to them. The Alsatians were fighting over their meat and sounded savage and fierce.

It was a cloudy, sultry evening. The children dragged their rugs out from under the awning to a place where the breeze blew more strongly. They lay down, trying to go to sleep. The two girls slept, but Jack lay wide awake, feeling worried about Kiki and Philip and the girls too.

He heard a noise far away in the distance and sat up. He knew what that was – it was a helicopter! There was no mistaking the noise now. Was it coming to the mountain?

He awoke the two girls. 'Dinah! Lucy-Ann! The helicopter's coming. Wake up and let's watch. Get back under the awning, in case it lands too near us.'

The girls dragged their rugs under the awning. They went to sit on the parapet and listened, wondering if Philip was awake and listening too. He was. He was lying on his tummy, looking out of his cave, watching and listening. It was too dark for him to see anything much, but he hoped he might share in the excitement.

The noise came nearer and at last sounded very loud. 'Look – there it is,' said Jack, excited. 'See – going round the mountain a bit above us. Aren't they going to flash a light here to show it where to land?'

As he spoke two of the soldiers appeared in a hurry on top of the mountain. They ran to the middle of the great rocky courtyard and did something the children could not see. Immediately a strong light flashed upwards into the sky, and in its beam the children saw the helicopter, its wheels poised almost above their heads.

'There it is! It's landing!' cried Jack. 'See how it's dropping down slowly, almost vertically! It's just the right sort of machine to land on a mountain-top!'

The helicopter came down to the courtyard and stopped. The vanes ceased to whirl above it. Voices hailed one another.

'It's a jolly *big* helicopter,' said Jack. 'I've never seen such a big one before. It must be able to carry quite a large cargo.'

The beam of light was now directed on the helicopter and the children could see what was going on quite clearly. Boxes and crates were being tumbled out of it on to the ground, and the hard-working men were all very busy handling them, dragging them about, opening some of them and taking the contents down the stone steps to the store-places.

A lean-faced young man with a scar right across his cheek was the pilot of the helicopter. With him was a swarthy fellow who limped badly. They spoke to the workers in curt tones, and then left their machine and disappeared into the mountain.

'Gone to report to Meier and Erlick, I should think,' said Jack. 'Come on – let's go and have a look at the helicopter. Wish I knew how to fly it! We could escape nicely in it now.'

'And hover outside Philip's cave and take him off too!' said Dinah. They all went over to the machine. Jack got into the pilot's seat and felt grand. How he wished he knew how to fly the helicopter!

He was still sitting there when Meier, Erlick, the pilot and his companion, and one of the paratroopers appeared. Jack tried to scramble out before he was seen but he was too late. Meier saw him and dragged him out so roughly that he fell to the ground.

'What are you doing? You keep away from this machine!' shouted Meier in a fury. Jack skipped off to the girls, rubbing his shoulder.

'Are you hurt, Jack?' asked Lucy-Ann anxiously. He whispered that he was all right. Then he said something that made the girls stare fearfully at the group of men in the centre of the courtyard.

'I believe that paratrooper is the next one to try those "wings." They've brought him up to show him the helicopter and where he's to jump from.'

Both the girls thought it would be dreadful to have to leap from a machine high up in the air – and trust to the king's extraordinary 'wings.' They wondered how many people had tried them and failed. Nobody would know if they were efficient or not until they had been tried.

The paratrooper looked the helicopter over thoroughly. He talked to the pilot, who answered him shortly. Jack thought that the pilot wasn't any too keen about the para-jumping part. He would probably have been content to fly the goods to the mountain and finish at that.

'Tomorrow night you leave,' said the voice of Meier, cutting through the night. 'Come and eat now.'

Leaving two soldiers to guard the helicopter from the curiosity of the children, the rest of them disappeared into the mountain. Tomorrow night! What would they see then?

23

The wonderful wings

The three children retired to their rugs. They were afraid to go near the helicopter again, because the obedient soldiers, they knew, would stand no nonsense. Snowy appeared from over the parapet, full of curiosity. He ran over to the helicopter, but the guards hit out at him.

'The beasts! How can they be cruel to a little kid?' said Jack. 'Snowy! Come here! These fellows would make you into soup as soon as look at you. You'd better be careful.'

'Oh, Jack – don't say things like that,' said tender-hearted Lucy-Ann. 'Would they really? Surely nobody would ever have the heart to hurt Snowy?'

Snowy retreated hastily to the children and skipped up and down the parapet, as sure-footed in the dark as in the daylight. The beam of the lamp showed up the helicopter, but the rest of the courtyard was in darkness.

The dogs howled in their enclosure. They had not liked the noise the helicopter made, and they were uneasy and restless. The soldiers shouted threateningly to them, but the dogs took no notice.

'I don't like this adventure at *all*,' said Lucy-Ann suddenly. 'In fact, I simply hate it. I want to get away. I want to go back to Bill and Aunt Allie and Effans and Mrs Evans. Why did we have to find another adventure in these nice, peaceful summer holidays?'

'It just happens to us,' said Jack. 'Something in us attracts them, I suppose – like animals are attracted to Philip! Some people attract good luck, some attract wealth, some attract animals, some attract adventures.'

'Well, I'd rather attract something harmless, like cats or dogs,' complained Lucy-Ann. 'Oh dear! I do wish Snowy wouldn't keep walking over us when we're lying down.'

They fell asleep at last. In the morning, when they sent some food to Philip by Snowy, they sent a note also, telling him all they had seen in the night. Snowy brought a note back.

I'm sorry for the paratrooper! I wonder how many they've used in trying out this mad experiment. I'm glad I'm not chosen for anything as crazy as that! Keep your chin up! I'm all right here. I've got Snowy most of the time and Sally Slithery is getting so tame she eats out of my fingers. She sleeps on a bit of warm rock at the edge of my cave. Tell Snowy not to tread on her when he comes bounding in!
So long!
Philip

The day seemed very long again. The dogs were not taken down into the mountain and let loose on the countryside, but were exercised round and round the courtyard by the diligent soldiers. The children were glad about that.

'If old Bill arrives today, the dogs won't be out on the mountain-side. He'll be safe. So let's hope he comes. Not that he can do much if he does. He won't know where the entrance is – and if he finds it, he won't know how to work the rope-ladder – and there's no other way of getting in.'

Lucy-Ann looked very dismal. 'Shall we have to stay here all our lives long?' she asked.

The others laughed at her. 'No!' said Jack. 'Bill will do *some*thing – but don't ask me what!'

The paratroopers had not appeared again that day, not even the one who was supposed to be going to use the 'wings' that night. The helicopter stood there in the middle of the courtyard, the sun glinting on its motionless shape.

Evening came. The children grew restive. The soldiers had brought them food as usual, but had not said a word. What were all the paratroopers doing? Having a ceremonial feast of something to celebrate their comrade's experiment?

And where, oh, where was Kiki? Jack was feeling very miserable about her now. He turned over and over in his mind all the things that might have happened to her. She had never been away from him so long.

That night the beam shone out again in the courtyard. Meier, Erlick, three or four servants and the paratrooper appeared, followed by the lean-faced, scarred pilot and his companion.

Then up the opening, stepping out majestically, came the king!

He was dressed in his grand robes and crown and was hardly recognizable as the poor, bald old fellow who had talked to the children a day or two back. He held himself proudly as he walked to the centre of the courtyard.

Behind came four uniformed guards, carrying a box. They laid it down at the king's feet. In silence he stooped down and opened it.

He took out a pair of wings! They glittered like gold, and

were shaped like a bird's outstretched wings, big and wide. Lucy-Ann gasped in delight.

'Oh! Look, Dinah! Real wings! Aren't they lovely?'

The king was speaking to the amazed paratrooper. 'These will hold you up when you jump. Press this button here as soon as you leap from the helicopter. Then you will find that you cannot fall. You will no longer feel the pull of the earth. You will be free and light as air. Then you may use the wings, for guiding yourself, for planing, for soaring, whatever you wish!'

'Doesn't it sound marvellous?' whispered Lucy-Ann, drinking in every word.

'The wings must be fitted to your arms,' said the king. 'Hold them out and I will fix them on.'

'Here – is this all I'm going to have to stop me falling?' said the paratrooper.

'You will not need anything else,' said the king. 'In these wings are imprisoned powerful rays. At the press of the button they are released, and shoot towards the earth, preventing its pull on you. You cannot fall! But when you want to come to earth, press the button once more – and you will guide down gently, as the earth exerts her pull on you once more.'

'Yes, but look here – I understood it was a new kind of parachute I was trying out,' said the paratrooper. 'See? I didn't think it was stuff and nonsense like this!'

'It is not nonsense, man,' said Meier's curt voice. 'It is a great invention by the greatest scientist in the world. You will find Erlick and me waiting for you to come to earth when you have flown a mile or two. We shall take the dogs and find you. Then – riches for you, and honour for the rest of your life! One of the pioneer flying-men!'

'Look here – I'm a heavy chap,' began the paratrooper again. 'See? Those flimsy wings won't hold *me* – rays or no rays! I don't know about any pull of the earth on me – all I know is I'll have to fall, once I jump out with only those things on my arms. Are you crazy?'

'Get him!' suddenly said Meier, in a furious voice. Erlick and the soldiers at once pinioned the paratrooper's arms. He had to stand whilst the king fixed on the 'wings.' The children watched with bated breath.

The paratrooper cried out and struggled, but the ape-like Erlick was far too strong for him. 'Put him in the helicopter and take off,' commanded Meier. 'Go too, Erlick. Push him out at the right moment. If he's a fool he'll not press the button. If he is wise he will press it – and then he will see how well he flies!'

But the pilot now had something to say. He spoke in a drawling voice, clear and contemptuous.

'I think this fellow's too heavy. The last one was too. You'd better think again, Boss, and get those wings made twice the size. I'm game for an experiment where there's a chance for everybody – but I reckon there's not much chance for a big fellow trying out those wings of yours.'

'Do you mean you refuse to take this fellow?' said Meier, white with anger.

'You've got it right first time, Boss,' said the pilot, getting angry too, so that his scar showed up very plainly. 'Try a little fellow! I guess the experiment worked all right last time – for a minute or two – and then it petered out. These paratroopers are hulking great chaps – the ones you try out with me, anyway – and I tell you plainly I'm not taking anyone who doesn't want to go. Got it?'

Meier went up to the pilot as if he meant to strike him. Erlick pulled him back. 'That's right,' said the pilot, who had not turned a hair. 'Don't try any funny business with me, Boss. I know too much – and there's others will know too much too, if I don't get back on time!'

He got into his machine, and the swarthy man, his companion, who had not said a single word all this time, got in beside him. The paratrooper watched them dazedly. The engine of the helicopter started up.

The pilot leaned forward and spoke again to Meier, who looked as if he was on the point of bursting with rage.

'So long! I shan't be coming next time – I'm going for a holiday! I'll be sending somebody who's not so pernickety as I am – but I warn you – try a little guy!'

The machine rose vertically into the air, circled round the mountain-side slowly, and then made off to the west. In a few minutes it could not even be heard.

The children had watched all this, the girls only half understanding what was going on. Lucy-Ann felt sorry for the frightened paratrooper and very glad he had not been forced to go off in the helicopter.

The little group left in the courtyard paced up and down. A lot of talk and argument went on, though the paratrooper did not seem to be joining in at all. He had stripped off the wings and was held securely by the soldiers. The king carried his precious wings all the time, but at last replaced them in the box and locked it.

'Very well,' he said, 'I agree. It may be that the men we choose are too heavy – but who else could we have asked? Only paratroopers are used to jumping from heights! Try someone lighter if you wish. It will make no difference to my ideas.'

And then the children heard a few words that made them gasp in horror. 'One of those kids will do,' said Meier. 'That insolent boy, for instance. We'll put the wings on him and he shall jump from the helicopter!'

24

The helicopter comes again

When the courtyard was completely empty, and the beam had gone out, leaving the mountain-top in darkness, Lucy-Ann began to cry bitterly. Jack and Dinah put their arms round her. They felt like howling too.

'He doesn't mean it,' said Jack, trying to think of something really comforting. 'Don't worry! He only said that to scare us. They'd never make Philip do a thing like that.'

'They didn't say it to scare us. They meant it, you know they did!' sobbed Lucy-Ann. 'What are we going to do? We've got to do *some*thing.'

It was all very well to say that – but what in the world was there to do? The children got very little sleep that night. They debated whether to tell Philip or not what had happened – and what was proposed.

They decided not to. It would be dreadful for him to lie alone in his cave and worry. So, when morning came and they sent Snowy to Philip with the usual sandwiches made from their own breakfast rations, they said nothing in the daily note about what had happened.

But to their great surprise, who should be ushered up the steps by the soldiers that morning, but Philip himself! He bounded forward to greet them, grinning.

'Hallo! They've let me out! Tired of starving me, I suppose, and seeing me get fatter and fatter. I say, did you see the helicopter last night? I heard it.'

Lucy-Ann and Dinah hugged him and Jack slapped him heartily on the shoulder. They were delighted to see him again. Snowy had come with him and acted like a mad thing, careering up and down the parapet as if he was in a circus.

They told him very little about the night before. He was rather puzzled that they said so little, even in answer to his questions. But Jack, by means of heavy frowns, had let the girls know they had better not say too much. He thought it would be wise to postpone saying anything in case Meier really hadn't meant what he said.

But it looked a bit odd, Meier letting Philip come up to be with the others, all of a sudden – and bringing them very much better food and plenty of it. 'Like victims being fattened for the sacrifice!' thought Jack. 'I wonder when the next helicopter's due? How long have we got? Oh, Bill, do make haste!'

Lucy-Ann and Dinah, fearing that poor Philip really

would have to jump from the helicopter, were most affectionate to him. Dinah even enquired after Sally the slow-worm and did not shrink away when Philip brought her out of his pocket.

'I say! What's up with Dinah?' asked Philip at last. 'She's gone all sweet and sugary. It's not like her. She'll be offering to nurse Sally Slithery for me next!'

Philip felt sure there was something up. He couldn't *imagine* what it was. He wondered if it was bad news about Kiki. No – if Jack had heard any, he would be much more upset than he was. Philip felt uncomfortable. It wasn't like the others to keep anything from him. He tackled Jack about it firmly.

'Look here, Jack – something's up. Don't say there isn't – I jolly well know there is. So come out with it – or I'll go back to my cave and sulk!'

Jack hesitated. Then he took the plunge. 'All right, Philip – I'll tell you. But it's not good.'

He told him all about it – how the helicopter had arrived – what had happened – about the frightened paratrooper and the angry pilot – and finally about Meier's wicked suggestion that one of the children should try the 'wings.'

'I see,' said Philip slowly. 'And I suppose the one they're going to try is me?'

'That's what they said,' said Jack. 'The brutes! That experiment is only half-way to perfection – the wings aren't a hundred per cent foolproof, nor even fifty per cent – though they may be one day!'

'Well, well – to think I'm going to fly with wings,' said Philip, trying to pass the whole thing off as a joke. He saw Jack's troubled face. 'Don't worry, old son. It won't happen! Something will turn up – and if it doesn't, I'm no coward!'

'I know. You don't need to tell me that,' said Jack. 'The girls are awfully upset. That's why we've seemed a bit funny with you. We just didn't want to tell you.'

Philip pranced up to the girls, flapping his arms like wings. 'Cheer up!' he cried. 'As soon as I'm out of that helicopter I'll fly off to Bill and give him the shock of his life!'

But it wasn't much use trying to make a joke of it. It was too serious. None of the children felt like playing with Snowy, who was very hurt and gambolled down the stone steps into the mountain to look for somebody with a bit more fun in them.

Three days went by. The children had almost given up all hope of Bill coming now. Surely he would have been along before, if he had come looking for them? They would have seen a search-party on the mountain-side, if one had come. But they saw nothing at all. It was most disappointing. They felt quite sick with watching and waiting.

They pondered whether to make a dash for freedom again and try for the rope-ladder once more. But Jack shook his head. 'No, they'll be on the watch now. There's always one of those soft-footed soldiers about. Meier will have put somebody on guard.'

There was one good thing, orders had evidently been given to feed the children well, and they had plenty of good food. Even their sad hearts did not take away their appetites and they tucked in well, helped by Snowy, who would devour every scrap of greenstuff or vegetable if he could.

And then, one night as they slept together under the awning, their rugs pulled round them, they heard the familiar sound of the helicopter! All four sat up at once, their hearts beating. Tears came into Lucy-Ann's eyes.

The helicopter circled round the moutain-top slowly. Then the bright beam came on and the courtyard was lighted up. The helicopter came slowly down and at last its wheels rested on the rocky yard.

There were two men in the machine, but neither of them was the same as before. The pilot had on big goggles and a peaked cap. The other man was bareheaded. He looked stern and grim.

Meier soon came up with Erlick and the soldier guards. 'You the Boss?' called the pilot. 'I've taken Kahn's place. He's on holiday. Had a job finding this place. This is Johns, my mate. We've got the goods you wanted.'

There was the same unpacking as before, and boxes and crates were piled on the ground. The pilot and his companion jumped down.

'There is a meal ready for you,' said Meier. 'You will start back tomorrow night?'

'No. Got to leave tonight,' said the pilot. 'They're making enquiries about some of our doings. Got to be back at once.'

'You have been told that – er – that er . . . ' began Meier.

'What – that some paratrooper wants a jump off the helicopter?' said the pilot. 'Oh, yes. That's okay by me. If a chap wants to do that, well, it's no business of mine.'

'You will be paid very very well,' said Meier's grim voice. 'This time it is double the price. We have a young jumper – it is necessary for our experiments, you understand.'

There was a pause. The pilot's voice came on the air, sharp and enquiring. 'What do you mean – a *young* jumper?'

'A boy,' said Meier. 'He is here.' Then he turned to one of the soldiers and said something to him in a foreign language. The soldier darted off down the steps into the mountain. 'I have sent to tell the inventor that you have arrived,' he said. 'Now will you come to have a meal?'

'No,' said the pilot. 'I must be off. Get this boy and make him ready.'

Lucy-Ann's knees were shaking so much that she couldn't stand. Philip felt calm but rather fierce. All right! Let them strap those wings on him then – let them take him in the helicopter! He'd jump out all right! And if those wings *did* act – *if* they did – but would they? Philip just couldn't bring himself to believe that they would.

The pilot had not seen any of the children, but now Philip had to go forward, fetched by one of the soldiers. The others followed, though Lucy-Ann had to hold on to Jack. Before the pilot could say a word to them, the king appeared. The children thought he must have dressed himself up very quickly! His crown was a little crooked, but otherwise he looked as majestic as ever.

The box with the wings in was carried by one of the soldiers. The king undid it and took out the wings. They really did look beautiful – and what was more they looked as if they *would* be able to fly! Lucy-Ann hoped fervently that they could.

Philip made no fuss at all as the wings were strapped to his arms. He was shown the two buttons and nodded. He flapped his arms a little and was surprised to feel the power in the wings, as they met the air. The others watched him in admiration. Jack warmed to him. What pluck he had! – he didn't in the least show that he was scared. Perhaps he wasn't.

But deep down inside Philip was a nasty little core of dread. He kept it clamped down. Not for worlds would he have let anyone know it was there.

Then Meier, the king, Erlick and the others got a surprise. Little Lucy-Ann stepped forward and laid her hand on the arm of the king.

'Your Majesty! I think *I* ought to try out your wings for you. I am much lighter than Philip. It would be an honour for me to try them.'

Philip and Jack looked thunderstruck. The idea of it! Philip gave the little girl a hug, putting his winged arms all round her.

'You're a brave darling! But *I'm* going! And what's more I'll fly back to this old mountain-top and just show you how well I'm doing.'

Lucy-Ann gave a sob. This was too much for her altogether. The pilot said nothing but got into the helicopter with his companion.

The king showed no hesitation at all in letting Philip go. It was pathetic the way he believed whole-heartedly in his extraordinary wings. His head was in the clouds. The people who performed his experiments for him, and tried out his clever ideas were nothing to him at all.

Meier watched grimly as Philip climbed into the helicopter, helped by one of the soldiers, for his arms were hampered by the beautiful wings. The man would have been better pleased if the boy had objected and made a scene. He did not admire Philip's pluck in the least. His piercing eyes looked into Philip's and the boy looked back at him mockingly.

'So long!' he said, and raised one of his winged arms. 'See you later! Look out for youself, Meier. You'll come to a bad end one of these days!'

Meier stepped forward angrily, but the helicopter's engine began to whir. The rotors went slowly round, gathering speed. Lucy-Ann tried to stifle a sob. She felt sure she would never see Philip again.

The helicopter rose straight up into the air. The pilot leaned forward and shouted something loudly. 'Don't forget Bill Smugs!' he called, and his voice was no longer the same as it had sounded before. It was quite different. It was somebody else's.

In fact – it was BILL'S VOICE!

25

A thrilling night

Only Lucy-Ann, Jack and Dinah knew what the last shout meant. Meier and the others had no idea at all. They hardly heard what was shouted.

But the children had heard all right! They gasped. Jack's hand found Lucy-Ann's and Dinah squeezed Jack's arm.

They didn't say a single word until Meier, Erlick, the king and the servants had all disappeared once more. Then they made their way to their awnings, linking hands to keep together.

'Jack! That was *Bill*! Bill himself!' said Lucy-Ann, her voice going all funny as she spoke.

'Yes. And he knew if he yelled out, "Don't forget Bill Smugs," that we'd know it was him,' said Dinah. 'He called himself Bill Smugs the very first adventure we had – do you remember? Gosh – I never had such a surprise in my life!'

'And Philip's safe,' said Jack, in intense satisfaction. 'That's one good thing. The other fellow with Bill must be one of his friends. Philip will just chuck those wings overboard and that'll be that.'

'I feel as if I simply must sit down at once,' said Lucy-Ann. 'My legs will hardly carry me. I feel so joyful!'

She sat down and the others followed suit. They all let out a terrific sigh of relief. A heavy load rolled away from them. Philip was safe! He didn't have to jump out of the helicopter to try out an experiment for a mad old scientist, or for Meier and Erlick. He was with Bill.

'What made Bill think of getting a helicopter?' wondered Jack. 'Landing on the mountain-top with it too – under the noses of Meier and Erlick.'

'Well, don't you remember, you put in your note something about the helicopter we thought was landing up here?' said Dinah. 'The note we left with Dapple.'

'Yes, so I did,' said Jack. 'Well, that looks rather as if old Bill did come along here then – and found Dapple. Good for him! Trust Bill to get going somehow!'

'What's he going to do next?' said Dinah. 'Do you think he'll come back for us?'

'You bet he will!' said Jack. 'He'll park Philip somewhere safe and he'll be back as soon as he can. Perhaps tonight!'

'Oh, how lovely!' sighed Lucy-Ann. 'I don't like this mountain. I like Mrs Evans' farm-house best. I don't like anyone here – that horrid Meier, and that awful fat Erlick, and those nasty little pussy-footing soldiers – and the king.'

'Well – I feel sorry for him,' said Jack. 'He's just got into the hands of rogues. No doubt they've made plenty of money already from his inventions. Now they're going all out for this one. I do wonder if there's anything in it.'

'Well, I'm jolly glad Philip hasn't got to find out!' said Dinah. 'Good old Philip – he was as plucky as could be, wasn't he?'

'Yes. And Lucy-Ann was jolly brave too,' said Jack. 'Whatever made you think of trying to go in Philip's place, Lucy-Ann?'

'I don't know. It sort of came over me all at once,' Lucy-Ann tried to explain. 'But I wasn't brave. My legs were wobbling like jelly.'

'The only thing that worries me is Kiki,' said Jack. 'I hope those men haven't done anything to her. She's never been away from us so long. I haven't heard so much as a hiccup from her!'

The others were worried too. Dinah couldn't help feeling pretty certain that Kiki had come to some harm. If Meier caught her that would be the end of her. Dinah shivered when she thought of his cold, piercing eyes.

Suddenly she gave a small shriek. 'Oh! Something's wriggling over my leg! What is it, quick?'

'It's the slow-worm,' said Jack, making a grab at it. 'Sorry, Dinah. You see, Philip didn't want to make poor old Sally share his jump – so he slipped her into my pocket when he thought you weren't looking. I didn't know she'd got out. Don't yell, Dinah. With everybody being so frightfully brave tonight, you might as well show your pluck too!'

And, surprisingly, Dinah did. After all, what was a slow-worm compared to Philip's jump – if he had had to jump? Nothing at all. Dinah drew her leg away, but made no fuss at all. Sally slithered round them for a little while and then went into Jack's pocket again.

'I just simply can't get over knowing it was Bill in that helicopter!' said Lucy-Ann for the twentieth time. 'My heart jumped nearly out of my body when he suddenly changed his voice to his own and yelled out, "Don't forget Bill Smugs!" '

'We'll have to be on the look-out for when he comes back,' said Jack. 'I'm sure it will be tonight. Perhaps no one will hear him but us, because we'll be the only ones expecting him. You can't hear a thing down in that mountain.'

'Oooh – wouldn't that be super, if Bill came back without being heard, and took us off?' said Lucy-Ann. 'What *would* Meier and the others think! They'd hunt all over the place for us!'

'And send the dogs out too,' said Jack.

'Shall we keep awake to look out for him?' said Dinah.

'No, you girls have a nap. I'll keep watch,' said Jack. 'I'm much too wide awake to go to sleep. I'll wake you as soon as ever I hear anything.'

'What about that beam of light that shows the helicopter where to land at night?' said Dinah suddenly. 'Can you turn it on when you hear it coming, Jack?'

'I expect so,' said Jack, and went into the middle of the courtyard to find the switch that turned on the powerful beam.

But he couldn't find it anywhere. He hunted all over the place and gave it up at last. 'Can't find where the wretched thing turns on,' he said. 'Sickening!'

'Well, I daresay Bill can land all right,' said Lucy-Ann, who had the utmost faith in Bill's ability to do anything, no matter how impossible. 'You keep watch, Jack. I'm going to have a nap.'

She and Dinah shut their eyes, and in spite of all the terrific excitement of that night, they were both asleep in half a minute. Jack sat up, keeping watch. It was a cloudy night, and only occasionally did he see a star peeping out from between the clouds.

Good old Bill! How had he got that helicopter? How did he know how to fly one? Jack felt very thankful indeed that they had had the sense to leave a note behind with Dapple, telling everything they knew. Otherwise Bill wouldn't have known a thing about the mountain or its secret, and certainly wouldn't have guessed that helicopters landed on the top!

From far away a noise came through the night. Jack strained his ears. Yes – it was the helicopter coming back. It hadn't been long then – just long enough to drop Philip somewhere, hear his story and come back for the others. What a sell for Meier to find them all gone – and not to know what had happened to the wonderful wings!

The boy went to try and put on the lamp again, but could not find the switch at all. This was not surprising, because it was set in a tiny trap-door, let into the yard.

The helicopter came nearer. It circled the mountain. It rose vertically to land on the courtyard. Jack shook the two girls.

'It's here! Bill's back!'

The girls woke up at once. Snowy, who was asleep by then, woke up and leapt to his feet. He could feel the terrific excitement of the others, and sprang about madly.

'Look – it's landing!' said Jack, and the three of them strained their eyes to see the helicopter, a big dark shadow in the blackness of the night.

There came a slight crashing sound, and then the helicopter suddenly swung over to where Jack and the girls were. They had to dodge out of the way.

Bill's voice came on the air. 'Jack! Are you there?'

Jack ran to the helicopter as Bill switched on a powerful torch. 'I'm here, Bill. The coast's clear. Nobody's up here. Gosh, it's good to have you! Is Philip all right?'

'Quite all right. He's down on the mountain-side with Johns, the fellow who came with me, waiting for us. Get into the helicopter, all of you, and we'll go while the going's good.' Bill switched his torch round to see where the girls were, and in a moment all three were being helped up into the machine.

'I couldn't quite see where to land,' said Bill. 'I must have hit something coming down. I felt a good old jolt, and the helicopter swung round like mad. I hope she's all right!'

'You went into part of the rocky parapet, I think,' said Jack, helping the girls in. 'Oh *Bill*! This is grand! How did you . . . '

'All explanations later!' said Bill, and began to fiddle about with something in front of him. 'Now – here we go!'

The helicopter rose a foot or two in the air and then swung round in a peculiar way. Bill put her back to earth again at once. 'Now what's wrong? She shouldn't do that.'

Lucy-Ann was so longing to be off that she could hardly bear this. 'Let's go, let's go,' she kept saying, till Dinah nudged her to stop. Snowy was on Lucy-Ann's knee, as good as gold. She held on to him tightly, tense with excitement.

Bill tried again. Once more the machine rose into the air, and then did its peculiar swing-round. 'Something's wrong with the steering,' said Bill, in an exasperated voice. 'Why did I leave Johns down there? He might have been able to put it right. But I didn't think this machine would hold him as well as you three!'

In deepening dismay the children sat whilst poor Bill tried his best to get the helicopter to rise and fly properly. But each time it swung round violently, and Bill could do nothing with it. He was secretly rather afraid that it would get completely out of control and swing right off the mountain-top. He could not risk an accident with the three children on board.

For at least an hour Bill experimented with the steering of the helicopter, but it would not answer to the controls at all. He made the children get out to see if lightening the load made any difference, but it didn't.

'It must have got damaged when you struck the parapet,'

said Jack. 'Oh, Bill – what are we going to do now?'

'What about the way out by the wall?' said Bill. 'Philip told me all about it – something about a rope-ladder and so on. As a matter of fact, I did go to find the entrance there, when I came to look for you the other day – you spoke of it in your note, you remember – and I went behind the green curtain, found the crack in the rock and went in. But I couldn't go any further than that curious cave with no roof and the black pool at the bottom.'

'No. Nobody would find how to get out of that cave except by accident,' said Jack. 'We discovered how to get the rope-ladder down from above – by turning a wheel under the water in the pool. Down came the ladder!'

'Well – it seems to me we'll have to try to get out that way,' said Bill. 'This pest of a helicopter won't answer to her controls now. I daren't try and take off. We'd crash – and we haven't any wonderful wings to save us, either!'

'Oh, Bill – can't we really fly off in the helicopter?' said Lucy-Ann, her heart sinking like lead. 'Oh, I don't want to go down into that horrid mountain again! We might lose our way. We might get caught!'

'We'll have to try, I'm afraid, Lucy-Ann,' said Bill. 'Never mind – I'm here to protect you now. And, after all, it's the middle of the night, and nobody is likely to be about.'

'If only that helicopter would go properly!' said Jack. 'It's a piece of real bad luck that it won't. It's such a giveaway too. As soon as anyone sees it, they'll know something's up and will come to look for us.'

'All the more reason why we should get a move on now,' said Bill. 'Come on. Gosh, what's this banging against me? Oh, it's you, Snowy. Well, if you come too, you'll have to keep at our heels or you'll give the game away! By the way – where's Kiki? I haven't seen or heard her tonight.'

'We don't know *where* she is,' said Jack miserably. 'We haven't seen her for days – not since we were captured. She may be caged somewhere – or hiding in the mountain – or even killed!'

'Oh, *no*!' said Lucy-Ann. 'Don't say that. Kiki's too clever to let herself be captured. Perhaps we'll find her tonight!'

'Where's the way out of this place?' asked Bill, switching on his torch. 'Over there? Are there steps that go down into the mountain? Well, come on then. Every minute is precious now.'

They left the damaged helicopter in the yard and went towards the stone steps that led down into the mountain. Lucy-Ann shivered.

'I hoped I'd not go down there again! Take my hand, Bill, I don't like this!'

26

Flight through the mountain

Soon they were right down inside the mountain. They had passed Philip's cave, passed by the stores, and gone down the steep spiral stairway, cut in the rock.

It was very difficult to choose the right way to go, because all the dim lamps that lighted the passages were out. It was quite dark everywhere. Bill's powerful torch sent a bright ray in front of them, but he had to use it cautiously in case someone saw the light, and was warned of their coming.

There was a lot of standing still and listening, a good deal of argument on Jack's part and Dinah's about the right way to go. Bill was very patient, but his voice was urgent as he told them to think hard and choose the right way.

'If we followed Snowy, we'd probably go right,' said Lucy-Ann at last. 'He would know the way.'

'Well – but he doesn't know where we want to go,' said

Jack. 'I mean, if he knew we wanted to go to the rope-ladder cave, he could lead us there all right – but we can't make him understand that.'

They ended up in being completely lost. They found themselves in a dark tunnel, with a very high roof that none of the children recognized at all.

Bill began to feel desperate. If only he had been able to land without damage, this long trek through dark, unknown passages wouldn't have been necessary.

They went down very deep, and, quite suddenly, came out on to the high gallery that overlooked the pit. Bill drew in his breath sharply when he saw the mass of brilliance suddenly showing when the curious floor slid back for a moment. He and the children felt the strange feeling of lightness at once, but it passed immediately the floor slid over the glowing mass again.

There was nobody in the pit. Apparently the floor worked automatically by machinery of some kind, though there was none to be seen. That was the curious thing about the works in the mountain – there was no heavy machinery anywhere. Whatever power was used was not conveyed by iron or steel machines, and there was little noise except for the heavy rumbling that sounded before the shaking of the earth.

'There's obviously some metal in this mountain that can be used for that fellow's experiments,' said Bill. 'Some rare metal or other – like uranium, which is used for splitting the atom. There are a few mountains in the world which contain various rare metals – but usually they are mined for it and the stuff is taken out. In this case they haven't mined it – they are using it where it is! It's possible that they have to do that – in order to use the enormous thickness of the rocks in the mountain to protect the outer world from whatever rays they are experimenting with. Very ingenious!'

'I think we know the way back now,' said Jack, quite thankful at having found some place they recognized, even though it was the frightening pit!

He pointed behind them, up the wide, uphill passage that he knew went up and up for a long way. Bill switched his torch on it. 'Is that the way?' he said. 'Well, come along then.'

They went up the wide, steep passage. They came to the narrow, twisty little tunnel they had been in before and walked along till they came to the fork.

'Left-hand fork,' said Jack, and they took that. Bill was amazed to see the beautiful silken hangings that decorated the walls further on, and hung across the entrance to a cave.

Jack put his hand on Bill's arm. 'That's the king's bedroom, beyond,' he whispered. 'Dinah, have you got Snowy? Don't let him rush on in front.'

Bill tiptoed to the curtains and parted them. A dim light shone beyond. Bill looked with interest into the king's bedroom – and then closed the curtains quickly. He tiptoed back to the children.

'There's somebody lying on the couch there,' he whispered. 'An old fellow with a colossal forehead.'

'That's the king of the mountain!' whispered back Jack. 'The Great Brain behind all these inventions. I think he is an absolute genius, but quite mad.'

'He seems to be asleep,' said Bill. 'Is there any way we can go round this cave without waking him up?'

'No. I don't know of any,' said Jack. 'We've got to go through it, and then through a cave where he eats his meals, and then into the throne-room.'

Bill thought for a moment. 'We'll have to risk it then,' he said. 'We'll go through the room one by one but for heaven's sake don't make a sound!'

They went through the king's bedroom one at a time, hardly daring to breathe. Dinah had tight hold of Snowy, praying that he wouldn't bleat when he went through the room!

Fortunately there were very thick carpets on the floor, so it was easy to make no sound. Lucy-Ann's heart beat so loudly as she tiptoed across that she thought it must surely wake the king with a jump.

Then they were in the room where the long table had held so much lovely food. But now it was empty and there was not so much as a dish of fruit on it.

Then on to the throne-room – and outside this, behind the lovely hangings patterned with the red dragons, the little company paused. A curious noise came to their ears – was it snoring? What was it?

Bill peeped through the hangings very cautiously. He grinned. In the throne-room, sitting or lying, were the paratroopers. A very long table had been set down the middle, and on it were the remains of a lavish supply of food and drink. Not a single man was awake!

'So that's where those fellows have been the last day or two!' whispered Jack. 'I wondered where they were. Gosh, they've fallen asleep where they are – what a pretty sight!'

Bill fumbled about in the hangings they were looking through. He was looking for a switch. He found one and whispered to the children. 'Now listen – I'm going to switch off the light so that we can get through the hall without being seen. Keep close to one side of it and get through as quietly as possible. Even if we do make a noise and some of those fellows wake up it won't matter – because they won't be able to see who it is!'

This was a good idea. The light went out with a slight click and the great hall was in darkness. The children, led by Bill, moved quietly along one side, their feet making no noise on the soft mats.

When they came to the immense laboratory Bill stood still in amazement. He knew a great deal more about these things than the children did, of course, and he could see what a brilliant, ingenious mind must be at the back of all the things at work there.

They stood in the gallery and looked down at the wires and wheels, the glass jars and the crystal boxes, and heard the quiet, purposeful humming going on.

'What is it all doing, Bill?' whispered Lucy-Ann.

'It's transmuting, or changing, one power or energy into another,' said Bill soberly. 'Making it into usable form, so that . . .'

'So that it can be imprisoned in those "wings," for instance?' said Jack.

'Something like that,' said Bill. 'It's an amazing set-up altogether.'

There was nobody there. It did seem extraordinary that all these humming, spinning, whirring things should go on and on seemingly of their own accord, with just the king wandering round them occasionally.

Bill was so fascinated that for a few moments he forgot the urgency of finding the way out of the mountain. There was something dream-like about all this – it didn't seem real.

He was brought back to reality again by feeling Snowy butting against him. He jumped a little. Then he took Lucy-Ann's arm. 'Come along! What am I thinking of, stopping like this!'

Jack had found the passage that led out of the laboratory. He led them down it and they came to the great cave they had seen before. Bill's torch swept round it but there was nothing to see. Then they went into the passage that led to the roofless cave! The children felt they really were getting near freedom again – if only, only, only they could find out how to get that rope-ladder out of its place in the wall!

They passed the dim lamps, which, for some reason or other, were lighted here. They came to the roofless cave, and Bill's torch picked out the pitchers of ice-cold water standing at the back to refresh those who had had the long and exhausting climb up the rope-ladder.

'This is the place where the ladder's kept,' said Jack, and he took Bill's torch and swung it to find the place in the rocky wall where they had seen it last.

But before he could spot it, Lucy-Ann tripped over something and fell with a thud. Bill picked her up. She had hurt her knees but she didn't make a sound. Bill told Jack to flash his torch on Lucy-Ann to see what she had fallen over.

She had stumbled over the rope-ladder itself! There it lay, stretching from its place in the wall, over the floor and then disappearing downwards over the edge of the cave – down, down, down to the cave with the pool far below!

'Look! The ladder's out!' cried Jack, forgetting to whisper in his excitement. 'Oh, Bill – let's come on down at once!

'Somebody must have gone out of the mountain tonight,' said Dinah, 'and left the ladder down to come back by. I wonder who it was. We'd better be careful we don't meet them!'

'Jack, you go down first,' said Bill, who had been examining with great interest the way the ladder was attached to the hole in the wall. It was extremely ingenious. Bill could see how wires must be run up from the wheel in the pool to a lever which released the ladder – whose weight then compelled it to run out over the floor to the edge of the cave, where it fell and then pulled itself undone until it had come to its last rung. What made it able to roll itself up again Bill could not imagine – but the brain that could devise all the amazing things inside that mountain would find that a very simple problem!

Jack went to the place where the ladder hung over the edge. He knelt down and put his feet one after another on a rung a little way down. The ladder felt as firm as before. It was very well made and strong.

'Well, here I go,' said Jack. 'Send the girls next, Bill, and then you come. Snowy's gone already, down whatever little hole he and the dogs use! I don't know where that is. I only wish I knew where poor old Kiki was. I don't like leaving her all alone in this beastly mountain.'

Bill shone his torch on him. The girls watched his head disappear as he climbed down.

'You go now, Lucy-Ann,' said Bill. 'Jack must be a good way down. You won't tread on his head. Then Dinah can go, and I'll follow last of all. Don't attempt to leave the cave below till I am down with you.'

Jack was going steadily down. What a long long way it was! And then a very peculiar thing happened. The ladder began to shake below him! Jack stopped climbing at once.

'Gracious! Somebody's climbing *up*! And I'm climbing down! Whoever can it be!'

27

Escape at last

No sooner had he felt certain that somebody was climbing up very steadily below him than Jack immediately stopped climbing down and began climbing back again at top speed. He didn't want to meet Meier or Erlick on that ladder.

Some way up he bumped into Lucy-Ann's feet. She gave a small squeal of surprise. 'It's all right, Lucy-Ann. It's only me,' said Jack in a low voice. 'There's somebody coming *up* the ladder. Go back again as quickly as you can!'

Lucy-Ann at once began to climb up as fast as possible, in a great fright. Gracious! How awful to feel that somebody was coming up the ladder just as they were going down! She felt certain it was that horrid Meier!

She in turn bumped into Dinah's feet and passed the urgent message on to the surprised girl. Dinah began to climb back again up to the cave at the top very quickly indeed. Lucy-Ann and Jack were immediately below her. Jack felt as if somebody might catch his ankles at any moment.

And, of course, the next thing was that Dinah nearly got her head trodden on by Bill's big feet. He was descending at top speed to join the others, and was most amazed to find Dinah just below him.

'What's the matter? Didn't I tell you to buck up?' he said, and then caught Dinah's agonized whisper.

'Somebody's coming up! Quick, before they get Jack. Quick, Bill!'

Muttering something under his breath Bill climbed back quickly. He pulled Dinah up, then Lucy-Ann, then Jack. The ladder still shook. The climber, or climbers, were coming up steadily.

'Back into the passages!' commanded Bill. 'We can't afford to be caught now. We'll wait till whoever it is has gone and then we'll try again.'

They came to where the passage forked into three, and Bill pushed them all up into the darkest one – but coming towards them were footsteps, and somebody's shadow at the far end! They all rushed back again.

But now the climber had reached the top of the ladder and was behind them. They tried the second passage and found themselves in a maze of funny little caves, all leading one out of another.

'Wait here!' said Bill. But they had been seen, and challenging voices now began to echo along the dark passages.

'Who's there? Come out at once!'

They didn't stir. They were all crouched in a dark corner, overhung by a rocky ledge. Bill wondered if the beam of a torch would find them. He was afraid it would.

The feet passed by in another cave. Then came more voices. The hunt was on! Bill groaned. It sounded as if four or five searchers were about now. They would separate and search until they had found them. And they had been so near freedom!

'Come,' said Bill after a moment. 'We'll try a better cave than this.'

But, before they could move, the flash of a torch shone into their cave. They all stiffened and stood absolutely still.

The beam came nearer and nearer. Lucy-Ann forgot to breathe, and stood with her hand firmly clasped in Bill's.

Just as the beam of the torch was picking out Jack's feet – or so it seemed to Jack – a surprising interruption came. A voice came from somewhere near by, a hollow, mournful voice, full of misery and despair.

'Poor Kiki! Ding dong bell! Peepbo!'

Jack's heart leapt. *Kiki!* She wasn't dead, then! She must have been wandering, completely lost, all about the passages and caves for days. She didn't know they were close to her. She had seen the light of the torch and heard voices, and as usual she had joined in the conversation.

Bill's hand squeezed Jack's arm warningly. He was afraid the boy might call Kiki, or exclaim out loud in delight. But Jack held his tongue. Kiki went on talking in the most melancholy voice imaginable.

'Send for the doctor! Musty, fusty, dusty, pooh, gah!'

Jack had never heard her so miserable before. Poor Kiki! She must have thought herself quite deserted.

A sharp voice rang through the cave. 'What in the world was that? Somebody's in this cave! Erlick, come here! Did you hear that?'

'What?' asked Erlick, coming in with another torch.

'A voice,' said Meier. 'Somebody's in here. Two people, probably. One talking to another. Stand there with your torch whilst I walk all round with mine.'

Meier began to walk round, examining all the walls carefully for hiding-places. Bill groaned silently. Now they had no chance to get to another cave at all.

Kiki gave a realistic sneeze and then a cough. Meier stopped his search and swung his torch in the direction of the sound.

'We can hear you! Come out or it will be the worse for you!' he shouted, in a furious tone.

Kiki was frightened. She had been without food for some time, and was hungry and unhappy. The man's angry voice filled her with panic and she flew off into the next cave, having no idea that her beloved Jack was so near her. It was just as well that she didn't know, for if she had known she would certainly have flown to Jack's shoulder and given their hiding-place away at once!

Her voice came from the cave further on.

'Polly put the kettle on! Send for the doctor!' Then came a loud hiccup, and an apologetic 'Pardon!'

'Good heavens! What's going on?' cried Meier, completely puzzled. 'It's that voice again that we've been hearing at intervals. Well, where there's a voice there's a body and I'm going to find it this time, if I have to shoot the caves to pieces!'

A loud report made Bill and the children jump in fright. Meier had drawn his revolver and fired wildly in the direction of Kiki's voice. Jack didn't like that a bit. He was afraid Kiki might be hit.

Meier and Erlick went into the next cave after Kiki's voice. It came to them from further away.

'Upsadaisy! Wipe your feet, you naughty boy.'

The children couldn't help smiling, scared though they were. Kiki always managed to say such ridiculous things in moments of urgency. There came another shot, which echoed all round the caves.

Kiki gave a cackle of scornful laughter, and then made a noise like a car changing gear. She came back to the next cave again, and the men followed. They still had not caught sight of Kiki because they were looking for a human being, running away in front of them, whereas Kiki flew high in the roof of the caves, and perched on small ledges, well hidden.

Somebody else ran through the cave where the children were, calling to Meier.

'Mr Meier, sir, sir! All children run away! Helicopter come back. All alone on mountain-top. No one there. Children run away!'

It was one of the numerous soldiers, who had evidently

discovered the returned helicopter, and the disappearance of the pilot and the children. There was an amazed silence.

Meier raised his voice and let forth a stream of furious foreign words, none of which Bill or the children could understand. Then came Erlick's voice.

'No good going on like that, Meier. Get out the dogs. The children must have gone down the ladder. You left it down when you went out tonight, didn't you? The dogs will soon round them all up.'

'What's happened to the pilot, though?' raged Meier, and lapsed into some foreign language again. The soldier came pattering back through the cave again, presumably on his way to get the dogs.

'Send for the doctor,' called Kiki mournfully. She screeched like an engine and made Meier flash his torch in and out of the caves again, almost beside himself with rage.

Erlick, Meier and one or two others with them then began a loud argument in many languages. Bill didn't wait to hear what it was all about. He pushed the children out of their hiding-place and towards the nearest passage. Very quietly and quickly they all fled back towards the cave with the ladder. Maybe there was a chance now of escape. Jack wished with all his heart that he could take Kiki too.

They went down the ladder in the same order as before, Jack wondering fearfully if he would find anyone coming up this time, ready to catch him by the ankles. But he didn't. He reached the bottom safely, his legs shaking with the effort, panting and exhausted.

Lucy-Ann almost fell off the last rung, weak with relief to find she was at last at the bottom. It had seemed an endless climb down to her. She sank to the ground beside the pool, her heart beating painfully.

Dinah followed and threw herself on the ground too. Then came Bill, not so distressed as the others, but very glad indeed to be at the bottom of the ladder.

'Phew! The bottom at last!' he said. 'What a climb! Now

come on – out we go on the mountain-side. We'll join up with Philip and Johns. If only those wretched dogs don't find us! Philip's told me about them and how you thought they were wolves. I don't fancy a pack of Alsatians on my trail, somehow, with Meier and Erlick urging them on!'

The dawn was beginning to come over the mountains. The sun was not yet above them, but a golden light was spreading upwards from the east. The children were very glad indeed to feel the fresh wind on their faces when they went out through the crack in the rock, and swung aside the big green curtain of creeper and bramble. They took deep breaths and gazed around them in the silvery light of dawn.

'Come on,' said Bill. 'I left Philip and Johns by a stream – where you left Dapple. We took Dapple back with us by the way, when David, Effans and I came with the rest of the donkeys to look for you. Philip said you'd know where the place was, even if we landed a little way from it in the helicopter – he thinks we're all coming through the air of course, to land on a good flat place where we left a light burning to guide me. It was a bit tricky landing in the dark with Philip and Johns! The helicopter nearly overbalanced. Still, we managed it.'

'Philip will be looking out for us by that light then?' said Lucy-Ann. 'Not by the stream.'

'No. I told him not to, in case anyone was roaming about there, saw the light and spotted him and Johns,' explained Bill. 'I thought Meier and Co. might possibly be on the lookout for Philip, if they thought he had jumped. I was supposed to radio back to them what had happened – but I didn't, of course!'

It was easy to find their way to the meeting-place, now that dawn was coming. But before they got there, a bit of good luck came to Jack – in the shape of Kiki!

She suddenly sailed down on him from the air with a cackle of delight, and a screech that nearly deafened them all. She flew to his shoulder and rubbed her head into his ear, giving it little pecks and pulls of love. Jack was so overjoyed that he couldn't say a word. He just scratched Kiki's head and made funny, loving noises, which Kiki immediately copied.

'Oh, *good*!' said Lucy-Ann in delight. 'Oh, Jack! Dear old Kiki, isn't it lovely to have her again. It's been awful without you, Kiki.'

Even Bill joined in the demonstrations of affection. 'You saved us, Kiki, old bird! You led those fellows such a song and dance that they let us escape. How did you know where we were? Did you fly out and follow us?'

Kiki didn't tell them, so they never knew, but Jack felt sure she had flown down into the roofless cave, and come out of the crack into the open air. Then she must have heard their voices and come to join them.

'God save the Queen,' said Kiki, in a happy voice, and gave a loud hiccup. 'Pardon! Pardon the queen pop goes Polly!

'Oh, Kiki! We thought you were dead,' said Dinah. She looked round, missing Snowy. 'And now Snowy's gone! Where is he?'

'He hasn't been with us for some time,' said Bill. 'He'll turn up, I expect – just like Kiki!'

'Dithery Slithery,' said Kiki suddenly, cocking her head on one side and looking at Jack's pocket. Sally the slow-worm was half in and half out, enjoying being out in the fresh air again. Dinah didn't even squeal!

They went on their way, with Kiki firmly on Jack's shoulder – and suddenly they heard a yell.

'Hie! Here we are! Jack! Dinah! Lucy-Ann! Bill! And oh, I say, there's Kiki too. Hurrah! You've escaped! But where's the helicopter? We've been waiting and waiting for it.'

It was Philip, of course, leaping up and down like a mad thing, with Johns standing stolidly behind him – and Snowy frisking about round them both. He had found Philip! So all the family were together again. They were full of delight – but wait – what was that howling noise in the distance?

'The dogs!' said Jack. 'They're after us!'

28

Trailed by the dogs

Lucy-Ann shrank back against Bill and Johns when she heard the savage howls and barks. She didn't at all like the idea of the dogs being after them!

Bill and Johns exchanged glances, and Bill said something under his breath and looked stubborn and angry. They had all been so pleased at their escape – and now here they were, about to be caught again! Nobody could do anything against ten man-hunting dogs!

'Bill! Get into the stream and wade up through the water,' said Jack suddenly. 'That's what the other man did when he wanted to break his scent. Dogs can't smell a trail through water. Let's all wade up the stream, and try and find a good hiding-place – a big tree, like Sam went up.'

'Well – it's a poor chance,' said Bill, 'but we'll try it! Blow that helicopter – behaving like that just when I wanted to take off to safety! We'd have been quite all right by now if it hadn't been for the damage to the steering.'

They all waded into the middle of the little stream. Up it they went, the water very cold to their feet. Lucy-Ann was between Bill and Johns. She felt very glad indeed that there were two grown-ups with them! In the distance the dogs barked again. They were certainly on the trail!

The little company went up the stream as quickly as they could, so that their scent was well broken. But they could easily be seen, and it was essential that they should get up into a tree, or find a cave as soon as they could.

And soon they found just exactly the thing! The stream disappeared into a large hole in the mountain. The clear water came bubbling out from there into the sunshine swirling round the feet of the two men and the children – and of Snowy too!

'Look – it comes from that big hole,' said Bill, pleased. 'We'll go in there and hope it will take us all. We ought to be able to hide here till the dogs give up all hope of finding us.'

They crawled in one by one. Bill switched on his torch. There was only just room for them all, because a few yards back the hole narrowed down to a tiny tunnel, out of which the stream gushed madly.

They sat down where they could, squeezed up closely against one another. Jack and Philip had their feet in the stream. They sat there, listening to the distant yelping of the Alsatians.

Bill pulled some chocolate out of his pocket. 'I forgot about this,' he said, and handed it round. It was very comforting to have something to nibble. Johns had brought some too, so there was plenty.

'Do you think the dogs have lost the trail now?' asked Jack, not hearing the barking coming any closer.

'Yes. Sounds like it,' said Bill. 'They're at a loss, I should think. They must have come to the stream, jumped over it and found the trail was at an end. They probably won't have the sense to realize we've gone upstream.'

'But I should think the men with them would guess,' said big stolid Johns, who was taking this extraordinary adventure with the utmost calm, as if things like that happened to him every day. 'I know I would! If I were hunting a man with dogs, and we came to a stop by a stream, I'd order the dogs up or downstream at once.'

'Oh dear!' said Lucy-Ann. 'Would you really? Well, I'm sure Meier will, then, when he catches up with the dogs, because he's terribly clever. He's got the most piercing eyes, Bill – honestly they go right through you.'

'Well, he'd better try looking right through *me*,' said Bill. 'He'd be sorry!'

'Pardon!' said Kiki. 'Sorry!'

'You forgot your hiccup, old thing,' said Jack, and Kiki solemnly produced one. Johns laughed suddenly. He said he'd heard plenty of hiccups without birds, and seen plenty of birds without hiccups – but when you got the two together it was worth a lot!

'The dogs are coming nearer,' said Jack suddenly. They all listened, straining their ears. It was true. Their howls were distinctly louder.

'Meier's caught up with them, then,' said Dinah. 'And he's guessed our trick, and they're all coming upstream.'

'Yes. And they're sure to smell us here,' said Philip. 'Absolutely certain to. We can't diddle dogs like that!'

'Hey diddle diddle,' said Kiki, and screeched.

'Shut up,' said Jack, and tapped her on her beak. 'Do you want the dogs to hear you?'

'Pooh,' said Kiki, and nipped Jack's ear.

'Listen! I can hear the dogs splashing in the stream!' cried Philip. And so he could. The sound came to everyone's ears, and Lucy-Ann clutched Bill's hand even more tightly. Would this horrid adventure never end?

And then they saw the first dog, his red tongue hanging out, his breath coming in excited pants. He was half leaping in the water, not wading – in and out he leapt, in and out, coming nearer and nearer.

Then came Meier's hateful voice. 'Go on! Get them! Find them!'

The leading dog came right up to the hiding-place. He could smell everyone in there, as he stood in the stream outside the hole. He did not attempt to go in. He had found what he had been told to find – he had not been told to capture and hold.

He lifted his head and howled like a wolf. Kiki was very surprised. She attempted an imitation but an Alsatian's howl was beyond her. She only produced a curious whirring noise that made the dog cock his big head on one side and listen.

Then the other dogs came up, panting too, their tongues all hanging out. They stood beside and behind their leader, sniffing. They looked very fierce indeed!

'Not a nice sight,' murmured Bill to Johns, who was staring stolidly at the dogs as if he was perfectly used to being hunted by a pack of Alsatians and didn't mind it at all.

'Keep still,' Bill commanded everyone. 'As long as we don't attempt to move or get away the dogs won't do anything more than stand there and stare.'

There came the sound of shouts and Meier and Erlick appeared, very red in the face with running. Meier stopped dead when he saw the pack of dogs standing looking in the hole where the stream poured out.

He pushed Erlick behind a tree quickly. It was plain that he feared Bill might have a gun. He shouted out loudly.

'Come on out! The dogs have found you. If you don't want them to set on you, come on out – and throw any gun you've got down on the ground, and put your hands up. We've got you covered.'

'Pleasant fellow, isn't he?' said Johns to Bill. 'It'll be nice to get hold of him. Do we go out, boss, or don't we?'

'We don't,' said Bill shortly. 'I doubt if he'll dare to set the dogs on us. He knows the children are here.'

'Meier wouldn't stick at anything,' said Jack. And he was right. When there was no answer, and not even a movement from the hole in the hill, Meier began to lose his temper as usual. He shouted out something in a foreign language, then changed to English.

'You heard what I said. You have one more chance. The dogs are ready to pounce. They'll round you up all right, and I warn you, their teeth are sharp, so don't resist!'

Still nobody moved. Lucy-Ann shut her eyes. She really couldn't look at the eager, panting dogs any more. She could see that they were just awaiting the word to rush into the cave and drag them all out.

And then Philip suddenly moved, and before anyone could stop him, he was outside the cave.

'Put your hands up!' called Meier, and Philip put them up. The dogs sniffed at him, and under his breath Philip talked to them.

'Don't you remember me? I'm Philip. You slept with me up on the rock. Fine dogs you are. We're friends, don't you remember?'

The dogs did not understand one word, but they understood his tone of voice. They remembered this boy. They felt his friendliness and his attraction. The leader began to whine a little. He longed to have this boy pat his head. But Philip had his hands above his head, and had only his voice to charm the dogs with.

He went on talking to them in a low voice, whilst the other children, and Bill and Johns, watched spellbound. They all thought the same. Philip, Philip, what is there in you that makes all creatures your friends? What gift have you got, so rare, so irresistible? 'Lucky boy!' thought Bill. 'And lucky for every one of us that you can charm these dogs!'

Meier called out angrily. 'Where are the others? Tell them to come too, or I'll give the order for them to be dragged out!'

The leader dog stood up and put his paws on Philip's shoulders. He licked the boy's face. It was a very wet lick, but Philip did not even turn away his face. That was the signal for all the other dogs to come round too. Quite forgetting Meier, they milled round Philip, trying to get near him, sniffing at him, giving him a lick when they got near enough.

He put down his hands. Meier would not dare to take a shot at him now in case he killed a dog! He ran his hands over their backs, patted their heads, rubbed their noses, and all the time he talked to them in the special voice he kept for animals.

Meier snapped out an order to the dogs. 'Fetch them out! Get them! Bring them here!'

The dogs turned their heads automatically at his commanding voice. They hesitated. The leader looked at Philip. 'Come with me,' said Philip. 'Come. You will find more friends in here.'

And, to Meier's everlasting astonishment, the boy actually led all the dogs to the cave, where at least four of them squeezed in to lick Lucy-Ann, Jack and Dinah! They sniffed doubtfully at Bill and Johns, growled at Snowy and Kiki, and then, when Philip laid a hand on Bill's arm and then on Johns', they accepted them as friends too.

'Philip! You're a marvel!' said Bill, in heartfelt admiration. 'It's magic you use – can't be anything else!'

'What a boy!' said the stolid Johns, allowing his face to change its expression for once in a way, and show great admiration.

'Meier's shortly going to have a fit, I think,' said Jack. 'He just can't understand all this!'

'Fetch them out, I say! I'll shoot the lot of you dogs, if you don't obey orders!' stormed Meier. 'What's come over you? Fetch them out!'

The dogs took absolutely no notice at all. Their leader had accepted Philip as master now, and they all followed his decision. What Philip said they would obey. They feared Meier, but they loved Philip.

Meier suddenly fired his revolver in a fury. He did not fire at the dogs, but over their heads. They jumped and growled, turning their heads towards him. Bill judged it was time to do something.

'Philip! Will the dogs obey you? Will they go for Meier and Erlick? If they will – order them to! We'll give that couple a taste of their own medicine!'

29

The tables are turned!

'Right!' said Philip. He pointed to the tree where Meier and Erlick were hiding behind its big trunk. 'See, boys! Fetch them out! Bring them here! Fetch them for me, then!'

Before Meier or Erlick knew what was happening the pack of Alsatians was speeding joyfully to obey. The whole pack flung themselves on the two rogues, and bore them to the ground. There was no chance to use a revolver. In fact Meier's gun rolled on the ground and was completely lost under the scrambling crowd of dogs.

'Don't hurt them! Bring them here!' ordered Philip in excitement, proud of his power to give commands to the pack of dogs.

Bill and Johns were now out of the cave, and Jack followed. The girls did not come out yet. They didn't want to! Lucy-Ann clutched Dinah's arm till she squealed. Both girls watched what was happening, breathless with intense excitement.

The dogs began to drag the two men over to Philip. Erlick, the great ape-like fellow, a real bully if ever there was one, was screaming for mercy, a coward, like all bullies. 'Call them off! I'll surrender! Call them off, boy!'

Meier fought savagely, not seeming to care whether he was bitten or not. He could not find his revolver and was beside himself with amazement, anger and fear.

The dogs were trained not to bite unless commanded, but one or two of them gave him a well-deserved nip – a little repayment for his callousness in dealing with them in their training. The leader got hold of him by the slack of his trousers, and, looking rather ridiculous, Meier was brought to where the boys and the two men were standing watching.

Then Erlick was brought too, trying to stand, almost weeping with panic. He remembered a gun he had in his pocket, and he reached to get it, thinking it was his last chance of escape.

But Johns was on the spot. 'Hands up,' he said. 'Any funny business on your part, Erlick, and the dogs can have you for all I care. Stand up, Meier, and put your hands up too.'

White with rage Meier put up his hands when the dogs allowed him to find his feet. He glared at the boys and Bill.

'What did you do to the dogs?' he snapped at Philip. 'They've never turned on me before!' He lapsed into a foreign language again and poured out streams of abuse.

'Shut up,' said Bill, who was now holding his own revolver in his hand. 'You talk too much.'

'Wipe your feet,' said Kiki's voice and she flew out of the hole and on to Jack's shoulder. 'Pooh! Gah!'

Meier glared at the parrot, recognizing the voice that had puzzled him for so long. If looks could have killed, certainly Kiki would have fallen dead at that moment. As it was she went off into one of her dreadful cackles, and Meier clenched the fists he was holding above his head, wishing that for one moment he could get hold of Kiki.

'What do we do now?' enquired Jack. 'It's a long way from home, Bill – and we've got no food to keep us going if we have to walk back.'

'Effans and Trefor and David are not far off,' said Bill. 'I told them to stand by somewhere near this mountain with plenty of donkeys, in case we needed them. I wasn't sure if the helicopter would fly very far with such a lot of you on board!'

'*Oh!* Will they really be near here?' said Lucy-Ann, gladly. 'Oh, Bill – you think of everything! Oh, *good*!'

'Can we take the dogs back with us?' asked Philip, who was still surrounded by furry bodies and wagging tails. 'I could look after them till we get them away somewhere. I daresay you'd like them for the police force, Bill. They're jolly well trained.'

'Thanks for the offer,' said Bill, with a grin. 'I'll accept it. And now – quick march! We'll leave this surprising mountain behind, and I and a few others will come back to it later. I feel it wants a little cleaning up. And we'll take that mad genius in charge before he does something dangerous. I wouldn't put it past him to blow up the mountain.'

'Good gracious!' said Lucy-Ann, in alarm. 'Well, let's get away before he does!'

They set off at a smart walk. Meier and Erlick walked in sullen silence. They had their hands by their sides now, for Johns had searched them both, and they were now weaponless. Jack and the others began to feel a familiar feeling of emptiness under their belts.

'I'm jolly hungry,' announced Dinah. 'Has Effans brought any food with him, do you think?'

'Well, Mrs Evans was so upset to hear that you were lost, that she immediately did an enormous baking,' said Bill, 'and I believe two of the donkeys are laden with the results. So let's hurry!'

'Where are they?' asked Jack.

'In the Vale of Butterflies, waiting for us patiently,' said Bill, with a grin. This was a most surprising thing to hear.

'The Vale of Butterflies!' cried Jack. 'Why, we couldn't find it! We began to think it was all Trefor's make-up!'

'Oh, no. It was really quite easy to find, if only David had known how to read a map,' said Bill. 'The name was on it in Welsh, so you wouldn't have understood it. But I don't believe David has ever learned to read a map properly! I shouldn't have let him go off with you as guide.'

'Did *you* find it then?' asked Lucy-Ann.

'Oh, yes. It's on the way here, actually,' said Bill. 'David took a wrong road, that's all – accidentally left the track. Anyway I told him to wait there with the donkeys, because I thought you'd rather like to see the butterfly valley, after having missed it and found a very strange mountain instead!'

'Oh! Everything's coming right!' said Lucy-Ann joyfully. 'The adventure is over, isn't it, Bill? Well – it doesn't seem nearly so bad now as it did!'

'Poor Lucy-Ann!' said Bill. 'You do have adventures thrust upon you, don't you? Never mind, you'll soon be back at the farm, enjoying Mrs Evans' wonderful cooking!'

'As soon as you came, things were all right,' said Lucy-Ann happily. 'It was super hearing you yell out, "Don't forget Bill Smugs!" last night. Gosh, was it only last night? It seems years ago!'

They went through a narrow pass between two mountains, feeling hungrier and hungrier – and there below them was the Vale of Butterflies!

They stopped in delight. The valley was a froth of coloured butterflies, red, yellow, white, pink, blue, copper, brown! There were thousands there, fluttering in the sunlight, darting erratically to and fro, hovering, dropping down to the millions of flowers. These made a carpet of brilliant colour, and the children thought they had never seen such a lovely sight before.

'Why are there so many butterflies, I wonder!' marvelled Dinah.

'I suppose because there are so many varieties of food-plants,' said Bill. 'This valley is apparently as famous for flowers as for butterflies, but because it is so much off the beaten track, it is rarely visited. I've no doubt the pack of dogs would have kept trippers away, anyhow!'

'There's Effans – and the donkeys!' cried Philip. 'Hey, Effans! Hallo, Trefor – and David!'

Dapple moved to greet Snowy, who ran in delight to his friend. Effans beamed. Trefor's blue eyes shone. Only David did not greet them eagerly. He kept his eyes on the ground and seemed ashamed.

'He got it hot and strong from Mrs Evans when he arrived

back alone with the donkeys chasing after him,' explained Bill. 'I also had a few words to say to him, as you can imagine! So he now feels he can't look anyone in the face. It won't do him any harm to feel like that for a while. He behaved foolishly!'

'Poor David!' said Lucy-Ann. 'I expect he's sorry now,' and she spoke to the old man kindly. He looked at her gratefully.

'It's good to see you again, indeed to gootness it is, whateffer!' said Effans in his singing voice.

'Whateffer, whateffer!' shouted Kiki in delight. 'Look you, look you, whateffer!'

'That bird!' said Effans in great admiration. 'Look you, it iss a marvel, that bird. I would give ten pounds for a bird like that, whateffer!'

'She's not for sale,' said Jack, stroking Kiki. 'No, not for a million pounds. Where's the food, Effans? We're starving!'

'All explanations after the meal!' said Bill to Effans. 'We'll have a talk then, Effans, whilst the children go mad over the butterflies! Meier, Erlick, keep over there. Philip, tell the dogs to look after them.'

Effans stared in surprise at the two sullen men. Meier glared back. Erlick was full of self-pity, and had even begun to reproach Meier for his carelessness in letting them be captured. Meier looked at Erlick as if he could snap at him like the dogs.

'A pretty couple,' said Bill. 'I think we'll turn our backs on them. They spoil the view.'

Joyfully the children settled down to the finest picnic they had ever had. Mrs Evans had indeed surpassed herself. There was roast chicken, tender tongue, spiced ham, hard-boiled eggs, cucumbers, tomatoes, potted meat, fresh fruit, home-made lemonade which Effans had cleverly left cooling in a near-by stream, and so many other eatables that the boys despaired of even being able to taste them all!

They sat there on the hillside, the carpet of bright flowers spread at their feet – unbelievably brilliant in colour! And the butterflies!

'They're like flying flowers!' cried Lucy-Ann in joy. 'Hundreds of them! Thousands of them! What are they, Philip?'

'Fritillaries, painted ladies, commas, peacocks, ringlets, coppers, skippers, heaths . . . ' reeled off Philip. 'My word, what a paradise of butterflies! I really will never forget this all my life long!'

It was a wonderful picnic – wonderful food, gorgeous butterflies, brilliant flowers – and plenty of laughter and jokes! Kiki was quite mad, and when she saw how Johns and Effans admired her, she showed off tremendously. She gave them her whole repertoire of noises, and Effans laughed till he choked.

The stolid Johns munched away, keeping his eyes on Kiki, and occasionally giving a slight smile at her more outrageous sayings.

'Indeed to gootness, whateffer! Wipe your feet and blow your nose. Pifflebunk! Pardon!'

Snowy wandered round taking titbits from everyone. The dogs watched from a distance, feeling certain that their friend Philip would not forget them. It was a very good thing that Mrs Evans had provided so much, because with two prisoners and ten dogs every scrap of food would be needed!

Bill, Johns and Effans exchanged news when the children had gone to wander through the clouds of butterflies. Effans listened gravely. Trefor and David tried to understand, but most of what Bill said was beyond their English. Effans told them the story in Welsh later.

'They are brave children, look you,' said Effans. 'Very brave children, whateffer!'

30

The end of it all!

They had to sleep out in the open that night. Effans gave the children the rugs he had brought, because all their sleeping things had been left behind in the cave, on the mountain-side. The prisoners slept apart, guarded by the dogs. It was very warm, and Snowy got pushed off by everyone when he tried to cuddle down first on top of Philip, then on Jack, and then on the girls.

They had had a very long talk with Bill and told him all their adventures down to the last detail. Bill had marvelled at their accidental discovery of the strange mountain and its even stranger secret. He had examined the 'wings' which Philip had given to Johns to take care of for him.

'I shall take those back to school with me next term!' he said. 'Won't the boys stare! I bet some of them will want to try them!'

'Well, all I can say is I should discourage anyone from jumping off the school roof or anything like that, and trusting to these wings,' said Bill drily. 'I have a feeling that the ingenious brain behind these things is failing a little – the old "king" will never discover how to make the wings he so much wants to make. But he certainly has invented some remarkable things. I have had a talk with Meier, and he has told me why he believed in Monally – that's the "king's" real name.'

'Why did he believe in him?' asked the children curiously.

'Well, apparently he has, at one time or another, produced the most remarkable inventions,' said Bill, 'and Meier has backed him and made a great deal of money out of them. How he came to find this mountain, and the rare metal in its heart, which the "king" wanted for his latest idea of conquering the pull of the earth, I haven't been able to find out yet. Some dirty work of some sort, I expect.'

'What are you going to do about everything?' asked Jack.

'Well – the paratroopers will be sent back home. The soldiers will be questioned and also sent back. I have a feeling there's something strange about them too. The "king" will be taken into safety,' said Bill. 'I shall send two or three scientists to the mountain to let them report on what they find there. I shouldn't be surprised if they advise us to destroy everything in it. The "king" has been meddling with dangerous things. With no one there to keep a guiding hand on them there might be a vast explosion.'

'It's a good thing we discovered it, isn't it?' said Lucy-Ann.

'A very good thing,' said Bill. 'And it's an even better thing you left that note with Dapple. If it hadn't been for that I'd never have found you.'

'What happened?' asked Jack.

'I came along to find you, complete with donkeys, after David's rush home,' said Bill. 'Instead I found only Dapple – and the note, which talked of very peculiar things indeed, and made me smell a very large rat.'

'Go on,' said Philip, interested.

'Well, I snooped round but couldn't find my way in through the roofless cave,' said Bill. 'So the only thing to do was to start finding out about helicopters. If somebody could land on that mountain-top, then so could I!'

'Good old Bill!' said Jack.

'And then,' said Bill, 'I found when I began making enquiries about all the helicopters in this country, who owned them and so on, that other people were also making enquiries about a few of them! Some of the helicopters had been flying off in suspicious circumstances, nobody knew where. So the police were even then enquiring into the matter – and I joined them, hotfoot!'

'And what did you find?' asked Dinah.

'I found a young pilot, with a terrific scar across his face!' said Bill. 'Ah – you know him, I see. And he spilt the beans, as we say! Told us he was worried about paratroopers jumping without proper parachutes and so on. And so, when he went on holiday, I took his place on the next helicopter trip – and hey presto, there I was on the top of the mountain!'

'Oh, Bill – it was heavenly to see you!' said Lucy-Ann.

Bill had told them all about Mrs Mannering too – how anxious she had been – how her hand had healed very well – and how she had begged in vain to be allowed to come with Effans and the others to meet the children, with the donkeys.

It was a long time before the children could go to sleep that night, for the day had been so exciting. The dogs lay and snoozed, one eye on the prisoners. The donkeys lay peacefully together. Snowy, sent off by each of the children, wandered off to Dapple and lay down beside him. Dapple was very pleased.

They got back to the farmhouse by dinner-time the next day, for Bill had got them all up very early the next morning. Mrs Mannering ran out in joy. She had been very worried indeed.

Mrs Evans followed. 'Indeed to gootness, it's grand to see you, whateffer! To think what you have been through, look you – as much danger as in war-time! It's glad we are to see you back!'

'It's well they are looking, too,' said Effans, in his up-and-down voice, beaming. 'And that bird, indeed, she is funnier than ever!'

'Whateffer, look you!' mimicked Kiki, also in a sing-song voice, and Effans went off into guffaws, imitated by Kiki. The two of them sounded so jolly that everyone else began to laugh too!

Mrs Evans, of course, had got another lovely meal ready for them all. And *what* a lot there were to feed that day too! She even found a fine supply of bones for the dogs, and

Philip had to take them a good way off because Mrs Mannering said she really couldn't bear to hear such a munching and crunching as the ten dogs made short work of the bones.

What a lot there was to tell! Mrs Evans' eyes nearly fell out of her head as she listened, and handed out food of all kinds to everyone.

'To think of the children doing such things, look you!' she kept saying. 'Inside that mountain, indeed! Down in that pit too, look you!'

'Pardon, look you!' said Kiki, and gave a loud sneeze. Effans choked and Kiki copied him, making such a dreadful noise that Mrs Mannering said she was to go out of the room if she couldn't behave herself.

'Oh, Aunt Allie – she's just so glad she's back again,' said Jack, tapping Kiki on the beak.

'Send for the doctor,' said Kiki, fixing her wicked little eyes on Effans, who was still choking with laughter. 'Send for the weasel! Send for the look-you!'

Nobody could help laughing. Jack gave Kiki a very large plum, hoping to keep her quiet. Holding it in one clawed foot, Kiki dug her beak into it, making juice squirt all over poor Effans.

'Pardon!' said Kiki in delight, and did it again. Effans felt that he would exchange every one of his sheep for a bird like that. He watched Kiki and quite forgot to eat.

Johns was to take the prisoners down to the town, with David, escorted by two of the dogs. Mrs Evans said she would keep the rest of them at the farm-house until the police had decided what to do with them.

'Mother – I suppose we couldn't possibly keep two or three of the dogs, could we?' asked Philip longingly.

'Good gracious, no!' said his mother. 'It's bad enough being landed with so many of your pets when you go back to school – but to have three great hungry Alsatians to look after would just kill me! No, they will be happier as police dogs.'

Bill was to stay until two or three scientists arrived to go with him to the mountain. Some police officers were to accompany them too, to round up the soldiers – though Bill did not expect any trouble from them at all. They probably had bad records, and had signed on with Meier to keep out of the way of the police for a while and to earn money.

'Can we go to the mountain too?' asked Jack hopefully. 'You might lose your way inside, Bill.'

'Oh, no I shan't,' said Bill. 'I found a nice little map of the inside of the mountain in Meier's pocket. I shan't lose my way – and you may as well give up all hope of coming with me, because you've been in quite enough danger these holidays. I'm afraid if I took you with me another adventure might blow up – I never saw such children for smelling out adventures! I believe if I took you to visit my dear old aunt, we should find she had suddenly been kidnapped in a submarine, and you were forced to go the other end of the world to rescue her!'

The boys were very disappointed not to go with Bill back to the mountain. Neither of the girls wanted to. Lucy-Ann was quite certain about that.

'I don't mind the adventure a bit now it's all over and we can talk about it,' she said. 'But I didn't like it at the time. I hated that rumbling old mountain. Bill, Philip's going to let me wear his wings this afternoon in return for when I offered to jump from the helicopter instead of him. I shall fly from that high rock up there down to the farm-house!'

'Indeed you won't!' said Bill promptly. Lucy-Ann laughed at Bill's shocked face.

'It's all right. I was only pulling your leg,' she said. 'But I'm going to wear them for a little while, and jump about flapping them. Won't the hens be surprised?'

'Very,' said Bill. 'You'll stop them laying eggs, I should think! Look after her, Philip. See she doesn't do anything mad.'

Philip grinned. 'Lucy-Ann's all right,' he said. 'She's the most sensible one of us all.'

He put his hand into his pocket to feel if Sally the slow-worm was there. An astonished expression came over his face. He gave a yell.

'Oh! Whatever's the matter!' said Lucy-Ann, jumping in fright.

'The most *wonder*ful thing has happened!' said Philip. 'Honestly, I never thought it of Sally.'

'What? What?' cried the others. Philip brought out his hand and opened it. It was full of what looked like little silvery darning needles, all wriggling about.

'Sally's babies! Mother, look! My slow-worm has got a whole lot of baby ones in my pocket. Oh, Mother, I don't believe any slow-worm has ever done that before to anyone! It's absolutely unique! Aren't they *lovely*?'

'Ugh!' said Dinah.

'Perfect!' said Jack.

'Do give me one for myself,' said Lucy-Ann. 'Oh, Philip! This is much, much more exciting than our adventure!'

'Much,' agreed Philip. 'Good old Sally! I've never had baby slow-worms for pets before – now I've got heaps.'

'You're not to keep them in your pocket, Philip,' said his mother. 'It's not good for them or for you.'

'But Sally will be so disappointed,' said Philip, in dismay.

The adventure was forgotten. All four heads bent over the silvery little creatures in Philip's palm. Snowy came to look. Kiki bent down from Jack's shoulders.

'Look you, whateffer!' she said, with her head on one side, and opened her beak to hiccup. She caught Mrs Mannering's eye and changed her mind.

'Pardon!' she screeched and went off into a cackle of laughter. 'Bad Kiki! Send for the doctor, look you! Wipe your feet and blow your pardon!'

Enid Blyton

The Ship of Adventure

Contents

1

A grand holiday plan

'Mother's got something up her sleeve,' said Philip Mannering. 'I know she has. She's gone all mysterious.'

'Yes,' said his sister, Dinah. 'And whenever I ask what we're going to do these hols she just says "Wait and see!" As if we were about ten years old!'

'Where's Jack?' said Philip. 'We'll see if he knows what's up with Mother.'

'He's gone out with Lucy-Ann,' said Dinah. 'Ah – I can hear old Kiki screeching. They're coming!'

Jack and Lucy-Ann Trent came in together, looking very much alike with their red hair, green eyes and dozens of freckles. Jack grinned.

'Hallo! You ought to have been with us just now. A dog barked at Kiki, and she sat on a fence and mewed like a cat at him. You never saw such a surprised dog in your life!'

'He put his tail down and ran for his life,' said Lucy-Ann, scratching Kiki on the head. The parrot began to mew again, knowing that the children were talking about her. Then she hissed and spat like an angry cat. The children laughed.

'If you'd done that to the dog he'd have died of astonishment,' said Jack. 'Good old Kiki. Nobody can be dull when you're about.'

Kiki began to sway herself from side to side, and made a crooning noise. Then she went off into one of her tremendous cackles.

'Now you're showing off,' said Philip. 'Don't let's take any notice of her. She'll get noisy and Mother will come rushing in.'

'That reminds me – what's Mother gone all mysterious about?' said Dinah. 'Lucy-Ann, haven't you noticed it?'

'Well – Aunt Alison *does* act rather as if she's got something up her sleeve,' said Lucy-Ann, considering the matter. 'Rather like she does before somebody's birthday. *I* think she's got a plan for the summer holidays.'

Jack groaned. 'Blow! I've got a perfectly good plan too. Simply wizard. I'd better get mine in before Aunt Allie gets hers.'

'What's yours?' asked Dinah, with interest. Jack always had wonderful plans, though not many of them came to anything.

'Well – I thought we could all go off together on our bikes, taking a tent with us – and camp out in a different place each night,' said Jack. 'It would be super.'

The others looked at him scornfully. 'You suggested that *last* hols and the hols before,' said Dinah. 'Mother said "No" then, and she's not likely to say "Yes" now. It *is* a good plan, going off absolutely on our own like that – but ever since we've had so many adventures Mother simply won't hear of it.'

'Couldn't your mother come with us?' suggested Lucy-Ann hopefully.

'Now *you're* being silly,' said Dinah. 'Mother's a dear – but grown-ups are so frightfully particular about things. We'd have to put our macs on at the first spot of rain, and coats if the sun went in, and I wouldn't be surprised if we didn't each have to have an umbrella strapped to our bike-handles.'

The others laughed. 'I suppose it *wouldn't* do to ask Aunt Allie too, then,' said Lucy-Ann. 'What a pity!'

'What a pity, what a pity,' agreed Kiki at once. 'Wipe your feet and shut the door, where's your hanky, naughty boy!'

'Kiki's got the idea, all right!' said Philip. 'That's the kind of thing that even the nicest grown-ups say, isn't it, Kiki, old bird?'

'Bill isn't like that,' said Lucy-Ann at once. 'Bill's fine.'

Everyone agreed at once. Bill Cunningham, or Bill Smugs

as he had first called himself to them, was their very firm friend, and had shared all their adventures with them. Sometimes they had dragged him into them, and sometimes it was the other way round – he had got into one and they had followed. It really did seem, sometimes, as Mrs Mannering said, that adventures cropped up wherever Bill and the children were.

'*I* had an idea for these hols too,' said Philip. 'I thought it would be pretty good fun to camp down by the river, and look for otters. I've never had an otter for a pet. Lovely things they are. I thought—'

'You *would* think of a thing like that,' said Dinah, half crossly. 'Just because you're mad on all kinds of creatures from fleas to – to . . . '

'Elephants,' said Jack obligingly.

'From fleas to elephants, you think everyone else is,' said Dinah. 'What a frightful holiday – looking for wet, slimy otters – and having them in the tent at night, I suppose – and all kinds of other horrible things too.'

'Shut up, Dinah,' said Philip. 'Otters aren't horrible. They're lovely. You should just see them swimming under the water. And by the way, I'm *not* mad on fleas. *Or* mosquitoes. *Or* horse-flies. I think they're interesting, but you can't say I've ever had things like that for pets.'

'What about those earwigs you had once – that escaped out of the silly cage you made for them? Ugh! And that stag-beetle that did tricks? And that—'

'Oh, gosh! Now we're off!' said Jack, seeing one of the familiar quarrels breaking out between Philip and hot-headed Dinah. 'I suppose we're going to listen to a long list of Philip's pets now! Anyway, here comes Aunt Allie. We can ask her what she thinks of our holiday ideas. Get yours in first, Philip.'

Mrs Mannering came in, with a booklet in her hand. She smiled round at the four children, and Kiki put up her crest in delighted welcome.

'Wipe your feet and shut the door,' she said, in a friendly tone. 'One, two, three, GO!' She made a noise like a pistol-shot after the word 'go,' and Mrs Mannering jumped in fright.

'It's all right, Mother – she keeps doing that ever since she came to our school sports, and heard the starter yelling to us, and letting off his pistol,' grinned Philip. 'Once she made the pistol-shot noise just when we were all in a line, ready to start – and off we went long before time! You should have heard her cackle. Bad bird!'

'Naughty Polly, poor Polly, what a pity, what a pity,' said Kiki. Jack tapped her on the beak.

'Be quiet. Parrots should be seen and not heard. Aunt Allie, we've just been talking about holiday plans. I thought it would be a super idea if you'd let us all go off on our bikes – ride where we liked and camp out each night. I know you've said we couldn't when I asked you before, but—'

'I say "No" again,' said Mrs Mannering very firmly.

'Well, Mother, could we go off to the river and camp there, because I want to find out more about the otters?' said Philip, not taking any notice of Dinah's scowl. 'You see—'

'*No*, Philip,' said his mother, just as firmly as before. 'And you know why I won't let you go on expeditions like that. I should have thought you would have given up asking me by now.'

'But *why* won't you let us go?' wailed Lucy-Ann. 'We shall be quite safe.'

'Now, Lucy-Ann, you know perfectly well that as soon as I let you four out of my sight when holidays come, you *immediately* – yes, *immediately* – fall into the most frightful adventures imaginable.' Mrs Mannering sounded quite fierce. 'And I am quite determined that these holidays you are not going off *any*where on your own, so it's just no good your asking me.'

'But, Mother – that's just silly,' said Philip, in dismay. 'You speak as if we go out *looking* for adventures. We don't.

And I ask you – what possible adventure could we fall into if we just went down to the river to camp? Why, you could come and see us for yourself every evening if you wanted to.'

'Yes – and the very first evening I came I should find you all spirited away somewhere, and mixed up with robbers and spies or rogues of some kind,' said his mother. 'Think of some of your holidays – first you get lost down an old copper mine on a deserted island . . . Then another time you get shut up in the dungeons of an old castle, mixed up with spies . . .

'Oooh yes – and another time we got into the wrong aeroplane and were whisked off to the Valley of Adventure,' said Lucy-Ann, remembering. 'That was when we found all those amazing, stolen statues hidden in caves – how their eyes gleamed when we saw them! I thought they were alive, but they weren't.'

'And the next time we went off with Bill to the bird-islands,' said Jack. 'That was grand. We had two tame puffins, do you remember, Philip?'

'Huffin and Puffin,' put in Kiki at once.

'Quite right, old bird,' said Philip. 'Huffin and Puffin they were. I loved them.'

'You may have gone to look for birds – but you found a whole nest of rogues,' said his mother. 'Gun-runners! Terribly dangerous.'

'Well, Mother, what about last summer hols?' said Dinah. '*You* nearly got caught up in *that* adventure!'

'Horrible!' said Mrs Mannering, with a shiver. 'That awful mountain with its weird secrets – and the mad King of the Mountain – you nearly didn't escape from there. No – I tell you quite definitely that you can never again go off anywhere by yourselves. I'm always coming with you!'

There was a silence at this. All four children were very fond of Mrs Mannering – but they did like being on their own for some part of each holidays.

'Well – Aunt Allie – suppose Bill came with us – wouldn't

that be all right?' asked Lucy-Ann. 'I do always feel safe with Bill.'

'Bill can't be trusted to keep out of adventures either,' said Mrs Mannering. 'He's grand, I know, and I'd trust him more than anyone else in the world. But when you and he get together there's just no knowing what will happen. So, these holidays, I've made a very safe plan – and dear old Bill isn't in it, so perhaps we shall keep away from danger and extraordinary happenings.'

'What's your plan, Mother?' said Dinah nervously. '*Don't* say we're going to a seaside hotel or anything like that. They'd never take Kiki.'

'I'm taking you all for a cruise on a big ship,' said Mrs Mannering, and she smiled. 'I know you'll like that. It's tremendous fun. We shall call at all sorts of places, and see all kinds of strange and exciting things. And I shall have you under my eye, in one place all the time – the ship will be our home for some time, and if we get off at various ports we shall all go in a party together. There won't be a chance of any strange adventure.'

The four children looked at one another. Kiki watched them. Philip spoke first.

'It does sound rather exciting, Mother! Yes, it really does. We've never been on a really big ship before. Of course, I shall miss having any *animals* . . . '

'Oh, Philip – surely you can go without your everlasting menagerie of creatures?' cried Dinah. 'I must say it'll be a great relief to *me* to know you haven't got mice somewhere about you, or lizards, or slow-worms! Mother, it sounds super, I think. Thanks awfully for thinking up something so exciting.'

'Yes – it sounds smashing,' said Jack. 'We'll see no end of birds I've never seen before.'

'Jack's happy so long as he's somewhere that will provide him with birds,' said Lucy-Ann with a laugh. 'What with Philip with his craze for all kinds of creatures, and Jack with his passion for birds, it's a good thing we two girls haven't got crazes for anything as well. Aunt Allie, it's a wizard plan of yours. When do we go?'

'Next week,' said Mrs Mannering. 'That will give us plenty of time to get our things ready and packed. It will be very warm on the cruise, so we must get plenty of thin clothes to wear. White's the best thing – it doesn't hold the heat so much. And you must all have sun-hats the whole time, so don't begin to moan about wearing hats.'

'Isn't Bill coming?' asked Philip.

'No,' said his mother firmly. 'I feel rather mean about it, because he's just finished the job he's on, and he wants a holiday. But this time he's *not* coming with us. I want a nice peaceful holiday with no adventure at all.'

'Poor Bill,' said Lucy-Ann. 'Still – I dare say he'll be glad to have a holiday without us, for a change. I say – it's going to be fun, isn't it?'

'Fun!' said Kiki, joining in, and letting off a screech of excitement. 'Fun, fun, fun!'

2

On the *Viking Star*

It certainly was fun getting everything ready – buying flimsy clothes and enormous hats, masses of films for the cameras, guide-books and maps. It was to be quite a long cruise, and the ship was to go to Portugal, Madeira, French Morocco, Spain, Italy and the Aegean Islands. What a wonderful trip!

At last everything was ready. The trunks were packed and strapped. The tickets had arrived. Passports had been got, and everyone had screamed in dismay to see how hideous they looked in their passport photographs.

Kiki screamed too, just for company. She loved screeching and screaming, but she wasn't encouraged in this, so it was a fine change to scream when everyone was doing the same.

'Shut up, Kiki,' said Jack, pushing her off his shoulder. 'Fancy screaming right in my ear like that! It's enough to make me stone deaf. Aunt Allie, will Kiki want a passport?'

'Of course not,' said Mrs Mannering. 'I'm not even sure she will be allowed to go with us.'

Jack stared at her in the greatest dismay. 'But – *I* can't go if Kiki doesn't. I couldn't leave her behind. She'd be miserable.'

'Well, I'll write and ask if you can take her,' said Mrs Mannering. 'But if the answer is no, you are *not* to make a fuss, Jack. I've gone to a lot of trouble to arrange this trip, and I can't have you upsetting it just because of Kiki. I can't imagine that she will be allowed to go – I'm sure passengers would object to a noisy bird like that.'

'She can be awfully quiet if she wants to,' said poor Jack. Kiki chose that moment to have a fit of hiccups. She hiccuped very well, and it always annoyed Mrs Mannering.

'Stop that, Kiki,' she ordered. Kiki stopped and looked reproachfully at Mrs Mannering. She began to cough, a small but hollow cough, copied from the gardener.

Mrs Mannering tried not to laugh. 'The bird is so *idiotic*,' she said. 'Quite crazy. Now, where did I put that list of things that I've got to do before we go?'

'One, two, three, GO!' shouted Kiki, and Jack just stopped her making a noise like a pistol-shot. Mrs Mannering went out of the room, and Jack spoke solemnly to Kiki.

'Kiki, I may have to go without you, old bird. I can't upset all the arrangements at the last minute because of you. But I'll do what I can, so cheer up.'

'God save the Queen,' said Kiki, feeling that it must be a solemn moment by the look on Jack's face. 'Poor Polly, naughty Polly!'

The last few days went by slowly. Lucy-Ann complained

about it. 'Why is it that time always goes so slowly when you're wanting something to happen quickly? It's sickening. Thursday will never come!'

Jack was not so excited as the others, because a letter had come saying that parrots could not be taken on board. All four children were very sorry about it, and Jack looked really worried. But he did not grumble about it, or worry Mrs Mannering. She was sorry for him and offered to arrange with a woman in the village to look after Kiki for him.

'She used to have a parrot of her own,' she said. 'I expect she'd enjoy having Kiki.'

'No, thanks, Aunt Allie. I'll arrange something,' said Jack. 'Don't let's talk about it!'

So Mrs Mannering said no more, and even when Kiki sat on the tea-table and picked all the currants out of the cake before anyone noticed, she did not say a word.

On Wednesday all five went off in Mrs Mannering's car to Southampton, followed by another with the baggage. They were in a great state of excitement. Everyone was in charge of something to carry, and Lucy-Ann kept looking at her package anxiously to make sure she still had it.

They were to stay at a hotel for the night and embark on the ship at half-past eight in the morning, to catch the tide. They would be away at eleven o'clock, steaming steadily towards France – what an excitement!

They all had a very good dinner at the hotel, and then Mrs Mannering suggested going to the cinema. She felt sure that not one of the children would go to sleep if she sent them to bed at the usual time.

'Do you mind if I go and hunt up a school friend of mine, Aunt Allie?' said Jack. 'He lives in Southampton, and I'd like to spring a surprise on him and go and call.'

'All right,' said Mrs Mannering. 'But you're not to be late back. Do you want to go and see him too, Philip?'

'Who's this chappy, Jack?' asked Philip, but Jack was

half-way out of the room. A mumble came through the door.

'What's he say?' said Philip.

'Sounded like "Porky" to me,' said Dinah.

'Porky? Who does he mean, I wonder,' said Philip. 'Somebody mad on birds, I expect. I'll come to the cinema. I'd like to see the picture – it's got wild animals in it.'

They went off to the cinema without seeing Jack again. He was home when they came back, reading one of the guide-books Mrs Mannering had bought.

'Hallo! See Porky?' said Philip. He got a frown from Jack, and was puzzled. What was Jack up to? He changed the subject quickly, and began to talk about the picture they had seen.

'Now, to bed,' said Mrs Mannering. 'Stop talking, Philip. Off you all go – and remember, up at seven o'clock sharp in the morning.'

Everyone was awake long before seven. The girls talked together, and Philip and Jack chattered away too. Philip asked Jack about the night before.

'Why did you shut me up when I asked you if you'd seen Porky?' he said. 'And anyway – who *is* Porky?'

'He's that fellow called Hogsney,' said Jack. 'We called him Porky. He left ages ago. He was always wanting to borrow Kiki, don't you remember?'

'Oh, *yes*, Porky, of course,' said Philip. 'I'd almost forgotten him. Jack, what's up? You look sort of secretive!'

'Don't ask me any questions, because I don't want to answer them,' said Jack.

'You're being jolly mysterious,' said Philip. '*I* believe it's something to do with Kiki. You kept putting us all off when we asked you what you'd done with her. We thought you were feeling upset about it, so we didn't press you.'

'Well, don't press me now,' said Jack. 'I don't want to say anything at the moment.'

'All right,' said Philip, giving it up. 'I know you're up to something, though. Come on – let's get up. It's not seven yet, but we can't lie in bed on a morning as fine as this.'

They were all on the boat at just after half-past eight. Mrs Mannering found their cabins. There were three in a row – a single one for her, and two double ones for the others.

Lucy-Ann was delighted with them. 'Why, they are just like proper little rooms,' she said. 'Jack, is your cabin like ours? Look, we've even got hot and cold water taps.'

'We've got an electric fan going in our cabin,' said Philip, appearing at the door. 'It's wizard – lovely and cool. You've got one too.'

'The water is only just below our porthole,' said Dinah, looking out. 'If the sea got at all rough it would slop into the hole!'

'It would be well and truly screwed up before that happened!' said Philip. 'I'm glad we're at the water-line – it will be cooler in this warm weather. I say, isn't this super! I'm longing to sail off.'

They all went to see Mrs Mannering's cabin, which was the same as theirs, but smaller. Then they went to explore the ship. She was quite big, but not trememdous, and was white from top to bottom – white funnels, white rails, white sides.

Her name was on each of the white lifeboats slung at the sides of the deck – *Viking Star*. Lucy-Ann read it a dozen times over.

'We shall have lifeboat drill tomorrow, I expect,' said Mrs Mannering, joining them on their exploration.

'There are big life-belt jackets in our cabin cupboards,' said Lucy-Ann. 'I suppose you tie them round you.'

'You slip them over your head, so that half the jacket is at your front and half behind – and then you tie it firmly round you with the tapes,' said Mrs Mannering. 'You'll have to put it on tomorrow for lifeboat drill.'

It all sounded very exciting. They went round the ship, thrilled with everything. There was the sports deck, where someone was already playing quoits with thick rings of rope, and two others were playing deck-tennis. 'Fancy being able to play games like this on board ship!' said Dinah.

'There's a cinema down below,' said Mrs Mannering, 'and a writing-room, and library and lounge, and an enormous dining-room!'

'And gosh, look – here's a swimming-pool on the ship itself!' cried Jack, in amazement, as they came to a beautiful pool at one end of the ship, shimmering blue with water.

The ship's siren suddenly hooted twice, very loudly. Lucy-Ann almost fell into the swimming-pool with surprise. Mrs Mannering laughed.

'Oh, Lucy-Ann – did it make you jump? It made me jump too.'

'What a terrific noise!' said Lucy-Ann. 'My goodness, it's a good thing Kiki isn't here. If she began to hoot like that siren she'd be impossible.'

'Shut up, idiot,' said Dinah, in a low voice. 'Don't remind Jack we're going off without her.'

Lucy-Ann glanced round for Jack, but he wasn't there. 'Where's he gone?' she asked Dinah. But nobody had seen him go.

'He's somewhere about,' said Philip. 'I say, we must be sailing soon. Look – they're taking up the gangways. We'll soon be off!'

'Let's stand at this side and wave to all the people,' said Lucy-Ann. She leaned over the rail and watched the people crowded together on the dock-side below. They were shouting and waving. Suddenly Lucy-Ann gave a squeal.

'Look! *Look!* There's somebody with a parrot *just* like Kiki! Honestly, it is. Where's Jack? I *must* tell him. Blow, he's nowhere to be seen!'

The engines of the ship had now started up, and the children felt a vibration under their feet. Lucy-Ann strained her eyes to look at the parrot that was so very like Kiki.

'It *is* Kiki!' she cried. 'Kiki! Kiki! Goodbye! I'm sure it's you!'

The parrot was chained to a young man's wrist. Whether it was making a noise or not the children could not tell because of the hullabaloo going on. It certainly was remarkably like Kiki.

'We're off! We've moved away from the quay!' cried Philip. 'Hurrah, we're off!' He waved madly to everyone. Lucy-Ann waved too, and watched the parrot. It was getting smaller as the ship moved away towards the open water. Its owner seemed to be having trouble with it. It was flapping its wings, and pecking at him.

Then it suddenly rose into the air – the chain parted – and the parrot sailed right over the stretch of water between quay and ship, screeching madly.

'It *is* Kiki, it is, it is!' yelled Lucy-Ann. 'Jack, where are you? JACK!'

3

Everyone settles in

Dinah, Lucy-Ann and Philip rushed to find Jack. The parrot had reached the ship, and they had lost sight of it. They were all certain it was Kiki, and Philip had a shrewd idea that Jack would not be quite so surprised about it as they themselves were.

Jack was nowhere to be found. It was most exasperating. They hunted for him everywhere, and at last Lucy-Ann thought of his cabin. 'He might be there,' she said. 'Though why he wants to go and shut himself up there just at the exciting moment when the ship is leaving Southampton, I really can't imagine! And where's the parrot? She seems to have disappeared too.'

They went down the stairs to the cabins and found their way to the passage where theirs were. They flung open Jack's door and crowded in. 'Jack! Are you here? What do you think we've just seen?'

They stopped in surprise at what they saw. Jack was sitting on his bed in the cabin, and Kiki was on his shoulder, making a curious crooning noise into his ear, pulling at it gently.

'Gosh!' said Philip. 'So she found you. I suppose it *is* Kiki?'

'Of course, idiot,' said Jack. 'What a bit of luck, wasn't it? Old Porky brough her down to the quay to see me off, chained to his wrist – and she broke the chain and flew over to me! Came into my porthole too – brainy old bird!'

'*Porky?* The boy you used to know at school! Did you give Kiki to *him* to mind for you?' said Lucy-Ann, amazed. 'But – how did she get down here?'

'I brought her in the car yesterday,' said Jack, putting one hand over his ear so that Kiki could not nibble it. 'She was in the picnic-basket I was carrying, as quiet as a mouse. I was terrified one of you would ask me to open the basket and get you out something to eat!'

'But I say – won't Porky be upset to have her escape like that?' said Dinah.

'And *how* did she know you were here, if you were down in your cabin?' wondered Lucy-Ann. 'Perhaps she heard me call her. That must have been it – she heard me yelling "Kiki! Kiki!", broke her chain in her excitement and flew over – and by a lucky chance she chose your very porthole!'

'You'd better tell Aunt Allie all that,' said Jack, with a grin. 'It makes a very fine story – better than mine!'

The three stared at him in silence. 'You're a determined old fraud, Jack,' said Philip, at last. 'You arranged it all; I bet you did! Yes, even arranged for the chain to snap and for Kiki to see or hear you at your porthole.'

Jack grinned again. 'Well, I think Lucy-Ann's idea is very good – shouting to Kiki like that and making her so excited that she flew across to the ship. Anyway, she's here, and here she stays. I'd better keep her down in the cabin, I think.'

They all made a fuss of old Kiki, who enjoyed it very much indeed. She couldn't understand the noise the vibration of the engines made, and kept cocking her head on one side to listen. She tried an imitation, but not a very good one.

'Now don't you do any funny noises,' Jack warned her. 'You don't want to be hauled up before the Captain, do you?'

'Pop goes the weasel,' said Kiki, and pecked his ear. Then she suddenly gave a most realistic sneeze.

'Don't,' said Jack. 'Use your handkerchief! Gosh, Kiki, I couldn't have gone without you.'

Everyone was pleased to know that Kiki was safely with them. They broke the news as gently as possible to Mrs Mannering. She listened in annoyance, but it did not seem to occur to her for one moment that Kiki's arrival was anything but an unfortunate accident. She sighed.

'All right. If she's here, she's here. But for goodness' sake, Jack, keep her locked up in the cabin. You really will get into trouble if the passengers complain about her, and she may be sent to the crew's deck and put in a cage if you don't keep a firm hand on her.'

So Kiki was locked into the cabin, and passed the first day wondering whether *she* was giddy, or whether there was a slight earthquake going on all the time. She had no idea she was in a big ship, and could not understand its movements, though she had many a time been in small boats.

The first day seemed lovely and long. The *Viking Star* slid easily through the calm, blue water, her engines purring sweetly, leaving behind her a creamy wake that seemed to have no end, but to stretch right back to the horizon itself. England was soon left behind. The first stop was to be Lisbon in Portugal.

It was fun to go down to meals in the big dining-room and choose what they liked from the long menu. It was fun to go up on the sports deck and play deck-tennis and try to keep their balance as they ran for the rubber ring. It was even fun to go to bed – because it mean snuggling down into a narrow, bunk-like bed, turning out the light, feeling the breeze from the electric fan cooling their hot bodies and hearing the plish-plish-plash of the water just below their portholes.

'Lovely!' said Lucy-Ann, before she fell asleep. 'I hope this trip doesn't turn into an adventure. I like it as it is. It's quite exciting enough without having an adventure.'

It wasn't quite so nice in the Bay of Biscay! The sea was rough and choppy there, and the boat pitched and tossed and rolled. Mrs Mannering didn't like it at all. She stayed in her cabin, but the four children were as right as rain. They turned up to every meal in the dining-room, and ate steadily right down the menu. They would even have gone up to try and play deck-tennis on the sports deck if one of the stewards had not firmly forbidden them to.

And then, quite suddenly as it seemed, everything changed. The sea grew blue and calm, the sun shone out very hotly indeed, the sky was brilliant, and every officer and man appeared in spotless white.

Mrs Mannering felt all right again – and Kiki grew very, very impatient at being kept in the cabin. She was already great friends with the steward and stewardess who looked after the cabins. They had soon got over their astonishment at finding her in Jack's cabin.

They had not seen her at first. She was sitting behind the little curtain that hung at the side of the porthole, which Jack had to keep shut in case Kiki flew out. It was the stewardess who heard her first. She had come in to make the beds.

Kiki watched her slyly from behind the curtain. Then she spoke in a firm and decided voice.

'Put the kettle on.'

The stewardess was startled. She looked round at the door, thinking that someone must be there speaking to her. But nobody was.

Kiki gave a loud hiccup. 'Pardon,' she said. The stewardess felt alarmed. She looked all round. She opened the cupboard door.

'What a pity, what a pity!' said Kiki, in such a mournful voice that the stewardess could bear it no longer and flew to find the steward. He was a dour and determined Scot, with very little patience.

He came into the cabin and looked round. 'What's to do, wumman?' he said to the stewardess. 'What's scairt ye? There's naught here.'

Kiki gave a loud cough, and then sneezed violently. 'Pardon,' she said. 'Where's your hanky?'

Now it was the steward's turn to look amazed. He stared all round the cabin. Kiki gave a loud and realistic yawn. She had a wonderful collection of noises. She couldn't resist looking round the curtain to see how her performance was going.

The steward saw her and strode over to the porthole. 'Now look ye here – it's a parrot!' he said. 'Did ever ye hear the like? A fine and clever bird it must be to do all that! Well, Polly – you're a clever wee bird, that's what you are!'

Kiki flew to the top of the cupboard and looked at the steward and stewardess, first out of one eye and then out of the other. Then she made a noise like the dinner-gong being beaten for the ship's meals. At the end she went off into one of her cackles of laughter.

'It fair beats ye, doesn't it?' said the Scots steward, amazed. 'A rare, bonny bird it is. The laddie that owns it should think shame on himself to keep it shut up here.'

'It scared me, right enough,' said the stewardess. 'I wonder if it would like a grape. My great-aunt's parrot loved grapes. I'll go and get some.'

Pretty soon Kiki was enjoying some black grapes, and when Jack came along to see her, he found the cabin floor scattered with grape-pips, and two admiring people gaping at Kiki in delight.

'Dirty bird!' said Jack sternly, looking down at the pips. 'You come down off that cupboard and pick up these pips.'

'Pips,' said Kiki. 'Pops. Pip goes the weasel.'

'I hope she hasn't been annoying you,' said Jack to the stewardess.

'Oh, she's wonderful,' said the woman. 'I never saw such a clever bird. You ought to take her up and show her off.'

It wasn't very long before Jack did take her up to the deck above on his shoulder, much to the surprise and amusement of all the passengers. Kiki had a wonderful time, showing off. The only thing she couldn't bear was the hoot of the ship's siren, which always startled her so much that she fell off Jack's shoulder in fright every time she heard it. She didn't know what it was or where it came from, and usually flew off to hide herself somewhere whenever she heard it.

She came to the lifeboat drill, and Lucy-Ann was certain she was upset because she had not a small life-jacket to wear. They all put theirs on, went to their right lifeboat and listened to a short talk from one of the officers about what they were to do if danger arose. Lucy-Ann hoped fervently that it wouldn't.

'We're going to land in Lisbon tomorrow,' said Mrs Mannering. 'But none of you is to wander off alone. I'm not going to have any adventure starting up. You'll all keep close to me – please understand *that*!'

4

Philip collects a pet

Soon the days began to slip by quickly. After Lisbon Lucy-Ann and Dinah lost count of them. They did not even know if the day was Monday, Tuesday or any other. They knew Sunday because everyone went into the big lounge then and listened to the captain taking a short church service.

For days they saw no land. Philip grew very excited when a shoal of flying-fish flew out of the sea and kept up in the air for some time. They were lovely little things.

'What makes them do that?' wondered Lucy-Ann.

'Just being chased by some hungry big fish,' said Philip. 'Wouldn't you leap out of the water and try and fly through the air if an enormous fish was after you, Lucy-Ann? Gosh, I wish one of the fish would fly on deck. I'd just love to see it close to.'

'Well, you couldn't possibly make it a pet, thank goodness, because it would die in your pocket,' said Dinah. 'It seems unusual for you to be without any pets at all, Philip. Very nice!'

But she spoke too soon, because Philip collected a pet two days later! They had called at Madeira, left that island, and gone on to French Morocco. It was there that Philip collected his strange little pet.

The children liked French Morocco. They especially liked the bazaars, although the air was so strongly scented that Mrs Mannering said it made her feel faint, and she walked along with smelling-salts pressed to her nose. The children soon got used to the air, though Kiki didn't, judging by the number of 'Poohs' she said. 'Pooh! Gah! Pooh!'

Dinah tried out her French on the black-eyed traders, and was pleased when they understood. She bought a tiny brooch, and Lucy-Ann bought a blue vase.

'Don't you see anything *you* like?' she asked Philip. He shook his head.

'I don't want things like that. Now if I could see something really exciting – say an old dagger – or, I tell you what! Something I've always wanted and never had.'

'What's that?' asked Lucy-Ann, determined to buy it for him if only she could see it.

'You'll laugh – but I've always wanted a ship in a bottle,' said Philip.

'I've never even seen one,' said Lucy-Ann, astonished. 'A ship in*side* a bottle, do you mean? What a peculiar thing? How is it put there?'

'I don't know,' said Philip. 'It's daft of me to want it, really – it's just one of those ideas you get, you know.'

'I'll be sure to look out for one for you, wherever we go,' promised Lucy-Ann. 'Oh, do look at Kiki. She's taking sweets from those little children there. She'll make herself sick again!'

Mrs Mannering insisted that they should all stay close to her, and keep with the ship's party. The four children wished they could explore by themselves, for they liked the people and their strange, dark, narrow little shops.

'Certainly not,' said Mrs Mannering. 'Why, didn't you hear what happened to the man at the next table to ours on the ship? He and his wife went off by themselves in a taxi to visit some place or other – and the driver took them to a deserted hill, and wouldn't take them back to the ship till they had given him all the money they had!'

'Gracious,' said Lucy-Ann, surprised.

'He brought them back just as the gangway was being drawn up,' went on Mrs Mannering, 'so they had no time to make any complaint. *Now* you know why I want you to keep with the ship's party. No more adventures for you, if I can help it! It would be just like you all to disappear somewhere, get into awful danger and put a few more grey hairs into my head!'

'You haven't *really* got very many,' said Lucy-Ann. 'Just about one for each of our adventures, that's all! I *will* keep near to you, Aunt Allie. I don't want an adventure either.'

The next day there was to be a trip by motor-coach to a famous place inland – an old town on the edge of the desert. 'The motor-coaches will be here on the quay at half-past ten,' Mrs Mannering told the four. 'Be sure to wear your sun-hats. It will be terribly hot.'

It was on that trip that Philip collected his new pet. The motor-coaches duly arrived and everyone crowded into them, feeling extremely hot. Off they went at top speed down a sandy road that for a time seemed to run through what looked like a bare desert. Large cactus-plants grew by the road-side. Lucy-Ann thought they looked ugly and spiteful with their numerous prickles and fat bulging bodies.

In two hours' time they came to the old town. Its ancient arches and towers seemed to spring up suddenly out of the sand. Little dark-eyed children, with hardly anything on, ran to meet them, their hands held out.

'Penn-ee, penn-ee,' they said, and Kiki echoed them at once. 'Penn-ee, penn-ee!'

They all went into the narrow street of the old town. The guide took them to an ancient building and began to drone its history. Then one by one the party climbed steep, winding steps up an enormous tower.

Half-way up Philip looked out of a great stone window. It had no glass, of course. The wall was so thick that he could sit on the window-sill with his legs stretched right out. He hung on to the side of the window and slid forward to look down.

Far below he could see a little crowd of excited children. They were pointing upwards and chattering. Some of them were throwing stones.

'Now what are those little scamps throwing stones at?' thought Philip. 'If it's something alive I'll knock their heads together!'

He slid down from the enormous window-sill and ran down the great winding stairs. A stone flew through a window-opening not far from the bottom, and he stopped.

He heard a small whimpering noise, and, hidden in a corner of the window-opening, he saw a little heap of brown fur. He went over to it. What could it be?

Click! A stone flew near him. Blow those kids! He stepped to the window and looked down sternly. 'You stop that!' he shouted. 'Do you hear me? Stop it!'

The small children looked in consternation at this sudden apparition. They disappeared in a hurry. Philip reached over to the brown bundle. A small wizened face peeped out at him, with mournful brown eyes. Then it was covered by tiny hands.

'Why – it's a monkey – a tiny monkey!' thought Philip. He knew how scared the small creatures were, and he was afraid of frightening this poor little stoned animal. He had seen plenty of monkeys in that part of the country already, but not near – they always kept well out of the way.

Philip spoke to the small creature in what Lucy-Ann called his 'special animal-voice.' It uncovered its funny little face again, and then, with one bound, was cuddling into the boy's shoulder, nestling against his neck, trembling. He put up a cautious hand and rubbed its soft fur.

No animal had ever been able to resist Philip's magic. Horses, dogs, cats, snakes, insects, birds – they came to him at once trustfully and confidingly. Not one could withstand him. It was a gift that everyone marvelled at and envied him for.

Philip sat down on the broad window-sill and talked to the scared and miserable little monkey. It chattered back in a high, cheeping little voice. It looked at him shyly out of child-like brown eyes. Its tiny brown fingers wound themselves round one of his. It was Philip's devoted slave from that moment.

When the others came pattering down the stairs in front of the rest of the party, they were astonished to see the small monkey cuddling up to Philip.

'There – I knew he'd get hold of something, sooner or later!' said Dinah. 'Ugh! A nasty, dirty, smelly little monkey, full of fleas too, I expect.'

'Well, it *is* dirty and smelly, and I'm sure it's got fleas,' said Philip. 'But it isn't nasty. It's been stoned by those wretched children down below. Both its legs are hurt.'

'Poor little thing,' said Lucy-Ann, almost in tears. Jack stroked the tiny thing's head, but that only made it shrink closer to Philip.

'You're not to take it back to the ship with you,' began Dinah. 'I shall tell Mother if you do. I won't have a monkey in our party.'

'He's coming with me,' said Philip sternly.

Dinah began to lose her temper. 'Then I shall tell Mother I won't have it. I shall—'

'Dinah, it's so *small*, and it's *hurt*,' said Lucy-Ann, in a shaky voice. 'Don't talk like that. It's so unkind.'

Dinah flushed, and turned away. She was cross, and horrified at the thought of having a monkey 'tagging along' with them, as she put it – but she did not want to go against all three of the others. She said no more, though she was unhappy for the rest of the day.

How Philip hid the monkey till he got back to the ship only he knew. The fact is that no one even noticed it. Jack and Lucy-Ann helped him valiantly by standing in front of him whenever they thought anyone might see the monkey. Dinah would not help, but on the other hand she did nothing to give the secret away.

Back in the cabin, the three children pored over the tiny creature. 'It's not even a grown monkey,' said Philip. 'How those children could stone a little thing like this beats me.

But I suppose in every country there are cruel and unkind people – after all, we've seen boys back at home throwing stones at a cat. Look – its legs are bruised and cut, but they're not broken. I can soon get those right. I wonder if it would let me wash it – it's so dirty.'

The little thing would let Philip do anything in the world he wanted to. The children spent two hours washing and drying it gently. Jack brought a small shoe-brush to brush its fluffy fur. It let Philip put iodine on its cuts and gave only a tiny whimper.

'There!' said the boy. 'You look fine. What's your name?'

The monkey chattered something, and the children listened. 'It sounds as if he's saying "Micky-micky-mick," ' said Lucy-Ann.

'Right. If he thinks his name is Micky, Micky it is,' said Philip. 'I wonder what Kiki will think of him.'

'She won't like him much,' said Jack. 'She'll be jealous. Good thing we left her in the girls' cabin. She'd screech the place down if she saw us washing and brushing Micky.'

Kiki certainly was most amazed to see Micky on Philip's shoulder that night. She stared, and then, just as Jack had said, she screeched – one of her very best express-train screeches. Mrs Mannering put her head in at the cabin door to protest.

She suddenly caught sight of the monkey and stepped forward in surprise, wondering if she had seen aright. 'Oh, Philip! You oughtn't to have brought it back to the ship. What a tiny thing!'

'Mother, some children were stoning it. I had to bring it away,' said Philip. His mother looked at him. It was just exactly the kind of thing Philip's father had done when he was alive. How could she scold him for something that was in his very blood?

'Well – I don't know if a fuss will be made if you keep him on the ship,' she said, stroking the monkey's head. 'What does Dinah say about it?'

'She was very cross at first, but she didn't say much,' said Lucy-Ann. 'She's still in our cabin, I think. She'll get over Micky. She'll have to.'

'Micky – Kiki – Micky –Kiki –Micky – Kiki,' said Kiki triumphantly, as if she had suddenly discovered something very clever. She loved words that sounded the same. 'Micky – Kiki, Micky – Kiki—'

'Shut up, Kiki,' said Philip. 'I say, what a pity he's called Micky – we'll never stop Kiki saying those two words now. But he *is* Micky. We can't alter his name now.'

So Micky he was, and in a day or two he was everyone's friend – yes, even Dinah's! He had such a dear, comical face that it was impossible not to like him when he looked at you out of mournful brown eyes.

'He's such a baby and yet he's got such a wise, wizened little face,' said Lucy-Ann. 'And I do like his tiny fingers – just like ours! Don't you, Dinah?'

'Well – he's not as awful as I thought he was at first,' admitted Dinah. 'I can't say I want him sitting on my shoulder all day long, like Philip – and I'm sure he's still got fleas – but he's really not bad.'

'He *hasn't* got fleas,' said Philip, annoyed. 'Don't keep saying that.'

Micky soon recovered his spirits, and from being a gentle, confiding little thing, he became a mischievous, chattering madcap. He leapt about the cabin as lightly as a squirrel, and Dinah was always scared he would take a flying jump on to her shoulder. But he didn't. He was wise enough not to do that!

Kiki was alarmed to see these acrobatics, and when the two were together in the same cabin she always turned to face Micky, so that she could jab him with her beak if he leapt at her. But he left her alone, and took very little notice. She didn't like that at all!

She took to calling his name in Philip's voice, which she could imitate perfectly. 'Micky! Micky!'

The monkey would look round at once, but would see no Philip. 'Micky!' Kiki would say again, and the monkey would begin to leap all over the place, trying to find Philip.

Then Kiki would cackle with laughter, and Micky would go off in disgust and sit on the porthole sill with his back to Kiki, looking through the thick glass out to sea.

Kiki certainly had the best of it because she soon found that she could make noises that terrified Micky. If she barked like a dog the little creature went nearly frantic with fright. He was puzzled too. He watched Kiki closely, and soon realised that no dog barked unless Kiki was in the cabin. Then was Kiki some kind of bird-dog?

The next time she barked she followed it by a fierce growl. This was too much for Micky. He picked up a tablet of soap from the basin and flung it at the surprised Kiki. It hit her full on the beak and she gave a squawk of alarm and nearly fell off her perch.

Micky sent a tooth-brush after the soap, and then the tooth-mug. He was a very fine shot, and soon Kiki was flying round the cabin trying to find a place to shelter from the volley of articles that Micky was sending after her – hairbrushes, combs, a roll of films, anything he could get hold of!

Philip stopped the battle when he came in. 'Micky! Pick them all up!' he said sternly. 'What did Kiki do to you to make you lose your temper like that? Bad Micky!'

'Naughty Micky, bad boy!' said Kiki at once, and went off into one of her cackles of laughter. Micky picked everything up humbly. Then he went to sit on Philip's shoulder as usual. Kiki was jealous. She flew to his other shoulder.

The monkey chattered at her. Kiki chattered back, in exactly the same monkey-voice as Micky used. He stared in amazement, and answered excitedly. Philip listened, amused.

'Well, I don't really know if you urderstand one another or not,' he said. 'But it's just as well you should. I don't want to find my cabin strewn with all my belongings each time I come into it. So just be friends! Do you hear, Kiki and Micky?'

'Pooh,' said Kiki, in a friendly voice, and nibbled at him.

'Pooh to you!' said Philip. 'And kindly stop nibbling my ear!'

5

Lucian arrives

The children soon felt that the *Viking Star* was their home – a floating home, containing everything they wanted except the open countryside. They got to know every nook and cranny on the ship, they explored the engine-room under the eye of Mac, the chief engineer, and they were even allowed up on the bridge by the first officer, a very great honour.

Mrs Mannering made friends on the ship with two or three people she liked. There were only a few children on board besides Jack and the others, and they were much younger and so spoilt that nobody wanted to have much to do with them.

'I rather wish there were more children of your own age,' Mrs Mannering said to her four. 'It might be more fun for you.'

'Well – *we* don't want anyone else, thanks,' said Philip. 'We're all right on our own. It's bad enough having those other spoilt kids around – always wanting to mess about with Micky, and trying to get Kiki to talk to them.'

'She's too sensible,' said Jack. 'Kiki just looks at them and says "Shut up!" whenever she sees them.'

'How rude of her!' said Mrs Mannering. 'I do hope you stop her when she talks like that to the other children.'

'Well, actually I don't,' said Jack. 'She only says what I

jolly well would like to say myself. Spoilt little brats! I'm going to push that nasty little yellow-haired girl into the swimming-pool one of these days – coming whining round me asking me if she can hold Kiki. *Hold* Kiki! What does she think Kiki is – one of her frightful dolls?'

'You mustn't push the child into the pool,' said Mrs Mannering, horrified. 'I do agree she wants slapping – but she's only a little girl, Jack.'

'She's a human mosquito,' said Jack. 'I just wish I had a fly-swatter when she comes near.'

'Well, all the kids are getting off at the next stop,' said Philip, fondling Micky, who, as usual, was on his shoulder. The boys looked a curious pair, one with a parrot on his shoulder, the other with a monkey. The passengers smiled whenever they saw them.

'I'm glad to hear those tiresome children will soon be gone,' said Dinah, who was not very fond of youngsters. 'But I expect some equally dreadful ones will embark in their place.'

She was wrong, as it happened. Only one boy embarked; no girls at all. All the spoilt youngsters left, stumbling down the gangway at Naples, screaming and complaining to the last, certainly a most unpleasant collection of small children. Jack and the others watched them go with pleasure, and Kiki screeched after them. 'Goodbye, good riddance, goodbye, good riddance!'

'Jack! She's never said that before,' said Mrs Mannering reproachfully. 'You must just have taught her!'

'Kiki only reads my thoughts, Aunt Allie,' laughed Jack. 'I say – look here – here comes Brer Rabbit!'

The children giggled as they watched a tall, gangling boy come up the gangway. His mouth certainly was exactly like a rabbit's. The front teeth stuck out, and his chin sloped backwards. He was about as old as Jack and Philip. He wore large, round glasses that magnified his eyes and made them look rather staring. He had a very amiable grin on his face as he came up the gangway.

He seemed very excited, and was talking in a mixture of English and some foreign language to a rather languid-looking lady behind him, and a short, burly man who wore dark sun-glasses that completely hid his eyes.

'Uncle, Aunt, we're off at last! Oh, I say, what a magnificent ship! I'm sure I shan't be seasick in her.' Then he went off into what sounded like a string of gibberish, but was really a foreign language. Kiki cocked her head when she heard this string of what sounded to her like complete nonsense.

As the boy passed she spoke to him in a conversational tone, pouring out the same kind of gibberish that she had heard. The boy looked at her in amazement.

'Oh, I say! A talking parrot. Oh, I *say*!'

'Oh, I say!' repeated Kiki immediately. 'Oh, I *say*! Oh, I SAY!'

'Shut up, Kiki. Don't be rude,' said Jack.

Micky leaned forward on Philip's shoulder and sent out a stream of excited chattering to Kiki. The boy stared in delight.

'Oh, I say! A talking monkey too! What's he saying?'

'He says he thinks he's seen you somewhere before, but he can't remember where, and he wants to know if Kiki the parrot remembers,' said Philip solemnly. Lucy-Ann gave a delighted giggle. The boy stared open-mouthed, then he laughed, showing all his big teeth.

'Oh, you're pulling my leg, aren't you! But I say – what fun – a parrot that talks, and a tame monkey! Aren't you lucky!'

'Get on, Lucian, get on,' said the burly man behind him, and gave the boy a push. Lucian went forward at a run, turning round to give the four children an apologetic grin for leaving them so abruptly. The man said something in an annoyed voice to the woman with him, but as he said it in a foreign language the children didn't understand a word. They guessed at once, however, that Lucian was not very popular with his uncle!

'Well – if Rabbit is the only boy to come on board here, I suppose he'll pin himself on to us all day long,' said Philip. 'What a weed!'

'Oh I say!' said Kiki. Jack groaned.

'Now we shall have Kiki saying that day and night. It's a good thing Micky can't talk properly – we'd never get a word in edgeways!'

The ship sailed off again into waters bluer than ever. It was pleasant to go to the bow of the ship and feel the breeze. Both Kiki and Micky liked this too.

Just as Jack and Philip had feared, the new boy tagged himself on to them whenever he could. The children always knew when he was coming because Kiki invariably gave them warning.

'Oh, I say!' she would squawk, and the four would sigh. Lucian again! He would come up grinning amiably, and settle himself beside them.

He told them all about himself immediately. He had no father or mother. His father had been English, but his mother was Greek, so he had plenty of Greek relations. He went to school in England, but spent most of his holidays with his relations. He was fourteen, nearly fifteen, he didn't like games, he loved history, and he wished his name wasn't Lucian.

'Why?' asked Dinah.

'Well – because the boys at my school change it to Lucy-Ann,' explained Lucian. 'I mean – fancy having a name that's as girlish as that.'

'It's *my* name,' said Lucy-Ann. 'I like it.'

'Well – it's very nice for *you*,' said Lucian. 'But awful for me. Especially when they shorten it and call me Lucy.'

'Juicy Lucy!' said Kiki at once, in delight. 'Juicy Lucy! Oh, I say!'

Everybody roared, even Lucian. Kiki cackled too.

'Juicy Lucy, goosey-Lucy, oh, I say!' carolled Kiki.

'Oh, I say really – that bird of yours is a regular comic, isn't she?' said Lucian in admiration. 'Gosh, I wish I could borrow her to take back to school. I say, do *you* take her to school with you?'

'I used to,' said Jack regretfully. 'But she kept telling our form-master to wipe his feet and shut the door, and when she yelled out "Don't sniff, use your hanky" to the Head, well, that was about the end.'

'Do you remember how you put her in a cupboard once, to hide her in class – and she went off like fireworks, fizzling and popping and exploding?' said Philip, with a grin. 'It was just after Guy Fawkes Day – she remembered the noises.'

Lucian listened in the greatest admiration, his wide mouth open as if he listened with that as well as with his ears.

'Oh, I say! What happened?'

'Well– we exploded too!' said Philip. 'And after that, the master did – in a different way, of course. We had to put Kiki out to live with someone in the village. We go to see her every day, naturally, and have her on half-holidays and weekends.'

'And she always goes to every school match and cheers like anything – doesn't she, Jack?' said Lucy-Ann.

'She's a wonder,' said Lucian. 'Let me have her for a minute.'

'Look out – she won't go to strangers,' warned Jack. But Lucian was already trying to get hold of the wonderful parrot. He soon let her go. She gave him a vicious nip with her curved beak, and he yelled. To Lucy-Ann's amazement she saw tears in his eyes!

He turned and went off without a word, sucking his

bleeding thumb. The others looked at one another.

'He was crying,' said Lucy-Ann, in sheer amazement that a boy of fourteen should do such a thing.

'He's a nit-wit,' said Jack, trying to calm down Kiki, who had put up her crest tremendously, and was dancing angrily from one foot to another.

'Nit-wit,' said Kiki, pouncing on the word at once, 'Nit-wit, wit-nit, tit-bit, bit-nit, oh, I say!'

'You're a bad bird, nipping people like that,' scolded Jack. 'That was a nasty nip.'

'Nip-wit,' announced Kiki.

'Yes, that's about what you are – a nip-wit!' said Jack, with a chuckle. 'Now don't you start, Micky! We've had enough rudery from Kiki.'

Micky had started off on one of his long strings of excited gibberish. It was comical to see how seriously and solemnly Kiki listened to this, with her head on one side.

She answered the little monkey gravely when he had finished his excited announcement, whatever it was.

'Rikky-likky-acky, icky, pop-pop-pop!' she said. The children roared. 'She thinks she's talking his language. Good old Kiki! You can't get the better of *her*,' said Philip. 'I'm glad she's more friendly with Micky now. He's such a dear.'

'He's getting awfully mischievous, though,' said Dinah, who now thought of the monkey much more kindly. 'He went into a dozen cabins yesterday, and collected all the soaps out of the basins and put them in one of the armchairs in the lounge.'

'Gracious!' said Jack. 'He'll be getting into trouble soon.'

'You mean *we* shall,' said Philip. 'I wish we could teach Kiki to keep an eye on Micky for us – but she encourages him. I'm sure it was Kiki who told the monkey to climb up the mast to the man in the crow's-nest there and give him an awful fright.'

'Micky's a dear,' said Lucy-Ann, and she tickled him

under his furry chin. He looked at her with wise, sad eyes. Lucy-Ann knew he was very happy now, but she was always worried because he looked at her sorrowfully. She only half believed Philip when he told her that all monkeys looked sad.

'There's the gong for lunch,' said Dinah thankfully. 'I feel as if it's about an hour late today, I'm so hungry. Come on, everybody!'

6

The tale of Andra's treasure

The *Viking Star* was now going off to cruise among the islands of the Aegean Sea. The water was a beautiful dark blue, and the children thought it was the nicest part of the trip, seeing the islands loom up out of the purple-blue sea.

Lucian proved himself quite useful here, because he knew that part of the sea very well. He was able to tell them about the different islands, and he was full of exciting stories of old pirates and robberies at sea, and the taking of treasure.

'See that island we're coming to,' he said. 'That's Oupos. It's only small, but it's got an old castle on it with one of the biggest dungeons in the world. The old sailors used to take prisoners at sea, and sail to Oupos, and dump their prisoners in the dungeons. Sometimes they left them there for years – till they were old men.'

'How horrible!' said Lucy-Ann. 'Have you been on Oupos?'

'Yes, once,' said Lucian. 'I saw the holes for the dungeons too. Nearly fell down one myself.'

'What do you mean – holes for the dungeons?' asked Philip.

'Well – the yard of the old castle was pitted with holes –

deep, very deep holes,' explained Lucian. 'And when a prisoner was landed on the island he was dragged to the great yard and popped down the nearest hole. He fell down, down into the dungeons below, and joined the other prisoners there.'

'How awful! Couldn't he get out again?' asked Jack, in horror.

'No. The only way out was up the steep, deep holes,' said Lucian. 'No one could climb up those.'

'But how were the prisoners fed?' asked Philip.

'Easy,' said Lucian. 'The guards just went to the holes each day and tipped food down.'

'I don't know whether to believe that or not,' said Jack.

'I tell you I've been on the island and seen the holes,' insisted Lucian. 'Of course, the dungeons aren't used *now* – the yard is all overgrown, and you can hardly see the dungeon holes. That's how I nearly fell down one.'

'Would you have been there till you were old?' asked Lucy-Ann.

'Of course not. My uncle would have got a rope and hauled me up,' said Lucian. 'I should probably have broken my leg, though.'

'Tell us some more tales about these old islands,' said Jack. 'I wouldn't mind visiting one or two!'

'Well, I dare say we could, if I asked my uncle,' said Lucian surprisingly.

'What do you mean? What's your uncle got to do with it?' demanded Philip. 'You talk as if he owned the islands.'

'He does own quite a few,' said Lucian. 'Didn't I tell you? It's a craze of his, I think. He buys this one and that one, explores it thoroughly – and then maybe he gets tired of it and sells it again.'

The four children looked at Lucian to see if he was telling the truth. It seemed extraordinary to them that anyone should buy and sell islands as if they were cakes or something.

'But – what does he do it for?' asked Jack. 'I mean – is he interested in old things – is he looking for antiques or something?'

'He's very interested in history,' said Lucian. 'Yes, and in old things generally. You should see his house in Athens. He's got the most marvellous collection of things from these old islands. He's crazy about them.'

The children thought about Lucian's uncle. They could not tell if he was crazy or not. He seemed an ordinary, rather cross grown-up to them, hard to size up because he always wore dark glasses and they could not see his eyes.

'You don't know what people are *thinking* if you can't see their eyes,' Lucy-Ann said, and it was true.

'I expect I get my liking for history from my uncle,' said Lucian. 'I'm always top in that. Bottom in everything else, of course. And I *loathe* games.'

'Yes, you've told us that before,' said Jack.

'But only about fifteen times,' put in Dinah.

'Oh, I say!' said Lucian. 'Sorry! It's just that I do detest them so much.'

'Sixteen times,' said Lucy-Ann.

'Goosey-Lucy,' remarked Kiki, very aptly, the children thought. They grinned at one another, Lucian *was* a goose, a silly, credulous, aggravating, tiresome goose, a nit-wit and a rabbit – but he was quite harmless and sometimes really amusing.

'To come back to your uncle,' said Jack. 'Do you honestly mean he owns some of these exciting islands?'

'Oh yes. He doesn't own Oupos now. But he owns the one we'll soon be passing. That'll be Helios. He's about finished with it now, though. He sent his men there to dig and explore, but they didn't find much.'

'What *did* they find?' asked Lucy-Ann, with interest.

'Let me see – they found three magnificent vases, but that was about all,' said Lucian. 'They were cracked, of course – they nearly always are, it seems to me. He found a pair of daggers too – frightfully old I think those were. And he got a lot of rubbish too – you know, bits of broken crockery, pieces of jewellery not worth anything – oh, yes, and he got a little carving of a goose. He gave it to me.'

'Goosey-Lucy,' put in Kiki again. She appeared to be listening hard to all this rigmarole of Lucian.

'Shut up, Kiki. Don't interrupt,' said Jack. 'Go on, Lucy – I mean Lucian.'

'Oh, I say! Don't you start calling me that, Jack,' said Lucian, looking hurt.

'Don't be an ass. Get on with your story,' said Jack. He had no patience with Lucian when he began getting hurt, which happened quite a lot.

'Do you know any more stories about the islands?' asked Lucy-Ann, seeing that Lucian still looked upset.

'Well – there's the story of the Andra treasure-ships,' said Lucian. 'That's supposed to be absolutely true. I've heard my uncle tell it many a time.'

'Go on – tell us,' said Philip, scratching Micky's back for him, as he lay cuddled in the boy's arms, fast asleep.

'Well, it happened hundreds of years ago,' began Lucian. 'I can't remember the exact date. There was a king called Panlostes who had a kingdom on one of these islands, a large one. I expect you know that most of them had rulers of their own. Well, Panlostes had a son.'

'What was he called?' asked Lucy-Ann.

'I don't know,' said Lucian. 'Anyway this son had an accident when he was small, and he lost one eye and hurt his foot so that he limped. He wanted to marry the daughter of a king on the mainland of Greece, a girl called Andra.'

'But she wouldn't have him because he was one-eyed and limped, I suppose,' said Jack. 'And there was someone else she liked and wanted to marry.'

'Well – if you know the story . . . ' began Lucian, half annoyed.

'I don't. But I know lots like it!' said Jack. 'Go on.'

'Andra's father said the girl should marry the one-eyed

prince, if King Panlostes would send him gold and arms and treasure worth half his kingdom,' went on Lucian, warming up again. 'So the King got ready a fleet of ships and stuffed them with riches of all kinds, and one morning they set sail from the island to go to the mainland.'

Lucy-Ann gazed out over the dark-blue sea, imagining the fleet of small ships, their sails filled with the wind, their holds packed with rich treasure. She heard the sharp commands, the creaking of the old wooden ships, the billowing, flapping noise of the sails. Lucian took another breath and continued.

'Well – the girl Andra sent word to the man she really wanted to marry to tell him about the ships. And he got ready some ships himself and set out to intercept the treasure-fleet.'

'Did he find them?' asked Lucy-Ann.

'Yes, he did. But when he attacked them and finally defeated the fleet – he found no treasure!'

'Gracious! Where had it gone?' asked Dinah. 'Had they dumped it into the sea, or something?'

'No. The captain of the fleet had never meant to deliver the treasure safely. He had made up his mind to take it to an island he knew of, land it there, hide it safely and come back for it when he could. He meant to tell both Kings that he had been attacked and robbed on the way to the mainland.'

'And he *was* attacked – but he had hidden the treasure!' said Jack. 'What happened next?'

'The captain was killed and so were half the men. The rest of them made off in their ships and scattered far and wide. Search was made for the hidden treasure, but it couldn't be found.'

'Golly – was nothing more ever heard of it?' said Philip.

'Oh yes. Some of the men thought they remembered where the island was where they had landed the treasure one night. They made up an expedition secretly and went to look for it. They quarrelled and fought – and in the end only two or three men were left. One of them had made a rough map.'

'A map of the island? Was it ever found?' asked Dinah, in excitement.

'Yes. Years later. A Greek merchantman got hold of it somehow and pored over the old map till he had made some sense out of it. He made up his mind that it could refer to only five out of all the islands in the Aegean Sea – and there are heaps and heaps, you know. So he began to explore them one by one.'

'Did he find the right one?' asked Lucy-Ann, her eyes shining. 'This is a lovely story, *I* think.'

'Yes – the old story says he did find the island – and found out where the treasure was too. But before he could do anything about it, he died.'

There was a disappointed silence. 'But who got the treasure then?' asked Jack.

'Nobody,' said Lucian. 'The old merchantman never told a soul. But it's said that *some*where there's a copy of the map and plan he made. Goodness knows where! He hid it before he died; or so people say. He lived about a hundred years ago.'

'What a thrilling story!' said Dinah. 'I wish *we* could find the map. Where did the old man live? Surely the map would be hidden in the house he had?'

'I should think it's been searched from top to bottom,' said Lucian. 'I know the island he lived on. We shall come to it in a day's time. It's called Amulis.'

'Oh! Are we going to land on it?' cried Lucy-Ann. 'I'd like to!'

'Yes. We usually do call there,' said Lucian. 'It's quite a big island, with towns and villages, and some good shops that sell antiques and things. Visitors often go in parties from the ships and buy things.'

'We'll go together!' said Dinah. 'I want to buy some things – I haven't nearly enough. Come with us, Lucian, you'll really be a very great help!'

7

Lucian is very helpful

Mrs Mannering was pleased to hear that the ship was to call at the romantic island of Amulis. She, like the children, had been fascinated by all the misty-purple islands that kept looming up in the dark-blue sea. She had been dipping into Greek history, and somehow it seemed as if the Aegean Sea belonged to the past, not to the present.

The children borrowed her books and read them too. How old these island were, and what stories they held! Lucy-Ann was fascinated by them. She stood at the deck-rail and watched all day long.

'Why are there so many?' she said. 'What do you call a collection of so many islands? It's a long name, I know.'

'Archipelago,' said Mrs Mannering. 'You know, Lucy-Ann, it's said that once all these islands were joined together, making a great mainland. Then something happened, and the sea rushed into what is now the Mediterranean basin, filled it up, and drowned a lot of this mainland. Only the highest parts, the hills and mountains, were left – and they show above the water as islands – the Aegean islands we are cruising among!'

'My goodness,' said Lucy-Ann, her quick imagination showing her a great sweep of water, rushing relentlessly over a land where towns and villages stood – swallowing them up one by one, drowning them – and at last leaving only the highest parts showing above the surface of the waters. 'Oh, Aunt Allie – do you mean that far below us, on the ocean bed, are the ruined remains of cities and villages? Did it happen long ago?'

'Thousands and thousands of years ago,' said Mrs Mannering. 'There wouldn't be a trace of them left now. But it explains the myriads of little islands in this sea. I'm glad we are to visit one of them.'

'You're not afraid of us falling into some exciting adventure now, are you?' said Lucy-Ann slyly. 'You think it will be safe to visit this romantic little island?'

'Quite safe,' said Mrs Mannering, laughing. 'For one thing I shall be with you.'

'We've asked Lucian to come too,' said Dinah. 'I know he's a nit-wit – but he really does know about these islands, Mother. He's told us all sorts of stories about them. His uncle owns some of them.'

'Yes, I heard that he did,' said Mrs Mannering. 'I've talked to his wife – quite a nice woman. I can't say I'd like a husband who did nothing but buy up islands and dig frantically for months, then sell them and start somewhere else. He's got a bee in his bonnet, I think. Still, he certainly seems to have made some interesting finds – finds that have made him a wealthy man!'

The *Viking Star* sailed into a small port the next day. The children were hanging over the deck-rail and were surprised when their ship came to a stop and anchored where she was, without steaming to the jetty.

'We can't get any closer in – the jetty isn't suitable for us. We're too big,' explained one of the officers to the children. 'You'll go ashore in a motor-launch.'

Sure enough a launch came out to the ship, and a score or so of passengers climbed down the ladder to the deck of the launch. The four children went, of course, and Lucian, also Mrs Mannering and some of the other interested passengers. Lucian's people did not go. They knew so much about the island that they had no desire to visit Amulis.

But to the children it was all very thrilling indeed. The motor-launch sped off to the jetty where they all landed. Lucian was quite at home on the island, which he had visited before with his uncle.

'You keep with me. I can show you all the interesting

things,' he said. 'And I can talk to the people too, and bargain for you, if you want to buy anything.'

Lucian was certainly very, very useful. He pushed off the flock of little children who came crowding round begging for money, and sent out such a fierce stream of odd sounding words that even Kiki was most impressed. He knew his way about and was quite good at explaining things.

'Here's the market. The people from the hills up there bring their goods down here – look at them on the stalls – then they spend the money they get at the shops in the town. Or they go to the cinema.'

The people were a picturesque lot. They wore big hats because of the sun, and a collection of nondescript white garments that might have been anything, but which suited them quite well. The children were beautiful, Lucy-Ann thought, with their dark eyes, beautifully shaped faces and thick curling hair.

Lucian took them to an old ruined castle, but the boys were disappointed because there were no dungeons to be seen. The girls were amazed to see people apparently living in parts of the castle, together with their goats and hens.

'They're very poor islanders,' explained Lucian. 'They've got nowhere else to live. Further inland, if I'd time to take you, you'd see people living in caves in the mountain-sides. They used to do that thousands of years ago, too. It's strange to think those caves have sheltered people century after century.'

'Do those cave-people go to the cinema in the town?' asked Dinah.

'Oh yes. They love it, though they can't read anything in English on the screen, of course. The speech is translated, of course,' said Lucian. 'They live in two worlds really – the world of long ago, when people used caves as shelter and scraped along with their goats and hens and geese, and in the world of today, where there are motor-cars and cinemas and so on.'

'A weird mixture,' said Jack. 'I shouldn't know where I was!'

'Oh, they know, all right,' said Lucian, and he paused to shout angrily at a small child who was trying slyly to pull at a ribbon Lucy-Ann was wearing in her dress. Kiki also began to scream excitedly, and Micky jumped up and down on Philip's shoulder, chattering. The child fled in terror. Lucy-Ann felt quite sorry for it.

Lucian took them to the shops. Some of them were small, scret shops, dark and full of strange goods. One shop, which was full of antiques to attract visitors, was quite big.

'You can go in here if you want to look round and buy something,' said Lucian. 'Oh, I say! Where's Micky gone?'

'Just to have a little exercise on the canopy over the shop,' said Philip. Micky was amusing, the way he often leapt off Philip's shoulder and hung on to all kinds of things near by, scampering here and there, flinging himself through the air to some fresh place, never once falling or missing his hold. He was now galloping over the sun-canopy, running from side to side, occasionally stopping to fling himself up to a window-ledge overhead and then drop back. But when he saw that Philip was going into the shop below he threw himself down from the canopy and with a flying leap was back on the boy's shoulder.

'Can't get rid of you, can I?' said Philip. 'You're a bad penny, always turning up – and you do make my neck so hot!'

The shop was fascinating to the four children. They had no idea which things were genuinely old and which were not. Lucian, with the knowledge he had picked up from his uncle, pointed out a few really old things, but they were far too expensive to buy. Lucy-Ann looked at her money. and asked Lucian if there was anything at all she could afford to buy.

He counted it up. It was Greek money, and Lucy-Ann had no idea of its value.

'Yes, you might buy one or two things,' he said. 'There's this blue carved stone, for instance.'

'No, I don't want that,' said Lucy-Ann. 'I really want to buy something for Philip. It's his birthday soon. Is there anything he would like? Don't let him see it – it's to keep for his birthday.'

'Well – what about this tiny carved ship?' said Lucian, holding out a miniature ship, exactly like some of the ships in the harbour. 'It isn't old, of course.'

Seeing the ship reminded Lucy-Ann of something. 'Oh! *I* know what I'd like to buy for him, Lucian. I've just thought. Something he badly wants.'

'What's that?' said Lucian.

'He wants a ship in a bottle,' said Lucy-Ann. 'I know it sounds a funny thing to ask for, but Philip says he always *has* wanted a ship in a bottle.'

'Well – I don't think I've ever seen one *here*,' said Lucian. 'It's not the kind of thing they sell. Wait a minute. I'll ask the johnny who's at the back of the shop. He'll know.'

He made his way through the masses of curious goods, and disappeared behind a screen, where he could be heard talking to someone. He appeared again a minute later.

'No, they don't sell things like that here,' he said. 'But he says he knows where there is one, though it's rather a dirty old thing, and he thinks it's cracked.'

'Where is it?' asked Lucy-Ann. 'I could clean it up, if it isn't *too* badly cracked.'

'He says he saw it on a shelf in a house belonging to an old fisherman, not far from here,' said Lucian. 'I'll take you, if you like. Would Mrs Mannering mind?'

Mrs Mannering was with the ship's party, but she was keeping an eye on Lucian and his little company. Lucy-Ann thought she had better go and ask permission. They went out of the shop and found Mrs Mannering with the rest of the party having a cool, fruit drink in a curious little court-yard overshadowed by an enormous tree.

'Aunt Allie – I want to give Philip a ship in a bottle for his birthday, and I've heard of one. Lucian says he'll take me to get it. May I go?' asked the little girl.

'Yes, but don't be long, Lucian,' said Mrs Mannering. 'It's not far, is it?'

'Oh no – just behind the market, that's all,' said Lucian, and set off with Lucy-Ann. They crossed the noisy market, falling over stray hens, and getting in the way of a herd of goats. They came to a tall blank wall and went round it. On the other side was a sloping courtyard, and round it were set several quaint little cottages made of stone.

Lucian went to one of them and shouted in at the open door. A croaking voice answered him. 'Want to come in?' he asked Lucy-Ann. 'It will be a bit gloomy, I expect.'

Lucy-Ann didn't really want to go in, but she thought it would be rude to refuse, so she stepped over a hen that was squatting on the step, and went into a small dark room that seemed to the girl to be full of laundry and the scents of smoke and cooking.

'There's the ship in a bottle. Look,' said Lucian, and he pointed to a stone shelf at the end of the room. There was a broken pot on it, an old bone – and the bottle! Lucy-Ann peered at the bottle to see if there was a ship inside. It was so sooty and dirty that she could not see through the glass.

Lucian said something to the old woman sitting on a stool, picked up the bottle and carried it to the door. He wiped it with his handkerchief, and held up the bottle for Lucy-Ann to see.

'There you are. You can *just* see the ship now. We'd have to wash the bottle in soapy water before we got the dirt off. It's quite a good ship – nicely carved. And I should think Philip would like it if he really wants one, though I can't imagine why anyone should long for a ship in a bottle.'

'Oh I can!' said Lucy-Ann, peering at the ship. 'I've often longed for things like this – you know, quite useless, but nice and unusual. I had a friend once who had a glass ball, and inside was a little snow-man – and when you shook the ball a whole lot of snow rose up inside the ball and showered itself down over the snowman. I loved that. So I know why Philip wants this.'

'Well – shall I ask the old woman if she'll sell it?' asked Lucian. 'The bottle is dirty and cracked, so it's not worth much.'

'Yes – ask her. You know how much money I've got. I can spend all that,' said Lucy-Ann. Lucian went back into the cottage with the bottle, nearly falling over two clucking hens on the way. A loud argument could be heard from inside. Lucy-Ann stayed out in the open air, listening, but not understanding a word. She felt she could not bear to brave the dark inside the cottage again.

Lucian came out, triumphant. He carried the bottle. 'Well, there you are. I've spent half your money. The old woman wanted the money badly, but she said she didn't know what her old grandad would think if he knew she'd sold a ship that had been in that bottle and in that family for years and years. However, as her grandad must have died long ago I don't expect he'll mind. Here you are.'

'Oh, thank you, Lucian,' said Lucy-Ann gratefully. 'I'll get a bit of paper and wrap it up. I do, do hope Philip will like it. It's an exciting present, isn't it?'

But it was going to be much, much more exciting than Lucy-Ann imagined!

8

The ship in the bottle

Lucy-Ann managed to get some paper and wrap up the bottle and ship before Philip saw it. The others were curious to know what she had got, but she would not tell them.

'It's something breakable, because you're carrying it so carefully!' said Jack. When they got back to the ship she unwrapped the bottle, when she and Dinah got into their cabin, and showed it to her.

'What a dirty old thing!' said Dinah. 'What is it? You haven't spent your money on that, surely!'

'Half of it,' said Lucy-Ann. 'It's for Philip's birthday. He said he wanted one. It's a ship in a bottle.'

'Is it really? Gosh, so it is!' said Dinah, interested. 'Let's clean it up and see it properly. Isn't it a big one?'

They rubbed soap on a flannel and proceeded to clean up the bottle. Once the glass was clean the ship inside could be plainly seen. It was a beauty, quite big, intricately carved, with carefully made sails. In contrast to the bottle, it was clean and free from dust. The colours it had been painted with were still bright.

'Look at that!' said Lucy-Ann in delight. 'It must be a model of one of the old Greek ships. How did it get into the bottle, Dinah? Look, the neck of the bottle is small and narrow – nobody could possibly push that lovely little ship through the neck. It would be quite impossible.'

'I can't *imagine* how it got into the bottle,' said Dinah, puzzled too. 'But it's certainly inside. Won't Philip be pleased? I rather like it myself.'

'Oh, so do I. It's wizard,' said Lucy-Ann. She stood it on a shelf. The bottle had a flat side, and stood on this, the lovely little ship sailing along, as it seemed, in the middle of the bottle, all its sails set.

'What's the ship called?' said Dinah, peering at it. 'I can't tell, can you? The letters on it aren't like ours. They must be Greek.'

The ship in the bottle was duly given to Philip two days later on his birthday. He was thrilled. Lucy-Ann glowed with delight when she saw how pleased he was.

'But *where* did you get it? Why, it's the nicest one I've ever seen!' he said. 'Quite the nicest. Really beautifully made. I wonder how old it is. I'm glad it's such a nice big one too. Most of the ships in bottles I've seen are much smaller than this.'

Micky and Kiki came to look at the ship in the bottle. Micky saw the ship through the glass and tried to get hold of it. He couldn't, of course, because of the glass, and it puzzled him.

'Happy Christmas,' said Kiki to Philip, every now and again. She had been taught to say 'Happy returns' but she kept mixing it with 'Happy Christmas,' which she said every few minutes.

'Thanks, old thing,' Philip said. 'Happy New Year to *you!*'

'Oh, don't muddle her any more,' said Dinah. 'Let's go and show Mother the ship in the bottle.'

They went up on deck and found Mrs Mannering. Her deck-chair was next to Lucian's aunt's chair, which she found rather trying sometimes, as she didn't very much like the uncle.

'Look Mother – see what Lucy-Ann's given me for my birthday – something I've always wanted,' said Philip.

It was admired, and then passed on to Lucian's aunt and uncle to see. Mr Eppy looked at it carefully. He seemed puzzled.

'The ship is very old – really old,' he said. 'But the bottle is modern. The idea of a ship in a bottle is a comparatively recent one, of course. But the ship inside is far older – almost an antique! Very interesting.'

'It's got a name carved on it, very small,' said Lucy-Ann. 'I can't read it. Can you, Mr Eppy?'

He peered at it and spelt it out. 'Yes – A-N-D-R-A – queer name for a ship! Never heard of one called that in Greek.'

'I've heard the name before,' said Lucy-Ann, and she tried to remember. 'Oh yes – wasn't it the name of the girl in that lovely treasure story of Lucian's – the girl who didn't want to marry a one-eyed man? Well, we often call our ships by the names of girls or women – look at our big liners, *Queen Mary* and *Queen Elizabeth*. I don't see why a Greek ship shouldn't be called after a princess too.'

Mr Eppy wasn't listening. He wasn't at all interested in any of the children, not even in Lucian, his own nephew. He yawned and settled himself to sleep. Mrs Mannering nodded to the children to go. Micky and Kiki were rather tiresome when anyone wanted to sleep. Kiki's squawks and Micky's chatter and tricks didn't appeal to the grown-ups as much as they did to the children.

They took the ship in the bottle back to the cabin – this time to the boys' cabin. Philip decided to put it on the shelf opposite his bed, where he could see it. He was very pleased with it indeed. It was quaint and strange, and beautiful, and he had always wanted it. Now he had it.

'Be careful that monkey of yours doesn't tamper with it,' Jack warned him. 'He's very curious about the ship inside – keeps trying to touch it through the glass, and he gets quite annoyed when he can't.'

The *Viking Star* cruised from island to island. Time did not seem to exist, and not one of the children had any idea of the days. It was all like a pleasant dream, where, fortunately, the food tasted very real and very nice. In fact, as Jack said, if the food had not tasted jolly real he might honestly have thought that he *was* dreaming.

And then a squabble blew up between Micky and Kiki that broke up the dream in a strange way, and made things very real and earnest indeed from that time onwards.

It happened one evening. The boys had gone up to play deck-tennis with the girls, and for once had left Micky and Kiki down below in their cabin. Micky was such a nuisance when they played deck-tennis because he *would* fling himself after the rubber ring, and, if he got it, tear up to the top of the nearest pole and sit there, chattering in glee.

So he had been relegated to the cabin that sunny evening, with Kiki as company. Kiki was cross. She did not like being left behind. She sat on the porthole-sill and sulked, making a horrible moaning noise that distressed Micky very much.

The monkey went to sit beside her, looking at her enquiringly, and putting out a sympathetic paw to stroke Kiki's feathers. Kiki growled like a dog and Micky retreated to the shelf, where he sat looking puzzled and sad.

He tried once more to comfort Kiki, by taking Jack's tooth-brush over to her, and trying to brush her feathers with it, chuckling with delight. Kiki turned her back on him, and finally put her head under her wing, which always puzzled and frightened Micky. He did not like her to have no head. He began to look for it cautiously, parting the parrot's feathers carefully and gently. Where had the head gone?

Kiki spoke from the depth of her feathers. 'Nit-wit, nit-wit, nit-wit, oh, I say! Grrrrrrr! Wipe the door and shut your feet! God save the Queen.'

Micky left her in despair. He would wait till she grew her head again, and became the jolly parrot he knew. He put the tooth-brush back into its mug and considered the sponge near by. He picked it up and sucked some moisture out of it. He sponged his little face with it as he had seen Philip do. Then he got tired of that and darted back to the shelf again.

What could he do? He looked down at the shelf. On it was the ship in the bottle. Micky cautiously put his hand down to the bottle. Why couldn't he get that little thing inside? Why couldn't he get it and play with it? He put his head on one side and considered the ship inside.

He picked up the bottle and nursed it like a doll, crooning in his monkey language. Kiki took her head out of her wing and looked round at him. When she saw him nursing the bottle, she was jealous and cross.

'Shut the door, shut the door, naughty boy,' she scolded. 'Where's your hanky, pop goes the weasel!'

Micky did not understand a word, and it would not have made any difference if he had. He shook the bottle hard.

Kiki raised her crest and scolded again.

'Naughty, naughty! Bad boy! Pop-pop-pop!'

Micky chattered at her, and would not put the bottle down. Kiki flew across to the shelf and gave the surprised monkey a hard peck. He gave an anguished howl and flung the bottle away from him, nursing his bleeding arm.

The bottle fell to the floor with a crash, and broke in half. The little ship inside was shaken loose from its base and fell over on its side. Micky saw it and leapt down to it. Here was that thing inside the bottle at last! He picked it up and retired under the bed in silence.

Kiki was shocked by the noise of the bottle falling and breaking. She knew it was a bad thing to happen. She made a noise like a motor-mower, and then relapsed into silence. What would Philip say?

Five minutes later the two boys came clattering into the cabin to wash and put on clean things for dinner. The first thing they saw was the broken bottle on the floor. Philip looked at it in horror.

'Look! It's smashed! Either Kiki or Micky must have done it!'

'Where's the ship?' said Jack, looking all round. It was nowhere to be seen. It was not till they hauled Micky out from underneath the bed that they got the ship. He had not harmed it at all. He got three hard smacks, and Kiki got three hard taps on her beak.

'My beautiful present!' groaned Philip, looking at the little carved ship. 'Look, isn't it a beauty, Jack? You can see it better now it's out of the bottle.'

Jack looked at it and pulled at a tiny knob in one side. 'What's this?' he said. To his great surprise the knob came out and he could look inside the ship.

'It's hollow inside,' he said. 'And there's something there, Philip – looks like paper or parchment. I say – what can it be?'

Philip suddenly felt excited. 'Parchment? Then it must be

an old document! And why should it be hidden inside the ship? Only because it contains a secret! I say, this is super. Goodness knows what the document is!'

'Let's probe it out and see,' said Jack. 'Look – this little section of the ship can be moved, now we've taken that knob out – and we'll just about have room to get out the parchment.'

'Be careful! It may fall to pieces if it's very old,' Philip warned him. Jack removed the loose section of the ship and put it beside the knob. Then, very carefully, he began to try and probe out the parchment. But he was excited and his hands trembled too much.

Then the gong went to say that dinner was ready. 'We can't go,' groaned Jack. 'We *must* find out what this is!'

'Look out – you're tearing it,' said Philip. 'Let's wait till after dinner, Jack. We won't have time now. And I think the girls ought to be here to see all this.'

'Yes. You're right. We'll wait till after dinner,' said Jack, with a sigh. 'Lock the whole thing up, Philip. We can't risk anything happening to the ship and its secret!'

So they locked the little ship up in a cupboard, and then, hot with excitement, went up to have their dinner. What a thrill! They could hardly wait to tell the girls!

The two girls could not imagine what was the matter with the boys that dinner-time. Jack kept grinning quite idiotically at them, and Philip did his best to do a little whispering, to give the news.

Mrs Mannering frowned at him in surprise. 'Philip! You forget yourself. Say what you have to say out loud, please.'

That was just what Philip could not do, of course. 'Er – who won at deck-tennis?' he said feebly.

'Well, really – I can't imagine why you had to say that in a *whisper*,' said Mrs Mannering. 'Don't be silly, Philip.'

'Sorry, Mother,' said Philip, not looking in the least sorry, but extraordinarily pleased. He simply could not help it. He kept thinking of the ship and its secret parchment. It was something really exciting, he was sure of it.

As soon as dinner was over the four children slipped away. When they got to a safe corner, Jack clutched at the girls. 'Lucy-Ann! Dinah!'

'What *is* it?' said Dinah. 'You both acted like lunatics at dinner. What's up with you?'

'Sh! Listen! You know that ship in a bottle,' began Jack, but Philip interrupted him.

'No. Let me tell. Well, Micky and Kiki broke the bottle between them, the wretches, and when we got down into the cabin, there it was, smashed on the floor – and the ship was gone!'

'Where?' said Lucy-Ann, upset.

'Micky had it, under the bed. We got it and looked at it – and will you believe it, there was a knob that came out, and then we could remove another section of the ship – and inside there's a parchment document of some sort!'

'*No!*' cried the girls, both together, thrilled to hear the news.

'It's true. You come down and see. Don't tell anyone though, especially Lucian. It's our own secret.'

They all tore down to the boys' cabin and nearly knocked over the steward, who had been turning down the beds.

'Sorry!' said Jack. 'Have you finished, steward?'

'Yes, I've finished – but what's all your hurry?' said the astonished steward. He got no answer. The door closed in his face, and he heard the latch being put across to lock it. Now what were those limbs of children up to?

Inside the cabin the light was switched on, and the cupboard unlocked. Philip took out the little carved ship. The others crowded round to look at it.

'See – you take out this knob – and that loosens this section of the side – and it comes right out,' said Philip. 'And now look – can you see the document neatly crammed inside? I'm sure it's parchment.'

The girls took a deep breath. 'Gosh – it's a thrill,' said

Dinah. 'Get it out, quick!'

'We'll have to be careful not to tear it,' said Jack. 'Stand back a bit, you girls. You keep jogging my arm.'

How the boys managed to wheedle the closely folded paper out of the inside of the wooden ship was a miracle. Little by little they edged it out, until at last it was completely out, and the inside of the ship was empty.

'There we are!' said Jack triumphantly, as he laid the yellow parchment carefully on the dressing-table. 'Now to see what it is.'

With gentle, careful fingers Philip unfolded the parchment. It spread out into quite a big sheet. The children pored over it, thrilled.

'It's a map!'

'A plan of some kind!'

'I can't read the words. Blow, they must be in Greek or something!'

'What *is* it? It looks like some island or something!'

'Look at these marks – they must be the bearings of the compass – look, would that be north, south, east, west?'

'It's *two* maps, that's what it is. Look, this bit must show an island, I think – surely that's meant to be sea round it. And that bit is a plan – a plan of some building, I should think, with passages and things.'

The excited talk went on and on, each of the four children trying to press closer still to the map. Philip remembered that he had a magnifying-glass and went to get it. Then they could see even better, and could make out a few strange words and marks too faded to see before.

'See this faint word here, at the left-hand side, right at the top,' said Lucy-Ann suddenly. 'Well, it looks exactly like the name on the ship, doesn't it? Let's compare them and see.'

They looked at both the words, first on the ship and then on the map. They certainly were the same.

'Well – Mr Eppy said the ship's name was *Andra* – and if the name on the map is the same, it must have something to do with an island or a person called Andra,' said Dinah.

There was a silence. Everyone was digesting this, and wondering if they dared to say what they thought it meant. No – it wasn't possible. It simply wasn't possible.

Lucy-Ann voiced their feelings first. She spoke in rather a breathless voice.

'Andra – the name of the girl who wouldn't marry the one-eyed prince. Do you suppose that one of the ships of treasure sent out and lost was called Andra in her honour? And do you suppose Andra was the name given to the search for the treasure – and that's why this ship and this map are marked Andra?'

'It can't be!' said Jack, under his breath. 'It isn't possible that we have hit on the old plan that was lost – the copy of the older plan made hundreds of years ago! It just isn't possible.'

'It's probably a hoax,' said Philip, feeling perfectly certain that it wasn't.

'No – it can't be,' said Dinah. 'Mr Eppy, who knows about old things, told us the ship was old, didn't he? He was puzzled about it, because he said the ship was far older than the bottle.'

'Well, I'll tell you what *I* think,' said Jack slowly. 'I think this may be the plan – and I think probably that old Greek merchantman who copied the original one and died, hid it in this ship – which he may have carved himself.'

'Yes – and after he died his family may have kept it as a curio, not knowing what was inside it – and later on somebody else got the ship and thought it would be a very suitable one for putting inside a bottle,' finished Philip.

'But *how* did it get inside?' wondered Lucy-Ann. 'That's a real puzzle to me.'

'It's quite easy, really,' said Jack. 'The masts are hinged – they lie flat on the hull with threads tied to them. The ship's hull is slipped through the neck of the bottle – then the threads tied to the mast are pulled, and up come mast and sails! The threads are drawn away and the bottle sealed with the fully-rigged ship inside!'

'Gosh – how clever!' said Lucy-Ann. She looked at the ship again, and at the map lying beside it, old and yellowed.

'To think we are looking at a plan that was first drawn ages ago by a Greek admiral in charge of a fleet of treasure-ships! And on this very map is shown where that treasure is still hidden – and we're the only people in the world that know the secret!'

It certainly was rather a tremendous thought. Silence fell on the four children. They looked at one another. Lucy-Ann spoke again, timidly.

'Jack! Philip! This won't be another adventure, will it?'

Nobody answered her. They were all thinking about the strange map. Jack voiced their thoughts.

'The thing is, as Lucy-Ann says – we may be the only ones in the *world* that know this secret – but it's all Greek to us! We can't read a word on the map, we don't even know what the name of the island is, that is marked here. It's maddening.'

'We shall have to find out,' said Dinah.

'Oh yes – run round to various Greek people – Mr Eppy, for instance – and say, "Please will you decipher this strange document for us?" That's not a very bright idea, Dinah. Anyone who knows anything would see there was something worth while in this map – and it would disappear like a shot!'

'Oh dear – would it?' said Lucy-Ann. 'Do let's be careful of it, then.'

'I know what we could do to make sure nobody could possibly steal it and use it,' said Jack. 'We could cut it carefully into four pieces, and each one of us could have a bit – then if anyone tried to grab our bits he wouldn't be any better off – he'd only have a quarter of the plan, which wouldn't help him much!'

'Yes – that's a good idea,' said Philip. 'Though why we are

imagining thieves and robbers like this I don't know!'

'Only because we've had a bit of experience in our other adventures,' said Dinah. 'We're getting to know how to handle them now!'

'And you know,' said Jack, still thinking of his plan, 'if we cut the map into four pieces, we could quite well go to *four* different people to ask them to decipher each quarter – without their seeing the other bits at all – so *they* wouldn't be any wiser, but *we* could fit their explanations together and get a complete picture of what the map means.'

'That's really a very clever idea, Jack,' said Philip, considering it. 'All the same – I vote we don't go to Mr Eppy about one of the bits.'

'I don't see why not,' said Jack. 'He won't be able to tell anything from one bit, and we certainly shan't say we've got the rest. In fact, it wouldn't be a bad idea to go to him first – he'd be able to tell all right if it was a genuine document. If it isn't we shan't need to waste our time trailing round to find three other people to decipher the other bits.'

'Do you think he might guess what *we* guess – that this map is a plan of the Andra treasure hiding-place?' asked Philip, still doubtful of the wisdom of asking Mr Eppy about the map.

'We won't give him the bit with the name "Andra" on,' said Jack. 'And we won't say a word about the other bits, or even where we found them. We'll just say we came across his bit in our explorations, but we don't know where. Lucy-Ann doesn't need to say a word. She's the only one who knows where the ship was bought – *we* don't. So we can truthfully look him in the eye, and say "No, sir – we haven't any idea where this bit of paper originally came from. It just – er – kind of appeared." '

'I hope he believes you,' said Dinah. 'He never seems to believe a word that Lucian says.'

'Oh, well – that nit-wit,' said Jack.

'Lucian's really nicer than you think,' said Lucy-Ann. 'It

was all because of him, don't forget, that I got this ship – I'd never have found the ship in the bottle if it hadn't been for him.'

'Well, he shall have a small share in the treasure if we find it,' said Jack generously.

'Oh – are we going to look for it, then?' said Lucy-Ann. 'What about Aunt Allie? What will she say? And will the *Viking Star* mind us going to hunt for a treasure island?'

'Don't jump ahead, Lucy-Ann,' said Jack. 'How can we possibly settle anything in the way of future plans till we know what the map says? I imagine Aunt Allie will be as thrilled as we are when she hears about this.'

'Well, I don't,' said Lucy-Ann. 'I think she'll hate it. She'll take us all straight back home! She won't have us rushing about looking for islands and treasure, *I* know. She's had enough of that kind of thing with us.'

'We shan't tell her, then, till everything is settled – and, when it is, we'll send for old Bill,' declared Jack.

Lucy-Ann cheered up immediately. As long as Bill Cunningham was there, nothing would matter. The four sat down on the two beds, quite tired out with their exciting talk. They wished the electric fan would go twice as fast because they felt so hot. It whirred away, turning this way and that, a real blessing in the warm cabin.

A terrible noise, far louder than the electric fan made, came to their ears. They jumped.

'That's Kiki – making her express-engine screech,' said Jack. 'Come on – we'd better get her or we shall have the captain himself down to see what's up. My gracious, there she goes again. We've left her too long in the girls' cabin. Little wretch!'

The children hurried to the cabin next door, anxious to stop Kiki before other passengers complained. Kiki was standing on the dressing-table in front of the mirror, screeching at herself. Although she knew mirrors very well indeed, there were still times when she flew into a rage at seeing another parrot there, one that she could not peck.

'Stop it, Kiki, bad bird!' cried Jack. 'I'll tie your beak up, I will! Bad bird, naughty Polly!'

'Happy returns,' said Kiki, speaking to Philip, and ignoring Jack. She made a sound like a cork being popped out of a bottle, and then another noise like the gurgling of a liquid being poured out.

'She wants a drink,' said Jack. 'Sorry, old thing. I forgot you'd be hot in here.' He filled a tooth-glass with water and Kiki sipped it thirstily. Micky came out for a drink too.

'We are awful,' said Philip. 'We forgot all about these two in our excitement. There's always water for them in our cabin, but there isn't any in the girls'. Poor Kiki, poor Micky!'

'Nit-wit,' said Kiki politely. She gave a realistic hiccup. 'Pardon! Micky, Kiki, Micky, Kiki, Micky, Ki—'

'That's enough,' said Jack. 'We don't think that's funny. Come along for a walk on deck. We'll all get some fresh air, and then sleep on our plans.'

They went up on deck with the parrot and the monkey. The other passengers smiled to see them. They liked the four children and their amusing pets. Kiki gave a hiccup every time she passed anyone, and immediately said 'Oh, I say! Pardon!' She knew that made people laugh, and she loved showing off.

It was cool on deck in the evening air. The children said very little, because they were thinking such a lot. The bottle – the ship – the old map – quartering it – deciphering it – hunting, hunting, hunting for – Andra's treasure!

Down in their cabins that night they all found it very difficult to go to sleep. They tossed and turned, wishing they could get cool. Micky and Kiki were on the porthole-sill for coolness. The boys had it open always now, because neither of the pets showed any sign of wanting to go out of the big round opening.

Lucy-Ann lay thinking in her bed. She had the old familiar

feeling of growing excitement and anticipation, mixed with a little dread. She knew that feeling! It was the one she got when an adventure was beginning. She called softly to Dinah.

'Dinah! Are you asleep? Listen – do you think we're beginning one of our adventures again? Do, do say we're not!'

'Well, if we are, whose fault will it be?' came back Dinah's voice, very wide awake. 'Who bought that ship?'

'I did,' said Lucy-Ann. 'Yes – if we plunge headlong into an adventure this time, it'll be all because *I* bought the little ship – the Ship of Adventure!'

9

The secret of the Ship of Adventure

When the morning came, the boys began to realize the difficulties in front of them concerning the strange document they had got hold of. The matter did not seem half so easy to tackle or a quarter so straightforward as they had imagined the night before.

Things the boys had pooh-poohed, such as Mrs Mannering's objections, suddenly seemed very awkward indeed. In fact the whole idea lost its rosy glow and seemed to recede into the realm of the impossible. It was very disappointing.

But when they got out the map again, which Philip had carefully put into an envelope and kept under his pillow all night long, the excitement of the night before swept over them again. *Somehow* they must get the map deciphered, they must find out for certain if it was genuine – and then, who knew what might happen!

They made their plans. The map must be carefully cut into

quarters. Each quarter must be placed in a small envelope, which in turn should be put into one a little larger. Each child must secrete his bit of the map either about his or her person, or in the cabin.

That was the first thing to do. Then one of them must take his quarter to Mr Eppy and see what he said. Not the bit with the name of the island on, of course, but one of the other pieces.

'And Lucy-Ann mustn't come with us when we ask him,' said Philip. 'Because if he asks us straight out where we originally got the paper we can all say truthfully we don't know – but Lucy-Ann can't say that – and she'd blush or something and give the game away.'

'I should *not*,' said Lucy-Ann, who did not want to miss any of the excitement.

'You would. You're such a truthful person,' said Philip. 'Don't look like that, Lucy-Ann – it's a very nice thing to be, and we wouldn't have you any different. It's only that this is important, and it just might spoil things if you show there's something up.'

'All right,' said Lucy-Ann, with a sigh. 'Perhaps you're right. I do wish Mr Eppy would take off his sun-glasses sometimes – I just don't know what he's really like if I can't see his eyes.'

'I should think he's all right, except that he's a bit short-tempered,' said Jack. 'He's nice to his wife, and he's always very polite to Aunt Allie. Of course, he's pretty awful to Lucian – but then if *we* had poor old Rabbit for a nephew we'd be pretty awful to him too.'

'We are now, sometimes,' said Lucy-Ann. 'Like when we go on and on and on at him to have a swim in the ship's pool, when we know he's scared stiff of the water.'

'It's only to see what excuse he'll think up each time,' said Jack. 'He's a marvel at excuses.'

'Well – what about this map – when shall we take it to Mr Eppy?' asked Philip. 'And if he says it's genuine, what do we do next? Is there anyone else on the ship we can ask about the next bit of the map?'

'Yes – there's the deck steward,' said Dinah. 'He's Greek. He could decipher it all right, I should think. And there's that little Greek woman who keeps the shop on the promenade deck – she'd be able to do a bit too, I expect.'

'Yes. We're getting on!' said Philip, pleased. 'Well – what about doing a bit of snipping?'

'I've got some very, very sharp scissors,' said Lucy-Ann. 'They're in my cabin. I'll go and get them. And I'll see what Micky and Kiki are doing there at the same time – up to some mischief, I expect!'

'Well, we couldn't have them here whilst we get out the map,' said Jack. 'Micky might quite well make a grab at it and throw it out of the porthole, like he did yesterday with the post-card I'd just written!'

'What a horrible thought!' said Dinah. She visualized their precious map sailing away out of the porthole and she got up to shut it. 'Just in *case*,' she said, and the boys laughed.

Lucy-Ann went to get her scissors. She was a long time coming back, and the others got impatient. 'What *is* she doing? She's been ages.'

When Lucy-Ann came back she had Kiki with her. 'I had to bring her,' she said. 'She had got Micky into a corner, and she was dancing in front of him from one leg to another – you know how she does when she's cross – and she was growling terrifically just like a dog. Poor Micky was scared stiff. I just had to stay and comfort him a bit.'

'What you mean is, you stayed and had a good game with them both,' grumbled Jack. 'Keeping us waiting all this time. Where are the scissors?'

'Blow! I left them behind after all!' said Lucy-Ann, and departed again in a hurry, looking rather red. She came back immediately, with the scissors in her hand. Kiki was now contentedly perched on her beloved Jack's shoulder, singing something that sounded like 'Humpty-Dumpty, three blind mice' over and over again in a very quiet little voice. She knew she had been naughty.

Jack took the scissors, and, very carefully and solemnly, cut the precious document in half. The parchment crackled as he cut it. The others held their breath and watched.

Then Jack cut the halves into half again, and there, on the boys' dressing-table, lay the four pieces – four exciting parts of a rare and unique document – if it was what the children imagined it to be!

'Now for small envelopes and then a bit larger ones,' said Dinah. She rummaged in the boys' writing-cases and produced four fairly strong little envelopes. Each bit of the map was carefully slipped into one. Then four bigger envelopes were found, and the small envelopes were slipped into those. Good! The first step was taken.

'We can easily paste the four bits together once we have got all the pieces deciphered,' said Philip. 'Now – what's the best time to interview Mr Eppy – and exactly how shall we set about it?'

'It would be quite a good time now,' said Jack. 'He's usually up in his deck-chair – and he'll probably be awake because it's not long after breakfast!'

'I say – are we to tell Lucian anything about this?' said Lucy-Ann.

'Don't be silly! Of *course* not!' said Jack. 'I wouldn't trust old Lucian with anything. His uncle has only got to bark a few words at him and he'd tell him everything he knew – and a lot more that he didn't, besides.'

It was decided that Jack's bit should be the one presented to Mr Eppy. It had not the name 'Andra' on it, neither had it the name of the island, so far as they could tell. It had one part of the island, with a few obscure hieroglyphics.

'What are hiero-something-or-other?' asked Lucy-Ann, when Jack used the word. 'It sounds like a medicine or something!'

'Hieroglyphics? Well – these squiggly marks that we don't understand,' said Jack. 'Marks that stand for words. Secret symbols, perhaps.'

'Secret symbols – it sounds thrilling,' said Lucy-Ann. 'Now – where shall I hide my bit?'

'*Not* in your writing-case or anywhere obvious like that, Lucy-Ann,' said Philip. 'I know where I'm going to hide *mine.*'

'Where?' asked the others, and watched as Philip rose and went to his dressing-table. It was fixed to the wall, of course – every bit of furniture in the cabins was fixed either to the wall or to the floor, so that it would not move if the ship rolled. Between the wall and the dressing-table was a thin space, no more than a crack. Philip bent down and slid his envelope into this crack.

'There!' he said. 'No-one will dust there – it's absolutely hidden between the bottom of the dressing-table and the wall. Where will you put yours, Jack?'

'I'll keep it on me,' said Jack. 'My shorts have got a thin lining. I'll take out a few stitches so that I can slip my bit in. I'll pin it up afterwards. But I shan't hide mine yet, because I've got to show it to Mr Eppy.'

Dinah had thought of a really excellent place. She took the others to the cabin. Behind the electric fan was a panel of wood, to which it was fixed. She slid her envelope neatly into the crack between the panel and the wall of the cabin. It hid it completely. She had had to turn off the fan to use the hiding-place, of course – now she turned it on again, and the others voted her hiding-place as first-class – no one would ever think there was anything hidden behind an electric fan that whirred round and round all day and night!

'Good for you!' said Jack. 'Now what about Lucy-Ann?'

'Think of somewhere that Micky can't get at,' warned Philip. 'He's watching you. He can't get Dinah's piece because he's afraid of the fan. He'd never dare to explore behind it!'

'Could I slip it under the carpet?' said Lucy-Ann.

'No,' said Jack. 'The stewardess might feel it there when she was doing the carpet, and get it out.'

'Well – I know – what about at the back of a drawer-space?' said Lucy-Ann. She pulled out one of the drawers in her dressing-table and set it on the floor. She got a drawing-pin from her pencil-box and pinned the precious envelope to the very back of the drawer-space.

'There!' she said. 'No one can possibly see it's there unless they pull the drawer right out – and why should they do that?'

'Yes. That's fine,' said Jack, and the others approved too. 'Micky's not strong enought to pull the drawer out, even if he wants to. Now what about going and tackling Mr Eppy?'

'Right. Lucy-Ann, you go up to the deck-tennis place with Lucian whilst we talk to his uncle,' said Philip. 'Then you'll both be out of the way.'

Lucy-Ann went off to find Lucian. He was mooning about by himself, wondering where they all were. He was delighted to see Lucy-Ann, and agreed at once to have a game with her. He liked her the best of the four – probably because he felt she didn't make fun of him as much as the others.

'Well, *they're* disposed of, all right,' said Jack, watching them go up the steps to the sports deck. 'Come on. We'll make for the deck-chairs. Kiki, do decide which of my shoulders you want to sit on – this flapping to and fro is most uncomfortable!'

'I wish you'd have Micky for an hour or two,' groaned Philip. 'He's like a hot-water bottle by my right ear this morning.'

The passengers watched the three children with their parrot and monkey as they passed by. They had got used to them by now, and enjoyed the antics of the two pets. Mrs Mannering was on the watch for them.

'I wondered where you'd got to,' she said. 'Where's Lucy-Ann?'

'Playing with Lucian,' said Jack. He sat down by Mrs Mannering. Mrs Eppy and her husband were the other side of her. Jack spoke loudly so that his voice would carry well.

'I've got an unusual thing here,' he said. 'An old, old document, I should think. Do you suppose Mr Eppy would be kind enough to look at it for me, Aunt Allie?'

'Well, ask him!' said Mrs Mannering. 'He's here.'

10

Hiding-places

Philip and Dinah were sitting on the edge of the same deck-chair together, next to Mrs Mannering's. Jack was on the foot-end of her chair, with his bit of paper. They all looked very innocent and unconcerned.

'I don't really like to bother Mr Eppy now,' said Jack. 'He's reading.'

Mrs Eppy heard. She tapped her husband on the arm. 'Paul,' she said. 'Jack wants to ask you something.'

Mr Eppy knew that perfectly well, but he had pretended not to hear. He looked up.

'Very well,' he said grudgingly. 'What is it?'

'Just some old bit of paper we found,' said Philip, joining in. 'Probably quite uninteresting. We can't understand anything on it, of course.'

'It mayn't be old at all,' said Jack, flipping his bit with his thumb.

'It *looks* old,' said Mrs Mannering, getting interested. 'Where did you get it?'

'I don't really know – picked it up somewhere on one of

the islands we visited,' said Jack. 'Do you know exactly where, Dinah?'

'No,' said Dinah truthfully. 'I've no idea.'

'Nor have I,' said Philip.

'Pass it over,' said Mr Eppy, sounding rather bored. His wife passed him the piece of parchment. He took it and glanced at it, meaning to pass it back with a scornful remark. What did these children know about old things? Nothing! It was probably a bit of an old letter, blown about by the wind, that they had picked up in the street. Or maybe they had bought something and this was part of the paper it was wrapped in. Mr Eppy looked at it and opened his mouth to say something contemptuous.

But he did not say a word. He went on looking and looking at the paper. Finally he took his dark glasses off and looked at it without them.

'Er – is it genuinely old, sir?' asked Jack, at last, not able to wait any longer.

Mr Eppy did not answer. He was feeling in his pocket for something. He took out a little black case and undid it. Inside was a strong magnifying-glass set in an eye-piece that could be screwed into the eye – something like watch-repairers wear sometimes when repairing watches. Mr Eppy screwed the glass into his eye, like an enormous monocle, and once more bent over Jack's piece of parchment.

He looked for a very long time. The children waited, almost breathless. Why didn't he speak? Why was he such ages? It was mean of him!

At last Mr Eppy took the eye-piece out of his eye and looked at the children. They got a shock, because they had never seen his eyes without dark glasses before. He had not nice eyes at all! They were decidedly cold. One was blue and the other was dark brown. Dinah felt a little shiver down her back. How very very peculiar! She couldn't help staring at him, looking first at one dark-blue eye and then at the other dark-brown one. Was one false? No – how silly! – he would have eyes that matched if one was false.

'Well,' said Mr Eppy, and paused as if he was thinking what was best to say. 'It's – er – quite interesting. Er . . . '

'But is it genuinely *old*, Mr Eppy?' insisted Jack. 'That's what we want to know.'

'The parchment isn't all here,' said Mr Eppy, and his eyes glanced from one to the other of the children. 'This is only a piece of it. And judging by the *edges* of the parchment it has been recently cut. Rather odd that, don't you think so?'

This was most unexpected. Jack answered at once, feeling that there must be no pause which might give them away.

'Gosh – how very strange! Well, I suppose we've just got hold of *one* bit, sir. Er – I wonder who's got the rest of it.'

'So do I,' said Mr Eppy, looking at Jack and swinging his eye-piece to and fro on his finger. 'I should be very – very – interested to know.'

'Why, sir?' asked Philip, looking perfectly innocent, much to Dinah's admiration.

'Well – I can't tell much from this one piece,' said Mr Eppy. 'It would be a help to have the rest.'

'What *can* you tell, Mr Eppy?' asked Dinah.

He looked at her with his odd eyes. 'I can tell that it shows part of an island,' he said. 'An interesting island – with some secret on it. I could perhaps tell what the *whole* secret is, if I had the other bit of the parchment.'

'What a pity you haven't got it, sir,' said Jack, holding out his hand for his piece.

'*Where* did you say you found this?' said Mr Eppy, snapping out the question so suddenly that the children jumped.

'We didn't say – because we don't know,' said Jack, at once.

Mr Eppy frowned. He put his dark glasses on again, and became the familiar, rather puzzling man they knew, with his peculiar eyes completely hidden.

'I'll keep this parchment for a while,' he said, and actually took out a wallet to place it there.

'I'd rather you didn't, sir, if you don't mind,' said Jack. 'I'm going to take it home – er – for the school museum – if it's genuinely old and all that.'

'Yes, it's genuine,' said Mr Eppy dryly. 'I'll buy it off you. I'm interested in old things, as you know.'

'We don't want to sell it, Mr Eppy,' said Jack, getting alarmed. 'It can't be worth anything, anyway. We want it as a curio.'

'Very well. But I should like to borrow it for a while,' said Mr Eppy, and he calmly slipped the parchment into his wallet, and put the wallet into his pocket. Then he picked up his book and began to read.

Jack looked at the others in dismay. He was angry and crestfallen – but what was he to do? He could not snatch Mr Eppy's wallet and grab his piece of parchment from it. And if he kicked up a terrific fuss, Mrs Mannering would be angry, and Mr Eppy would get suspicious – if he was not suspicious already!

Philip and Dinah were dumbfounded. The cheek of it – taking their parchment like that! Would he give it back? They wished they had taken a tracing of it. If only they had! Now they might never get back their treasured bit of parchment.

They got up and went, feeling that they must talk about it. Mr Eppy took no notice of their going. Jack did not dare to say anything more to him, but he glowered at Lucian's uncle as if he could tear his wallet out of him.

They went to their cabin. 'Beast!' said Jack. 'Surly fellow! What sauce to pocket our parchment like that!'

'Hope we get it back,' said Dinah gloomily.

'There's one thing – we jolly well know it's old – and genuine – and holds something most interesting to Mr Eppy,' said Philip, cheering up a little. 'We do know that. He was quite knocked out when he first looked at it – even had to get that eye-piece arrangement out. I bet he knows it may be part of a treasure-plan.'

'I don't think, somehow, it was a very good idea to take it to Mr Eppy,' said Dinah. 'There may be markings on it that tell a man like that – who knows about old things – far more than they would tell anyone else.'

'I hope he doesn't guess we've got the other bits,' said Jack.

'He does,' said Philip. 'I bet he does.'

Lucy-Ann came bursting into the cabin. 'Hallo!' she said. 'How did you get on? I had to stop playing with Lucian because that uncle of his came up and called him. He took him off somewhere.'

'He did, did he?' said Jack. 'I suppose he's going to ask him what *he* knows, then. Good thing he knows nothing!'

'What happened?' said Lucy-Ann. 'You all look rather down-in-the-mouth. Wasn't it genuinely old?'

'Yes. But Mr Eppy has taken it and put it into his wallet,' said Jack. 'And I bet we don't get it back!'

Lucy-Ann was horrified. 'But why did you let him take it, you *idiot*!'

'Well, what would *you* have done? Knocked him off his deck-chair, grabbed his wallet and run off with it?' demanded Jack, going through a performance of knocking somebody down and grabbing something. Kiki was astonished and rose into the air in fright, squawking. She settled on top of the cupboard in alarm. Jack took no notice of her. He was really crestfallen at what had happened – after all their wonderful, careful, clever plans, too!

'We'll just have to hope he gives it back, that's all,' said Philip. 'And if he does – it will probably mean he's got a very nice copy of it!'

'We'll have to find out what he has said to Lucian,' said Jack. 'He'll probably tell him to try and pump us about this bit of parchment – and find out if we have the other bits – and where we got the thing from – and when – and where the rest of the plan is.'

'Yes. And we'll make up a perfectly marvellous tale and

stuff him up like anything!' said Dinah, her eyes sparkling. 'Come on – let's think of one! If Mr Eppy's up to some game, we'll be up to one too. Now – what shall we say if Lucian pumps us?'

'Well, we said *we* didn't know much about it, so perhaps we'd better pretend that Lucy-Ann knows *all* about it,' said Jack, looking more cheerful, as he considered the idea of pulling Lucian's leg, and perhaps Mr Eppy's as well.

'Oh dear,' said Lucy-Ann, in alarm. 'Have I got to tell a whole lot of fairy-tales to Lucian?'

'No. We'll do that for you,' said Jack, with a grin. 'Now then – let's think. How shall we say that Lucy-Ann got hold of that parchment?'

'She was standing on the sports deck one day,' began Dinah, 'and she was feeding the gulls that live round about these islands.'

'And a great big gull came up with something in his beak,' went on Philip. 'He flew round Lucy-Ann's head, and . . . '

'Dropped a paper at her feet, when he swooped down for bread,' said Jack. 'She picked it up and showed it to us – and we thought – aha – only a very clever man like dear Mr Eppy could decipher this strange document handed over by a generous gull. . . . '

'And so we took it to show him,' finished Dinah. She giggled. 'It's too silly for words. Lucian will never swallow that.'

'He will. But his uncle won't!' grinned Philip. 'Serve him right. He'll expect to get the goods from Lucian when he's pumped us – and he'll find he's got rubbish!'

'Well, don't make *me* say it,' said Lucy-Ann. 'I'd go scarlet the whole time.'

'Listen – isn't that Lucian now?' said Jack. 'You go off, Lucy-Ann. Look, take this book, and say you're taking it to Aunt Allie. Go on. That will get you out of the way. It *is* Lucian. I know his idiotic humming.'

Lucy-Ann snatched a book and went to the door. It

opened as she got there, and Lucian's rabbit-face came round it.

'Hullo, hullo!' he said. 'Can I come in?'

'Yes, do,' said Lucy-Ann, squeezing by him. 'I'm taking this book to Aunt Allie. But the others are here. They'll *love* to see you.'

11

Lucian in trouble

'Hallo, Lucian,' said Jack. 'Come in. Have a sweet?'

'Oh, thanks,' said Lucian, and sat himself down on the bed. He took a large piece of peanut-crunch out of the tin Jack offered him. 'I say – this is jolly good stuff.'

'Like a game of deck-tennis?' asked Philip.

'Er – well – actually I only like playing with Lucy-Ann,' said Lucian, who was so very bad at the game that even little Lucy-Ann sometimes beat him hollow. 'Can't give you others much of a game, you know. I say – my uncle's been telling me about that bit of parchment you showed him.'

'Has he? What did he say?' said Jack.

'Well, he thinks it may be the genuine goods, all right – but he can't tell without the other piece or pieces,' said Lucian, munching away. 'Oh, I say – look at that monkey. He's taken an enormous piece of nut-crunch!'

'Yes – almost as big as your bit!' said Dinah, who noticed that Lucian invariably took the largest piece of crunch from the tin.

'Oh, I say – did I really take a big bit?' said Lucian. 'Have to watch myself! You never told me about that bit of parchment. Why didn't you? I'd have liked to see it.'

'Well – it isn't very important, is it?' said Philip. 'I mean – we never thought you'd be interested.'

'Oh, but I *am* – like anything!' said Lucian, crunching hard. Micky was crunching, too, and Kiki was watching him balefully. She didn't like nut-crunch, but she couldn't bear to see Micky enjoying his. 'You might tell me all about it, you really might. Where you got it, and – er – everything.'

'Didn't your uncle tell you where we got it?' asked Dinah innocently. Lucian looked surprised.

'Gosh, no,' he said. 'Did you tell him? Well, why on earth did he ask me to find out?'

He had given himself away properly. The others winked at one another. 'Well, perhaps we *didn't* tell him,' said Jack solemnly. 'Did we, or didn't we?'

'Didn't, did, didn't, did,' remarked Kiki, thinking it was time that someone took notice of her. But nobody did.

'It's a shame not to tell old Lucian,' said Dinah, in a kind voice. Lucian beamed.

'Yes. After all, he's a friend of ours,' said Philip.

Lucian was so overcome by this remark that he swallowed a bit of nut-crunch and choked. Kiki immediately had a choking fit too. She did that kind of thing remarkably well. Jack thumped Lucian on the back, whereupon Micky actually went to Kiki and thumped her too. The children roared with laughter, but Kiki was furious with Micky and chased him all over the cabin.

'Oh dear,' said Dinah, wiping tears of laughter away. 'Those creatures will be the death of me. Now – what were we talking about?'

'About me being a friend of yours, and so you'd tell me about that bit of parchment,' said Lucian promptly. 'Oh – may I really have another bit of crunch? I say, thanks awfully.'

He took a bit, remembering not to take the largest there this time.

'Oh yes,' said Jack. 'We were saying it was a shame not to tell old Lucian. Well, old chap, it happened to Lucy-Ann, actually. Let's see . . . er . . . '

'She was standing on the deck, ready to feed the gulls that fly over from the islands,' said Jack. Lucian nodded. He had often seen Lucy-Ann feeding them.

'And suddenly a very large gull flew round her head, holding something in its beak,' went on Philip. 'That's right, isn't it, Jack?'

'Absolutely,' said Jack, with a solemn face.

'And lo and behold – when the gull came down for its bread, it dropped the parchment at Lucy-Ann's feet!' said Dinah. 'What do you think of that, Lucian? That's right isn't it, Jack?'

'Oh, definitely,' said Jack, in a firm voice.

Lucian stared. His mouth dropped open. 'Oh, I say!' he said. 'Isn't that amazing! I mean to say – whoever would have thought of that?'

As the three of them had thought of it quite easily, they did not answer. Dinah felt a dreadful urge to giggle, and turned her face away. Lucian seemed quite overcome with the story.

'I mean – honestly, it's like a fairy-tale or something, isn't it?' he said. 'That gull dropping it at Lucy-Ann's feet.'

The others agreed that it *was* exactly like a fairy-tale. 'Most extraordinary,' said Lucian, getting up and swallowing the last of his nut-crunch. 'Well, I must be off. Thanks awfully for telling me all this. Oh, I say – what's happened to the bottle that the ship was in? You've got the ship without the bottle now!'

'Yes. Micky and Kiki broke it between them,' said Jack. 'Little wretches! Still, it's a nice ship, and doesn't need its bottle.'

Lucian went out. The others grinned at one another. What a leg his was to pull! Poor old Lucian – he just *asked* for his leg to be well and truly pulled!

'I can just see him spouting that all out to his disbelieving uncle,' said Jack. 'Come on – if I don't get up into the fresh air and have some exercise I shall expire. Let's find Lucy-

Ann and have a game of quoits or something. It's too hot now for deck-tennis.'

They played games all the morning, and then went down to lunch, feeling very hungry indeed. To their surprise Lucian did not appear at lunch. They wondered if he was ill. Mrs Mannering asked his aunt about him.

'No – he's not ill – just a touch of the sun I think,' said Lucian's aunt. 'He's lying down and keeping quiet.'

'I vote we go down to Lucian's cabin and see if he's all right,' said Jack. 'He's never minded the sun before.'

Down they went, and knocked quietly. There was no answer. Jack turned the handle and went in. Lucian was lying on his bed, his face in his pillow.

'Are you asleep, Lucian?' said Jack softly.

Lucian turned over abruptly. 'Oh – it's you,' he said. Jack saw that the boy's face was blotched and tear-stained.

'What's up?' he said. 'I say, can the others come in? They're outside.'

'Well – if they want to,' said Lucian, who obviously was not welcoming visitors, but did not like to say so. All four children were soon in the cabin. Lucy-Ann was distressed when she saw Lucian's blotched face.

'What's the matter?' she said. 'Is your sunstroke very bad?'

'It isn't sunstroke,' said Lucian, and, to the children's horror his eyes began to fill with tears. 'It's my beastly, horrible uncle!' He buried his face in the pillow again to hide his tears.

'What's he been up to?' said Jack, not very sympathetically, because he thought it was too feeble for words for a boy of Lucian's age to behave like that.

'He called me all kinds of names,' said Lucian, sitting up again. 'He – he called me a nit-wit – and a nincompoop—'

'Poop!' said Kiki. 'Nit-wit!'

'Now don't *you* start,' said poor Lucian to the parrot. 'He said I was a born idiot and a fool and—'

'But *why*?' asked Lucy-Ann, astonished.

'Well, I told him how Lucy-Ann got that silly bit of parchment,' Lucian told them. 'You know – just how you told me. I thought he'd be so pleased to think I'd found out what he wanted to know. But he wasn't.'

'Wasn't he? That was too bad,' said Philip, thinking that Lucian deserved his scolding for running straight to his uncle with the fairy-tale they had made up – they had meant him to, of course, but what a tittle-tattler he was!

'I said to him, "A gull brought the parchment down to Lucy-Ann and laid it at her feet," ' related Lucian, in a dramatic manner. 'And Uncle said "WHAT?" So I told him again.'

'And what did he say the next time?' asked Jack, trying not to laugh.

'All the things I told you. He was very insulting and offensive,' said Lucian. 'After all, he believed all the other things I told him. I can't think why he didn't believe *that*!'

'What other things did you tell him?' asked Jack at once.

'Oh, nothing much. He just wanted to know if I'd been shopping with any of you – and where – and all that. I told him I'd been shopping with Lucy-Ann – and how we'd found that old ship in a bottle for her. And he said, "Ah – of course – the *Andra*! The *Andra*!" Just like that. I tell you he was most peculiar altogether.'

The others listened to this in silence. Mr Eppy had certainly pumped Lucian to some purpose. He knew they had bought the ship and where – he remembered seeing the name when they asked him what it was – the *Andra*. He was putting two and two together. Probably he already guessed that the parchment had been found in the ship, because that ass Lucian would be sure to have told him that the bottle was broken and the ship free of it.

'Did you tell your uncle the bottle was broken, that the ship was in?' asked Jack.

'Er – yes, I think I did,' said Lucian. 'I say – I haven't done anything wrong, have I? I mean – you don't mind my telling my uncle all this?'

'We didn't mind your telling him about the gull and the bit of paper in the least,' said Philip truthfully. 'I'm sorry your uncle is so disbelieving. It was wrong of him to call you names like that.'

'It was, wasn't it?' said Lucian plaintively. 'He's got no right to. He called *you* a few names too.'

'Well, don't repeat them,' said Jack. 'You really ought to learn to respect people's confidences, Lucian. I mean – it just isn't *done* to go round repeating to somebody else the things you've been told, possibly in confidence.'

'Now *you're* angry with me too!' wailed Lucian. Jack got up in disgust. This kind of behaviour was too much for him altogether. He did not even feel sorry for Lucian for getting into trouble because of a cock-and-bull story that they had made up specially for him. Lucian just walked into trouble as fast as he could!

The others got up too. Only Lucy-Ann was sorry about Lucian. Still, even she was disgusted at his tears and self-pity – really, he ought to pull himself together.

They went out without a word, leaving Lucian feeling miserable, upset, angry – and very, very hungry!

'Come to our cabin for a minute,' said Jack. 'We ought to have a few words about all this. Mr Eppy is putting two and two together a bit too fast. What an idiot Lucian is! Why did he have to blab about that ship so much? We'd better put it in a safe place, in case Mr Eppy borrows it as he did our parchment.'

They went into the boys' cabin, and Philip gave a cry that made them all jump. 'Look – he's borrowed it already! It's gone!'

12

The second piece of the map

It was true – the beautiful little carved ship was no longer in its place of honour on the shelf. It was gone.

The four children stared at one another in exasperation. Blow Mr Eppy! What right had he to 'borrow' things like this? Would he give it back?

'What's he borrowed it for, anyway?' wondered Dinah. 'If he goes so far as to suspect that we found the parchment there I still don't see why he should borrow it. He's got the parchment, anyway!'

'A *bit* of it, only – and he knows it,' corrected Jack. 'He probably thinks the rest of it is still in the little carved ship – either that we haven't noticed it, or that we have kept it there. And he's borrowed it to see.'

'Stolen it, you mean,' said Lucy-Ann scornfully. 'Horrid man! I think he's awful.'

'Shall I go and ask him if he's got it?' said Philip. He was feeling very angry – quite ready to beard any lion in its den!

The others considered this. 'Suppose he *didn't* take it?' said Jack. 'It would be jolly awkward, accusing him of it.'

'Who else would have taken it?' demanded Philip. 'Nobody!'

'Look – let's go and have a swim in the pool and forget it for a bit,' said Dinah. 'If you still feel like bearding the lion afterwards, you can go. It's so awfully hot. I'd love a swim.'

'All right,' said Philip reluctantly. 'But I might not feel so keen on going after Mr Eppy afterwards.'

However, he was still of the same mind after his swim. The others couldn't help admiring him – they really thought it was a brave thing to do, to go and tackle Mr Eppy and accuse him of 'borrowing' their ship!

He went off to find Mr Eppy. He was not in his cabin. He was not in his deck-chair. Where could he be? Philip began to hunt over the ship for him, determined to find him. He saw him at last coming out of the radio office.

'Mr Eppy,' said Philip, marching boldly up to him. 'What have you done with our ship?'

Mr Eppy stopped. Philip wished to goodness he did not wear those dark glasses. He had no idea if Mr Eppy was surprised, angry or what.

He soon knew. Mr Eppy spoke in a very snappy voice indeed. 'What do you mean, boy? What ship do you speak of?'

'The little carved ship we showed you – the one in the bottle – called *Andra*,' said Philip, wishing more than ever that he could see Mr Eppy's eyes, and read what was in them. 'What have you done with it?'

'I think you are mad,' said Mr Eppy coldly. 'Quite mad. As mad as Lucian, who comes to me with a fairy-tale about a little girl, a gull and a piece of parchment. What nonsense, what fiddlesticks! And now you come to me with a question about a toy ship! You think I have taken it to float in my bath, perhaps?'

'*Did* you take it, Mr Eppy?' persisted Philip.

'No! And do not dare to insult me with your fairy-tales and your crazy questions any more!' thundered Mr Eppy.

He strode off, his mouth very grim. Philip was a little shaken. Well – he had not got much change out of Mr Eppy, that was certain. Blow the man! Philip felt absolutely certain he had got the ship. He went down to meet the others in his cabin. They would be waiting for him there.

He opened the cabin door and went in. 'Well,' he said, 'it's no go. He says he hasn't got the ship – but I bet he has. I feel it in my bones!'

'Then your bones tell you wrong,' said Jack, and he pointed across the room to the shelf on the wall. 'Look there.'

Philip looked, and gasped. The little carved Ship of Adventure was back in its place again!

'Where was it?' he asked. 'Gosh, what an idiot I've made of myself, accusing Mr Eppy of having it! Where on earth *was* it?'

'We don't know,' answered Dinah. 'We all came in here a few minutes ago after we left you on your way to tackle Mr Eppy – and the first thing we saw was the ship!'

'There it was, on the shelf – just where we left it this morning,' said Lucy-Ann.

'Who put it back?' asked Philip.

'Aha – if we knew that we'd know who took it,' said Jack. 'I still think it was Mr Eppy. If you remember, he came in to lunch *after* we did – he could easily have slipped down here, and taken the ship then. And he could just as easily have put it back whilst we were having our swim. If he saw us in the pool, which is quite likely, he'd know that he had plenty of time to slip down here and replace it.'

'The knob's a bit loose,' said Dinah. 'We think he found how it worked all right, and removed that wooden section, and examined the inside of the ship thoroughly.'

'I see. And when he found there was nothing there he generously brought it back!' said Philip. 'I don't like that man. He'll be hunting round all our cabins looking for our other bits of parchment, if we don't look out.'

Lucy-Ann felt alarmed. 'Oh dear – will he find them, do you think?'

'He might,' admitted Philip. 'They seem jolly good hiding-places to us, but they probably would be easy enough for him to discover.'

'I say – are we going to get the other bits deciphered now?' said Dinah suddenly. 'You know, we thought we'd ask the little Greek woman who keeps the shop on the ship, and the deck steward. Suppose Mr Eppy gets to hear we've been showing other people more bits of parchment. He'll soon be after them.'

'Yes, that's a point,' said Jack. 'But if we don't get them deciphered, we're no better off than we were. Hidden treasure is no use to anyone if they don't know in the least where it is. Anyway, we don't even know if the plan *does* show hidden treasure – all we know is that it is a genuine old document, and that Mr Eppy is distinctly interested.'

'I think we could trust the little shopwoman not to say a word,' said Lucy-Ann. 'She's nice, and she likes us. If we told her it was a secret, wouldn't she keep it? After all, we've got to ask *some*body!'

They debated whether the shopwoman was trustable or not. They decided that on the whole she was.

'She said she'd show me some photographs of her children,' said Lucy-Ann. 'She's got three on some little island or other. She leaves them with her grandmother when she goes on the ship. Couldn't we all go and see the photographs, and then ask her about the parchment?'

'Trust Lucy-Ann for knowing everyone's life-history,' grinned Philip. 'It beats me how she does it! She already knows the names of the second officer's children, and she knows everything about the stewardess's old mother and what illnesses she suffers from, and she even knows how many dogs the captain himself has kept during his whole life!'

'I *don't*,' said Lucy-Ann indignantly. 'I simply wouldn't *dare* to ask him about dogs. Anyway, he can't have had any on board ship.'

'I'm only pulling your leg, Lucy-Ann,' said Philip. 'Actually I think your idea of looking at the shopwoman's photos, and then springing our parchment on her – or a bit of it – is a good one.'

'Let's go now, then,' said Lucy-Ann, looking at the clock. 'Everyone always has a sleep in the afternoon at this time – no one is ever in the shop. She'll be alone.'

They went off together. Philip had the idea of first finding out where Mr Eppy was – just in *case* he should be snooping round!

He came back and reported. 'He's asleep in his deck-chair on the promenade deck. His head's well back, and he's not reading or anything.'

'How do you know he's asleep?' demanded Jack. 'You can't tell if his eyes are open or shut behind those awful dark sun-glasses.'

'Well – he *looked* asleep,' said Philip. 'Sort of limp and relaxed. Come on – we'll go to the shop now.'

They went to the little shop. The Greek woman who kept it showed all her white teeth in a pleased smile when she saw the children with Kiki and Micky.

'Ah, Kiki, Micky, and what mischief have you done?' she asked, tickling the little monkey and poking Kiki in the chest. 'One, two, three, GO!'

Kiki immediately made a noise like a pistol-shot, which was just what the little Greek woman meant her to do. She was quite familiar with Kiki's ways, and always roared with laughter when the parrot hiccupped, coughed or sneezed.

'Tell him to snizz,' she begged. 'I like when he snizzes.'

So Kiki obliged with a fine variety of 'snizzes', much to Micky's amazement. Then out came the photographs and the children were treated to a life-history of each of the three little girls she possessed. Dinah thought that surely never in this world had there lived such children before – so sweet, so good, so loving, so religious, so incredibly beautiful – and so extraordinarily boring!

Then Jack thought it was *their* turn to talk. He nudged Philip, who at once brought out his piece of the map. 'Look,' he said to the shopwoman. 'Can you make head or tail of this for us? It's an old old document we found. What does it say – and what does it show?'

The Greek woman looked at it sharply with her bright black eyes. 'It is a plan of some sort,' she said. 'But you have not got the whole of it here – what a pity! It shows part of an island called Thamis or Themis, I cannot tell which. See, here is its name, in Greek – but you will not understand the letters, of course. Your alphabet is different. Yes, it is part of an island, but where it is I do not know.'

'Can't you tell anything else from the map?' asked Dinah.

'There is something of importance on the island,' said the woman. 'Perhaps a temple? I do not know. There is a building marked here – or maybe it is meant to be a city. Again I do not know. I could tell you more if I had the whole of the map.'

The children had been so engrossed in all this that they had not heard the soft footsteps of someone coming. A shadow fell across them. They looked up and Lucy-Ann gave a gasp. It was Mr Eppy, his dark glasses hiding his eyes as usual.

'Ah – something interesting. Let me see,' said Mr Eppy coolly, and before anyone could stop him he had twisted the parchment out of the Greek woman's fingers and was looking at it himself!

Philip tried to twist it out of *his* fingers, but Mr Eppy was on his guard. He held it aloft and pretended to joke.

'He won't let Mr Eppy see! Bad boy!'

'Bad, naughty boy!' echoed Kiki at once. Micky, thinking it was a game of snatch, suddenly leapt up in the air, and lunged out at the paper. He got it in his little paw, fell back to Philip's shoulder – and then, still with the parchment in his hand, leapt to the top of the shop and sat there, out of reach, chattering excitedly.

Mr Eppy knew when he was beaten. 'What a funny little creature!' he said, in an amiable voice that managed to sound quite angry too. 'Well, well – we'll have a look at the parchment another time!'

And with that he left the dumbfounded children, walking off rapidly, back to his deck-chair.

13

Good-bye, Mr Eppy!

'*Well!*' said Dinah, finding her voice first. 'Of all the cheek! Philip, he *couldn't* have been asleep when you saw him in his chair! He must have seen you looking at him and guessed you were up to something – and looked about till he found us.'

'Blow him,' muttered Philip. 'Now he's seen *two* of the bits. He knows what the island is too because the name was on that second bit. That's an awful bit of bad luck.'

They left the surprised little shopwoman and went moodily up to the bow of the ship, glad to feel the wind in their faces. Micky had come down as soon as Mr Eppy had left them, and Philip had his bit of parchment back in safety. But the damage was done – Mr Eppy had seen it!

'If there *is* anything in our idea, Mr Eppy has seen enough to cotton on to already,' said Jack gloomily. 'I can't say that we have been at all clever over this. Anything but.'

'Simply *given* our secret away,' said Dinah. 'We're losing our grip!'

'Anyway – I don't really see what we could have *done* about the treasure,' said Lucy-Ann suddenly. 'I mean – we can't possibly go hunting for it, even if we knew exactly where it was. So we might as well give it up, and if Mr Eppy wants to go hunting after it, let him!'

'Well, I must say you're very generous, giving up what might have been *our* treasure – and just saying Mr Eppy can have it!' said Jack, exasperated. 'All because you don't want an adventure again!'

'Oh, I say!' cried Kiki, and the children stopped talking at once. Kiki had given her usual signal for the approach of Lucian. Up he came, grinning amiably. He appeared completely to have forgotten his last meeting with them in his cabin, when he had been in tears. His face still looked a bit blotched, but otherwise he seemed very cheery.

'Hallo!' he cried. 'Where on earth have you been the last half-hour? I've been looking for you everywhere. I say, look what Uncle's given me!'

He showed the children some pieces of Greek money. 'I expect he was sorry for going for me like that, don't you?' he chattered on. 'Anyway, he's in a very good temper now. Aunt can't understand it!'

The children could understand Mr Eppy's sudden good spirits very well indeed. They grinned wryly at one another. Mr Eppy had got what he wanted – or some part of what he wanted – and he was pleased. It struck Jack that Mr Eppy probably always got what he wanted, in one way or another. He wouldn't much care *which* way. He thought uneasily that they ought to find safer hiding-places than the ones in the cabins, for the remaining pieces of parchment.

He felt very gloomy. What was the use of bothering? *They* would never be able to do much about the treasure! How could they? Aunt Allie would not hear of it, he knew. And there would *have* to be some grown-up in charge. If only Bill had come on the trip with them!

An idea came into his head. 'I'm going off by myself for a little while,' he announced. 'See you later.' Off he went with Kiki, thinking about his idea. What about looking up the island Thamis or Themis, whichever it was, on a modern map, and seeing if it was shown there? It would be interesting to see whereabouts it was. Why, it might be quite near where they were cruising!

He went down to the ship's little library with Kiki and asked for a good map of the islands. The librarian gave him one and looked disapprovingly at Kiki. He did not like parrots in his quiet library.

'Blow your nose,' Kiki advised him. 'Wipe your feet! How many times have I told you to shut the door? Pooh! Gah!'

The librarian said nothing at all, but looked down his nose. He had never in his life been spoken to like that before – and by a parrot, too! He was most irritated.

'One, two, three, GO!' said Kiki, and made the noise of a pistol going off. The librarian almost jumped out of his seat.

'Sorry about that,' said Jack hastily, afraid that the librarian would turn him out. He tapped Kiki on the beak. 'Manners, Kiki, manners. Shocking!'

'Shocking,' repeated Kiki, in a mournful voice, and began to sniff in exactly the same way that the librarian did.

Jack pored over the map of the islands, forgetting all about Kiki in his interest. For a long time he could not see Thamis – and then there it was, under his eyes! It was not a large island, and was marked with what seemed to be a city or town, just on the coast. One or two small marks seemed to indicate villages – but there was only the one town.

So that was where the legendary fleet of treasure ships went, years and years ago! They put in at that city by the sea, sailing into the port at dead of night. How did they unload the treasure! Were there people there in the secret? Where was it put? It must have been hidden remarkably well if no one had ever found it in all the years that had gone by.

Jack pored over the map, his imagination giving him picture after picture, and making him stirred and excited. He gave a deep sigh, which Kiki immediately echoed. If only he could go to Thamis – to that city by the sea – if only he could just have a *look* at it!

But it would be Mr Eppy who would do that – Mr Eppy who knew all the islands by heart, and who could afford to hire ships to go from one to the other, exploring each one as he pleased. Jack folded up the map with another sigh. He put the whole idea away from him, once and for all. You couldn't go on treasure-hunts unless you were grown-up – his common sense told him that all the plans he and the others had made were just crazy dreams – lovely dreams, but quite impossible.

Jack strolled out of the library and up on deck. They were heading for another island. They were to go close by it, so that the passengers might see the romantic coast-line, but they were not calling there.

At least, so Jack had thought. As they came near, he saw that he must have been wrong. The ship was either going into the port there, or people were going off in a motor-boat that had come out to meet the ship. The ship's engines stopped at that moment, and Jack leaned over the side to watch the motor-boat nose its way near.

It soon lay alongside the big ship, rising and falling gently on the waves. A ladder was shaken down the side of the *Viking Star*. Someone began to climb down, someone who waved back to others on the ship, and called out in a foreign language.

And then Jack got a shock. The someone was *Mr Eppy*! He was calling good-bye to his wife and nephew. He climbed right down to the motor-boat and jumped deftly to the deck. His big suitcase was lowered on a rope, and swung down on the deck beside him. He looked up and waved again, his dark glasses showing clearly.

Jack scowled down angrily and miserably. Blow Mr Eppy, blow him! Jack felt sure he knew why he was leaving the boat. Mr Eppy knew enough to set things in motion for the grand Andra treasure-hunt. He was going to Thamis. He would smell out the treasure that Jack and the others had happened on, in that old map. It would be his.

And probably Jack would never even know what happened about it – never know if it was found, or what it was, or anything. It was like reading a tremendously exciting book half-way through, and then having the book taken away and not knowing the end of the story.

The motor-boat chugged away from the ship. Mr Eppy and his sun-glasses disappeared. Jack turned from the deck-rail and went to find the others. He wondered if they knew about Mr Eppy.

He found them in the cabin. Micky had eaten something that disagreed with him, and had been sick. They were looking after him anxiously. They had not even noticed that the engines of the ship had stopped, and were now starting again.

'There!' Dinah was saying as Jack came into the cabin. 'He's all right now – aren't you, Micky? You shouldn't be so greedy.'

Jack came in looking so gloomy that everyone was startled. 'What's up?' said Philip at once.

'It's *all* up,' said Jack, sitting down on the nearest bed. 'Who do you think's gone off in a motor-boat – suitcase and all?'

'Who?' asked everyone.

'Mr Eppy!' said Jack. 'Hotfoot after our treasure! He knows the island, he's guessed the Andra treasure may be there – and he's gone to set things going. At least, that's how *I* see it!'

'That's a blow,' said Philip. 'We've messed everything up properly. He certainly doesn't let grass grow under his feet,'

'We may as well give up all our grand ideas,' said Dinah. 'What a shame! I did feel so terribly thrilled.'

'I bet he had just been sending a radio message for a motor-boat to take him off here, when I met him coming out of the radio office,' said Philip, remembering. 'Just that first bit of parchment must have got him going. Now he's seen the second and he's certain!'

'It's bad luck,' said Lucy-Ann. 'We don't usually mess up things like this. Hallo – who's that?'

'Oh, I say!' said Kiki at once – and sure enough the door opened, and in came Lucian with his everlasting cry. 'Oh, I say! What do you think's happened?'

'You've got rid of your uncle,' said Dinah at once. Lucian grinned.

'Yes. He's gone. Said he had had an urgent business message and couldn't fool about cruising around with

Auntie and me any longer. Gosh, I'm glad he's gone.'

'Yes, he's not a pleasant person,' said Jack. 'I'm glad he's not *my* uncle. Some of his little ways are not what you might call attractive.'

'They're *not*,' said Lucian, who felt he was quite free now to speak his mind about his uncle. 'Do you know – he wanted me to take your little carved ship to him and not say a word to you about it? What do you think of that?'

'Not much,' said Jack. '*Did* you take it?'

'Of course not!' said Lucian, with such indignation that everyone felt he was telling the truth. 'What do you take me for?'

Nobody said what they took him for. They felt that it would be a pity to spoil his pleasure. Lucian beamed round at them.

'Now we can have a jolly good time, without my uncle, can't we?' he said.

'I can't say your uncle makes any difference to us one way or another,' said Jack. 'I don't want to talk about him any more. He's an unpleasant subject for discussion. There's the gong to dress for dinner, Lucian. You'd better go. You had no lunch and you must be ravenous.'

'I jolly well am,' said Lucian and went, looking quite delighted with life. The others, however, looked anything but delighted. In fact, they looked distinctly gloomy.

'Well – that's the end of what looked like a most promising adventure,' said Philip.

But he was wrong. It was not the end. It was really only the beginning!

14

Things begin to happen!

Things began to happen the very next day. The ship was cruising along as usual in a purple-blue sea, and the sun shone down from a sky spread with dazzling white clouds and patches of brilliant blue.

Gulls glided by, and all kinds of other seabirds bobbed on the water, or soared high above the ship. Everyone was peaceful in their deck-chairs, reading or snoozing, waiting for the mid-morning drink of iced lemonade brought by the stewards. Even the children were lazing in their chairs, tired after their strenuous morning game at deck-tennis.

Kiki sat on the back of Jack's chair, snoozing too. She had been chasing gulls, calling to them in a voice so like theirs that the poor things were completely bewildered. Now she was tired out. Micky was curled up in the shade of a lifeboat, fast asleep.

A small page-boy appeared, the one who ran messages, and fetched odds and ends for the passengers. He carried a long envelope on a salver.

He called out loudly as he went. 'Radiotelegram for Mrs Mannering, please. Radio for Mrs Mannering, please.'

Philip nudged his mother, and beckoned to the call-boy. Mrs Mannering looked up, startled to hear her name shouted out. The boy came up to her and presented the radiotelegram.

She tore it open, wondering who it was from. She read it out loud to the listening children.

Your aunt seriously ill and calling for you. Fly back if you can, and I'll take over the kids. Radio me, please.
Bill

There was a silence. 'Oh dear,' said Mrs Mannering. 'This *would* happen on a cruise. What shall I do? It's all very well for Bill to say "Fly back". But where from? And how can I leave you all?'

'Don't upset yourself, Mother,' said Philip. 'I'll see to things for you. I know the second officer very well and he'll tell me what you're to do.'

'As for us, you needn't worry at *all*,' said Jack. 'You know we're all right on the boat. You wouldn't want us all to fly back with you, surely!'

'Oh no. Of course not. Especially after I've paid such high fares for you all on this cruise,' said Mrs Mannering, still looking worried. 'Oh dear – I do hate sudden things like this. I really do.'

'Mother dear, it's all right,' said Dinah. 'You can get a plane from the very next place we stop at, if there is an airfield. You'll be in England tomorrow. And Bill will take over, as he said. He'll probably meet you at the airport, when the plane lands there, see you safely on to your train, and then catch a plane to join us. He'll enjoy the rest of the trip. Maybe you'll be back too.'

'Oh no, I shan't – not if Aunt Polly has got one of her really bad turns,' said Mrs Mannering. 'She's been so good to me – and to you too – that I *must* stay with her till she's quite herself again. Oh, I do hate leaving you four by yourselves.'

Mrs Eppy could not help overhearing all this. She spoke to Mrs Mannering. 'I can keep an eye on the four for you till your friend comes, you know. After all, I have to look after Lucian, and he's much the same age. I shall be pleased to do what I can.'

'Well, that's good of you,' said Mrs Mannering, getting out of her deck-chair, helped by Philip. 'I suppose it's idiotic of me to worry about them – they're all quite big now – but they do seem to get into such awful scrapes sometimes!'

She went off with Philip. He was very useful indeed. He

found the second officer, and very soon he had worked out all the details with him. The ship would go out of her way a little, and call at an island that had an airport. A radio message would be sent immediately, so that a plane would be waiting. In no time at all Mrs Mannering would be back in England.

'We could wait at the island till your friend comes on *his* plane,' said the second officer, after consulting with the captain. 'It would only mean altering our programme a very little – it is a very free-and-easy one, as you know. Now – do you want to radio instructions to Mr Cunningham, so that he will know what time to meet your plane at the airport?'

It was amazing how easily everything was arranged after all. 'I was silly to get upset and flustered,' said Mrs Mannering to the children. 'Thanks to Philip, it's all been arranged beautifully. I'll be away tomorrow, and Bill will arrive later – probably that evening. It's wonderful!'

The girls helped her to pack. The *Viking Star* steamed to a large island, where there was a good airport. The children saw aeroplanes taking off as they came near, for the airport was on the coast.

A motor-boat came out to take Mrs Mannering off. She kissed all the children good-bye. 'Now don't get into any scrapes,' she begged them. 'Be good. Keep away from danger and trouble. Give Bill my love and tell him if he leads you into anything I'll never, never forgive him!'

They waved good-bye as the motor-boat chuffed away to the port. They watched it through their binoculars and saw Mrs Mannering getting out on to the jetty, with a porter carrying her cases.

'She's got into a taxi,' announced Jack. 'Now she's off to the airport. She'll soon be away!'

Half an hour later an aeroplane took off from the airport on the coast, and rose into the air. It flew towards the ship, circled it twice and made off to the west.

'That was Mother's plane,' said Philip. 'I think I even saw

her waving. Well – safe journey to her! And now we must look out for old Bill.'

A curious silence fell on the children. They were all thinking the same thing, but nobody quite liked to say it. Jack cleared his throat.

'Er – you know – now that this has happened – er . . . ' He stopped.

Everyone waited politely. 'Well, go on,' said Dinah.

'Er – I was just thinking,' said Jack, 'just thinking that now – well – with old Bill coming and all. Er . . . '

He stopped again. Dinah gave a little giggle. '*I'll* say it for you,' she said. 'It's what we've all been thinking, I know. Dear old Bill is coming – and we can tell him all about the map and the Andra treasure – and Mr Eppy. And maybe – *maybe*, he'll do something about it!'

'Gosh, yes,' said Jack. 'I didn't know how to put it without seeming a bit heartless, as Aunt Allie has only just gone. But things are a bit different now. Bill may think we *ought* to do something.'

'How – simply – super!' said Philip, drawing a deep breath. 'Just as we'd given up hope!'

'We couldn't *possibly* drag Mother into an adventure,' said Dinah. 'But Bill's different. I mean – he won't want us to plunge into an adventure, I know – but he may quite well think *he* ought to do something about it.'

'And we shall at least know what's happening,' said Jack. 'Won't it be grand to show him the little carved ship – and the map – and tell him everything! Good old Bill!'

Lucian came up, with rather a solemn expression on his face. 'I say! I'm awfully sorry about all this. I do hope your mother arrives safely, Philip, and that her aunt will get better. I hope all this won't spoil the rest of the cruise for you. I am most awfully sorry.'

'Thanks,' said Philip. 'We shall get over it.'

'Oh, I say, I quite forgot to give you this,' went on Lucian. 'I'm so sorry. My uncle gave it to me before he left, and said I was to hand it to you. I can't imagine what it is.'

Jack took it. He guessed what it was, and he was right. It was the piece of the plan that Mr Eppy had 'borrowed'. He had put it into a sealed envelope with a little note.

Thanks. Not very interesting after all.
P. Eppy

Jack laughed. 'Not very interesting, says he! I bet he's got a careful tracing of it. Much good may it do him!'

He went off to put it into its safe place – in the lining of his shorts. He was glad that Mr Eppy hadn't seen all the other pieces of the plan. Still, probably he did not need to. He might guess where the treasure was, if he knew the island. If so, it wouldn't be there long!

The day went by rather slowly. Mrs Eppy was rather annoying, because she took very seriously her promise to look after the children. She hunted them out at meal-times, and even told the table steward to seat them at her table.

But Jack was not having that. 'No, Mrs Eppy,' he said firmly, but politely. 'We expect our friend, Bill Cunningham, tonight – or at the latest, tomorrow morning. We will keep our own table and eat with him. Thank you all the same.'

Lucian was disappointed, and sulked. He did not even smile when Kiki and Micky had a fight over a banana and ended by pulling it in half.

After the evening meal the children went up on deck, hoping against hope that Bill would arrive that night. The second officer had had no message, so thought he probably *would* arrive.

'He would surely have radioed me if he was coming tomorrow,' he said. 'He knows we're holding the ship here for him. All the same, I'd go to bed, if I were you kids – he may come in the middle of the night!'

They would not hear of going to bed! They sat up on deck

and watched the sun go down in a blaze of gold. They saw the clouds turn rosy-pink. Then they watched night creeping over the sea from the east, and saw the water turn more and more purple, till at last they could hardly tell it from the sky. Then the stars came out brilliantly, and the water sparkled again.

Lucy-Ann was almost asleep in her deck-chair when Jack nudged her. 'Wake up! There's a plane. It may be Bill's!' She was awake at once, and went to the deck-rail with the others.

The plane went down to the airport landing ground. It must be Bill's! After about half an hour they heard a motor-boat starting up its engine in the port.

'It's Bill coming out now!' cried Lucy-Ann in excitement. 'Dear old Bill!'

The motor-boat came nearer and nearer. It stopped by the ship, and a ladder was thrown down. Someone began to climb up. Lucy-Ann could contain herself no longer.

'Bill!' she cried. 'Is it you, Bill? BILL!'

Up came a familiar voice. 'Ahoy, there! Bill it is!'

And Bill it was. He came climbing on to the deck, and the four children ran to him at once. They smothered him, hugged him, and were bear-hugged back.

'Dear Bill! Good old Bill! It's grand to see you. *Now* everything's fine.'

'Yes, everything's fine!' said Bill, swinging Lucy-Ann right off her feet. 'Gosh, it's good to see you all! *Now* we'll have some fun!'

15

Bill hears the tale

Bill was hungry and thirsty. The children, excited and happy, took him down to the lounge, where he ordered chicken-and-ham sandwiches and a drink for himself, and, for a treat, some sandwiches for the children.

'Though, let me tell you, you'll have awful dreams tonight, having a meal so late,' he warned them. 'So if you are chased by bears, fall out of aeroplanes or get ship-wrecked in your sleep, don't blame *me*!'

'We shan't,' said Lucy-Ann. 'Anyway, now I know you're here, I shan't even *mind* having nightmares – you'll turn up in them to rescue me!'

The steward brought the meal, smiling. He had also brought a banana each for Micky and Kiki, on two separate plates. Kiki was very much impressed with the plates – it wasn't often *she* had a plate! She insisted on putting her banana back on her plate each time she had taken a bite, which amused the children immensely.

'Kiki's gone all polite, I see,' said Bill, taking an enormous bite of his sandwich. 'Gosh, this is good. I haven't had anything to eat for hours. Well, kids, how's things?'

'We've a lot to tell you, Bill,' said Jack. 'Jolly interesting, too. We've happened on something very exciting.'

'You would, of course,' said Bill. 'But don't think you're dragging me into any hare-brained escapade this time! I've had enough of you and your adventures! I've come out for a nice, quiet, restful trip.'

Kiki gave a tremendous squawk and made him jump.

'Micky! You've taken Kiki's banana!' said Jack. 'Philip, smack him. There'll be a fight soon, if you don't. All right, Kiki, I'll get you another. Poor old thing, that's what your good manners brought you – you put your banana down politely on your plate after each bite – and Micky goes and takes it!'

'Nice little monkey,' said Bill, tickling Micky under the chin. 'Yours, I suppose, Philip. It beats me how you collect pets wherever you go. Let's see – you've had a fox cub – a lizard – a slow-worm – a snowy-white kid – two puffins – white rats – and now a monkey. Well, well – so long as you don't collect a hippopotamus or a flock of lions I don't mind!'

The children were bursting to tell him about the treasure-plan, but they felt they ought to let him eat his sandwiches first. He told them how he had met Mrs Mannering at the airport in England, and had seen her safely off to her aunt. Then he had taken his own private aeroplane and set off.

'Alone?' asked Jack.

'No. With a friend of mine – Tim Curling – don't think you've met him,' said Bill. 'Don't you want all your sandwiches, Lucy-Ann? Right, I'll help myself. Yes, Tim came too, and I've left him with the plane. He's going to hire a motor-boat and do a bit of cruising.'

'Oh! I wish we could, too,' said Dinah.

'*Do* you?' said Bill, in surprise. 'But I thought you liked being on this big, comfortable ship. You're used to rowing-boats and sailing-ships and motor-boats – this big ship must be a real change.'

'Yes, it is. But – well, shall we tell you our news, Bill?' asked Jack eagerly.

Bill ate the last vestige of the sandwiches and finished his drink. He yawned a vast yawn and Kiki immediately did the same. 'I suppose it can't wait till morning, can it?' he said. Then he saw the disappointed faces of the children and laughed. 'Oh, all right. Out with it.'

'Fetch the little carved ship, Lucy-Ann,' said Jack. 'I've got the four bits of the map. Hurry. We'll wait till you come back before we begin.'

Lucy-Ann sped off. She came back very quickly, panting, with the little ship in her hands. Bill took it. 'What a beauty! This is valuable you know. Where did you get it?'

Then out came the story of how Lucy-Ann had discovered the ship in the bottle, with Lucian, and had bought it for Philip's birthday. In low, excited tones, so that no one else could hear, the children told of the breaking of the bottle and the unexpected finding of the parchment inside the ship. Then Jack produced the parchment, still in its four quarters. Bill glanced at it with great interest. Then he stood up.

'Come on down to my cabin,' he said. 'I think it would be wiser to talk there. This is all rather extraordinary.'

Very pleased with Bill's reception of their tale, the children trooped down the stairs to the cabins. They all crowded into Bill's. They knew it well because it had been their mother's. They managed to squash themselves on the bed, with Bill in the middle.

'Move Micky up a bit, will you?' said Bill. 'He keeps breathing down my neck. Now then – what's this map? It's very old, I can see that. Why is it in four pieces?'

They told him. They told him the old legend of the lost Andra treasure. They told him of Mr Eppy's strange behaviour. They told him of his departure – and all that they feared.

Bill listened intently, asking one or two curt questions now and again. When they had finished he took out his pipe, and began to stuff it very slowly with tobacco. The children waited. They knew that Bill was thinking hard. Their hearts beat fast. What did Bill think of their tale? Would he take it seriously? *Would he do something about it?*

'Well,' said Bill, putting his pipe into his mouth, and speaking out of one side whilst he hunted in his pocket for matches. 'Well – I think you've got something there – but I'm basing my feelings on Mr Eppy's behaviour, not on your map, which I don't know enough about to decipher. You've been very ingenious in trying to get it explained to you, and you've fitted various curious facts together very well – such as finding the name Andra on the little ship, and noticing it again on the map.'

'Yes – that was a bit of luck,' said Jack. 'You really *do* think the map is genuine, Bill? I mean – do you think there's any hope of its really showing where the old treasure is?'

'I can't say,' said Bill, puffing away at his pipe. 'Can't possibly say. I'd have to take the map to an expert, get it deciphered properly, find out all I can about the old Andra legend – it may be just a tale, you know – and see if there really is an island called Thamis, and what it's like.'

'There *is*,' said Jack triumphantly. 'I found it on a map.'

Bill began to laugh. 'I don't know how it is that you children always seem to happen on something extraordinary,' he said. 'Just when I thought we were in for a lovely, peaceful trip I shall have to go hunting about for an expert on old documents, and get him to translate Greek so old that it's probably impossible to read correctly. And if there's anything in it I suppose we'll have to see this island called Thamis.'

'Bill! Will you really?' cried Jack in delight, and Philip bounced up and down on the bed, nearly upsetting everybody. Dinah clutched Lucy-Ann, her eyes shining. They were all so pleased because Bill had not pooh-poohed the whole idea.

'We'd better get to bed now,' said Bill. 'It's very late. We'll talk about all this in the morning – but don't get excited! We can't possibly do more than give this map to an expert, and then maybe run over to Thamis and back, if it's near enough, just to give it a look over. After all – we're on a cruise, you know.'

The children got up reluctantly. Bill went with them to their cabins. 'I'm going up on deck to smoke my pipe,' he said. 'Happy dreams!'

In the early morning Jack and Philip woke up with a jump. They sat up in bed. Light was just filtering through their porthole, and a curious noise was coming from far below them.

'It's the engines of the ship,' said Jack, in relief. 'I wondered whatever in the world it was. What a weird noise they're making! What's happening?'

'They've stopped,' said Philip, after listening for a minute or two. 'No – there they go again – clank-clank-clank. They don't sound a bit right. They don't purr like they usually do. I hope nothing's wrong.'

'Now they've stopped again,' said Jack. 'Well – if there's any danger we shall hear the ship's siren hooting and hooting and the steward will come along and bang on our door.'

'Yes. And our life-jackets are ready in the cupboard, so we've nothing to worry about,' said Philip, feeling sleepy again. 'It's nothing. Let's go to sleep.'

But in the morning they found that the ship was still not using her engines. She lay there on the purple-blue sea, rocking a little, with the airport island lying not more than a mile or two off.

'Funny!' said Jack, and dressed quickly. He banged on the girls' door as he went by with Philip. The two boys tore up on deck, and found their friend, the second officer.

'What's up?' they asked him. 'Why have we stopped?'

'Mac's got trouble with his engines,' said the officer. 'Soon be all right, I expect.'

They saw Bill coming along. He had been up for some time, walking round the deck for exercise. They rushed to him, and he grinned. 'Hallo! Ready for breakfast? I'm ravenous. Hallo, Micky, hallo, Kiki.'

'Micky-Kiki-Micky-Kiki, Micky-Ki . . . ' began Kiki. Jack tapped her on the beak.

'That's enough. Take a bit of exercise. Go and chase the gulls!' But Kiki did not want to. She was bored with the gulls now. Besides, she wanted breakfast. Breakfast was nice on board ship because there was always grapefruit, and Kiki liked that. She loved the cherries on top of the grapefruit halves, and the children took it in turn to give her one.

When breakfast was over they took Bill all over the ship. They were not allowed down in the engine-room because of the trouble with the engines. Mac was in a fearful temper, and had been up all night long working on them.

A message was put up on the ship's notice-board that morning.

Owing to engine-trouble, the *Viking Star* is putting back to port. Passengers will be notified further at six o'clock this evening.

With a curious clanking and labouring the *Viking Star* made her way slowly to the island with the airport. Motor-boats came roaring out to meet her and find out what was wrong. In one of them was Bill's friend, Tim. He was soon on board, and Bill introduced him to the children.

'Tim, here are the four children I've told you about. Be careful of them, or they'll pull you into a perilous adventure. That's the kind of children they are. Put them in the middle of an iceberg and they'll find an adventure somehow!'

The children liked Tim. He was younger than Bill, had a mop of unruly curly hair which the wind did what it liked with, and eyes as green as Lucy-Ann's. He had as many freckles as she and Jack had, and a most infectious laugh.

'You'd better come off in the motor-boat with me, hadn't you?' he said to Bill. 'Come back to the island. It's interesting.'

'Right,' said Bill. 'We'll have the day together. Come on, you four – down the ladder with you!'

16

Bill makes a few enquiries

They had a wonderful day on the island. Tim hired a car and away they went to explore. They had lunch in a big town set in the centre of the island, a proper town with shops and buses and cinemas.

After lunch Bill disappeared. 'I've heard of an old chap who's a real expert at old documents,' he told the children. 'One of the greatest experts there are. It's a bit of luck. I'll go and see him. You've got the four bits of the map with you, haven't you, Jack?'

Jack nodded. The children had decided that it would be safer to bring them than leave them behind. He gave them to Bill in an envelope. 'I *do* hope the expert will say it's genuine,' he said earnestly. 'I say – shall we tell Tim?'

'You'd be quite safe to,' said Bill. 'Tim is all right! Whether he'll believe you or not is another matter!'

So, whilst Bill was gone, the children told Tim their secret. He was inclined to grin at first, and laugh it all off as a tale. But they were so serious that he saw that they, at least, believed in it all. He tried to be serious too.

'Well, it's marvellous,' he said. '*I* believed in all these treasure tales when I was a kid too. Jolly nice of Bill to take it seriously and go off to have your map explained.'

The children saw that he did not really take their tale seriously, and they dropped the subject, polite but disappointed. A little doubt crept in Lucy-Ann's mind. *Was* it all a tale? No – surely Mr Eppy wouldn't have behaved so oddly if there had been nothing in it.

Bill was a long time gone. The children were tired of waiting, and Tim was just suggesting they should take a run in the car to a strange-shaped hill in the distance, when he came back.

'Sorry to have been so long,' he said. 'I found the old boy – looks as if he'd come out of the fifteenth century, he's so old and dusty – and so slow I could have screamed. But he knew his stuff all right.'

'What did he say?' asked Jack, crimson with anticipation.

'It's genuine. No doubt of that at all,' said Bill, and everyone breathed loudly in relief. 'He doesn't know if it's a copy of any older map, or a fresh one made by a Greek sailor a hundred or so years ago – probably a mixture, he says. The island is Thamis. It is shown clearly on the map, and even if the name had not been there it could have been recognized by its shape – it's curiously formed at one end.'

'Yes. I noticed that,' said Philip. 'Go on, Bill!'

'The map is in two distinct parts,' went on Bill. 'One shows the island, and on it is marked a city or a port. He doesn't know the island himself so he can't tell. The other part shows this same city or port, and is apparently a guide or directions to some spot in the city where something valuable is placed. He says it isn't clear if this valuable thing is treasure of a temple or even a tomb – he only knows it was something of value to the person who first drew the map.'

The children were listening, all eyes and ears. This was marvellous!

'But – doesn't he think it's the Andra treasure?' asked Jack.

'He apparently doesn't know that tale very well – he says there are hundreds of old legends of pirates and treasure-ships and kidnapping and so on – most of them untrue. He hadn't much to say about that. He is inclined to think it's a temple.'

'*I* think it's the Andra treasure,' said Lucy-Ann, her eyes shining. 'I really do!'

'I got him to re-draw the whole map for us, with the Greek words in English – he speaks English extraordinarily well,' said Bill, and he spread out a nice new sheet of paper on his lap, drawn with fine lines, and marked with words. The children pored over it, too thrilled to speak.

Yes – there was the old map re-drawn – put into English – the faded marks shown clearly. How simply wonderful! Even Tim was intensely interested, and almost began to believe in it.

Jack read some of the words out in a whisper. 'Labyrinth – Catacombs – Two-Fingers – Goddess – Bird – Bell – gosh, what does it all mean? Are the labyrinths and catacombs in this city or port? Was the treasure taken down them?'

'We don't know. All we know is that a way is shown here to a certain place in the city where a certain valuable thing can be found – if it hasn't already been found and taken away or destroyed,' said Bill. 'But you must remember that the original of this map is probably hundreds of years old – the way shown on this map possibly no longer exists. In fact the probabilities are that it doesn't.'

'Oh, Bill – do you really believe that?' asked Dinah reproachfully.

'Well – to be perfectly honest – I do,' said Bill disappointingly. 'I think the map is genuine – no doubt about that at all – but I also think that as all this happened so long ago there's no hope of finding the secret way shown here. It would either have been built over, or destroyed, or even completely forgotten, so that there may not even be an entrance to the labyrinths or catacombs, whatever they are.'

'But – Mr Eppy obviously thinks there's some hope,' said Philip.

'Oh, that reminds me – this old chap, the one I've been to see, knows Mr Eppy. He says he's a real crank about these things – quite dippy about them – and goes off on all sorts of hare-brained schemes,' said Bill. 'Buys and sells islands as if they were books or carpets or pictures! He admits that Mr Eppy knows a lot about the islands, and about the antiques that can be found in them – but he doesn't think that because he believes in the map, for instance, that necessarily means there is anything to get excited about. Rather the other way about, I gathered.'

'Blow!' said Jack. 'So there may be nothing in it after all. In fact, probably not.'

'In fact, probably not, as you say,' agreed Bill. 'All the same, if we had the chance, which we shan't have, of course, I wouldn't mind hiring a motor-boat and chugging off to have a look at Thamis, wherever it is.'

'Oh, I do wish we *could*,' said Lucy-Ann. 'It would be lovely just to *see* it.'

'I could run you over there,' said Tim unexpectedly. 'That is, if it's not too far away.'

'No time,' said Bill, folding up the map. 'We've got to be back by six, as you know. Thanks all the same, Tim. Now, we'd better be off, I think.'

By the time they got to the port it was half-past five. The *Viking Star* had been piloted right in to the pier, and was lying there looking very white and beautiful, but with no sign of the bustle about her that usually meant she was soon sailing.

The gangway was down, and passengers were trooping along it. Lucian was among them with his aunt. They had not seen him all day, except in the distance, and then they had taken no notice of him, not wanting him to tag himself on to them now they had Bill. He waved to them and shouted.

'Oh, I say! Where have you been all day? My aunt wanted you to come with us and have lunch with one of my relations on the island.'

'Sorry! We had other plans!' called back Jack. 'See you some time.'

'Who's the boy?' enquired Bill. 'Oh – it's Lucian, I suppose, the nephew of your Mr Eppy. He must be a bit of a nuisance to you!'

'We can manage him, all right,' said Philip. 'Look – here's

the notice-board. There's a big notice up. What does it say?'

The notice was printed in chalk on the big black notice-board.

Passengers are regretfully informed that the *Viking Star* will have to remain in port for a day or two until damage to her engines is repaired. Passengers may remain on board, if they wish, or stay in a hotel provided by the Company, or may use the motor-boats which the said Company will provide for the use of any passengers wishing to explore this romantic part of the Aegean Sea.
(Signed) L. Petersen, *Captain*

The same thought struck all four children at once. They turned to one another, their eyes shining.

'We could, couldn't we?' said Lucy-Ann, and the others understood at once. Jack nodded, his eyes bright. He slipped his arm through Bill's.

Bill looked round at the children. He smiled broadly, and then laughed out loud to see the four eager faces looking at him, all with the same question in them.

'Can we go to Thamis, after all – that's what you want to know, isn't it?' he said. 'Well, I don't see why not. It looks as if we'll be here a few days, and if the Company provide us with a motor-boat, well, we'll agree to their kind proposal, and off we'll go in one!'

'*Bill!* BILL! How marvellous!' cried everyone, and Jack and Philip began to thump one another on the back, and the girls squeezed Bill's arms till he yelled. Kiki and Micky flew off the boys' shoulders in a hurry, and retired in surprised annoyance to the top of the notice-board.

'Come on – stop this pantomime,' said Bill, still laughing to see the children's excitement. 'Let's get up on deck and make a few plans before we change into clean things for dinner. Get Micky, look – he's beginning to rub out the top part of the notice with his tail.'

They went up to a favourite corner on the promenade deck and sat down. 'It's too good to be true,' said Jack, delighted. 'We keep on thinking things are no good, we'll have to give them up – and then something happens and everything's all right.'

'Yes. We knew we couldn't do anything without Bill, and he wasn't here – and then he suddenly came,' said Lucy-Ann.

'And then we knew we still couldn't do anything, because we'd have to go with the ship on her cruise,' said Dinah. 'And now she's held up, and we can go off by ourselves!'

'Extraordinary how you children get what you want,' said Bill. 'Now about this motor-boat tomorrow. I rather think we'll hire one on our own. If we take one that the Company provide we'll have to go with some of the other passengers – and they certainly won't want to go to Thamis, wherever it is.'

'And we wouldn't want them to, either,' said Jack. 'No – let's have a boat of our own. Can Tim come too?'

'He's got other plans,' said Bill. 'But we'll tell him, just in case he'd like to come. Well – it certainly will be a thrill. I must find out exactly this evening where this Thamis is. I'll get hold of the second officer and ask him if there's a sailor on board who can tell me anything. We'll have to find out the precise route or we might go cruising among these islands for weeks!'

'Oh, Bill – isn't it grand?' said Lucy-Ann. 'I can't wait for tomorrow. Jack, Philip – we're really going to see the treasure island after all! We really are!'

17

To Thamis at last!

Bill soon got all the information he wanted. 'That's the best of being grown-up,' said Dinah. 'Grown-ups always seem to be able to find out anything, and get things cut and dried in no time.'

'Yes – Bill's found out where Thamis is, has ferreted out a map of the route, and has even got the name of a Greek sailor who owns a motor-boat and knows the way!' said Jack, in admiration.

'How did he find all that out?' asked Lucy-Ann.

'Got hold of a Greek sailor below decks, and found he had a brother who runs one of the motor-boats,' said Philip.

It was the following morning. The children had had a big breakfast, and had been provided with enormous packets of food to take with them, by the steward who looked after them so well at table.

'I've packed a whole grapefruit, two cherries and four bananas for Master Micky and Miss Kiki,' he said, with a twinkle in his eye. Lucy-Ann went off into giggles.

'Oh – it does sound funny to call them that! Miss Kiki! Kiki, did you hear that? Miss Kiki!'

'Misskiki, kickmissy, missmicky,' began Kiki, and cackled loudly.

They all walked down the gangway to the pier. They found Tim waiting for them. He had heard the news.

'Hallo, sir,' he said to Bill. 'Can I do anything for you today?'

'Well, we're going off to have a look at Thamis,' said Bill. 'I've hired a motor-boat from a Greek who apparently knows the route. Like to come with us?'

'Well, if you've made your own plans, sir, I won't come

today,' said Tim. 'I've got a chappy here who wants a spot of flying. Can I take the plane up?'

'Yes, of course,' said Bill.

'And if you fly over Thamis, wave to us,' said Jack.

'Right,' said Tim, with a grin. 'I'll look it up and see where it is. Look out for us!'

He went off, and Bill turned to find the boat he had hired. A small, dark Greek came up, with brilliant eyes and a shy smile. He saluted, and spoke in broken English.

'I'm Andros, sir, please. My brother, he say Mister want my boat. Mister, sir, she here.'

'Right. Thanks, Andros,' said Bill, and he looked at the spick-and-span little boat lying alongside. 'Very nice boat. Now, you know the way to Thamis, don't you?'

'Thamis. Yes, Mister. But Thamis poor place. Andros take you find islands.'

'No, thanks. We want to go to Thamis,' said Bill firmly.

Andros seemed surprised at their wanting to go to Thamis. 'Poor island,' he said again. 'Visitors not go there, Mister, sir. I take you fine place.'

'Look here – don't you know the way to Thamis?' said Bill. 'Sounds as if you don't. Oh, you do. Then, to Thamis, please, and let's get on with it.'

'Thamis, Mister, sir,' agreed little Andros. 'Yes, yes, Thamis. Old, old island, but nothing there now, Mister, sir.' He glanced with interest at the parrot and the monkey. 'They come too also?'

'Of course,' said Jack, stepping into the boat, and helping the girls in. 'Come on, Bill, Mister, sir!'

'Mistersir, mistersir, mistersir,' screamed Kiki. 'Pop goes the weasel! Bang, pop, God save the Queen.'

Andros gaped at her, open-mouthed. Micky leapt on to his shoulder and back to Philip's, chattering. He was excited. He even pulled Kiki's tail, a very silly thing to do, because Kiki would now watch for a good chance to nip Micky's – and Micky had quite a long tail to nip!

Andros started up the engine. The motor-boat nosed out of the little harbour, leaving behind the great *Viking Star*, beautiful but silent. Soon they were out on the open sea, skimming along, bobbing up and down on the white horses that reared themselves every now and again. The sun was hot but the wind was strong. The girls' hair streamed out straight, and they laughed in delight to feel so much wind in their faces. After the heat on the ship it was lovely.

'How far is Thamis?' asked Jack. Andros turned his curly head.

'Four hours, five hours,' he said.

'Do you go there much?' asked Bill.

'No, no, Mister, sir. Poor island. I go to Janos, the next one, where my sister lives,' said Andros. 'Thamis dead island, Mister, sir.'

'What does he mean?' wondered Jack. 'A poor dead island! Doesn't sound much of a place, does it?'

'Well, there must be some sort of port or town there,' said Philip. 'The one marked on the map. It looked quite a big one. There must be plenty of people living there, and that means shops and things. It can't be quite dead!'

It was a lovely journey to Thamis. The sea was choppy, and yet was full of glints and sparkles. The boat sped along like a live thing, the engine purring away. At twelve o'clock they all had a picnic lunch and blessed the steward who had packed them such a fine one.

'Five different sorts of sandwiches – four different kinds of cake – half a pound of sweet biscuits – rolls and butter and cheese and tomatoes – and the grapefruit, cherries and bananas for Kiki and Micky,' said Jack.

Lucy-Ann sat contentedly eating, with the wind in her face. She looked very happy. The others looked at her and nudged one another. They waited. They knew exactly what she was going to say. She opened her mouth, and at once all the others chimed in together.

'You know, we always think food tastes *much* nicer when

it's eaten out of doors!'

Lucy-Ann stared at them in surprise. 'How very peculiar! – I was *just* about to say exactly the same thing,' she said.

The others chuckled. 'We knew you were,' said Philip. 'You always do say it, Lucy-Ann. We watched for you to open your mouth and begin, and we said it for you!'

'Idiots,' said Lucy-Ann, and laughed. Andros laughed too. He liked these children and their funny pets. He had refused to share their food, and was eating his own lunch. It was made up of black bread, some very high-smelling cheese and a jug of some kind of drink.

Kiki and Micky ate their dinner solemnly together. Micky was not very pleased with the terrific breeze that blew every hair on his body backwards or forwards, depending on which way he sat. Nor was Kiki pleased when her feathers blew round her like an umbrella turning inside out. The two of them sat together in a little sheltered place, sharing the grapefruit, the cherries and the bananas. Micky politely peeled a banana for Kiki and handed it to her.

'He skins it just like we do,' said Lucy-Ann. 'I always think he's so clever at that.'

'Clever,' said Andros, pointing to Micky. 'Good and clever.'

Micky unfortunately spoilt Andros's good opinion of him by throwing away the banana skin so carelessly that it landed on the sailor's head, hanging ridiculously over his right eye. Kiki gave one of her rich chuckles, and was just about to add her banana skin to Micky's when Jack took it away from her.

'Mistersir, mistersir, mister Pollysir,' squawked Kiki, trying to snatch it back.

The boat went on and on, occasionally passing other islands, one or two large ones, but most of them small. Finally Andros raised his hand and pointed to the east.

'Thamis,' he said. 'Mister, sir, Thamis.'

Everyone looked eagerly to where he pointed. They saw a

small island, purple in the distance, rearing itself out of the waters as they sped nearer. Thamis! Was it really Thamis, the old island marked on the treasure map?

Eagerly the children leaned forward and watched it take shape as they raced nearer. Lucy-Ann's imagination began to work. Long long ago, she thought, this is where the fleet of treasure-ships stole up to in the night. Soon we shall see the city marked on the map – the treasure-city!

'Perhaps,' she thought, 'one of the ships was called the *Andra* like our own little Ship of Adventure. Perhaps it sailed into the very spot we're making for now. We're getting quite near. We shall see the city soon – the one marked on the map.'

'Is there a good harbour?' asked Bill, turning to Andros. The man looked surprised.

'Oh no, Mister, sir. No harbour now. Only two places to land. I, Andros, know them both. I take you to old city port.'

'Good,' thought Jack. 'Now we shall soon be there – in the old city marked on the map. I hope it won't be *too* modern, like the towns we've seen on some of the islands. Ah – now we're getting in close.'

They were. They could see rocky beaches. The waves pounded on them. They looked for the town, and saw buildings coming down to the water's edge. It seemed strange that there was no proper harbour. City ports always had a harbour.

The boat ran in gently, Andros looking out for rocks, and taking a course he seemed to know. He was making for a little channel that led inland.

The children fell silent as they neared the island. Their eyes were fixed on the city. It did not look right, somehow. Something was the matter with it. It looked – well – *dead*, Lucy-Ann thought.

Jack remembered his binoculars and put them to his eyes. He gave an exclamation. 'Gosh! Would you believe it!'

'*What?*' said everyone at once impatiently.

'It's all ruins,' said Jack, and he lowered the glasses and looked at the others. 'It's a *ruined* city! I never thought of that!'

'I, Andros, told that,' said the sailor. 'I tell you poor island, dead island. One farm, two farms, perhaps. City gone. Nobody there. All gone to other islands now.'

They nosed into the little channel. It was deep and calm. 'You get out, and I wait?' enquired Andros. 'Not see much. All dead and poor this island. Yes, Mister, sir. I take you better places.'

'We'll get out, Andros,' said Bill. 'Bring the rest of the food, Jack. We may as well explore now we're here, and we'll picnic in the old ruins. They will be quite interesting, I expect.'

Not knowing quite what to think, the children leapt off the boat on to a ledge. They climbed up some old worn steps, and came into what must have been the main street of the ruined city. It was overgrown now and difficult to walk in. There were ruins everywhere. Bill looked at a few of them closely.

'These are hundreds of years old,' he said. 'I wonder what made the people leave Thamis and go elsewhere. I suppose the island couldn't keep them in food. What a place!'

'It's got such a weird deserted feeling about it that I feel I'm living hundreds of years ago,' said Lucy-Ann. 'I wish the city would come alive – be full of the long-ago people, walking and running here along the street, looking out of the old broken window-openings, going down to whatever harbour there was to see the ships!'

'Well, I hope the city *doesn't* come alive,' said Dinah. 'I'd be scared stiff. I don't like it much as it is, either.'

It was built on a steep hill, and the ruined buildings rose one above another, some just a wall or two, others a hollow shell, and still others looking fairly habitable until the children peeped inside and saw the holes in the roof and the walls.

Almost at the top was an old ruined temple, one or two graceful arches still remaining. Its massive columns stood in a broken row, with one or two gulls perched on the jagged tops. Bill scraped aside some of the grass that grew on the floor of the temple, and pointed out lovely mosaic stones to the children.

'Bill, is there anything here at all that's on the map?' asked Jack. Somehow it was all so different from what he had imagined that the idea of hidden treasure now seemed ridiculous. Bill got out the re-drawn map.

'Look – this is where we came in with our boat, surely,' said Philip, pointing. 'It says "CREEK". Well, wouldn't you call that channel a creek? And look – the entrance or beginning of the way to the treasure is somewhere near the creek.'

'Oh, Bill – let's go back and explore along there!' said Dinah.

Bill laughed. 'We've certainly got a bee in our bonnet about this! All right. Come on. It'll be on the way to the boat, anyway.'

'Just let's get to the top of the hill,' said Jack. 'We could see over the rest of the island then. It's not very large.'

'Right,' said Bill, and they climbed to the very top. They could see away over to the other side of the island, where the dark-blue sea was tipped with white horses. It was a bare, rocky place, but here and there were green patches, and small buildings could be seen.

'The farms Andros spoke of, I suppose,' said Bill. 'My word – he was certainly right when he called it poor and dead! It's not quite my idea of a treasure island!'

They turned to go down the hill on which the ruined city was built. They made their way carefully. Half-way down Lucy-Ann stopped and listened. 'I can hear something,' she said.

'So can I,' said Dinah. 'It's a bell ringing! Whatever can it be?'

18

A few surprises

It seemed so very unusual to hear a bell ringing in that dead and silent city that the little company felt really startled. The sound came nearer.

'Dong-dong-dong.' Kiki didn't like it either and crouched against Jack's cheek. Micky chattered quietly.

'Dong-dong-dong!'

'Something's coming round that corner,' said Jack suddenly. And something did.

It was a donkey, a little grey donkey with a big bell hanging from his neck! With him was a small boy, an imp of a boy, riding astride, with panniers each side of the donkey, great baskets that were full of something covered in white cloths.

'Good gracious!' said Dinah, and she sat down on a big stone, most relieved to see that it was just a donkey-bell that had startled them all. 'I don't know *what* I thought was coming!'

'I suppose the boy's from one of the farms,' said Bill, looking puzzled. 'But why has he come here? There is nobody living here.'

Then an even more surprising thing happened. The boy caught sight of the five people watching him, and grinned a welcome. He leapt off the donkey, pointed to the pannier baskets and shouted out something that sounded unlike anything they had heard before, but which the children imagined must be Greek spoken in the local accent of Thamis. Then he brought the donkey right up to them, and began to throw back the cloths that covered whatever was in the panniers.

'It's food,' said Bill, in amazement. 'Bread – cheeses – meat. Gosh, he's unpacking the lot.'

The boy unpacked everything, chattering all the time. He evidently could not understand why nobody helped him, and addressed quite a few cutting remarks to the two boys, who, of course, could not make head or tail of them.

'Here, boy,' said Bill. 'What's all this?'

He pointed to the pile of food. The boy sent out another explanation, pointing to Bill, and then pointing to the food.

'Anyone would think he had brought all this for *us*,' said Bill, exasperated. 'I can't understand it at all.'

The boy mounted his donkey again. He held out his hand to Bill, palm upwards. That was plain enough. He wanted money!

'Well, well – it beats me,' said Bill, astounded. 'A very fine welcome to Thamis, I must say – but most unexpected. We don't want the food, sonny. WE DON'T WANT IT. TAKE IT BACK!'

No amount of shouting could make the boy understand. He got very angry, and tapped his palm smartly to make Bill understand he wanted money. In the end Bill tipped a handful of coins into his hand. He counted them carefully, nodded his head, grinned brilliantly, and then very unexpectedly spat at Micky. Micky spat back, and Kiki growled like a dog.

The donkey backed away from Kiki and began to bray. 'Eee-yore! Eee-eee-yore!'

Kiki was extremely startled, but she soon recovered, and produced a very good bray herself. The boy gave a yelp of surprise, kicked his donkey hard with both his bare heels, and galloped away round the corner, the donkey's bell ringing hard. 'Dong-dong-dong-dong-dong!'

Bill sat down and scratched his head. 'Well, what do you make of *that*?' he said. 'A present of some very fine country food, sent by somebody we don't know, who can't possibly have known we were here.'

'It's a puzzle,' said Jack. 'I wouldn't mind one of those rolls.'

They all had one. They were very good. They sat and munched them, wondering about the boy. They could not make head or tail of his appearance.

'What are we going to do with this food?' said Philip. 'It won't keep if it's left out in the sun. It seems an awful waste of good food to leave it mouldering here.'

'It does,' said Bill. 'Well – the only thing we can do is to carry it into a cool place somewhere – and hope that boy will come back!'

They picked up the food and went into a near-by building. There was a hole in the floor, shaded by a half-ruined wall. They packed all the food there, wondering what would happen to it.

'Now we'd better go down to the creek and see if we can find the entrance, or whatever it is, shown on the map,' said Bill. He pulled it out of his pocket and looked at it. The children looked too. 'We shan't find it, so don't think it!' said Bill, who was secretly of the opinion that there was nothing to be discovered in this poor, 'dead' island.

They went down the overgrown, stone-strewn street, and came to the rocky creek. The motor-boat was there, rocking gently. Andros was fast asleep on the shady side of the boat.

The little party walked down the rocky ledge to the boat. Then they looked up the creek. Bill gave an exclamation. 'Of course! That's it!'

'*What*, Bill?' said the children at once.

'Well, "Two-Fingers" is marked on the map, apparently for no reason at all. The expert swore that's what the old Greek word meant. I just thought it might be an old name for someone – but now I see what it meant. Look up there.'

The children looked where Bill pointed – and above their heads some way away to the left they saw a peculiar rock. It was like a clenched hand – with two fingers raised! Yes – two fingers. There they were. And 'Two-Fingers' was marked on the map!

'Come on. That's a guide of some sort,' said Bill, and they climbed along till they came to the queer two-fingered rock. They found a hole behind it, a hole that would quite easily allow a person to step into it. Bill fumbled for a torch. He switched it on.

'There may be a passage of some kind,' he said. 'Yes – there is! This is really extraordinary! I think, Jack, you'd better go back to the boat and get a lantern or two, if you can find them. My torch isn't too good.'

Jack sped down to the boat. Andros was still asleep. Jack spotted two lanterns and brought them carefully up to the two-fingered rock, handing them at awkward places to Philip, who had come to meet him.

'Good,' said Bill. 'We'll light these. I'll take one, and you can take the other, Jack. I'll save my torch.'

They lighted the oil lanterns inside the hole. It wasn't big enough for a cave. It really was just a large hole behind the strange-looking rock – but at the back was what looked like an entry into the hill. Could it possibly be the entrance shown in the map?

'Do you think it is, Bill?' asked Lucy-Ann eagerly, when the lanterns were lighted and Bill held one up to peer into the narrow rocky passage behind the hole.

'No. I can't believe it is,' said Bill. 'It must have been known for years by everyone in the city, when it was alive with people. It's just a coincidence, I expect.'

The children, of course, didn't think it was. They felt very thrilled indeed as they made their way along the dark little passage. It went for a hundred yards and then came out into a wide space. Bill held up his lantern. It shone on to rocky walls – but what was that at the back? The wall looked different there.

He took his lantern over to it. The beam shone on to large blocks of stone built like a great irregular door. 'I wonder why that was built here,' said Bill, surprised. He swung the lantern round to light up the rest of the cave. The walls were of smooth, shiny rock. There was not the smallest opening there at all. The only opening was the one they had come in by, from the narrow passage.

He swung the light on to the built-in stones again. Then he put the lantern down.

'This was built to block up some other opening,' he said at last. The children's hearts sank. 'It is immensely strong, as you can see for yourselves – a door of great blocks of stone, a door that can't possibly be opened, or got through in any way.'

'Bill – do you think it's blocking up the entrance shown on the map?' asked Jack, dismayed.

'Well, yes – I do,' said Bill. 'It's been built many, many years – it's old, as you can see. Why it was built, goodness knows! Anyway, there it is – and we're stopped right at the very outset! If this is the way shown on the map, the way that one must follow to get to wherever the treasure was hidden, it's impossible to follow it. Quite impossible!'

'Oh, Bill!' said Lucy-Ann, almost in tears. 'It's too bad. Isn't there *any* way through?'

'Well – send Micky to see,' said Bill. 'If there's even a small hole Micky will find it. You know what monkeys are. Send him, Philip.'

'Go, Micky – go and hunt about,' said Philip. Micky looked at him enquiringly. He did not like this business of exploring dark passages, but he leapt off Philip's shoulder and obediently went off on an exploration of his own. Kiki watched him and then flew to a ledge at the top of the immense stone doorway.

'Send for the doctor,' she said in a hollow voice. 'Polly's got a cold. Send for the doctor.'

Micky bounded up to join her. He scurried about, putting his paw here and there, into crannies and crevices. But obviously there was nothing to find, for he soon came back and leapt on to Philip's shoulder, nestling closely to his neck.

'No go,' said Bill. He set the lantern down on the floor, meaning to put the map away. Just as he was folding it up

Lucy-Ann gave an astonished cry.

'What's the matter?' said Jack, startled.

'Look – what's that over there – on the floor? Surely, it's – it's – a *torch battery*!'

Philip saw the thing she meant and went to pick it up. He brought it to the light of the lamp. 'Yes – that's just what it is – an old worn-out battery from a torch rather like Bill's. Bill – you haven't dropped a battery, have you?'

'Of course not,' said Bill. 'Yes, this is certainly an old battery – somebody must have thrown it down and put a new battery into his torch – whoever he may be! We are obviously not the only ones to know this place!'

Lucy-Ann shivered. She was sorry she had spotted that battery now. It made her feel uneasy. Who had been in this walled-up cave, and why?

'Let's go, Bill,' she said. 'We can't do any good here – it's all walled up. Let's go back to Andros. I don't like this.'

'Right. We'll go back,' said Bill. 'In any case, we ought to go now. We've been here ages, and we've got to get back to the ship tonight. Come along.'

They made their way out of the cave, down the narrow passage in the rocky hill and came to the hole. They climbed round the two-fingered rock and made their way to the creek.

And then they got a terrible shock. The motor-boat was gone! They stared as if they could not believe their eyes.

'Where's the boat?' said Dinah feebly.

They looked up the creek and down. No sign of the boat at all. How very extraordinary! And then Jack gave a cry, and pointed out to sea.

'Isn't that it? Look – right out there?'

They all strained their eyes, and Bill nodded his head grimly. 'Yes – that looks like it. What on earth made Andros go off without us? What an astounding thing to do!'

'He was fast asleep in the boat when I got the lantern,' said Jack. 'Never stirred. Everything seemed all right then.'

'Blessed if I understand it,' said Bill, looking bewildered.

'He seemed a good trustworthy chap – and I haven't even paid him. What in the world has possessed him to act like that?'

'That boat's going pretty fast,' said Philip. 'Almost out of sight now. Well, well, well – here we are marooned on our treasure island, sure as eggs are eggs!'

Lucy-Ann was very much alarmed. She took Bill's arm. 'What are we going to do?' she said. 'Are we to stay here, Bill?'

'Lucy-Ann, of course we are,' said Jack, before Bill could answer. 'Where are we to go if we don't stay here? Have you got an aeroplane stowed away somewhere, ready for this emergency?'

'Shut up, Jack,' said Bill, putting his arm round Lucy-Ann. 'We shall be all right, don't fret, Lucy-Ann. It's only one of our adventures!'

19

All kinds of shocks

They stood there for a little while, not certain what to do. It was all so very unexpected. Then Bill shook himself and grinned round at the others.

'Well – it looks as if we've got to spend the night here, doesn't it? – and get our supper ourselves. Thank goodness we've got the food that extraordinary boy brought on his donkey! And Jack's got the rest of our picnic lunch as well.'

'Oh *yes* – I'd forgotten that!' said Dinah, pleased. She had been thinking they would have nothing to eat.

'We can go and tuck in straight away,' said Bill. 'We'll find somewhere to sleep all right – it's very warm, and we shan't take any harm. I don't particularly want to go and find one of those farms we saw, in case Andros takes it into his head to call back for us. He must have gone crazy.'

It was a curious evening that they all spent on Thamis. They went to find the store of food and had a very good meal indeed. They put the rest of it safely back in the cool place they had stored it in at first. Then they went wandering round the silent, ruined old city again. Lucy-Ann found an old pot with a broken neck, which she was very pleased with. Jack found some kind of metal fork – at least that is what he took it to be – with two of its prongs gone.

Bill had been hunting about for some place to sleep in. He had not been very successful. At last he chose a room not far from the ruined temple, one that had three walls and a little roof left. It was overgrown with thick grass and would have to do for a bedroom.

The sun was going down. It would soon be gone. Bill decided to put the food in the 'bedroom' too, then it would be handy if they wanted any. He and the boys removed it from the place it was in and put it carefully in some thick, cool grass. They were glad there was such a lot!

When the sun disappeared everyone felt tired. Lucy-Ann was yawning her head off, and so was Kiki. Micky explored the ruined little room thoroughly, approved of it and settled down on Philip as soon as the boy had made himself a fairly soft bed in the thickly growing grass.

The four children fell asleep at once. Kiki perched herself quietly on Jack's middle as soon as she knew he was asleep. He had pushed her off two or three times, but this time he did not wake, and she remained where she was, her head tucked under her wing.

Bill lay and looked up at the stars he could see through the holes in the roof. He was angry with himself for bringing the children to Thamis. Now they had landed in difficulties again – all because of a legendary and most elusive treasure, one that certainly had not existed for years – if it had ever existed at all!

He puzzled over the boy on the donkey, who had brought the food. He puzzled over the blocked-up entrance and the battery Lucy-Ann had found – but more than anything he puzzled over the sudden disappearance of Andros.

He was just about to fall off to sleep when he heard a noise. Micky must have heard it too, because he stirred and his small head looked round the 'bedroom.' Bill lay and listened, holding his breath. *Was* it a noise he had heard?

Then he heard the unmistakable sound of a voice! Then another voice, deep and complaining. Where did they come from?

He sat up cautiously and listened again. The voices came once more, and then Bill heard footsteps – footsteps coming down the ruined city street! He did not like it at all. Who on earth was walking through the old dead city in the middle of the night?

Kiki had heard the voices too. She flew out of the room she was in and hid herself under the ledge of an arch, waiting. The footsteps came nearer. The voices came too, talking together. Bill silently posted himself beside a broken window-opening and watched. There was only starlight to see by, but he might be able to make out something.

Two dark figures came up the street. They stopped every now and again. It seemed to Bill as if they were looking in the ruined buildings to find something. Would they look into this one and find the children? Bill debated whether he should go out and accost these people? Who were they, anyway?

Then he decided that people who walk the streets of a ruined city at dead of night are not perhaps the best people to ask help from, and he remained where he was.

The two dark figures arrived near by. He heard their voices again, but they spoke in a foreign language – Greek, probably – and he could not understand a word. They were obviously looking for something, Bill thought – and then he suddenly guessed what it was.

The food, perhaps! Maybe the boy had brought it for *them* – and they had not been there – but Bill had, and had got it instead. Now the men were looking for it, sure that the boy had dumped it somewhere.

'They'll look in here then, sure as anything,' thought Bill. But they didn't. Just as they got to the broken doorway, near where the parrot was perched, Kiki went off like a pistol-shot.

CRACK!

The children all woke up at once and sat up. They were too startled to make a sound, and as soon as they heard Bill's 'Sh!' they sat silently waiting.

The two men were most alarmed. Bill could see them clutching one another. They said something rapidly, obviously asking each other what that noise was.

Kiki considered them. She didn't like them. She began to cackle with laughter, and this horrified the men more than anything else could have done. Kiki's laughter was so completely idiotic that it froze them to the marrow.

Kiki stopped. She swelled out her throat and began to make her famous noise of an express train screeching through a tunnel, getting louder and louder and louder. It was a magnificent effort, and had very satisfactory results.

The men yelled too, in panic, and set off as fast as they could, certain that something terrible was coming after them. Kiki sent another pistol-shot after them and then relapsed into cackles.

'Well, really, Kiki,' said Bill, when the two men were completely gone. 'What a performance!'

'Who was it out there, Bill?' asked Dinah.

'I've no idea,' said Bill. 'But I have a feeling it was two hungry fellows come to look for the food the small boy presented us with today. Anyway they've departed in a great hurry.'

'Kiki was marvellous, wasn't she?' said Jack. 'Good old Kiki! Clever bird!'

Kiki gave an out-size hiccup. 'Pardon! Send for the doctor! Pop goes the weasel.'

'Yes. Very nice. But that's enough now,' said Jack. 'Bill, who do you think those men were?'

'I've just told you – I've no idea,' said Bill. 'This place

beats me. Come on, let's go to sleep again. I don't somehow think those fellows will come back – and if we have any other visitors I've no doubt Kiki will deal with them!'

They settled themselves off to sleep again. Bill lay awake wondering a little more, then he too fell asleep. He did not wake till morning.

The others were already awake. Jack had awakened very thirsty and had gone to look for water. He found a well beside a tumbledown house some way down the hill, and saw water in it. It was not long before he had rigged up a way of bringing up the water, which was crystal clear and cold.

He tied string round the broken pot Lucy-Ann had found and lowered it down the well. It did not hold much water because the neck was broken, but it was enough for them all to quench their thirst. They had breakfast off the rolls and cheeses, and hoped the boy would come again that day!

'Go down and see if there's any sign of the boat, Jack,' said Bill, when they had finished. So off he went, and soon came back to report that the creek was empty. No boat was anywhere to be seen.

'Well – we shall just have to wait about, that's all,' said Bill. 'It will only be a question of time till we are taken off. Tim will wonder what's happened for one thing. Or Andros will discover he's done a crazy thing, and come back for us!'

At about twelve o'clock they heard the dong-dong-dong of the donkey's bell again, and round the same corner came the imp of a boy. Bill knew what to do this time! He and the others unpacked the food, the boy was paid, and, with the donkey's bell ringing loudly, he departed, much better pleased with his reception. Everyone stared after him.

'Really very extraordinary,' said Bill. 'Let's hide the food quickly, before the real recipients come along. We'll have a meal ourselves too. I'm hungry!'

They dragged it to the room in which they had slept the night before, and had a good meal before they hid it. Bill wondered if he should find his way to one of the farms for help. But what help could they give? And what kind of a reception would he get? Anything might happen to him on this lonely island. He might be robbed and kept prisoner, or even killed.

Jack asked Bill to give him the map to study – the re-drawn one. 'Not that it's going to be much use,' said Jack, with a grin. 'Now that I'm on Thamis I don't think so much of it as I did. And it's difficult to believe in treasure when all you can see around you is a lot of ruins.'

Bill gave him the map. Jack took it into the space once occupied by the temple, and sat down in a corner. Lucy-Ann came to sit with him. Kiki settled between them, murmuring companionably.

The two red heads bent over the map together. 'It's got so many things on it that I can't make out the reason for,' said Jack. ' "Two-Fingers" – well, we know what that means, all right – and now look here – a lot further on, it says "Bell." Well, what does that mean? Bell! What has a bell? A donkey, of course – and schools have bells – and . . .'

'Churches,' said Lucy-Ann. 'I expect this old temple had a bell once upon a time. I wonder where it was.'

She looked round and about but could see no place where a bell could have hung.

Jack looked at her suddenly. 'Lucy-Ann – of *course* – a temple *would* have a bell. The temple may be one of the clues, one of the guides to the treasure.'

'Do you think so?' said Lucy-Ann doubtfully. 'But – surely the treasure would have been hidden deep *underground* somewhere – not in the temple, up here. We know the entrance to the secret passage was far *down* the hill, just above the creek.'

'Would it be hidden *under* the temple, perhaps?' said Jack. 'Or somewhere near? Maybe the temple had vaults. I say – that's an idea! If this one once had vaults, they must still be there. *Vaults* don't become ruins, like buildings. They're not exposed to wind and rain and sun. Vaults! Yes – going deep down into the hill – reached by an underground passage from the creek – a passage that could be approached easily enough from the sea – could be used by sailors who wanted to smuggle in goods. Lucy-Ann – there must be vaults! Come on – we'll look for them.'

Lucy-Ann, half excited, half disbelieving, got up and followed Jack. He began to hunt all over what must have once been the courtyard. It was too overgrown to tell if any way could be found underground.

They leaned against a great half-broken column to rest themselves. There was a large piece out of the column just above their heads, and Kiki flew up there to perch. At that moment Micky came bounding into the old courtyard of the temple, followed by the others. He saw Kiki and leapt up beside her.

She wasn't expecting him, and was startled and angry. She gave him such a violent nip that he lost his balance on the ledge – and fell backwards into the inside of the enormous column!

He shrieked with fright as he fell, and Kiki poked her head inside the hole to see what had happened to him.

'All gone,' she announced in a hollow voice. 'All gone. Ding-dong-bell.'

'You idiot, Kiki!' shouted Philip. 'Hey, Micky, Micky! Come on up!'

But there was no Micky. Only a little whimpering cry came up. 'He's hurt,' said Philip. 'Here, Jack, give me a leg-up. I'll go down into the column after him. He can't have fallen very far.'

Jack gave him a leg-up. He got on to the broken place, swung his legs in and was about to jump down when he stopped and looked in cautiously.

'Hey, Bill!' he called. 'Hand me your torch. I'd better look before I leap, I think. There's something odd here!'

Bill handed him up his torch. Philip switched it on and looked down into the hollow of the great column. He turned and looked back at the others.

'I say – it's amazing. It looks as if there's steps at the bottom of this column! What do you think of *that*?'

20

Exploring the treasure-route

Everyone was amazed. Steps! Stone steps leading downwards at the base of the hollow stone column! Jack gave a loud whoop.

'I bet they go to the vaults!'

'*What* vaults?' asked Dinah, in astonishment. But Jack was too excited to tell her.

'Bill – let's go down. Come on. We're on the track of the treasure. Didn't the map say "Bell"? Well, the temple must have a bell. I bet the treasure's somewhere underneath!'

'You're talking double Dutch,' said Bill, not following this at all. 'Philip – come down. Don't attempt any scatter-brained exploration till we get the lanterns, and till I have a look myself. Do you hear me?'

'Yes; right Bill,' said Philip reluctantly, and jumped down. 'Micky's down there somewhere – he must have fallen on the steps and gone bumping down. I can still hear him whimpering.'

'I expect he got a bit of a shock,' said Bill. 'Go and get the lanterns and also the food, you boys. If we are going underground, we'd better prepare ourselves!'

Before the boys returned, Micky had come back; a Micky very frightened and sorry for himself indeed. He looked for his beloved Philip but he wasn't there, so he went to Lucy-Ann, and let her nurse him like a baby. He whimpered all the time, and Lucy-Ann was very distressed.

'Now, now – you haven't really hurt yourself,' she consoled him. 'Just a bruise or two, I expect. It was very, very naughty of Kiki. Still, you've make a wonderful find, Micky. Really wonderful!'

Kiki was very ashamed of herself. She went into a corner

and put her head under her wing. Nobody took any notice of her at all.

The boys came back. Bill had had a good look down the hollow column with his torch. It puzzled him how the ancient folk, who had used the column as a way of getting underground, had made an entry in it. He could see no way of entry at all – except, of course, through the great hole broken in the column.

'It's a narrow spiral stairway,' he told the girls. 'Probably Jack is right. It may lead down to the vaults of the temple – a very secret way to them, possibly known only to the head priest. Come on, boys – help the girls up. I'll go down first.'

He dropped down deftly to the head of the steps. He shone his torch down. Yes – it was a spiral stairway as he had thought. It would be very narrow here, but probably got wider lower down. He had almost to crawl down the first twelve steps, and two or three times nearly slipped, because the treads were so narrow and steep.

The girls followed, helped by the boys. Dinah took one lantern, finding it very difficult indeed to manage with it, and at last had to hand it down to Bill, because she needed both her hands at the top of the stairway. Lucy-Ann went down by the light of the second lantern, held by Jack.

The food was dropped in behind them. 'Might as well leave it there,' called back Bill. 'We can fetch it if we need it – and it's as good a hiding-place as anywhere else.'

So they left the food at the top of the stairway, on a stone ledge there, and pretty soon all five were a good way down. As Bill had thought, the stone steps grew very much wider and easier a little further on.

Micky was now on Philip's shoulder again. Kiki had followed Jack into the column, very quiet and subdued. Down they went and down.

They came to the end of the stairway. It finished in a vast cave or vault that stretched out endlessly in the rock of the hill. The lanterns only lit up a small part of it.

'Yes – here are the vaults all right,' said Jack. 'The way we've come to them must have been a very secret one, I should think. Look – there's another way up, Bill – over there – more stone steps – straight ones this time, not spiral – going quite steeply upwards.'

'Yes. I should think that was the ordinary way used up and down to the vaults,' said Bill. 'The way we came is very well hidden. See, from here you can't even see it, hidden behind that enormous rock.'

He swung his torch up the wide sweep of steps to which they had now walked over. 'I'll go up and see where they lead to,' said Bill, and up he went. They heard his steps going up and up, and then they stopped. They heard them coming down again.

'Came up against a stone ceiling!' he reported. 'Probably there's an exit there, closed up by a great stone trap-door – overgrown now with weeds and grass. That was obviously the ordinary way in and out. Well – where do we go from here?'

'Bill, let's look at the map again,' said Jack. 'I'm sure we must now be at the place marked "Bell". "Bell" for temple, you know.'

By the light of Bill's torch they all pored over the map again. Bill traced the 'Treasure-path' with his finger. ' "Two-Finger Rock",' he said. 'We were there, and were stopped by the walled-in place.'

'Yes – then the next thing marked is "Goddess",' said Philip. 'Can't think what *that* means!'

'Something on the way from "Two-Finger Rock" to here, perhaps,' said Jack. 'We could go and see. Then look – there comes "Tomb". I suppose that's where someone was buried.'

'Yes – in a stone cell, I should think,' said Bill. 'And then we come to "Bird," which seems rather strange.'

'Then to "Bell," ' said Jack triumphantly. 'And that's where *we* are, I bet!'

'Yes – but not where the treasure is,' said Bill. 'Look – you go on to here – marked "Labyrinth". Not so good, that.'

'What's a labyrinth, exactly?' asked Lucy-Ann.

'A maze – a place where it's so winding and muddling that you can easily get lost,' said Dinah. Lucy-Ann did not like the sound of that at all!

'Labyrinth,' she said. 'Well, what's next?'

' "Catacomb",' said Bill. 'And that, apparently, is where the treasure was put! What a way to bring it!'

'Let's go and find it!' said Jack cheerfully. He folded up the map and put it into his pocket. 'Come on – we've got nothing else to do. I must say it's nice and cool down here after the heat up above in the sun!'

'The thing is – which way do we go?' said Bill. 'One way goes to the "Labyrinth," the other to the "Tomb". But although the points of the compass are marked on the map to make things easy, we're not able to see the sun, so we have no idea of direction. Anyone got a compass?'

Nobody had. 'Well – we'll have to guess,' said Bill. 'There's only two ways to go, apparently – to the right – or to the left. Let's go right.'

So they set off to the right of the vault. Bill with his torch, the two girls holding hands and each boy carrying a lantern. The shadows were weird, and the hollow echo of their feet strange and rather alarming. Kiki and Micky did not like it at all, and each sat silent on the boys' shoulders.

They went for some way and then came to a wide passage that led downwards in a smooth slope. It went for a good way, and then stopped short at what appeared to be a door. It was a wooden door and had once been immensely stout and strong. Even now it was still good, but one of the hinges had given way, and, as the children first pushed and then pulled it, the other hinges gave way too, and the door fell inwards, almost on top of Bill. He just leapt away in time.

He shone his torch on it. Carved right across the door was an enormous bird. 'There you are – "Bird",' said Jack, pleased. 'That was one of the clues, wasn't it, Bill? It's an eagle – beautifully carved, too.'

'Now we know which way we're going – the wrong way!' said Bill. 'Still, we'll go on now – this is amazing!'

Leaving the fallen Bird-door behind, they went through the opening. Looking back, they saw that the passage they were now following forked into two by the door – evidently there were two ways to go there – and the right one was the Bird-door – hence the clue called 'Bird'.

They went down a very narrow passage indeed. It ran downwards, as the other had done, until it opened out into a narrow chamber. There was a smooth stone ledge at one side. At each end were wooden slabs, carved with intricate symbols. The little company stopped to look at them.

'This must have been a tomb,' said Bill. 'Possibly where a priest was buried. There are many old burying-places like this.'

'The sailors who carried the treasure must have had to carry it through this tomb,' said Philip. 'Perhaps they knew this way because they robbed tombs.'

There was no door to the tomb, but the doorway was cut out smooth and level. Possibly there had once been a door. Beyond it the passage began again, sloping downwards more steeply still.

'Now for "Goddess",' said Jack. 'I say – it's a pretty good guide, this map, isn't it, Bill? If we had been able to make our way through "Two-Finger Rock" – where the hole was, you know – we could have used the map as an absolutely accurate guide.'

'Look out – there are steps here, now,' said Bill. 'Cut in the rock. It gets pretty steep here.'

They went carefully down the steps. At the bottom was a beautiful archway. It was made of some kind of marble, set into the natural archway of the rock. Beynod the arch was a marble floor, still smooth and shining, for there was no dust underground.

The walls were carved too, the solid rock itself chipped out into figures and symbols. Eagles, doves, foxes, wolves – curious designs and patterns decorated the whole of the strange little cave.

'This must be "Goddess",' said Bill. 'A place to worship some little-known goddess, I imagine – hidden under the ground, only to be visited in secret.'

'Yes – that must be it,' said Philip. 'Isn't it strange? I suppose those carvings are hundreds of years old!'

'And now for the last clue – or first, whichever you like to call it,' said Bill. ' "Two-Fingers"! We know what that is, anyway. But we shall come up against the other side of the stone door, I've no doubt. Here we go. My word, it's steep now, isn't it? No steps either. Be careful, you girls!'

They made their way, stumbling, down a very steep passage – and, just as Bill had said, they came up against the other side of the walled-up doorway they had seen when they had gone into 'Two-Fingers' hole. They stopped and considered.

'Yes – we've found the treasure-route all right,' said Bill. 'Now – we'll start from here again – "Two-Fingers" – and we'll work our way back – past "Goddess" and "Tomb" and "Bird" till we come to "Bell" – the temple vault.'

'And *then* we'll go on!' said Jack, almost trembling with excitement. 'On to "Labyrinth" and "Catacomb" – and "TREASURE"!'

21

Kiki is very tiresome

Back they all went, through the curious little cell that must once have been a marble temple underground, dedicated to some strange goddess – through the old tomb, and over the fallen door carved with the bird – and soon they were back in the temple vault.

'Now we start off the other way – to the left,' said Bill, who was now almost as excited as the four children. 'Come along – down this passage here. Hold up your lantern, Philip. My torch isn't very strong.'

'Does this passage lead into the labyrinth – the maze where people get lost?' asked Lucy-Ann, a little fearfully. 'Shall *we* get lost?'

'No. We'll find some way of keeping safe,' said Bill. He and Jack looked closely at the map. 'Although this part is marked "Labyrinth", it shows only one route or passage – but every now and again the letter "R" turns up – for Right, I suppose. We seem to have to turn to the right six times. Well, if we come to a fork, we shall know what to do – right every time! Come along! Put the map back in your pocket, Jack.'

They went down the low-roofed, winding passage for a little way, and then Jack called out to the others. 'I say – anyone got Kiki?'

They all stopped. 'I haven't,' yelled back Lucy-Ann. 'Nor has Dinah.' Bill said he certainly hadn't, and as for Philip, he only had Micky on his shoulder.

'She flew off my shoulder when we got into the vault,' said Jack, remembering. 'Kiki! KIKI! Where are you?'

There was no squawk or screech in reply. 'Blow!' said Jack. 'I'll have to go back and get her. I'll catch you up.'

He ran back. The others went on. Jack had a lantern and could easily catch them up.

They soon came to a fork. 'We take the right-hand one,' said Bill. 'This way!' The passage twisted and turned extraordinarily often, and it was impossible to know if they were going forwards, or by so much turning and twisting, were going in the opposite direction.

'One right turn – two – and this is the third,' said Philip. 'Three more right turns and we'll be at the catacomb!'

'Ooooh,' said Lucy-Ann. 'I hope it won't be long! I'm tired of these dark passages. This one is stony – I keep hitting my toes against some stone or other.'

'I wish Jack would catch us up,' said Philip, who was last. 'I keep thinking I hear him behind me – and when I turn, he isn't there. Ought we to wait for him, Bill?'

'Yes – perhaps we ought,' said Bill, and they stopped. But no Jack came. Gracious, what *could* he be doing? Lucy-Ann began to feel worried.

'Jack!' she called. 'JACK! Are you coming?'

'Better go back for him,' said Bill, puzzled. 'I hope to goodness he hasn't missed the way. He knew we had to turn right each time.'

They went back for some way – and then Bill stopped. 'I suppose *we're* right?' he said. 'I don't somehow remember this passage – it's got such a very, very low roof. I've just bumped my head against it, and I certainly didn't do that coming along!'

'Oh dear – surely we haven't missed our way – it seemed so easy – turn to the left each time going back,' groaned Dinah. 'It *must* be right, Bill.'

Bill was uneasy. He certainly did not remember this low-roofed passage. He made up his mind. 'We'll go back,' he said. 'I think we missed the last left-turn, somehow.'

So they went back – but soon they came to a dead stop! The passage grew narrower and narrower, and at last nobody could squeeze through. *That* couldn't be right, either!

'Wrong again,' said Bill, much more cheerfully than he felt. Secretly he was scared and horrified. How big was this labyrinth? How far did it go into the hill? On the map it looked a short route – but the labyrinth itself might spread for miles, intersected by mazes of passages, criss-crossing, wandering round and round.

'It's a real maze,' thought Bill. 'And probably there are only one or two direct routes across it – and we've missed the one we ought to have taken. Goodness knows how long we'll be wandering about here!'

'I wonder where Jack is,' said Lucy-Ann anxiously, as they wound in and out of the curious passages of the labyrinth. 'I do hope he's all right.'

Where *was* Jack? He had gone back to get Kiki, and had heard her talking mournfully to herself in the temple vault, perched on the spiral stone stairway that led up to the broken column. He called her.

'Kiki! What are your doing there? Why didn't you come with us, idiot? Now I've had to come all the way back for you!'

Kiki was tired of being underground. She wanted to go up into the sunshine. Also she wanted a drink, and there seemed to be no water below the ground.

'Kiki! Come along! I want to get back to the others,' called Jack.

'Send for the doctor,' said Kiki, preening her wings. 'Polly's got a cold, send for the doctor.'

'Don't be so *tiresome*,' said Jack, exasperated, and he went over to where Kiki sat. She flew up a few steps and cocked her head at Jack. He could see her plainly in the light of his lantern, and he was cross.

'You're behaving very badly,' he scolded her. 'Come down and sit on my shoulder, bad bird.'

'Naughty Polly, send for the doctor,' said Kiki, who seemed to have got the doctor on her brain. She flew up a few more steps. Jack had to follow. Blow Kiki! She *would* behave like this just when he wanted to catch up the others.

He reached the parrot and she flew higher again. Finally she disappeared.

Jack yelled up the stone steps angrily. 'You wait till I get you, you bad bird! Playing me up like this! For the last time, come down!'

A mocking voice floated down to him. 'Wipe your feet, don't sniff, pop goes the doctor!'

That was really too much for poor Jack! He climbed the spiral stone stairs as fast as he could, finding it very difficult indeed at the top, where they came up at the bottom of the broken column. At last he stood inside the column. He could see very well now, for the sun shone in through the hole in the stone. Kiki was sitting on the broken edge of the hole, preening herself in the sun. She kept a look-out for Jack, knowing he was very cross.

'Oh, I say!' she said loudly. 'Oh, I say!' She flew off the edge of the hole and disappeared from Jack's view. He could still hear her calling out, though. 'Oh, I say! Oh, I say!'

Saying all kinds of rude things about Kiki under his breath, Jack found a rough foothold in the inside of the column, and heaved himself up to the hole. He swung himself through the hole and jumped down into the sunshine, looking round for Kiki.

There she sat, not far off, in a tree of some kind, peering down the hill. 'Oh, I say!' she cried, in a shrill voice, and then went off into a cackle of laughter.

Jack ran to the tree angrily – and then he stopped. Someone was coming up the hill – someone quite familiar – astonishingly familiar! Someone with teeth that stuck out in front, and with a chin that was hardly there at all!

'*Lucian!*' said Jack, too much astonished to move. And Lucian it was. No wonder Kiki had suddenly gone off into a stream of 'Oh, I says!' Lucian stopped and stared at Jack as if he really could not believe his eyes.

'Oh, I say!' he said. 'Oh, I SAY.'

'Hallo,' said Jack feebly, and grinned. 'Er – what in the world are *you* doing here?'

'Well, I might say the same to you,' said Lucian. 'Of all the extraordinary things! Well, I never! I can't believe it!'

'How long have you been here?' asked Jack. 'Why are you here?'

'I only came today,' said Lucian. 'My uncle's here, you see – goodness knows why! I don't know when he came, exactly. Anyway, he got here and then sent for another motor-boat to come to him here on Thamis, bringing some men he wanted, and some goods – and I thought I'd come along too. The *Viking Star* is held up, as you know, and I was bored stiff. I suppose my uncle's going to get some antiques here or something.'

Jack digested all this in silence. Oho! So Mr Eppy was there too, was he? He was hot on the track after all. Jack thought quickly. What a pity he had met Lucian! Now the boy would tell Mr Eppy.

'Jack, what are *you* doing here? You really must tell me!' said Lucian insistently. 'It's *too* extraordinary. And Kiki too! Where are the others?'

'Why should they be here?' said Jack. He did not want to tell Lucian about them – or where they were – or how to get to them. That would never do. He thought hard, but he could not make any plan that seemed good – except that if he could get rid of Lucian he would pop down the broken column, get down the spiral stairway to the vaults – and warn Bill. Bill would know what to do.

How could he get rid of Lucian? Lucian wasn't likely to let him out of his sight at all. And blow, blow, blow! – there was Mr Eppy coming up the hillside now, with three other men!

Mr Eppy was too surprised to speak, when he suddenly caught sight of Jack and Kiki. He stopped dead and stared through his dark glasses. He took them off, rubbed them, and was about to put them on again when Lucian went off into one of his silly fits of giggling.

'Oh dear! Oh, I say! You can't believe your eyes, can you, Uncle! Nor could I. But it really *is* Jack – and Kiki the parrot too.'

For one wild moment Jack wondered if he should run for it – run from the surprised men, and hide somewhere, till he could manage to get back to Bill and warn him.

But there was no time. At a word from Mr Eppy the three

men with him ran up and stationed themselves behind Jack. Then Mr Eppy came up, and stood in front of him.

'And what exactly are *you* doing here?' he said, in such a peculiar, menacing tone that Jack was astonished and scared. 'Where are the others?'

'We came to explore a bit,' said Jack, at last. 'That's all. Anyone can come and explore these islands. The *Viking Star*'s engines broke down, and the passengers were told they could hire motor-boats and cruise among these islands.'

'Why did you come to *this* one?' asked Mr Eppy, still in a fierce voice. Lucian answered unexpectedly for him.

'Oh, Uncle! I expect he came hunting for the treasure you told me about.'

'Hold your tongue, idiot of a boy,' said Mr Eppy, almost spitting at poor Lucian. 'And now *you*' – he turned to Jack again, 'how dare you come trespassing on *my* island!'

'It isn't yours,' said Jack.

'It is. I have just bought it!' said Mr Eppy. 'Ah – you didn't know that – but you know *why*!'

22

Mr Eppy again

Yes, Jack did know why Mr Eppy had bought the island. He stared at the man miserably, his heart sinking. If the island was Mr Eppy's, then the treasure would be his too. Once again it looked as if the adventure had come to a sudden end.

'You know *why* I have bought it?' repeated Mr Eppy. 'Tell me, boy.'

'Well – I suppose you wanted to look for treasure on it,' said Jack, in a low tone. 'But you won't find it. You only saw two pieces of the map, remember!'

'Then you will tell me what was on the other pieces,' said Mr Eppy, in a dangerous tone.

Lucian was by now looking distinctly frightened. 'Here, I say, Uncle,' he began. 'I don't think you ought to talk to old Jack like that, you know. I mean to say . . .'

Mr Eppy took a step backwards, and slapped Lucian neatly across the mouth. His hand made a noise like a whip-crack and Kiki immediately imitated it. Then she scolded Mr Eppy. 'Naughty boy, naughty boy, nit-wit, mister-sir!'

Lucian burst into howls. He put his hand up to his mouth, and stumbled away to a corner. The three men did not turn a hair.

'That is how I treat foolish boys,' said Mr Eppy, turning back to Jack. 'Are you going to be foolish too?'

Jack said nothing. Mr Eppy put his face close to him, and hissed at him so startlingly that Jack took a sudden step back, and trod on the foot of one of the three men.

'Where are the others?' demanded Mr Eppy, with his face close to Jack's. 'They must be here too. I sent away your boat yesterday. I threatened the man with prison for daring to land people on my island!'

'Oh – so *that's* why Andros ran away,' said Jack, in disgust. 'What a foolish thing to do, Mr Eppy! Don't you know he'll come back again, probably with help?'

'He won't,' said Mr Eppy. 'He knows I shall put him in prison if he opens his mouth. No, no – I knew what I was doing. When I saw the boat there I guessed you and that big friend of yours were interfering here. I have heard of him! This is *my* island! Everything on it is mine.'

'All right, all right,' said Jack. 'But why send the boat away without us? Why not send us off too? If you had told us it was yours – and I know you do buy and sell islands – we wouldn't have trespassed without permission.'

'I wanted you here,' said Mr Eppy. 'You have the plan – have you not? You did not leave it behind you? Ah, no – you would bring such a precious thing with you!'

Jack was silent. Of course – that was why Mr Eppy had sent the boat away without them – he meant to get the plan! And as he thought of that, Jack also thought of something else – something absolutely maddening.

He had the plan on him – the re-drawn one. He had looked at it with Bill, underground, and had not given it back! Suppose Mr Eppy searched him? He would most certainly find it. How could he destroy it before he was searched?

'It was you, I suppose, who met the farmboy yesterday, and today too, and took the food I had sent for,' said Mr Eppy. 'A most extraordinary thing to do! I am not pleased with things like that – they make trouble for me.'

'Well – goodness gracious – how in the world were we to know that the food was for *you*, when we didn't know you were here, and couldn't understand a word the boy said?' cried Jack. 'Your boat wasn't in the creek. We didn't know anyone else was visiting the island.'

'I came to the other creek,' said Mr Eppy. 'But I shall not tell you where it is. No – not till you tell me where the others are – and then, when I have the plan, maybe, I say *maybe*, I will set you free from this island – all of you, who have come to interfere with my plans.'

'It's ridiculous,' said Jack, in disgust. 'We haven't come to interfere. Bill would be the first to say we'd all go, if he knew you had bought the island.'

'Where are the others?' barked Mr Eppy suddenly.

'Somewhere about,' said Jack indifferently. 'Why don't you look for them? And don't shout at me like that. I'm not Lucian.'

'Has this Bill the plan?' asked Mr Eppy, his voice getting sharper.

'Why don't you find him and ask him?' said Jack. 'Call him! See if he answers! If I'm here why shouldn't he be?'

Mr Eppy gave Jack such a sudden box on the ears that the

boy had no time to dodge it. Kiki almost got the slap too, but rose into the air in time. She pounced down on the angry man, and gave his ear such a vicious nip that he yelled in agony.

Jack suppressed a smile. Serve him right! Good old Kiki! The parrot sailed to a high branch and perched there, scolding hard.

'Bad boy, naughty boy! Gr-r-r-r-r! Go to bed, go to the doctor, go to the weasel!'

Mr Eppy said a sharp sentence to the three silent men behind Jack. In a trice they had him pinioned by the arms, laid flat on the ground. Then with a practised hand one of the men searched him. He drew out the plan at once.

Mr Eppy took it. Jack could imagine how his eyes gleamed behind the dark glasses!

'And so! *You* had it,' said Mr Eppy. He unfolded it, and saw that it was not the original plan. He looked at it closely. 'What is this? It is drawn by someone who has seen the other – drawn for you – it has been deciphered and translated?'

'Find out for yourself,' said Jack, still lying on the ground. He expected a kick or a blow, but Mr Eppy was so intent on the re-drawn plan that he did nothing. Jack remembered that the man had seen only two parts of the map before – enough to tell him which island to come to, and that there was treasure there – he must now be studying the other parts with eager interest.

' "Two-Fingers",' he muttered. Then he looked at Jack. ' "Two-Fingers",' he said. 'That showed on the piece I saw before – and I found the two-fingered rock. But there is no way through.'

'Oh – so that was your old battery we found in the hole, I suppose,' said Jack, sitting up. 'We wondered whose it was.'

Mr Eppy did not answer, or seem even to hear him. He was studying the map again. He was muttering something to himself. ' "Two-Fingers" – "Goddess" – "Tomb" – "Bird' – "Bell" – "Labyrinth" – "Catacomb" – that is the route they took. The whole of it!' Then he began to mutter in Greek, and Jack could no longer understand him.

Lucian was still holding his hand up to his mouth, and his face was tear-stained. Kiki was down by him, pecking at his shoe-lace. 'Oh, I say!' she was repeating. 'Oh, I say!'

'Have you found the way at all?' demanded Mr Eppy.

'What way?' said Jack innocently.

'Pah! The way to the treasure-chamber!' spat Mr Eppy.

'Pah!' spat Kiki at once. 'Pah!'

'I'll wring that bird's neck,' threatened Mr Eppy. 'Answer my question, boy.'

'No. We haven't found the way,' said Jack, truthfully, feeling quite glad that they had gone the wrong way and not the right one, in their following of the route! All the same, he wondered if Bill and the others had managed to find the way by now, without him. But surely they would have waited for him? They must be wondering what in the wide world had happened to him! Jack hoped fervently that they would not all come climbing out of the broken column. If they did they would be taken prisoner by Mr Eppy and his men, and Bill would find it extremely difficult to keep his secret. In fact it would not be any good his trying, now Mr Eppy had the map.

'Once Mr Eppy knows the way down the broken column the treasure is as good as his!' thought Jack. 'What a good thing Lucian didn't spot me getting out of it! I only hope the others don't make a sudden appearance. I'm sure they will soon!'

But they did not, for the very simple reason that they had lost their way in the labyrinth! They were still wandering about the passages, getting more and more anxious. They had lost Jack, and had lost their way too.

'This awful maze!' said Dinah, in despair. 'Look, Bill – I'm *sure* we've been in *this* passage before. I remember the way this horrid piece juts out – it knocked my elbow last time, and this time too. I'm sure it's the same.'

'We're going round and round and in and out and goodness knows whether we're near the vault or near the catacomb!' groaned Philip.

Bill was very worried. He stood and thought for a moment, trying in vain to get a sense of direction. It was so difficult underground! He set off again, and soon came to a fork.

'Well,' he said, 'I vote we go right here. It may be one of the places where we're supposed to go right. So we'll hope for the best! Come on!'

They trailed after him, Lucy-Ann getting very weary of it all. They reached another fork, and turned right once more. Then they came to where the passages branched into four ways. Again they took the right-hand fork. Bill was feeling a little more cheerful. Perhaps they were on the right road now. They no longer came to blind ends and had to turn back as they had been doing before. Ah – here was another fork. Well, to the right again!

The passage ended abruptly in a downward flight of steep steps. Bill swung the lantern up high and peered down the steps.

'We've come the right way at last!' he said. 'These must be the catacombs – underground caves and passages all joined together that were once used as hiding-places, burial-places and goodness knows what!'

'Oh, Bill – have we really come right?' said Lucy-Ann, in joy. 'I thought we were lost for ever and ever! Do we go down the steps?'

'We do,' said Bill. 'I'll go first. Come on.'

Down he went and the others followed carefully. There were about thirty steps, and it seemed to the children as if they really were going down into the bowels of the earth. At the end was a strange place, stretching out into the darkness. Lining its walls were stone shelves, rocky niches, hollowed-out places that looked as if they had been used for storing things in, or for people to hide in and sleep.

They came to a hole in the floor of this extraordinary place. Bill shone his torch down it. It was a shaft leading downwards, and there were footholds in the rock. 'I'm going down,' said Bill. 'I've got a hunch this is the place!'

He disappeared down the shaft with his torch, and soon his voice came back, excited and loud.

'This is it! This is the treasure-chamber – the TREASURE'S STILL HERE!'

23

Treasure – and trickery!

The three children and Micky almost fell down the shaft, they were in such a hurry. They handed Bill the lantern, and, by the light of that and of Bill's torch, they looked in wonder round the curious treasure-chamber.

It was perfectly round, as if it had been hollowed by machinery from the rock – though actually, of course, it had been done by hand. Thrown higgledy-piggledy into this enormous round cave – perhaps flung down the shaft in a hurry – were mouldering barrels and boxes and brass-bound chests.

Bursting out of them was a perfect medley of strange and amazing goods – chains of some kind of metal, set with precious stones – brooches, armlets, anklets – combs for the hair made probably of gold, and set with tiny stones – beautiful vases of metal, perhaps gold, perhaps brass, but too tarnished to tell. Beautifully wrought daggers lay in one corner, and what looked like armour of some kind in another – all fallen from the mouldered chests and boxes, or possibly burst out of these when they were thrown down the shaft so long, long ago.

There were broken models of figures and articles that

looked like drinking-cups and bowls, and yet other things whose use the children simply could not guess.

'Well, well, well,' said Bill, as thrilled as the children. 'What a treasure hoard! Andra's treasure, maybe – we shall never really know. But whether it is or not, it is certainly worth half a small kingdom, because of its priceless age! Look at this dagger – it must be hundreds of years old – perfectly preserved down in this dry shaft. I should think only our museums can show things like this now.'

'Bill! It's super!' said Philip, his eyes shining in the lantern-light, as he picked up treasure after treasure, everything beautifully modelled and carved.

'I suppose the things like robes and cloaks and shoes have all mouldered away,' said Dinah regretfully. 'I'd like to have dressed up in those. Oh, Bill – we've really found it!'

'I wish Jack was here,' said Lucy-Ann, with tears in her voice. 'He would have loved it so. Where *can* he be, Bill?'

'I should think he probably took a long time finding Kiki and decided he wouldn't risk coming after us by himself,' said Bill. 'I'll tell you what we'll do – we'll go back and find him, and then we'll bring him here to have a look at the greatest treasure in the world!'

'But shall we be able to find our way back?' said Philip doubtfully. Bill was very doubtful about this too. Also his torch was giving out and he was sure the oil in the lantern would not last much longer. It was very necessary to find their way back, pick up Jack, and also – have something to eat! Excitement had kept them going, but now all of them were feeling very hungry indeed.

'If we manage to get back quickly and find Jack we'll all have a meal,' said Bill. 'Then if Jack's lantern is all right we'll use that to come here again – but this time we'll be sensible and mark the walls as we go along! Actually I think we could find our way here easily enough if we concentrated on going right, right, right, all the time. We must have missed one of the right turns.'

They climbed back up the shaft, leaving the extraordinary hiding-place behind them – what a strange treasure-chamber! How old was it? Had anyone else seen it since it had been put there?

They found themselves in the catacombs again. It was easy to get back to the steep flight of steps. Up they went into the labyrinth, and began to make their way through the passages. 'Now we must keep left, left, left,' said Bill. 'Then we shall be quite all right.'

But no – once more they missed their way and began the everlasting wandering round and round and in and out of the maddening underground maze. Lucy-Ann was almost crying with weariness.

All this time Micky had been quietly on Philip's shoulder, clinging to his head at awkward places. He too was tired of the curious dark walk that everyone was taking. He wanted to be out in the open, he wanted something to eat and even more he wanted something to drink.

He suddenly leapt off Philip's shoulder and landed on the floor of the passage. He began to scud along by himself. Philip called out to him.

'Hey, Micky, Micky! Come here! We don't want to lose you too!'

Micky slowed down, but he still went on. Bill called to Philip. 'Leave him, Philip! I believe he knows the way out. Animals have a good sense of direction, you know – a kind of homing instinct. Maybe he can take us straight to the broken column!'

Micky did not know what Bill was saying, but if he had known he would most certainly have agreed. Of course he knew the way! Of course his instinct told him exactly the right way to go – left, left, left, without any silly mistake such as the humans had made. Why, he, Micky, could have taken them straight back to the vaults at any time if only they had told him they wanted to go!

'Well, here we are in the vault again!' said Philip thankfully, when, in a very short space of time indeed, they came out into the enormous temple vault. Lucy-Ann was so thankful that she began to cry very quietly to herself. Nobody could see. She wiped away a few tears, then stopped her crying, feeling rather ashamed. She slipped her hand into Bill's. He squeezed it comfortingly.

'We're all right now,' he said. 'We've found the treasure and found our way back – now we'll find Jack! As we haven't heard or seen anything of him, I imagine he's out in the open, waiting for us!'

Jack was still in the courtyard with Mr Eppy, Lucian and the three men. It was some time later, and the boy had not been having at all a nice time. Mr Eppy had been on and on at him, trying to find out where the others were, and whether Jack knew the route to the treasure.

He had threatened Jack, had boxed his ears several times, and had boxed Lucian's too, when he had tried to come to Jack's help. Jack had been surprised at Lucian for that. He had always thought him such a feeble boy. He looked at Lucian gratefully.

'Thanks, Lucian,' he said. 'But don't interfere, old chap – you'll only get hurt. I can look after myself. Your uncle will get into trouble for ill-treating me, don't you worry!'

Jack had begun to feel extremely hungry. So had the others, presumably, because Mr Eppy changed the subject suddenly and began asking Jack where they had put the food they had got from the farm-boy. Jack remembered perfectly well where it was – inside the broken column, on the stone ledge at the base of it, where the stone stairway began – but how could he say that? It would give the secret away completely!

So he sat silent, shaking his head to Mr Eppy's exasperated questions, getting more and more hungry – and getting really rather anxious about the others too. Where in the world could they be? The sun was going down already, and soon it would be night.

And then Kiki began to talk excitedly. She left Jack and flew to the broken edge of the hole in the column. She peered down it. Jack bit his lip. Oh, Kiki, Kiki, don't give the game away!

Kiki had heard the others coming. She had heard Bill's deep voice, as he came up the spiral stairway, she had heard Lucy-Ann's high voice, just behind. She had gone to welcome them.

'Kiki!' called Jack. 'Come here.'

'Shut the door, shut the door, wipe your feet, beg your pardon!' shouted Kiki excitedly, her head inside the column. And then an answering call came from inside too.

'Hallo, Kiki, old bird! So there you are! Where's Jack?' It was Bill's cheery deep voice.

Mr Eppy sprang to attention at once. He gave a short sharp order to his three men, and they ran to the column, waiting. Jack gave a yell.

'Look out, Bill! Danger! Look out!'

There was silence from inside the column. Then Bill's voice came up again.

'What's up?'

'Mr Epp . . .' began Jack, and was silenced as Mr Eppy placed a heavy and very rough hand over his mouth.

Bill shouted again. 'What's up?' As he got no reply, he appeared at the hole in the column, and swung himself astride the edge. The men were at the other side, hidden, waiting to spring.

Bill saw Mr Eppy apparently holding down Jack, and he leapt off the broken edge of the hole in the column at once. The three men sprang on him and bore him to the ground.

One sat on his head so that he could not shout. Jack squirmed under Mr Eppy's hand, kicking and trying to bite, but the man was very strong indeed.

Then up the column came Philip, wondering what had happened to Bill, and when he saw him being well and truly sat on he sprang to his rescue. Mr Eppy shouted a few words and the men released Bill. He sat up at once, feeling his nose, and wondering if any of his teeth were loose!

'What on earth is all this?' he began. But before he could go on, a call from inside the column came to him. It was Lucy-Ann.

'Bill! Oh, Bill! What's happened? Can we come out?'

Bill considered. 'I'm going to help the girls out,' he said to Mr Eppy, who nodded, and very soon both girls, and a very scared Micky, were standing in the old courtyard with Philip, Jack and Bill.

'What's happened?' said Lucy-Ann. 'Oh, I'm so glad to see you, Jack. I was dreadfully worried about you. Gracious, there's *Lucian*!'

'Oh, I say!' said Lucian, trying to put a brave face on things. 'Fancy meeting *you* here!'

Mr Eppy said something snappish in Greek and poor Lucian collapsed again. Then Mr Eppy turned to Bill, who was now eyeing him with a very sinister look indeed. Bill was extremely angry, and his injured nose was swelling rapidly.

'Look here, Eppy, or whatever your name is,' he said, 'you're going to run into serious trouble. You can't roam round with a posse of shady fellows like these, acting like gangsters. What are you doing here, anyway?'

'It's *my* island,' said Mr Eppy, with a note of triumph in his voice. 'I've bought it. You can clear off – *when* I've found the way to the treasure with your help. Otherwise I shall have you arrested for trespassing and for trying to steal what is mine.'

'You're mad,' said Bill, in scorn. 'Absolutely crazy. I don't believe a word of it! You only heard of the island a day or two ago – you haven't had time to buy it. That's a wonderful tale – but you won't get *me* to believe it. Now, you keep your hands off all of us, and behave yourself – or you're the one that's going to land in prison and pretty quick too!'

Mr Eppy gave an order – and Bill was pounced on again

by the three men. He was down on the ground in no time, and one of the men was tying his wrists and ankles together. Bill was strong, but his strength was no use against the three. Mr Eppy had Jack by the wrists so that he could not go to Bill's help, and as soon as Philip ran to help, he was struck by one of the men and sent spinning. Lucy-Ann began to cry with fright.

Lucian did nothing. He was trembling in a corner. Kiki and Micky were high up in a tree, watching in amazement. What was all this to-do? Kiki swooped down and gave Mr Eppy a nip on the ear again, and he nearly let Jack go, the pain was so sharp.

After Bill was tied up, the boys were tied too. 'Don't touch the girls,' threatened Bill. 'If you do you'll get more then you bargain for when we get out of here!'

It was no use. Dinah and Lucy-Ann were also tied. Dinah was angry and mutinous, and Lucy-Ann was very frightened.

'And now,' said Mr Eppy, 'now *we* go to find the Andra treasure. *My* treasure! You had only the plan – I have the island, and I shall soon own the treasure! Thank you for showing me the way down!'

He went inside the column, and the three men followed him. Lucian was beckoned over and made to go down just behind his uncle. He looked very frightened.

'Well!' said Bill. 'Of all the scoundrels! Can we possibly get free whilst they're down there? It's our only chance!'

24

Prisoners!

Everyone waited till the last man had disappeared down the column. Then Bill spoke.

'Well, I'm blessed if I'll ever look at a treasure map again, or listen to anything you kids have to tell me! It's fatal. We plunge into trouble immediately. Jack – Philip – can you possibly loosen your ropes?'

'I've been trying,' said Philip, and Jack said the same. 'Those beasts know how to tie knots all right. The rope is biting into my ankles like anything, and I can hardly move my hands.'

All of them had their hands tied behind their backs, and it was really impossible to get free. Bill rolled himself over and over to the girls. He was very sorry for poor Lucy-Ann. Dinah was as tough as a boy – but Lucy-Ann could not help being scared.

'Lucy-Ann, don't be upset,' said Bill, ending up just by her. 'We'll think of some wonderful way to get even with these rogues.'

'I hope they'll get lost in the labyrinth,' said Jack fiercely, still struggling with the rope that tied his wrists.

'They probably will,' said Bill. 'In any case they'll be a long time gone. We must somehow get free before they come back.'

'The first thing *I* do when I get free is to hop inside the column and get some of the food we put down there,' said Jack. 'That's if the brutes have left us any! I bet they've taken most of it with them.'

Bill privately thought they probably would have taken it, but he didn't say so. He gave up trying to loosen the rope round his wrists. It only made it cut into his flesh unbearably.

He looked round to see if there was a sharp stone he could perhaps rub his ropes on. He saw one and rolled over to it. But as his hands were behind his back he could not see what he was doing, and cut his fingers on the stone till they bled. He gave it up.

Kiki was up in the tree, muttering to herself. All the shouting and struggling had frightened her. She cocked her head down at Jack and decided it was safe to go to him. She flew down and landed on his middle.

'Send for the doctor,' she said, her head on one side. 'Send for the doctor, mistersir.'

'Good idea, Kiki,' said Jack, with an attempt at a grin. 'Tell him to come quickly! Telephone him at once!'

Kiki at once gave an imitation of a telephone bell ringing. It sounded queer in that old ruined courtyard! Even Lucy-Ann gave a little laugh.

'Hallo, hallo!' said Kiki, pleased at the attention she was getting. 'Hallo!'

'She's telephoning now!' grinned Jack. 'Good old Kiki. Got the doctor yet? Tell him we're all suffering from a nasty attack of Eppy-itis!'

Micky leapt down from the tree to join in the fun. He too had been badly scared, but now that everyone was talking and laughing, and the noisy men had gone, he felt safer. He landed on Philip, and tried to cuddle on to his shoulder. Philip was sitting up, his hands tied behind him.

'Sorry I can't stroke you, old thing, and make a bit of fuss of you after your scare,' said the boy. 'But my hands are tied! Yes, that's right – go and look for them. I've still got them – but they're behind me!'

Micky badly wanted to be nursed, but he could not find any arms to cuddle into! He went behind Philip to investigate. What had the boy done with his hands and arms? Ah – there they were behind him! Micky pulled at Philip's hands with his tiny paws. He wanted to be stroked and petted.

'Sorry, Micky – nothing doing,' said Philip. He grinned round at the others. 'Micky can't understand why I don't use my hands to pet him! He's pulling at them!'

Micky had discovered the rope that bound Philip's wrists together. He was puzzled. What had Philip done with this rope? Why was it so tightly round the boy's hands? Micky tugged at the rope, and pulled at the knot.

Philip sat very still. 'That's right, Micky,' he said, in a caressing voice. 'That's right! You tackle those knots. Then I can pet you all you like!'

Everyone pricked up their ears at once. They looked eagerly at Philip. 'I say, Philip – is Micky – can Micky – do anything?'

'Don't know,' said Philip. 'He's fiddling about like anything. Go it, Micky. Pull those knots undone!'

But Micky couldn't. His tiny paws were not strong enough to undo the tightly tied knots of the rope. He gave it up. But he thought of something else!

He put his mouth down to the rope, and tried to gnaw it with his teeth!

'What *are* you doing, Micky?' cried Philip, feeling the wet little mouth against his wrist. 'Gosh, Bill, the clever little thing is trying to *gnaw* through the rope now!'

Everyone watched Philip intently. His face showed clearly all he was thinking. 'That's it, Micky – bite away!' he said. 'Good little monkey! No, go away, Kiki – don't interfere with Micky!'

Kiki had gone to Philip and was now getting behind him to see what Micky was up to. She watched him.

'One, two, three, GO!' she said, for all the world as if she was encouraging him.

'Come here, Kiki. Leave Micky alone in his good work,' ordered Jack, and Kiki came obediently.

'How's Micky getting on?' asked Bill.

'Fine, I think,' answered Philip, trying his hands to see if they felt any looser. 'I think the rope doesn't feel quite so tight. Go it, Micky.'

It was a long job, but Micky was patient and perservering. Once he knew that he was doing what Philip wanted, he went on and on. Bill marvelled at the way Philip understood animals and animals understood him. Any creature would do anything in the world for Philip!

'They're getting loose!' exclaimed Philip. 'Go on, Micky – just a bite or two more!'

And, sure enough, after another bout of patient gnawing, the rope snapped when Philip pulled on it. He brought his freed hands round to the front of him, groaning.

'My word – they're painful! Thanks, Micky, old thing – you did a very good job of work. Wait till my hands feel a bit better and I'll pat you from head to tail!'

The rope was still dangling from one of his wrists, the knots in it tied as tightly as ever. Philip picked it off with the other hand. He opened and shut his numb fingers, and then proceeded to pet the little monkey, who, delighted to be fussed, snuggled into Philip's arms with contented little grunts.

Nobody hurried Philip. Nobody begged him to be quick and undo *their* bonds. Every one knew that it was right for Micky to have his reward.

'Now, that's enough, old fellow,' said Philip, at last. 'I must see to the others. You come and help!'

Philip put Micky on to his usual place on his shoulder. He felt in his pocket for a knife. His hands still felt queer and stiff, but they were rapidly getting more life into them. He brought out his knife and clicked it open.

He cut the rope round his ankles, and then he tried to stand up. His feet felt numb, for his ankles had been tied very tightly. But he was soon able to walk steadily. He went straight over to the girls.

He cut their bonds with his knife and Lucy-Ann gave a groan of thankfulness. 'Oh, Philip – thank you! That's better. Dinah, are your hands all right?'

'Bit stiff and numb,' said Dinah, rubbing them together. 'Wouldn't I like to tie up Mr Eppy! And wouldn't I make the ropes tight! The brute! He must be mad.'

Soon everyone was free. Bill found it hardest to stand because his ankles had been tied very viciously, and so had his hands. It took him some time to get the blood flowing freely in them, and it was a very painful process at first.

Everyone made a fuss of Micky, and the little monkey enjoyed it all thoroughly, chattering softly. Jack kept an eye on Kiki. She was jealous, and was looking out for a chance to nip Micky's long tail.

'I'll tie *you* up if you try any tricks, Kiki,' warned Jack, and tapped her smartly on the beak. She put her head under her wing, muttering to herself. 'Poor Polly, poor Polly, don't sniff, use your hanky!'

'She's irrepressible!' said Bill, still massaging his wrists. 'Well, I feel better now. What about some food, lads? *If* it's still there, of course!'

Jack was half-way to the column already. He had to get Philip to give him a good leg-up, because his ankles still felt weak. Up he went, and dropped down inside. He looked about for the food. It was dark inside the column now, for the sun had gone. He felt about and to his delight found some bread, and what felt like cheese. He called to Philip.

'Look out, Philip. I'm throwing the food out.'

Philip waited. Out came bread, cheese and a packet of some kind of meat. 'Wait a bit – here's some more bread,' shouted Jack, and out it came.

Jack climbed out again, grinning. 'They must have been in such a hurry to get to the treasure that they didn't even stop for a snack!' he said. 'They *must* have seen the food there.'

'Bill, is it safe to sit and have a meal?' asked Lucy-Ann anxiously.

'Quite safe,' said Bill. 'I'm going to sit here by the column and I shall be very, very sorry for anyone who tries to get out whilst *I'm* here!'

25

What happened in the night

It was getting quite dark now. The sun had gone a long time ago, and the children could hardly see one another as they sat together in the courtyard, munching hungrily.

'I've never known bread and cheese to taste so lovely,' said Dinah. 'Actually I didn't think this cheese was terribly nice yesterday – sort of sweetish – but today it's heavenly.'

'Only because you're so hungry,' said Jack, giving Kiki some of his. 'It's goat-milk cheese, isn't it, Bill? I say, look at Micky stuffing himself.'

'Pop goes Micky,' remarked Kiki, coming in at the right moment as usual. 'One, two, three, POP!'

'Idiot,' said Jack. 'Well, Bill – what are you thinking about?'

'Quite a lot of things,' said Bill soberly. 'We've had an extraordinary day. And I'm just planning what to do about it.'

'Wasn't that treasure wonderful!' said Lucy-Ann, her eyes shining.

Jack had, of course, heard all about their adventures underground by now, and was very envious because he was the only one who had not seen the treasure-chamber, with its remarkable collection of riches. He had listened with amazement, and had wished and wished he had been with the others.

'What are your plans, Bill?' asked Philip, feeling that he could think sensibly again, now that he was free and had had a good meal. 'I suppose we can't do much tonight.'

'No, we can't,' said Bill. 'That's quite certain. We've been through enough today without taking on any more adventures. Besides, the girls are nearly asleep, poor things!'

So they were. Excitement and exercise had completely tired them out. Lucy-Ann lay cuddled against Dinah, her eyes closed.

'Well, I'm pretty sleepy myself,' said Jack. He yawned loudly. 'I wouldn't mind a nice long snooze!'

'Anyway, Bill – what *could* we do, even if we *wanted* to do anything tonight?' asked Philip, beginning to yawn too. 'We can't escape! Andros won't come back, that's obvious, if Mr Eppy has threatened him with prison. After all, he's only an ordinary boatman! I expect Mr Eppy gave him plenty of money too, to make up for us not having paid him.'

'Yes – money and threats combined would soon send Andros away,' said Bill. 'In any case, Andros would know, of course, that Mr Eppy had his own boat here – possibly two boats, as he sent for more men and goods. So we shouldn't be absolutely stranded, as Mr Eppy could always bring us back.'

'Gosh, yes – his boats must be *some*where, mustn't they?' said Philip, waking up considerably. 'We've only got to find them, Bill – and we're all right! Hadn't we better snoop round now, before the others come back from underground?'

'No. Nothing more tonight,' said Bill firmly. 'I've already planned to do that tomorrow. When we find Mr Eppy's boat or boats, we'll be all right, I hope. Now listen – I'm going to be on guard for the first four hours, and, after that, you, Jack, and then you, Philip, will have a two-hour watch, and by that time it will be morning.'

'What are we going to watch for? Are we to wait for dear old Eppy to pop his head out and say "Hallo, there"?' asked Jack, with a grin.

'Exactly,' said Bill. He had now lighted one of the lanterns, and it gave a weird light to the scene. 'You two boys are tired – you won't be any good at watching till you've had a sleep. You can have your turn when I wake you.'

'Right,' said Jack, settling himself against Philip. 'We'll let the big tough guy watch first. As a matter of fact, I believe

I'm asleep already.'

'What will you do if the others appear?' asked Philip, with interest. 'Knock them on the head as they come out of the hole?'

'Probably,' said Bill, and he lighted his pipe. 'You don't need to worry about that. Good night! I'll wake you in four hours' time.'

The two boys were asleep almost before he had finished his sentence. The smell of Bill's tobacco wandered round the courtyard. Micky smelt it in his sleep and cuddled closer to Philip. He did not like the smell of tobacco. Kiki was standing on Jack, her head under her wing. The girls were absolutely still, sleeping soundly although they had such an uncomfortable resting-place.

Bill put out the lantern. Only the glow of his pipe shone in the courtyard now and again. He was thinking hard. He went over all the happenings of the last two days. He considered Mr Eppy's assertion that the island was his. He puzzled over the whereabouts of the other creek, where probably Mr Eppy's boat or boats were. He wondered how the little party underground was getting on. He hoped fervently they were well and truly lost in the labyrinth.

He made his plans for the next day. They would find the boats. That would be the first thing. Where on earth would the creek be – the second creek that Andros had spoken about? Perhaps it would . . .

A noise stopped his thoughts at once. He put down his pipe and stood up, a silent figure close beside the broken column. He listened. The noise had come from underground, he was sure of that.

Well– if it was the company coming back, he was in for a wakeful night! Bill picked up a large piece of wood that he had had his eye on all the evening. It had probably been part of a door or window-frame – now it would make a very good weapon!

He stood by the column, listening intently. A scraping

noise came up to him – someone was climbing up the last part of the stone spiral. The noise stopped. The Someone was evidently in the column now. What was he doing? He appeared to be feeling about for something. 'The food!' thought Bill, with a grin. 'Well – it's gone!'

A little whimper came up to him, and then a shaking voice said, in a low tone, 'Jack! Philip! Are you there?'

'Why – it's Lucian!' thought Bill, in astonishment. 'Well – he can't be alone!'

He listened again. The whimpering began once more, rather like a miserable dog's. There was no sound of any other voice, or of anyone else coming up the stairway. Bill made up his mind. He leapt up to the broken edge of the hole in the column, switched on his torch and looked down.

Lucian was standing below him, his terrified face looking up, dirt caked on his cheeks. He put up his hand as if he expected Bill to aim a blow down at him.

'Lucian!' said Bill. 'What are you doing here? Where are the others?'

'I don't know,' moaned poor Lucian. 'They only took me down as far as that vault place at the bottom of these steps. They wouldn't let me go any further with them. They told me to stay there till they came back, and not stir. My uncle said he'd half kill me if he didn't find me waiting for them when they came back.'

'Didn't they come back, then?' said Bill, keeping his torch flashed on to Lucian's face.

'No. And it's hours ago,' cried Lucian. 'I don't know what's happened to them. And I'm so hungry and cold and tired – and I'm frightened down there, too. I didn't dare to have my torch on all the time in case the battery gave out.'

Bill believed the frightened boy. 'Come on up,' he said. 'Here – take my hand and jump. Go on, Lucian, *jump*! Surely you can leap up here.'

Poor Lucian couldn't. In the end Bill had to get into the column and shove him up to the hole. Even then Lucian looked about to fall off. He was in a terrible state of nerves.

At last he was safely down in the courtyard, and Bill gave him some bread and cheese. He fell on it as if he hadn't eaten for a month.

A thought suddenly struck him. 'I say – how did you get free? I mean – weren't you all tied up?'

'Yes,' said Bill grimly. 'We were. But fortunately for you, we got free – yes, all of us – the boys are asleep over there – and the girls near by. No, don't wake them – they're tired out. If we'd all been tied up still, you would have stayed in that column all night. Not a nice thought, Lucian!'

'No,' said Lucian, and shivered. 'I wish I hadn't come to this horrible island. What's going to happen? Are you going down to look for my uncle? He must be completely lost, you know.'

'He can stay lost, as far as I'm concerned,' said Bill. 'In fact, it will do him good. Your uncle is not a man I've any kindly feelings for, at present.'

'No. He's horrible,' agreed Lucian. 'Once he'd found the treasure he'd planned to leave you stranded here, all of you, and go off by himself to get more men to come and remove it.'

'Nice, thoughtful fellow,' said Bill. 'Well, young man, you'd better get some sleep. And tomorrow you're going to help us, to make up for the misdeeds of your nasty-minded uncle.'

'Oh – I'd be very glad to help you,' said Lucian, at once. 'I would really. I'm on your side, you know that.'

'Yes, I expect you are,' said Bill. 'You'll have to be from now on, anyway!'

'How can I help you tomorrow?' asked Lucian.

'By taking us to the creek where your uncle's boats are,' said Bill, at once.

'Oh, of course – if only I can remember where it is,' said Lucian anxiously. 'I'm not awfully good at remembering routes, you know. But I dare say I'll remember that.'

'You'll have to,' said Bill grimly. 'And now, go to sleep. No – don't go over to the boys. Just stay where you are. And mind – if your precious uncle arrives during the night, there's to be no warning to him from *you*. Otherwise some unpleasant things will happen to you.'

'Oh, I tell you I'm on *your* side now,' protested Lucian, and settled himself as comfortably as he could. 'Good night, sir. See you in the morning!'

26

Next morning

In four hours' time Bill awoke Jack. In a few sentences he told the surprised boy about the arrival of Lucian. 'He keeps saying he's on our side now, but you never know with a nit-wit like that,' he warned Jack. 'So keep your eye on him. And if you hear the *slightest* sound from underground, prod me awake at once, Jack!'

'Right, Bill,' said Jack, fresh from his sound sleep. 'I say – they've been a long time underground, haven't they? They *must* be lost!'

'I sincerely hope so,' said Bill. 'I don't imagine they will be lost for ever, however, desirable as that might be – that labyrinth isn't a frightfully big one. Well, I'm going to sleep, Jack. Keep your wits about you!'

Jack was still sleepy. He was afraid he might find it difficult to keep awake, so he lighted the lantern, and walked about round the courtyard. He shone the light on to Lucian. He was so fast asleep that he did not even stir. Philip was soundly off too, and as for the girls, not an inch of their faces was to be seen, they were cuddled up so closely to one another.

Kiki accompanied Jack on his rambles round the courtyard. She knew she had to be quiet, so she whispered all the time. She wasn't very good at whispering, and tickled Jack's ear till he could not bear it any longer. He took her off his shoulder, and made her perch on one of his arms.

His two hours went by without anything happening at all. He awoke Philip. It took a long time because the boy was so very sound asleep. As fast as Jack rolled him over to wake him, he rolled back again, his eyes still shut.

Jack took off one of Philip's shoes and tickled the soles of his feet. That woke him up all right! Philip sat straight up and glared round at the lantern Jack held.

'What are you . . .' he began, in a loud voice, and Jack shushed him at once.

'Sh, idiot! You'll wake the rest! Sorry about tickling your feet, but I simply *couldn't* wake you! It's your turn to watch now.'

Philip put on his shoe, saying something uncomplimentary to Jack under his breath. Micky woke up too, and looked in astonishment round the yard. He had forgotten where he was.

Jack told Philip in whispers about Lucian's arrival. Philip was amused. 'So Lucian is on our side now!' he said. 'Well – he's not a bad sort really – only he's *such* a nit-wit! Poor Lucian – I guess he was scared out of his life! Right, I'll keep my eye on him – though honestly he wouldn't have the nerve to do anything he shouldn't. And if our dear Mr Eppy pops his head up out of the column, I shall have the greatest pleasure in conking him good and hard.'

Jack grinned. 'Well I'm off to sleep again,' he said. 'Good hunting, Philip!'

Philip's eyes persisted in closing, as he sat there keeping watch. He got up and walked about, as Jack had done. It would be an unforgivable thing to sleep whilst he was on guard. Quite unthinkable. He wondered what the time was, and glanced at his watch. The hands were phosphorescent, and showed him the time. Five o'clock – or getting on that way. He looked at the eastern sky. It was already silvering with the dawn.

It was almost at the end of Philip's two hours that the noise came. By this time the sun was up and the sunlight was on everything, clean and new and beautiful. Philip was enjoying the warmth of the first slanting beams, when he heard the noise.

He pricked up his ears, and Micky began to chatter softly. 'Sh!' said Philip. 'I want to listen.' Micky was silent at once.

The noise came again – the scraping of boots on stone. 'They're coming!' thought Philip, and he ran to where Bill was sleeping, face down in the grass that grew over the yard. 'Bill! Wake up! They're coming!'

Bill woke up at once. He sprang to his feet, all sleep gone in an instant. Jack awoke too, and so did the girls. Only Lucian slept on, but nobody took any notice of him.

Bill ran to the column. He took the big wedge of wood from Philip. 'Stand back,' he said to the girls. 'I don't expect for a moment I'll have much trouble, but you never know. I'm not standing any nonsense from Eppy and Co.'

He stationed himself just under the broken edge of the hole in the column. He listened. Voices came up to him. Someone was evidently now standing inside the column, having come up to the top of the spiral stairway. Bill heard what was said, but couldn't understand it.

However, he recognized Mr Eppy's voice, and took a firm hold of his piece of wood! Mr Eppy stood still for a moment and listened to someone shouting up to him from the stairway below. Then he called up in a low voice.

'Lucian? Are you there, Lucian?'

Lucian *was* there – but he was fast asleep, so of course he didn't answer. Mr Eppy called again softly. 'Lucian!'

Bill answered, in a grim voice. '*I'm* here – Bill Cunningham – and I'm waiting for you, Mr Eppy! The moment you try to get out of there I shall knock you back – with this weapon!' Bill banged his wedge of wood down on the column with such a noise that everyone jumped violently, and Lucian woke up.

There was a dead silence inside the column. Then there was a scraping noise, as if someone else was coming up the stairway. Voices spoke together, very low.

'How did you get free?' came Mr Eppy's voice again. 'Did Lucian free you? He's not here.'

'No, he didn't,' said Bill.

The voices spoke together again. Then Mr Eppy called up urgently.

'Mr Cunningham! My men tell me that they have just found poor Lucian down here – badly hurt. He needs help. Let us come up at once.'

This was a most astonishing piece of news, especially to Lucian, whose mouth fell open in amazement. He was about to speak when Jack nudged him to be quiet. Bill was handling this!

'Sorry to hear that, Mr Eppy,' said Bill. 'Hand him up and we'll look after him. But you remain below. That's definite.'

Another conference took place in low voices. Then Mr Eppy spoke again.

'I must ask you to allow us to come up with the boy. He is seriously hurt. I am very distressed about him.'

Lucian's face was a study. Dinah almost giggled as she watched him. Bill answered at once.

'Nothing doing. Nobody comes up except – er – Lucian. Hand him over.'

As Lucian was even then sitting on the grass in the courtyard it was quite impossible for Mr Eppy to hand him over. Lucy-Ann whispered to Dinah, 'Isn't he a terrible story-teller!'

Bill began banging idly on the column with his wedge. 'Well, you don't seem to want to part with Lucian,' he called. 'Now I warn you – if anyone appears at the hole in this column they're for it!'

Bang, bang! That was Bill's piece of wood on the column

again. It couldn't please Mr Eppy very much. He was not a brave man, and it was easy to imagine his feelings down in the column!

'Can we have some food?' he called, at last.

'No,' Bill shouted back hard-heartedly. 'There is barely enough for our breakfast.'

Judging by the scraping noises that could then be heard, Mr Eppy and the others had decided to go back down the stairs and have a conference. Bill jerked his head at Jack.

'Give out the food that's left to everyone. I'm staying here in case any of these fellows try something funny. I have a feeling there's a revolver or two among them, so whatever happens I can't let them appear at the top.'

Jack and Philip shared out the remaining food. Bill gulped down his share, keeping eyes and ears open for any movement or sound from the broken column. But there was none.

He beckoned the others over to him at the end of the rather unsatisfactory meal. 'Now, listen,' he said in a low voice. 'I must stay here, you can see that. What you have to do is to go with Lucian and find the creek where the boat or boats are, belonging to Mr Eppy. Be careful there are no men left in them.'

'There are two men with two boats,' said Lucian. This was disappointing news. Bill considered again.

'Well – the thing to do first of all is to find the creek with the boats,' said Bill. 'Don't show yourselves. Just find the creek so that we shall know the way. Then come back here. We'll hope that farm-boy arrives with more food at twelve o'clock, as he usually does.'

'We could do with it,' said Jack.

'So could our dear Mr Eppy and his friends,' grinned Philip. 'Bill, what do we do after we've found the creek and the boats, and come back to report?'

'We send Lucian down with a message supposed to come from his uncle, to tell the men to come along up here,' said Bill, 'and we pop down and go off in the boats!'

'But, I say – you'll go on the rocks!' protested Lucian, at once. 'You can't come to these islands without a boatman who knows them. You'll be wrecked!'

This was a problem to be faced. Bill considered again. 'Well – we'll have to make up our minds about that when the time comes. In the meantime, off you go. Lucian, lead the way.'

Lucian, looking rather doubtful, went to the sloping city street. He set off down it, and turned off to the left half-way down.

'You seem to know the way, all right,' said Jack approvingly. Lucian looked at him uneasily.

'I don't,' he said. 'I'm absolutely no good at this kind of thing. I never can find my way anywhere. I've no bump of locality at all. I shall *never* find the boats!'

27

Unexpected visitors

Lucian was perfectly right. He did not know the way, and he could not find the boats. He was completely hopeless. He simply wandered here and there, making towards the sea, but arriving at a rocky beach where no boats could possibly lie.

'You're a mutt,' said Jack, in disgust.

'Mutt!' said Kiki, pleased with the word. 'Mutty! Send for the doctor.'

Nobody smiled even at this. They were all too disappointed and disgusted with poor Lucian. He looked ready to cry.

'It's not my fault,' he said with a sniff. 'If I'd known it was going to be so important I'd have taken careful note of the way. But I didn't know.'

'Now, look here – if you start to moan again I'll push you down a rabbit-hole, and stuff it up with seaweed,' said Jack, in disgust. Lucian looked alarmed.

'I *would* remember if I could,' he said dismally. 'But I do tell you this – nobody can come or go from these islands in a boat without a seaman who knows the way. There are hundreds of rocks just below the surface of the sea. Even an experienced seaman finds it difficult. I know, because I've so often visited them with my uncle.'

Jack looked at him. 'Well – I believe you about that,' he said. 'I shouldn't care to navigate a boat myself without a sailor who knew the way. Gosh – we're really beaten now – no boats – and if we had them we'd probably wreck ourselves. A very poor outlook indeed!'

Lucy-Ann immediately had a vision of themselves and Mr Eppy and his friends remaining on Thamis Island for years and years! She sighed.

'I wish I'd never bought that ship in a bottle for Philip,' she said. 'If I'd known it was going to bring us such an adventure I'd have thrown it away!'

They began to make their way back to the city. As they went, Jack stopped and looked up at the sky. 'What's that noise?' he said. 'Sounds like an aeroplane!'

They all stopped then, and listened, looking for the plane. Soon it came in sight, a small speck coming in from the north.

'Pity we can't make a signal of distress,' said Dinah. 'Anyway I'm going to wave my hanky!'

She took out a small hanky, and, much to the others' amusement, waved it wildly in the air.

'Do you really suppose for one moment that the plane can see your dirty little hanky, and would come down here if it did?' demanded Philip.

'You never know,' said Dinah, still waving vigorously.

'You're daft,' said Philip, and Dinah, gave him one of her best scowls. Leaving her waving madly, the others went on, still keeping an eye on the plane, which by now was over the island. It flew over it – and then made a wide circuit and flew back!

'It's seen my hanky!' shrieked Dinah. 'It's coming back!'

'Don't be an ass,' said Philip. But the plane certainly had come back – and what was more it was coming down low, too, making another circuit of the whole island as it flew.

'There's a flat space over there. Look! look!' screamed Dinah to the plane, as if she really thought it could hear her. 'Come down there! Oh, don't pass it!'

The plane swooped down still lower and came round again. It seemed to see the flat place that Dinah had yelled about, and it came down neatly, as slowly as it could. Its wheels touched the ground, and for one awful moment it looked as if the rough ground was going to tip the plane over on its nose. But it righted itself and came to a stop.

Dinah looked at the others with flushed cheeks. 'There you are! It saw my hanky – and it heard my yell!'

The others were staring in delight at the plane. 'It can't be friends of Mr Eppy's!' cried Philip. 'It must be someone sent to look for us. Come on!'

Their feet flew along over the rough paths. They saw two men getting out of the plane. They waved to the children and went to meet them.

Lucy-Ann's sharp eyes recognized them first. 'It's TIM!' she squealed. 'Tim, Bill's friend. And isn't that Andros the boatman with him?'

She was right. It *was* Tim, and beside him was a rather shamefaced Andros. Tim hailed them.

'Hallo, hallo! Where's Bill? Are you all safe? Andros here came to me with such a wild story I had to come along and investigate!'

'Yes, Bill's all right!' cried Jack, and he pumped Tim's arm up and down in sheer delight at seeing him. 'I say, it's good to see you. Did Andros really come and tell you about us?'

'He told me a most extraordinary tale,' said Tim. 'He

apparently chewed it over for a day or so, and then decided he'd better tell someone. When he saw me down at the quayside, trying to spot you all, he recognized me and came up. He said that he took you to Thamis and dropped you there. Then he fell asleep waiting for you.'

'That's right,' said Jack.

'And then someone came and woke him up in a hurry, and told him he'd no right to be there, and threatened him with prison,' said Tim. 'Andros replied that he'd left a party there, a man, and four children, a parrot and a monkey – and this fellow raved at him, said it was his own island, and if Andros didn't clear out then and there he'd have him arrested straight away.'

'Mr Eppy in a rage, evidently,' said Jack.

'Andros then pointed out that he hadn't been paid and this fellow poured money into his hands and then pointed a revolver at him. So Andros fled, comforting himself by thinking that as the fellow had a boat somewhere he could at least bring you all off in his own good time. That right, Andros?'

'I do not understand all, Mister, sir,' said Andros. 'Bad man here. Very bad. Andros very sorry, Mister, sir.'

'Well, now *you* tell your tale,' said Tim to Jack. So between them the children poured out their story – and it was such an astonishing one that Tim listened open-mouthed. Good gracious – what a tale! He had never heard anything like it in his life.

He soon grasped everything, and grinned to think of old Bill standing patiently by the broken column, waiting for Mr Eppy or his men to come out and be dealt with.

'I wouldn't mind dealing with them myself,' said the young man cheerfully. 'Biff, thud, ker-plonk – very nice, too!'

'Oh, Tim – you do make me laugh!' said Lucy-Ann, with a giggle. 'I wonder if Bill has been doing any biffing.'

'Well, if he has, I hope it's Mr Eppy that's getting the biffs, so say nothing of the ker-plonks,' said Tim, grinning. 'Well, now – what's our plan to be?'

'We've got to find the other creek and the boats,' said Jack. 'That's the first thing to do. Then we've got to get the two men out of the way – the ones who are with the boats. Then somehow we've got to get the boats going and sail off safely without being wrecked on the rocks.'

'Well, Andros will know where the creek is – in fact, I know myself,' said Tim. 'I saw it from the plane – and saw the boats there too. And Andros and I will account for the two men all right.'

'No. We know a better way than that to get them out of the way,' said Philip, and he told Tim his plan to send Lucian to them with a fake message. Tim nodded.

'Yes, that's better, really. Saves a lot of rough stuff. Not that I mind that, but I'm not sure about our friend here. He's not made of such stern stuff as he might be.'

'I think we'd better get back and see Bill before we do anything,' said Jack. 'And anyway we don't want to get the two boatmen out of the way yet, and turn them on to old Bill. That wouldn't be a very good plan. Come on – let's get back to Bill.'

So off they all went, Kiki chattering merrily, knowing that the children were now feeling very much more cheerful. 'Mistersir,' she said to Andros. 'Mistersir, mister!'

They got back to the temple courtyard, and Bill stared in surprise to see Tim. 'Hallo!' he said. 'Well, well, well – so it *was* your plane I saw coming over the island. I couldn't see it come down from here, but I hoped it had. Bit of luck you meeting with the children. I suppose they've told you all the news.'

'Yes, rather,' grinned Tim. 'Pretty adventurous lot, aren't you? Any trouble with the chappies down the column?'

'Just a biff or two a little while ago,' said Bill. '*Not* on Mr Eppy's head, unfortunately – one of the other fellows, I fear. I haven't heard so much as the flick of an eyelid since.'

The sound of a bell came echoing up the ruined street. 'Dong-dong-dong!'

'Pussy's down the well!' screeched Kiki, suddenly remembering ding-dong-bell. 'Who put her in, who put her in?'

'What on earth's that bell?' asked Tim, startled. 'Are we late for school or what?'

'Don't be silly!' said Lucy-Ann, laughing. 'That's our food. It comes every day regularly at this time. And I'm jolly glad – I'm still hungry after our poor breakfast.'

Tim was amazed to see the imp of a boy coming along with the panniered donkey. Bill did not leave his post by the column, but handed out money to Jack to pay for the food. The boy emptied the panniers, winked at Tim and spat once more at Micky. The monkey immediately spat back, and his aim was a lot better than the boy's. 'Pah!' said the little imp, in disgust.

'Pah!' echoed Kiki. 'Pooh! Dong-dong-dong, pop goes the pah!'

The boy gave her a look of amazement and climbed on his donkey's back. He sent a stream of comments at Kiki, who copied him at once, ending with one of her pistol-shots. The donkey reared in fright, and then galloped off with the boy at top speed.

'You'll be the death of me, one day, Kiki,' said Bill, weak with laughing. 'Now then – hand out the food, Jack – and I suppose we'd better throw a bit down the column, or our friends below will starve to death!'

Fortunately the boy had brought a great deal of food, so there was plenty for everyone. Bill yelled down the column in a stentorian voice:

'If you want food, there's some coming. But don't try any funny tricks, or you won't get any more!'

Somebody evidently came up to get the bread, cheese and meat that Bill threw down. He also threw some fruit, feeling that the men must be as thirsty as he was. There was no word of thanks from anyone in the column, and no sound after the food had been taken.

'Wonder if they found the treasure,' said Jack, munching hard. 'Wish I'd seen it! I bet I shan't now – and if I don't, it'll be the disappointment of my life!'

28

Escape!

Plans were made whilst they ate. 'Tim, I want you to take the two girls off in your plane,' said Bill. 'I don't want anyone exposed to danger here one moment longer than necessary. Andros, once we have got rid of the two men down in the boats, you are to take charge of the better boat of the two, and go off with the rest of us.'

'What, Bill! Do you mean to say we're going to leave a boat for those scoundrels to escape in?' cried Jack indignantly.

'No. I'm going to ask Andros if he will kindly remove some small thing from the engine of the other boat – so that it won't start up when the men want it to,' said Bill, with a laugh. 'I think it would be a very good thing to leave them here, prisoners, till we report them, and find out whether Mr Eppy has bought the island or not. If he has, he's in a strong position, of course, and nothing we say will be listened to with much attention.'

'He's always buying and selling islands,' put in Lucian. 'I expect he has bought this all right. He's well known for that.'

'You may be right,' said Bill. 'Do you want to come with us, Lucian, or stay and welcome your uncle out of the column?'

There was no doubt about what Lucian wanted to do. He was going with Bill and the others!

They all felt a lot better after the meal. Tim set off for the plane with the two girls, who hugged Bill before they went and begged him to keep himself safe.

'I shan't set off in the plane till I hear your motor-boat starting up and going off,' said Tim. 'Good-bye for the present. Come on, girls. What people are going to say when I land with you at the airport I cannot imagine. You're too dirty for anything – regular little grubs!'

Andros, Lucian, Jack and Philip set off for the boats. It was decided that only Lucian should go right up to the boats and give the false message. He was to say that the men were wanted up in the temple courtyard, and give them directions as to how to get there. As soon as Bill spotted them coming he was to leave the broken column where he was on guard, and go to the boats, keeping himself out of sight of the two men.

'Then we'll be into one of the boats in a jiffy, and off and away!' said Jack joyfully. 'What a sell for Mr Eppy!'

Andros led the way. He knew the other creek well, though he did not consider it so good as the one he had landed in. When they got near to the boats, Lucian went on alone, whilst the others hid themselves behind bushes.

Lucian was nervous but tried not to show it. He went up to the boats and shouted loudly: 'Ahoy there – where are you?'

The two men appeared. Lucian began to say something loudly in Greek, and the two men nodded. They leapt from the boat to the beach, and made their way up the shore. Lucian was telling them where to go, pointing this way and that.

'Well, I hope he's telling them correctly,' thought Jack, remembering how hopeless Lucian had been at trying to find the way to the boats that morning. 'Let's hope he has been more careful at marking the way this time.'

The men soon disappeared. Andros raced to the boats. He chose the smaller one of the two as being the better. He went to the other boat and tinkered with the engine. He withdrew something from it and threw it into the other boat, where it fell with a thud.

He grinned at the boys. 'That boat no good now,' he said. 'Engine dead. We get in here quick.'

They all got in. Andros tinkered about with the engine there too. It started up quickly and he stopped it at once.

The boys wondered how old Bill was getting on. Had he spotted the two boatmen? Was he even now coming down to the boat, keeping himself unseen? They hoped so.

Suddenly they heard shouts, and they all sat up straight in their boat. What was that?

Bill was tearing down to the shore at top speed. Behind him were the two men, also running at top speed. Andros acted quickly. He started up the engine at once, and called to the boys to give a hand to Bill when he came.

Red in the face and panting hard, Bill tore up to the boat. Willing hands dragged him in, and almost as he touched the deck of the boat it was off and away, its engine making a terrific noise in the calm of the little creek.

The two men leapt into the other boat at once, shouting angrily. Andros gave a malicious grin. Bill saw it and knew what it meant. The other boat was useless!

No amount of trying would make the second boat start up. Its engine was dead. The two men realized that Andros must have tampered with it, and they stood up, shaking their fists and shouting unintelligibly. Jack and Philip enjoyed it all thoroughly, but poor Lucian was as white as a sheet.

'Well – we're off,' said Bill, getting his breath again. 'Gosh, I had a narrow escape. I was watching for the men, but they came on me unawares. They must have guessed there was some trickery about, because they suddenly made a bee-line for me and gave me a jolly hard run. I was glad I'd got all directions from Andros as to where the creek was. I nearly missed my way as it was.'

'Any sound from Eppy and Co.?' asked Jack. Bill shook his head.

'No, but they'll have heard the shouts and I expect they'll be out of the column by now and having a good snoop round. They'll join up with the other two men and then Mr Eppy will have a few choice things to say to the two men who left the boats, and so gave us the means of escape. I expect he is thinking of quite a lot of things to say to Lucian too, for giving them that fake message.'

Lucian gave a feeble smile. He was still very white. 'I shall get a fearful beating,' he said.

'You won't,' said Bill. 'I'll see to that. I'll give your uncle something to think about, when I get back to the airport island. He's going to find himself in hot water very, very soon. I don't care whether he's bought the island or not. He's a rogue.'

The sound of an aeroplane's engine attracted their attention. 'It's Tim's plane!' cried Jack, and he stood up in the motor-boat and waved. 'Ahoy there, Tim!'

The plane swooped down low, and Kiki gave a squawk of terror. Micky hid his head under Philip's arm. The boys cheered and yelled. 'Good-bye, good luck, Tim! Hello there, girls.'

At about six o'clock in the evening the motor-boat arrived at the airport island. The first thing they saw was the *Viking Star* in the harbour, still lying silent. The second thing they saw was Tim on the quayside – and the girls with him! They had landed a long time ago, had had a good meal, and then had come down to the quay to wait for the others.

'I've been to the police,' said Tim. 'Told the chief you had something to report and would he please not go home till he'd seen you. He's all hot and bothered – it isn't often anything happens here!'

Bill laughed. 'Well, I expect the report will really have to go to the mainland to be dealt with – but as Andros comes from here, and Mr Eppy hired his boats from here, and presumably saw lawyers here if he bought the island, it's best to see the chief of police of this island.'

The chief was a small bird-like man with an intelligent face, and quick, darting eyes. He spoke English very well. He was very thrilled to think there might be some important news for him.

He listened intently to Bill's remarkable story, asking a few questions now and again. The children added little bits. When the inspector heard of the treasure he almost fell off his chair.

'We must find out if this man Eppy did buy the island,' he said. 'I know him. He is always buying islands and selling them. I do not like him. He is crazy.'

A good deal of telephoning then went on, with a few 'Hallos' from a rather bored Kiki, and some 'Mistersirs' and 'One, two, three, pops!'

At last the little man turned to Bill, his face beaming. 'Paul Eppy *did* try to buy the island. But it is not for sale. It is not his – it belongs to our government.'

'*Good!*' said all the children together.

'What a sell for Mr Eppy!' said Dinah.

'I hope he will not get away with any of that unique treasure,' said the inspector. 'He is not an honest man.'

'He can't,' said Jack, with a grin. 'Andros tampered with the only motor-boat there – he can't use it. He's a prisoner there, and so are all the rest of them.'

'Good. I think that is *very* good,' beamed the bird-like man. He turned to Bill. 'If you will be kind enough to put in a report, sir – a detailed one – for me to forward to the mainland – I would be very much obliged. The children should read it, and sign it. And Andros here should sign the part of it that refers to his doings in the matter.'

'Right,' said Bill, and got up to go. 'Well, that's that. I've had some thrilling adventures with these four – but this beats the lot. I only wish we could have a bit of that treasure!'

'Sir, you shall,' said the inspector earnestly. 'I will see to it personally. My government will be very honoured to allow you to choose what you want from it.'

'A carved dagger for me!' said Philip, at once. 'Gosh, what would the chaps at school say!'

'Come along,' said Bill. 'We'll go on board the *Viking Star*, and take Tim to dinner there with us. I want a good bath, a good shave, a good meal and a good sleep in a comfortable bed.'

And off they all went on board the *Viking Star*, happy and excited, talking nineteen to the dozen!

29

Happy ending after all!

In the night the *Viking Star* sailed once more. Bill did not hear the engines starting up, nor did any of the five children. Kiki woke up, poked her head out from under her wing and then put it back again.

It was astonishing to find themselves at sea again. They were making for Italy. 'Oh dear – we've left the treasure island far behind,' said Lucy-Ann mournfully.

'Don't be a humbug,' said Jack. 'You know you're jolly glad you escaped from it.'

'Yes, I know that,' said Lucy-Ann. 'But I just hate leaving all that treasure.'

'I never even saw it,' Jack reminded her. 'I feel I've been done out of something – all because that idiot of a Kiki took it into her head to fly off my shoulder just as we were going to look for the treasure. Nit-wit!'

'Nit-wit,' echoed Kiki pleasantly. 'Tit-bit!' She flew down and looked at a plate of grapes.

'No, you don't,' said Jack, and removed it from her. 'No

tit-bits for a nit-wit – and anyway you've helped yourself to about two hundred grapes already. You're a greedy pig, Kiki.'

'I suppose the rest of this cruise will be as dull as ditch-water,' said Philip. He glanced at the little carved ship on the dressing-table of his cabin. 'Golly – weren't we thrilled when we found the treasure map inside! Bill says we've got to give that up to the Greek museum, but we can keep the re-drawn map, the one we used – if we can get it back from Mr Eppy!'

'I wonder what Mother will say to all this,' said Dinah suddenly. 'She won't be a bit pleased with Bill, will she? She'll never speak to him again!'

'Well – that would mean we'd never even *see* him again!' said Lucy-Ann, horrified at the thought. 'I simply love Bill. I wish he was my father. It's horrid not having a father or a mother. You're lucky, you and Philip, Dinah, you *have* got a mother, even if you haven't a father.'

'Well, you share our mother with us, don't you?' said Philip, at once. 'You call her Aunt Allie – and she treats you as if she was your mother.'

'Yes, I know. She's a darling,' said Lucy-Ann, and said no more. She was worrying about Bill. Suppose Aunt Allie really kept her word, and refused to speak to Bill again because he had taken them into danger? That really would be dreadful.

It was maddening to sail away from all the romantic little islands, just as they had had such an adventure – all the children longed to know what had happened after they had left. What did Mr Eppy do? What happened to him? How did he eventually get off the island – or was he still there? And what about the treasure, that fabulous, amazing treasure hidden in the round treasure-chamber deep down in the heart of the old ruined city?

Bill promised to let them know all he heard – and he was as curious as the children! The *Viking Star* put in at Naples, and then went on to Spain. It was there that Bill got the first news. He came straight to the children.

'Well, you'll be glad to know that Eppy and Co. couldn't get off the island, and almost went mad with rage about it. Then that police inspector chap sent a boat there – and what's more went in it himself – and had the whole lot arrested then and there. What a shock for Mr Eppy!'

'What about the treasure?' asked Dinah eagerly.

'It's all been brought out of the round rock-chamber, and is being sent to the mainland to be examined and valued. A list of the things will be sent to us – and we are each to choose a memento!'

'Gosh!' said Jack. 'I'll have a dagger, like Philip, then. I bet the girls will have jewellery.'

'*Is* it the Andra treasure?' asked Lucy-Ann.

'They seem to think so,' said Bill. All their eyes went to the little ship on the dressing-table. There it stood, its sails set, its Greek name showing on its side. The *Andra*. What a Ship of Adventure it had been!

'What's going to happen about Lucian?' asked Dinah. Lucian was still on the *Viking Star*, but with *them*, not with his aunt and uncle this time! His aunt, in hysterical tears, had remained on the airport island to be with her husband. Bill had offered to take Lucian back to England, and park him with a school friend till it was time for him to return to his school.

'Lucian is to go to other relations in future for the holidays,' said Bill. 'That is – unless *we* can occasionally put up with him. I feel sorry for that lad.'

There was a silence. 'It's awful when you feel you've got to do something you don't like doing just because you're sorry for someone,' said Lucy-Ann, with a sigh. 'I don't know whether Aunt Allie will like to have him, anyway. And oh, Bill – do you think she's going to be very cross with you about all this? This adventure, I mean?'

'Yes. I think she is,' said Bill. 'I telephoned her from Italy, and told her a little. Perhaps I should have waited till we saw her. She wasn't at all pleased.'

'Oh, dear – we shan't have a very nice time the rest of the hols,' said Lucy-Ann. 'I don't like it when Aunt Allie is upset or cross. She'll be tired, too, after looking after her Aunt Polly. I do wish this adventure was going to have a nice end, not a nasty one!'

Everyone was quite glad when at last the *Viking Star* arrived at Southampton, at the end of her long cruise. After the exciting adventure in the middle of it, things had seemed very tame and dull. It was lovely to be on firm land again, going home. Mrs Mannering was not going to meet them. She was leaving her aunt the day before and going home to get things ready for the family. Lucian was to be left with a school friend of his on the way. They were all going home in Bill's car.

The boy was sad to say good-bye when the time came. He stammered and stuttered as he held out his hand to each of them in turn. 'Good-bye – er – I do hope I'll s-s-see you all again. I've had – er – er – a lovely time – and er – I'm sorry for anything I did you didn't like – and – er . . .'

'Er-er-er,' copied Kiki, in delight. 'Pah! Send for the doctor. Er-er-er-er-er-er . . .'

'Shut up, Kiki, and behave yourself,' said Jack, vexed. But Lucian didn't mind.

'I shall miss old Kiki,' he said. 'And Micky, too. Good-bye, Micky – er think of me sometimes, all of you.'

He almost ran from them, and Lucy-Ann stared after him, rather distressed. 'Poor old Lucian – he was almost crying,' she said. 'He's really rather a nice old – er – nice old . . .'

'Nit-wit,' said everyone, and Kiki yelled out too. 'NIT-WIT! Send for the doctor!'

'Well, he's nice for a nit-wit, then,' said Lucy-Ann. She settled down in the car again. 'Now for home – and dear old Aunt Allie. I've got a frightfully big hug saved up for her!'

Mrs Mannering was delighted to see them all, though she

was rather cool to Bill. She had a wonderful tea ready for them, and Kiki screeched with delight to see a plate laid for her and Micky, with a lovely fruit salad.

'One, two, three, GO!' she said, and settled down to eat, keeping an eye on Micky's plate, hoping she could snatch a titbit from it.

After tea they all sat in the comfortable sitting-room, and Bill lighted his pipe. He looked rather gloomy, the children thought.

'Well, Allie,' he began. 'I suppose you want to hear it all – the hunt for the Andra treasure – and all that happened.'

'We had some jolly narrow escapes,' said Jack, stroking Kiki. 'And you'll be glad to know, Aunt Allie, that Kiki got two grand nips at Mr Eppy's ear!'

They began their tale. Mrs Mannering listened in amazement. Her eyes went continually to the little carved ship on the mantelpiece, put proudly there by Philip as soon as he reached home.

'There!' said Philip, when they had finished their tale. 'What do you think of that?'

Mrs Mannering did not answer. She looked at Bill. He would not meet her eyes, but knocked out his pipe very hard on the fender.

'Oh, Bill,' said Mrs Mannering sadly. 'You promised me – and you broke your word. I shall never trust you again. You promised faithfully not to lead the children into any kind of adventure again. I wouldn't have asked you to look after them if I hadn't trusted you. I can't trust you any more'

'Aunt Allie! What do you *mean*, you can't trust Bill any more!' cried Lucy-Ann indignantly, and she went to Bill and put her arms round him. 'Can't you see he's the nicest, most trustable person in the whole world?'

Mrs Mannering could not help laughing. 'Oh, Lucy-Ann – you're very fierce, all of a sudden. It's just that every time I leave you alone with Bill you get into horrible danger. You know you do.'

'Well, why can't you and Bill always be with us together?' demanded Lucy-Ann. 'I don't see why you can't *marry* each other – then we'd always have Bill, and you could keep an eye on him to see he doesn't lead us into adventures.'

Bill exploded into an enormous shout of laughter. Mrs Mannering smiled broadly. The others looked at one another.

'I say!' said Philip eagerly, 'that's a wizard idea of Lucy-Ann's! We'd have a father then – all of us! Gosh, fancy having Bill for a father. Wouldn't the other boys envy us?'

Bill stopped laughing and looked soberly round at the four beaming children. Then he looked at Mrs Mannering. He raised his eyebrows enquiringly.

'Well, Allie?' he said, in a curiously quiet voice. 'Do *you* think it's a good idea, too?'

She looked at him, and then smiled round at the eager children. She nodded. 'Yes – it's really a very good idea, Bill. I'm surprised we've never thought of it before!'

'That's settled, then,' said Bill. 'I'll take these four kids on – and you'll see to it I don't lead them into any more adventures, Allie? Is that agreed?'

'*Well!* This adventure had a wonderful ending after all!' said Lucy-Ann, drawing a deep breath. Her eyes shone like stars. 'Good old Bill! Oh, I'm so happy now!'

'God save the Queen,' said Kiki excitedly. 'Polly put the doctor on, send for the kettle. Pop goes Bill!'